SAVING 6
CHLOE
WALSH

PIATKUS

PIATKUS

First published in Great Britain in 2023 by Piatkus

7 9 10 8

Typeset in Garamond by M Rules

Printed and bound in Great Britain by
Clays Ltd, Elcograf S.p.A.

Papers used by Piatkus are from well-managed forests
and other responsible sources.

MIX
Supporting
responsible forestry
FSC® C104740

Piatkus
An imprint of
Little, Brown Book Group
Carmelite House
50 Victoria Embankment
London EC4Y 0DZ

An Hachette UK Company
www.hachette.co.uk

www.littlebrown.co.uk

For my children.

Earthside and in heaven.

Glossary

Bluey:	Porno movie.
Jammy:	lucky.
Jammiest:	luckiest.
Corker:	beautiful woman.
St. Stephen's Day:	Boxing Day/ December 26th.
Bonnet:	hood of the car.
Boot:	trunk of the car.
Pound Shop:	Dollar store.
Burdizzo:	castration device
Messages:	groceries.
Mickey/Willy:	penis.
Spanner:	idiot.
Feis:	a tradition Gaelic arts and culture festival/event.
Hole:	often said instead of ass/bottom.
Solicitor:	lawyer.
Daft:	silly.
Daft as a brush:	very silly.
Poitín:	Irish version of moonshine/illegal, home-brewed alcohol.
Wheelie Bin:	Trash can.
Jumper:	sweater.
Cracking on:	hooking up.
Runners:	trainers/sneakers.

Wellies:	rubber boots worn in the rain.
Fair City:	Popular Irish television soap.
On the hop:	skipping school.
Cooker:	Oven/Stove/Hob.
Rolos:	Popular brand of chocolate.
Eejit:	fool/idiot.
Gobshite:	fool/idiot.
Lifted:	arrested.
Sap:	sad/pathetic.
Rebel County:	nickname for County Cork.
Primary School:	elementary school – junior infants to sixth class.
Secondary School:	high school – first year to sixth year.
Leaving Cert:	the compulsory state exam you take in your final year of secondary school.
Junior Cert:	the compulsory state exam you take in third year – midway through your six-year cycle of secondary school.
Playschool:	pre-school/nursery.
Junior Infants:	equivalent to kindergarten.
Senior Infants:	equivalent to second year of kindergarten.
First Class:	equivalent to first grade.
Second Class:	equivalent to second grade.
Third Class:	equivalent to third grade.
Fourth Class:	equivalent to fourth grade.
Fifth Class:	equivalent to fifth grade.
Sixth Class:	equivalent to sixth grade.
First Year:	equivalent to seventh grade.
Second Year:	equivalent to eighth grade.
Third Year:	equivalent to ninth grade.
Fourth Year:	Transition Year: equivalent to tenth grade.
Fifth Year:	equivalent to eleventh grade.
Sixth Year:	equivalent to twelfth grade.

GAA:	Gaelic Athletic Association
Culchie:	a person from the countryside or a county outside of Dublin. Usually used as a friendly insult.
Jackeen:	a person from Dublin. A term sometimes used by people from other counties in Ireland to refer to a person from Dublin.
Dub:	a person from Dublin.
Frigit:	someone who has never been kissed.
Gardaí Síochána:	Irish police force.
Garda:	policeman.
Shades:	police.
Hurling:	a hugely popular, amateur Irish sport played with wooden hurleys and sliotars.
Camogie:	the female version of Hurling.
Scoil Eoin:	the name of Johnny, Gibsie, Feely, Hughie, and Kevin's all-boys primary school.
Sacred Heart:	the name of Shannon, Joey, Darren, Claire, Caoimhe, Lizzie, Tadhg, Ollie, Podge, and Alec's mixed primary school.
St. Bernadette's:	the name of Aoife, Casey, and Katie's all-girls primary school.
Grinds:	Tutoring.
Fortnight:	two weeks.
Chipper:	a restaurant that sells fast food.
Craic:	fun.
Gas:	funny.
Mope:	idiot.
The Angelus:	Every evening at 6pm in Ireland, there is a minute silence for prayer on the television.
The craic was ninety:	Having a lot of fun and banter.
On the lash:	going out drinking.
On the piss:	going out drinking.

Swot:	nerd/academically gifted.
Spanner:	idiot.
Yolk:	nickname for an illegal drug.
Hatchet craic:	Great fun.
Langer:	idiot.
Fanny:	Vagina.
Scoring:	Kissing.
Shifting:	Kissing.
Shifting Jackets:	Lucky piece of clothing, usually a jacket, when trying to pick up a girl.
Langers:	group of idiots and/or to be extremely drunk.
Tog off:	change into or out of training clothes.
Child of Prague:	a religious statue farmers place out in a field to encourage good weather. (An old Irish superstition)
Rosary, Removal, Burial:	the three days of a Catholic funeral in Ireland.
Spuds:	potatoes.
A slab of beer:	a box of 24 bottles of beer.
Get your hole:	have sex.
Ridey:	a good-looking person.
Strop:	mood-swing/pouting/sulking.

Name Pronunciations

Aoife:	E-fa
Aoif:	(like reef without the r)
Sean:	Shawn
Gardaí:	Gar-Dee
Caoimhe:	Kee-va
Sadhbh:	Sigh-ve
Sinead:	Shin-aid
Neasa:	Nasa
Eoghan:	Owen
Tadhg:	Tie-g (like Tiger but without the 'r' at the end)

Author Note

Saving 6 is the third installment in the Boys of Tommen series, the first book for Joey Lynch and Aoife Molloy, and has a cliffhanger ending.

Some scenes in this book may be extremely upsetting, therefore reader discretion is advised.

Because of its extremely **explicit** sexual content, mature themes, triggers, violence, and bad language, it is suitable for readers of 18+.

It is based in the south of Ireland, set during the timeframe of 1999 to 2004, and contains Irish dialogue and slang and phrases popular for the times.

A detailed glossary can be found at the beginning of the book.

Thank you so much for joining me on this adventure.

Lots of love,

Chlo xxx

Preface

I never knew devastation until he walked into my world and gave me a glimpse into his.

I never knew demons until I stood beside him and watched him battle monsters more frightening than my imagination could ever concoct.

I never knew heartbreak until he decimated my heart by decimating his body.

I never knew hurt until he walked away from me.

I never knew.

I never . . .

PROLOGUE

The meet-cute

August 30th 1999

JOEY

"All you need to do is keep your head down and your temper reined in. You're a smart kid. You've got this. Just keep that tongue of yours in check and don't react to any nonsense. Do you want me to walk in with you?"

"Do I fuck."

"It's okay to be nervous, Joe."

"I'm not nervous."

"And it's okay to be scared, too."

"Do I look like I'm scared?" I growled, aggravated by his incessant coddling. "I'm not a baby, Dar."

"I know you're not," my big brother conceded, as we walked up the path to Ballylaggin Community School – a journey he had taken every weekday for the past six years. His time at secondary school was over now, while mine was just beginning. "I just *need* this to go well for you."

"Yeah," I snorted. "Well, we both know that's not going to happen."

"This is your fresh start, Joey," he said. "Whatever happened in primary school is behind you now. Don't carry any of that trouble with you."

"There's no such thing as fresh starts," I drawled. "Just different locations filled with the same bullshit."

"You're too young to be this cynical."

"And you're too smart to waste your time and breath on this pep talk," I countered. "I'm not Shannon, lad. I don't need the words or the hand-holding."

"Is it so wrong of me to want to see you off on your first day of secondary school?"

"You could have done that back at the house," I reminded him. "You didn't need to walk me to school. I'm not a baby."

"You're my baby brother."

"I've never been a baby anything, Dar."

"Always so self-sufficient." Shaking his head, he gave me a sad smile. "Well, maybe I wanted to spend some extra time with you."

"We share a room," I deadpanned, shifting the ton of bricks that was my school bag onto my other shoulder. "We already spend enough time together."

"I love you, Joe," he threw me by saying. "You know that, right?"

"You *love* me?" Feet faltering, I turned to look up at him. "What the hell is wrong with you?"

"Nothing," he replied, tone thick with emotion. "I'm just . . . I need you to know that."

"Why?" I demanded, feeling unnerved by his sudden declaration. It was out of place and felt all wrong to me. "What's happening?"

"Nothing." Smiling, he reached down and ruffled my hair. "Nothing's happening, shithead. I just wanted to tell you."

"Okay . . . " I eyed him suspiciously, not sure if I entirely believed him. "But if you even *think* about hugging me in front of all these people, I will kick you in the nuts."

"Your voice is starting to break," he chuckled. "My baby brother is growing up."

"I don't need a deep voice to kick your ass," I shot back, hackles rising.

He rolled his eyes. "Sure thing, squeaky."

"Do all the girls here wear skirts that short?" Eyes widening, I watched as a group of girls filed out off a school bus and onto the footpath in front of us. "I take it all back, Dar." Delighted with life, I grinned up at my brother. "I think I'm going to like secondary school."

"Don't even think about it," Darren chuckled, ribbing me with his elbow. "Those girls are in sixth year. You're a baby first year to them."

"Already told ya that I've never been a baby anything," I shot back with a wink before turning my attention back to the glorious view of bare legs and peachy asses.

"Aren't you a bit young for getting notions about girls?"

"I'm thirteen."

"Not until December."

"I bet I've seen more tits than you."

"Mam's don't count."

We both laughed, causing a few of the girls in front to turn around.

"Oh my god! Darren Lynch!" one of the blondes squealed, giving my brother a warm smile as she moved straight for him. "What are you doing here? Didn't you get like a thousand points in your leaving cert last June? There's no way you're repeating sixth year?"

"No, not repeating. Just walking my little brother in for his first day," Darren replied, receiving the half-hug the girl offered him. "And I could ask you the same question. What are you doing slumming it in a BCS uniform, Tommen girl?"

"I, uh, transferred over here. I'm going to finish up sixth year at BCS," the blonde replied in a strained tone. "It's, ah, sort of for the best, all things considered, you know?"

"Yeah." My brother nodded and sympathy filled his eyes, which confused the fuck out of me. "I do."

"So, how's everything going, Dar?" She was quick to push on from whatever the hell had them eyeing each other *meaningfully*. I rolled my eyes and forced back the urge to hurl. "I haven't seen you since that weekend."

"I've been around," he told her, scratching the back of his neck. "Just dealing, you know?"

"Yeah." Another meaningful look passed between them. "I know."

"I don't," I decided to interject, because why the hell not? "Care to explain what the hell you're both talking about?"

My brother sighed in resignation before reeling off introductions. "Caoimhe, this mouthy shit is my little brother." He turned to me and gestured to the girl. "Joe, this is Caoimhe Young. You were probably too young to remember her in primary school, but her little sister is friends with Shannon."

Her blue eyes landed on my face, and she smiled. "So, you're the next Lynch in the pecking order, huh?"

"Apparently so." I shrugged noncommittally before turning back to Darren. "Are ya done with the trip down memory lane, or do I need to stand around for another ten minutes?"

"Oh boy, Dar," she laughed. "You're in trouble with this one, huh?"

"Tell me about it," my brother replied with a sigh. "It was good seeing you, Caoimhe." Catching hold of the back of my neck, he steered us around the group of girls and up the path towards the school. "Take care of yourself."

"You, too, Dar," she called after us. "Keep in touch."

"Keep in touch?" I shook my head and wrestled free from his hold. "What the hell does that mean?"

"Who knows," Darren muttered, steering me towards the gates of the school. "You know the way girls are."

"Did you have sex with her?"

"What?" He stopped walking and swung me around to look at him. "No, I didn't have *sex* with her. Why would you even ask me that?"

"Don't get all high and mighty on me," I laughed, playfully shoving his chest. "I know you've been with girls in the past."

Darren sighed heavily. "Not like that, I haven't."

"Well, I think she likes you," I offered up, falling into step alongside him once again. "She was looking at you with those gooey eyes."

"Gooey eyes," Darren chuckled. "You're a dope."

"She *was*," I laughed. "I'm surprised she didn't swoon when she saw you." Clearing my throat, I pressed a hand to my forehead and mimicked, *"Oh, Darren Lynch. Is that you my eyes can see? Be still my beating heart!"*

"You're such a little shit," my brother laughed.

"And you're a dark horse," I shot back with a wink, ribbing him with my elbow. "Got anymore blondes lurking around school, waiting to fall at your feet? Because I'll be happy to take them off your hands."

"Pack it in," he chuckled, with a rueful shake of his head. "Honestly, it's not like that. She's just a good friend."

"Don't worry, Dar," I laughed. "I know you're gay. I'm only messing with ya—"

"Jesus Christ, Joey!" Darren hissed, clamping a hand on my shoulder. He looked around us, eyes wild and panicked, before he released a breath and muttered, "Not so loud, okay?"

"Why do you do that?" I demanded, good mood forgotten, as I shook his hand off, feeling my temper rise. "Why do you hide who you are?"

He shook his head, blue eyes laced with pain. "Joey."

"No, it's bullshit, Dar," I pushed, unwilling to let it go. "I'm not ashamed of you, and you shouldn't be either."

"I'm not ashamed of myself," he replied quietly.

"Well, good," I snapped. "Because you don't have shit to be ashamed of."

"Yeah, well, according to Dad, I have."

"Yeah, well, fuck Dad," I spat. "He's the one who should be ashamed of himself, not you."

"You do realize that up until six years ago, being gay was a punishable crime in this country?"

"Yeah, and so were condoms and any other form of birth control," I growled. "Which just goes to show that the laws are bullshit."

"Joe . . . "

"This country is backwards, Darren, you know that," I argued. "Yeah, it's getting better now, but we both know that the foundations on which our laws are built have a lot less to do with common sense than religion."

"I really don't want to talk about it, Joe."

"Well, I don't want to see you walking around the place with your tail between your legs when you have no reason to," I countered. "It's bullshit, Darren. Every word that comes out of that man's mouth is utter bullshit, so don't let him make you feel bad about yourself. Dad's living in the dark ages, so don't you dare let him drag you back there with him."

"What do you propose I do, Joey?" he asked in a weary tone. "Go toe to toe with him?"

Yes. "You can take him."

"No, I can't," he replied. "Besides, not every disagreement in life has to result in a dog fight."

"In our lives it does," I corrected hotly. "So, you better get your head in the fight and make damn sure that you're the biggest dog."

"Like you, squeaky?"

"I might not be the biggest dog in the fight," I begrudgingly conceded. "But I always have the sharpest teeth."

"Kind of like the saying, it's not the size of the dog that matters, it's the fight in the dog?"

I nodded. "Now you're speaking my language."

Darren gave me a strange look. "So, in your mind, it's a dog-eat-dog world that we're living in?"

"It's not in my mind, Dar. It's a fact."

"You know," he mused in a melancholy tone, "I can't figure out if that backbone of yours will be your saving grace or your downfall."

"Whichever way it goes is fine by me," I said with a shrug. "Because I couldn't care less."

"That's not true," he argued. "You care."

"No," I laughed humorlessly. "I really don't."

"I need you to start caring, Joey."

"I care," I grumbled. "I care about you, and Shan, and Tadhg, and Ols—"

"I need you to start caring about *you*, Joe—"

"Holy *shit*."

My feet came to an abrupt stop the minute my eyes landed on a tall blonde, with the face of an angel, sitting on the wall at the entrance of the school.

"What?" Darren demanded, looking around us. "Where's the fire?"

"There." Struck dumb at the sight of her, and with all notions gone of continuing any further conversation with my brother, I pointed to the girl whose long blonde hair was splaying all around her in the breeze. "*Her*."

"I don't know her," my brother noted. "She must be a first year."

Looking like nothing my eyes had ever seen, I watched as she sucked on a Chupa Chups lollypop, entirely uninterested in the lad attempting to talk to her, while her long legs dangled from the wall.

"Jesus Christ." I blew out a breath. "I don't care if you're gay or not, lad. You can't deny that girl is the best-looking thing your eyes have ever seen."

At that exact moment her gaze flicked to mine.

The second our eyes collided, I felt a pang of heat shoot straight to my chest.

Holy fuck.

When I met her gaze head on, I fully expected her to blush and look away.

She didn't.

Instead, she tilted her head to one side and studied me with a similar look to the one I was sure I was sporting.

Arching her brow, she slowly removed the lollypop from her mouth, and gave me an expectant look.

My gaze flicked questioningly to the dark-haired lad still trying and failing to garner her attention before returning to her face.

With a defiant tilt of her chin, she gave me a look that said *what are you waiting for?*

Well shit.

What *was* I waiting for?

"Steady up, baby brother," Darren chuckled, as he forcefully walked me up the path towards the main building and *away* from the blonde. "She's cute, but don't throw your hat in the ring just yet. I promise there will be fifty more girls in your year that look just as lovely."

Doubtful.

"I don't want fifty more girls," I replied, twisting back to find her still watching me. "I want *that* girl."

"Oh, to be a first year again." Laughing, Darren dragged me along with him until she was out of sight. "If I've taught you nothing else these past twelve years, then remember this; keep your temper in check, your head in the books, your ass off the streets, and your hands off girls that look like that."

"Like what?"

"Like they have heartbreak written all over them."

"So, in other words, spend the next six years of secondary school living like a priest," I grumbled, breaking free of him when we reached the school. "Where do I sign up?"

"Hey, that's what I did," my brother chuckled, thoroughly amused by my disgust. "It worked well for me."

"Because you're shit craic," I told him. "Seriously, Dar. It's a wonder we're related at all."

"Well, we are," he reminded me before pulling me in for a hug. "I'll always be your brother, no matter what, okay? Don't ever forget it."

"What did I tell you?" I hissed, scrambling away from him before anyone saw me hugging my *brother* of all people. "I should follow through and kick you in the nuts for that."

"Take care of yourself." His voice was thick with emotion as he watched me scowl at him. "I love you."

"Jesus, relax with the love bullshit," I grumbled, feeling acutely uncomfortable. "I'm starting secondary school, asshole, you're not sending me off to war."

He nodded stiffly. "I know."

Feeling off-balance, I eyed him warily before shaking my head and walking off in the direction of the entrance.

Stop.
Don't go.
Something's wrong.

Turn back.

This is all wrong.

"Dar?" Hovering uncertainly, I turned back to find him already walking away. "I'll see you after school, yeah?"

My brother didn't answer.

"Dar?"

He didn't turn back to look at me, either.

"Darren?"

Instead, he pulled his hood up and kept walking away from me.

"So, is that guy your keeper, or can you think for yourself?" a female voice asked, and I spun around to find none other than blondie from the wall standing in front of me – and holy fuck if she wasn't even better looking close up.

With all notions of Darren's weird farewell long forgotten, I focused entirely on the face looking up at me.

High cheekbones, pink pouty lips, big eyes, and hair that looked like something out of a magazine, she was, hands down, the best-looking thing my eyes had ever seen. "I can definitely think for myself."

"You saw me back there," she stated evenly, green eyes snaring me.

"I did."

"You kept walking."

I nodded like a fool. "I did."

"Don't do that again."

Fuck me. "I won't."

She looked me over once more before nodding in approval. "You're beautiful."

Well shit. "Likewise."

"Hm." Her lips tipped up. "So, do you have a name, boy-who-can-think-for-himself?"

"Does it matter?" I countered, needing to regain some ground I had lost to this powerhouse of a girl. "We both know that you'll be calling me baby by the end of the day."

She licked her lips to bury her smile. "Is that so?"

I stepped closer. "You tell me, blondie."

Now, she did smile, and it was a glorious sight. "Okay, that was seriously smooth."

I smirked. "Thanks."

"I'm Aoife," she laughed, holding her hand out to me.

"Joey," I replied, accepting her small hand in mine.

"Joey." Shaking my hand, she tilted her head to one side, and studied me without a hint of shyness. "Your name suits you."

"I could say the same thing about you," I replied. "Your name means radiance and beauty, right?"

She grinned. "You know your Irish."

Yeah, I knew my Irish, but not *that* well.

There had been a girl in my class at primary school named Aoife, who had constantly droned on about how she had been named after an Irish warrior queen, with a level of beauty that was rumored to rival that of Helen of Troy.

I wasn't, however, about to tell *this* particular Aoife that.

Not when I needed every advantage I could get.

"So, what class have you been assigned to?" she asked, retrieving her folded-up timetable from the pocket of her short, pleated skirt. "I'm in First Year 3."

Fuck if I knew.

I straightened out the crumpled-up ball of paper that was my class timetable for the school year. I was fucking thrilled when I read the words *First Year 3* on the page. "Same here."

She was in my class.

Get in there!

Maybe my luck was changing.

"So, you're as mediocre a student as I am," she laughed. "My brother got assigned to First Year 1. That's the class for the brainiacs."

"You're a twin?"

She nodded. "For my sins."

"So, we're the third smartest class?"

"Or the third thickest," she laughed. "Whichever way your glass is filled."

"Why? How many classes has our year been split into?"

"Four."

"Jesus," I laughed. "That doesn't say much for us, does it?"

"Nope." She grinned back at me. "Not a whole pile. So, what primary school are you coming from?"

"Sacred Heart," I replied. "You?"

"St. Bernadette's," she said with a grimace. "That's the—"

"All-girls primary school run by the nuns outside of the town?" I winced in sympathy. "Well, that's shit luck on you, huh?"

"Yep. Eight years with the nuns. Can't you see my halo shining?"

"Oh yeah, it's blinding."

"According to Sister Alphonsus, I should be continuing my education in an all-girls environment," she mused with a devilish smile. "Apparently, I have a wild streak in me, with a penchant for the *male form* that no amount of prayer can eliminate." She rolled her eyes. "All because I said I thought the guy playing Jesus in a movie they showed us was gorgeous."

I arched a brow. "Gorgeous?"

"What?" she laughed. "He *was*."

"Well, it sounds to me like you need to spend less time on your knees praying and more time—"

"Don't say it," she warned, reaching up to cover my mouth with her hand.

"With the *male form*," I chuckled, peeling her fingers off my lips with my hand.

"So, should I spend more time with the male form in general?" she laughed, and somehow our fingers were entwined now. "Or with you? Because it's safe to say that I'm impressed with the male form standing in front of me."

"Is that your way of telling me that you don't have a boyfriend?"

"No, it's my way of telling you that I *will* have a boyfriend once you ask me."

"Jesus." My heart rate sped up. "You're not backwards about anything, are you?"

She winked and slid her school bag off her shoulder. "Where's the fun in that?"

Thrown off-kilter by this girl, I took the bag she held out for me and slung it over my free shoulder.

"There," she said with an approving nod, admiring her bright-pink bag on me "That should do it."

"Should do what?"

"Warn the other girls away."

"Warn the other girls away?" My brows rose up. "Did you just *mark* me with your bag?"

"I sure did," she replied, smiling sweetly up at me before turning on her heels and sauntering off in the direction of the school. "Now, let's go, *baby*."

I laughed, because, in all honesty, what else could I do?

I had a distinct feeling that I would be doing a lot of following after this girl.

Still, my feet moved after her.

FIRST YEAR

The monsters under my bed

November 30th 1999

JOEY

With the sound of my own pulse thundering in my ears, I kept my eyes trained on my bedroom floor, and concentrated on my breathing, on the cracks in the skirting board, on the freshly burrowed hole in my sock, on anything *but* the asshole pounding and demanding to get in.

"Open this door, boy, and I'll put manners on ya!"

"Useless little cunt, just like your brother."

"Not such a big man now, are you, ya little prick!"

"Get your hole out here, ya little bollox, before I break the fucking door down!"

My heart was racing violently in my chest, every inch of my body was battered and bruised, and while I knew my mam was out there and defenseless, I honest to God didn't have it in me to go another round with the man she called her husband.

Not when he'd gotten the better of me so easily tonight.

Swallowing the blood that was trickling down the back of my throat, I twisted my head to the side, and considered my options.

Fight.

Die.

Run.

Die.

Tell.

Die.

Hide.

Die.

Die.

Die.

After spending a selfish amount of time contemplating taking a knife to my wrists, I clenched my eyes shut and locked every muscle in my body tight until my entire frame shook from the tension.

Don't do it, lad.

It's not your turn yet.

Don't give him the satisfaction of checking out.

Think of the others.

Desperate to distract myself from the temptation, I held my breath and concentrated on why I couldn't leave this house.

On why I had to stay.

Shannon. Tadhg. Ollie ...

Shannon. Tadhg. Ollie ...

Shannon. Tadhg. Ollie ...

Slowly, as my mind resigned to the fact that there was no way I could leave three innocent children with the monsters that had created us, I felt my muscles unlock, causing me to sink deeper into depression.

Trapping me ...

Resentment bubbled to life inside of me, with my mind honing in on one face.

On one name.

Fuck Darren for leaving me alone in this.

Mam was crying in her room, with her clothes strewn everywhere, and her dignity smeared all over his dick, and I couldn't do shit for her.

And just like last time, I couldn't save her.

And just like all the times before that, I couldn't stop him.

The deep timbre of my father's voice echoed through my bedroom walls, as the threats he had been doling out to me late into the night slowly morphed into frustrated snarls and then eventually drunken slurs.

"Fucking prick," was the last thing I heard him call me before his heavy footsteps clumsily retreated from my door.

Minutes later, his voice could be heard again, but at the other end of the landing this time, with my mother, once again, the target of his whiskey tantrum.

Heart hammering violently in my chest, I reached for the alarm clock on my bedside locker and squinted, trying to make out the time with only the dull hue of the street light outside my window to guide me.

02:34

For fuck's sake.

Setting the clock back down, I released a frustrated breath, drummed my fingers against my chest, and tried to calm the fuck down.

It wasn't coming easy, though.

Not tonight.

Because Darren was still gone, and *he* was still here.

The one person I depended on in times like this – on nights like this – had walked away without as much as a backwards glance.

I should know.

I watched him go.

Dad never hit Darren like he hit me.

He was the firstborn, the golden boy.

I was the spare.

Darren got open-palmed slaps.

I got closed-fist punches.

Darren was diplomatic.

He could talk our father around better than anyone else in the house, and bring him back to his senses – well, most of the time.

Glowering at his empty bottom bunk, untouched since his departure, I felt the familiar swell of bitterness wash over me, taking with it another piece of my childhood.

I had just started first year, for Christ's sake, wouldn't turn thirteen for another month; what hope had I against a man twice my size?

I didn't. Darren *knew* that, and he still left me here defenseless.

I was twelve-years-old and a frontline soldier in the war that raged within my family home. The enemy I found myself up against was bigger and stronger, and my ally had abandoned me when I needed him most.

I'd known something was wrong that morning he walked me to school. I could feel it in my bones as I watched him walk away from me – as I called after him like a fucking child.

For the first few days after my older brother's abrupt departure, I had waited with bated breath, praying that everything would somehow blow over and Darren would walk back through the front door.

The move was completely out of character for me.

I didn't *pray*.

But the evening I came home from my first day of secondary school, and discovered he was gone, I found myself whispering oaths and promises to the man in the sky, offering up anything and everything I could think of, in exchange for the safe return of my brother.

My ally.

My prayers went unanswered, and I had lost more ground than I could afford to in the weeks that had since passed.

Disgusted with myself for hiding behind a locked door, I tried to reason with my pride, knowing deep down that going back out there tonight would be the equivalent of signing my own death warrant.

You barely made it out alive . . .

Loud sniffles filled my room just then, and I bit back a growl, letting my head smack against the bedroom door I was perched against, hurley in hand.

"Don't listen to it," I instructed my sibling – which one, I had no clue, because the three that still resided in this shithole were currently hiding under my duvet. "Block him out."

"It's so scary, Joe," Tadhg sniffled, appearing from beneath my quilt on the top bunk. "What if he's hurting Mammy again?"

"He's not," I snapped, lying through my teeth to my six-year-old brother. "She's grand. Now go to sleep."

"I can't," he croaked out.

"You have to," my ten-year-old sister whisper-hissed. "You know what will happen if he realizes that we're awake."

"Shut up, Shannon," Tadhg wailed. "I'm scared . . . "

"I know you are, Tadhg," she continued softly, appearing from beneath the covers with our three-year-old brother, Ollie, curled up on her lap. "That's why we have to stay quiet."

"The lot of ye need to go the fuck to sleep," I ordered, taking on the protector role that I had unceremoniously been thrust into. "You're grand. Mam's grand. We're all grand. Everything's fucking grand."

"But what if he is hurting her again?"

I had no doubt that he *was*, in fact, hurting her again.

Problem was, I couldn't do shit about it.

God knows I'd tried.

The broken nose I was sporting from earlier tonight proved just how little I could do about the animal we called our father.

Thankfully, Tadhg and Shannon didn't seem to understand the way in which our father was hurting our mother.

I, on the other hand, had been ten years old when I learned the meaning of the word rape.

It wasn't the first time I'd seen him force her down, nor was it the first time I'd heard the word tossed around in conversation, but it *was* the first time that I managed to connect the word to the action and make sense of what had been happening to my mother.

Make sense of what that animal had forced her to take into her unwilling body.

Repeatedly.

My intervention had been a futile one that ended in my mother – battered, bruised, bloodied and naked from the waist down on the kitchen floor – dismissing me from the room. Blaming me with her eyes for something I had no control over, but not before my father got a few good hits in on my prepubescent frame.

After I registered what rape meant, what it really and truly meant, my resolve to keep my mouth shut about what happened at home only strengthened further.

I knew Darren had been raped when we spent those six months of senior infants in foster care. I'd heard enough about it – had been made feel guilty enough about it – to know that it was bad enough to keep my mouth shut and keep our family's private business to myself.

"Remember, Joey, remember that no matter how bad Dad gets, it will never be worse than that . . . "

"You think that's bad? You don't know how fucking lucky you have it . . . "

"You got ice-cream and cake with your foster family, I got ruined . . . "

"You have nothing to complain about, not compared to me. You had it easy, so stop feeling sorry for yourself . . . "

"Do you know what happens in those care homes? Do you want Tadhg to end up like me? Do you want that for Shannon? Keep your mouth shut. Nothing is bad enough in this house to merit going back there. Nothing . . . "

Once I saw it for myself, I knew there was no way I would ever put my siblings in a position where that could happen to them.

I would rather die first and that wasn't me being dramatic.

I meant it.

For years after that, I didn't sleep at night. I didn't dare. The noises – the fucking sound of her – was burned into my memory, repeating over and over on a loop of mental destruction.

And even when it was quiet, I was on edge. The silence unsettled me almost as much as her screams.

Because her screams meant she was still breathing.

Her silence meant that she was dead.

I could remember lying in my room, not unlike tonight, body rigid, as I strained to hear every squeak in the mattress, every disgusting grunt and groan coming from the closed door at the other end of the landing.

Panic would consume me then and, nine times out of ten, I would spring out of bed and stand guard outside my sister's bedroom, terrified that she possessed something an animal like our father would eventually come looking for.

At least when we were all together under the same roof, I could protect her, I could protect them all, take some of the pain for them, and let them have some semblance of a childhood.

If I told, we would be put into care. And if we were put into care, there was a good chance we would be separated. And if we were separated, then I couldn't protect them from the predators that Darren warned me were everywhere.

"You think it won't happen to you, but it does. It happens all the time . . . "

"Not everyone lucks out like you and Shannon did when you were placed with the same foster family . . . "

"I can still feel him inside of my body, tearing me apart, ripping me open, and it makes me want to die . . . "

The very thought of something happening to Shannon, Ollie, or Tadhg made my skin crawl and my mouth clamp shut.

I could take the pressure.

I could take the blows.

I could handle his whiskey tantrums.

I could take it all if it meant that *they* didn't have to.

Like a revered blood oath, I mentally reaffirmed the vow I had made to myself the night after Darren walked out, and that was to protect my brothers and sister with everything I had in me.

I would never allow them to be beaten like I had been, or be abused like our mother, or defiled like our brother.

With whatever I had inside of me, I would protect and defend them from harm.

They would never have to sit behind a barricaded bedroom door with a hurley in hand.

I would be here to do it for them.

I knew what it felt like to have my protector abandon me, and I would *never* allow that to happen to them.

I would die first.

Yeah, fuck Darren for leaving our brothers and sister to fend for themselves against a monster.

Fuck him for making me our father's number one punching bag.

You've always been that, lad . . .

Fuck secondary school, too, for that matter. My gaze drifted to my unopened school bag that contained a mountain of homework. I hadn't the slightest intention of completing shit given by teachers whose opinions on me were the least of my worries.

Yeah, it was safe to say that secondary school was another bust.

Understatement of the century, lad . . .

According to my new principal, Mr. Nyhan, I was *short tempered* and *unresponsive to authority*. If he had to put up with half of the crap I did, he wouldn't be so responsive to authority himself.

Asshole.

I reveled in pissing him off.

The reason for my blatant dislike of him was simple; he had played hurling with my father back in the day.

Hurling.

A shiver rolled through me.

It was both my saving grace and my living nightmare.

Forced to play by my father from the age of four, and terrified of having that weight dropped onto Tadhg's shoulders like it had been dropped on mine when Darren quit, I pushed myself to keep it up.

And I was good.

I was better than my father or Darren ever were, and I think it made him hate me more – the fact that I wasn't completely useless like he constantly reminded me.

Dick.

It was because of thoughts like these, and fucked up nights like the current one, that when Shane Holland, a lad a few years above me at BCS, offered me my first hit from a joint in fifth class, I took it.

When he promised that it would relax my racing mind and help me sleep, I sucked that shit so deep into my lungs that I almost choked myself in the process.

And do you know what happened?

It *worked*.

I went home that night and slept like a baby, blissfully unaware of anything outside my locked bedroom door.

After my first night of unbroken sleep in years, I was instantly converted, and decided that weed was for me.

After a smoke, I could relax, better than I'd ever been able to. I could close my eyes at night and not hear *her* in my head.

I could ignore the burning pain of betrayal and rejection that crippled me every time I thought of Darren leaving me to fend for the family alone, or what would happen if I tried to leave.

I had peace.

Last Saturday after work, for example, I'd met up with Shane and a few of the older lads from school for a few hours.

I already knew most of the lads, having grown up in the same area. They were all fairly harmless; well, most of them, at least.

It wasn't like I was naïve enough to believe that Shane and any of his asshole friends were *my* friends.

They just offered me an escape from the biggest asshole in my world.

My father.

Besides, the prospect of getting stoned had been a hell of a lot more appealing than the prospect of taking a hiding from my old man for missing a 65 – hurling's equivalent of a corner kick – during my match earlier that morning.

So, with the last twenty euro I had left from the job I had recently acquired, I jumped at the chance to escape for the night.

To escape.

To just make it all stop . . .

All hell had broken loose the following morning, when I was rumbled for my midnight venture, but I had zero regrets. I couldn't remember getting home. I had been too strung out on a fucked-up concoction of weed, Devil's Bit, and tablets to notice.

Or care.

Hell, I would do it again in a heartbeat if it meant that I was spared from the reality of my life – spared from them – for a few short hours.

Jesus, I wish I had a smoke right now . . .

"I think he is hurting her again," Tadhg croaked out, dragging me from my thoughts, when the sound of our mother's pained wailing wafted through the air, followed by feral grunting.

Oh, I know he is. "For the last time, he's not hurting her."

"Are you sure?"

No. "Yep."

"You promise?"

No. "Yep."

"Thanks for letting us stay with you, Joe."

"No problem."

"Do you want to squeeze in here with us?"

And have two thirds of you piss on top of me during the night? "No thanks."

"Are you sure you don't want to—"

"Sleep. Now."

Mood darkening, I let my thoughts wander back to Darren, as I bedded down for the night, with only my resentment to keep me company – and my hurley.

Dick.

Anyone but her

February 14th 2000

JOEY

"And then you just reconnect the wires together like this, and bob's your uncle," Tony Molloy explained on Thursday evening after school, as he passed me a pair of wire cutters.

The engine of the car he had been rewiring roared to life.

I grinned. "That's fucking mental."

He arched a greying brow. "I'm only showing you this in case of an emergency, not for a midnight joyride or any of that shite young fellas around here are up to."

"Obviously."

"Here, hand me that face-tester."

Thoroughly intrigued, I did as the older man asked, soaking in everything he taught me, and feeling beyond grateful that he had gone out on a limb for me last year – even if it meant that the role that I had been given made me Tony's glorified lackey.

Filling petrol in the garage's adjoining forecourt wasn't exactly thrilling stuff, but the chance to work on engines was something I discovered I enjoyed. More than just enjoyed, it was *exactly* the distraction I needed.

The money wasn't brilliant, at a fiver an hour, but I was too young to get a job on the books, not to mention too hot-headed to hold one down even if I was old enough.

I couldn't seem to help it. I had a problem with keeping my shit together. The rage that built up inside of me whenever I was confronted with an altercation, or an asshole determined to argue with me, was uncontrollable.

There was something inside of me that demanded I fight back, no matter how small or unimportant an argument may be.

I couldn't get ahold of it.

It was like there was a demon living just beneath the surface of my skin, one that had taken too many kicks lying down, and refused to take a single other.

Besides, the relief on my mother's face when I handed up my wages every Friday night made it all worth it.

If I could take only a tenth of the pressure off her frail shoulders, put there because of the useless bastard she married who refused to find a job, then I would gladly slog it out for a fiver an hour.

Taking all of the hours they would give me, I worked most evenings after school until around nine or ten at night, and all day on Saturday, unless I needed to take a few hours off for matches.

"So, how's school going, lad?" Tony asked, climbing to his feet. "Keeping the head down after that suspension last week, I hope?"

I wasn't a fan of school and my boss knew it.

I fucking hated it at the best of times, but when I weighed up my options, I would have lived in the place – or here – if it meant I didn't have to go home.

"I already told ya about that," I said, following Tony into the office that doubled up as a staff room. "That prick Rice was out of line."

"And you were only more than willing to put him back in his place," Tony mused. Flicking on the kettle, he gestured to the black eye I was sporting. "Keep showing up to work looking like that, and you'll scare off all the old biddies coming in for their petrol."

I shrugged.

"You know, Joe, you really need to learn how to keep your head," he continued, pouring two mugs of tea. "A hot temper like that makes you a liability, boyo. It will hold you back in life."

Or it will keep me alive just long enough to grow up and get out of this town.

"Maybe," I agreed, running my tongue over the recently healed cut on my bottom lip.

"It's already holding you back," he said, handing me one of the mugs, before diving into one of his frequent '*you have so much potential*' pep talks.

Sinking down on a chair at the table opposite him, I took a sip from my mug and tuned his voice out, making sure to nod and agree at the right cues, having heard every fucking word before, but knowing deep down inside that Tony wasn't the enemy.

Every word he spurted was a familiar one that had been echoed before.

From him.

From Nanny Murphy.

From my principal at BCS.

From my coaches and trainers.

Blah fucking blah, blah, blah . . .

"Hi, Dad," a female voice called out from the office doorway, causing Tony to pause mid-lecture, and my heart to jackknife in my chest.

My eyes landed on the familiar, leggy blonde, standing in the doorway, sporting the same uniform I had worn earlier today, and I bit back a groan.

For fuck's sake . . .

This girl.

Yeah, this girl was a pain in my hole.

"Aoife." Tony's eyes lit up. "What are you doing here?"

"I was studying at the library with Paul," his daughter replied, cheeks flushed, as she dropped her school bag on the floor, and walked towards her dad. "We have midterm exams next week. I lost track of time, and you said I wasn't to walk home in the dark." Smiling angelically at her old man, she batted her big green eyes and asked, "Any chance of spin home?"

"Lost track of time at the library?" Tony cocked a disbelieving brow. "At half-seven on Valentine's night? Do you think I came down in the last shower?"

I snorted, also finding her excuse fucking laughable.

Her green eyes narrowed in warning at me, and I shrugged.

Like I gave a shit if she got into it with her old man or not.

She should've come up with a better lie.

That one was pathetic.

"Midterm exams?" Tony looked to me. "Joey, son, you're in the same year as my twins. Did you hear anything at school about midterm exams?"

"Not a word," I replied, vaguely recalling hearing something about upcoming exams, but enjoying her discomfort too much to hand her the shovel she clearly needed to dig herself out of this hole.

"Like he'd even know," Molloy shot back with a growl. "Don't mind a word he says, Dad. Joey Lynch spends more time in the office with the principal than he does in class with—"

"You and *Paul*?" I offered.

Tony's brows rose. "Is that Paul the boyfriend?"

"More like Paul the prick," I scoffed.

"Wow, Joey." Her eyes narrowed on me once more. "I'm surprised you took your head out of your ass long enough to learn your classmates' names."

"We're on the same hurling team."

She folded her arms across her chest. "Yeah, and?"

"And that's how I know his name," I drawled, leaning back in my seat. "No heads-up-asses required. And Paul Rice *is* a prick."

Tony laughed and quickly backpedaled. "Hold up, isn't that the lad you were suspended for fighting with last week?"

"That's the one," I confirmed.

"Because you hit him for no reason," Molloy growled, quick to defend her boyfriend.

"That's what you think," I shot back.

"Ugh. Whatever," she snapped. "Can I have a spin or not, Dad? I need to get home. I've a ton of homework to get finished."

"Why didn't you get it done at the library?" I mocked, enjoying riling her up a little more than I should. "While you were doing all of that important *studying* with Paul."

"Why don't you shut your mouth?" she countered huffily. "And mind your own business."

"And more importantly, why didn't this Paul walk you home?" Tony interjected, tone serious now. "What kind of a young fella leaves his girlfriend in town on her own at night?"

"His mam collected him for training," she explained with a shrug.

Tony looked to me. "Training?"

I shook my head. "There's no hurling training tonight."

"Tai chi," she correctly hotly. "Not everything revolves around hurling."

"Tai chi?" Tony frowned. "I thought that had something to do with house decorating."

"That's *feng shui*, Dad."

I choked back a laugh.

Molloy glared at me.

"And his mother didn't give you a lift home?"

She shrugged, flustered. "I didn't ask her for one."

Her father glowered. "And he didn't ask her for you?"

"See," I drawled, giving her father a knowing look. "Prick."

"Dad," she snapped, dutifully ignoring me now. "Can I have a spin or not?"

"Not."

"What? Dad, I need to get home. I told you; I have a ton of homework."

"Sorry, love, but I have a Corolla that needs a full servicing before I close up. I'll be here another few hours at least."

"Dad."

"Daughter."

"Father!"

"Fruit of my loins."

"Fine," she huffed dramatically, reaching for her school bag. "Don't bother driving your defenseless teenage daughter home in the dark of the night. I'll take my chances and walk."

"You'll do no such thing," her father commanded. "Sit down. You can get your homework done while I'm finishing up and I'll take you home then."

"I'm not staying here until you close," she shot back, affronted at the thought. "It's only a couple of miles of a walk. Twenty minutes, tops. Besides, it's cold in here, and boring, and I need—"

"To do your homework," her father filled in for her. "Yeah, I think you've said that already. Well, you're not walking on your own."

"Well, I'm not staying," she shot back defiantly, her blonde ponytail swinging over her shoulder, as she hoisted her bag up, and headed for the door. "I'll be fine."

"Jesus Christ," Tony grumbled, shaking his head. "Joey, son, do me a favor and make sure that headstrong daughter of mine gets home in one piece. You can knock off afterwards."

"I don't need a chaperone," Molloy argued, looking horrified, but her father cut her off.

"Either he walks you home, or you wait here for me to finish up work. Your choice."

Balking, she seemed to ponder her choices before locking her eyes on mine. "Well, are you going to walk me home or not?"

For fuck's sake . . .

I was supposed to be learning how to replace the spark plugs in Danny Reilly's old Corolla, but, instead, I was walking a furious teenage girl home against her will.

How I got roped into this shit, I would never understand.

If Tony knew me, really fucking knew me, he'd quickly realize that his daughter was hell of a lot better off on her own than with me.

I was a bad bet; my mother had as good as told me so on several occasions.

With my hands in the front pocket of my hoodie, I walked alongside Aoife Molloy, listening to her rant on about sexism, differential treatment because she was a girl, the double standards of us being the same age and her father having no problem with me walking back alone, not to mention a whole host of other bullshit since we left her father at the garage.

In all honesty, her dramatic raving should be driving me nuts by now. Instead, I was mildly amused by her.

"It's a disgrace," she hissed, power walking down the footpath in her high-heeled school shoes, her bare thighs on show beneath the scrap of grey fabric she called a skirt. "He's being totally unreasonable—"

"Can I just stop you right there?" I interjected, holding a hand up.

"Yeah," she said, turning to look at me with an expectant look. "Why?"

"No reason," I replied. "I just wanted you to stop talking."

"You know, Joey, you can be such an asshole sometimes." Frustrated, she shook her head and marched on ahead of me. "*Such* an asshole."

Fine by me.

I didn't up my pace and chase her like I suspected she was used to fellas doing.

When she realized this, she swung back around to glare at me.

"You threw me under the bus tonight with the whole library thing," she burst out, looking more emotionally invested in this argument than was necessary. "You could have backed me up, or just said nothing at all. Instead, you egged my dad on, made him worry about my relationship with Paul, insinuated that I was getting up to no good with him instead of studying."

"Weren't you?" I quipped, gesturing to the purplish mark on the side of her neck – curtesy of Paul the prick's lips, no doubt.

"That's not the point," she shouted, stamping her foot. "You could've said nothing, you could've ignored me like you usually do. Instead, you tried to cause trouble for me."

I shrugged, not entirely disagreeing with her statement.

"You don't want to be here with me right now. It's obvious. I'm the very last person you want to walk home, so why bother?"

"Your father asked me to."

"Well, I'm asking you not to."

"You don't pay my wages."

"Ugh." She blew out another frustrated breath. "You are so annoying."

"And you are such a fucking princess," I shot back, unapologetically. "Pissing and moaning because your father cares enough about you to want to make sure you get home safe." I rolled my eyes. "Yeah, I can see that you're having a real hard day, Molloy."

Her feet came to a grinding halt and she swung back to face me. "Why don't you like me?"

"Why does it matter to you?"

My words stumped her and she shook her head again. "We're in the same class – have been for almost a year now, and still you act like I don't exist. I'm a nice person, okay. I have never said a bad word to you, but you avoid me like the plague. You're never nice to me at school, and I don't get it." She blew out a heavy breath. "What changed?"

"Nothing."

"Bullshit," she snapped. "You were into me on that first day, and then suddenly you weren't. So, what changed?"

My life fell apart and I realized you were my boss's daughter.

"Nothing."

"You are such a liar!" she argued, unwilling to back the hell down like I needed her to. "We hit it off and you know we did."

"It's not a crime for a fella to change his mind, Molloy," I deadpanned. "Take it on the chin and leave it alone, will ya?"

"Maybe I could if you didn't purposefully avoid me."

"I don't avoid you."

"You *constantly* avoid me," she corrected. "You only speak to me when you have to – and that's usually only when my father's around to mock and tease me. You talk to all of the other girls in our class, Joey. *All* of them. But not me. Never me."

Be glad, I thought to myself.

"You have a fella," I reminded her, the thought souring my mind. "Why would you *want* me to talk to you?"

"How about to be nice?"

"I'm not nice."

"Yes, you are."

"No, I'm not."

"Say something nice to me."

"Molloy."

"Come on," she demanded. "Do it. I dare you."

"You have nice legs," I offered flatly. "There, happy now?"

"You can be nice to the other girls in our class, but not me," she argued. "Molloy . . ."

"I've seen you be nice to Danielle Long, and Rebecca Falvey – and a ton of other girls from our year."

I gave her a pointed look that said all I needed to say about that.

"You were with *all* of them?" she demanded and then groaned. "That's disgusting."

"No more disgusting than you letting Paul Rice put his hands in your knickers last week."

Her face flushed bright pink. "Excuse me?"

"You heard me." With a concoction of fucked-up feelings swelling up inside of me, I couldn't help but taunt her. "Lace pink thong, from what I hear. How long have you been going out with him? A week now? He sure found a way into your knickers quickly enough."

"He *told* you?"

"He told everyone, Molloy."

"Who?" Her face fell and I felt like a piece of shit. "Who did he tell?"

The look of sadness in her eyes made me want to hit the prick all over again.

It had been worth the suspension.

Hearing Ricey tell half of the lads in our PE class about how Tony's daughter was so tight he could barely get a finger inside her had caused me to flip the fuck out on him in the changing rooms.

I did it for Tony because he wasn't there to do it himself.

At least, that's what I continued to tell myself.

"He's a prick, Molloy," I bit out. "Prick's talk, so word of warning: never do anything with one that you don't want his entire circle of friends knowing about."

"You don't."

"I don't want?"

"Talk."

"That's because I'm not a prick. I'm an asshole, remember?" Stepping around her, I crossed the street towards her house, not looking back to see if she was following. I could tell she was by the sound of her high heels clicking on the ground.

"So, come on, since you're so forthcoming tonight, tell me why you don't like me anymore?"

"That's a desperate question to ask a fella."

"Don't you mean an asshole? And you know I don't mean it like that."

"It's still desperate."

"Answer me anyway."

"No."

"Why not?"

"Because."

"Because? Come on, Joey. Please."

"We're not compatible," I said, blowing out a frustrated breath.

"To have a conversation together?"

"To have anything together."

"So, what you're basically saying is that you think you're too good to be my friend?" She planted her hands on her hips. "To hang out or be seen with me?"

The opposite.

"You asked me a question," I told her, opening her front gate and gestured for her to go inside. "I answered you. Take it whatever way you like."

"That's not good enough."

"I don't care," I replied, hand on the gate. "Now, I walked you home, safe and sound, with plenty of time to get your precious homework done. You're welcome."

She made no move to go inside, choosing to stand under the street lamp and glare at me, while I continued to hold the gate open for her like a tool.

"It's because of my dad, isn't it?" she pressed, ponytail blowing in the night breeze. "Is that why you changed your mind? Why you don't even want to be friends with me? Did he say something?"

"Go inside, Molloy."

"Don't tell me what to do, Joey."

"Fine. Suit yourself." Shaking my head, I let go of the gate, and turned to walk away. "What do I care?"

"You know what? I think you *do* care," she called after me. "In fact, I think you do like me. You like me and that's why you act how you do. That's why you riled my father up about Paul tonight. I'm right, aren't I? You like me."

Of course I fucking liked her.

She was the first thing my eyes had landed on when I walked through the entrance of Ballylaggin Community School last September, and the only face I consistently sought out since.

"*. . . She's a good girl, is our Aoife," Tony said, dark eyes watching me warily. His agitation had been slowly rising since I arrived at work from my first day at secondary school and mentioned that his daughter and I had been assigned to the same class. "She's a bit on the wild side, but what young one isn't these days? She's not backwards in coming forwards, either, but she's a good girl at heart. And innocent, too . . . "*

"*I hear you, Tony," I quickly intercepted, needing this job more than I needed to get myself caught up in anymore unnecessary drama. Besides, I had responsibilities at home, shit that came before anything else. Even pretty blondes with long, long legs. "I don't have any intentions of going near your daughter."*

"*Good lad yourself," came his relieved reply. "It's not that I don't like ya, boyo, you know I do. It's just that I don't want the two of you going out together and complicating things at work. Especially when she's . . . "*

Too good for the likes of you.

"*Don't worry," I interrupted. "I know the way the land lies. I won't go there. You have nothing to worry about when it comes to me."*

I knew Tony was fond of me. I was a good worker, just not good enough for his daughter . . .

"*Good man,*" he said with a chuckle. "*But if you could keep an eye on her for me, make sure she's not being taken advantage of, or losing the run of herself, I'd owe you one.*"

"*Will do . . .*"

"You're delusional, Molloy."

"And you're in denial, Lynch." Planting her hands on her hips, she gave me look of pure frustration. "I waited for you; you know."

I arched a brow. "You waited for me."

"Uh-huh." She nodded and blew a strand of hair out of her face. "I waited for *months* for you to get your shit together and ask me out." She looked me right in the eye when she said, "Paul wasn't my first choice, you know."

"Meaning?"

"Oh, I'm *sorry,*" she drawled sarcastically. "I wasn't aware that you needed me to write it down for you, asshole."

Well shit.

The truth was, if Tony wasn't her father, and I didn't have so much riding on my job, then she wouldn't have had to wait for shit. She sure as hell she wouldn't be fucking around with that pretentious prick, Paul Rice, that was for sure.

But I had responsibilities that she could never understand. I had a sister to protect, brothers to feed, and a mother to keep me up late into the night worrying about. I didn't have the luxury of time to piss away like Paul had; nor had I the credentials, or reputation, any father would want in a lad for his daughter.

I didn't blame Tony for wanting me to steer clear of his baby girl.

I would feel the same way about me, too.

"Well, it looks like you got bored of waiting," I heard myself say, mentally kicking myself for not ending the conversation and walking away like I *knew* I should. "You've managed to shack yourself up with a Garda's son from a nice side of town, so I reckon it's safe to say that you came out on top, Molloy."

"Yeah." She blew out a frustrated breath. "It looks like I did, huh?"

I didn't know what to say to that.

To her.

Fuck me.

"Go on inside and finish your homework like the good little girl you are," I finally decided on, ignoring the weird ache in my chest, as I turned to walk away. "Oh, and don't forget to wash the smell of Paul the prick off ya."

"Ha. I *knew* it." Reaching out, she grabbed my hand and dragged me back to her. "I *knew* you liked me."

"Hey!" Snatching my hand away from hers, I shoved it back in the front pocket of my hoodie, feeling unnecessarily rattled by her touch. "Don't do that again."

Confusion filled her eyes. "Don't do what?"

"Touch me."

"Why not?"

"Because."

"Because?"

"Because I don't like you."

"Liar."

"How about because I don't know where those hands have been."

Her eyes narrowed. "Excuse me?"

Dick move.

Take it back.

Take it back, asshole.

"Hey." I shrugged, unwilling to listen to common sense. "For all I know, you could've been pulling on your saint of a boyfriend with those hands."

"You did *not* just say that to me."

Yeah, I did, and the fact that she was standing here challenging me meant that I couldn't take it back.

Jesus, I had problems.

Like a defiant child, Molloy reached up and patted my chest, trailing her hands up my neck to my face. "Here, asshole, have some germs."

Pushing my hood down, she ruffled my hair before trailing her hands down my chest and into the front pocket of my hoodie. "Mm, mm, mm," she taunted, before entwining her fingers with mine. "Feels nice, huh?"

"You're such a brat," I muttered, shaking my head, as I repressed the urge to shiver from the wonderful fucking feeling of having her warm skin on mine.

"And you're such a tool," she came right back with, unwilling to give an inch. "Now, are you going to walk me inside, or do I have to tell my dad that you abandoned me in the dark?"

My mouth fell open in disgust. "I walked you to your *gate*."

"My gate is not my door." She arched a brow in challenge. "Anything could happen to me."

"*Sure* it could." I rolled my eyes. "In the ten seconds it will take you to walk inside?"

When she made no move to back down, I relented with a frustrated sigh.

"Fine." Shaking my head, I followed her into her garden. "I'll walk you to your fucking door."

"So chivalrous," she teased, as she grinned victoriously up at me. "And *sweet*."

"I'm not sweet."

"And gentlemanly."

"I'm not that, either – and let go of my hands."

Cackling evilly to herself, Molloy turned the handle of the front door and pushed it inwards. "You coming in?"

Was she mental?

"No, Molloy," I deadpanned. "I'm not coming in."

"You sure?" Leaning against the door, she waggled her brows and said, "There's a full box of Coco Pops in the kitchen with my name on, that I'm willing to share with you."

"I'm not coming . . ." my words broke off when my brain registered what she had said. "Coco Pops?"

She nodded. "The good kind."

Well shit.

Rubbing the back of my neck, I heard myself ask, "Is there milk in the fridge?"

"Always."

My stomach rumbled loudly at the concept of getting fed tonight because, let's face it, the odds of finding anything in the kitchen on a Monday night at my house weren't in my favor.

"This doesn't mean we're friends," I warned, as I took an uncertain step inside her front hall. "This changes nothing, Molloy."

Hit me with those green eyes

February 14th 2000

AOIFE

Okay, so inviting a boy who *wasn't* my recently acquired boyfriend into my house on Valentine's night might not have been my brightest idea, but in my defense, sharing a box of Coco Pops with Joey Lynch wasn't exactly the crime of the century.

It was a harmless, platonic, random act of kindness/show of gratitude to the boy who had walked me home in the dark.

See, I could be chivalrous, too.

"Pull up a chair," I instructed, as I strode into the kitchen ahead of him. "I'll grab the bowls."

Looking wary and mistrustful, my classmate shuffled towards the kitchen table and slowly pulled out a chair. "I mean it, Molloy. This doesn't mean we're friends."

"Yeah, yeah," I drawled, humored by his pathetic attempt to shield himself from my irresistible charm. "Whatever you say, Joey Lynch."

Setting to work, I grabbed bowls, spoons, milk from the fridge, and a box of cereal from the cupboard before setting them down on the table in front of him. "Dig in."

He didn't move an inch.

"Tea?" I offered then.

Joey looked at me like I had grown an extra head. "*Tea*?"

"Tea," I confirmed, fighting back at smile at his discomfort. "It's something us regular folk drink from time to time."

"I know what tea is," he muttered, shaking his head. "And no, I'm, uh, I'm not thirsty."

Realizing that he had no intention of touching anything on the table until I joined him, even though he hadn't stopped eyeing the cereal box since I placed it in front of him, I set the kettle down and moved for the table, taking the seat opposite his.

"Seriously, Joe," I encouraged, pouring two bowls of chocolatey goodness, and then filling both bowls to the top with milk. "Tuck in."

With a deep frown set on his face, he steered the overflowing bowl towards him, and reached for a spoon. "Thanks."

"You're welcome," I replied around a spoonful of cereal, feeling a swell of something strange in the pit of my stomach, as I watched him wolf down his bowl of cereal like he hadn't eaten in days. "Mam's out with a few of the girls tonight, and I don't cook, so it's the best I can come up with."

"You don't cook?"

"No, do you?"

Joey shrugged. "A bit."

My brows shot up. "What can you cook?"

Another shrug. "Depends."

"Depends?" I pressed, as I reached across the table and refilled his empty bowl. "On what?"

"Thanks," he replied, dutifully waiting for me to remove the box before his wolfing resumed. "It depends on what's in the cupboard."

"Well, I know you're good at home economics," I decided to add, having sat in a classroom with him for the past few months. "The dishes you prepare are always the teacher's favorite."

"Only because it's edible," he snorted, keeping his head bowed as he ate. "I've had a lot of practice."

"With your mam?" I asked, thoroughly intrigued by this boy, as I rested my elbow on the table and watched him. "Did she do a lot of cooking with you growing up?"

"Something like that," he replied, reaching for the cereal box. "Do, ah, do you mind if I . . ."

"Go for it."

"So, where's your brother?"

"Knowing Kev, he's probably inhaling the books in his room."

"He's a fair bit of a brainbox, isn't he?"

"Just a tad," I reluctantly conceded, grimacing when I thought about my twin and his superior academic brilliance. "He's my mother's golden boy."

"Hm." Joey nodded in understanding. "I know that feeling."

"What?" I teased. "You're telling me that you're not the pet at home?"

He arched a brow. "More like the pest."

I laughed. "I don't believe that for a second, mister hotshot hurler."

He smirked. "You'd be surprised, Molloy."

"So, how many siblings do you have?"

"Four," he muttered before quickly correcting himself and saying, "three."

"Four, three?" I laughed. "Which is it?"

"I *had* four, I *have* three," he replied in a flat tone.

"Oh my god," I croaked out, feeling a pang of sympathy hit me. "Did one of your siblings pass away?"

"He's still breathing," Joey deadpanned. "But he's dead to me."

Well crap . . .

"Okay," I replied, watching him warily. "Tell me about the others."

Joey shrugged. "Two brothers, one sister."

"How old?"

"Ten, six, and almost four."

"You're the eldest?"

"I am now."

Okay . . .

"What's it like having younger siblings?" I heard myself ask. "It's only me and Kev here."

"It's exhausting."

"I can imagine."

He looked up at me through hooded lashes. "You have no idea."

"Which one's your favorite?"

He gave me a hard look. "You don't pick favorites, Molloy."

"Bullshit," I laughed. "Everyone has a favorite. That doesn't mean that you love any of them more or less than the other. It only means that you're more compatible with one and prefer their company."

He thought about it for a long moment before mumbling, "I suppose I'm closest to Shannon."

"Your sister?"

He nodded.

"Is she the one who's ten?"

Another nod. "She'll be eleven next month."

"She's the next one in line after you, right?"

Another nod.

"So, the dead brother must be the oldest?"

He glared at me. "Don't push it."

"Oh, don't get all cranky with me."

"Stop asking so many questions and I won't."

"Fine." I smiled sweetly back at him, knowing that a person caught more flies with honey, and said, "You have nice eyes."

"Nice eyes."

"Uh-huh." Reaching for the cereal box, I refilled his bowl and then added some more to mine. "You said stop asking questions, so I'm paying you a compliment instead."

"Why?"

"Why not?"

"Why, though?"

"Because it's nice to be nice, Joey."

"You are a really weird fucking girl," he grumbled, looking thrown off-kilter, before begrudgingly adding, "With nice legs."

I grinned back at him. "*Thank* you."

He eyed me in disbelief. "You're welcome."

"What about the rest of your family?"

"What about them?"

"Who are you closest to?"

"Myself."

"Oh come on." I rolled my eyes. "You can't say yourself."

"Why not? It's true."

"Well, do you have a secret rich aunt, or some cool cousin you love hanging out with at family functions?"

"No."

"Come on, Joe." I smiled. "Humor me. There has to be someone."

He stared at me for a long time before releasing a breath. "I have a great-grandfather."

"Yeah?"

He nodded warily.

"What's his name?"

"Anthony."

"Same as my dad." I beamed. "Is he your mother's father or your—"

"My mother's."

"And is he nice?"

Another slow nod. "I, ah, don't see him much anymore, but I spent a lot of time with him growing up."

"Why don't you see him much anymore?"

"Shit happened in the family." He shrugged. "And I got busy with work and school and hurling."

This was the longest I had managed to get Joey Lynch to stay and talk to me since we met at the start of the school year, and I was willing to do just about anything to keep him in my kitchen – and keep him talking.

To say that I felt drawn to him would be a major understatement.

I felt it that very first day of first year – that epic wave of familiarity, lust, and camaraderie – when our eyes locked, and I felt it now.

There was something about this boy that I found impossible to ignore, and I knew he felt it, too.

Joey could deny it until the cows came home, and throw up all the walls he wanted, but he wasn't fooling me with his blasé bullshit indifference.

The arctic reception I received from him on the second day of first year – and every day since – had nothing to do with him not liking me and everything to do with the fact that he worked with my father and didn't want to piss him off.

As the school year unfolded, I had watched as Joey made his way through the girls at school like they were going out of fashion.

Danielle Long.

Amy O Donovan.

Samantha McGuinness.

Laura Callaghan.

Nicole O Leary.

Denise Scully.

Saoirse Dooley.

Neasa McCarthy.

Neasa *Murphy*.

The list went on and on – a*nd it didn't include me.*

He never *once* flirted or made a pass at me after that first day, and it pissed me the hell off.

In no way was I one of those self-absorbed or conceited teenage girls, but I had enough confidence and wherewithal to know that I was a damn good catch.

Annoyed at myself for wasting almost six months of my life waiting around for Joey to get his shit together and ask me out, I'd accepted our fellow classmate's offer.

Once again, I found myself annoyed, but this time, my anger was projected towards my shitty sense of judgment.

I had never been short of offers from the lads since starting at BCS but had agreed to go out with Paul because he was comfortable to be around and a relatively safe bet.

Joey was thinner than Paul – he was taller, too. He had muscle, that I could vouch for, having seem him shirtless many times after PE, but he was seriously lean.

Like a runner.

Or someone hungry . . .

But I knew with Paul I wouldn't get my heart broken.

And while my heart certainly wasn't broken, my pride was definitely wounded.

Knowing that his friends knew what we got up to, knowing that *Joey* knew, only made the humiliation that much harder to swallow.

"You look pissed," Joey noted, watching me from across the table with those sharp green eyes.

"I am."

"I can leave."

"No, it's not you," I replied. "I'm pissed with Paul for talking about me."

"Oh." Setting his spoon in his empty bowl, Joey leaned back in his chair and gave me a hard look. "Well, if it's any consolation, he won't be talking about you again."

"Because you set him straight, right?" I joked.

Joey didn't laugh.

"Oh my god." Awareness crashed down on me. "You set him straight, didn't you?" I whispered, feeling my heart rate spike, as I thought back to their fight the other day. "That's why you hit him, isn't it?"

"Someone had to."

"And that someone was you, right?"

He shrugged.

My heart leapt. "Joe . . . "

"Thanks for the food, Molloy." He pushed his chair back and stood up. "I should be going."

"No." Disappointment soared to life inside of me. "You don't have to go yet."

"Yeah, I do." Grabbing his bowl and spoon, he walked over to my sink and quickly rinsed them both off before setting them on the draining board.

Meticulous, he walked back to the table with a dishcloth in hand and wiped down where he had eaten. Tossing the cloth in the sink once he was finished tidying up, he moved for the front door. "Again, thanks for the food."

"No problem," I replied, holding the door open for him.

He pulled his hood up, concealing his face, and stepped into the night. "I'll be seeing ya, Molloy."

"Yeah, Joey Lynch." I blew out a shaky breath. "You will."

You are just like him

February 25th 2000

JOEY

My youngest memories began around the time of my third birthday. I couldn't say for sure if the events that occurred before that day had been particularly good because all I seemed to remember was the bad.

And right now, at ten o clock on a Friday night, after breaking up another shitstorm between my parents, all I could remember was the bad.

Aching in places I didn't know existed, I couldn't stop my brain from rehashing some of the more disturbing memories from my childhood . . .

"You can cry, Joey," Mam whispered, fingers curling around my skinny arm. Her touch was soft and warm and the feel of her made something twist inside of my stomach. "It's okay to feel, baby."

Nope.

She was wrong.

Again.

Furious with her and the whole fucking world, I swallowed my pain, pushed my feelings to the back of my mind, and concentrated on my job – a job I was fairly certain no other boy in my school was doing for their mam.

Rocking baby Ollie in my arms, I held the bottle to his lips, watching carefully for any sign of wind just like Mam showed me to do.

She couldn't do it herself.

Nope, of course she couldn't.

Postpartum hemorrhage, my hole.

More like postpartum battery.

He beat her the other night because the baby wouldn't stop crying.

It was the closest I'd seen her come to dying in a long time.

The image was still at the forefront of my mind.

The blood.

The wailing.

The feeling of hopelessness.

"Where are the nappies?" I asked when the cranky little shit was finally finished guzzling the four-ounce bottle I'd made for him. "He smells."

"I can do it," Mam started to say as she pulled herself into a sitting position.

"Stay down," I ordered, shivering at the memory of what I'd seen come out of her body just a few short days ago. "I can look after him."

Eyeing the nappy bag in the corner of her room, I balanced my baby brother in my arms and reached for it.

"Come on, ya little fatty," I muttered, lowering him back onto her bed and gently pulling his wriggling body out of his onesie. "Let's get this over with."

He stared up at me, all big eyes and cuteness, and I frowned.

"Don't look at me like that," I warned. *Like I can keep you safe.* "And don't piss on me either."

"You'll make a great father in years to come," Mam said with a tremble in her voice.

"I'd rather die," was all I replied . . .

"Joey."

I wished she would stop talking to me.

Her voice made it hurt.

All of it.

"Joey, please."

Reluctantly, I forced myself to look at her, feeling my heart shrivel up and die in my chest when my gaze took in the sight of my mother.

She was ruined.

Again.

She usually hid it well, but not today. Like a fresh coat of paint on the wall, my father had layered her in a fresh coat of blueish-green bruises.

I'd never seen anything like it, and that wasn't an understatement.

She looked like a corpse.

Guilt churned inside of me, and I honestly wanted to die.

What could I say to her?

How could I form the words to tell her just how sorry and mad I was all in the one breath?

I wanted to hold her and shake her all at once.

As my lungs expelled the air I'd been holding in, I let every harmful feeling and thought of tonight's events seep inside my head, hoping that they could somehow spark the flame of self-preservation inside of me.

Hoping my thoughts could fuel my anger and my anger could help me flip the switch and *not* care anymore.

Because caring was killing me, and I honestly didn't think I could hold on much longer.

"What do you want from me, Mam?" I heard myself ask, tone hoarse, heart cut to shreds.

Her blue eyes widened. "Wh-what do you mean?"

"I mean what do you want?" I snapped, running a hand through my hair. "You call me out of bed to fight him off you? I did. To barricade the door? I've done that, too. What do you want from me now, Mam? What do you want me to do?"

"He's gone this time," she whispered. "He won't be back. I p-promise."

"You don't believe that any more than I do," I replied, too weary to fight with her. It had taken everything in me to go toe-to-toe with her asshole husband earlier. I had nothing left in the tank, not even my hatred to chug on. "He'll be back, and he'll be worse the next time."

"Joey . . ."

"He's going to *kill* you, Mam," I choked out. "Don't you get that? Can't you hear me? You're going to die in this house. If you don't get away from him, you're going to die here. I can feel it in my bones . . . "my voice cracked, and I choked back a sob, unwilling to shed tears. "Don't you love yourself? Don't you love me?"

"Of course I do," she sobbed softly, reaching across the table to place her small hand on my torn knuckles. "I love my children so much."

'I love my children' not *'I love you, Joey'*.

Typical.

She might think that she loved all of her children, but she certainly didn't, or couldn't, love me.

Darren was her firstborn and favorite, Ollie was her sweet and affectionate baby, Tadhg was her mischievous rogue, and Shannon was her only daughter.

That left me.

The spare.

Blinking back the wet in my eyes, I glared at her small hand as she attempted to comfort me with minimal contact. "Why?"

"Why what?"

Why don't you love me?

Inclining my head, I nodded towards the wedding band on the fourth finger on her left hand, and asked instead, "Why do you keep wearing that thing?"

Jerking her hand back, Mam cradled it to her chest and whispered, "Because that's what I'm supposed to do."

Temper rising, I glowered back at her. "And he's supposed to *not* kick the living shit out you, or did ye not have that particular promise in your wedding vows?"

"Don't, Joey."

"Don't what?" I sneered. "Tell you the truth?"

"I'm too tired to fight with you."

"And I'm too tired to clean up any more of your messes," I hissed. "You keep us here in this fucking house of pain. It's your choice, and you choose *him* every single time. Darren was right to get the fuck out of this place."

Flinching as if I had struck her, Mam slowly rose from the table, looking like she was seconds away from collapsing.

Against my will, I felt myself rise, feet moving straight for her. "Here," I said, gently reaching around her back. "I'll help you upstairs . . . "

"Don't!" Jerking away from my touch like it had burned her, she dragged in several shaky breaths. "Please d-don't."

Bewildered, I stood there with my palms up, unsure of what the fuck I had done to cause this kind of a reaction from my own mother.

"Mam," I placated in as gentle tone as I could muster. "It's me. Joey. I'm not going to hurt you. You know this."

"I know exactly who you are," she whispered, trembling.

"What does that mean?" I ran a hand through my hair, feeling my whole body vibrate with a fucked-up mixture of desperation and resentment. "Look," I said, trying to soothe her. "I know I'm not as diplomatic as Darren was, okay. I know he was the one you could talk to about shit like that, and I'm sorry for throwing him leaving in your face, but I'm—"

"Don't," she choked out, tears falling freely down her cheeks. "Don't talk about Darren. You are *nothing* like Darren!"

"Because I'm still *here*?" I hissed, feeling my resentment overtake my despair. "Newsflash, your precious fucking Darren is gone. The saint himself walked away. He left us. But I'm still here, Mam. I'm right fucking *here*."

"I know you're here," she cried. "Shouting and ordering and laying down the law just like—" Clamping her mouth shut, she shook her head. "Never mind."

"Just like what?" I pressed in confusion, watching as she slowly walked towards the kitchen door. "I'm just like what, Mam?"

"It doesn't matter."

"It does. Tell me what you meant. I'm just like what, Mam?" Shaking from head to toe, I strangled out, "Him? Is that what you were going to say? I remind you of him?"

Please say no.

Please say no.

Please say no.

"Yes," she confirmed with a pained expression on her face. "You remind me of your father." Shuddering, she clenched her eyes shut as a tear fell from her cheek. "I know it's not your fault, I know, okay, but you just remind me so much of him. More and more each day."

"In what way?" I choked out, chest heaving. "In looks? Because if it's in looks then that's not my fault. I can't help who I look like, but I am nothing like that man in any other way."

"You are," she said before leaving the room. "In every way."

And with those words, my mother cut me deeper and more viciously than my father ever had.

Ever could.

And that moment, I knew deep in my bones, was the beginning of the end for me.

The switch I had been so desperate not to flip these past few years had finally tripped.

And I felt nothing.

With a trembling hand, I reached into the pocket of my sweats, and retrieved my phone.

Dialing the familiar number, the one I'd been trying to avoid, I pressed the call button and held the phone to my ear.

He answered on the third ring. "Well, well, well, if it isn't my favorite little kid."

"I'm not a kid," I bit out, chest heaving. "I need something."

Shane chuckled down the line. "I thought you were on the straight and narrow these days, kid. Isn't that what you told me after the last time?"

Clenching my eyes shut, I ran a hand through my hand and exhaled. "Yeah, well, there's been a change of plan."

"Meet me at the green over at Casement Avenue in half an hour."

I sagged in relief. "I'll be there."

"And kid?" he added in a warning tone. "No more freebies."

Now you know why

February 25th 2000

AOIFE

"I don't get it," Paul said down the line on Friday night, tone impatient. "I told you that I wouldn't do it again. Why can't you let it go and meet up with me?"

"Because the last time I met up with you, you told people about our private business," I shot back, rolling my eyes at his new ground-breaking level of stupid. "I'm still mad at you. You broke my trust. And if I can't trust you, then I can't be with you—"

"You can! You *can* trust me," he urged, quickly changing his tune from hard to groveling. "I'm sorry, babe. I am. It will never happen again."

"No," I agreed wholeheartedly, only half-mad because the truth was I only half-cared. "It won't happen again, because your hand will never get that close to my knickers again, Paul Rice."

"But I love you."

"Oh my god." I rolled my eyes to the heavens. "Get a handle on yourself. We've only been going out for a few weeks."

There was a long pause before the sound of soft laughter filled my ear. "Too far?"

"Just a tad," I shot back, grinning. "*I love you*," I mimicked his earlier declaration. "You big sap. What if I was one of those girls who actually believe the crap boys tell them?"

"Then I might be one step closer to getting my hand back in your knickers?" he asked hopefully.

"Not so much as your pinky finger will get anywhere near my knickers again."

He laughed down the line before saying, "Listen, there's an underage disco at the GAA pavilion tomorrow night. Come with me. Let me make it up to you."

"So, you want to make up for being a sleaze-bag to me by taking me to a sleezy underage disco, where girls line the walls for boys to grope them?" I arched a brow. "Gee, that is so tempting, but no thanks."

"You're really going to make me suffer, aren't you?"

"Yes," I wholeheartedly agreed. "Yes, I am."

"You liked the necklace I bought you, didn't you?"

"It was okay," I mused, reaching up to thumb the shiny stud around my neck. "But buying me presents won't win me over, Paul."

He sighed down the line. "Aoife."

"Now off you go, I'm busy."

"Doing what?"

"People-watching."

"You're out?" His tone was curious and laced with jealousy. "With who?"

"My other boyfriend," I countered, dangling my legs, from my perch on my front garden wall. "Didn't I mention him before? He's *very* trustworthy."

"Not funny."

"It was a joke."

"Who are you with, Aoife?"

"Nobody," I laughed. "Night, Paul."

"No, wait, who are you really with—"

Hanging up, I slid my phone back into my dressing gown pocket and sighed as a familiar wave of strange frustration settled over me.

It had been almost two weeks since Joey Lynch dropped the pink-lace-thong bomb on me, and I wasn't really angry with Paul anymore.

I wasn't even that irritated about the whole debacle to begin with.

Sure, I was far from happy with him for discussing me with his buddies, but I knew enough about lads my age to know that was what they did.

They talked shit.

A lot of it.

My best friend, Casey, thought I should be raging about what Paul did, and maybe she was right, but I didn't seem to care enough about it – or my relationship – to wrangle up the necessary feelings.

Besides, being with Paul was nice. He was good-looking, clever, and, for the most part, we had a lot of fun together.

Still, though, I couldn't help but feel restless.

For what, I couldn't fathom.

Yes, you can, you little liar . . .

"What are you doing out here, Aoif?" Katie Wilmot, my next-door neighbor, asked, dragging me from my daydream.

Friends since childhood, our paths had changed course last year when I left her behind in primary school for BCS. Next year, she would be pushing the bar out further by heading off to Tommen, the private school outside of Ballylaggin, but living next door to each other meant that our friendship would remain intact.

Hoisting her small frame onto my garden wall beside me, she slipped her arm through mine and rested her head on my shoulder. "It's freezing out here."

"Yeah, I know." I let out a heavy sigh and rested my cheek on her red curls. "I'm just people watching."

"You mean you're *boy* watching," Katie corrected with a smirk.

Not bothering to deny something we both knew was true, I turned my attention back to the commotion occurring across the road from our row of houses.

It was half past eleven on Friday night and the Gardaí were making an arrest – which was nothing new for this area of town.

Lately, they had been cracking down on underage drinking, and had scored a coup for themselves in the form of a gang of teenage boys.

I knew them all.

Some were from my street, more were from my school, and then there was *him.*

"Hey, isn't that the lad who works with your dad?" she asked, voicing my thoughts aloud, as we watched one of the male Gardaí pin Joey Lynch to the side of the paddy wagon.

Instead of keeping his mouth shut like the others, Joey laughed and taunted the Garda, who was roughly patting him down.

Dressed in his usual attire, an oversized navy hoodie that concealed his blond hair, he continued to talk back to the Garda, goading him into losing his cool.

"Joey Lynch," I replied with a heavy sigh. "And yep. It sure is."

Snatching the cigarette that was balancing between Joey's lips, the Garda tossed it on the ground before stamping on it.

The move earned him a slew of verbal abuse from my classmate.

"What an idiot," I grumbled with a shake of my head, feeling sourly disappointed in his behavior, mostly because I knew he could do better.

Never mind do better, he *was* better, dammit.

I thought that sharing a box of cereal with him two weeks ago had somehow melted those arctic walls erected around him, but I was sorely mistaken.

He had shown up to school the following day more closed off than ever, sporting one hell of a nasty shiner, and an even nastier attitude to match it.

Joey never mentioned it to his friends either, something I knew for sure because Paul would have taken leave of his senses, had he gotten wind of my *cereal* encounter with our classmate.

"He's a walking red flag," Katie agreed, before adding, "Isn't he a little young to be hanging out with Shane Holland? Isn't Shane like seventeen—"

"Shane's eighteen," I corrected, glaring at the biggest scumbag in Ballylaggin.

Shane was bad news, and everyone knew it. He was in sixth year at BCS and the worst kind of wrong to be knocking around with.

It was common knowledge around here that he was a dealer, and while he might be small time, his brothers were not. Apparently, the older Holland brothers were in deep with some of the big-time dealers from the city.

Joey was only in first year.

If he was hanging around with Shane, then he was playing with fire.

It was a bad move.

A really bad move.

I watched the Gardaí shove three of the older boys into the back of the paddy wagon and released a sigh of relief when they *didn't* take Joey – his young age, no doubt, the deciding factor.

"Why do you think he does it?" I asked, verbalizing aloud the question I'd been asking myself since I first laid eyes on him.

Tonight wasn't the first time I'd seen the boy get collar-boned by the authorities.

It happened frequently.

"Why do you think he self-destructs like that?"

Self-destruction. It was the only way I could describe his reckless behavior.

"Who?" Katie asked. "Joey?"

"Yeah," I replied, eyes trained on the Garda van, as it drove past my house.

"Because he's a teenage boy?" Katie offered with a shrug.

"Yeah, but it has to be more than that," I replied, my gaze returning to my classmate, who was staring after the van with a look of frustration etched on his face. "You just saw how he reacted with the Garda back there, Katie. It was almost as if he *wanted* them to take him away."

"What?" my neighbor laughed. "That's crazy talk. Nobody wants to be taken away by the Gards."

"Most don't," I whispered. *But he does.*

"I don't know, Aoif," she said, worrying her lip. "He seems like kind of a bad guy to me."

I shook my head. "He's not a bad guy."

"How can you be so sure?"

No clue. "I just am."

"How?"

"Okay, so here's the deal." I heard myself blurt. "I know he's a walking disaster, okay? I know he takes drugs and gets into fights, hangs out with all the wrong people, and can be a real dickhead like we've just witnessed."

"But?" Katie interjected with a teasing smile.

"Just *look* at him, Katie." Sighing heavily, I threw a hand up and gestured towards him. "Take a good look."

"Yeah," she agreed quietly. "He's sort of beautiful."

"More than sort of," I corrected with a shiver. "But it's more than that." Chewing on my bottom lip, I tried to find the words to explain my feelings. "There's just something about him that intrigues me. I don't know what it is, but from the first day I saw him, I was just, sort of . . . curious?"

"Of course you are," Katie laughed. "It's the age-old trope. There's always a reason why the good girl lusts after the chemically dependent bad boy."

I smirked. "Funny."

"Well, intriguing or not, messing around with a guy like that is a recipe for disaster," she added. "Seriously, Aoif, he looks dangerous. You should steer clear of him if you don't want to end up getting hurt."

And just like that, his head turned in our direction; green eyes meeting mine.

And just like every time I felt his eyes on me, my heart, the traitorous bitch, thundered violently in my chest.

He didn't look happy to see me.

He never did.

He stood on the corner of my street, unmoving, eyes never leaving mine.

Nostrils flaring, he continued to stare at me boldly.

With what I knew *wasn't* a cigarette now balancing between his lips, he tilted his head to one side eyes glazed over, but still sharp and full of mistrust. "You got a staring problem, Molloy?"

Okay, so we were back to throwing insults.

I arched a brow. "No worse than your attitude problem."

His brows narrowed. "Enjoying the show?"

"More like a shitshow," I taunted back. "And hey, looks like you snagged yourself one of the leading roles. Congrats. Stellar performance."

"What are you *doing*, Aoife?" Katie whisper-hissed, digging me in the ribs with her skinny elbow. "Don't *talk* to him. I thought we established that he's bad news – oh great, he's coming over."

I knew he was trouble, or maybe just troubled.

Either way, I knew he wasn't going to be anyone's knight in shining armor.

Casey always joked that Joey Lynch would never reach his twenty-fifth birthday. His latest antics only stacked the odds even further against him. It should have been a warning enough. And still, something about the boy made me want to jump off the ledge.

With my stomach doing somersaults, I watched as Joey crossed the road, closing the space between us.

His lips were puffy and swollen. Whether that was a natural attribute or from constantly fighting, I couldn't tell, but those lips were almost too pretty to belong to a boy.

And so damn tempting . . .

"You're out late," he said, coming to stand in front of me. Because of my height advantage from sitting on the wall, he had to look up at me, and when he did, I swear I felt the air whoosh from my lungs.

Not because he was insanely sexy – something he very much was – but because the left side of his face was a dark shade of purple, with his left eye swollen almost entirely shut.

"Your face," Katie gasped, voicing my thoughts aloud. "What happened to you?" Her eyes drifted to his hand. "Oh my god, are you smoking a—"

"I asked too many questions," he interrupted, giving my friend a menacingly cold glare. "Do you do that, too?"

I could feel Katie wilt beside me.

"No," she croaked out. "It's just that the Gards are around and I don't want to be seen with . . . drugs."

"Drugs?" Joey stared at her like she had two heads. "It's a joint, not a line. Relax, will ya?"

"Hey." I narrowed my eyes in warning. "Don't be a dick."

"I'm going to go inside now," Katie whispered, clearly unnerved by his words, as she hopped down and practically legged it towards her front door. "Night, Aoif."

"Was that necessary?" I asked when my friend had hurried inside. "You scared her off."

He shrugged noncommittally and steered the conversation towards my attire. "Nice housecoat, grandma."

"Nice face, Rocky," I shot back, tightening the knot on my robe.

A faint trace of a smile teased his lips. "Shouldn't you be inside catching up on all of your soaps?"

"Nah," I replied breezily. "Nothing on Fair City could ever be as entertaining as your earlier spectacle."

"Happy to oblige."

"So, what are you doing hanging around with Shane Holland and the rest of those dopes?"

"What's it to you?"

I shrugged. "Call me curious."

"You know what happened to the curious kitty," he replied coolly, giving me his best mind-your-own-business glower.

"Don't even bother with those scare tactics," I countered, feeling a flash of heat below my navel. "I'm not my friend. I don't scare easily."

"Good for you," Joey muttered. Taking one final drag from his smoke, he exhaled a cloudy puff of sickly-sweet smelling smoke before tossing the butt away. Shoving his hands into his front pocket, he retreated a few steps. "Don't tell your father about tonight."

"Fine," I agreed, jumping down from the wall, partially because my ass was numb from the cold concrete, but mostly because I wanted to stop him from leaving. "What are you going to do for me in return?"

Pausing, he turned back to face me. "What do you want?"

Your attention, I thought to myself, as I closed the space between us, only stopping when I was standing right in front of him.

He was a lot taller than me now that I had lost my wall advantage.

"I'm not sure yet."

Tilting his head to one side, Joey stared down at me for the longest time.

Mistrust, wariness, and reluctant curiosity were all emotions evident on his face when he asked, "What are you doing, Molloy?"

I wasn't one hundred percent sure.

On the one hand, I had a boyfriend, who, aside from suffering from the rare case of loose lips, treated me well enough. But on the other hand, I found myself drawn to this boy much more than was good for me.

I had felt it, the weird invisible pull, the very first day he walked into my world, and it hadn't let up since.

"My friend thinks you're dangerous," I told him with a smile. "She thinks I need to steer clear of you." Tilting my head to one side, I added, "She's thinks that messing around with boys like you will get a girl like me hurt."

"Wise friend," he replied coolly. "You should listen to her."

"That's the thing about me, Joe," I pushed back and said, "I don't like being told what to do."

I watched him watch me, his gaze trailing down my body.

When his eyes locked on mine, I swear I saw something shift inside of him. "Then I guess we have something in common after all."

"Yeah," I blew out a shaky breath. "I guess we do."

With a dark look etched on his beautifully bruised face, he took a step towards me, and I desperately attempted to feign nonchalance as a shiver racked through me. "But that still doesn't make us friends."

"I get it," I replied, breath hitching in my throat, as I continued to poke the bear. "It's too hard for you to be friends with someone when you want them as badly as you want me."

"Is that so?" Smirking, he took another step closer and I found myself backing up with every step he took, until my back hit against my garden wall. Resting a hand on the wall next to me, he leaned in close. "You think I like you, Molloy?"

"I know you do," I breathed, heart galloping recklessly in my chest.

Reaching down with his free hand, he tucked a tendril of hair behind my ear and whispered, "You think I *want* you?"

The air left my lungs in an audible whoosh, and I knew that I was standing in the face of danger.

This boy possessed all of the terrible traits that mothers warned their daughters about.

Trouble.

It should have been his middle name.

Every bad, wrong, and dirty teenage boy characteristic wrapped up in a perfect, fucked-up package.

Physically, he trumped me in every way.

Taller.

Stronger.

Darker.

Meaner . . .

Still, I wanted him to come *closer*.

"Go inside, Molloy," he said in a softer tone now, as his green eyes searched and found in mine something that had put the fire out for him. "You don't belong out here in the dark with someone like me."

"Yes, I do," I was quick to blurt, before quickly adding, "I live on this street, remember?"

"Aoife!" My father's voice echoed from our front doorway. "What are you doing outside at this time of night? The Gards are crawling all over the terrace, pet."

"Jesus." Jerking away from my body like I had scalded him, Joey shoved his hands into his pocket and muttered a string of curse words under his breath, as he shook his head and blew out a ragged breath.

My father's confused gaze flicked to Joey, and he blinked for a moment before a look of resignation settled on his face.

"Joey," he acknowledged with a heavy sigh. "I hope you weren't in that crowd I saw the Gards taking away. You're a good lad, and you know I'm fond of ya, but those lads are bad news. I'm not comfortable having someone who knocks around with that kind talking to my—"

"He wasn't with them," I answered before Joey could. "He was dropping Katie home," I quickly added, feeling the lie roll surprisingly easy off my tongue. "They went to the cinema together, isn't that right, Joey?"

"Uh, yeah." Joey nodded slowly, his green eyes wary and locked on mine. "That's right."

"Yourself and young Katie?" My dad frowned at Joey. "You kept that one quiet."

Joey shrugged. "It's ah, early days?"

"Ah, mighty stuff. Good lad yourself," Dad called back with a cheerful grin before turning around to go back into the house. "Aoife, don't be long outside now, ya hear? Only the bad types are out at this time of night."

"Yeah, Dad, I'll be two minutes," I called back and then sagged in relief when the door closed behind him.

"You lied for me." Joey's tone was cold and full of unspoken accusation. "You covered for me."

"Yeah." My heart hammered against my chest bone, as if it was trying to beat its way out of my body and join forces with his. "I did."

"Why?" His green eyes were laced with a mixture of heat, annoyance, and reluctant curiosity. "What do you want from me?"

"I'm not sure yet." My gaze locked on the recently healed cut on his bottom lip. "I guess you'll just have to owe me for now."

"For now?" Breathing hard, he stepped closer until there wasn't an inch of space between our bodies. "I don't like owing people."

"Well, that's too bad," I replied, snaking my tongue out to wet my lips. "Because you're not in control of this situation."

He tilted his head to one side and a ghost of a smile teased his full lips. "And you are?"

"Answers," I blurted out then, feeling the heat of his stare entirely too much to handle. "I want answers."

"If it's answers to homework, then you're barking up the wrong tree," he drawled lazily. "In case it skipped your attention, Molloy, I'm far from a scholar."

"That's a lie." Nothing to do with Joey Lynch skipped my attention, which was how I knew that he was far more intelligent than he led the teachers at school to believe.

"You think I'm a scholar?"

"I think you're smarter than you let on." He might have a horrible attitude and rarely turned in his homework on time, if at all, but he had a sharp mind.

"How'd you figure that one, Molloy?"

"Your work in class is never wrong, it's your homework that's lacking," I stated unabashedly. "You never have a problem completing any assignment we're given in any of our subjects. Maths, English, Science, Home Economics. None of it phases you. When you're in class, that is."

What he seemed to be lacking wasn't brains.

It was time.

"Jesus," he muttered, rubbing his jaw. "Stalker much?"

"Fuck-up, much?" I shot back before adding, "And it's called being perceptive. So no, I don't want to copy your homework, I have my swot of a brother to copy that from, but I do know what I want."

"Which is?"

"I want to know why you're so hell-bent on insisting that you don't like me when we both know you do. I want you to explain why I'm the only girl in our year that you go out of your way to *not* flirt with. And while we're at it, I want you to admit the real reason you blew cold on me in September?"

"Jesus Christ." Rubbing a hand over his bruised face, Joey muttered a string of curse words. "You're not back to this shit again."

I shrugged. "Either tell me why you don't like me or admit that you do."

"I just don't like you anymore, okay?"

"Anymore suggests that you once did."

"Just stop, okay!" Throwing his hands up, he took several steps backwards, putting space between us. "I thought I liked you, but I changed my mind. I have zero interest in you. None. And last time I checked, that wasn't a crime. So let it go – and stop watching me. Christ, you're like my own personal little stalker."

"And you're like my own personal little fuck-up." I reclaimed the space he put between us. "So, let's have it, huh? The truth, this time. Why'd you hit Paul if you don't like me?" I cocked a brow. "He told me that you threatened to cut his fingers off and shove them up his own ass if you caught him talking about putting his hand in my knickers again." I dragged that particular confession out of Paul when he was groveling and begging my forgiveness. "Well, Joe?" Blowing out a shaky breath, I added, "Why'd you do that if you have zero interest in me? Why bother fighting my battles, defending my honor, if you don't care?"

"I did that for your dad," he replied, jaw ticking. "Because he's been good to me."

"And because he told you not to go there with me, right?"

He shook his head but made no reply.

"I'm right, aren't I?" I pushed, unwilling to let it go. "That's why you don't look at me at school. Why you're so determined to pretend that I don't exist. Well, I'm not going to make it that easy for you."

Fury danced in his eyes as he stalked back to where I was standing. "Listen carefully to me," he said in a deathly cold tone, as he walked me backwards until my back was flush against my garden wall again. "When I hit your prick of a boyfriend, I was defending your father's honor, not yours." Eyes narrowing, he leaned so close that his nose brushed against mine. The move caused a jolt of electricity to rock through my body, predominantly the parts of my body south of my bellybutton. "I was thinking that your dad's a good guy, who doesn't deserve to find out that his daughter is so—"

"Finish that sentence," I warned, beyond furious, as I reached up and fisted the front of his hoodie. "I dare you."

"Easy," he spat, glaring down at me. "You want to know why I don't like you, Molloy?" Narrowing his eyes, he added, "It's because you're too fucking *easy*. I could have had you like *that* on the very first day." He snapped his fingers for emphasis. "Do you know how boring that is? Do you know how incredibly uninteresting that makes you?"

Shoving him roughly away, my hand swept up of its own accord, slapping him hard across the side of the face. "Screw you, Joey."

His head twisted sideways from the contact and for a moment I held my breath, not daring to move an inch, as I waited for him to retaliate.

It didn't come.

He never touched me.

Instead, he nodded sharply, more to himself than me, and whispered, "Now, you get it." Backing away slowly, he locked eyes on me and said, "That's why, Molloy."

"That's what?" I called after him. "That's why you don't like me?"

"No," he called over his shoulder, as he walked away from me. "That's why you shouldn't want me to."

And then he was gone.

SECOND YEAR

She's not your problem, lad

October 10th 2000

JOEY

At half past nine, on a Wednesday night, in the middle of January, I could think of better places to be than freezing my bollocks off in a jersey and shorts, battling it out with fifteen less than mediocre opposition players for dominion over a leather ball.

The floodlights surrounding the GAA pitch were so bright they illuminated the rain that was lashing down on us, as we played down the last few minutes of the clock, having long since ran away with the match.

I'd lost count of the score in the first half when we'd gone sixteen points ahead.

At this point, it was uncomfortable to continue playing hard when it was such a landslide.

Still, I pucked the ball around with my teammates, knowing that it would be an even bigger insult to the lads on the opposite team to call the game.

They still had their pride, after all.

"Lynchy, over here, over here," Paul Rice called out, embarrassing himself by screaming for the ball like we were playing in the All Ireland final. "I'm open, lad."

What a langer.

Shaking my head, I repressed the urge to tell him to fuck off and dutifully pucked the sliotar towards him, only too willing to relinquish control in this instance.

Wanting to win a competitive match was something I fattened on.

Wanting to annihilate and humiliate an inferior team gave me no pleasure whatsoever.

Catching the ball mid-air, my eejit of a teammate ploughed up the pitch, over-powering and out-skilling his opposition number, before sinking the ball in the back of the net and celebrating like it was going out of fashion.

Ugh.

Biting back a groan, I dropped my head, feeling a huge dollop of second-hand embarrassment for the fool wearing the same-colored jersey as me.

"What's the story with him, six?" the lad marking me asked, using my jersey number to address me, while looking as unimpressed with Ricey as I felt. "We're clearly out of the game. No need to rub it in."

I couldn't give him an honest answer without revealing the discord between us, so I muttered something unintelligible under my breath and shrugged, deciding to leave it at that for the good of the team.

The final whistle blew a moment later, and I sprinted to the sideline, unwilling to participate in any hole-blowing celebrations that were occurring on the pitch.

Ripping off my helmet, I tossed it on the grass with my hurley and reached for a bottle of water.

Thankfully, several of my teammates felt the same and, after a few handshakes, headed off to the changing rooms to tog off.

"Good sportsmanship, six," the coach from the other team said, coming over to clap my shoulder. "Fantastic bit of hurling out there, boy."

"Thanks." Repressing the urge to rip his hand off my shoulder, I forced a nod and swallowed down several mouthfuls of water before adding, "Appreciate it."

"You're Teddy Lynch's young fella, aren't ya?"

Now I did shrug his hand off. "That's right."

"Pure class was your father, back in the day," the man said with a wistful sigh. "A true legend. Played against him myself a few times. Cork lost one of their finest hurlers when he did his knee in."

"Yeah," I bit out, knowing full well that my father's dependency on alcohol, not to mention his inability to keep his dick in his pants, had a lot more to do with his demise from hurling than any knee injury.

"I can tell that he trained you up," the man continued to piss me off by saying. "You're a lucky young fella to have a father like that."

"Yeah," I deadpanned, giving him my back to let him know that I was done with this conversation. *I'm so fucking lucky.*

Thankfully, he seemed to get my drift and fucked off to back to his own team, leaving me alone to stew in my resentment.

Knowing there was no point in following the rest of my team off the pitch until the *legend* himself got his pound of flesh, I waited on the sideline, knowing that he would eventually rear his ugly head.

If tonight's match had been held on a Thursday or Friday, I wouldn't have to suffer his presence. He was paid his social welfare every Thursday and would be too busy getting hammered in his local to bother me.

In a sick way, I preferred it like that.

Having him here, sober and broke to the ropes, with only my performance to focus on until he got his next fix, made everything ten times worse.

"Joey!"

The familiar sound of his voice drilled through my ears, and I flinched, feeling every muscle in my body lock tight in panicked anticipation.

Reluctantly turning around to face the crowds on the hilly green at the side of the pitch, I channeled in on my father, who was heading straight for me.

It was hard to miss him, I begrudgingly conceded, when everyone knew who he was, and stopped to shake his hand and salute him.

"What was that?" he demanded, swinging the gate open and stalking onto the pitch towards me.

"What was what?" I asked flatly.

"That was your ball," Dad growled, closing the space between us. "That was your fucking goal, and you passed it off to that eejit in the forwards."

"I scored three goals, Dad," I reminded him, tone hard and laced with bitterness. "And twelve points." Shrugging, I added, "It was enough."

"Enough?" He looked at me like I was insane. "*Enough*?"

"Yes, enough," I snapped. "Jesus Christ, you were watching the game. Tadhg and the under-6s would've given us a harder challenge."

"You listen to me, boy," my father barked, planting his beefy hand on my shoulder. "This is no place for consciences. When you're on that pitch, you keep going, do ya hear me?" His fingers dug into flesh as he spoke. "You run those legs into the ground. You don't stop until your body gives up. Until you're puking and bleeding and your legs can't hold ya any longer." He narrowed his eyes when he said, "And you sure as hell don't show *pity*."

I clenched my jaw. "The game was *over*."

"It's not over until the final whistle blows," he snapped. "If you want to make a name for yourself in this sport, then you need to heed my warning, boy. I know what I'm talking about."

"I'm *not* you."

"And you never will be if you don't start being more ruthless on the pitch."

"Then I guess I never will be."

"Where's the killer instinct, boy?"

Saved up for when I'll need it against you.

He released my shoulder then and gave me quick once-over before shaking his head, his disappointment blatant. "You're not big enough."

"I'm the tallest one on the fucking team," I shot back, hating myself for feeding into his bullshit. "What do you want from me?"

"You're too fucking skinny," he snapped. "I was twice as built as you when I was your age. You need to start bulking up, boy. Your sister has bigger muscles than you."

Lovely.

"Your brother was a good stone heavier than you when he was playing U-16s."

Of course he was.

"Darren had serious conditioning about him back in the day."

Furious, I straightened my shoulders and silently seethed, as the insults kept coming.

"Darren didn't look like the wind could topple him, either – unlike you."

Obviously.

"You might have the height and speed, boy, but you're too fucking light."

Tuning his voice out, I concentrated on what was happening just over his shoulder, on the hilly bank behind him.

From my standpoint, I had a perfect view of Molloy, who was having a heated conversation with Ricey.

She didn't look happy.

In fact, she looked downright miserable.

Either completely oblivious to his girlfriend's bad mood, or just plain indifferent,

Ricey waved a hand around as he spoke, turning back to gesture to a car full of our teammates. Shaking his head at something she said, he moved in to kiss her, only to be met with a hand to the chest, and a furious-looking Molloy warning him off. Throwing his hands up in frustration, he said something in response before jogging over to the car and climbing into the back seat, leaving her alone.

With her hands folded across her chest, I watched her watch the car drive away and shook my head in frustration. Why she was still with that selfish prick, six months later, was beyond me. He wasn't even remotely good to her, and he damn sure wasn't loyal, either. I had it on good authority that there had been least two occasions during the summer where he'd messed around behind her back. In fact, Podge had seen him with his own two eyes mauling the face off some young one from the convent secondary school.

If Molloy didn't know, she was stupid.

If she *did* know, and still stayed with him regardless, then she was pathetic.

"Are ya listening to me, boy?" my father barked, dragging my attention away from the blonde and back to him.

"I'm listening," I bit out, having no clue what he'd just said, as I reluctantly met his gaze head on.

I hated looking at him. I *despised* his eyes. He had cold, dead eyes that felt nothing and only came to life when he was inflicting harm on someone.

"Grab your shit," he ordered. "You can shower at home. We can finish this conversation in the car."

So you can get me alone?

Yeah, fucking right.

Climbing into the car with my father when he was in a mood like this would be the equivalent of following a stranger into the back of their van on the promise of sweets. I knew exactly how he finished conversations and I *always* came out worse off. I sure as hell wasn't going to offer myself up like a sacrificial lamb by climbing into his car, with nobody around to stop him.

He could keep his spin home.

I wasn't *that* suicidal.

"I can't," I heard myself lie, as I stepped around him and moved for the gate. "I have to stop in at work before I go home."

"Why?" he called after me, sounding impatient. "Have you wages to collect or something? Because I can drive you over."

Oh, you'd love that, wouldn't you? "No, I left my school bag at the garage."

"Then you can walk your hole over there," he barked. "I'm not your lacky, boy."

Ignoring him, I kept walking and moved for the changing rooms, needing to put some distance between his fists and my body.

"Hey asshole," Molloy called out when I stalked past her, letting me know in no uncertain terms that I still wasn't entirely forgiven for calling her easy back in first year.

I had thrown the word out as a roadblock, a diversion, to send her running in the opposite direction of me.

It didn't work.

Instead of avoiding me, like I needed her to do, like any normal girl would, she gave me hell. With smart-ass comments, and witty one-liners,

Molloy continued to throw her version of shade at me, determined to get me back for offending her.

"Molloy," I acknowledged with a small nod.

"Nice game."

"Nice legs."

"Want to be a gent and walk these nice legs home?"

"Why?" With my hand on the changing room door, I turned back to glare at her. "Is he not coming back for you?"

Red-faced, she shook her head.

Fury erupted inside of me. "He just *left* you here?"

She nodded.

"He's an asshole."

Another embarrassed nod.

"Where's your father?"

"Gone out with my mam for the night." She waved her phone at me. "Phone's off."

"Jesus." I released a frustrated growl. "The fuck are you doing with a tool like him, Molloy?"

"Will you walk me home or not?"

No.

No.

Fucking no.

She's not your problem, lad.

Just walk away.

"Give me ten minutes to shower and get changed," I heard myself mutter, mentally kicking myself in the balls.

Her eyes flashed with relief. "Thanks, Joey."

"Hm," was all I replied before slipping inside the changing room and heading straight for the showers. *You're absolutely not welcome.*

Unwilling chaperones

October 10th 2000

AOIFE

Sitting on the wall of the GAA pavilion, I waited for my reluctant chaperone to emerge from the changing room, while furiously tapping out a text to the asshole who had upped and left me on my own in the dark.

> AOIFE: I REALLY HOPE YOU ENJOY CELEBRATING THE WIN WITH YOUR LITTLE PALS BECAUSE YOU WON'T BE CELEBRATING ANYTHING WITH ME EVER AGAIN, ASSHOLE.

> PAUL: DON'T BE MAD, BABE. I'LL MAKE IT UP TO YOU. XX

> AOIFE: MAKE IT UP TO ME? YOU LEFT ME ALONE TO GO BOWLING WITH YOUR TEAMMATES, PAUL! YOU DIDN'T EVEN OFFER ME A SPIN HOME!

> PAUL: IT'S NOT MY FAULT THERE WASN'T ANY ROOM IN THE CAR. COME ON, AOIF. DON'T MAKE A BIG DEAL OF THIS. IT'S NOT LIKE YOU LIVE IN THE COUNTRYSIDE. YOU KNOW THE TOWN BETTER THAN I DO. YOU'LL BE GRAND. I'LL SEE YOU AT SCHOOL TOMORROW, K? I'LL BUY YOU LUNCH. Xx

"Ugh!" Furious, I powered off my phone, unwilling to deal with him a second longer.

I didn't want him to buy me lunch or anything else.

I wanted him to *walk me home*.

I didn't think that was a lot to ask for, considering the only reason I had traipsed across town in the first place was because he had badgered me to come and watch him play.

It was a good forty-minute walk from the GAA grounds to my terrace on the other side of town, and while my parents were fairly chill, if my dad found out that I walked home alone, I would be grounded for a month. *Minimum.*

No way was I losing my freedom over some asshole boy.

When Joey finally emerged from the back of the building, his hostility was obvious.

With a gear bag slung over his shoulder, his helmet and hurley in hand, and a cigarette balancing between his lips, he inclined his head to where I was sitting and said, "Let's go."

Resisting the urge to taunt or goad him like I usually would, I hopped down from my perch and joined him on the footpath, knowing that having him walk me home was the safest way out of getting hell from my dad.

My dad loved Joey.

What's more, he trusted him.

Having Joey walk me home would be an improvement on Paul in my father's eyes.

Looking wholly unimpressed with the position I had put him in, my classmate pounded the footpath beside me, silently seething, while he smoked his cigarette.

"Aren't you a little young to be getting hooked on smoking?"

"Aren't you a little nosey to be asking for answers to questions that are none of your business?"

"Seriously?" I laughed humorlessly. "You're this pissed off because I asked you to walk me home?"

"No, Molloy," he bit out. "I'm pissed off because that prick put you in a position where you *had* to ask me to walk you home."

His answer was sharp, cutting, and precisely to the point.

"Listen, I'm embarrassed enough about it," I heard myself admit. "No need to layer it on, Joe."

"You *should* be embarrassed," he snapped, tossing his cigarette butt away. "Embarrassed for giving an asshole like Paul Rice the chance to treat you like an option."

"Whatever," I grumbled. "I'm not fighting with you on this."

"Because you know I'm right."

"What's it to you?" I demanded.

"Nothing," he hissed, tone laced with venom. "It's *nothing* to me, Molloy."

Yes, it *was*.

It was *everything* to him, just like it was *everything* to me, but he was too damn stubborn to ever admit it.

"Well then, shut up about it," I snapped, folding my arms across my chest protectively. "Damn."

Joey was quiet for about half a minute until he blew out a frustrated breath and said, "All I'm saying is if some asshole treated my sister the way I watched him treat you tonight, he sure as hell wouldn't be getting another chance to pull that stunt on her again."

"Wow," I deadpanned. "Keep it up, Joe, and I'm going to start thinking that you have *actual* feelings."

"I do," he shot back, not missing a beat. "For the people I *actually* care about."

"Like your sister."

"Like my sister," he confirmed without a hint of embarrassment, which wasn't something most guys our age would admit. "Although Shan's not thick enough to fall in with a prick like Rice."

I narrowed my eyes at him. "Like you're such a saint when it comes to girls."

Joey shrugged nonchalantly. "I've never left my girlfriend alone in a dodgy side of town so I can fuck around with my buddies."

"Because you refuse to have a girlfriend."

"Which is a good thing for Ricey," he snapped. "Considering I seem to spend most of my time looking out for *his* one!"

"Oh please." I rolled my eyes. "So, you've walked me home a few times. Big deal."

"A *few*? You might want to count again." He gave me a hard look. "How many times has your old man had me walk you home from the garage?"

Half a dozen or more.

"How many times has that prick treated you like an afterthought?"

My cheeks reddened. "Oh, shut up."

"All I'm saying is think about the way he treated you tonight. Especially when he shows up at school tomorrow with some bullshit apology and a flashy new bracelet, or whatever crap he locks you in with."

"I'm not a magpie, Joey," I snapped, seriously annoyed now. "I can't be bought with shiny new jewelry."

"No, you're just a doll," came his hurtful response. "Ricey's personal fucking mannequin to drape in jewelry and stand by his side, looking pretty and saying *nothing*."

I stopped walking.

I stopped breathing.

His words cut me to the bone.

"Move your legs, Molloy," he growled, several feet up the road, as he turned back to glare at me. "I'm not waiting around all night for you. I have shit to do after this, ya know."

"You asshole."

"*Me*?"

"Yes, you!"

"How am I the asshole?"

"Because you hurt my feelings."

"No, I didn't."

"Yes, you did, Joey!"

"Fine," he growled. "I'm an asshole. Now let's go."

I shook my head.

"Molloy."

"I am *not* a mannequin!"

"Fine." Joey shook his head. "I take it back. You're not a mannequin."

"That was really mean."

He stared at me for a long time before finally blowing out a breath. "Yeah, I know."

"Apologize."

"For what?"

"For calling me a mannequin."

"I *just* said you're not a mannequin."

"That wasn't an apology."

"Yeah, it was."

I gaped at him. "No, it wasn't, Joey."

"How was that not an apology?"

"Because it didn't contain the word *sorry*, asshole."

Looking thoroughly confused – and thoroughly fed up – my class-mate released a furious growl. "Let's just walk, okay? Just move your legs, Molloy. *Please.*"

Relenting because he used the word '*please*', I closed the space between us, and fell into step beside him once more. "Haven't you ever apologized to someone?" I asked, morbidly curious now.

"I just did."

"Oh my god." I studied his side profile. "You haven't."

With a deep frown etched on his face, Joey concentrated on the road ahead of us, but didn't respond.

We walked in silence for the rest of the way, and it wasn't until we turned the corner of my street that I heard him mutter the words, "I'm sorry."

"Wow." My heart fluttered around in my chest. "Is that your first time saying that word to anyone?"

He shrugged, clearly uncomfortable. "Probably."

"Well, thanks," I replied, nudging him with my shoulder when we reached my gate. "I forgive you."

"Hm," he grunted in response. "I'm thrilled."

A reluctant smile spread across my face, and I asked, "Do you want to come inside?"

"That's not a good idea," he replied, dutifully walking me all the way to my door. He might be bad tempered, this boy, but he was a real quick learner, and hadn't left me at my gate since the night I pitched a fit.

"Why not?" I asked, unlocking the front door, and stepping into the hall to switch on the light.

"You know why."

"No, I don't."

"You have a boyfriend."

"So?" I argued. "I asked if you wanted to come inside, not marry me. Does having a boyfriend suddenly mean that I can't be friends with boys?"

"I'm not your friend, Molloy."

Releasing a frustrated growl, I caught ahold of his hand and dragged him into my house. "Well, I'm yours, asshole." Closing the door behind us, I reached up and pushed his hood down. "See; that wasn't so hard, was it?"

"No."

"Besides, you've been in my house a million times with Dad."

His jaw ticked. "That's different."

"Because he's your *friend*?" I taunted. "Shut up and feed me."

"Feed you?"

"I can't cook, remember?" Leading him by the hand into my kitchen, I walked him over to my fridge and smiled. "And you can."

Joey gaped at me. "You think I'm going to cook for you?"

"For us," I corrected, giving him my sweetest smile.

"Don't do that," he warned.

"Do what?"

"Give me that butter wouldn't melt smile," he growled, pointing a finger at me. "It won't work on me, Molloy. I'm immune."

Of *course* it was going to work. "I love steak."

"Steak?"

I nodded. "Uh-huh."

"You have steak."

"I have two steaks."

He eyed me for a long moment, clearly weighing up his options, before blowing out a frustrated breath. "Get the frying pan."

"Yay." Clapping my hands in delight, I did a little shimmy dance before bouncing off in the direction of the cupboard where Mam kept the pots and pans. "I like my meat well done."

"You'll take your meat whatever way I give it to you," Joey grumbled, rummaging in my fridge for what he needed. "This doesn't mean anything, Molloy," he added. "You didn't win this round."

I threw my head back and laughed. "I always win, Joe."

This is not a date

October 18th 2000

JOEY

Don't ask me how it had happened but sitting on my boss's couch in front of a roaring fire, with a full stomach and an empty plate on my lap, with his daughter's shoulder touching mine, was exactly how I found myself ending what had, otherwise, been a very shitty day.

Not only had I cooked for the girl, but she had somehow wrangled me into bringing in buckets of coal and slack, and lighting the fire for her, too.

Persuasion was certainly a skill that Molloy had honed to perfection.

Knowing that I shouldn't be here, but not wanting to eat and run like a prick, I decided on half an hour being a reasonable amount to time to linger.

"Right." When the thirty minutes was up, I set my plate down on the arm of the couch and slapped my thighs. "I'm going home."

"No, you're not," she grumbled, hooking her arm through mine.

"Molloy."

"No." Shifting closer, she rested her cheek on my shoulder and returned her attention to the film playing on the television. "Now shush."

"I can't be here when your parents get home," I argued, trying and failing to pry my arm free from her freakishly strong hold.

"Why not?"

"Because your dad will flip the fuck out."

"No, he won't," she scoffed. "We're friends, Joe. I'm allowed to have friends over anytime I want."

"We're not friends, Molloy. And stop snuggling me."

"Friends snuggle."

"Friends do not fucking snuggle."

"I snuggle with Casey all the time."

"Well, I can assure you that I have never snuggled with Podge."

"Then you can practice with me." Shifting closer, she curled up in a small ball, and burrowed her head under my arm. "See. You're already a pro."

"Okay, how is this normal?" I demanded, glaring at my arm that she had somehow managed to drape over her shoulders. "You're a real slick mover, aren't ya?"

"Just chill, Joe," she coaxed, resting her head against my chest now, as she draped her arm over my stomach. "Watch the film."

"I don't watch films."

"Yes, you do."

"No, I don't."

"Well, you do now."

"Fine." I blew out a frustrated breath. "What's the film called?"

"It's a grisly horror called *Wrong Turn* about this group of twenty-something-year-olds who take a wrong turn and end up getting hunted by these really creepy cannibal people. It's all blood and gore, with minimal sexy time, but it's a good movie."

"Kind of like how I took a wrong fucking turn tonight and ended up in a nightmare," I drawled sarcastically. "Not quite as grisly as your film, but once my boss gets home and sees me snuggling his daughter, I'm sure it'll be a bloodbath."

"Listen here, Joey Lynch." Sitting upright, she grabbed my chin and turned my face to look straight at her. "I saw you first. You're *my* friend, not his. So, stop worrying about my dad, and start focusing on me."

"Technically, your dad saw me first—"

"You're *mine*, okay?"

"I'm not yours, but whatever." Huffing out a breath, I attempted to fold my arms across my chest, only for Molloy to loudly clear her throat expectantly. "I'm here, like you want, I'm staying for the fucking film, like you want, but I draw the line at *snuggling*."

"Snuggle me."

"No."

"Do it."

"It's not happening, Molloy."

"Snuggle me, Joey."

"I said no."

"Snuggle me or I'll scream."

"For fuck's sake, fine," I snapped, lifting my arm up for her to nestle into my side. "There. We're *snuggling*. Are you happy now?"

"I will be," she cackled, shifting closer to drape her long legs over my lap. "Once you do one more thing for me."

"Oh Jesus, what?"

"Tell me that we're friends."

"Molloy."

"Say it, Joe."

"Why?"

"Because it matters."

"To who?"

"To me."

Jesus Christ. Shifting uncomfortably, I let my shoulders sag before mumbling, "We're friends."

"What was that?"

"We're *friends*."

She laughed. "I was hoping for something more along the lines of 'Aoife, you're my dearest, sexiest, most lovable, bestest friend in the whole wide world'."

"Don't push your luck."

"But I'm your favorite, right?" With a teasing lilt to her voice, she said, "Your favorite friend?"

"Yes, fine! Whatever. Christ," I grumbled, rolling my eyes. "You're my favorite friend, with my favorite legs."

"Well, now see, that wasn't so hard, was it?" she laughed, reaching up to pat my cheek. "And just so you know, Joe?" She leaned in close and pressed a kiss to my cheek. "You're *my* favorite friend, with my favorite everything."

Well shit.

Take it easy, lad, it's not that deep

March 11th 2001

JOEY

You know the saying about idle hands being the devil's workshop?

Yeah, I thought that might be true.

Sunday was the one day of the week that I didn't have work, school, or training. Aside from the occasional match, I was a free agent.

Problem was, doing nothing didn't come easy to me.

I was never *less* in control than when I found myself at a loose end.

With my hands hanging, and nothing to occupy my racing mind, I went looking for trouble, and found it in the form of sharing a few lines of coke with Shane and the lads.

The temporary high was fantastic.

I felt on top of the world.

I felt like I could run a marathon and *win* it.

I felt like there wasn't anything I couldn't do.

The only snag to an otherwise perfectly planned out Sunday was that I forgot about the match I had to play.

And now, several hours later, after crashing hard, I felt like shit.

Throughout the entire game, my heart continued to race violently, thundering so loud and hard against my chest bone, that I could hear it in my ears.

Distracted and on edge, I messed up all over the pitch, either pucking the sliotar too long or not being in the right position for defense and had only managed to score two measly points in the whole sixty minutes.

There was an underage county selector for Cork in the stand, and I'd blown it.

Knowing that my father was also somewhere in the stands, watching my piss-poor performance, and plotting my punishment for disappointing him, only made me feel ten times worse than I already did.

Thoroughly depressed and thoroughly fucking stressed, I whipped my helmet off the minute the referee blew the final whistle and stalked off in the direction of the changing rooms, ignoring several claps on the shoulder from my teammates.

Tossing my hurley and helmet on top of my gear bag, I reached a hand behind my head and whipped my jersey off, ignoring all of the chatter around me.

Burning the fuck up from running around a pitch for the past hour, I blew out a harsh breath and snatched up my water bottle.

"Mighty stuff, lads," Eddie, our club trainer, declared with a clap, when he walked into the changing room a few minutes later. "That was a solid win. Those lads from St. Pats are a hard bunch. They were never going to go down without a fight, so be proud of yourselves for a hard-earned victory."

Unscrewing the cap on my bottle, I poured the contents over my face and neck, feeling immediate relief when the water began to cool my overheated skin.

"Good game," a familiar voice said, and I turned my head just enough to see none other than Molloy's boyfriend, Paul Rice. He was taking up perch on the bench beside me, freshly showered, and with a towel slung around his waist. "I thought you were in for that goal in the second half."

"Yeah," I agreed, tossing my bottle back into my bag, and reaching for a towel. "Me too." The ball I'd put narrowly wide would come back to bite me when I got home, no doubt.

"You had a good game, though," Ricey offered, as he got dressed. "Nice shot at the end. I thought at one stage, they were going to run away with it—"

"I played poorly," I cut him off by saying. "Don't try to dress it up as anything else."

"What's your problem?" he demanded, running a hand through his dark hair. "We won, didn't we?"

"You're my problem," I came right out with, bristling with tension. "I thought I made that clear last year?"

"What the hell?"

"I don't like you, asshole. I don't like how you talk; I don't like how you act, and I sure as shit don't like how you treat your girlfriend. We might share a team and a classroom, but that's it," I added. "Don't misconstrue my tolerance of your presence as an invitation to speak to me about anything other than hurling."

"Seriously?" I watched as recognition flashed across his face. "You're still holding on to that fight we had?"

Damn straight I was.

"Jesus, Lynchy." He shook his head in frustration. "That was a year ago, and Aoife let it go, so why can't you?"

"More fool her," I replied flatly. "I guess she doesn't know you as well as I do."

His brow furrowed. "What's that supposed to mean?"

"It means that I know you're a dog," I replied, deciding against taking a shower. Fuck it, I would have one at home later. Stuffing my gear into my bag, I grabbed a pair of sweats and dragged them on. "And not a very discreet one at that."

His dark eyes widened like saucers as awareness dawned on him. "Are you talking about Danielle Long? Because nothing happened with her, I swear—"

"Only because she didn't want it to happen." Pulling a fresh t-shirt on, I kicked on my runners, and tossed my gear bag over my shoulder. "Yeah, dickhead, I saw the sex-texts you sent her over the February midterm. The many, *many* texts you sent her." Sliding my hurley through the earholes of my helmet, I gripped the middle of the handle and gave him a seething look. "I have your card marked, ya little perv."

"What were you doing going through Danielle's phone?"

"She showed them to me," I replied. "Right around the same time she asked me to give you a message of her own." Offering him a menacing glare, I said, "Do you need me to explain the message in detail or have you gotten the gist?"

"Those texts were only a joke," he defended with a fake laugh. "A piss-take with the lads."

"Sure they were," I deadpanned. "I already told ya before that Molloy's old man is a good friend of mine. Fuck her over and I'll take it as a personal insult."

"Take it easy, lad. It's not that deep," Ricey huffed defensively.

"Does Aoife know that?" I shot back.

"I haven't done anything wrong," he growled. "It was a few texts. I didn't ride the girl, and, besides, myself and Aoife were off at the time."

"Going by those messages you sent her friend, I think it's pretty clear that you and Aoife should be off permanently."

"Oh yeah, because that would suit you down to the ground, wouldn't it?" he argued back. "You'd only love that, wouldn't you, Lynchy?"

"Does she know about the many *many* other girls that you've been messing around with when her back is turned?"

He narrowed his eyes. "Bullshit."

"Bull-true," I hissed, pointing a finger at him. "I see you, Ricey. I *see* right fucking through you, asshole."

"And I see you right back," he snarled, shoving to his feet. "At least have the balls to admit why you're so interested in my love life."

Bristling, I stepped towards him, and then had to take a breath in order to stop myself from lashing out, from springing forward and throttling the bastard, but it wasn't coming easy to me.

"It's so fucking obvious, lad." He narrowed his eyes. "You're jealous because I'm with her."

"Keep it up," I warned, chest rising and falling quickly, as my temper rose. "I dare you."

"Whoa, whoa, whoa," Eddie said, clearly noticing the tension, as he came to stand between us, with several of the team joining him – Podge included. "What's going on here, lads?"

"None of this grudge you're holding against me has anything to do with being friends with her dad," Ricey said with a smirk. "You've got a problem with me because I got the girl that you've wanted since day dot. She's with me, not you, and it drives you fucking nuts."

"That's enough, lads, we're all on the same team here."

Fury emanated from every pore in my body, as I balled my hands into fists at my sides and willed myself to not react. "If I wanted your girlfriend, asshole, she'd be with me."

"She'd be with *you*?" Rice threw his head back and laughed; Billy-brave-bollocks now that the coach and half the team were around to save him. "You're talking out of your hole, Lynchy. My Aoife wouldn't give a fuck-up like you a second glance. She's one of the nice girls, too nice for her own good sometimes. So, don't mistake her friendliness for anything other than taking pity on some washed-up drunk's pathetic scumbag son. It's bad enough you've got her father throwing you scraps; like meat to a half-starved stray—"

"You're a fucking dead man! "

"Don't do it," Podge was quick to say, perceptively stepping in front of me and pushing me away from the prick with a death wish. "He's not worth it, Joe."

No, but she is.

Fuck, where'd that thought come from?

"Come on, lad," Eddie interjected, grabbing ahold of the back of my neck with his beefy hand, and steering me towards the door. "You need to cool down."

"Don't do that," I snarled, breaking free from his hold, chest heaving now, as my skin crawled from the touch – from the surge of memories that came with a touch like that. "Don't ever fucking touch me like that again!" I warned, trembling, as I reached up and cupped the back of my neck. "Ever again."

"It's all good, Lynch," Eddie replied calmly, holding his hands up in retreat. "I just want you to go outside and take a breather, lad. For your own good, that's all. There's a selector outside looking to talk to you, and it won't do your chances of being called up to the minors a bit of good if he sees you losing the head like this."

"Like I give a fuck about the minors," I hissed, backing up towards the door. Raising the hand still clutching my hurley, I pointed it right at Ricey. "Next time you see me, you won't have a roomful of people to protect you."

"I'm shaking."

"No need to shake, asshole. Just make your peace with God, because I'm going to bury you."

Having said that, I turned on my heels and stalked out of the changing room, slamming the door loudly behind me.

I turned back three times towards the changing room, twice to go back to kill Ricey, and the other to go talk to that selector, before finally wrangling my temper into check.

Releasing a furious growl, I kicked at the gravel, and forced myself to walk away.

I didn't have the patience or the mental capacity to handle any types of conversations about my future.

Besides, hurling was an amateur sport, and while I understood how big an honor it was to be chosen to play for your county, it wasn't going to pay any bills.

Now, if I'd been born into money, I could've played rugby like those posh pricks over at Tommen College and had the opportunity to make some decent money for putting my body on the line.

"So, you survived the match without maiming anyone," a familiar voice called out, dragging me from my thoughts. "And you managed to score, too. What an overachiever."

I swung my gaze around only for my eyes to land on Molloy's fantastic fucking legs, as they dangled from the wall she was perched on.

Shielding my eyes from the evening sunshine, I squinted up at her.

Dressed in an oversized white jumper and tight denim jeans, she sucked on a red freezer ice pop, and smiled down at me. "Nice winning score, by the way."

"Nice legs."

Grinning, she took another lick from her freeze pop, before saying, "Do you have any plans for the rest of the evening?"

"Why?"

"What do you mean why?"

"Why means why, Molloy."

"Do you want to hang out?"

"With you and *him*?" I snorted. "No fucking thanks."

"Come on, Joe," she said in a playful tone, green eyes dancing with mischief. "Paul can be third wheel."

"Funny."

She rolled her eyes and cackled. "Oh, don't be so cranky."

"Joey!" a chorus of young voices echoed out, and I watched as my younger brothers, Ollie and Tadhg, came thundering towards me.

"You were class, lad."

"Yeah, you were the bestest," Ollie agreed, wrapping arms around my waist. "Good job, Joe."

"Thanks, lads." Patting Ollie's small shoulder, I let go of the hold I had on my hurley so Tadhg could snatch it up to inspect for cracks or damage – something he did after every game.

"Who are these little mini-images of you?" Molloy asked, curious green eyes locked on my brothers. "Don't tell me you've been hiding a secret wife and family from me."

I rolled my eyes. "They're my brothers, genius."

"I'm Ollie," my little brother piped up before I had a chance to answer. "And that's Tadhg," he added, pointing to where Tadhg was messing around with my hurley. "This is Joe. He's our big brother." Arching his head back, he asked, "Who are you?"

"I'm Aoife," she replied with a little laugh. "And, yeah, I already know your big brother. He's in my class at school."

"Is she your friend, Joe?" Ollie asked, looking back to me. "She's pretty."

"I sure am his friend, Ollie. And aren't you just adorable to call me pretty." Her gaze flicked to me, and she winked. "Joey thinks I'm pretty, too."

"Pretty fucking annoying," I muttered under my breath.

"That's 'cause it's true," Ollie with a lopsided grin. "Whoa, she's really *really* pretty, Joe."

"Settle down, stud," I grumbled, reaching into the front pocket of my gear bag for the emergency tenner I always kept in there. "Here," I said, thrusting it into his hand, trying to buy myself a minute's peace. "Go up to the shop and get yourself and Tadhg a bar of chocolate."

"Whoa, thanks, Joe – hey, Tadhg!" Ollie roared, running off in the direction of our other brother, who was pucking a sliotar against the wall further up. "Joey gave us a tenner!"

"Sweet," I heard Tadhg say, hurley forgotten, as he and Ollie ran off in the direction of the pavilion tuck-shop.

"I want my change back," I called after them.

"They're adorable," she said, drawing my attention back to her. "They didn't come here on their own, did they?"

"They're something alright," I muttered, as my eyes searched the dispersing crowd, while the familiar feeling of impending doom settled deep in my stomach. "And no, they came with our father."

"Is your dad the big guy I see you talking to after games sometimes?"

"That would be him."

"Babe?" I heard Ricey call out, and we both turned our heads in unison to find him standing outside the changing room, with a mutinous look about him. "Are you coming or what?"

"Yeah, give me a sec," she called back, jumping down from the wall, and landing far too fucking close to me for comfort.

"You sure you don't want to come?"

"Yeah, Molloy, I'm sure."

"I want you to."

I want you, too ... "Not interested."

"Fair enough, Joe." Sighing heavily, she patted my shoulder. "I'll see you tomorrow at school, okay?"

"Yeah. I'll see you then."

Frowning, I stared after her as she skipped off in the direction I'd just come from.

To him.

Which just so happened to be the same direction my father was now coming from, with a thunderous expression on his face.

Fuck.

Congratulations

May 15th 2001

JOEY

"The weather was shit, and I wanted to die ... "
"The sky was black, and I was pissed off ... "
"None of it matters because it won't put food on the table ... "

Tossing my English copybook across the room, I gave up on the essay I had been attempting to write.

Glaring at my homework journal like it was the devil incarnate, I bit back the urge to roar.

What the hell was I doing?

Sitting on my bed doing fucking homework, of all things, I glowered at the wall opposite my bed and sighed in defeat.

Who was I trying to fool?

Didn't matter whether I finished tonight's essay or not. I wasn't going to college, I wasn't going anywhere, and the teachers couldn't do shit to make me feel worse about that than I already did.

The sound of my stomach growling in hungry protest stirred me from my depressing thoughts, and I stood, knowing that I would have to face him sooner or later.

Besides, I had to be at work in an hour.

Later, Joey.

Later is always better when it comes to him.

"Fuck it," I grumbled to myself, "you're going to die young anyway; might as well put an expedited stamp on your forehead."

Changing out of my school uniform, I threw on my work clothes before stepping into the landing. Ignoring the stench of piss and whiskey, I stalked down the staircase, needing to seem as aloof and unaffected as I could when facing the parentals.

It was my saving grace.

My only way of protecting myself from the prick whose prick I had been conceived from.

If you don't care, then nothing he does can hurt you.

The minute I stepped off the last step of the staircase, I could hear them arguing in the kitchen.

Surprisingly, I wasn't the hot topic of disappointment.

Today, it was Shannon's turn.

"She's not going, Marie," my father barked, balling up a bunch of papers and tossing them across the table at Mam. "It's out of the question."

"But she's so quiet, Teddy," Mam attempted to coax. "So shy. She'll never manage it. She's already struggling to cope with primary school."

"She'll have to get over it," Dad replied, not batting an eye. "She's no better than the rest of them. I won't have her sent to private school when the boys are in public."

"I can take extra shifts at work," Mam hurried to say. "I don't mind. I will pay for it myself—"

"I said no," Dad barked. "It's not happening. Get it out of your head."

"What's going on?" I asked, walking into the kitchen.

"Your mother thinks your sister needs to go to private school next year when she finishes up primary," Dad, who was sober for a change, told me. "Thinks she's too sensitive for BCS."

She was.

Shannon had a hard time fitting in with people, a very fucking hard time, and I often wondered what would happen to her when she eventually started secondary school.

To be honest, it was a thought that terrified me to my core, so I tried not to think about it.

Because they kept her back in baby infants, Shannon was three years below me at school, so when we went our separate ways at the school gates of BCS next year, with her as a first year and me as a fourth year, she wouldn't have anyone to look out for her – something that she badly needed.

The girls in her class at primary school were septic, and had given her hell since baby infants, and those were pubescent girls.

The teenage girls she would face when she started secondary school would be a different kettle of fish to handle.

My sister did have a couple of friends – one nice girl called Claire, I remembered in particular, who, would, no doubt, be heading off to Tommen College after primary school to join her rugby-head brother, Hughie.

Unfortunately for Shannon, she would be heading for BCS with me.

There wasn't much I could do for her, besides get myself suspended defending her honor, which I had no doubt would happen.

One of these days, my sister was going to have to fight back.

"How much is Tommen?" I asked, raiding the fridge for a packet of ham.

"Several thousand a year," Mam replied. "But it looks to be a fantastic school. And I have an entire year to save up for the tuition. She's only finishing fifth class now, so I have plenty of time to make it work. I really think it would be the best place for her—"

"There's nothing wrong with the local community school," Dad rebuffed with a snort. "It's free and we both went there, Marie. And would ya look at Joey. He's doing just grand there. He's flying road with the hurling. He's already training with the underage team and didn't need a fancy fucking education from Tommen to get there, either."

"Yes," Mam said carefully. "But Shannon isn't Joey."

"Thank Christ for that," Dad muttered.

I tensed, unsettled by the rare compliment, before finishing preparing a ham sandwich and grabbing a can of Coke from the fridge.

I tried to keep a cool head, a calm disposition, and a handle on my temper. It never came easy to me, though, and was growing more impossible with every extra second that I spent in his company.

It didn't sit well with me when my father complimented me or spoke like a civilized human being.

In a messed-up way, I preferred his drunken slurs and angry slaps.

At least I knew where I stood with those.

He'd been on the dry for three weeks now, and I knew it was only a matter of time before he fell off the wagon.

Because my father was an alcoholic.

Addiction ruled his life.

That was the pattern his life had taken, and I hated him for it.

But not as much as I hated myself for following in his footsteps.

A smoke to sleep, a line to function, and whatever else I could get my hands on to escape.

It had been my mantra for a long time now.

I knew I was too young to be walking this particular line, but in all honesty, I didn't have any other options available to me.

In my head it was die or get high.

And I had too many people depending on me not to die.

Fuck.

Pushing all thoughts of self-loathing out of my head before I snapped and did something reckless, I turned to my parents and said, "I think ye should send her."

"To Tommen?" Mam asked, tone hopeful.

"Yeah." I nodded, chewing down a mouthful of my sandwich. "It'd be good for her. You're right, Mam. Shannon will get swallowed up at BCS."

"And how do you propose we fund this 'several thousand euro each year' private school?" Dad demanded, turning his glare on me.

"Gee, I don't know," I shot back, gesturing to my oil-stained overalls. "Maybe by getting off your hole and getting a job like the rest of us."

"Oh, Joey," Mam sighed, dropping her head in her hands, as my father jerked to his feet so fast it caused the chair that he'd been sitting on to slide across the kitchen tiles.

"The fuck did you say to me, ya little bastard?"

"Do you need a hearing aid? I said get off your hole and get a job." Unwilling or just plain unable to keep my mouth shut, I continued to sign my own death certificate. "Believe it or not, there's plenty of them out there. Granted, I'm yet to hear of one that pays well for your qualifications. I suppose, in your defense, it won't be easy to find a pub that'll pay you to prop up their bar – expert that you are and all that."

I didn't duck or try to avoid the fist that crushed into my jaw.

There was no point.

He wouldn't stop until he got his pound of flesh.

It was either take my beating now or later.

I chose to get it over with now.

I did, however, regret not putting my can of Coke down first as it flew out of my hand across the kitchen.

That shit was expensive.

My head snapped back from the force, the pain from his knuckles took the air clean out of my lungs, but I didn't let him see it. I would rather die than expose an ounce of vulnerability to the man I had the misfortune of calling my father.

Breathing hard and fast, I quickly ran my tongue over my teeth, assessing the damage, as the familiar tangy taste of blood filled my mouth.

My body was a map of cuts and bruises, scars and distortion. Nothing would change. Nobody would ask and I wouldn't – couldn't – tell.

Taking it on the chin seemed to be the norm for me. Besides, if I took the brunt of his bad mood, it meant that they were spared – that she was spared.

My father was a powerful man, and there was a hell of a lot of force behind those punches he threw. They were hard enough to knock me sideways, but not enough to shut me up.

"Is that it?" Like a suicidal masochist, I laughed into his face. "You're getting soft, old man."

"Teddy, don't," Mam begged, rushing over to intercept her husband's arm before he could rear back once more. "He's only a boy."

"Don't do me any favors," I sneered, hating her for defending me.

She didn't fucking love me. She thought I was the same as him. "I don't need you to do shit for me."

"Watch your mouth, ya little fucker," Dad warned, knotting his beefy hand in my t-shirt. "Don't talk to your mother like that. Not in her condition."

"Like what? Like you do?" I laughed, roughly shoving him away, quickly backpedaling once I registered what he said. "Wait, what do you mean in her condition . . ." I held up a hand, feeling like I was suddenly suffocating as the walls closed in around me. "Don't say it." Feeling lightheaded, I glanced between them before my eyes reluctantly settled on her stomach. "Don't fucking say it."

Mam placed her hand on the small swell of her stomach, and I wanted to die. "We're having another baby, Joey."

No.

"I'm due in November."

No.

"The doctors reckon it's another boy."

Please God fucking no.

"It'll be different this time, Joey," Mam hurried to add, almost jumping out of her skin when Dad wrapped his arm around her. "You father is off the drink. For good, this time. We're working through everything—" her breath hitched, and she cleared her throat before whispering, "This baby is our fresh start."

Liar.

Liar.

Liar.

Babies weren't supposed to be made in order to plaster over cracks in marriages, but that's what this one would be. That's what each one of us were, temporary plasters to cover the cracks in our parents' dysfunctional relationship.

Numb, I stared at my mother's face, as a new level of devastation washed over me. "You planned this?"

Mam opened her mouth to reply, but he got there first.

"We both did," Dad snapped. "Now, aren't you going to say anything to your mother and me?"

"Congratulations," I replied in a dead tone – a lot like how I felt in that moment. Shaking my head, I stepped around them and moved for the door, grabbing my training bag as I moved. "I'm working until half six, and I've a match after, so I'll be late home."

"It will be different this time, Joe," Mam called after me, voice thick with emotion. "I promise."

"Yeah," I agreed, before closing the front door behind me. Because this time, I had no intention of remembering any of it.

Not a damn second.

By the time I had made the walk to work, my mood had darkened to the point where I honestly didn't think I could handle another ounce of bullshit.

However, that's exactly what I got the second I walked into the garage and locked eyes on none other than Molloy, hand in hand, with her lapdog of a boyfriend.

Wonderful.

Just fucking *wonderful*.

"Hey, Joe," Molloy said with a beamer of a smile, noticing me the second I walked into the building.

I nodded stiffly. "Molloy."

"Joey, lad," Tony said with a warm smile. "How are you?"

"Grand, Tony. Sorry I'm late," I muttered, stalking past them to store my hurley, helmet, and gear bag in the office.

I was in no mood to play a match tonight, but sometimes the matches I wasn't in the form to play ended up being the best ones.

I was certainly riled up enough for it.

Returning to her conversation, Molloy laughed and chatted to her father, while Paul the prick stood alongside her like a, well, like a spare prick.

Her blonde hair was loose today, flowing freely down the middle of her back, and I swear I'd never seen anything like her.

Like an angel with dirty wings, she batted her long lashes at her father, concealing that sharp tongue I knew she possessed, as she played the role of darling daughter and all-round good girl.

But she knew better.

So did I.

She reminded me of one of those beautiful, exotic caged birds you'd see in a backstreet pet shop; out of place and itching for freedom.

Somehow, I doubted she got that by walking around holding hands with a stiff like Paul fucking Rice.

In the beginning, I had assumed that Molloy was trying to get one up on mè by going out with my teammate. My lack of attention had pissed her off, and she wasn't the type of girl to lie down to anyone. I had been positive that their relationship was her way of goading me.

Problem was, fifteen months had passed since she agreed to go out with him, and while they were off more than they were on, and he treated her like shit, she *always* went back to him.

That unsettled me.

It fucking stung.

I knew I had no right to feel any type of way about it, but that didn't stop me from feeling *every* type of way about it.

The hell was she doing with a fella like Paul Rice?

He was too boring for her and had a shit right hook.

She needed excitement and to be challenged.

It was written all over her face.

She waited for you, remember?

He wasn't her first choice.

Pretending that it didn't hurt me to see her with him was something that I had no choice but to master.

So, like I did every other time she came into the garage, flaunting her fantastic fucking boyfriend, I handled the knife-in-the-gut sensation like a trooper, and went about my business.

Thrumming with tension, I quickly set to work, sorting through a pile of tires that needed their tread tested.

Ignoring the couple playing happy fucking families behind me, I let my thoughts wander to my mother.

Another baby.

Due to be born in November.

That meant, he or she would only be three when I turned eighteen.

I would be leaving a toddler behind when I got the fuck out of that house.

Jesus.

A shudder rolled through me, and I clenched my jaw so tight it hurt my teeth.

You see, I had made a deal with myself; I'd promised myself that I would see it out until I finished school. I'd be eighteen and a half by then. I would stay in the house and look after my brothers and sister until then. I could do it. I could hold on until then. But afterwards, once I finished my leaving cert, I was getting the hell out of there.

I had a whole plan thought up in my mind.

I would get a second job, something that was full-time and made good money, and with it I would put a deposit down on a cheap one-bedroom flat. Shannon would come with me. She could have the bedroom and I would take the couch. It would be small and basic, but it would be ours.

A few months would pass by and, as I made more money, we would upgrade to bigger place, where Ollie and Tadhg would join us. They would be eleven and thirteen by then, old enough to look after themselves.

Nowhere in the blueprint of my mind did I foresee having another sibling to care for, let alone a potential toddler.

I wouldn't be able to do it.

I would have to work during the day, and maybe some nights, too.

I couldn't look after the baby.

But I couldn't leave them look after the baby, either.

For fuck's sake.

THIRD YEAR

THIRD YEAR

New bathrooms and old mistakes

September 1st 2001

AOIFE

"Where'd you want me to toss the old one?"

Jerking awake at the sound of the familiar voice, I sprang up in my bed and craned my neck to hear better.

"Throw it out in the yard." That was my dad's voice. "I'll load it into the van later and take it to the dump."

"You sure?" My eyes widened in horror. "It's a cast iron tub. Could be worth something if ya take it to Timmy Murphy over in Glenmore? He wheels and deals in scrap."

"He has a young one in the same year as yourself and the twins, doesn't he?"

"Neasa. Yeah, she's in my class. Listen, I could give him a buzz, if you want? He might throw ya a score for it."

"Nah, the thing is on its last legs. It's red rotten underneath. It wouldn't make the price of the diesel it would cost me to drive it over there."

Oh my god.

"Fair enough."

He did not!

"Good man, Joey, can you carry that downstairs on your own?"

He did!

"Yeah, Tony, it's not a bother. I'll have to head off around three today, though. I've a match at the pavilion."

Dad brought him home.

"Jesus, son, you're as strong as an ox. And that's not a bother. We'll have it finished by then."

Again!

And I looked like something that had been dragged through a ditch. *Perfect.*

The prospect of seeing Joey, after spending a whole summer of not seeing his face every weekday morning in class, had me throwing the covers off my body, and springing off my bed, only to face-plant the floor in epic fashion, stubbing my toe on the metal corner of my bed as I fell.

"Jesus, Mary, Joseph and the donkey," I cried out, along with an array of colorful curse words. Twisting onto my back, I let out a strangled keening noise, as I grabbed my foot and held it to my chest. "Ow, ow, ow . . ."

My bedroom door swung inwards then, revealing my worried-looking father standing in the doorway.

"What in the name of Christ are ya doing, Aoif?" he asked, pressing a hand to his chest. "I thought there was a cat on heat in your room with the noises you were making."

"No cat on heat. Just . . . me," I mumbled, letting my head fall back against my bedroom carpet, pride – and toe – wounded. "What are you doing?"

"Joey's giving me a hand to replace the old bathroom," Dad explained. "Your mother wants the bath taken out, and an electric shower put in instead."

"Sounds expensive," I replied, wondering how we could afford a new bathroom. "What's wrong with what we already have?"

"You know your mother," Dad said with a weary sigh.

Yeah, I did, and I knew my father, too.

What Mam wanted, Dad got for her, regardless of whether he could afford it or not, usually as a form of compensation for his latest slip.

A new bathroom was a small price to pay for his wandering eye, I suppose.

It wouldn't do me an ounce of good to know the name of my father's latest mistake.

Not when I already knew the names of too many of the ones that had come before this one.

Frowning, Dad said, "Ah, Jaysus, Aoife, throw some clothes on, will ya?" He gestured to my bare legs. "Your brother's downstairs with his friends, and I've the young fella over from work."

"I was in bed," I shot back defensively, pulling at the hem of my string top in a piss-poor attempt to conceal my thighs. "And I'm in my own room. I don't make a habit of walking around in my knickers, Dad."

"Still," he grumbled, looking embarrassed, as he quickly turned on his heels and disappeared into the bathroom. "Did you ever hear of pajamas? And it's ten o clock in the morning. Shouldn't you be out of bed and doing something productive?"

Did you ever hear of doing something productive like keeping your dick in your pants?

"In case it slipped your attention, it's like twenty-three degrees outside, which is freakishly rare for us, hence the knickers," I tossed back. "And as for the lack of productivity, I have two days left of my summer holidays before school starts back up on Monday, and I'm thrown into revising for the Junior Cert, father dearest, and I have every intention of making the most of said days."

"So?" I heard him call out from the bathroom. "That's no excuse to laze around all weekend. You should find something productive to do."

"And you should find yourself a moral compass."

"What was that, love?"

"Nothing." Feeling my heart sink into the pit of my stomach, I climbed to my feet. "Nothing at all, Dad."

What a lovely way to end the summer holidays, I thought to myself dejectedly, as I padded across my room to close my door. *Your father's fucking around again, and instead of dealing with your father's infidelity, your mother's spent the savings on a new bloody bathroom.*

"That's loaded into the van, Tony. Do you want to strip that Lino flooring while we're at it? That way, we only need to make the one trip to the dump . . ." Joey's voice trailed off when he stopped short in the landing, just outside my bedroom door, and right in front of yours truly.

The minute his eyes landed on my bare legs; I felt a flush of heat wash over my skin. I didn't feel the need to hide my body, not when I was thrilled that he was finally looking.

Besides, I wasn't the self-conscious type. I had a nice body, and I wasn't about to convince myself that I hadn't, especially when the rest of the world was more than willing to chip away at a teenager's self-esteem.

"Enjoying the show?" I teased, planting my hands on my hips, when his eyes continued to trail over me. I thought it was quite poetic that I returned the same sarcastic question he'd asked me once before.

In equally unapologetic fashion, he took his sweet time returning his gaze to my face. "It beats the view of your father's ass crack, that's for sure."

I arched a brow. "It?"

Humor danced in his eyes, a rare change from the usual, generic fuck-the-world-and-everyone-in-it glower he doled out to just about everyone. "You."

It wasn't like we hadn't seen each other during the summer. I'd swung by the garage on many the occasion to torment him when he was working with Dad, and I'd been to most of his and Paul's matches, but we had been surrounded by friends or my dad.

Ridiculous as it sounded, I missed our little one-on-one moments.

Sure, they might have occurred against his will at times, but I knew that he enjoyed my banter as much as I enjoyed his.

Heart bucking wilder than necessary, given the fact that it was only the boy's eyes that were on me, and not his hands, I reached up and brushed my thumb over his swollen bottom lip, addicted to tormenting him. "What's that on your mouth, Joe; drool?"

"Don't do that." His green eyes darkened. "Not here."

"Don't do what?" Tone heavily laced with sarcasm, I traced his bottom lip with my thumb and grinned. "This?"

"Play your games when your father is across the landing."

"Why not?" I teased, hell-bent on playing games. "Are you afraid he'll catch you looking at his daughter like you want to eat her up." I stepped closer, waiting for him to crack and be the first to move away. "Do you, Joe? Do you want to eat me up?"

Reaching up, Joey snatched my wrist with his big hand, but instead of pushing me away like I was prepared for him to do, he pulled me towards him – so close that my body was pressed against his.

"Don't try to fuck with my head, Molloy." His voice was low and heated, and held the hint of warning. "I indulge you by playing your little games, but don't push your luck."

"My luck?" I breathed, heart racing violently, as I watched him watch me.

"Your luck," he confirmed. "There's only so far you can push me."

I could do nothing but stare at his face and resist the urge to slap it – or kiss it.

I wasn't sure which.

"I'm not Ricey. I won't kiss your cheek and hold your hand," he added, tone heated. "You keep goading me into touching you and that's exactly what I'm going to do." His pupils dilated and my heart hammered recklessly against my ribcage. "You might think that you're brave enough to take me on, to go toe-to-toe with me, but make no mistake about this." Leaning in close, he pressed his lips to my ear, and whispered, "You're not the wolf in our story, Molloy." His breath fanned my cheek, causing my pulse to skyrocket. "You're the lamb."

"What's that, Joey, lad?" my father called out from where he was kneeling in the bathroom, with his back to the landing.

"Nothing, Tony," Joey called back, not moving one muscle, as he turned his attention back to me. "You're the sweet, innocent lamb that's hell-bent on playing with fire," he said, walking me backwards until my legs hit my bed. "So, you might want to stop hunting me, Molloy." His hands moved to my hips, and he literally tossed me down on the mattress. "Because if you don't?" With my wrists pinned to the mattress above my head, he stepped between my legs and leaned in close, so close that his nose brushed mine. "Then one of these days, I'm going to hunt you back."

Oh fuck.

"You got that?" Releasing one wrist, he swiftly cupped my chin and forced me to look at him. "*Friend*?"

"I've got it." Breathless and feeling faint, I felt myself nodding. "*Friend*."

"Good girl."

I narrowed my eyes. "You dick."

He grinned victoriously down at me before releasing me and walking out of my room to rejoin my father in the bathroom.

On shaky legs, I hurried towards my bedroom door and slammed it shut, before blowing out a ragged breath. "Holy shit."

Did that just happen?

A few hours later, after a whole lot of soul-searching and not a lot of job hunting, I found myself sprawled out on a towel on the lawn in our back garden, soaking in the last of the sun-rays from the unusual heatwave, with the family dog curled up on the grass beside me.

Still mentally chewing over my earlier altercation with my classmate, I had been ordered by my father to go downstairs and stay out of their way.

My father had hit his limit this morning, when I had continued to hover in the bathroom doorway, making smart-ass comments about their shoddy work, and tormenting his precious apprentice.

It wasn't my fault.

The boy was too damn distracting to not stare at, and too sharp-tongued to not play with, but that didn't matter to Dad.

Banished from my own bedroom doorway for distracting my father's, and I quote, "poor young fella", I had retreated to the garden with the dog.

Ugh.

"What do you think, Spud?" Reaching down, I stroked his neck. "Hmm? I'm not a lamb, am I?"

Spud, who was a mix between a boxer and at least three other breeds, let out a groan of contentment, rolling onto his back and kicking wildly when I scratched his ear.

"Exactly," I cooed. "A lamb could never give you such good ear scratches. That boy is full of crap." *And sexy as hell.*

"Do you mind?" A dark shadow fell over me, blocking the sun. "My friends are here."

"And?" I drawled, using my foot to kick my brother out of my way of the sunshine.

"And I'm trying to play WWE," Kevin growled, shoving me back with his foot. "But they keep coming downstairs for drinks."

"Don't touch me with your freaky fungus feet," I warned. "And so? What do your creepy little friends have to do with me?"

"It's called athletes foot," Kev shot back defensively. "And they're not coming downstairs for drinks, dickhead; they're coming down to gawk at you."

Sliding my sunglasses off, I pulled myself onto my elbows and glared up at the scrawny little shit. "Don't call me a dickhead, dickhead."

"Aoife, come on," he said, gesturing to where I was sprawled out. "Can't you do that inside?"

"Can't I sunbathe inside? Why no, Kevin, sorry but I can't. That's not how sunbathing works," I deadpanned, readjusting the strap of my yellow bikini top.

"Then cover yourself up."

"That's not how sunbathing works either, Kev."

"Aoife," he groaned, tone whiny now. "Come on, you're embarrassing me. Just go inside or put some clothes on."

"How many days of sunshine do we get in Ireland, Kev?" I asked my half-twin.

Yeah, we might have shared a womb for nine months, but that was all we had in common. The truth was that we couldn't have been any different from each other.

"The answer is not enough," I told him. "Not enough by half. Besides, Dad's upstairs, putting a new bathroom in with Joey, and I've already been banished."

"Yeah, I saw he brought him over again," my brother grumbled. "He could have asked me to help him with the bathroom."

"Ha," I laughed. "Like you know the first thing about manual labor."

"He could show me," Kev snapped in a defensive tone. "I'm a faster learner than that thick fucker upstairs."

"Don't call him thick," I warned, hackles rising. "He's more world-wise than you'll ever be."

Kev rolled his eyes. "Oh yeah, because knowing where to score drugs takes a real genius."

"So, he smokes weed occasionally," I heard myself defend. "Big deal, Kev. So do a lot of other people in our year. It doesn't make him a bad person."

"It doesn't make him a good one either," he shot back. "Why are you always defending him?"

"Because he's my friend, Kevin."

"Yeah? Well, your friend does a lot more than smoke weed."

"Like you'd know."

"I *would*, actually," he replied. "I'm in his year, too, remember. I know what goes on just as well as you do."

"Yeah, in the swot class," I snorted. "And *sure* you do, Kev. You're right in there with the big guns, aren't ya? Mister popularity himself."

"You think your looks and popularity are going to get you far in life?" he laughed. "You're so stupid that it's pitiful."

"Look at you, getting all riled up and catty." I grinned. "No need to pity me, dear brother, because I'm doing just fine for myself."

"No, Aoife, *I'm* doing fine. *I'm* the one going places. The only way you're getting out of this council estate is if you marry up," he sneered. "Because you sure as shit won't make it on your own. So, you might want to hold on to Paul Rice, because he's looking like your best shot."

"Oh, whatever, you dick."

"It's the truth."

"Keep talking shit to me and I just might have to take my top off and give those gamer buddies of yours a real special show."

He narrowed his eyes. "You wouldn't dare."

"Try me." Narrowing my eyes right back at him, I reached for the string behind my neck and said, "I'm told I have perky nipples."

"You're such a bitch," he spat before storming back to the house.

"Takes one to know one, you little pussy," I called after him and then sighed in contentment, thrilled to have gotten the better of him. "Good one, huh?" I cooed, tickling Spud on his belly. "Yeah, I know you think he's a dope, too. I don't need a boy, do I? No, I don't. I'll make my own way in life."

"Aoife Christina Molloy!" my mother called out a few minutes later. Pushing the kitchen window open, she leaned out and shook a wooden spoon at me. "Get into the house and cover yourself up before I come out there and drag you inside."

"Are you serious?" I growled, giving Spud one final belly rub, before reluctantly climbing to my feet. "He *told* on me?"

"There are teenage boys in this house, Aoife," Mam shot back. "And you're sprawled out in the garden like Pamela fecking Anderson herself. Do you want to be the cause of giving them a turn?"

"I know how old they are, Mam. Most of them are in my year at school." I laughed. "And you're afraid I'll give them a turn? More like a horn—"

"Don't you dare finish that sentence," Mam warned, still waving around the wooden spoon like a demented housewife.

"Yeah, well, Dad told me to stay out of his way," I shot back. "So, guess what I'm doing?"

"Enough of the cheek, young lady. Inside right now, or you're grounded for the rest of the month. And that also includes having friends over. No phone, either. And no—"

"Jesus, fine," I huffed, stalking to the back door. "Relax, would you. It's not that serious."

"Thank you," Mam said when I stomped into the kitchen. "Now, go upstairs and throw on some clothes, like a good girl, before your brother has a conniption fit."

"Is it okay if I get a drink before I'm exiled from the family home for possessing a pair of boobs?" I asked sulkily, as I reached into the fridge and grabbed a carton of orange juice. "Or is rehydrating a crime now, too?"

"Drama queen." Rolling her eyes, Mam smirked and turned back to her ironing. "Pour me a glass, too."

Grabbing two glasses out of the press, I poured a glass of orange juice and quickly gulped it down before refilling my glass and pouring one for Mam.

"Thanks, love."

"You're not welcome," I teased, setting a glass down on the counter beside her.

"Trish, we've the bathroom just about done, love. I'm off to the dump with that old bath before they close," my father called from the front hall. "I won't be long."

"I'll see ya, Trish. Thanks for the sandwich."

"You're welcome, Joey, love."

Resisting the urge to rush out into the hallway and take one last look at Joey Lynch before he left with my dad, I held firm, and took another sip of orange juice instead.

"Make sure you take that old Lino with you, Tony," Mam called back, not bothering to look up from her ironing board. "And there's a few bags of rubbish at the side of the house that could do with being cleared out."

"Already taken care of."

"Good man yourself."

"A little heads up that Joey was coming over would've been nice," I said once as the front door closed behind them.

"Ah, he's a lovely boy, isn't he? Such a hard little worker," Mam gushed, smiling into her ironing. "I thought you'd be delighted to see him. The two of you are great little friends at school, isn't that right?"

"Yeah, we're buds," I agreed, suppressing a laugh. "A head's up would've been nice, though."

"It's a shame that he and your brother don't seem to gel," Mam added with a sigh.

"That's not on Joey, Mam. Kev doesn't gel with anyone," I snorted, resting my hip against the counter. "He's too stuck-up."

"Aoife."

"What?" I threw a hand up. "It's true."

"It would do your brother no harm to get off that computer and spend some time at the garage. I'm sure if he gave it a chance, they'd find some common ground."

"Common ground with who? Dad or Joey? Because, no offense, Mam, but your darling baby boy thinks he's above the both of them. Kev doesn't have any intention of getting his hands dirty. He has too high of an opinion of himself to slum it with us normal folk."

"He does not," she scolded. "Don't be mean."

"So, what's the story with the new bathroom?" I decided to change the subject by asking, unwilling to give my dope of a brother another second of airtime.

"What do you mean?"

"You know what I mean, Mam."

"Nothing, love." My mother, who looked a lot like what I presumed the forty-something-year-old version of me would look like, smiled brightly. *Too brightly.* "It was just time for a change."

"Mam," I sighed, reaching over to stroke her leg with my foot. "Are you okay?"

I knew she wasn't.

Her heart had been broken by my father for what had to be the fourth time in a matter of years – that I was aware of.

"I will be," she replied, tone forcefully cheerful, as she tucked a blonde wisp of hair behind her ear. "I'm looking forward to a nice hot shower tonight."

"So, who was it this time?" I asked then, poking the bear. I didn't really want to know, or at least, I shouldn't want to know, but I asked her anyway because I was a glutton for punishment. Reaching into her pile of neatly folded ironing that was stacked on the kitchen table, I retrieved a t-shirt and pulled it on. "Was it a one-off, or was it going on for a while?"

"I don't want to talk about it, Aoife," Mam replied quietly. "And I don't want you to think badly of him, either. He's a good man, deep down, and a wonderful father."

"Yeah, he is a good father," I agreed, setting my empty glass in the sink. "But he's a shitty husband, Mam."

She, on the other hand, was a good wife, and a great mam, but that didn't change the fact that her constant stream of forgiveness looked an awful lot like weakness in my eyes.

Sure, they seemed to have a decent relationship – when Dad wasn't letting his wandering eye get in the way. In a weird way, they were pretty stable, and never seemed to let any discourse in their marriage interfere with mine or Kev's lives.

"He makes a lot of mistakes," Mam agreed, handing me the denim shorts she had just finished ironing.

"Too many mistakes," I offered, stepping into my shorts and dragging them up my hips. "Too many times."

"I know you have your own thoughts and opinions on how I should react to this," she said evenly. "But it's a lot easier to know what to do when it's another person's life you're judging."

"It seems pretty black and white to me."

"That's because you're young." She smiled. "The whole world isn't black and white, Aoife. There's a whole lot of grey in the middle."

"I don't understand," I admitted with a frustrated sigh. "I don't get how you can stay with him when he's proven that he can't be trusted." I shook my head and pointed to her. "Look at how ridey you are, Mam."

"Ridey?"

"It means desirable," I explained. "Beautiful, gorgeous, fuckable—"

"Okay," Mam laughed softly. "Thank you for compliment, but that's enough of the bad language."

"Well, it's true. You are stunning, Mam," I pushed. "Kev thinks his weirdo buddies are coming downstairs to see me, when half of the time it's to sneak a peek at you."

"Aoife," she chuckled.

Sighing, I asked, "Why do you put up with it, Mam?"

"I love him," she replied. "I have invested more than twenty years of my life into the man and had my children with him. And believe it or not, he loves me, too."

"Then maybe he needs to love you better," I told her. "Because his words and his actions aren't exactly aligning, Mam."

"No marriage is perfect."

"No," I agreed. "But not all wives are cheated on, either."

"What about Paul?" Mam asked, steering the conversation towards me, tone defensive. "You love him, don't you? Imagine having spent most of your life raising a family together and then having to—"

"No."

Mam blinked in surprise. "No?"

"No," I confirmed, with a shake of my head. "I don't love Paul, and I have no plans on that status changing."

"Why not?"

"Because I have no intention of giving a boy that kind of power over me," I replied simply. "From my viewpoint, men let you down – even the good ones like Dad can't be trusted. So, why would I ever expose myself to that kind of pain? It would be emotional suicide."

Mam looked flabbergasted as she let out a small laugh. "Aoife, if you don't have feelings for the poor boy, then why in God's name have you been going out with him for the past year and a half?"

"Because I *choose* to," I explained. "Not because I *need* to."

"And what about Paul?" she demanded. "Have you spared a thought for his feelings?"

"I never said I didn't care about him, Mam; of course I care." Shrugging, I added, "I'm fond of him – obviously. I just don't have those crazy deep feelings that cloud common sense."

She arched a brow. "Fond?"

I shrugged. "What's wrong with fond?"

"Fond isn't a word a girl normally uses to describe her feelings towards her boyfriend."

"Well, that's all I have, Mam."

"But—"

"And if you think that Paul Rice is in love with me, then you're wrong," I was quick to point out. "His feelings are as replaceable to him as I am. If we broke up in the morning, I could guarantee you that it wouldn't take him more than a week, two tops, to move on to someone else."

"Aoife," Mam gasped.

"What? It's true." Laughing, I waved a hand idly in the air. "That's how fleeting boys' feelings are – and I don't just mean Paul, either. That's all boys. Sure, he might be pride-hurt, but he would forget about me pretty quickly."

"But—"

"Come on, Mam, it's like you've just said; you've been married to Dad for twenty years, and that hasn't stopped him from forgetting about you every time he strays."

"So, this way of thinking is because of our marriage?"

"Maybe?" I shrugged. "I don't know."

"I hope not."

"But even if it is, I'm glad because it prepared me for the inevitable. Don't catch feelings and you won't get hurt." I smiled. "Simple."

"So, you're saying that you never want to fall in love and get married?"

"It's not like I'm one hundred million percent opposed to the idea of marriage and motherhood. If the right guy came along and proved me wrong, then sure, I could do it," I admitted. "But I could never cope with the crap you've had to deal with. I could never do that, Mam. And certainly not with your grace. If I loved a man, and I mean truly, madly, deeply loved him, then I could never handle knowing that he was with another woman. It would destroy me. I would go insane. I could never forgive that level of betrayal. Hence why taking that chance seems too risky to me. So yeah, I'm probably going to remain ring-free for the foreseeable forty plus years."

"So, you wouldn't care if, say, Paul went off with another girl?" Mam questioned. "You know, since you don't love him and all?"

"Honestly, I'd probably be pissed off, but mostly relieved."

Mam gaped. "Relieved?"

"Yeah," I replied. "Because he would have proven what I've known all along; that no man can be trusted."

"Oh, I don't know, Aoife, love," Mam said, worrying her lip. "That's an awfully cynical way of thinking."

"Practical." I winked. "It's a *practical* way of thinking – and clearly the right way of thinking, considering the rumors I've heard."

Mam gave me a disconcerting look. "What *kind* of rumors?"

I arched a brow and gave her a *what do you think* look.

"He *cheated* on you?" she demanded, immediately catching my drift. "Then what are you doing with him?"

"Ha!" I folded my arms across my chest. "Pot, meet kettle."

She sighed heavily. "Aoife, love, you don't have to put up with that sort of thing."

"I know that I don't," I agreed. "And don't worry, I've confronted Paul about the rumors."

"And?"

I shrugged. "He says it's all a pack of lies."

"But you don't believe him?"

"Would you?"

Mam gave me a sympathetic look.

"I don't believe a single word that comes out of a single boy's mouth," I told her.

That's not technically true.

You believe one *boy.*

"And how long have these *rumors* been circling?"

Longer than I cared to admit to my mother. "A while."

"Do you know for sure that he hasn't cheated on you?"

"Can anyone know that for sure?"

"No, I suppose not."

"Exactly."

"Then why would you stay with him, Aoife?"

"Why do you stay with Dad?"

"That's not a fair comparison," she replied. "We're married."

"Exactly," I agreed. "You're *married, committed, in love, invested* in one another, and it *still* happens. He still fucks you over *repeatedly*. So, if I've learned anything from you and Dad, it's that no man, no matter how perfect he seems, can be trusted."

"You shouldn't be afraid to love a boy, Aoife." Sadness filled her voice as she spoke. "Please don't let our mistakes hold you back in life. It would break my heart to think that our relationship affected you to the point where you struggle to commit your heart to someone."

"I'm not afraid of loving a boy," I told her honestly. "I'm afraid of losing myself in one."

"I hate to tell you this, but more often than not, the two go hand in hand."

"I know." *That's what scares me.*

"Aoife."

"Enough of the heavy." Patting my mother's shoulder, I gave her a bright smile before heading for the door. "I'm hot and sticky and in dire need of a shower."

"Don't you dare use that shower before I do," Mam called after me. "I mean it, young lady, I'm having the first go of it."

"Understood," I replied as I hurried up the staircase, with every intention of doing just that.

Whipping off my t-shirt, I snatched a towel out of the hot-press, and legged it into the bathroom, cackling mischievously to myself.

"I mean it, Aoife Molloy, don't even think about it!"

"I won't," I laughed, closing and locking the door shut before my mother could finish her threat.

Feeling smug, I stripped off the rest of my clothes and rubbed my hands together in gleeful anticipation, as I stepped into the fancy new shower and switched it on.

The motor roared to life, but nothing came out.

Not so much as a drop of water.

"What the hell?" I growled, twisting and turning the knobs in front of me. "Work, dammit, work."

A knock sounded on the bathroom door then, and I blew out a frustrated breath.

Stomping over to my towel, I quickly wrapped it around my body, and unlocked the door before swinging it open. "I know what it looks like, but I swear I wasn't going to use it before you . . ."

My words trailed off when my eyes landed on Joey.

"You're back."

"I'm back."

"Well good." Tightening my hold on my towel, I gripped the door and tried to play it cool. "Because you've done a crappy job installing this shower. The stupid thing doesn't even work."

"I know," he replied, as he stepped around me and walked over to the toilet. "That's why I'm back." Crouching down in front of the toilet, he reached behind the cistern. "Forgot to switch the stopcock back on."

"The stopcock?" I laughed. "What the hell is that?"

Twisting the knob on a valve, Joey reached up and flushed the toilet and then hovered over the bowl, watching the water circle. Seemingly satisfied with that, Joey stood up and walked over to the shower and switched it on. This time, when the motor roared to life, it was accompanied by a steady spray of water coming from the jets. "Ta-da."

"Yay!!" I clapped in delight. "My hero."

"Easy to please you, Molloy."

"That's impressive, Joe."

He snorted. "I turned the water back on."

"I wouldn't have known how to do that."

He shrugged and moved for the sink, turning on the tap to wash his hands. "Well, enjoy your shower."

"Oh, don't worry, I plan to. Thanks again, Joe."

"Anytime."

Switching the tap off, he looked around for a towel, and when he couldn't find one, he walked over to where I was standing and dried his hands on the bottom of mine.

"Hey," I growled, slapping at his hands. "Rude."

"Nice towel," he shot back with a cheeky wink before moving for the door. "I'll be seeing ya, Molloy."

"Hold up." My heart pounded loudly in my chest as I followed him to the door, slipping around him to press my back to the wood. *And keep him for a little bit longer.* "Are you going to your match now?"

He didn't look happy when he said, "That's the plan."

"Do you even want to play?"

My question seemed to throw him because he furrowed his brow in confusion. "Why would you even ask that?"

"Because you never look happy on the pitch," I replied, readjusting my hold on my towel. Looking up at his face, I offered him a sad smile. "You never look happy anywhere."

"And you'd know all about that, wouldn't you?" he was quick to counter, immediately on the defense, as his walls shot up around him. "Watching everything I do like a fucking stalker."

"Lower the gun, Joe." Knowing every one of his tricks, I kept my tone even when I said, "I'm not the enemy."

Joey glowered at me for a long moment before the hostility in his eyes eventually gave way to resignation. "I know." Blinking, he released a harsh breath and shook his head. "I know, Molloy."

"I know you do," I replied, reaching up to rub the prickly fucker's shoulder. "It's okay. I forgive you."

Heat blazed in his dark eyes when he snapped, "I'm not sorry."

Yes, he was.

"I know." Reaching up, I ruffled his blond hair and grinned. "I still forgive you."

Unable to conceal his discomfort, or his agitated state in general, he ran a hand through his hair and gestured to where I was standing. "Can you move aside so I can leave? I'm going to be late for the match."

"I'll move aside," I told him. "If you promise to wait for me."

He frowned. "Wait for you?"

"Yeah." I smiled. "I'm coming with you."

"Coming with me?" Another frown. "Where?"

"You're going to the GAA pitch. I'm going to the GAA pitch. We can keep each other company on the walk."

"No."

"Yes."

"You're not coming with me."

"Oh, yes I am."

Joey stared at me in horror, walls shooting back up at a rapid rate. "In what alternative universe did I give you the impression that I would want you to come with me?"

"How about the universe where you quit pretending that my mere presence irritates you and admit that you adore the ground I walk on."

His mouth fell open. "I do not."

"You do, too." Smiling up at him, I patted his shoulder. "*Friend*."

"I'm not your—"

"Don't even think about finishing that sentence."

Swiftly clamping his mouth shut, he swallowed. He stared at me for the longest time before growling, "You have five minutes and then I'm leaving."

Grinning in victory, I patted his chest before stepping aside and moving for the shower. "I'll be ready in twenty minutes."

"Ten," he bit out, swinging the bathroom door open. "Or I'm leaving without you."

"Twenty," I called over my shoulder as I dropped my towel and climbed into the shower. "You can wait in my room."

The bathroom door slammed behind him, and then I heard him say, "Fifteen and that's final."

"Twenty," I crooned, thoroughly enjoying his agitation.

"You're a pain in my hole."

I laughed.

Clash of the ash

September 1st 2001

JOEY

I was beyond agitated, and the worst part was knowing that it had very little to do with the slating we had taken in the first half of our match, and everything to do with *her*.

My annoyance didn't stem from the fact that Molloy had, once again, inserted herself into my life by tagging along to the pitch with me.

Nor did it come from the play-by-play she had given me on the walk over of the day trip that she had taken with Casey earlier this summer, to the Aqua Dome in Tralee.

Yeah, apparently, Molloy deemed me to be a good enough friend of hers to subject me to a detailed account of her misadventure with a rogue tampon string.

Much of the conversation had consisted of the perils of swimming pools, unexpected periods, and skimpy white bikinis, and had left me feeling slightly disturbed and eternally grateful to possess a dick.

The driving force behind my agitation was the fact, when he had arrived at the pitch, she had allowed that piece of shit boyfriend of hers to talk down to her like she was a child.

When we rocked up to the GAA grounds, Ricey had all but shit pebbles.

He didn't want her anywhere near me. I wouldn't have blamed him for feeling that way if he treated her even remotely good enough.

But he didn't.

He was a sanctimonious prick, who, when he wasn't speaking over her, was speaking down to her, or abandoning her like she was a suitcase he couldn't fit in his car, and decided he no longer needed.

Ricey looked at Molloy and saw a pretty face and a smoking body.

And for him, that was enough.

He didn't care to scratch the surface.

Meanwhile, I knew what she was about, and had her personality pegged to a tee.

His girlfriend was a mischievous, self-assured, free-spirited, good-time girl, with a pure heart and a penchant for trouble.

Her easy-going, playful nature meant that she didn't take a lot of his jibes to heart, but I did.

I fucking took them to heart *for* her.

Watching her tolerate his less than stellar treatment of her irked the hell out of me.

It evoked feelings in my chest that had no business being there in the first place.

"Lynch!" Eddie snapped, dragging my attention away from the screen of my phone, where I was attempting to play a game of Snake to calm myself down and distract myself from the very strong urge I had to lunge across the changing room and pummel Paul the prick.

"Shit," I grumbled when his interruption caused me to die in my game, and quickly snapped my head up to look at my coach, who was pacing the changing room floor. "Yeah?"

"Put the phone away," he instructed. "You're on my time now. You can text your girlfriend after the match."

"Girlfriend." I shook my head in confusion. "What girlfriend?"

"That blonde young one you're always knocking around with," Eddie snapped. "The one perched on top of the dugouts, driving me half mental with all the cheering. Do me a favor, lad, and leave her at home for the next match. She's a distraction. Texting you and tormenting you when you're trying to play. You can be doing all the loving you want with her on your own time – *after* you win this game for me."

"Oh shit," Alec laughed, pressing his fist to his mouth, as he gestured between myself and Ricey with his free hand. "He thinks she's your—"

"Shut the fuck up," Ricey seethed as he flung his helmet across the room at Alec, before rising to his feet and storming out of the room.

The changing room erupted with laughter.

Feeling an immediate shift in my mood, I smirked to myself, thrilled that Eddie had unintentionally riled Paul up, and finding it even more humorous that he thought she was mine.

She is *yours.*

"Have I missed something?" Eddie asked, looking around to each of us. "What's the matter with Rice?"

"That smoking hot distraction you're talking about?" Alec snickered. "Yeah, that would be Ricey's girlfriend." He waggled his brows before adding, "But don't worry, Eddie, lad, I reckon Lynchy will be doing plenty of *loving* with her in the near future."

"Jesus Christ, Al," I chuckled, as the team laughed and bantered around us. "You just can't help yourself, can you?"

"Right, right. That's enough of that," Eddie grumbled, looking embarrassed. "Get your holes out on that pitch and put us in the running for some silverware."

Sore and uncomfortable, I slid my helmet back on, grabbed my hurley, and made my way out of the changing room and back onto the pitch.

"Woo! Would you look at the ass on number six!" a familiar voice called out when I slipped through the metal gate of the fencing that separated the supporters from the field and moved to join the rest of my team.

Sitting on top of our team's dugout, inside the fencing where she had no business being, Molloy winked down at me. "Nice moves."

"Nice legs," I replied, feeling much more sated now than ten minutes ago.

She beamed down at me from her perch, with her long legs dangling off the edge of the steel roof. "Stay out of trouble out there, okay?"

I nodded slowly. "I'll try my best."

"Make sure you do," she laughed. "Because I've put an awful lot of effort into saving you, six."

A confused laugh escaped me. "What does that mean?"

Molloy winked. "It means what it means, my friend. Now, go play with your stick and ball—"

"Aoife," Ricey snapped, stalking towards her just as the referee blew his whistle. "What the hell are you doing?"

Reluctantly, I jogged back onto the pitch and took up my position as the second half went underway.

I couldn't concentrate for shit, though.

Not when my gaze kept drifting back to where Ricey, who had been subbed off for the second half, was arguing with Molloy.

"Run, Joey, lad!" Eddie screamed from the sidelines, when I caught a sweet ball mid-air.

Usually, I didn't need to be told to do anything.

When I got a sliotar in my hand, I moved on instinct.

Not today, though.

Not as I watched that prick grab Molloy's arm and drag her off the roof of the dugouts.

She fell onto her knees, and I lost it.

Abandoning the sliotar on the ground, I stalked towards them, ripping my helmet off as I moved, feeling a level of fury that was almost inhuman.

He had his hand clamped around her arm and was trying to pull her towards the gate, shouting something that I was too far away from them to hear.

"Joey!" Eddie was screaming. "What are you doing? Go back!"

"Lynchy!"

"Number six, get back on the pitch, or you're booked."

Ignoring them all, I kept moving, not stopping until that bastard was within reach.

Tossing my hurley aside, I caught ahold of the back of his jersey and ripped him away from her.

"What are you—" Ricey began to warn, but was quickly silenced by the fist I implanted in his jaw.

Staggering backwards, he cupped his jaw and tried to steady himself. "What the hell is your problem?"

"You," I roared, chest heaving. "You putting your hands on her like that."

"Jesus Christ!" Ricey roared back at me. "When are you going to get it through your head that she's *my* girlfriend, asshole, not yours!"

"Don't you ever touch her like that again, do ya hear me?"

"Or what?"

"Or I'll put you in a body bag."

"Oh, fuck off back to the tramp whose legs you came out of, you filthy scumbag."

"Joey, no!" Molloy screamed, hurrying to step in between us, but it was too late.

Because I had well and truly taken leave of my senses.

Boy-friends and boyfriends

September 3rd 2001

AOIFE

"What did you do?" Casey demanded, bright and early on Monday morning, sliding into the seat next to mine in tutorial. "The whole school is talking about it."

It was our first day back to school after the summer holidays and our teacher was late, leaving the class in disarray.

Everyone was chatting loudly to each other, while I slowly withered in my seat.

"Oh god." Dropping my head on the desk, I resisted the urge to wail. "You mean the fight, right?"

"Obviously," Casey replied, eyes wide. "Spill the beans."

"Where do I start?" I groaned.

The fight that had broken out between Paul and Joey at the weekend could only be described as a vicious dog fight that, had they not been dragged off each other, I had no doubt would have resulted in someone being taken away by ambulance.

And that was *not* me being dramatic, either.

Never in my life had I seen such violence up close and personal.

I could still remember the sound of bones crunching.

The white t-shirt I had been wearing was now in the wheely bin, having been sprayed with blood that Mam couldn't get out in the wash.

Whose blood, I couldn't say for sure, because by the time they were pulled apart, both boys had been doing quite a bit of bleeding in their own rights.

Two desks to my left was a badly bruised Paul, while six rows behind me, at the back of the class, was a slightly less bruised Joey.

Neither one would look at the other – or me.

"I don't know how it got so out of hand, Case," I groaned, after giving my best friend a detailed report on the weekend's shenanigans. "But apparently, it's all my fault."

They had both been suspended from the hurling team, something they were clearly furious about, and the blame was being placed at my feet.

"Well, it sort of is," my best friend laughed, offering me zero sympathy for my ordeal.

"Wow," I grumbled. "Thanks a lot, bitch."

"Oh, stop," she said, making a psssh noise. "You know I'm right. I'm just saying what you already know out loud."

"Ugh," I groaned, knowing that she was right. "I just . . . "

"Want to have your cake and let Joey eat it?" she teased.

"He's just my friend, Case."

"Yeah, he's just your fuckable friend, who can't play nice with your equally fuckable boyfriend," she corrected with a chuckle. "All the while, your most fuckable friend of all – moi – had to spend the last weekend of summer listening to the sound of her mother's headboard crashing against the bedroom wall, because you're too busy chasing boys to hang out with your bestie."

I winced. "Sorry."

"Whatever, bitch." She rolled her eyes again. "Just take me with you next time. I would have paid good money to see those boys throw down." Grinning, she added, "Was it hot? It was hot, wasn't it? Did they rip each other's jerseys off? Was there skin on show? Did you see abs? Tell me."

"You're a perverted freak."

"And you're a greedy bitch keeping them both for yourself."

I glared at her for a moment before blowing out a breath. "There was skin on show."

Her blue eyes lit up with excitement. "Whose?"

"Joey's."

"*Yes*." She pretended to bite her fist. "Give me more."

"The coaches ripped his jersey trying to pull him off Paul," I whispered, leaning in close so we weren't overheard by any nosey bodies. "I've never seen anything like it, Case. It literally took three fully grown men to drag him away."

"He's a scary boy, Aoif," she replied. "Sexy, yes, but downright terrifying."

"No, he's not."

"Yes, he is," she corrected, tone serious now. "You know I'm from Elk's Terrace, too. I grew up on the other side of the estate from him. Hell, I even went to the same playschool as him. In fact, I specifically remember him being stood in the corner for fighting most days. I've seen him in action on way more occasions than you, babe, so trust me when I tell you that Joey Lynch is a *very* scary boy."

"Not to me," I heard myself whisper. "To me, he's just Joey."

"And Paul?"

"Paul is . . . Paul."

"You're playing with fire, Aoif," she replied, eyes full of concern. "You need to cool this friendship with Joey or end it with Paul. This can't continue."

"I'm *not* doing anything with Joey. I care about him, okay. It's okay to *care* about a person."

"Maybe you're not doing anything with him physically."

"Physical is the line. I have not crossed the line, Case."

"It's supposed to be the line," she agreed, tone uncertain.

"What does that mean?"

"It means that you're my best friend, and I don't want to see you get hurt," she said. "And messing around with Joey Lynch is going to get you hurt."

"I'm not hurt—"

"You're not hurt *yet*," she interrupted. "But you will be, if you don't start protecting that heart of yours." She sighed heavily before whispering, "For what it's worth, I don't blame you for holding back with Paul. He's not exactly a knight in shining armor but jumping from Paul's ship to Joey's is the equivalent of jumping out of the pan and into the fire. I know you care about him, Aoif. I get that, okay? But boys like that can't be fixed. Not with friendship, or love, or anything else, because they are just not fixable."

"I can't walk away from him," I admitted, voice torn. "I don't know why, but I just can't do it."

"From who? From Paul?" Her gaze flicked to the desk behind us, and she winced before saying, "Or from Joey?"

Following her line of sight, I turned around in my seat just in time to get an eyeful of Neasa Murphy slipping her hand under the desk she was sharing with Joey.

Twisting sideways in her seat, she leaned in close and whispered something in his ear.

Whatever they were whispering to each other had Joey giving her a heated look, and Neasa rising from her seat and walking out of class.

Not missing a beat, Joey stood up and followed her out of the room, completely ignoring me when he passed our desk.

My heart sank.

Forget sinking; it shattered in my chest.

It didn't take a genius to know where they were going, or what they planned to do when they got there.

"Still can't walk away, Aoif?" Case asked sadly. "Because he doesn't seem to have the same problem."

A minor disagreement

September 24th 2001

JOEY

"Whose fist did your face get on the wrong side of?" were the first words Podge Kelly said to me, when I slid into the desk beside his at the back of the classroom for Monday morning tutorial. "You look like you went ten rounds with Tyson."

Yeah, and I felt it, too.

I could still remember the feel of my father's steel-capped boot as he drove it into my ribcage on Friday night. I could remember the smell, the sensation, the pain, all of it. It was ingrained in my memory in vivid technicolor.

"That's right, ya little bastard," he laughed cruelly. "Hide behind a locked door like your sister! Do I have a son or two daughters in there?"

"Fuck you!" I roared back, as I staggered to my feet, with a lifetime's worth of beatings urging me on.

"No, Joey, don't," Shannon cried, as she tried and failed to pull me to safety. "Don't go out there."

Dragging the chest of drawers away from the door, I clumsily unlocked the door and swung it open, knowing that I wasn't quite big enough to get the better of the bastard yet, but not giving two shits either way.

I would rather take another lifetime of beatings than let him think he got the better of me.

Refusing to curl into a ball like a wounded animal would, like my mother would, I had pushed onto my hands and knees, trying and failing to climb back up with every forceful hit of his boot.

*

With one hand slung across my aching chest, I had taken comfort in the feel of the frantic thump of my heartbeat against my ribcage, while silently counting my teeth with my tongue.

Forcing myself to swallow down the steady trickle of blood that was coming from my lip, I remained perfectly still, as my mind wildly pondered my predicament.

When he had me on the ground, good and beaten, the bastard had spat in my face.

Broken and barely breathing, I'd laid on my bedroom floor like a child, listening as his footsteps slowly retreated from my room.

You can go, *a voice deep inside of my mind hissed*, you don't have to put up with his shit a second longer. Pack your bags, do a Darren, and run!

Refuting the notion, I shook my head and released a pained groan, feeling groggy as shit, and about three kicks to the head away from the grave. If you don't get out of this house, you're going to die in it . . .

Yeah, I had a real stellar weekend.

Shrugging, I dropped my bag on the floor beside me, and quickly tugged my hoodie off, knowing if I didn't, I would be taking the familiar trip to the office. "Got it in a match."

"We didn't have a match at the weekend."

"Training then."

"We didn't have training either, lad."

"Who are you, my mother?" I snapped, bristling. "Do you want a list of my whereabouts? Fuck off with your questions, ya spanner."

Leaning over, he pulled at the collar of my shirt. "Jesus Christ, Joe, your neck is black and blue."

"Touch me again and you won't have a hand to wank yourself off with," I warned him, shoving his hand away before quickly fixing the collar of my grey school shirt.

Frowning, Podge ran a hand through his bright-red hair and

mumbled, "Relax, lad, I was only asking out of concern," under his breath. "Sorry for caring."

"Well don't."

"What? Don't worry about my friend? Don't ask questions when you come into school looking like you've had the living shite beaten out of you?"

"Exactly," I shot back, reaching into my bag for my homework journal. "Don't ask and don't care."

"Fine," he snapped, and for a brief moment I wondered what would happen if I told him the truth, before mentally flinching when Darren's words of warning reverberated in my mind.

"Go ahead and tell your teacher. See what'll happen when you do. See what'll happen to the rest of them. They'll take us all away; split us up. Maybe your conscience can live with them having their innocence stolen, but mine sure as hell can't."

I'm trapped, I thought to myself, feeling my resolve seep back into my veins at a rapid pace, *I'm all alone.*

I felt snared, fucking cornered.

Surrounded by liars and cheats, I couldn't turn my back for a goddamn second.

Exhausted from fighting a war I would never win, and cut open from betrayal, I struggled to rein in my tumultuous thoughts.

Nothing made sense anymore.

It felt like everyone was out to get me.

I couldn't trust a goddamn soul, that was for sure.

Help wasn't available for people like us, with families like ours.

We were fucked, royally screwed, and I was too broken to keep these kids alive any longer.

Not when I wanted to die.

It was at that exact moment that my phone vibrated, signaling a text message. Sliding it out of my pocket, I quickly glanced at the screen.

HOLLAND: SMOKE @ LUNCH?

Mentally sagging in relief, I quickly tapped out a response and pressed send.

LYNCHY: I'LL BE THERE.

Shaking my head, I bounced my knee as I quickly typed out another message.

LYNCHY: GOT ANYTHING ELSE?

HOLLAND: LIKE?

LYNCHY: SOMETHING STRONGER. SOMETHING TO SHUT MY BRAIN OFF.

HOLLAND: IT'S YOUR LUCKY DAY. GOT A BATCH OF 512S WITH YOUR NAME ON THEM.

LYNCHY: 512S? WILL THAT DO WHAT I NEED IT TO DO?

HOLLAND: LIKE YOU WOULDN'T FUCKING BELIEVE, MY FRIEND.

LYNCHY: THEN I'M ALL IN.

Somewhere in my mind, I knew I was behaving in a self-destructive manner, bringing on unnecessary pain, inflicting harm upon my own body and mind, but I couldn't stop myself – the depression eating me from the inside out forbade me to.

My body was in pilot mode. I was going through the motions, just trying to get from A to B by any means necessary.

A smoke used to do that for me, but not anymore. I could feel my love affair with cannabis beginning to wane, because, as the beatings from my father continued to intensify, my control continued to slip, and my desperate need to escape grew to epic proportions.

I needed something stronger.

Something to make it all stop.

Something to help me make it through the days.

"What's the story with the two of you?" Podge asked then, obviously trying to clear the air, as he gestured across the classroom. "And don't feed me the same line you give everyone else."

"Who?" I replied flatly, sliding my phone back into my pocket.

"Who?" Podge gave me a '*don't piss down my back and tell me it's raining*' look. "Aoife, ya bollox. Who else?"

The minute he said her name, I found myself searching the room for her familiar blonde hair, only to discover that she was already staring at me.

With my brow cocked, I stared back at her, and mouthed the word *stalker*.

Proving, once again, that she was unlike any other girl in our year, who would blush and look away under scrutiny, Molloy arched a brow right back at me and mouthed *fuck-up*.

I winked. *Nice legs*

Grinning, she scratched her nose with her middle finger. *Asshole.*

Biting back the urge to laugh, I shook my head and turned away, knowing all too well how distracting she could be. Somedays, she wasted entire classes worth of my time with her playful, bullshit antics.

While we never actually cleared the air after the fight I had with her precious prick of a boyfriend a few weeks back, she had somehow wormed her way back into my good graces. Something I had vowed would never happen after witnessing her once again go back to *him*.

My attempt at ignoring her had lasted three days, because, in all honesty, staying away from Aoife Molloy was almost as difficult for me as staying mad at her was.

She was my boss's daughter, and I shared a classroom with her for seven hours a day. Some of our classes had mandatory seating plans, where I was given no choice but to endure her witty banter for forty minutes at a time.

On Wednesdays, we had four classes in which we were partnered up. That was a hard damn day to ignore her, which was how I had only lasted three days in the first place.

I didn't know what to make of her, if I was being completely honest. She was like the sweetest fucking smell that wouldn't go away.

A part of me was terrified that she would keep digging, somehow manage to break through my walls, through every one of my rotten layers, until she got to the ugly center of me, and then run for the hills.

A bigger part of me refused to care.

Why should I?

What the fuck did it matter to me if she walked away or not?

I wasn't losing any sleep over her.

I refused to.

She meant nothing to me, and she never would.

Plagued with an immeasurable weight of responsibility from the moment I fell out of bed in the morning until I collapsed back into it at night, I struggled to maintain anything more than a casual friendship or hookup in my personal life, which was fine by me.

I didn't know how to trust people and I didn't want to learn how. I had plenty of acquaintances, so-called friends to fuck around with at school and training.

Besides, I didn't need the hassle of having any extra people draining from steadily depleting supply of energy.

My family did enough of that on the daily.

"There's no story, Podge," I said, clearing my thoughts. "She's got it in her head that we're friends."

"Aren't ye?"

I don't know what we are.

Bumming a pen from his pencil case, I quickly forged a week's worth of my mother's signatures on my homework journal, and bad behavior report book, signing off on every note of warning I'd received from my teachers and year head, and then admired my handy work.

Marie Lynch

I arched a brow and smiled to myself.

Not bad.

"Did you score with her?"

"Who?" I asked, distracted, as I carved my initials into the desk with his compass.

"The Virgin Mary," Podge replied drolly. "Who'd you think?"

"Did he score with who?" Alec Dempsey asked, turning back in his seat to talk to us. His curious gaze flicked from Podge's face to mine. "Who'd ya score with, Lynchy?"

"No one."

"Aoife Molloy."

"Oh shit, lad. I thought that was just banter. You actually rode her?" Alec's eyes widened. "Is that why the fight broke out?"

"No."

"No?"

"No," I repeated slowly. "What part of the word no is so hard to grasp?"

My gaze flicked to Ricey then, and he quickly turned his attention to the front of the class, avoiding eye contact.

I smirked, enjoying his discomfort.

Now this piece of shit, I had no problem ignoring, and with the exception of a few passing comments when we had to play together, I went about my business pretending that he didn't exist.

I'd shown him with my fists how I felt about him that day, and he had the good sense to keep a wide berth of me since.

"Of course he did," Podge accused, winking at Alec. "That's why she's always staring at him."

"Lad, she is by far the best-looking girl in our year," he groaned. "Maybe in the whole school."

There was no maybe about it.

Molloy's claim on that particular title was undisputed.

"That's why Ricey's so obsessed with her. He has to have the best of everything and be the best at everything. He hardly ever lets the girl out of his sight," Alec offered, and then his eyes bulged in his head. "Seriously, lads, he's fairly obsessed with Aoife and would lose his shit if she went behind his back . . . Holy fuck, did you score with her at the garage? That's where you work with her da, isn't it?"

"She'd be there without Ricey," Podge offered. "It's a good opportunity to get some alone time."

"Oh my god, lad, it's perfect," Alec agreed with an enthusiastic nod. "That's how you fucked her without him catching you, isn't it?"

I narrowed my eyes in disgust. "See, this is exactly how the rumor mill gets started around here."

"I'm surprised you could pry her legs open," Mike Maloney laughed, as he joined in the conversation. "From what I hear, she's tighter than a—"

"Finish that sentence," I said coldly. "Go on, I dare you. See what happens."

"And you'd know a lot about prying a girl's legs open, wouldn't you, Mike, with that big frigit head on ya," Podge chuckled, trying to steer the conversation back to warmer waters – back to safety. "If you say that you weren't with her, then I'll take your word for it, Joe."

"There's no other way to take the truth," I said flatly.

"Jesus, she's a serious ride, though," Mike added, sighing. "Ricey is some jammy fucker to have managed to convince her to go out with him."

"Tell me about it, lad," Alec agreed. "I swear I've had dreams about her legs."

"The length of them."

"And that skirt."

Swallowing down a surge of bitterness, I forced myself to block out their voices, because if I didn't, there was a very good chance I would lose my shit.

For once, luck was on my side.

"Joseph Lynch," Mrs. Falvey, our year head, announced when she walked into the classroom a beat later. "You're wanted in the office." She clicked her tongue, disapproval etched on her face. "And bring your red book with you."

"What did you do this time?" Mike whispered, nosey as usual.

"Fuck if I know," I muttered, quickly rising to my feet.

Only delighted to be getting away from the conversation unfolding around me, I grabbed my bag and headed for the door.

"I am so disappointed in you," Mrs. Falvey said when I passed her desk. "I thought we had gotten a handle on your behavioral issues last year. And what with it being a new term and all, I was willing to give you a clean slate, but then, four weeks in and I come to find that you've been fighting again."

"With *who*?" I asked, tone laced with confusion, as I scratched the back of my head.

"Marcus Shorten."

"Marcus *who*?"

"He's from Kilcock community college," she bit out. "Ring any bells?" I stared blankly.

"You *broke* his finger, Joey," she said with a frustrated sigh. "With your hurley. *On purpose*."

"When?"

"Last Friday," she hissed. "His mother phoned the school this morning. As you can imagine, she was very upset about the matter. She wants to take it to the board."

"Oh yeah," I mused, vaguely recalling the incident on the pitch last Friday when our schools met in a league game. "His mother actually phoned the school?"

"Yes, she did. She was very upset."

"That wasn't a fight," I scoffed.

What a sap; telling his mammy on me.

The teacher's eyes narrowed. "And what would you call it?"

Fucker nearly took my knuckles off with the steel band on the bas of his hurley. I was only returning the favor. "A minor disagreement."

"Well, that minor disagreement has earned you your first suspension of the school year," she snapped. "Congratulations." Clapping her hands together mockingly, she asked, "Is there anything you'd like to say for yourself?"

"Yeah. We won the game last Friday," I replied with a shrug. "And I was man of the match."

Suspensions and stilettos

October 18th 2001

AOIFE

"Fifty euro, Dad," I tried to plead my case on Thursday evening, after school. "It's for a good cause."

"Since when is a new pair of shoes a good cause?"

I shrugged. "Would you prefer if I lied and told you that I would put the money in the poor box?"

"*Aoife.*"

"Please, Dad," I begged. "I'll never ask you for anything else ever again."

"Until you need a skirt to go with the shoes? Like every other time you've asked me for money."

"Okay, fair point," I conceded, holding a hand up. "But you don't understand how badly I need these shoes, Dad. They're perfect for the costume I'm planning on wearing for Halloween."

"What's your mother saying about it?"

I rolled my eyes. "You know Mam."

Dad frowned. "If your mother doesn't think—"

"Come on, Dad," I coaxed, and then pulled out my trump card. "Kev gets any computer game he asks for and never has to jump through hoops, either. It's almost as if you guys don't want me."

A laugh erupted from beneath the car I was leaning against. I glared down at the culprit, who was sprawled out on a creeper, with only the lower half of his body available to kick.

"Aoife," Dad sighed. "Of course we want you."

"I'm only asking for a pair of shoes, Dad," I wailed, tone forcefully soft and frail. "Please?"

"Jesus," Dad muttered, wiping his hands on an oil rag. "Fine. I'll get my wallet. It's in the office."

"You are *the* best. I swear that you will live with me forever and will never see the inside of a nursing home," I crooned, throwing my arms around him with glee. "But yes, get your wallet," I added, steering him in the direction of his office. "Because they're the last pair on the shelves and I will *die* if Danielle Long beats me to the counter with them."

Waiting until my father had disappeared inside his office, I turned my attention back to Joey.

With one leg on either side of his body, I reached down, fisted the front of his overalls and yanked hard, causing him to roll out from under the car, spanner in hand.

"Do you mind?" he drawled, looking up at me from his perch, with his baseball cap slung on backwards, and oil smeared on his cheek. "I'm kind of in the middle of something here."

"Do *you* mind?" I shot back, hands on my hips, as I stood over him and glared. "You could have blown that for me with your snickering."

"You're a manipulative little witch, aren't ya?" He laughed again. "Playing your old man like that?"

"Only when I have to," I huffed, unwilling to feel bad about it. "You didn't see the *shoes*."

"Shoes," he snorted, shaking his head. "And you wonder why we're not compatible."

"Oh, get you, mister *I have no problem throwing my money away on weed*," I tossed back. "I guarantee if you saw me wearing those shoes, you'd understand."

"If they look as good on you as that yellow thong you're wearing, then I'm going to have to agree," he replied, gesturing to the perfect view up my skirt that I had unintentionally given him.

"Close your eyes."

"Close your legs."

"No." Heat flamed inside of me. "I'm not embarrassed."

"Neither am I."

"You're looking up my skirt."

"You're flashing your pussy in my face."

"Oh my god," I choked out. "You did *not* just say that."

Chuckling softly, he moved to roll back under the car.

"Wait." Stopping him from disappearing under the car by pressing my foot to his stomach, I wheeled him back out, unwilling to let him win this particular round of banter. "So, you like the color yellow?"

"It recently became my favorite."

"Is that so?"

"That's so, Molloy."

"My favorite color is yellow, too."

"It's a good color on you."

"I look even better when I take it off." Feeling mischievous, I purred, "You're so sure of us being incompatible, but I wonder if that might change if I sat on your lap? Hm? Do you think we'd find common ground there, Joe?"

"Why don't you take a seat, and we'll find out."

"Wh-what?" Thrown off-kilter by his flirtatious attack, I frowned at him. "What are you doing?"

"What are *you* doing?"

"You're flirting with me."

"*You're* flirting with me."

"So?" I huffed. "I always flirt with you."

He grinned. "Well, maybe I've decided to change tactics."

"By flirting?"

"Well." He shrugged. "Being an asshole doesn't seem to be working in my favor, does it?"

"But you're so *good* at being an asshole."

"Come closer and I'll show you how good I can be in other ways."

"Okay, now you're freaking me out," I choked out, springing away from him. "Stop this right now and give me back my asshole."

Laughing, Joey wheeled himself back under the car. "You lost that round, Molloy."

"I didn't lose," I huffed. "You changed the rules."

"Yeah, yeah," he called out from under the car. "Go and buy your shoes, princess."

My costume is better than his

October 31st 2001

JOEY

"One more street, Joe," Ollie begged, hands clasped together, as he stared up at me with those big brown eyes that usually made me cave in and give him whatever he wanted.

Not tonight.

There was an underage disco happening at the GAA pavilion tonight to celebrate Halloween, and as soon I got these two fuckers home to bed, I had every intention of attending – and getting shitfaced.

It was the only thing that was keeping me going; knowing that there was a naggin of vodka, and a joint with my name on them, waiting for me across town.

"You've a carrier bag full of sweets, lad." Leaning against some ran-domer's garden wall, I played another mindless round of Snake on my phone, ignoring the hordes of trick or treaters running up and down the street. "You have plenty."

"Tadhg gots more than me," Ollie whined. "He gots a whole bag more than me – see, Joe!" He pointed at our brother, who was carting around an overflowing plastic bag of sweets in one arm, and an equally overflowing pillowcase thrown over his shoulder. "It's not fair."

"Give it a rest, ya big moaner," Tadhg shot back with a snicker. "Maybe if you stopped trying to have a conversation with every old biddy that answers the door to ya, then you'd have gotten more houses done."

"I was being nice," Ollie shot back, tone hurt. "I was using my manners."

"And I was using my brain," Tadhg countered. "So quit complaining."

"But he gots more than me," Ollie complained again. "Look, Joe, look . . ."

"That just means that Tadhg's going to be a whole lot fatter than you," I replied, distracted, and then muttering a string of curses under my breath when I got killed in my game.

"Yeah, well, my costume is better than his," Ollie grumbled, gesturing to the makeshift cape and mask that Shannon had made for him. "I'm Robin."

"Don't get carried away with yourself, Ols," Tadhg shot back. "You've a black bin bag wrapped around your shoulders. You look more like a bag of shit someone dragged out of a wheely bin than Robin."

"Tadhg," I warned. "Pack it in. He's only small."

"Yeah, well, I look better than you," Ollie huffed, folding his skinny arms across his equally skinny chest. "You're a crappy Batman."

"Maybe, I am," Tadhg agreed. "But I still got more sweets than you."

"Right," I said, shoving my phone into my pocket. "Come on, lads, we've been out for almost two hours. Time to get ye home. I've things to do."

"What things?" Tadhg demanded, eyeing me warily, as I herded them across the road, grabbing ahold of Ollie's hand when he almost ran out in front of a car.

Smirking, I gave him a wink. "A Gard wouldn't ask that question."

"Uh-oh," Ollie grumbled, plodding along beside me. "That sounds like trouble."

You have no idea, kid.

"I already know where you're going anyway," Tadhg huffed. "That disco in the Pav."

"Then why'd ya ask?"

He shrugged. "Don't know."

"Is it fancy dress?" Ollie's face lit up. "Do you gots a costume?"

"It's *got*, not *gots*," Tadhg sighed. "Learn how to speak, will you?"

"Tadhg," I said in a warning tone before answering Ollie. "I don't know, kid. I suppose some of the girls will dress up."

"In scary costumes?"

More like as slutty angels and devils. "Some of them," I offered instead, distracted at the possibility.

Without my brain's permission, my imagination conjured up a fantastic fucking visual of Molloy; with her long legs on full display in red, fishnet stockings, and her tits pressed together in a skimpy white nurse's dress with one of those little nurse's hats perched on top of her long, blonde hair.

Jesus.

But then my imagination went all Judas on me by envisioning Paul the prick all over her on the dancefloor, and I physically balked.

Thoroughly disgusted now, I pushed all thoughts of Molloy to the back of my mind and concentrated on getting the boys home.

When I brought my brothers home after trick or treating, Shannon greeted us at the front door, waiting patiently for her cut of the loot – an agreement she and the boys had shaken on when she agreed to make their costumes.

Leaving them to their arguing, I hurried upstairs to take a shower and change my clothes.

When I walked into the kitchen twenty minutes later, Mam was at her usual perch at the table.

"You smell nice," she said, nursing a cup of tea. "Are you going out?"

"There's a disco over at the Pav, tonight. I'm meeting Podge and a few of the lads from school there," I replied, tone civilized, something that was always easier to do when the old man was out of the house.

A massive blowup last week had sent my father temporarily packing.

"Any sign of him?" I asked, reaching into the fridge for a can of Coke. "Did he phone?"

Because let's face it, we all knew he would.

Once he grew bored of whatever flavor of the week that he'd decided was better than the mother of his children, he'd come crawling back.

He always did.

"No." Shaking her head, she released a small sigh. "I told you last week, he's gone—"

"For good this time," I finished for her, reeling off the same line I'd heard at least half a dozen times a year since I was old enough to remember. "Will you be okay on your own with the kids?" I eyed her swollen belly and a swell of concern gnawed at my gut. "I can stay home if you need me to."

"No, you should go," she said, pulling herself to her feet. "I'll be fine here."

"Mam, if I go out, I'll be late." *In other words, I won't be back if you change your mind and decide you need me.* "Are ya sure you'll be alright?" I frowned, uncertain. "What about the, uh, the baby?"

"I'm not due for another three weeks," she replied. "And I've Shannon here to keep me company." Smiling, which was a rare sight these days, she added, "we might get a Chinese and watch a film once the boys go to bed."

"Yeah, I wouldn't count on them going to sleep anytime soon," I told her, thinking about the bags of sweets they'd collected. "Here ..." Pausing for a moment, I reached into my jeans pocket and pulled out a twenty euro note. "Get your takeaway with that."

"No, no, no," Mam argued, shaking her head. "That's yours. I have enough money."

No, she didn't.

I knew this because I'd watched her put her last tenner in the electric meter earlier.

"It's grand. I got paid yesterday," I told her, thrusting the money into her hand. "I still have money for myself."

She stared at the money in her hand for a long moment before shakily stuffing it into her dressing gown pocket. "Thank you, Joey."

"It's grand. Just make sure Shannon eats something, will ya?" I said, grabbing my keys and moving for the front door. "She's skin and bones these days." *You both are.*

"I will, I promise," Mam replied, following me to the front door, and then lingering awkwardly in the doorway when I stepped outside. "Have a good night."

"Yeah," I replied. "You too, Mam."

"Joey," she called out when I was standing at the garden wall. Wrapping her dressing gown tightly around herself, Mam hurried towards me.

Frozen to the spot, I didn't move a muscle when she reached up and pressed her small hand to my cheek.

Blue eyes watering with unshed tears, she leaned up on her tiptoes and pressed a kiss to my cheek. "Be safe."

"Yeah," I replied gruffly, clearing my throat, as guilt filled me for the sins that we both knew I would commit tonight. "I will, Mam."

Slut drops and alcopops

October 31st 2001

AOIFE

The Pavilion was packed to the rafters on Halloween night, with people grinding and sweating all over each other in their hunt for a good time, and I was no exception to the rule.

Throwing shapes to Flip & Fill's 'Shake Ya Shimmy' in my fancy new shoes – courtesy of daddy dearest – with my best friend by my side, I let loose and threw myself into the moment.

With our costumes coordinating, Casey was the slutty devil to my equally slutty angel. With her horns and my halo, we made quite the pair on the dancefloor, enjoying the attention we were receiving from the lads in our year almost as much as the music.

"Cop on, Aoife," an angry voice growled in my ear, as a big body pressed up against me from behind, and a pair of big hands clamped down on my hips. "Everyone is looking at you."

"So?"

"That's the point," Casey laughed.

"So, I don't like it," Paul snapped. "You're with me, which means you're mine to look at, not every fella in this place. Enough of the fucking peep show."

"One; you don't own me," I slurred, grinding my body against his. "Two; I'm only dancing."

"Yeah, like a slut."

"Are you serious?"

"Yeah, I'm serious," he shouted. "Do you want everyone to think that I'm going out with a slut?"

"Oh my god." I shook my head angrily and swung around to glare up at him. "You did *not* just say that to me."

"My whole fucking team is looking at ya," he argued, cheeks reddening. "It's embarrassing for me having my girlfriend shaking her ass like that."

I narrowed my eyes. "Go fuck yourself, Paul."

"No, babe, wait—"

Shrugging out of his hold, I grabbed Casey's hand and sexy danced towards her, ignoring the killjoy behind me.

"What's his problem?" Casey shouted over the music, gesturing to where Paul was scowling behind me.

"Apparently, I'm embarrassing him."

Narrowing her eyes, she sucked on her middle finger before using it to flip him off. "Asshole."

DJ Aligator Project's 'The Whistle Song' blasted all around us then, drawing every teenager within a ten-mile radius onto the dancefloor.

"Screw him," Casey ordered, dragging me deeper into the crowd. "Let's just have a girls' night."

"Excellent plan."

Drunk off the good time – and the vodka flushing through our veins – we ground against each other, shaking our asses like we were contesting for the role of the next member of Destiny's Child.

Spying one of the lads from our class, who was dressed as the funniest Marilyn Monroe I'd ever seen in my life, throwing shapes in the middle of the dancefloor, we quickly closed in on him.

"Angel-legs! Devil-tits!" Alec cheered, throwing his arms over our shoulders when we reached him.

Off his head on drink, drugs, and mischief, he bumped and grinded along to the unofficial blow-job song, not giving two shits how ridiculous he looked in his cheap, knock-off relic of her *Seven Year Itch* white dress and fake blonde wig, with his hairy legs on full display.

"I can't cope with him," Casey half-laughed, half-slurred, gesturing to the big eejit grinding his ass against us. "I can't tell if I want to slap him or kiss him."

"Both," I choked out through fits of laugher, as Al ripped the top half of his dress off in dramatic fashion, and pinched his own nipples, eyes rolling in equally dramatic fashion.

"Cover those tits up, Marilyn," Casey laughed, reaching up to hide our classmate's nipples with her small hands.

Not missing a beat, Alec's hands shot out to cup Casey's barely concealed breasts.

"Are you seriously touching my tits?"

"You're touching mine," Alec shot back, waggling his brows at her. "Seems like a fair trade to me."

"You have some pair on you, boy."

"I was about to pay you the same compliment."

"This is the part where they neck on," a familiar voice shouted over the music, and I turned to find an amused-looking Podge. "Told ya." Winking, he pointed back to where Casey and Alec were now mauling the lips off each other. "So predictable."

Laughing, I shimmied over to one of my favorite lads from our year and held my hand out to him. "Help a loner out, will ya, Podge?"

"The things I do for friends," he chuckled, taking my hand and pulling me in for a dance. "Don't be getting any notions now, ya hear?"

"I'll try my best." Grinning, I wrapped my arm around his neck and danced along to the music. "So, where's your friend tonight?"

"Which friend would that be, Aoif?" he teased, knowing full well who I was referring to me.

I rolled my eyes. "Funny."

"Lynchy's in here somewhere."

"So, he actually knows how to dance?"

"I don't know about dancing, but he definitely knows how to get a naggin of vodka past the bouncers."

"Aoife!" Ripping me clean out of Podge's arms, my boyfriend clamped his hand around my arm and roughly pulled me back to him. "Come here for a sec—"

"Hey," I snapped, yanking my arm free, as I turned around to glare at him. "That hurt." I reached up to rub my arm. "Don't do that."

"Don't be such a drama queen," he protested with a roll of his eyes. "Come outside with me." He reached for my arm again. "I want to talk to you."

"No." Yanking my arm free once more, I glared up at him. "You called me a slut."

"I didn't mean that the way it came out." Pulling me into a hug, he leaned down and planted a kiss on my lips. "Come on, babe, it was a slip of the tongue. Don't fall out with me over it."

"You said that I look like a slut," I hissed, shoving at his chest in order to escape his hold.

"Look at you," he shouted back at me, losing his cool. "You're practically wearing underwear and rubbing yourself against another fella!"

"Hey," Podge warned, coming to my defense.

"Stay out of this, Podge."

"Don't grab her like that, lad."

"It's okay, Podge, I'm grand," I told him before turning my glare back on Paul. "This is a Halloween costume, and Podge is my *friend*. I'm allowed to have friends, Paul."

"It's too revealing," he argued. "I can see the cheeks of your ass under that thing you call a dress. It makes you look like a whore. You're better than that."

"Whore?" Drunk and furious, I shoved at his chest. "You prick."

"Aoife—"

"I was dancing with my friend – enjoying myself. I wasn't doing anything wrong, and you insulted me." I glared at him. "Twice. That's a hard fucking limit for me, Paul."

"Yeah, but you've been drinking."

"And?"

"And I'm not comfortable with it."

"With what exactly?" I demanded, voice slurring. "Me drinking or dancing?"

Paul opened his mouth to reply but I quickly cut him off.

"You know what? Don't answer that. Don't even speak to me. In fact, why don't you consider yourself relieved of boyfriend duties for the night. At least that way you won't feel embarrassed by me."

"Don't do this, Aoife," he warned, snatching my hand up. "Not here. Not like this."

"You started this, Paul." Pulling my hand back, I wagged a finger in his face. "You called me a slut, remember? And a whore." Shaking my head, I backed up a step or two, bumping up against a hard chest. "Whoops."

"How are ya, Aoife?" Mack, one of the lads from my class, asked, offering me a friendly smile. "You're looking well."

"Hey, Mack." I smiled back at him before returning to glower at my boyfriend. "You're going to eat your words, asshole."

With that, I turned back to dance with my smiling classmate, who was only too happy to dance with me.

"Yeah, girl," Casey hooted in support, as she and Alec danced over to us. "You show that prick who's boss."

"Jesus Christ," Paul growled, grabbing ahold of my arm and roughly yanking me back towards him. "You're a messy fucking drunk."

"And you're just plain messy," I snapped. "Now leave me alone before you ruin my whole night."

"Let her go, Ricey, lad," Mack said in a concerned tone. "She was only dancing with me. We're friends, lad. No harm done."

"Yeah, prick," Alec interjected, with Casey's red lipstick smeared all over his face. "I wouldn't put hands on her, if I were you."

"She's making a fucking show of herself," Paul seethed before dragging me away from our friends. "I'd call that a lot of harm done."

"Hey," Casey called out after us. "Let go of her arm, Paul!"

"No," he bit out, as he began to make his way through the crowd, dragging me along after him. "You're going to sober up and we're going to talk about this."

"I don't want to talk," I complained, digging my heels into the floor. "I want to dance."

"And make an even bigger show of me?" He shook his head and continued to drag me towards the exit. "Yeah, that's not happening, babe."

"Stop," I argued, trying and failing to break free from his hold. "You're squashing my wings – my halo! Stop, I've dropped my halo on the floor."

One minute, I was pulling with all of my might to break away from Paul's hold, and the next, I was on my hands and knees on the floor, having lost my balance when he abruptly let go of my arm.

"My halo!" I half-slurred, half-cheered, reaching out a hand to retrieve it. "You bastard," I wailed, when someone's big foot stomped down on it, cracking the plastic in half. "You broke my halo!"

"Put your hands on her like that again and see what'll happen," a familiar voice threatened, as the owner of said voice hooked an arm around my waist and pulled me to my feet. "She's not a fucking ragdoll, asshole."

Bleary-eyed, I let my gaze wander up to the owner of said voice and beamed when his familiar green eyes landed on mine. "Well, hey there, Joe!"

"Molloy," he acknowledged in his usual deep timbre. "Causing trouble again?"

"Always." Grinning wolfishly, I hooked an arm around his neck for balance, feeling my pulse skyrocket at the sight of him. "What are you doing here?"

"Looking out for you, apparently," Joey muttered, keeping one strong arm hooked around me.

"She's mine, dickhead, back off," Paul growled, running a hand through his hair. "I'll look after her."

Joey cocked a brow. "Looks like you were doing a real stellar job at that."

"She's drunk. She's a handful when she's like this."

"So, that's your excuse for almost pulling her arm out of its socket?"

"Someone broke my halo, Joe," I wailed, waving a broken piece around aimlessly in front of his face. "I'm a fallen angel now."

"Don't worry about it," he replied with a shrug. "No one likes a saint, Molloy."

"Aoife, come on."

"So, what are you dressed as?" I asked, batting a random hand away, as my gaze trailed over the fitted white shirt and blue jeans Joey had on. "Let me guess," I teased, reaching up to fluff his perfectly styled hair and then letting my hand move to the silver chain hidden beneath the collar of his shirt. "You're a fallen angel, too."

"Come on, Aoife," Paul interrupted, catching ahold of my waist, and pulling me roughly to his chest. "We're leaving. Now."

"No," I growled, huffing out a breath. "I don't want to go with you. I want to stay and dance with Casey."

"Now, Aoife!"

"It doesn't look like she wants to go anywhere with you," Joey interjected coolly, stepping in front of us when Paul carted me towards the exit.

"I don't," I agreed, nodding vigorously, as I slipped out of his hold. "I want to stay."

"Stay out of it, Lynchy," Paul warned, reaching for my arm again. "She's my girlfriend, not yours. I'll look after her."

"Then why don't you start by asking her what she wants?" Joey countered, taking a protective step in front of me. "Not fucking telling her." Piercing green eyes locked on mine, when he turned back to me and asked, "Molloy, do you want to leave with him?"

"No," I replied, and then hiccupped loudly. "He called me a slut."

"You called her a slut?"

"I did *not* call her a slut," Paul quickly defended, pulling on my arm. "I told her that she was dancing like one."

"Same thing," I shot back, yanking my arm free from Paul's overly tight grip, as I leaned heavily against my protector's tall frame. "I'm not dealing with you tonight, so just go away and leave me alone."

"Aoife."

"No, stop. I'm not going with you, Paul."

"You're drunk and that prick is off his head on god knows what," Paul snarled. "If you think I'm leaving you alone with him, then you're out of your mind."

"I'm not leaving with you," I screamed, losing my patience. "I'm mad at you, remember?"

"So, what?" he demanded. "You'd rather stay here?" His disgusted gaze flicked to Joey. "With *him*?"

"Why not?" I slurred, patting his stubbly cheek with my hand. "He's my friend."

"Your *friend*?" Paul deadpanned. "He's not your friend, Aoife. He's a fucking druggie who's only out for a good time. *I'm* your friend. I'm the one who cares about you. I'm your *boyfriend*. You're mine, dammit!"

"I'm not your property, Paul," I screamed over the sound of Micky Modelle's dance version of 'I'll Tell Me Ma' as it blasted from the DJ booth.

His eyes bulged in his head, and he looked like he was about to lose his mind.

"Yes, you fucking are, now let's go," he roared, losing his cool with me. "Because there's no way in hell that I'm allowing you to stay here with him."

"*Allowing* me?" I hissed, outraged. "You don't get to *allow* me to do anything, Paul. Who the hell do you think you are? I'm my own person. I make the rules for me."

"Fine," he attempted to coax. "We can talk about all of it and more outside." He reached for me again, but this time it was the boy I was leaning against who batted Paul's hand away – and not gently, either.

"You heard her," Joey warned in a dangerously cold tone, reaching up to pry my hand off his cheek. How it had got there, I had no clue. "Walk away."

"Oh, you're just loving this, aren't you?" Paul narrowed his eyes.

"You must have a serious death wish, prick-face," Joey replied in a heated tone, as he took a menacing step towards Paul. "Walk the fuck away before you restart something that I'll be only too happy to finish."

"Try it," Paul snarled back. "You remember who my father is, don't you?"

"Threatening me with your daddy the Gard?" Joey threw his head back and laughed. "Like I give a fuck."

"He's a lot higher up the pecking order than just a Gard," Paul hissed. "You'd do well to remember that the next time you think about crossing me, Lynchy."

"Whoa, whoa, whoa," I mumbled, shaking my head, as I squeezed my body between them, feeling the heat emanating from both boys as I pressed a hand to each of their chests. "Don't even think about starting a fight in here."

"Who's trying to cause a fight here, Aoife?" Paul hissed back at me, tone accusing. "Because from where I'm standing, all I'm trying to do is take my drunk girlfriend home. You're the one making a scene, draped all over the school's scumbag like he's your savior. Classy, Aoif, real fucking classy." Running a hand through his hair, Paul glowered at Joey. "If you think that you've one-upped me tonight, Lynchy, you're wrong. Because this right here," he paused to wave a hand between us, before sneering, "doesn't count. She's not thinking clearly, and if you have a shred of anything decent about you, then you won't take advantage of the situation."

"Hey." Joey held his hands up and smiled darkly. "All I'm doing is being a good *friend* to my favorite *friend*."

"She's not your anything."

"Uh, yes, I am."

"Hear that, Ricey?" Joey replied, with a shit-eating grin etched on his face. "Your girl here *is* my anything."

"Hey," I snapped, glaring up at Joey. "Not cool."

He shrugged in response, unapologetic.

"And this is what you want to stay with instead of letting me take you home?" Paul demanded, giving me a look of such disgust that it made me wither. "A year and a half, Aoife. A year and a fucking half and you pick that piece of shit over me?"

"No, Paul, I'm not picking him over you, I'm picking *me* over you," I snapped in a shaky tone, as I shook my head, and staggered away from the both of them. "This is over, Paul. Congratulations, you're a free agent. We're done."

"Aoife!" Paul called after me, but I didn't turn back.

Screw him.

Screw them both.

Shoving my way through the mob, I tried to retrace my steps back to Casey, regretting my decision to come tonight almost as much as the alcohol running through my veins.

My phone was vibrating next to me.

Narrowing my eyes, I glared down at my phone and quickly pressed end when Paul's name lit up the screen.

He could go to voicemail, along with the other dozen unanswered calls he'd made, not to mention the seven unread texts.

Thoroughly depressed, I sat on the bonnet of a random car outside of the Pavilion, with a bag of chips balancing on my thighs, as my fishnet-stocking clad legs dangled loosely.

Frozen to the bone, but too drunk to truly appreciate how cold the night air was, I muttered angrily to myself as I chomped on my vinegar-coated chips like a demented lunatic.

I was so fucking mad; I could taste it on my tongue, as I swung my legs so furiously that one of my heels slipped off.

"Fuck," I slurred, staring down despondently at my shiny white stiletto when it landed in a puddle of muddy rainwater on the ground. "Well, now you can just stay there, you traitorous slut," I hissed, glaring down at the knock-off leather. "That's right. I said it. This is all your fault."

"Well, if it isn't the angel with her dirty wings," a familiar voice drawled, and I groaned loudly.

Great.

That's just great.

Twisting my head, my bleary-eyed gaze locked on none other than Joey Lynch, phone in hand, as he swaggered towards me.

"Fighting with your shadow again, Molloy?"

"I'll fight you," I grumbled, reaching behind me to check that my wings were still intact. "My wings are fine, asshole."

"Got a spare chip?"

"Nope, not for you," I growled, stuffing a fistful of chips into my mouth in a very unladylike way. "They're all mine."

"What are you doing out here on your own?"

"What does it look like I'm doing, jackass; I'm clearly sulking," I huffed, voice still slightly slurred from the alcohol in my belly. "What are you doing?"

Shrugging, he slid his phone into his jeans pocket. "Waiting for a friend."

"Oh, so you *have* friends?" I rolled my eyes. "I thought you were opposed to the idea."

With an amused expression etched on his sickeningly good-looking face, Joey strolled over to where I was sitting. "Ah, that's not entirely true." Winking, he reached into my bag and swiped a chip. "I'm only opposed to you, Molloy."

That small act of theft caused an unreasonable surge of violence to grow inside of me.

"Oh, look at me," I heard myself grumble as I made a terrible attempt to mimic his voice. "I'm Joey Lynch. I'm so hard, I'm so tough. I'm not friends with girls, even though I like to steal their chips and pick fights with their boyfriends." Frowning, I held up a hand and swiftly corrected myself. "Ex. That's right. He's my *ex*-boyfriend, because he sure as hell isn't my current one. Dick."

Laughing at my reaction, Joey shook his head and said, "You're a messy little drunk, aren't ya?"

"No," I corrected, slapping his hand away from my chip when he reached for another. "I'm a woman on the edge."

"The drama's that deep, huh?"

"Yes, and here's why," I snapped, grabbing another chip from his hand when he sideswiped me. "I have been very publicly labeled a slut tonight by my former boyfriend, that's right ..." I paused for dramatic effect, before continuing, "my *former* boyfriend, who, for your information, has never had the privilege of being even remotely slutty with me." Huffing out a breath, I muttered, "And that's not for the want of him trying, either." *Constantly.*

Joey's brows shot up as he stood in front of me. "You and Ricey aren't ..."

"No, we're not sleeping together," I spat, narrowing my eyes. "God, what do you take me for?" I quickly reached up and clamped a hand over his mouth. "You know what, don't answer that. I don't need any relationship advice from you."

Rolling his eyes, Joey reached up and peeled my hand from his mouth. "Jesus, Molloy," he growled, tongue snaking out to taste his bottom lip. "How much vinegar did you put on those chips?"

"The perfect amount," I replied, slipping a finger into my mouth to sample what he clearly had when I put my hand on his mouth. "Okay," I conceded, holding my finger back up. "I may have been a little overly generous with the bottle."

"You don't think?" His tone was laced with sarcasm.

"Hey, don't judge me," I defended huffily. "I already told you that I'm a woman on the edge. I can't be held responsible for my lack of judgement when it comes to pouring vinegar. Clearly, if tonight's anything to go by, I'm not a very good judge of anything."

"Well, my judgement's just fine, Molloy, and I can tell you that it's your boyfriend who's the prick in this situation." Shoving his hands into the front pockets of his jeans, Joey added, "If he's pressuring you, then walk. You have all the time in the world for that bullshit."

"Ex." My face burned with heat. "And by bullshit, you mean sex?"

"Would you prefer if I said fucking?" he offered, not missing a beat. "Look, do whatever you want, but if you want my advice, you shouldn't give yourself away to the likes of him."

"The likes of him?"

"Someone who's supposed to care about you, but then puts hands on you and calls you a slut when he doesn't get his own way."

"As opposed to the boy who once called me *easy*."

"There are a few big differences between us," came his amused reply, as he leaned closer, so close that I could smell the distinct fragrance of his Lynx. "Look, all I'm saying is you can do better than Paul Rice."

"Oh yeah?" Desperately trying to remain composed, and not reveal just how deeply this boy affected me, I kept my eyes locked on his when I asked, "Well, since you're in such a chatty mood, would you care to oblige me by sharing those *differences*?"

"If that's what you want."

"That's what I want."

"Fine," he replied, not missing a beat. "First difference: I may have had a momentary lapse in my own judgment when I called you easy." He placed his hands on either side of me as he spoke. "It's something that, on many occasions since that night, I've come to feel somewhat regrettable about."

"Wow. Is this another version of an apology?" I breathed, feeling my body sway closer to his. "Because it's as shitty as the last one."

"Not an apology," he corrected. "More like a rare admission."

"Well then," I breathed, feeling my heart buck wildly against my ribcage, as I leaned back on my elbows. "If it's a rare admission then it must have hurt you to say it?"

"You have no idea," he agreed, hands planted on either side of my body, as he stared down at me with dark, hooded eyes. "Will I keep going?"

I nodded. "Yes."

"Second difference," he said. "I'm not your boyfriend, Molloy. I'm not *supposed* to care about you, remember?"

"No, you're not *supposed* to," I agreed with a shiver, as he pinned me to the bonnet of the car. Excitement thrummed to life inside of me. "But you still do."

Heat flashed in his eyes, but he made no move to deny it.

What the hell was wrong with me?

Goading this boy was the same as putting my hand in the cheetah enclosure at Fota Wildlife Park.

A risky move.

"Is there a third difference?" I breathed.

"Yeah, there's a difference," he replied. "Do you want it?"

"I want it."

"You sure?"

"I'm sure."

"Third difference," he whispered then, leaning so close that I could feel his alcohol-scented breath on my face. "I'm not pressuring you to spread your legs for me." Rearing back, he made a point of glancing between us. "You did that all by yourself."

My gaze followed his, and my breath hitched in my throat when I saw that he had deftly stepped between my legs.

Not only that, but my legs had wrapped themselves around his hips of their own damn accord.

"Well shit," I whispered, breathing hard and fast, as I watched him watch me. "I have no idea how they got there."

"Yeah," he agreed, closing the space between us once more, his lips a hair's breadth from mine. "Me either."

He's going to kiss you.

Oh my god, Aoif, he's going to put his mouth on yours.

Be cool, don't freak out.

The sound of tires screeching tore his attention from me, and I wanted to cry.

No, God, *why*?

With Puddle of Mudd's 'Control' blasting from the car stereo, I watched as a souped-up, black Honda Civic came tearing up the road towards us, spitting gravel from the speed in which the person was driving.

Beeping on the horn, he flashed his lights at us, and my heart sank into my ass when I noticed who was driving.

Shane Holland.

"Shit," Joey groaned, momentarily dropping his head on my shoulder. "I better go," he finally said, voice strained. "He's here for me."

"Wait – no, Joey, don't go with him!" I strangled out in horror, catching ahold of his hand when he straightened up and took a step back. "Please don't go anywhere with him," I urged, scrambling to my feet, as I entwined our fingers and squeezed. "Stay here with me instead."

"Listen, Molloy; about us," he began to say, and then paused, like he was thinking carefully about what words needed to come next. His entire focus was on our joined hands, as his thumb gently brushed over my knuckles.

"About us?" I croaked out, shivering from the feel of his thumb tracing my skin.

"You're my friend," he finally settled on.

"You're finally admitting it without needing to be coerced?"

Nodding, he forced a small, humorless laugh. "Only took a few years, right?"

"Only a couple."

"Yeah." Clearing his throat, he looked behind him to where the car was waiting and then back to me. "I like you."

"Wow," I breathed. "Another admission."

"The hardest one yet."

"I bet."

"I know what you want us to be," he added, tone gruff. "But that can't happen."

"Joe—"

"No, listen to me," he urged, giving my hand a small squeeze. "I can be your friend, okay? I can do that. But you need to know that I've got some bad genes running through my system. Some seriously fucked up DNA."

"Nobody's perfect, Joe."

"It's not about being perfect, Molloy." Releasing my hand, I watched as he crouched down and retrieved my heel from the mud. "It's about being dangerous," he added, wiping it clean with the side of his jeans before slipping it back on my foot. "And that's what I am, okay? I'm a bad bet."

"No, you're not."

"Yes, I am."

"Then I don't care," I blurted out.

"You should."

"Well, I don't."

"Nice shoes," he said in a soft voice, tapping my foot. "You were right, they were worth hounding your father for."

"See?" I forced a smile when I felt like crying. "Told you."

"I'm not a good friend for you," he added quietly, still crouching, with his hand on my foot. "I wouldn't even know where to start."

"You're better at it than you think."

"I need my job, Molloy."

And there it was.

Finally.

"So, you're finally admitting it?" I heard myself whisper. "You blew me off because of my dad?"

"And because you can do better than me." Releasing my foot, he slowly stood up. "But you can do better than him, too."

"Joe."

"Lynchy!" one of the lads called out, swinging the back door of the car open. "Let's go, lad."

"Yeah, I'm coming," he called over his shoulder, causing a surge of panic to rack through me.

"Listen, we can just chat," I hurried to say. "Hang out, whatever. As friends. Friends is fine. Just please don't go with him, Joey."

Please don't let him sink his claws into you.

Releasing a pained breath, he leaned in close and pressed a kiss to my forehead. "I could go a fair bit crazy over you, Molloy." His lips brushed against my brow as he said, "Stay out of my head now, ya hear?"

"Don't, Joey," I called after him, voice thick with reckless emotion, watching his back as he walked away from me. "Don't go with them."

Turning back, his green eyes flicked to mine, and it was clear that the shutters had been firmly clamped shut, blocking me and the rest of the world out. "I'll be seeing ya, Molloy."

What did you take?

JOEY

Molloy was a distraction to me on a normal day.

Throw in a sexy angel costume, and a belly full of booze, and the girl was a recipe for disaster.

I had found myself watching her for most of the night for two reasons.

The first reason being that she was a fucking delight to look at. All long legs, curved hips, blonde hair, and braless tits barely contained beneath that scrap of white silk she called a dress, as she danced like nobody was watching – which brought me to the second reason why she owned my attention.

Everyone was watching.

Well, everyone with a dick and a penchant for pussy.

I wasn't the only one to notice the attention she'd been receiving, either.

I'd always thought she was too good for him, and I'd been proven right by the way he conducted himself tonight. Stamping his feet like a fucking toddler because his girlfriend was garnering more male attention than his ego could handle.

Ricey's behavior didn't exactly vouch for his faith in Molloy – or their relationship when he bulldozed onto the dancefloor like he was the fun police and spat the proverbial dummy in epic fashion.

I knew that Molloy was far from a wilting flower, and could handle herself up against just about anyone, but when I saw the way her asshole boyfriend manhandled her on the dancefloor, I lost my shit.

I knew it wasn't my place to intervene, I had no business sticking my nose into their relationship, but I physically couldn't stop myself from doing exactly that.

I did what I always did: dived in headfirst and to hell with the consequences.

And just like always, it backfired on me.

Because I had come this *close* to fucking everything up.

And in all honesty, if it hadn't been for Shane and the lads pulling up, I wouldn't have given it a second thought.

I would have done a lot more than kiss those pouty red lips of hers. I would have taken from her, something I had no right to have.

In the end, it was just as well that we had been interrupted, because when I came back to the Pavilion after settling up with Shane, she was with *him*.

After that, my mood had darkened to the point of no return.

Only Jesus Christ himself knew how irrationally jealous and hopeless I'd been feeling when I crushed and snorted the oxy that I'd scored from Shane, but it had given me exactly what I'd wanted.

An escape.

Higher than Everest, I swayed from side to side, as my mind drifted in and out of reality. The fantastic fucking feeling of nothing claiming my consciousness, taking me to a place I never wanted to leave.

Was I breathing?

I couldn't tell.

I couldn't care if I wanted to. And I didn't.

I just wanted to stop feeling.

To stop caring.

To stop, period.

"You're so gorgeous."

Eyes closed, I leaned heavily against the cool concrete at my back, with my hands hanging limply at my sides, as a stranger's hands pulled at my flesh.

"Your six-pack is insane."

Tonight, I wanted to float away, to just disappear, and have nobody depend on me for a few short hours, but then the voice kept talking in my ear, and dragging me away from oblivion.

"Joey . . . are you with me?"

No, I wasn't with her.

"I thought you were into this?"

I was floating the fuck away.

"Joey."

Nothing.

"Joey."

Numb.

"Joey."

Let me go.

"Joey, isn't that your mother?"

"Oh my god, what's his mam doing here?"

"Hey – snap out of it, fucker."

A hard smacking noise vibrated through my thoughts, bringing with it a burning sensation to the side of my face.

"What's wrong with him?"

"Nothing, he's grand."

"Grand? Look at him. He's out of his mind – get away from my son."

"Get it together, Joe."

"Joe, lad, your mam's here."

"Joey, wake up, I need you."

Mashing my lips together, I forced my eyes to blink open, and watched as a familiar face drifted in and out of focus.

"What did you take?" I heard my mother demand, as she held my face between her small hands. "What did you take, Joey!" Releasing a pained grunt, she breathed hard and fast for minute or two before turning her attention back to me. "What did you do to yourself?"

Fuck if I could remember.

"I'm grand," I slurred, reveling in the fucking fantastic feeling of warmth rushing through my body. "Where are ya . . . Mam, you're here."

"Yes, I'm here," she snapped, catching ahold of my hand like I was a small child. I hadn't been one of those in a very long time. "I came to get you because I need to go to the hospital," she choked out, as she pulled me along after her. "I wanted you to look after your brothers, so Shannon could be with me, but it's clear that you can't even look after yourself."

Freewheeling, I allowed her to lead me wherever she had decided I needed to be.

It didn't matter to me where that was.

Nothing mattered now.

"Are ya having the baby, Mam?" I asked, mashing my lips together, as I tried and failed to brush the hair out of my eyes. "Another one?"

"Yes, Joey, I am." The sound a car door opening filled my ears, and then I was being pushed inside, landing on my face in the back seat. "You're a disgrace."

"I know," I agreed drowsily, feeling her slide into the seat alongside me. "I'm sorry, Mam . . . "

"Don't speak," she snapped before she instructed who I presumed was a taxi-driver to take us to the hospital.

"Stop crying, Mam." Dragging myself into a sitting position, I attempted to pull at my seat belt before giving up entirely and letting her do it for me instead. "I'll, ah, it's all grand . . . "

"You're breaking my heart." Her voice cracked. "You're killing yourself."

The feelings I knew I should have weren't present inside the gaping hole in my chest. I was fucked. There was no point in denying it. No point in fighting it, either. Not when my own mother didn't have faith in me.

"You're just like him. In every way."

What was the point in fighting my DNA?

This was who I was, and I had a horrible feeling that I couldn't be fixed or put back together again.

I couldn't reset my life. I was paralyzed and trapped in a body that resembled the person I despised most of all.

Well, almost.

I was starting to despise myself just that little bit more these days.

It killed me to know that I was hurting my mother, though.

To think that I was making her feel the way he did.

"Yeah." Closing my eyes, I dropped my head on her shoulder and sighed. "Okay, Mam."

Angel with her dirty wings

October 31st 2001

AOIFE

"I am so damn sorry about what happened in there." Catching ahold of my hand, Paul led me away from a crowd of nearby partygoers, as he tried to weasel his way back into my good books.

Out of the corner of my eye, I watched as a black Honda Civic tore back up the entrance of the pavilion, causing my heart to hammer violently.

He was back.

The car door opened, and out fell a laughing Joey, with a cigarette dangling from his lips, and a can of Dutch Gold in his hand.

Unsteady on his feet, he banged the roof of the car to signal goodbye, before waving the car off.

Laughing to himself, he took a drag of his smoke and looked around, eyes finally landing and staying on me.

I waved at him.

He raised his hand to wave back but stopped when his gaze flicked to Paul.

His smile disappeared.

"You were only dancing," Paul continued, drawing my attention back to him. "I get it now. I was being a tool. I'm sorry, Aoif. I am." Blowing out a frustrated breath, he let go of my hand to run his hands through his hair. "I'm a jealous asshole, okay? I can't help it. Look at you."

"Look at me?" Folding my arms across my chest, I leaned against the parked car at my back, and gave him a hard look. "What the hell is that supposed to mean?"

"It means you're beautiful and I lose my head around you."

"Flattery won't get you out of this," I warned, flicking my gaze back to find Joey had disappeared from sight. "You called me a slut *and* a whore."

"Aoife, come on," he tried to plead. "You know I didn't mean it. I don't really feel that way about you."

"If you don't mean it, then you shouldn't say it," I snapped, unable to mask the emotion in my voice.

Because it *hurt*.

Having him think that way about me was not a good feeling.

Our relationship was a goddamn trainwreck, but it hurt to hear him say those things to me because before we hooked up, we were friends.

I'd always known that Paul was materialistic and vain. It never used to bother me that much because I had plenty of flaws myself.

I was loud and outspoken, could entice an argument from a silent monk – as my father liked to remind me – and I was especially slow to get intimate.

He always tolerated my flaws and therefore I tolerated his.

But lately, I was beginning to think that being able to mutually tolerate one another wasn't a good enough reason to stay in a relationship.

Especially when said relationship was starting to weigh heavily on my shoulders.

"Look, I think it's pretty clear that we're not working out," I heard myself finally work up the courage and tell him. "I'm not happy, and you're not happy, so I don't see why we should continue—"

"Don't say it," he warned, eyes wild with panic, as he grabbed my hands and pulled me towards him. "We're not breaking up, Aoife. It's not happening, so get it out of your head."

"Get it out of my head?" I slapped his hands away. "You don't get to make all of the decisions here, Paul. I have a say in whether or not I want to be in this relationship. You can't force me."

"You want him."

"What are you talking about?"

"You know exactly what I'm talking about." He narrowed his eyes in disgust. "*Who* I'm talking about."

I released a heavy breath. "This isn't about Joey."

"It's always about him, Aoife," he practically roared, losing his cool with me. "It will always come back to him because you are all about him. Don't bother denying it. It's written all over your face."

"He's my *friend*, Paul."

"Bullshit."

"I'm not fighting with you about this," I growled. "I have a friendship with Joey, and I'm not giving that up for anyone."

"You mean you're not giving *him* up," he corrected and then choked out a humorless laugh. "Jesus Christ, how blind can you get? The asshole doesn't want you. When are you going to get it through your thick skull? He doesn't give two shits about you, and it's fucking pathetic to see you fall over him like this."

"Paul!"

"Look!" he demanded then, physically turning me around so that I had a perfect view of the side of the pavilion. "Look at him," Paul ordered, catching ahold of my chin and forcing me to watch as Danielle Long pinned Joey against the wall of the pavilion and thrust her tongue inside his mouth. And even though his hands hung limply at his sides, he rocked his hips and kissed her back.

Oh yeah, he was definitely into it.

Into her.

My breath hitched in my throat, and it took everything I had inside of me to stand my ground and *not* break down.

"Look," Paul reiterated, forcing me to take it all in. "That's how much he's thinking about you, Aoife. He doesn't give a damn."

I'll stay with you

October 31st 2001

JOEY

"You can be such a . . . fuck-up, Joey," Mam screamed, heaving in pain, as she gripped the side rail of the bed and released a high-pitched, feral scream. "You're . . . just . . . like . . . him . . . sometimes."

"I said I was sorry," I strangled out, as the high I'd been floating on quickly gave way to a severe case of the shakes. "Stop looking at me like that."

Reality was crashing down around me in huge tsunami-sized waves, as I continued to plummet back down to earth.

Still, I was here, wasn't I?

I was the one holding her hand.

Where the fuck was he?

"Okay, Marie, on the next contraction, I want you to give me a big push," the midwife instructed. She pushed me out of her way, as she settled between my mother's legs with an array of medical supplies and instruments that my mind could not comprehend. "You're nearly there, pet. I can see the head. Another big push and you'll be crowning."

"Just, ah . . . " Feeling woozy, I backed away from my mother's hospital bed, needing to do something, needing to be just about anywhere other than *there*. "I'll be back . . . "

"No – Joey, don't go!" Mam cried out, catching ahold of my hand with a death grip. "Please don't leave me on my own."

"Mam, I don't . . . " Shaking my head to clear to my vision, I felt her squeeze my hand. I tried to make sense of my surroundings while attempting not to puke. "I'm just, ah—" Blinking rapidly, I wiped my brow with my sleeve and forced myself to concentrate on her face. "Please don't make me do this."

"I need you," she cried out, trembling. "I don't have anyone else."

Through the haze of withdrawal, I could see the terror in her blue eyes, and it was sobering.

"Please . . . I'm scared."

"Okay." Returning to her side, I gave my hand up to her, never saying a word when she squeezed my fingers so tight, they almost cracked. "I won't leave you."

"It's coming!" Mam screamed, as her face distorted in pain.

"Pant, Marie, just pant."

Jesus fucking Christ . . .

Never mind telling her to pant; I was about to pass the fuck out.

"That's the head out," the midwife announced. "Good girl yourself. The next contraction and he'll be born."

"Joey, don't go, please don't go," Mam cried out, tone panicked. "I'm all alone. I need you . . . please . . . "

"Yeah." Swallowing deeply, I steeled what resolve was left in me, and choked out the words, "Okay, Mam."

Less than a minute later, Mam's face contorted in pain.

She turned a dark shade of red as her entire body racked with tremors.

And then I heard it.

The sound of high-pitched wailing.

Stunned, I watched as the midwife lifted a small infant, caked in bloodied mucus, out from between her legs. "Congratulations," she said with a smile. "It's another boy."

I watched as they clamped the umbilical cord that connected him to our mother, and I wondered if the cord that attached me to her had ever been truly severed. It was invisible but still connecting me deeply to the woman who bore me. I wanted to let it all go. To just let the pain and pressure fall from my shoulders.

The midwife wiped the screaming baby down before bundling him up in a towel and placing him on my mother's chest.

"Jesus," I choked out, feeling my own body shake, as I stared down at the tiny purplish creature in her arms. "He's tiny."

"Is he okay?" Cradling the tiny bundle to her chest, Mam continued to cry and ask, "Is he okay?" over and over, as she pressed her cheek to its head.

"He's perfect, Marie," the midwife assured her. "A little on the small side, but then again, he's a couple of weeks early. He's more than making up for that with the pair of lungs on him."

"What are you doing?" I demanded then, watching in horror as one midwife stuck a syringe into my mother's thigh while the other began pushing down hard on her stomach. "Stop it, will ya? She's only had a baby. You'll hurt her."

"It's okay, Joey," Mam said. "This is normal."

"The fuck?"

"I promise your mother is perfectly fine," the midwife explained calmly. "This is all very normal. We're helping her uterus to contract so that she can deliver the placenta as quickly and as easily as possible."

"The pla-what-a?" I gaped at the nurse and then swung my gaze to my mother. "There's more?" I shook my head, horrified. "How the fuck can there be *more*?"

He called me fat

December 18th 2001

AOIFE

"It's not true."

"That's what you said last time."

"It wasn't true last time, either."

"I don't believe you."

"Listen, just come over to my house after school. We can talk properly there."

"So you can think up another bullshit lie to feed me?"

"Aoife, come on. We're supposed to working through this. How can we do that if you won't talk to me."

"Why don't you drag me to your house? You're getting pretty good at forcing things."

Blowing out a frustrated breath when I refused to relent, Paul stalked over to his desk at the far side of the classroom.

Almost two months had passed since the Halloween disco at the Pavilion, and to say that Paul and I were back on track would be a drastic overstatement – if we ever had been on track to begin with.

I wanted to end it on Halloween night and Paul didn't.

In the end, we had agreed upon taking a temporary break from each other, which had actually helped our cause for a grand total of three weeks until I caved and agreed to try again.

After that, everything went back to exactly how it had been.

Within a matter of days, we were back to basics, and I was pretty fucking fed up with the whole damn thing.

I knew that Paul was sorry for being rough with me that night and calling me names and had been trying to make it right. Problem was

I couldn't seem to muster up the energy required to join him in fixing our relationship.

Because I wasn't sure if I still wanted to have one with him.

I missed Paul the boy.

I wanted to stick around for that boy.

I did not miss Paul the boyfriend.

I wanted to run for the hills from that handsy, possessive bastard.

The only time I seemed to meet the former version of Paul was when we were on the outs.

Only then did he show me affection, take interest in what I had to say, and most importantly of all, treat me with respect.

When he was *that* version of himself, he was a pretty great guy.

The only problem was that great guy disappeared the minute he slapped a girlfriend label on my forehead.

The minute I had given him what he wanted, the controlling, self-absorbed asshole resurfaced.

Furious with myself for not holding firm but letting him sweet-talk me back into a half-hearted relationship, I fought his shitty behavior at every hand's turn. I knew deep down that I needed to woman up and end it for good, and to hell with the consequences. Because being stuck in this limbo, waiting around for things to change, was making me miserable.

Paul's latest display of assholeness, and the issue that I was currently fuming over, was the fact that there was one rule for me in our relationship and an entirely different one for him.

Flipping out at every hand's turn if I so much as smiled too long at one of the lads in class, he had no problem doing the same with girls.

The double standards and hypocrisy set my teeth on edge.

He didn't believe me when I told him that I wasn't messing around behind his back, but I was supposed to turn right around and swallow every bullshit line he fed me when another rumor about him arose.

This morning, for example, Casey heard from Mack, who heard from Dricko and Sam, that Paul had been seen hooking up with some girl from Tommen College when we were on our break.

When I confronted him about the rumor, he swore it was lies, which led us to our current predicament.

I didn't know what to believe anymore, but if it was true, I knew that I would respect him more if he would just be *honest*.

This latest rumor almost felt like the final nail in the coffin for our relationship. If Paul was sneaking around kissing other girls, and I was holding on to my heart for dear life, too afraid to part with it for fear of missing out on a never-was never-will-be relationship with Joey, then we were doomed.

Therefore, it was safe to say that I was coming to the conclusion that I would be better off alone.

Deep down in my heart of hearts, I knew that my giving our relationship another shot had a lot more to do with the hoe-bag who was supposed to be sitting next to me than any of Paul's apologetic proclamations.

And when I said hoe-bag, I meant Joey.

After our parting of ways at the disco that night, he had wholeheartedly thrown himself into contention for the school slut award.

Unlike before, when he seemed to have a little class and discretion about his conquests. Since that night, he didn't seem to give a damn about who was watching.

Or that I was watching.

In the weeks that followed since the Halloween disco, we had resumed our comfortable little routine of throwing shade and exchanging banter.

Joey literally never brought up what had *almost* happened, and acted like nothing had so convincingly, that I sometimes wondered if I dreamt the whole thing up.

I knew I hadn't, though.

The image of him kissing our classmate was scored on the inside of my eyes.

According to the rumor mill at school, Joey and Danielle had slept together the night of the Halloween disco.

Well, I suppose comparing 'fucking each other's brains out against a brick wall at the back of the GAA Pavilion' to sleeping together was a bit of a stretch.

What I had felt when I first heard about it was worse than bitterness. It had almost felt like heartbreak.

Rumors had continued to circle through the halls at BCS, horrible, vicious rumors about how they regularly hooked up. Rumors which shredded me every time they came my way.

Sick with jealousy every time I had to endure watching her fawn and paw at him during class, I didn't even try to fight the murderous feeling that ignited inside of my chest when I saw them together.

Because the truth of the matter was that I felt something for him.

Something I shouldn't, and something that definitely wasn't good for me.

But I still felt it.

To Joey's credit, and contrary to the rumors, he was explicitly tight-lipped. He might have been a fuck boy, but at least he didn't run his mouth, which meant that however far they had gone that night was never going to be confirmed on his end.

In fact, he treated her no differently to how he always had.

He was the same slightly aloof, a little flirty, and a whole lot of pissed-off Joey.

And while our friendship had remained reasonably intact since Halloween, I couldn't hide my hesitance – or my hurt.

Witnessing him share one kiss with another girl had both crippled and alerted me to the fact that I needed to stop.

Stop wishing.

Stop hoping.

Stop wondering.

Stop willing.

I needed to just *stop* when it came to this boy.

The realization that Joey could indeed inflict some serious carnage on my heart had me pushing down every feeling that tried to burrow its way to the surface.

Determined to move past my weird infatuation with my classmate, I avoided the places I knew I might run into him outside of school and kept my wits about me when I was in his presence.

Reconciling with Paul had been a lot easier when I had such a bitter taste in my mouth. Besides, he might say the wrong thing sometimes, but at least I didn't need to worry about him decimating his brain cells with every drug known to mankind.

He couldn't hurt me like that.

Only one person had the ability to do that.

A shadow fell over me then, as a pair of perfectly manicured hands landed on my desk. "Where's Joey?"

"Hello to you, too, Danielle."

"Sorry." She blushed and offered me an embarrassed smile. "I meant to say hi."

Not bothering to answer her, I resumed my post of doodling in my homework journal, drawing cute little spider webs, while I waited for our teacher to show up.

"Do you know where he is?" she asked in a much more persuasive tone. "He sits with you for history, doesn't he?"

"He sure does."

"So, where is he?"

"Joey's not here right now, but I can take a message and see that he gets it." I rolled my eyes and gestured to his empty seat. "Come on. Danielle. How the hell am I supposed to know? I'm not his keeper."

"I'm sorry, I just thought you would know since you guys are—"

"Friends," I filled in dryly. "Well, I don't know." Lies. "I have no idea where he is." More lies.

"He didn't come back to class after big lunch."

No shit, Sherlock. "I don't know what to tell you." Except that she need only take a gander around the back of the sheds to find lover boy. No doubt that's where he would be, along with Rambo, Dricko, Alec, and all of the other potheads in our year. "He'll show up when he shows up."

"But this is our last class of the day."

Nothing gets past you, does it? "Your guess is as good as mine."

Perfectly timed, the man of the moment himself decided to stroll into the classroom, and I didn't need to look at his eyes to know that he was high as a kite. The smell of weed coming off his uniform was strong enough to give me a buzz.

Danielle beamed at him. "Hey, Joey."

"Dan," Joey acknowledged, dropping his bag on our desk before sliding past me to take his seat on the inside.

Sinking down on the chair next to mine, he rested his elbow on the back of my chair and flicked my ponytail to get my attention. "Molloy."

"Joe," I acknowledged, keeping my gaze trained on my homework journal.

"I've been looking for you, Joe," Danielle said. "I wanted to talk to you."

"About?"

"Are you free after school?"

"I'm never free after school."

Oh, burn.

I bit back a snicker.

"Oh, that's okay." Her tone was forcefully bright. "Maybe lunch tomorrow."

"Maybe," Joey replied before flicking my ponytail again. "Got any more of those chocolates you keep in your pencil case?"

"Don't know why you keep asking when you already know the answer."

He moved for my pencil case, and I quickly slapped his hand away. "Don't touch my Rolos."

"Jesus," he muttered, pulling his hand back. "You can't spare one?"

"I could," I replied, refocusing on my spider web doodle. "But not for you."

"Not for me?" Snatching up my pencil, he asked. "Why not for me?"

"Because you don't even like chocolate," I grumbled, snatching my pencil right back from his hands. "You have the munchies, and I refuse to feed or enable your bad behavior."

"I'll, uh, I'll see you later, Joe," Danielle mumbled before retreating from our desk."

"Yeah, sure." He poked my shoulder. "My bad behavior?" Grinning like a dope, something that usually happened when he came back from lunch with the stoners, he leaned in close and nudged my shoulder with his. "Come on, Molloy, don't hold out on a friend."

"I have a Wham bar in my bag. It's yours if you want it but stay away from my pencil case stash."

"A Wham bar?" Joey gave me a disgusted look. "No fucking thanks. I'd rather starve."

"Then go right ahead, my friend."

"Jesus, who pissed in your cornflakes?"

You did, asshole. "I'm sorry, Joe, did I push a button? I was just looking for a way to mute you."

His brows shot up and he choked out a laugh. "Shit, that was a good one."

"I know." A reluctant smile spread across my face. "I was saving it up all day."

"For me?"

"Can you name another person I would rather mute?"

Another laugh. "Jesus, you're on fire."

"And you're on my last nerve."

"What's the matter, Molloy? Are you on the rag or something?"

"Oh my god." I snapped my gaze to his. "You did *not* just say that to me."

He grinned sheepishly. "Don't we share those details?"

Deciding on making him suffer, I narrowed my eyes and said, "Why yes, Joe. As a matter of fact, I am on my period." Smiling sweetly up at him, I added, "In fact, I'm having a real hard time getting my tampon out – what with all the blood and all. Care to help a friend out, you know, since that's your area of expertise and all?"

"I could give it a shot."

I glared at his stupid head for a long beat before relenting with a laugh. "You're sick."

"You said it, not me," he laughed, still grinning like a dope.

"I was trying to psych you out, asshole."

"You can't psych me out, Molloy. I'm immune to your antics," he shot back, eyes alight with humor. "But you're definitely psyching someone out."

I turned my head in the direction Joey was looking and locked eyes on a furious-looking Paul.

Great.

Just great.

"Looks like Paul the prick is about to have a coronary over there."

"Apologies for being late," Mrs Falvey announced, hurrying into class with a stack of books in her arms. "I was on a call to a parent."

Sure, she was.

More like she couldn't be bothered to turn up.

"Can everybody take out their textbooks and turn to page 112. Today, we're going to be revising the 1916 Easter Rising. It *will* come up in the junior cert paper in June and you *will* learn The Proclamation of the Irish Republic off by heart."

Pulling my book out, I set it down on the table between us, knowing full well that Joey wouldn't have his copy with him as per usual.

He rarely arrived at school with the required booklist, and spent most of his time bumming hand-me-down copies off teachers, or sharing with whoever was sitting next to him.

I never minded sharing with him, though, because as reckless as he was with his body, he had clear, neat handwriting, and took down notes that were far more useful and to the point than anything I had ever stolen out of my brother's school bag.

The fact that he could remain so efficient in class while his brain was clearly in an altered state made me even more envious.

"Joe," I whispered, after spending twenty minutes revising and taking down notes in companionable silence.

"Hm?"

"If I asked you a question, would you tell me the truth?"

"Depends."

"Something important to me."

"Like I said, Molloy, it depends," he whispered, not looking up from his copybook, as he scribbled something down, and then flipped the page over.

"On what?"

"On whether or not you needed to know the truth."

"Fine," I grumbled. "Forget it."

Joey sighed heavily and turned to look at me. "Ask your question."

"Will you give me the truth?"

"Just ask your question, Molloy."

"Have you heard any rumors?"

"Rumors."

"About Paul." Releasing a shaky breath, I added, "Messing around with some girl from Tommen."

Joey tensed for a moment before flicking his gaze to where Paul was sitting. A beat passed before he turned his attention back to me. "No."

My heart sank in my chest.

He was withholding.

I *knew* he was.

"I never thought you'd lie to my face, Joe," I muttered, feeling thoroughly disappointed in him. "It hurts worse than I thought."

"I didn't lie," he was quick to reply, tone hard. "You asked me if I heard anything about Ricey messing around with some girl from Tommen, and I haven't heard anything about some girl from Tommen."

"What does that mean?"

"It means what it means, Molloy."

I stared at him for a long moment before finally getting his drift. "You're being semantical."

He turned his attention back to the open book in front of us. "Do you want me to write down the notes for you?"

"I want you to be real with me," I whisper-hissed. "Joe, if you know something and aren't telling me, then I'm going to be really hurt."

Blowing out a frustrated breath, he rubbed the back of his neck and reached for his pencil. "It's not my business."

My heart plummeted into my ass. "Yeah, well, it's my business." I reached across the desk and grabbed his forearm. "Tell me, Joe."

He remained stone-faced when he said, "I'm no rat, Molloy."

"But you are my *friend*."

Tossing his pencil back down, he muttered something unintelligible under his breath before turning to face me. "I don't know about anyone from Tommen, and I'm not going to stand over anything I haven't seen with my own two eyes, but I know he exchanged some messages with one of the girls from here."

"You saw those?" My breath hitched. "With your own eyes?"

He nodded slowly.

"Who?"

"Molloy."

"Who, Joe?"

"Danielle."

My heart sank.

Of all the girls in our year, I felt threatened the most by her.

Knowing that not only Joey but Paul had both succumbed to her allure was gutting.

"What happened between them?"

"Nothing."

"Don't lie to me, Joe."

"Nothing happened," he repeated. "There were a few text messages exchanged a while back, but that's as far as it went."

"And you didn't *tell* me?"

"The fuck was I supposed to say?"

"How about 'hey, Aoife, your boyfriend is cheating on you'."

"Like I said before," he growled, "it wasn't my business."

"Yes, it was," I snapped. "You're my friend, Joey. You're more *my* friend than you are hers. Your loyalty should be with me."

"I don't know what to tell you, Molloy."

"The truth," I snapped. "But apparently, you can't do that, so you might as well not talk to me at all."

"I didn't send any damn messages behind your back," Joey hissed, eyes flaring with heat as his temper rose "So, pull your head out of your ass and place your anger at the right person's door. Don't take your shit out on me, Molloy. I warned you about him. I told you what kind of an asshole he was, but you took him back repeatedly, so don't fucking start with me."

Yeah, he did tell me, but that didn't make this easier.

Pulling my phone out of my skirt pocket, I quickly tapped out a text and glared across the room until the asshole recipient answered me.

AOIFE: DANIELLE?

PAUL: DANIELLE WHAT?

AOIFE: YOU WERE TEXTING HER.

PAUL: NO, I WASN'T.

AOIFE: DON'T DENY IT. I'VE HEARD IT ALL BEFORE.

PAUL: AOIFE, I SWEAR TO GOD I HAVEN'T LAID A FINGER ON DANIELLE. X

AOIFE: I DIDN'T SAY YOU TOUCHED HER, ASSHOLE. I SAID YOU TEXTED HER.

Paul glanced across the classroom at me and shook his head.

I narrowed my eyes in warning as if to say *don't you dare lie to me this time.*

PAUL: LISTEN, NOTHING HAPPENED WITH HER. THOSE TEXTS WERE A JOKE. I SENT THEM AGES AGO. THEY

MEANT NOTHING, BABE. I CAN EXPLAIN EVERYTHING.
I SWEAR XXX

Glowering, I shook my head and shoved my phone back into my pocket, ignoring when it vibrated to alert me that I had received another text.

"Are you okay?" Joey whispered from beside me.

"No," I snapped, feeling hurt, betrayed, and a million other emotions. "My boyfriend is a lying whore and my best friend's an even bigger one!"

"You shouldn't call Casey a whore, Molloy."

"I was referring to you, asshole."

"I didn't lie to you."

"You didn't tell me the truth, either."

"It wasn't my—"

"If you tell me that it wasn't your business one more time, I swear to God I will scream," I choked out, feeling my eyes water.

"Don't you dare," Joey warned, releasing a frustrated growl. "Don't you even think about playing the girl card and spilling tears on me."

"Don't worry, asshole, any tears I spill won't go to waste," I snapped, sniffling when I reached up to bat a traitorous tear away. "I'm planning to save them up to drown you with."

"You asked me to tell you the truth and I did," he whisper-hissed. "And now you're mad at me for doing what you wanted me to do in the first place."

"Because what you should have done in the first place was tell me when it happened," I choked out, digging him in the side with my elbow. "Not leave me in the dark, looking like a fucking idiot."

"You don't need me to help you with that," he spat. "You get plenty of practice every time you go running back to that asshole boyfriend of yours."

"Oh, go choke on a clit."

"Fuck you, Molloy."

"Fuck you back."

Feeling vengeful, I held my hand up and waited for the teacher to notice me.

"Yes, Aoife?"

"Joey called me fat." Sniffling, I batted another tear away. "I'm really upset about it. Can I please be excused?"

His mouth fell open. "You *bitch*."

Fuck you, I mouthed back at him.

"Joey!" Mrs Falvey snapped, looking horrified. "Yes, Aoife, go on outside and get some air."

"I didn't call her fat," I heard him defend, as I stalked out of the classroom door. "It's not her weight she has a problem with. It's that deranged vindictive streak in her."

I was dawdling outside of the girls bathroom, wasting the last few minutes of class until the final bell rang, when a sour-looking Joey came stalking down the corridor towards me.

"Thanks a bunch, Molloy," he called out, green eyes narrowed, as he closed the space between us. "Falvey put me back on a red book for the foreseeable."

"Oh please." I rolled my eyes. "When aren't you on a report book?"

"Do you know how big of a hassle that fucking book is? Having to get it signed before and after every damn class, and then having to meet up with Nyhan at the end of every day to be bitched at?"

"No," I drawled, tone laced with sarcasm. "Because, unlike you, I know how to behave myself."

"No," he corrected, stopping short when he reached me. "You're just sneaky enough to not get caught."

"That, too."

"Here." He dropped my school bag at my feet. "You left your bag."

"Thanks."

"I cleared the stash of chocolate in your pencil case."

I sucked in a horrified breath. "You asshole."

"Yeah, well, I'm not sorry," Joey shot back with a shrug. "You deserved it for pulling that stunt on me." Releasing a frustrated growl, he added, "But I *am* sorry for not telling you about prick-face sooner."

Anger dissipated, and feeling sheepish, I leaned in close and nudged his shoulder with mine. "And I'm sorry for telling Mrs. Falvey that you called me fat."

"And?" Joey pushed.

"And for you getting the red book back."

"And?

I blew out an aggravated breath and muttered, "And for threatening to drown you."

"Hm," Joey grumbled, nudging my shoulder back. "If it was anyone else, Molloy. If it was anyone else."

"But it's me."

"It's you," he confirmed. "Pain in my hole."

You have a baby

January 7th 2002

AOIFE

Joey was late to school on our first day back after Christmas break. When he finally showed up, fifteen minutes into the third class of the day, the circles under his eyes had my anxiety rising at a rapid pace.

"Jesus," I whispered, when he slumped down beside me. "You look like shit."

"Thanks," he grumbled, dropping setting his elbows on our desk and dropping his head in his hands. "You look like dinner."

I flamed with heat at the compliment. "Thanks."

"No problem."

"What happened to you?" Glancing around class, I checked to see that our teacher was looking elsewhere before leaning in close and whispering, "Are you high again?"

"No, Molloy," he mumbled, slumped over our desk. "Not high. Just tired."

"Why?"

"Because I haven't closed an eye all night."

"Again, why?"

"Because—" he paused to yawn. "Sean's cutting a tooth."

"Sean?" I stared blankly at his head. "Who's Sean?"

"He's my baby—"

"Your *baby*?" I interrupted, eyes widening.

"Brother." He lifted his head to glare at me. "Give me some credit, will ya?"

"Sorry." I winced. "I just ... I didn't know that your mother had another baby."

"Yep."

"When?"

"Halloween."

"*Halloween*?" My mouth fell open. "Joe, we legit talk every day and you never once mentioned that your mam had another baby."

"Why would I?" he asked, confusion etched on his face.

"Because that's the sort of thing that friends tell each other," I explained. "Friends tell each other personal details like that."

"Molloy, my mam had another baby."

I rolled my eyes. "Not two months after the event."

He shrugged in response.

"So, tell me about Sean?" I asked, resting my elbow on the desk, and twisting sideways to face him.

"What's to tell?" Joey replied, mirroring my actions. "He's small, he's cute, he shits everywhere, and he screams the house down."

"And he kept you up last night crying?"

"I told you," he growled defensively. "He's cutting a tooth. It's not his fault."

"I know that," I coaxed, resting my hand on his forearm. "I wasn't blaming him. I was just thinking that the walls of your house must be paper thin if he kept you up all night."

Joey looked at me for a long time before shaking his head.

"What?" I asked. "What does that look mean?"

"Nothing."

"Liar."

"Maybe I'll tell you in another two months."

I bit back a smile. "You look like you could use a pick-me-up."

"Yeah, I know, but I don't get paid until Friday."

"I was talking about chocolate, Joe."

"Do you have some?"

"I always have some."

Back to him

January 23rd 2002

JOEY

"Are you going to the disco at the weekend?" Sam, one of the girls from my terrace, asked at lunch on Wednesday. She leaned a hip against the railing at the back of the PE hall and took a second hit from a spliff before passing it back to me.

"At the Pav?" I asked, taking a deep drag, as I balanced on the metal railing.

"Yeah." She exhaled a cloud of smoke. "From what I hear, that blonde in your class has some big plans for you."

"Who?" My heart did a flip in my chest. "Aoife?"

"Yeah." Sam snorted. "You wish."

Yeah, I did.

Regularly.

"No, what's her face … Danielle," Jason O Driscoll aka Dricko offered, taking the spliff. "She's got it bad for ya, Lynchy."

"Jesus," I muttered, rubbing my jaw, as the familiar wave of warmth and dizziness washed over me like a warm blanket. "Then no, I won't be going to the Pav at the weekend."

"Are ya mad, lad?" Dricko laughed. "You've got pussy on call with that one."

"Nice, Jason," Sam huffed, elbowing her boyfriend in the rib. "Real nice."

"What?" he purred, hooking an arm around her and pulling her into his chest. "He's the one fucking her. My baby's right here."

"I'm not fucking her," I growled, shifting in discomfort.

"*Again*," Alec chimed in, taking the spliff from Dricko. "Because you've been there already, haven't you, lad?"

"Did you, Joe?" Sam laughed, joining in the fray. "Have sex with Danielle?"

"No," I bit out, lying through my teeth. "So pack it in, the lot of ye."

"Because there wasn't much sleeping happening," Dricko snickered. "When he was giving it to her up against the back of the pavilion on Halloween night."

"Nice, asshole," I grumbled.

"Oh my god, you didn't!"

"He did, and he can't even deny it because half the school was there." Alec erupted in a fit of laughter beside me and I swiftly leaned over the railing and smacking the back of his head. "Ow, Jesus, what was that for?"

"Being a tool."

"I heard your ma showed up, lad?" Dricko continued to torment me. "Shit luck, huh?"

"Ah, no, she didn't?" Sam groaned, covering her face with her hand. "Oh my god, Joe, you poor boy."

"Well, I'm off." Disgusted with myself more than the topic of conversation, I sprang down from the railing, threw my bag over my shoulder, and sauntered off with my middle finger in the air. "Fuck the lot of ye."

Ignoring the laughter and taunting behind me, I strolled back into school, dutifully ignoring a smiling Molloy and glowering Paul as I walked.

Knowing that she had once again taken the prick back made me want to erupt like a goddamn volcano.

I couldn't look at her when she was with him.

I couldn't fucking bear it.

Seeing her with him made me want to bleach my eyeballs.

It made me fucking ache.

"Hey." Breathless, Molloy caught up to me at my locker a few minutes later. "Didn't you see me back there?" she asked, reaching up to grip my arm to steady herself, as she panted.

"Jesus, you need to do something about your fitness levels," I stated. "You legit ran from the entrance to the lockers."

"So you *did* see me?"

"Yeah, I saw you." Grabbing what I needed from my locker, I slammed the door shut and snapped the small silver lock back into place. "But don't expect me to talk when you're with him." Zipping my bag closed, I threw it over my shoulder and turned to look at her. "I refuse to enable your bad behavior."

Now, she smiled. "Are you feeding me my own lines, Joey Lynch."

"Absolutely," I replied. "And you should take your own advice."

"Joe." She blew out a heavy breath. "About Paul—"

"I don't want to hear it," I quickly cut her off. "You're back with him. Fair enough, Molloy. Good for you. I'm not going to say another word to try to dissuade you, but don't expect me to pander. I don't like him, and I won't pretend to."

"And I don't like when you're swapping girls like they're sweets in a tub of Quality Street, but you don't see me turning my back on you."

"Who said I was turning my back on you?" I demanded. "Because I sure as hell didn't."

"You hate me."

"No."

"You're mad at me."

"Yes."

"You want to scream at me."

"Because I—" Stopping short before I blew a head gasket, I released a furious growl and tried to regain some control before speaking again. "I'm not turning my back on you, Molloy."

"Prove it."

"How?"

"Give me a hug."

"Molloy."

"Hug me, Joe."

Exhaling heavily, I hooked an arm around her shoulders and pulled her to my chest, knowing that there wasn't any point in fighting this girl when she set her mind to something. What she wanted, she got.

"Don't hate me for trying to move on," she whispered, wrapping her arms around my waist, and burying her face in my chest. "I'm doing what I have to to move past *this*." A shaky breath escaped her. "Same as you."

"Yeah, Molloy." Feeling my anger dissolve, I sighed heavily and dropped my chin to rest on her blonde hair. "I know."

Choke on this

February 1st 2002

AOIFE

"Oh, my Jesus, that's disgusting." Trying not to gag, I watched in horror as my home economics partner dislocated his wrist in such a way that the back of his fingers touched his wrist. "What the hell is *wrong* with your *hand*?"

Chuckling softly, Joey snapped his wrist back into place with a loud popping noise that caused me to gag.

"Blarghhh!" I grabbed his shoulder and tried not to hurl. "Blarghhh."

"What's that, Molloy?" he taunted, right before popping his wrist out of joint *again* with a loud bone-crunching crack. "You want me to go it again?"

"Stop, asshole," I wailed loudly. "Stop, I – Blarghhh!"

"Aoife! Joseph!" Mrs. Adams barked from where she was tasting a dire-looking chili con carne in the kitchen station opposite ours, while a frazzled-looking Podge hovered over her shoulder, waiting for the ultimate verdict. "That's not the sound of food tasting that I'm hearing."

"Cop on, lads," Dricko snapped, as he stood next to Podge, looking just as flustered as his partner, while they studied their bowl of slop. "She's scoring our dish. This is the practice run for the junior cert."

"Your dish is shit. I wouldn't serve it to my dog, zero stars for presentation and an F for effort," Alec chimed in, swinging the string dangling off the end of his pink, frilly apron. "And no, Miss, that's the sound of choking that you're hearing from sexy legs over there. So, Lynchy definitely fed something back her throat to make her gag like that—"

"Choke on this, asshole," Joey chuckled, flinging a soup ladle overflowing with our own batch of chili con carne across the classroom at his friend.

Chopped peppers and mince flew everywhere, as red chili stained the walls and floor.

"Joseph Lynch, get your backside over here right this minute and clean up your mess!" Mrs. Adams shouted, stalking across the room to confiscate the rogue ladle. "Right this instant, young man. Don't you ever again throw your utensils at other students in my classroom. And, for the love of God, stop making that poor girl gag, will you? It's not very gentlemanly."

"Waaahhhh!" Alec screamed, inconsolable now, as he threw himself on top of a less-than-impressed looking Paul, and howled laughing.

My eyes locked on Paul, and I gave him a hard look, daring him to open his mouth and give me crap.

Instead, he swallowed down his disapproval and offered me a half-hearted smile.

I nodded my approval.

After our latest bust up, I had laid it all on the table for him, letting him know in no uncertain terms that I wasn't going to be pushed around anymore. That I had a friendship with Joey and if he couldn't accept that then he needed to let me go. I also made it perfectly clear that I had no intention of holding him back if he wanted to pursue other girls, nor would I hold it against him. All he had to do was let me off the proverbial ride first.

Surprisingly, Paul had agreed to my terms and had mostly followed my rules since. The rumors had quietened down, right along with his controlling tendencies, and he wasn't losing his mind every time I spoke to a boy.

It was progress.

I turned my attention back to my classmate, who had narrowly avoided another trip to the lion's den.

The only reason Joey wasn't being sent to the office by our elderly teacher was because he was her best student by a country mile.

Looking ridiculously adorable in his stripy apron, with his cap slung backwards, Joey skulked over to where our teacher was standing and took the dishcloth from her outstretched hand.

"Good boy," the old woman said in an approving tone when my partner got down on his hands and knees and mopped up the mess.

If anyone in our class had a hope of taking home an A in their Home Economics exam in the Junior Cert then it was the brooding boy beside me, who had returned to the sink in our little station to rinse out a chili-stained dishcloth.

Knowing it was a terrible idea, I looked to the top of the classroom, to where Danielle was partnered up with Mack. Yep; there she was, ogling the strip of golden skin on display, as Joey stretched his arm up to wipe chili off the classroom wall.

Beyond frustrated, I quickly snatched up a spoon and busied myself with stirring our pot of chili, all the while deciding that it was a good thing Mrs. Adams had confiscated our soup ladle. Otherwise I might be inclined to fling another batch at Danielle's bleached-blonde head.

Ugh.

The sound of laughter filled my ears then and I regrettably turned just in time to see my so-called partner wiping a smidge of chili off her bare leg.

"Nice aim, Joey," Danielle laughed, holding on to his shoulders for balance, as he crouched in front of her and cleaned her fucking leg.

"Nice legs."

Oh no he did not!

He did.

He fucking did!

I wanted to scream.

I wanted to throw up.

The jealousy that rose up inside of me was so intense that I could physically feel my body temperature rising.

As a matter of fact, if someone was to take my temperature right that second, it wouldn't have surprised me to discover that I was spiking a fever.

Keep the head, I mentally instructed myself. *Do not pick up this pot of chili and throw it at them. Don't do it, Aoife. You are too much of a princess for prison. Think of your nails. Just keep stirring.*

"So," the flirtatious bastard himself said when he rejoined me at our station, "what's your party trick?"

Deciding it was safer to remain quiet than to explode in front of everyone, I refocused on the pot of chili con carne that I had been attempting to stir, and forced out a clipped, "Hm?"

"Your party trick," Joey repeated, coming to stand beside me. "And don't say puking on demand, because I will go out in sympathy with you."

Tucking my hair behind my ear, I strived for calm and managed to strangle out a blasé, "I don't have one."

Reaching around me, he grabbed the salt and sprinkled a pinch into the pot. "I don't believe that for a second." His chest brushed against my back as he spoke and the smell of grass, and Lynx, flooded my senses. He always smelled so good. It was so *annoying.* "A girl like you always has a trick up her sleeve."

"A girl like me?" I deadpanned, trying to keep my freshly manicured nails *away* from the red-staining goo, while also trying to keep my emotions in check.

"Stop." Stilling my wrist with one hand, Joey took the teaspoon I was holding with the other and replaced it with a longer-handled wooden spoon instead. "Use this."

I narrowed my eyes and glared at the wooden spoon in my hand. "Why?"

"Because you might actually stir something with it."

"Asshole," I grumbled, shoving him with my hip.

He laughed under his breath. "What's with the mood, Molloy?"

"I'm not in a mood."

"Says the girl with a face like thunder." He nudged my shoulder with his. "You were all shits and giggles a minute ago."

"I am *not* in a mood."

"Fine." Holding his hands up, he shook his head and moved to the sink. "Suit yourself."

"I will."

"You do that."

"That's what I'm going to do."

"Good."

"Asshole."

"Crank."

"Prick."

"Witch."

"Shut up," I spat, furious. "I mean it. Don't say another word to me."

"Fine," he shot back and then sprinkled me with a handful of dirty dishwater. "Don't say another word to me, either."

"My hair!" I screamed, abandoning the chili to pat myself down. "Do you have any idea how long it takes me to wash and blow-dry this?"

"*My hair*," he mimicked in a high-pitched tone. "Relax. It's water. You'll survive."

Beyond livid, I could see the repercussions of my actions playing out in front of me before it even happened and decided that a few days in detention was well worth taking this asshole down a peg or two.

Deciding against scalding him with chili, I walked over to the sink and reached around Joey to retrieve the bottle of green washing-up liquid.

Without a word, I retrieved my stool, set it down behind him, and quietly climbed on top of it.

Reveling in the drama I was about to inflict, I unscrewed the cap, ripped his cap off, held the bottle over his head, and dumped the contents of the bottle on top of him.

The minute the green slime plopped onto Joey's head; his entire frame stiffened.

"You're fucking dead," he growled, slowly turning around as green slime dripped down his hair, face, and shoulders.

"Bring it on, bitch," I growled, tapping the bottom of the bottle to make sure that every ounce of liquid drained out.

"Aoife!" Mrs. Adams screeched. "What in the name of—"

"Put me down!" I screamed, hands and legs flailing wildly, when Joey threw me over his shoulder, and turned back to the sink. "Don't you dare – ahhhh!"

"Paul, go and fetch Mr. Nyhan immediately!"

"But she's—"

"Now, Paul. Hurry."

"You want to throw down?" Depositing me, ass first, into the sink full of dirty water, Joey reached up and smeared his hands with washing-up liquid from his own hair before coating my poor hair snot green. "Then let's go, Molloy."

Cheers and laughter erupted around us, but I was too furious to take into account anything other than my thirst for revenge.

"*Joey*," I seethed, teeth chattering, as I tried and failed to heave myself out of the sink. "You are so dead."

"I'm right here," he taunted, narrowly dodging my nails when I tried to scratch at his chest. "Come and get me, witch."

"Stop it, the pair of you, right this instant!"

"I swear to all that's holy, when I get out of this sink, I am going to inflict the world of pain on you, Joey Lynch."

"Aoife Molloy!"

"Sounds like you need to cool down, Molloy," he shot back, before reaching for the cold tap and turning it on full blast, soaking whatever parts of my body that had previously been spared from his assault. "Better?"

"Joseph Lynch!"

"Oh my god, help me, you bastard!" I screamed, with my ass thoroughly wedged in the sink, as water sprayed and ricocheted everywhere. "I'm stuck."

"Good," he roared back at me, as he scooped clumps of washing-up liquid off his chest and face. "Stay there."

"D-dammit J-Joey." Gasping, and spluttering, I scrambled to turn off the tap that was spraying arctic water on top of me. "I'm c-cold."

"And I'm warm?" Depositing the goo on the tiled classroom floor, he repeated the move several times, trying and failing to rid himself of green gunk. "You're a pain in my hole, Molloy."

"Jo-jo-joey!" I screamed, teeth chattering violently. "H-help!"

"Fine," he snapped, exasperated, as he moved to come get me. "But I'm warning ya now—" Slip sliding on the floor, he righted himself before he fell and regained his balance. "Jesus Christ, the floor's a death trap."

"Sh-shut up and s-save me, asshole."

"Don't you take that tone with me," he warned, pointing a finger at me, as he hastily skated the rest of the way over to me. "I'm warning you, Molloy, if you pull anymore stunts, you're going straight back in the sink for a timeout."

Ignoring our classmates who were all reveling in my misfortune, I wrapped my arms around Joey's neck, and tried to help him free me from the sink.

"Shit," he muttered. "You really are stuck."

"I t-told y-you," I strangled out, clinging to him like a drowned cat. "G-get me o-out of he-here!"

"I'm *trying*," he bit out. "It's your ass."

"If you s-say that m-my ass is f-fat, I'm g-going to s-scream."

"Your ass is perfect." Reaching up to grease his hands with washing-up liquid from his hair, he tried and failed to un-wedge my hips. "It's this goddamn sink that's the problem."

"Jo-joe . . ."

"Hang on a sec; I have an idea."

"What the h-hell are you d-doing?" I choked out, when he pushed his hand between my clamped thighs and cupped me *there*. "Joey!"

"My bad." With a deep frown etched on his face, he slid his hand in further until he was gripping my ass cheek. "Okay, now clench."

"Wh-what?"

"*Squeeze* your ass, Molloy. You squeeze and I'll pull. On three, okay? One, two, three—"

"Ugh!" I squealed, clenching my ass cheeks so tight they went into spasm. Thankfully, it did the trick, and I was propelled out of the sink and into his arms.

"Wah-hey!" Several of our classmates cheered, erupting in a chorus of clapping.

"I'm f-free." I released a sigh of relief. "Oh th-thank Jesus."

"Yeah, I thought that might work—" Losing his balance on the floor that had become a glorified ice rink, Joey collapsed in a heap on the ground, taking me with him.

There were only three options available to me in this moment; laugh, cry, or keep fighting.

I chose the first one, and surprisingly, so did my partner in crime.

"Fuck," he choked out a laugh from beneath me. "That was . . ."

"Stupid." Lifting up on elbows, I grinned down at him. "I won."

"No, I won."

"Who came out on top?"

"You, Molloy." Shaking his head, he stared up at my face and released an amused sigh. "Always you."

"They did *what*?" A booming male voice echoed through the air, and I bit back a groan, when our principal came pounding into the classroom, looking like he was fit to be tied.

"And that's how you know you fucked up," Alec laughed.

"Why am I not surprised to see the two of you up to no good – *again*," our principal seethed, face turning purple in color, as he glowered down at us. "In my office. *Now*!"

"Aw crap," I groaned, dropping my head on his chest. "It was nice knowing ya, Joe."

"Yeah." Joey sighed heavily and patted my head. "Right back atcha, Molloy."

We are nothing!

February 1st 2002

JOEY

Dressed in matching plain grey tracksuits – the ones they kept in the office for students that shit themselves – and looking like we'd been released from Cork prison on compassionate leave, Molloy and I sat in the front row of detention, without a single other student to take the shine off us.

With her hands folded across her chest, and her long, wet hair pulled back in a tangled braid, Molloy glared at the chalkboard in front of us, clearly having resumed whatever grudge she had on me.

She'd been given a week's worth of lunchtime detentions, while I had been told by Nyhan to show up every lunch for the foreseeable future. In other words, the rest of third year.

Stinking of chili and cheap washing-up liquid, I leaned in close and took a whiff of her, unsure which one of us smelled worse.

"It's you," Molloy bit out, reading my mind.

"No, it's definitely you."

I felt a small amount of regret for the parts of her blonde hair that were sporting the color snot green, but not enough to apologize.

She started it.

Flipped the fuck out on me for no goddamn reason.

And while I was more amused than annoyed now, I wasn't about to cave in.

It was her turn to bend.

Drumming my fingers on the desk, I looked around the room, all the while racking my brain for a possible trigger for our fight.

I didn't do anything different.

She was happy, smiling, *enjoying* herself.

We were having a laugh together, and then she just *flipped*.

The defiant side of my personality demanded that I pay no heed to her bullshit.

She's not your problem.

That feeding into her drama would only lead to more.

The only problem with ignoring her was that I didn't *want* to.

After spending an innate amount of time trying to push her away, having her actually go did *not* feel good.

Not good at all.

"How are your hips, Aoife?" Mrs. Adams announced, slowly rising from her chair, at the front of the room. "I can't imagine that was comfortable for you."

"Sore."

I immediately felt like a tool. "You're hurt?"

Ignoring me, Molloy focused on our teacher when she said, "I'll survive."

"Back in my day, we called those child-bearing hips," Mrs. Adams stated, causing me to choke out a laugh and Molloy to glower.

"Are you calling me fat, Miss?"

"Dear God, no," our teacher hurried to soothe. "I wasn't saying anything of the sort."

"Retract the claws, Molloy," I tossed out, feeling sorry for the old lady. "She was paying you a compliment."

"How?" Molloy deadpanned. "By implying that I have wide hips to go with my even wider ass?"

Yeah, and you look so fucking sexy for it.

"Exactly," Mrs. Adams said, offering me a grateful smile. "Do you think the two of you can behave yourselves for five minutes, while I pop to the bathroom?"

"Yeah, Miss," I replied, waving a hand around aimlessly. "Whatever."

She gave me a worried look. "Joseph."

"I mean it." I held my hands up. "I'll be good."

"Good boy," she crooned before pottering out of the classroom, leaving us alone.

"Teacher's pet," Molloy muttered, still glaring at the board.

"Do you want to tell me what I did?" I asked, twisting in my seat to face her. "I clearly did something to piss you off."

"No." Sighing in resignation, she dropped her head in her hands and groaned. "It's fine. I'm just . . . It's fine. I need to get a grip."

"What's wrong?"

"It's stupid."

"Tell me."

"You'll think I'm crazy."

"I already think you're crazy, Molloy."

"Well, crazier than normal then."

"Try me."

"No."

"Molloy." Reaching across the desk, I grabbed her shoulders and turned her to face me. "*Try me.*"

Her big green eyes locked on mine, and I fucking hated the lonesome look in them. "Joe."

"Tell me."

Chewing on her lip, she glanced down for a long moment before blowing out a breath and whispering, "You said she had nice legs."

I waited a beat to hear the rest of it, but when it didn't come, I found myself staring at her in confusion. "Huh?"

"You said she has nice legs," she repeated, still looking down at her lap. "You *told* her that she has *nice legs.*"

"Who?"

"Danielle."

"I did?"

"Yeah, Joe, you did."

"When?" I asked, beyond fucking confused.

"In class."

Oh shit, I did. "And that's bad because . . ."

"Forget it." Shrugging my hands off her shoulders, she turned back to staring at the chalkboard. "It doesn't matter. I'm over it."

"You're *over* it?" I shook my head, feeling at a loss.

She blew out a pained breath. "Forget it, Joe."

"Can you just stop with this wounded girl act and be straight with me," I growled, frustrated with this coy version of my friend. "Come on. This isn't you. You don't talk in riddles, Molloy. Tell me straight."

"Wounded girl act?" She shook her head in disgust. "Wow, you really know how to talk to girls don't you?"

"No, I really fucking don't," I tossed back, aggravated. "Because the only girl I talk to is you."

"Liar," she spat. "You talk to Danielle."

"Oh, give it a rest, Molloy."

"You said she had *nice legs*, Joey," she snapped, erupting on me. "*Nice legs.*" She turned to glare at me. "Ring any bells, asshole?"

"That's what *this* is about?" I gaped at her. "You're mad at me because I used the words *nice legs*?"

"On another girl."

"They're just words."

"No, they are not *just* words, Joey."

"Jesus Christ, Molloy, what the fuck else was I supposed to say to the girl?" I demanded, throwing my hands up. "I'd just sprayed chili all over her legs. I was trying to make it right. What did you want me to say? Nice ankle*s*? Nice kneecaps? Nice fucking calf muscles? What?"

"You don't say *that*," she shouted back at me. "You don't feed her *my* line."

"I didn't mean anything by it."

"That makes it even worse."

"How?"

"Because it just does, okay."

"Well, it honestly meant nothing."

"Like it meant nothing when you were touching her legs?"

"Don't," I warned, shaking my head. "Don't even go there."

"Right in front of me, Joey," she strangled out, voice thick with emotion.

"Right in front of *you*?" I choked out a humorless laugh. "Am I hearing this right? You have the audacity to sit here, on your high horse, and give me shit for *talking* to a girl, when you've spent every day since first year flaunting that prick in my face?"

"But you haven't just *talked* to Danielle, have you, Joey? You've been with her!"

"You mean while you've been with your *boyfriend*? So what if I have?"

"Oh my god," she cried, reaching up to clutch her face with her hands. "You don't get it. You just don't fucking *get* it!"

"Get what?" I roared, losing my cool. "You know what? I don't know why I'm even listening to this shit." I shook my head and turned away, furious with myself for letting her get under my skin. "We're not a couple, Molloy. I'm not your boyfriend. We are *not* together. Do you hear me? We are *nothing*."

"That's fine, Joe, we're not together. We're nothing," she choked out. "So why don't you go right ahead and fuck Danielle, with her nice legs and shop-bought bottle-blonde hair!"

"What gave you the impression that I *haven't* fucked her?"

Molloy's sharp intake of breath assured me that I had gone too far.

"Listen, I didn't mean to," I began to say, but she didn't stick around to listen.

Instead, she pushed her chair back and stood up, walking silently from the room.

The fact that she didn't even slam the classroom door behind her let me know that I had, indeed, fucked up in a colossal way.

Dropping my head on my desk, I clutched the back of my neck and groaned. "Fuck."

At least that

February 1st 2002

AOIFE

Mr. Nyhan could suspend me for walking out of detention if he wanted to.

Hell, he could threaten me with expulsion, and it wouldn't matter a damn because there was no way that I was ever willingly walking back into that classroom.

I made it to the carpark before I broke down.

Releasing a pained cry, I slumped down on the concrete footpath and dropped my head in my hands, crying hard and ugly.

I hated him.

I wanted to hate him so much.

I *needed* to hate *him*.

You need to stop loving him first . . .

"Aoife," a familiar voice said, and I stiffened.

No, no, no, not now . . .

"Go away."

"What's wrong?"

"I said *go away*!"

Doing the complete opposite of what I wanted, Paul sank down on the footpath beside me. "What's wrong?"

"Nothing." Sniffling, I reached up to wipe my eyes with the back of my hand. "I'm fine."

"Did he hurt you earlier?"

"No." I sniffled again. "I hurt myself."

"How?"

I gave my heart to the wrong person. "It doesn't matter."

"It clearly does."

"Just leave it alone, okay?"

"Talk to me, Aoife."

"I can't."

"You can."

"You don't want to hear this, Paul."

"Try me."

"I like him, okay!" I heard myself choke out. "I *like* him."

I felt Paul stiffen beside me. "Joey."

Exhaling a ragged breath, I nodded once and then dropped my head in my hands, feeling a flurry of guilt and relief. "I'm really sorry."

"Since when?"

Since day one. "I don't know."

"Were you with him?" he asked quietly.

I shook my head. "No."

He eyed me uncertainly. "No?"

"No," I confirmed, swallowing deeply. "*No.*"

He stared at me for a long moment before releasing a shaky breath. "At least that."

"Yeah," I croaked out. *At least that.*

"Do you still care about me?"

"Yes," I replied honestly.

"Do you care about him?"

I didn't answer his question.

I couldn't.

I wasn't that cruel.

"Do you like him more than you like me?"

"It's different."

"So, what are you telling me, Aoif?" His eyes searched mine and I was incredibly impressed with how calm he was remaining. It actually made this harder because he was being the sweet guy he was when we first met, which made me feel like the biggest dick in Ballylaggin. "Are you saying that you want to be with him?"

"No." I shook my head. "That's not going to happen."

"I don't understand." His brows furrowed. "If you haven't been with him and don't plan on being with him then why?"

"I just needed to tell you, okay?" I wiped my cheek and exhaled shakily. "I needed to get it off my chest."

Paul was quiet for a very long time before speaking again. "I need to tell you something."

"Is it going to hurt?"

"It could."

"As bad as what I just told you hurt?"

"Maybe a bit worse."

Oh god. "Is it about those rumors?"

"Sort of."

Exhaling a shaky breath, I nodded for him to continue.

"I, ah . . ." Exhaling a pained breath, he looked down at his feet and said, "I slept with someone."

Well crap.

"You lost your virginity?" That hurt worse than I had expected it to. "To who?"

"A girl from Tommen."

"So it was true." My breath caught in my chest, and I forced myself to remain calm and show him the same decency that he had shown me. "What's her name?"

"Bella." He dropped his head in his hands and groaned, "Bella Wilkinson."

"When?"

"*After* you broke up with me at Halloween."

"How long after?" I asked, surprising myself with how level my tone was.

"Aoife."

"How long, Paul?"

"Does it matter?"

"I gave you my truth."

"That same night."

"At the disco?"

He nodded once.

"Wow," I breathed, shoulders sagging.

Well, that was just perfect.

Joey was fucking Danielle, Paul was fucking this Bella, meanwhile, I was fucking myself over.

Perfect.

"I'm sorry, Aoife," he hurried to say. "It was a huge mistake. It meant nothing, and I honest to God felt like the worst piece of shit on the planet afterwards."

"Was she blonde?"

"Huh?"

"Blonde," I croaked out. "Was she blonde?"

"No," he replied, tone gruff. "She had black hair."

"At least that."

"I'm so sorry, Aoif."

"Yeah." I dropped my head on his shoulder and sighed. "Me, too, Paul."

"Can I ask you a question?"

I nodded.

"Why haven't you?"

"Why haven't I what?"

"You and him." He cleared his throat. "We were off. You had the perfect opportunity to get him out of your system."

"Get him out of my system?"

"You know what I mean."

I turned to look at him but didn't have an answer. "It's not going to happen," I offered instead, physically recoiling at the memory of hearing those godawful words coming out of Joey's mouth. All mixed with the memory of seeing him with her that night. "I need to get over him."

"Well, I don't want things to be over between us," he said, reaching out to take my hand in his. "I care a lot about you, Aoif."

"I care about you, too," I replied, feeling numb.

"This is just a bad patch," he continued, lacing our fingers together. "We can come through it. We always do."

"How?" I whispered. "How can we make this work?" And more importantly, why should we?

"I suppose by telling each other the truth," he offered quietly. "Today was a good start."

"I don't know if I'm invested in this," I admitted weakly. "My head is all over the place, Paul."

"We'll figure it out," he replied, wrapping his arm around my shoulder. "It'll be okay."

No, it won't.

Valentine's Day

February 14th 2002

AOIFE

With my hands full, and my phone ringing in my skirt pocket, I used my elbow to open the front door and then swiftly deposited my school bag, PE bag, and stack of post I'd collected on the floor, before reaching into my pocket for my phone.

"Yes, Casey, I'm home," I mused, balancing my trusty Nokia 3310 between my shoulder and ear, as I stepped over the pile of crap I'd dropped in the hallway, kicked off my heels, and moved for the kitchen. "And no, before you ask, I haven't opened my Valentine's cards yet."

"Well hurry up, bitch," she groaned down the line. "And at least tell me who the huge teddy bear, holding the cute heart, is from?"

"You already know who it's from."

"Okay, are you opening them yet?"

"No, I'm going to make a sandwich."

"Sandwich? What happened to your mam's Thursday stew?"

"Dad took her away to that big fancy hotel in Kilkenny for the night, remember?"

"To screw?"

"*No*, to test the mattress," I shot back sarcastically. "Obviously to screw."

"Where's that hot little nerd for the night?"

"He's gone to Nana's to tune the channels into her new television, and please don't call my brother hot. I think I might puke."

"He is a little ridey, Aoif, with that blond quiff and black-rimmed glasses—"

"No, he's not." I gagged. "He's an irritant."

"A sexy irritant," she teased before adding, "Okay, let's open your cards. I've opened all of mine and I'm bored."

"Who'd you get this year?"

"The usual," she sighed down the line. "Mack, Charlie, Dricko, and Alec from our year. Sticky-Dicky from sixth year, a couple of anonymous ones, and some kid called Tim from first year."

"Aw, you got a baby first year. That's so sweet," I cooed mockingly. "And as for Richard Murphy—"

"Sticky-Dicky," she interrupted me to correct.

"Calling him that only lets people know that you've touched his dick, Case."

"His sticky dick."

"Sticky from what; your lip-gloss?"

"Bitch."

"Ha," I cackled.

"By the way, he invited me to his debs in July, too."

"Are you going to go?"

"Am I going to go to Sticky-Dicky's debs with him? *Obviously.*"

I laughed. "You can borrow a dress from me."

"Thanks, bestie, because I don't have anything formal. Now open them."

"Alright, alright." Walking back out into the hallway, I grabbed my school bag and returned to the kitchen table to unzip it and then turn it upside down.

"How many did you get?"

"A few."

"How many?"

Scanning the selection of cards on the table, I mentally tallied them all up and said, "I think there's fourteen?"

"Fourteen!"

"No, sorry, I counted one twice. There's thirteen."

"Okay, I hate you."

"Oh please," I laughed. "You know this holiday is total bullshit."

"Okay, so we know one of them is from Paul," Casey said, morphing into a detective on the other side of the line. "Who are the rest from? Start opening."

Ripping through more than a dozen envelopes, I stacked them neatly in front of me and put the phone back to my ear. "You ready?"

"Since yesterday."

"Finny O' Shea, Dermot Keane, and Luke Twomey from sixth year."

"Hey, Luke is Sticky-Dicky's friend."

"Danny Collins and Trev Mulcahy from fifth year."

"Trev Mulcahy?" she swooned down the line. "Lord Jesus, he's a pretty one."

"Okay ... there's one from fourth year."

"Who?"

"Liam O Neill."

"Oh, I've scored with him," she informed me. "He has a tongue like a washing machine stuck on a fast spin cycle."

"Nice mental image, Case."

"Be glad you only have to imagine it."

"Okay, no baby first years for me – no second years, either, which means the other cards are from lads in our year."

"Ooh," she squealed. "I'm intrigued."

"Okay, so we've got ... Rich, Keith, Mike, Jack, Ruairi, Alec—"

"That cheeky little shit," Casey grumbled. "He gave me one, too. What does yours say?"

"To the girl with the best legs at school. Here's a Valentine's card. If you are reading this card, it means that you opened my folds, so it's only fair that I get to open yours. From Alec." I laughed. "Yours?"

"To the girl with the best tits at school. Please wear the white vest for PE next week. The visual of your bouncing tits has given me endless hours of joy. Feel free to flash a nipple. From Alec."

"That sounds like Alec, alright," I laughed. "Okay, so the last card's the biggest one."

"Paul?"

"Yep."

"What did he say?"

My heart stopped when I opened the card, and I exhaled a shaky breath.

"Aoife?"

"Case, he's after putting fifty euro in the card."

"Are you serious?"

I stared at the note in my hand, feeling a swell of different emotions. "Why would anyone put money in a Valentine's card?"

"Because he thinks he can buy a night of your company?" she laughed, but the joke hit a little too close to a nerve for me to laugh.

"I don't want his money, Casey."

"Give it to me," she replied, not missing a beat. "I'm poor. I both need and want his money very much."

"I'm pissed off."

She sighed down the line. "You are sitting in front of a stack of cards from boys who adore you. There is nothing to be pissed off about."

"But—"

"Do I need to come over there and slap some sense into you? Come on, Aoif. He probably put that in there because he's panicking."

"Panicking?"

"Yeah, babe. You two have been all over the place for months now, so the poor eejit is probably shitting pebbles in case you change your mind and run off with the Lothario of BCS."

"Don't." I shivered. "That is never going to happen."

"You really haven't spoken to Joey since the fight?"

"I really haven't, and I really have no desire to."

"Well shit," she said quietly. "You know, I really thought he might send you a card to break the ice between you guys."

Yeah, me, too. "He's not the type to give cards."

"No," she agreed. "But I thought that he would make an exception for you."

"I don't want his cards," I replied flatly. "I don't want anything from him."

"What *happened* between you guys, Aoif?"

"Nothing."

"Yeah *right.*"

"Nothing happened, Case," I deadpanned. "And nothing ever will. Besides, I'm *this* close to swearing off boys for life."

She snorted down the line. "That's because you haven't found yourself a Sticky-Dicky yet."

"Does yours have any brothers?"

"He has cows," she laughed. "His family are farmers."

I threw my head back and laughed. "Okay, you need to get off the line. I'm going to go take a shower and grab something to eat."

"Need to cool yourself down from all that Sticky-Dicky talk, huh? Fair enough, babe. Just don't get too carried away in the shower. Otherwise, I'm going to have to rename you—"

"Bye, Casey," I laughed, cutting her off before she could finish her sentence and destroy what was left of my innocence.

Leaving the cards on the kitchen table, I headed for the staircase, pulling off my school jumper, shirt, and tie as I went. Tossing them in the laundry hamper at the top of the landing, I reached behind my back, unzipped my skirt and shimmied it down my thighs before stepping out of it.

Grabbing a towel out of the hot-press, I strolled into the bathroom, still laughing to myself about Casey and Sticky-Dicky.

My laughter, however, quickly died in my throat when I came face to back with none other than *Joey?*

My blood ran cold at the sight of him kneeling over our toilet, with a line of white powder on the toilet lid, and a rolled-up fiver pressed to the inside of his nostril. In the blink of an eye, the powder disappeared up the makeshift funnel and into his nose.

"Oh my *god*," I strangled out, words finally finding me. "What are you *doing?*"

I hadn't spoken a single word to him since our fight two weeks ago. Too upset and hurt to deal with my feelings, I had avoided him like the plague, unable to go another round after he hit me with a knock-out blow to the heart.

With his elbows resting on the toilet lid, Joey dropped his head in his hands and muttered, "Fuck."

"Are you serious?" I whisper-hissed, glancing back at the door, and suddenly feeling like the authorities were about to charge into my house and arrest the both of us. "You're doing *drugs* in my house?"

"No."

"Yes," I argued. "I just *caught* you!"

"I know, I know." Sniffing and twitching his nose, he muttered, "don't worry." Like it was no big deal that I had just witnessed him ingesting a Class A drug.

"Don't *worry*?" I gaped at him. "Joey!"

"What?"

"You're *in* my house?" I shook my head in confusion. "What the hell?" Blowing out a ragged breath, I closed the space between us and grabbed his chin, forcing him to look at me. "What are you doing in my house and why did you bring *drugs* here?"

"Your dad asked me to stop by," he mumbled, eyes unfocused. "Gave me a key. Said the shower motor wasn't running." He shrugged. "I fixed it."

"You fixed it?" I choked out a growl. "You fixed it? I don't give a shit about the shower motor, Joey. Why were you doing drugs?"

"You weren't meant to see."

"Clearly," I hissed, forcing him to look at me when he tried to pull away. "Are you completely insane? What the hell are you doing getting yourself involved in this crap?"

"I don't know."

"Was that cocaine?"

"No."

"Liar! Since when are you taking cocaine?"

"Doesn't matter."

"Yes, it does," I snapped. "Talk to me, dammit!"

"Why?" Jerking free of my hold, he stood up and quickly backed away. "The fuck has it got to do with you?"

"You brought *cocaine* into my house, Joey," I repeated my earlier words, hoping that this time he would understand how wrong his behavior was. "Into my father's house." I pushed at his chest, trying to evoke a reaction out of him. "You remember my dad, don't you? He's the one who gave you that job at the garage. The one who trusted you to—"

"Get out of my face, Molloy," he growled, trying and failing to sidestep me in his pointless bid to escape an interrogation. "I know I fucked up, okay?"

"Get out of your face? You're lucky I'm not tearing strips out of your face, asshole," I snapped, pushing at his chest, forcing him to back up until he was pressed up against my bathroom wall.

I kept my hand on his chest, feeling an abnormal amount of heat emanating from beneath his uniform.

"What the hell?" I muttered, reaching up and pressing my hand to his neck and then his cheek. "Jesus, Joey, you're burning up."

Panicked, I watched as his green irises disappeared right in front of me, overtaken by pupils so dark and dilated that it made him look like a completely different person. "I'm okay."

"You're okay?" I stared at his ridiculously gorgeous face, feeling nothing but terror. "Joey, I just caught you snorting a line. I think it's safe to say that you are absolutely *not* okay."

"That was a mistake," he was quick to say. "I shouldn't have done that here."

"No, you shouldn't have done it at *all*," I corrected, concern filling me at a rapid pace.

"It was a mistake." A shudder racked through him. "Your father trusts me. I shouldn't have . . . I let him down." The more he spoke, the faster the words flew out of his mouth, and the looser his tone became. "It's all good, though, Molloy." He reached up and snatched up my hand that I was still cupping his chin with. "It's a mistake. I, ah, I make a lot of those. I'm just so fucking tired sometimes and I, ah, well, it helps, ya know. Fuck it."

He shook his head again but didn't let go of my hand. "Joe?"

"I don't know what I'm trying to say." His entire frame pulsed with energy as he rolled his shoulders and looked around the room like it was the first time that he was seeing it. "I've a match over at the GAA pitch in an hour, it's against St. Pats, they've a serious defense, and I haven't slept in days." He blew out a shaky breath, "I'm just so fucking tired and I needed something to give me a boost . . . but it won't happen again. It won't happen again."

"Days?" I shook my head. "Why haven't you slept in days?"

"Night feeds."

"Night feeds?" What was he talking about? Was he rambling? Was this a side effect of taking cocaine? I had no clue. "Joe, are you with me?"

I could feel the tremors racking through his body.

They *terrified* me.

"Again, I'm, ah, I'm sorry about what you saw there. I don't make a habit of, well, you know." Shrugging, Joey suddenly dropped my hand like it had scalded him and shoved a hand through his blond hair before moving for the door. "It's really not a big deal, though, so no worries, yeah? There's not a bother on me."

"Not a bother on you?" The boy had spoken more words to me in the past three minutes than he had in the past three years. He was clearly bothered. "You're going to a match *now*? Like this?"

"Yeah, I sort of have to. Don't really want to be playing, but it's, ah, well, it's not worth the hassle of trying to get out of." Nodding vigorously, he yanked the bathroom door open. "Tell your father that I, ah, I sorted the shower. It's running perfect again." He turned back and gave me one final clipped nod. "I'll be seeing ya, Molloy."

As I watched him walk away, it took me a moment to get my bearings, and then a couple more to stop my head from spinning off my shoulders, as I registered what the hell I had just witnessed.

This was more than sharing a spliff and a flagon of cider with *the boys* on a Friday night.

This was cocaine.

It was serious.

Trouble.

Yeah, the boy was trouble with a capital T.

"Oh no, you don't!" Bolting out of the bathroom, I caught ahold of his hand before he could reach the staircase and quickly dragged him into my bedroom.

"You're not going anywhere," I warned, swiftly closing and then locking my door behind us. "You're staying right here with me."

"Open the door."

"No."

"Let me out."

"No."

All jittery and with his hands shaking at his sides, he reached for the key in my door. "Let me out of this fucking room, Molloy."

"I said *no*." Snatching up the key, I slipped it into my bra and glared up at him. "You're staying with me."

"I have a match."

"I don't care. Sit down."

"I can't sit down!" he snapped, running his hand through his hair, as he paced my bedroom floor. "I need to move."

"Then move," I agreed. "In here."

"I'm fine," he snapped, body trembling, as he closed the space between us, backing me up against my bedroom door. "Let me out."

I shook my head, heart racing wildly. "No."

"Stop fucking with me," he ground out, chest heaving against mine, as the heat from his body scorched my skin.

He was fully clad in his school uniform, while all I had on was a pair of pink knickers and a black bra. I wasn't even matching, dammit.

"I'm not fucking with you," I growled. "I'm *trying* to *help* you."

"You don't need to do that."

"Apparently, I do."

"I'm fine," he crooned, acting both irrational and erratic, as he placed his hands on my shoulders. "It's all good." His hands were trembling

235 • CHLOE WALSH

so much that I could feel the vibration right down to my toes. "Shh," he coaxed, and then burst into a fit of laughter. "We're grand, okay?"

He actually *laughed* at me.

Oh, yeah, he was definitely high.

"Fuck." Laughing manically, he let his forehead smack against the wooden door frame right next to my head. "You're killing my buzz, Molloy."

He hit his head against the doorframe again, causing another pained laugh to escape him.

And then he did it again and again.

And again.

I debated calling Casey for help, before swiftly shutting that notion down, unwilling to get him into any more trouble.

Besides, it wasn't fear for myself that I was feeling.

I wasn't afraid of Joey.

No, I was afraid *for* him.

"Now, you listen here, asshole." Snatching up his chin, I pulled his face down to mine, forcing him to look at me. "You are going to wait this out in my room, and you are going to do it without banging your head off any more doors." With my hands on his shoulders, I walked him over to my bed and pushed him down. "You are going to sit down and take a breath."

"I can't sit down."

"You can," I argued, pushing him back down when he tried to stand.

"I need to move."

"You need to do what you're told."

"I can't breathe."

"Yes, you can."

"Something's wrong," he groaned, shaking his head, as he reached a hand behind his head and yanked his jumper off. "I can't breathe."

"Joe."

"I can't fucking breathe," he strangled out, chest heaving, as he sprang back up and tried to side-step me. "Let me go."

"Yes, you can." Pushing him down on my bed, I stepped between his bopping knees and pulled his chest flush against my belly. "Look at me."

"I'm suffocating."

"Joey?" Holding his face between my hands, I tipped his chin up and forced him to look at me. "Breathe."

"Molloy—"

"*Breathe*, Joe," I coaxed, feeling panicked now that he was panicking. "Just breathe, okay?"

Blowing out a frustrated breath, he attempted to inhale a deep breath, but stopped midway to say, "I can't. I can't. I need to move—"

"Shh." Lowering myself down on his lap, I took his hands in mine and placed them on my waist. "Just breathe." With my eyes on his, I inhaled deeply, held it there for a moment, and then slowly let it out. "Just like that."

He never took his dark eyes off mine as his hands tightened on my hips, and he mirrored my actions, taking a deep breath and then slowly letting it out.

"Good," I praised, settling my hands on his shoulders. "Again."

Still trembling, Joey took another deep breath, held it there, and then slowly released.

"Just like that." Threading my fingers through his sun-bleached hair, I stroked his cheek with more affection than was appropriate and continued to breathe in and out with him over and over again, never once taking my eyes off his.

The more he watched me, the harder I felt *him* grow beneath me.

From my perch on his lap, I could feel all of him straining against me, and I would be a liar if I said it didn't make me ache.

"How are you feeling?"

"Like I want us to get naked and fuck."

Jesus.

"Well, that's not happening," I whispered, feeling my entire body tremble. "So, stop thinking about it."

"I know it's not." Looser with his actions now that his mind was hazed, he pulled me closer to him, fingers kneading the fleshy part of my hips, as he slowly rocked his hips against me. "But we will."

My breath hitched in my throat.

He nuzzled my breasts with his nose. "Not today."

I released another shaky breath.

"But we will."

Oh Jesus.

"Shh. Focus, Joe. Keep your breathing even," I instructed, when I could do anything *but*.

Inhaling a deep breath, he leaned in close and buried his face in my chest. "I'm trying."

"Good,' I breathed, shivering. "Keep trying."

Achingly aware that my bra was the only thing that separated his lips from my breasts, I hailed on every ounce of self-restraint I had to help me in this moment.

His voice was muffled, and his lips brushed against the piece of fabric that concealed my pebbled nipple, when he groaned, "I miss you."

My heart thudded violently in my chest. "I miss you, too."

"I'm sorry," he whispered, nuzzling the outline of my nipple with his nose. "For feeding her your line."

"It's okay." Knotting my fingers in his hair, I cradled his head against my chest and released a shaky breath. "Everything's going to be okay."

Several minutes ticked by, but neither one of us moved.

Instead, I remained on his lap, holding both his head *and* my breath, while he focused intensely on his.

Slowly, the tremors racking his hands, racking his entire body, lessened, and I felt a mountain of relief flood my body.

Repressing a shiver, I reached down to feel his clammy forehead and found that temporary relief abandon me. "Joe, you're burning up worse than before."

"Hm?"

"You're too hot." Concerned, I let my hands trail to his damp neck, and even damper school shirt. "Holy crap, Joe, you're drenched."

"It's grand," he mumbled, still dutifully concentrating on his breathing. "It'll pass."

Yeah, I wasn't so sure. "Hang on. I'll open a window."

I moved to climb off his lap, but he swiftly wrapped his arms around my body and pulled me back to him. "Don't move."

"Joe, you're literally piping hot." Panic began to set in when I watched a bead of sweat trickle down the side of his neck. "I could fry an egg on you. Seriously. I need to cool you down."

"I don't care." He buried his face back in my chest and inhaled another deep breath. On the exhale, he whispered, "Don't leave me."

"Joe . . . "

"Please just stay." He paused to release another slow breath, before continuing, "This is the only time it's ever stopped. Please don't break it."

"This is the only time what's ever stopped?" I croaked out, feeling my heart thunder wildly in my chest. "And don't break what?"

"My head," he mumbled, before adding, "The quiet."

I don't understand, I wanted to cry, but I held firm and remained *calm*.

"I promise I won't leave you," I told him, gently removing his tie from his neck. "I'll stay right here. But I need to not be on your lap right now because my body is heating yours up."

When he made no move to comply, I leaned back, causing his head to fall forward, and reached for the buttons on his shirt.

"Something's wrong," he groaned, hands slumping at his sides. "I don't feel right."

"How could you feel right after doing what you just did?" I argued, quickly unbuttoning his shirt and sliding the fabric off his shoulders, only to be greeted by the sight of dark purple bruising all over the left side of his chest, reaching all the way up to his collarbone. I sucked in a sharp breath at the sight. "Jesus, what happened?"

"Fight."

Joey had a gorgeous chest; lean and strong, with light brown nipples and tightly carved abdominal muscles. His hips were narrow and sported those epic V-shaped sex lines that all the athletically gifted seemed to possess. A dusting of golden-brown hair trailed south from his navel, disappearing beneath the waistband of his grey school trousers.

And while his golden skin was littered with scars, I was certain that I had never seen anyone more perfect in my life.

"A fight?" Shivering, I gently placed the palm of my hand on the bruise that was covering his heart. "With who?"

"Some asshole." Blowing out a pained breath, he covered my hand with his and whispered, "You should let me go."

"I know I should." With my heart hammering violently in my chest, I quickly clenched my eyes shut and willed my heart to just *calm* down. "But I can't."

"There's something wrong," he groaned then, shifting uncomfortably. "With my dick."

"Is this your way of getting me to look at your dick?"

"No," he groaned, slipping a hand into the waistband of his grey school trousers. "This is me telling you that there is something *really* wrong with my dick."

"What is it?"

"I don't know." He hissed out a pained breath and flopped back on my bed, groaning like he was in genuine pain. "Fuck."

"Did you twist a nut?" I asked, deadly serious. "Because Kev did that once, and it's actually really serious. If you don't seek medical treatment, you can lose the whole testicle, Joe—"

"No," he groaned, and then covered his face with his hands. "Fuck, it's too much."

"Okay, that's it!" I threw my hands up in panic. "Take off your clothes and let me see."

"Not a good idea."

"Oh, just shut up and strip, dammit." Concerned, I reached for the button on his school trousers, and snapped it open before undoing his fly. "Lift up your hips."

"Molloy."

"Lift up."

"Fuck." Shifting upwards, he hissed out another pained groan when I dragged his trousers down his hips. "Oh Jesus Christ, don't touch it—"

"I'm sorry!" Wincing, I carefully peeled the waistband of his black boxers over what had to be the biggest damn dick I'd ever seen. "What the fuck is *that*?"

Springing to attention like a front-line soldier, his fully erect penis bopped around mere inches from my face. "Why is it so—"

"I don't know!" he bit out, pulling up on his elbows to glare at it like it was the enemy. "It won't go the fuck down. I keep getting harder."

"Is that supposed to happen?"

"*No*."

"Then why—"

"I don't fucking know, Molloy!"

"Okay, okay, why don't we both just calm down!" I shouted, more to myself than him, as I stood in my bedroom, in my bra and knickers, with Joey Lynch's dick glaring angrily up at me. "Jesus, that's a big damn dick, Joe."

"Shut up, Molloy," he snapped. "Don't fucking say that. It makes it worse."

"Why don't you ... well, you know?" I shrugged. "Give it a pull? You know, see if it goes down?"

"Oh, my fucking god," he growled, and then hissed out a pained breath. "I'm not wanking myself in here."

"Obviously, you don't have to do it with me *in* here," I argued. "I can go downstairs and make us a sandwich or something."

"A *sandwich*? Really, Molloy?"

"I don't know," I strangled out. "I haven't eaten since lunch and you're ... and I'm ... Look, I'm just trying to help, okay?"

"Get my phone."

"Huh?"

"My phone," he bit out. "Please. Pass it up to me."

"Where is it?"

"Pocket."

Scrambling to retrieve his phone, I managed to fish it out of his pocket without making eye contact with *it*.

"Got it," I said, climbing onto the bed to kneel beside his slumped frame. "Here."

"Thanks."

"No problem."

Erectile malfunction

February 14th 2002

JOEY

I couldn't explain what had possessed me to do something as incredibly reckless as doing a line in my boss's house.

The only valid excuse I had to hand was that exhaustion had taken over my body to the point that it was crippling me.

Pitiful as it was to admit, I hadn't slept in months.

Fifteen weeks, to be exact.

Ever since the latest of my father's spawn was inserted into my life.

From the minute he came home from the hospital, Sean was inconsolable.

No joke, he was off his goddamn head 24/7, while our mother was off her head right along with him.

If she wasn't working, or pawning the baby off on Nanny, she was hiding in her room, crying into her pillow, and doing everything humanly possible to avoid having to handle him.

Nanny mentioned something about how the reason Mam didn't seem to be bonding with Sean was because of something called postnatal depression.

I didn't understand it.

How could I fix it if I didn't know a damn thing about it?

I couldn't, and the old man was no fucking help, either.

She refused to nurse him.

She wouldn't give him a bottle.

She rejected the idea of holding him.

Every time he cried; she looked like she wanted to peel the skin from her bones.

It was fucking horrible.

After getting his feet back under the table when she came home with the baby, the old man hung around for a few weeks, treading water, and somewhat behaving himself.

It didn't last long, of course.

Three weeks after she gave birth, Dad had lost his shit with Mam, and physically dragged her out of the bed.

Depositing her on the floor next to the crib, he'd roared and screamed in her face until I couldn't take another damn second of it. Eruptions had occurred, resulting in us having one of our worst ever fights.

In the end, the old man had gotten the better of me, but at least I'd gotten a few good punches in to make him pay for hurting my mother, who was still bleeding after the baby, for Christ's sake.

Livid that she point-blank refused to take the baby, Dad had grabbed the crib, with Sean inside of it, and walked it out of their bedroom and *into* my thirteen-year-old sister's.

After that, the old man stopped trying, and of course, my mother laid the blame for his withdrawal at my feet.

Unable, or just plain unwilling, to take care of his responsibilities, Dad went straight back into his usual pattern of drinking, fucking, and smashing the house up, leaving me to clean up his mess.

With school, work, hurling, and Ollie and Tadhg to look after, I didn't object when Shannon took on the role of caring for Sean.

Because the truth was, I didn't want to do it.

I didn't *want* to love another one.

Not when his age and vulnerability would keep me shackled to this house for longer.

Regardless of my aversion to getting attached to the colicky little shit, that's exactly what had ended up happening.

Because, as willing as my sister was, she didn't know what to do with a newborn, and, after three nights of non-stop screaming, I'd taken the crib into my room, unwilling to let that kid cry it out another minute.

Three and a half months had passed since then, and while Mam was slowly warming to Sean, changing his nappy, and taking him for walks on her day off, his crib was still in *my* bedroom.

Falling asleep standing up these days, I had started to buy a couple of grams every payday from Shane, needing the pick-me-up to just function.

Today was far from the first time I'd dabbled with uppers, but it was the first time I felt like my heart might actually beat its way out of my chest. The high was all fucking wrong, and I was raging with Shane for selling me a lemon, because whatever the hell I had put up my nose, was *not* cocaine.

My head was all over the place, my body was burning the hell up, and all I wanted to do was *fuck*.

The urge to get off was almost unbearable, leaving me with a raging hard-on, which was a problem because the girl who'd taken on the role of my personal chaperone was the one girl I *couldn't* have.

And I wanted to have her.

I wanted to have her so fucking bad, it was painful.

While the haze in my mind was clearing, the pressure in my dick only seemed to be mounting.

"Got it," Molloy declared, and she climbed back onto the bed in her tiny pink thong that was doing nothing to help the cause. "Here," he she said, thrusting my phone onto my stomach.

"Thanks."

"No problem." Patting my shoulder, a sign of solidarity, no doubt, she shifted closer, settling on her knees beside me. "I've got your back."

Considering she hadn't looked in my direction in weeks, I should be thrilled to hear those words coming out of her mouth.

But in my current state, it was hard to focus on anything other than the glorious visual of her scantily clad body.

If it weren't for the fact that I was seriously concerned for my dick, I would have reveled in this moment.

Stop looking, asshole.

Looking makes it worse.

Shaking my head, I unlocked my phone and quickly tapped out a text.

LYNCHY: WHAT DID YOU GIVE ME?

HOLLAND: ???

LYNCHY: WHAT THE FUCK DID YOU DO TO ME?

HOLLAND: NOTHING, ASSHOLE, WHAT'S WRONG WITH YA?

LYNCHY: I CAN'T GET MY DICK TO GO THE FUCK DOWN!

HOLLAND: AH SHIT. WRONG BAG, KID. MY BAD.

LYNCHY: YOUR BAD? WHAT DOES SHIT MEAN? WHAT DID I TAKE?

HOLLAND: BLOW WITH A TWIST. WASN'T MEANT FOR YA. I'VE AN AUL FELLA IN HIS 50'S WHO COMES UP WEEKLY FOR IT.

LYNCHY: WHAT. THE. FUCK. IS. THE. TWIST?

HOLLAND: SILDENAFIL.

LYNCHY: WHICH IS ...

HOLLAND: A CHEAP VERSION OF VIAGRA. CRUSHED AND MIXED WITH SNOW, IT'LL BLOW THE HEAD OFF YA. LITERALLY.

LYNCHY: JESUS CHRIST, ASSHOLE. I HAVE A MATCH LATER!

HOLLAND: RELAX, YOU'LL BE GRAND IN A COUPLE OF
HOURS. RIDE THE WAVE AND ENJOY IT, LAD.

HOLLAND: MIGHT WANNA SKIP THAT MATCH, THOUGH.

HOLLAND: FIND YOURSELF SOME NICE WET PUSSY TO
BURY THAT COCK INSIDE.

"Oh fuck," I choked out, clenching my eyes shut, as my frantic brain
tried to absorb what the hell was happening to me.

"What?" Molloy demanded, wide-eyed. "What is it?"

Unable to voice an answer, I tossed my phone on her lap and slung
an arm over my face.

"You mixed erectile dysfunction medication with cocaine?" she
screeched. "Are you insane!"

"I didn't fucking know, did I?"

"No wonder your dick is trying to levitate off the bed. It's been set
on ready-steady-fuck-mode, Joe!" Shaking her head, she re-read the
messages on my phone before tossing my phone on the mattress. "Well,
I can tell you one thing right now, and it's that this area right *here*—"
she paused to point at her pussy, before quickly adding, "is off-limits to
that leaning tower of *penis*!"

"Did I *ask* you to get me off?"

"*No*, but I can clearly see that you *want* me to," she argued, pointing
to the head of my cock. "No wonder you're in pain, carting that thing
around. I'm in pain *thinking* about—"

"Molloy."

"Okay, okay." Grimacing, she held her hands up. "Not helping. Got it."

"Can I . . . " Blowing out a pained breath, and feeling totally fucking
degraded about what I was about to ask, I forced the words, "use your
shower," out of my mouth?"

Her brows furrowed. "My shower?"

I gave her a meaningful look.

"Oh," she replied, eyes widening. "My *shower*. Yeah, of course. No problem." Nodding, she quickly clambered off the bed and yanked my jocks and school trousers the rest of the way off my legs. "Can you stand?"

"Yes," I bit out. "Can you not kneel in front of me like that. *Please*."

"Oh, shit, sorry." Springing away from me, Molloy pottered over to her dresser, attempting to give me privacy, while she turned back to look every three seconds.

"I am sorry about this," I muttered, climbing to my feet.

"Meh." She shrugged, as she fingered through a stack of CD cases on her dresser. "It's been an interesting Valentine's Day."

"Yeah, I bet." Standing bollocks naked in her bedroom, I hobbled towards her door, with every inch of me on full view. "Molloy."

"Yeah?"

"The door." Resting my head against the timber, I repressed the urge to roar, and bit out, "You have the *key*."

"Ah crap." Stepping around me, she reached inside her bra and withdrew a key. "Do you want soap?" she asked, with her ass way too close for comfort. "Or a magazine—"

"Just *open* the door."

"Got it."

Calling a truce

February 14th 2002

AOIFE

Fifty-eight minutes.

That's how long the shower motor hummed above me.

That's how long it took for Joey to tame the beast.

Another ten minutes passed before he finally emerged from the bathroom.

Re-dressed in his school uniform, with his blond hair cocking up in forty different directions, and his cheeks noticeably flushed, he stepped into the kitchen, towel in hand. "Thanks."

"Better?" I asked, unable to suppress the laugh that escaped me, as I flipped a piece of French toast in the pan. "Feeling *relieved*?"

"Funny," Joey growled, but the reluctant smile on his face assured me that he wasn't mad.

"Did it go down?"

"Eventually," he admitted, with a wolfish smile. "I thought I was going to have to go to A&E for a while there."

"Imagine if you had," I snorted, switching off the hob and plating up the French toast. "We would have needed to hitch a trailer onto the taxi to cart that stallion between your legs."

"I'm never going to hear the end of this, am I?"

"No, probably not," I agreed, still laughing. "Here." I handed him a plate stacked with my homemade goodness. "You need to replenish your life force."

"You cooked all by yourself." His brows rose in surprise. "I'm impressed."

"I have a pretty decent home economics partner who taught me a thing or two," I replied, moving to the table with my own plate. "He's an asshole, but he knows his way around the kitchen."

"So, this home economics partner," Joey said, following me over to the table. "Is he your friend?"

My heart flipped in my chest. "He was."

"Was?"

Nodding, I sank down on my chair and took a bite or toast. "He used to be my best friend."

"What changed?"

"We had a fight."

"Is that right?"

"Uh-huh. He broke my heart."

Pain flicked in Joey's eyes. "Molloy."

"Joke."

Relief flooded his features when he swallowed my lie. "Well, I hear this partner of yours feels shit about the fight the two of you had."

"Does he now?"

"Yeah." Joey nodded. "He misses his friend."

My heart flipped. "He should miss her. She's amazing."

He smirked. "He wants her back."

"She never left." I swallowed deeply. "She just needed a timeout."

"Good." He nodded. "Because if she did leave, he wouldn't like it."

"He wouldn't?"

"No." His green eyes locked on mine from across the table. "He wouldn't."

Exhaling a shaky breath, I reached across the table and laid my hand, palm up. "Nice moves."

He stared at my hand for a long beat before slowly placing his hand on top of mine. "Nice everything."

FOURTH YEAR

FOURTH YEAR

I'll be with you

September 2nd 2002

JOEY

Holding my breath under the water, I remained motionless with my hands gripping the sink, until my lungs turned to fire in my chest and my thoughts became muddled and blurry.

That shitty human survival instinct instilled in all of us, the one that programed us to search for oxygen, forced my face to the surface of the water.

Numb, I breathed slowly through my nose, purposefully torturing my lungs that demanded I gulp in as much air as I could.

Fuck my lungs.

Fuck the world.

The circles under my eyes were darkening to the point where, when I woke up this morning, I actually looked like I had two black eyes.

A million sleepless nights, combined with a million fucking mistakes this past summer, had taken its toll on my body.

Cutting a line with my bank card, I leaned over the windowsill that held the mirror – and what would get me through the next six hours – and quickly snorted the powder up my nose.

I had a pain slap bang in the center of my chest.

The ache was fucking terrible, and I couldn't seem to shake the damn thing off.

I was going out of my mind worse than ever lately.

And I was raging.

I was so fucking mad that I could feel the burning and bleeding from somewhere so deep inside of me, I knew couldn't be found to be patched up.

I was a mess.

Jesus . . .

Shuddering, I leaned over the sink for another half an hour, waiting for my stomach to settle, and my brain to cooperate, before I could manage to go back into my room and throw on my school uniform.

The hurley and helmet in the corner of my room taunted me with a whole host of demands and expectations that I wasn't sure I could live up to for much longer.

"Hey." Shannon's voice filled my ears and I stilled for the briefest of moments before turning to face her.

"Hey." I offered her what I hoped what a supportive smile. "Are you ready for your first day?"

"No," she whispered, chewing on her lip.

Yeah, me either. "You'll be grand," I said instead. "I'll be with you."

"Do I look okay, Joe?" Shannon asked in a small voice, as she hurried along beside me, swamped in her BCS uniform.

"You look grand, Shan," I told her, keeping my gaze fixed straight ahead. If I looked at her, if I saw the fear in her blue eyes, I would crack.

Jesus Christ, I was a nervous wreck.

Seriously, if anyone that didn't know me saw me in this moment, they would swear that *I* was the one starting secondary school this morning, and not my baby sister.

With my palms sweating, and my heart racing rapidly, I had to force my legs to slow down so she could keep up.

Schooling my anxiety, the best I could, I walked Shannon up the path to BCS, while discreetly glowering at every motherfucker who dared look in her direction.

Maybe an offensive strike was the best form of defense when it came to protecting her this year.

Maybe, that way, I could get her through this school year unscathed.

"I'll always be your brother, okay? No matter what."

*

Darren's voice infiltrated my mind and I balked, swiftly burying the memory of that last time I'd taken this walk with a sibling.

Burying him.

He's gone.

He's dead.

He doesn't exist anymore.

"You okay, Joe?" my sister asked, reaching up to touch my shoulder. "You look sad."

"It's okay." I forced a smile. "Everything is going to be okay."

"Yeah?"

I nodded. "Yeah, Shan."

Because I won't ever leave you.

Meet the gobshites

September 21st 2002

AOIFE

I didn't want to be here tonight, much less on display like a prettified porcelain doll, but that's exactly what I found myself doing on Saturday night, as I sat opposite the Rice family at Spizzico's, one of the more uppity restaurants in Ballylaggin.

"Just bear with me for another hour," Paul coaxed, giving my hand a squeeze under the table, as Paul's father, Garda Superintendent Jerry Rice, drawled on about his upcoming golf tournament in Kerry. "I promise, we can do something you pick after this, okay?"

I slapped on a smile for his mother's benefit, when I was screaming on the inside.

I'd tried.

I really had.

When we decided to try again, I promised myself that I would put to bed any notions of my father's apprentice and concentrate on making it work with the boy who *actually* wanted to be with me.

And to be fair, that's exactly what I had done for months.

I kept it friendly and jovial with Joey in class, but I steered clear outside of school.

For months, I had thrown myself into our relationship, giving Paul one hundred and fifty percent of my time, attention, and effort, only to find myself still feeling *empty*.

Because it didn't seem to matter how much I avoided, distracted myself or denied it, my thoughts *always* returned to the place they shouldn't.

To the person they shouldn't.

"Please get me out of here," I hissed through clenched teeth, still smiling like a creeper at my boyfriend. "Because if I have to listen to your father talk about his impressive handicap or pretentious golf match for another second, I'm going to scream."

"It's a tournament," he corrected, fake smiling right back at me. "Not a match, babe."

"I don't care," I replied, still grinning. "Please."

"Give it a rest," Paul bit out. "You're getting a free meal in a restaurant your family could never afford to eat at, and all you have to do is smile and nod in exchange."

My mouth fell open. "You did *not* just say that to me."

"I beg your pardon?" Mrs. Rice asked, setting her fork down. "Aoife, dear, did you say something?"

"Yeah," I replied. "I said that I'm—"

"Tired," Paul cut me off and said, reaching over to pat my hand like a little child. "She just said that she's a bit tired. Aoife started working at The Dinniman during the summer," he continued as by way of explanation. "She's finding it hard to adapt to work *and* school."

"What?" *No, I'm not.*

"The Dinniman?"

Paul nodded. "It's a restaurant across town."

"It's a pub that serves food," I corrected, ignoring Paul's warning glare. "I'm waitressing there a few evenings after school, and on weekends."

"Well, good for you." Mrs. Rice smiled warmly. "It will be nice to have a bit of pocket money for yourself."

I smiled back at her. "Yeah, I like it so far, and most of the locals are from my own area, so it's grand really."

"I'm always telling Paul that he should get himself a little Saturday job now that he's in fourth year," Mrs. Rice offered. "I think it's important that a young person learns the value of a euro."

"And I think it's important that he concentrates on his studies," Mr. Rice interjected. "He has all the money he needs from us, Rita. The law degree he has his heart set on will be earned by working hard at school, and not waiting tables in The Dinniman. Of course, I mean no offense, Aoife."

Offense taken.

"It's grand." I tucked my hair behind my ears. "Fourth year isn't a heavy workload year," I heard myself add. "Most people in our year have jobs by now."

"Perhaps, but surely not in pubs?"

I shrugged. "In lots of different places."

Mr. Rice frowned. "And you wouldn't consider finding work elsewhere?"

"Where would you suggest?" I bit out, flustered from his interrogation.

"Somewhere more appropriate for a girl of your age," he offered with a wave of his hand. "Maybe a little babysitting job on Saturdays."

"I like it at The Dinniman," I replied, feeling my cheeks burn from the effort it was taking to restrain myself. "I make more money there than any babysitting job would pay."

"I didn't think a waitressing job would pay that well?"

Shows what you know, you big posh prick . . .

"Would you look at her, Dad," Paul interjected with a chuckle. "She's an asset to the place."

"Thanks, Paul." I beamed, feeling my stomach flip from the compliment. "I appreciate that."

"No problem, babe," he replied, slinging an arm over the back of my chair. "Besides, one look at her with that little white shirt and short black skirt, and the owners are guaranteed to fill the bar," Paul continued, clicking his fingers for emphasis. "Of course they're going to pay well to keep her."

I take it back, Paul, you big eejit.

Silently seething, I glowered at the side of his handsome side profile.

Swallowing down my discomfort, I smiled and nodded along as the conversation switched to plans of the future.

My future looked drastically different to Paul's. There would be no University of Limerick for a degree in law on the map for me, that was for sure.

I was more than likely headed to a local further education and training college after secondary school, where I would train in hairdressing or beauty.

At least, hairdressing was the only career piquing my interest at that moment in time.

"I have to say, both of my sons have exquisite taste in the company they keep," Mr. Rice declared then, holding his tumbler of whiskey up, and gesturing first to me and then to his oldest son Billy's new girlfriend, Zara.

"Yeah." I raised my water glass and resisted the urge to gag. "Here, here."

Meanwhile, Zara smiled sweetly back at him. "Thank you, Mr. Rice."

Poor innocent fool, I thought to myself, *give it time. You'll learn.*

She was just the latest in a long line of beautiful women Billy had brought home to show off.

Paul's older brother was nineteen and I had counted no less the seven different girlfriends accompany him to these family meals since we had started going out back in first year.

"Quick," I whisper-hissed in Paul's ear. "Call my phone and I'll take it from there. I can't take another minute of him."

"What, no." He balked. "Just wait it out."

"Paul."

"Aoife."

Making a point of looking at my watch, I quickly feign-gasped. "Oh my god, is that the time?"

Lame.

Lame.

Lame.

"Paul." I turned to look at my boyfriend, all wide-eyed and full of crap. "My dad wanted me home an hour ago."

"Are you sure?" he asked, narrowing his eyes.

"Yes," I replied, giving him a look that said *go with it or I'll cut your dick off*.

Turning back to his family, I offered them an apologetic smile, as I stood. "I am so sorry about this." Smiling brightly, I added, "hopefully, we can do it again soon," while knowing on the inside that I would never allow myself to get roped into another one of these my-dick-is-bigger-than-your-dick dinners.

Hell to the no.

"That was beyond fucking rude, Aoife," Paul admonished, as I power-walked away from the restaurant, and he hurried to keep up with me. "What were you thinking?"

"I was thinking that you duped me into having dinner, *again*, with people I have nothing in common with, *again*."

"They're not people, they're my parents."

"Parents are people, Paul."

"Don't get smart with me. You know I hate it when you're sarcastic," he snapped, running a hand through his dark hair. "You really fucking embarrassed me back there. You're sixteen, not six. Don't you think it's time that you learned how to act your age?"

"You know what, maybe we should just call it a night," I snapped, shoving my hands into my coat pockets. "Since my personality is clearly rubbing you up the wrong way so much tonight."

"What? No, don't be stupid," he growled, retracing the steps he'd taken.

"I'm not stupid, Paul."

"You know what I meant." Slinging an arm over my shoulder, he said, "Come on, babe, it's Saturday night. I don't want to spend it on my own."

And what about what I want?

"So, where do you want to go?" he asked, pulling me close to his side.

"I'm thinking about just going home."

"No, that's boring," he replied.

"I wasn't aware you had been invited?"

"Your house doesn't have internet, or a flat screen, or anything decent to watch," he added, with a dismissive wave. "And no offense, but it's kind of a tight squeeze when your family are all in the sitting room with us."

"Wow." I shook my head. "We can't all have Gards for fathers."

"Amy Murphy is having a house party at her place tonight," he offered then. "I told her that both of us would swing by for a bit."

"Amy?" I gaped at him. "She's a sixth year."

"Yeah, so?"

"So. why did you tell her that I'd come?" I looked up at him. "I barely know the girl, Paul, and I never agreed to go."

"Because you're with me," he replied, like this would somehow answer my question.

It didn't.

"I'm not sure I like where this is going, Paul," I said, eyeing him warily.

"Come on, babe," he said, with a megawatt smile. "It's just a party."

"Yeah."

That wasn't what I was referring to.

The demons in your head

April 11th 2003

JOEY

"Where the fuck have you been?"

It was a question I had expected Tony to ask me when I walked into work twenty minutes late, having been kept late after training to talk to selectors.

It wasn't, however, a question I had expected my father to ask.

And definitely not here.

"What's going on?" My gaze flicked to Tony, who was leaning against the tool drawer, with a cup of tea in his hand, and a sympathetic gaze on his face.

Instantly, my back was up.

There was only reason my father would come here.

"Is she dead?" It was the first thought I had, and surprisingly, I managed to ask it without collapsing in a heap on the floor. "Is Mam ..."

"Your mother's grand," Dad growled. "It's your mother's grandfather. He's on the way out."

I sucked in a sharp breath. "Granda Murphy?"

"How many great-grandfathers do ya have, boy?"

Just the one.

Not that I'd seen much of him for a while.

Fuck.

Guilt swarmed me.

I'd been so busy with life that I'd pretty much checked out on my great-grandparents for the last few years.

Sure, I still saw Nanny regularly when she handed off the smaller boys, but I'd be a liar if I said that I had spent any decent chunk of free-time with either one of them since first year.

Since Darren left.

I just ... put them on the back burner, thinking they would always be there.

You're a prick, Joey.

"What's wrong with him?" Panic gnawed at my gut. "Where's Nanny? Is she okay?"

"I just told ya, boy. Are ya hard of hearing now, as well as thick stupid? He's fucking dying," Dad snapped. "The man's nearly ninety. It can't be that much of a surprise to ya," he continued. "Your mother was trying to ring ya about it. If you want to see him, you'd want to go now before he kicks the bucket."

Stunned, I just stood there, unblinking, as I tried to digest the words coming out of his mouth.

The man who took on the role of raising my mother and aunt when his own daughter died, only to then have to take on the role of sheltering my mother's children from the raging storm that was our father.

He was the first man whose touch I didn't fear.

He was the man who taught me how to ride a bike.

He was the man who took me to the cinema for the first time.

He was the man who was never supposed to go anywhere because we needed him to stay right here and not fucking leave!

"Where is he?" I strangled out, feeling my heart thud so hard in my chest, I thought it might burst. "Is he at their house?"

"He's at the hospital," Dad replied. "And I'll give ya a spin over now, if you sub me a tenner until I get paid at the post office."

I stared blankly at him. "My grandfather's dying, and you want me to give you money to take me to see him?" I shook my head in disgust. "I'd rather slit my wrists than feed your drinking habit, old man."

"Nah, because you're too busy feeding your own habit, aren't ya, boy?" Dad sneered. "The apple doesn't fall far from the tree. You'd do well to remember that." Stalking past me, he yanked the door of our car open and hissed, "Keep your fucking money – and find your own way to the hospital while you're at it!"

"Are you alright, Joey, lad?" Tony asked me when my father had driven away. "Do you want a spin to the hospital?"

"I, ah ..." Shaking my head, I ran a hand through my hair and exhaled a ragged breath. "No, I should get to work." I looked around aimlessly. "I'm supposed to work, and I'm already late ..."

"None of that matters right now," Tony said, steering me to his parked van. "Hop in and I'll take you to see your grandfather."

"Ah, right, Tony, cheers," I mumbled, feeling shook to my core, as I climbed into the passenger seat of his white transit. "Thanks."

"Anytime, son." He gave my shoulder a squeeze. "Anytime."

Granda had contracted pneumonia, Nanny Murphy explained, when I found her in the hospital corridor a little while later.

Apparently, he'd been sick for a few weeks, and they never told us. Instead, she continued to help me with the boys, even though her husband's health had taken such a massive decline and had to be going through the mill herself.

My mother wasn't present at the hospital due to a rift in the family a few years back, caused by my father, but her sister Alice was, and so was Shannon.

I didn't want to go inside the room that my great-grandfather was dying inside.

"Go in and see him, pet," Nanny begged, squeezing my hands in hers. "He's been asking for his little Joe."

A tremor racked through me. "I don't think I can do it, Nan."

"You can," she promised, reaching up with her small hand to stroke my cheek. "I promise."

Fuck ...

Sucking in a sharp breath, I forced myself to open the hospital room door, and walk inside.

He didn't look one bit like the formidable man from my childhood as he laid in the bed, with tubes and wires all around him.

He looked so small and frail.

"Joey," Aunty Alice said with a weary smile, as she slowly stood and offered me the chair by his bedside. "I'll give you a minute alone with Granda."

You don't have to go, I wanted to scream, but I just nodded and said, "thanks," instead.

"How are ya, Granda?" I heard myself say in a shaky tone, when I finally grew a pair, and walked over to him. "I hear you're not feeling great."

"Joseph," he wheezed, gingerly raising his hand. "Your name is Joseph."

"Yeah, Granda," I whispered, sitting down on the edge of his bed. "It's me." Scooping his frail hand up, I gently squeezed. "It's Joey."

"Your birthday is on Christmas Day," he whispered, breathing labored. "A holy day."

"Yeah," I agreed. "That's me." Winking down at him, I said, "You have the right grandson."

"My favorite grandson," he wheezed, and then gave me a tiny smile. "My Joseph."

"Ah now, don't let the rest of them hear ya say that," I said with a smile, as tears burned the back of my eyes. "Tadhg would be well pissed off."

A labored cough escaped him and my guilt roared to life inside of me.

"Listen, I'm sorry I haven't been around, Granda." Jesus, I was a piece of shit. "I should have come to see you more often."

"Nonsense," the elderly man croaked out. "My Joseph. You're not Noel, Christian, Christopher, Klaus," he continued to ramble, breathing ragged. "Not, Casper, Gabriel, or any of the Christmas names they had in mind."

"Casper? Klaus?" Reaching up, I wiped my eyes with the back of my free hand. "Thank fuck for that."

"Because you're Joseph," he urged in a raspy voice, covering our joined hands with his other one. "You're my Joseph."

"Are you feeling alright, Granda?" Frowning, I reached over and touched his clammy forehead. "You're rambling."

"Loyal, kind, forgiving, fearless, nurturer, protector." He smiled up at me. "Joseph acted ... He took on a role .... He was the father of the lost."

I frowned, confused. "Granda, it's *me*. Joey."

"I named you Joseph," he croaked out, swallowing hard now. "Did you know that?"

"No." I shook my head. "I didn't know. How'd that come around?"

"Your father wanted to name you Theodor after him," he strangled out, breathing labored. "He said you were going to be just like him ..." he paused to cough wheezily. "But you were no Teddy. You were *Joseph*." He coughed again. "So, I bribed him with a tenner for the pub, and called you what I wanted you to be called." He smiled up at me. "My Joseph. My brave, brave boy. Terrible burdens. A cursed cross to carry. But always rising from the ashes. Always getting back up. Always the ... protector."

"Yeah." Panicked, I looked around the empty room, feeling at a loss. "Granda, I'm just going to go and get the nurse for you, okay?"

"Don't give in to them," he rasped, holding on to my hand with strength I was surprised he was capable of. "Promise me that you'll ... never ... give in to them."

"Give in to who, Granda?" I croaked out.

Gasping and wheezing for air, he looked me right in the eyes, green eyes on green and whispered, "the demons your father put in your head."

I'll be seeing ya, Molloy

April 14th 2003

AOIFE

Joey's great-grandfather died on a Friday, and the following Monday, I sat with my father, in one of the pews at the back of St. Patrick's church, as he and his family prepared to lay him to rest.

Dad went to show support to his apprentice that he was so fond of.

I went for the exact same reason.

Keeping our distance, we watched as Joey wrangled his brothers and sister into a pew behind who I knew was their great-grandmother. Their mother and father didn't come, so the Lynch children sat alone.

Sitting in the second row from the front, Joey sat on the edge of the pew, with a baby on his lap, and his sobbing sister beside him.

The two younger boys sat beside Shannon and spent the entire service nudging and poking each other in the ribs, only stopping when their older brother leaned over and threatened violence.

Afterwards, at the graveside, I watched as he parented his four younger siblings with a proficiency that a grown man would struggle to master.

It was so impressive, so heartbreaking, and so incredibly hot all in one breath.

I waited behind my father in the queue to pay my respects to the family, dutifully shaking each one of their hands and mumbling the age-old *"I'm sorry for your troubles"* funeral line that was ingrained in every Irish person to grace the earth.

"Aoife!" Ollie squealed when I reached him in the queue. "Thanks for coming."

"No problem," I replied, offering him a warm smile and a handshake. "I'm very sorry to hear about your grandfather, Ollie."

"Me too," he agreed with a solemn nod. "It's real sad, huh? Poor Granda gots the die-mone-ia."

"Pneumonia," Tadhg corrected, elbowing in his younger brother before reluctantly shaking my outstretched hand. "When are you going to learn how to speak, asshole?"

"Stop swearing, Tadhg," Shannon whisper-hissed, as she balanced Sean on her hip, and gingerly took my hand. "Thank you for coming."

"I'm sorry for your loss," I told her, giving her small hand a soft squeeze. "You too, little buddy," I added, unable to resist the urge to ruffle the blond-haired infant's curls, before moving on to the next sibling, which just so happened to be the one I had come for.

"I'm very sorry for your troubles, lad," my father said, clapping Joey on the shoulder before moving along to the next mourner.

"Thanks, Tony," Joey said, and then he flicked his surprised green eyes on me. "Molloy."

"Joey."

"You came."

"I did."

He stared hard at me for the longest moment before blowing out a ragged breath, and muttering the word, "Thanks."

"Of course." Sliding my hand into his, I squeezed and leaned in on my tiptoes to press a kiss to his cheek. "I'm so sorry, Joe."

Nodding stiffly, he squeezed my hand back and then leaned away, gaze flicking to where my father was, clearly checking to see if he was watching us.

"Well, bye," I whispered, moving along the queue, when all I wanted to do was stay right there in front of him.

"I'll be seeing ya, Molloy," he replied, with a small wink that was just for me.

"Yeah." My heart hammered in response, and I quickly turned on my heels, and walked straight back, not stopping until I had my arms wrapped around his waist, and my face buried in his neck. "You will."

Joey was rigid for a long moment before his arms came around my body and his pulled me tightly against him.

Gripping the back of his shirt, I released a shaky breath and kissed his cheek once more before forcing myself to leave.

"I'm telling you, Trish, that young lad's father is septic," I heard my father say when I walked into the kitchen later that night. "A good-for-nothing drunk. You should have seen the way he told the poor lad about his grandfather dying the other week. It was heartless, love. The man is heartless," he continued, not noticing me – or my pricked ears – as I hovered in front of the fridge, pretending to busy myself with rearranging a tray of eggs. "You should have seen the look in his eyes."

"Poor Joey," Mam said with a sad sigh.

My heartbeat quickened at the sound of his name.

"Poor lad is right," Dad agreed. "And then he tried to bribe a few bob out of the boy for the pub."

"You're joking?"

"I'm not, love. He actually asked the young fella for money."

"Jesus, that's desperate, Tony."

"Tell me you're joking," I demanded and then quickly stifled a groan when I realized that I had outed myself. *Ah crap.*

"What are you doing ear-wigging over there, young lady?" Mam asked. "It's after eleven. Don't you have school in the morning?"

"I'm only in the door from work," I explained, gesturing to my uniform. "Am I not allowed to eat something before I go to bed?"

"There's a pot of stew on the stove," Mam said, as she continued to iron – yes, the woman never stopped – the corner of one of Kev's shirts.

"How are ya, my little pet?" Dad smiled warmly up at me from his perch at the table. "Was it busy down the pub tonight?"

"It was packed for a Monday night," I replied, kicking off my heels, and untucking my white shirt from the waistband of my black, mini pencil-skirt. "Mam, I need a new pair of black tights," I added, gesturing to the hole in the ones I had on, while I grabbed a bowl off the draining board and half-filled it with my mother's stew. "I snagged my leg on the corner of a table I was serving, and some old fella asked me if it was a ladder I had in my tights or a stairway to heaven."

Dad narrowed his eyes. "I hope you gave him a good clip around the ear."

"Didn't have to," I replied between mouthfuls of stew. "His wife did it for me."

"The cheek of some of those old men," Mam sighed. "There's a spare pair in my wardrobe. I'll fish them out for you later, pet."

"Thanks, Mam." Turning my attention back to my dad, I asked, "So, you've met Joey's dad?"

"Met him?" Dad shook his head. "I went to school with the man."

My eyes widened, curiosity piqued, as I quickly slurped down what was left in my bowl. "I never knew that?"

"Ah, he was in the same year as myself and your mother," Dad explained with a nod. "We weren't in the same circle of friends, but we knew him well enough." Frowning, he added, "I'm sure he played hurling with your principal, what's his name . . ."

"Eddie Nyhan," Mam offered.

"That's the one," Dad agreed with another nod. "They hurled together back in the day."

"Sounds like you know a lot of him?" I offered, trying to sound as nonchalant as possible, when I was desperately feeding my Joey Lynch addiction with all of the juicy details. "Do you know his mam, too?"

"Marie Murphy?"

I nodded. "She's Marie Lynch now, but yeah."

"She was years younger than us," Mam explained and then turn to Dad. "Do you remember, Tony? Wasn't it awful when he got that poor girl pregnant when we were in sixth year."

"Do I what?" Dad grumbled, rubbing his jaw. "She was only a baby herself at the time." He flicked a glance to me and said, "She was a couple of years younger than you when she had a baby on her hip, Aoife."

"Really?"

"She was only in second year at the time," Mam interjected "Do you remember the scandal, Tony? It was desperate."

"Do I what, Trish?" Dad replied grimly. "It was terrible business."

"Why?" I asked. "How old was Teddy?"

"Too old to be looking at a fourteen-year-old girl, that's for sure," Mam muttered, tutting. "Nevermind marrying the poor girl off to him, they should have thrown him behind bars for getting a child pregnant."

My mouth fell open. "Joey's mam was only fourteen when she got pregnant with him?"

"No, no, no," Dad corrected. "Not with Joey. With the older lad. What's his name?"

"Derek?" Mam offered. "Daniel?"

"*Darren*," Dad declared, slapping his hand on his knee. "That's the one. Darren. Joey came later down the line."

Darren.

The brother that was dead to Joey.

Interesting.

"Where'd he go?" I asked.

"Over to the U.K., from what I hear," Dad replied. "Took off the minute he came of age."

"Well, I'm sure if I had to live with Teddy Lynch, I'd take off, too," Mam interjected. "He's a horrible man. His father and brother were the same. Rotten to the core, the lot of those Lynch men."

"Joey's not rotten," I heard myself blurt out before I could stop myself. "He's the opposite of rotten," I clarified, ignoring the burn in my cheeks. "He's really sound, actually."

"Exactly," Dad agreed, turning to look at my mother. "I know the lad is a bit of a hot-head, but he has the world of potential inside of him if his father would only take an interest in guiding him down the right path."

"Sure, aren't you after doing that already by taking him on at the garage, Tony?" Mam replied. "You're very good to him."

"I've been to a few of his hurling matches too, you know, Trish, and

I've never seen anything like him. Put a hurley in his hand and a sliotar in front of him, and it's something special to see."

"It's true," I heard myself agree. "He plays on the same team as Paul. He's phenomenal."

"His father was the same at that age," Mam offered then. "You remember Teddy Lynch back in the day at school. He was a gifted hurler."

"Teddy was good back in the day, but on his best day, he couldn't hold a torch to that young fella of his," Dad replied. "If he was mine, I'd be shouting about him from the rafters. I wouldn't be letting him wander off the rails, that's for sure."

"Don't you already, love," Mam said with a smile. "It drives our Kevin mad to hear you always praising young Joey."

"Ah, I don't mean any harm to poor Kev," Dad was quick to say. "He's a great lad, is our son, but he has no interest in cars or sports. He's all about the computer and the books, Trish, which is grand by me. But I don't have a notion of what he is talking about half the time with those big words."

Mam laughed in response.

"Dad?" Curious, I poured myself a glass of water from the tap, and asked, "Why weren't Joey's parents at the funeral today?" Turning back to face my own parents, I rested a hip against the sink as I spoke. "I mean, it was pretty bad form to see only the kids there and not their parents."

"As far as I know there was a big falling out between the Murphys and the Lynchs."

"The Murphys?"

"Marie's side of the family," Dad explained with a sigh. "The grandfather was Murphy, so I can only presume they weren't there because Teddy wasn't welcome to attend, and his wife wouldn't go without him."

"It's sad, really, when families are at loggerheads like that," Mam said. "It's the children I feel sorry for."

"Yeah," I whispered, mind drifting straight to Joey. "Me too."

FIFTH YEAR

LIGHT YEAR

You don't hit girls

August 16th 2003

AOIFE

My parents were going through another rough patch, and it didn't take a genius to figure out why, especially when my father's check book was out.

The compensation for this latest hiccup turned out to be something that benefitted all of us.

Built-in wardrobes.

Yay!

"Jesus, Molloy," my father's favorite laborer – and mine – growled, as he tossed another pile of clothes from my old wardrobe on to my bed before dragging the wardrobe into the middle of my room. "Where are you going with all the clothes?"

"Rule number one," I said, sitting in the middle of my bed, rummaging through a mountain of clothes and shoes. "You never judge the size of a girl's wardrobe."

"No judgment from this end," Joey replied with a resigned shake of his head. "Just confusion."

Yeah, Joe, me too, I thought to myself, as I shamelessly watched him work, taking in every tight muscle under his white t-shirt, and the golden strip of skin he flashed when he stretched.

His body truly was a sight to behold, considering by the time this summer had ended, he had racked up almost as many tattoos as he had scars from fighting.

We were back to BCS in a couple of weeks, our fifth year, and as good as Joey looked in a school uniform, and damn did he look good in our uniform, I was thoroughly enjoying the visual of him in his work clothes.

"You planning on giving me a hand anytime soon?" he asked, dragging me from my thoughts, as he dropped another heap of clothes on my lap. "Or do you plan to just sprawl out on your bed for the evening."

"Sprawl," I said with a lazy sigh, flopping back on my pillows. "Definitely sprawl."

"You're a pain in the ass," he grumbled, but sounded more amused than annoyed.

"What's that? You like my ass?" I teased. "Why thank you, Joey. It's my pride and joy."

"Your legs should be your pride and joy, Molloy," he tossed over his shoulder, and the compliment thrilled me.

My heart skipped. "So, you don't think I have a nice ass?"

"I can't remember what it looks like," he replied, quick as a cat. "Why don't you take off your pants and I'll tell you."

"Funny."

He glanced over his shoulder and gave me a devilish smirk. "It was worth a shot."

Fuck.

"You'd get such a surprise if I dropped my pants," I taunted, throwing a rolled-up pair of socks at his head.

He deftly caught them midair. "Not as big as the surprise you'd get if I dropped mine," he shot back.

My mouth fell open and he winked.

"Now, get off that pride and joy of yours and show me where you want the dressing table area."

"Fine. Oh wait! Yay, I forgot I had these," I practically cooed with glee, as my gaze landed on a pair of itty-bitty jean shorts. "I can't wait to wear them again."

"*Wear* them?" Joey cocked a brow. "You're telling me *those* are shorts?"

"They sure are," I confirmed, climbing off the bed to hold them up to my waist. "Shit," I grumbled in dismay. "I think they might be too small now."

"They didn't fit you when you were ten," my brother mocked from the doorway, where he was holding a pile of his own clothes. "They're hardly going to fit you now – not with that fat ass you're dragging around after you."

"You mean *this* ass?" I replied mockingly while slapping my ass. "The one your pervy friends keep trying to get a look at?"

"No, they don't," Kev argued. "They don't even like you."

"Uh-huh." I rolled my eyes. "*Sure* they don't."

"My friends have better taste in girls," Kev spat, which caused Joey to chuckle. Turning to glare at him, my brother demanded, "What's so funny?"

"Nothing, lad." Shaking his head, Joey continued to measure the height of my floor to ceiling with a measuring tape, marking off certain parts of my wall with a pencil as he worked. "Nothing at all."

"He's laughing because of how hilarious your denial is," I pissed my brother off even further by chiming. "Because he knows damn well your buddies are only too happy to get a close-up look of this bad boy." I tapped my ass again and choked out a laugh when my brother threw his pile of clothes at me.

"You're literally the female version of Shrek," he hissed. "You don't even—"

"And don't forget these babies," I interrupted, giving my braless boobs a jiggle. "Isn't that right, Joe?"

"He doesn't agree with you," Kev snapped and then turned to Joey and asked, "Do you?"

"Your sister's right, Kev," Joey said with a sigh. "Trust me, lad, you might be in her year, but I'm in her class, and they're looking."

I grinned in victory. "See?"

"Only because she acts like such a fucking tease," Kev hissed, barging into my room, and snatching the shorts out of my hand. "I don't know how Paul puts up with you."

"Hey, give those back," I ordered, chasing my brother around the room. "Oh, you wouldn't dare," I whisper-hissed, when he yanked my bedroom window open and dangled my shorts over the window ledge. "Put the shorts down, fuck face."

"Make me, fatty."

"Oh, you're a dead man," I warned, lunging across my mattress, only to get there a second too late.

"Noooo!" I cried out, shoving my brother out of my way just in time to see my rediscovered shorts land on the roof of our garden shed, before blowing away once again only to reach their final destination in a pile of Spud's shit in our garden.

"Wear them now," Kev taunted smugly. "When they're covered in one of Spud's giant shits."

"Oh, you think you've won, huh?" I arched a brow, challenge accepted. "Well, just you wait and see, little brother. I look forward to wearing nothing but the skimpiest bikini I own when I come downstairs tonight during your weird sleepover with your even weirder buddies."

"You wouldn't dare." His eyes bulged. "And who are you calling little brother? You're like three minutes older than me, dickhead. Also, they're not weird sleepovers," he said, before turning to Joey to explain. "We watch pay-per-view."

"Porn," I interjected with a snort.

"Hey." Joey held his hands up. "Whatever works for ya, lad."

"Wrestling," Kev corrected, face turning purple. "We watch *wrestling*. It's a sport, in case you haven't heard, Aoife."

"Fat lot you'd know about wrestling," I snickered. "Unless it comes in the form of a video game."

"As opposed to you," he sneered. "The Olympic fucking champion of lying on the flat of her back like a slut."

Bullseye.

Ouch.

"Hey," Joey warned, turning to glare at my brother. "Come on, Kev. Don't say shit like that to your sister."

"What?" Kev threw his hands up. "Have you not been listening? She's a complete—"

"I'm a virgin, wank-stain!" I screamed, feeling that one hit a little too close to a nerve.

"Yeah," Kev snorted, with a shake of his head. "You're a virgin, and I'm Santa Claus."

"That's it," I snarled, choosing violence, as I lunged for my brother. "Make your peace with Jesus, dick brain, because I'm about to become the only child I should have been before your shitty egg gatecrashed Mam's womb!"

Like two gladiators poised for battle, we lunged at each other.

Prepared for my onslaught, Kev swiped a clothes hanger off the floor and flung it at me. "Oh, bring it on, fatty-bang-bang."

"You're going to have to do better than that, sir-wank-a-lot," I snarled, bending like one of the fellas from *The Matrix* to avoid a hanger to the face.

"You mean like this?" Kev hissed, spearing me to the ground with a loud thud. "How's that for a wrestling move?"

"You . . . won't . . . defeat . . . me," I strangled out, as I attempted to use my hips to buck him off my chest. "And . . . you . . . called . . . me . . . fat."

One minute, my brother was sitting on my chest, and forcing me to slap myself with my own damn hands, and the next he was pinned to my bedroom wall.

"The hell are you doing?" Kev wheezed out, as Joey pressed his forearm harder into his throat. "Lynchy, stop, I can't . . . breathe . . . "

"You think it's okay to touch her like that?" he snarled, completely livid. "You think I'm going sit back and do nothing? I don't fucking think so, asshole—"

"Whoa, whoa, whoa, Joey, stop!" Springing up, I raced over to them. "Let go," I instructed, grabbing ahold of his arm. "Joey, let go. It's okay. He wasn't hurting me."

"He put his fucking hands on you, Molloy," he roared, shaking with temper, as he continued to put pressure on my brother's windpipe. "I saw him with my own goddamn eyes."

"We were just playing around," I hurried to explain, as I slid between both boys, and forced him to release his death grip on my brother's throat. "That's what we do, Joe. It's a game we play."

"But he put his *hands* on you." Joey's eyes bulged. "I fucking saw."

"I was messing with her," Kev choked out. "I wouldn't really hurt my sister like that, you thick bastard."

"Shut up, Kev," I hissed, shoving him out of way, before turning my attention back to my classmate. "Joey . . . , shh, shh, Joe, look at me." Reaching up, I cupped his face between my hands. "*Look* at me."

Reluctantly, he did, and I sucked in a sharp breath at the sight.

His eyes were wild and feral looking.

He was visibly shaking with barely restrained anger, as he clenched his fists to the point where his knuckles had turned white.

"He. Hurt. You."

"No, he didn't."

"I *saw* him."

"I'm okay," I heard myself sooth, thumbs smoothing over his stubbly jaw. "And you're okay. It's okay. Everyone's okay."

"I'm not!" Kev wheezed, clutching at his throat, as he staggered from my room. "I'm not okay, Aoife."

"Kev, wait, don't say anything to Dad," I called out, chasing after my brother. "He didn't mean—"

"He could've killed me, Aoife," Kev strangled out, as he stormed into his bedroom, still clutching his throat. "That psycho nearly killed me."

"But he didn't?" I offered lamely, only to receive a door slammed in my face for my troubles. "Dammit."

Shaking out my trembling hands, I drew in a steadying breath and hurried back to my room.

"Yeah, so Kev's beyond pissed." I slammed the door shut and glared at my rogue protector. "What did you that for, Joe? He's going to tell our parents and you're going to end up getting in trouble with Dad."

"Let him tell them," was all Joey replied, as he crouched down and quietly loaded up all of his tools into his bag. "It doesn't matter."

"Yes, it does matter," I argued, stalking towards the beautiful eejit. "You love working at the garage."

"Doesn't matter," he repeated, keeping his head down, as he filled his bag and zipped it shut. "I'm sorry for causing trouble for you," he added, as he stood up and threw the bag over his shoulder. "I'll be seeing ya, Molloy."

"No, no, you're not walking out of here," I warned, hurrying to barricade my bedroom door and keep him in here with me. "We can sort this out."

"What's to sort, Molloy?" he said flatly. "I hit my boss's son. I think it's pretty clear that I'm done here."

"No, you're not done here. You're not even close to being done, here. So, just cool your jets and let me think about this," I ordered, shoving his chest, and feeling a swell of excitement when he let me walk him backwards. Because let's face it, after the display he'd just put on, there was no way anyone could make this boy do anything he didn't want to do.

Walking Joey over to my bed, I pushed on his shoulders, and watched as he obligingly sank down on the mattress.

"Why'd you do that, Joe?" I croaked out, standing in front of him. I was physically shaking from head to toe as my earlier adrenalin deserted me.

"Because he hurt you," he replied, looking up at me with the most lonesome expression I'd ever seen. In this moment, Joey Lynch looked like the quintessential lost boy. "Because he put his hands on you."

"But he's my brother, Joe," I heard myself explain softly. "We were only messing. It was play-fighting."

Joey looked up at me like I was speaking a foreign language, and the rare vulnerability caused me to do something incredibly reckless.

"I don't . . . " He blew out a sharp breath. "I fucked up."

Nudging his legs open, I stepped closer. "Yeah, you kind of did, Joe." I reached out and ruffled his blond hair, and then, unable to stop myself, I cupped his face between both hands, and I looked down at him. "Picking fights with my brother, of all people," I admonished softly, thumbs grazing over his cheekbones. "Spud packs a bigger punch with his tail."

"I thought he was . . . " Shaking his head, Joey let his head fall forward to rest against my stomach. "I just saw you on the ground and he was . . . and I just . . . " The move was incredibly intimate, and I sucked in a sharp breath from the contact. "Fuck."

"I'm okay," I coaxed, unable or just plain unwilling to stand back and not comfort him. With trembling hands, I held his face to my stomach, and whispered, "You're okay."

He didn't respond, but he didn't pull away either, so I remained right there in my bedroom, with his cheek pressed to my belly and my hands stroking his hair.

Finally, after what felt like an age, I felt the tension slowly leave his shoulders, and then his arms came around my waist. "He hurt you," he croaked out. "You don't hit girls."

New school year, same old me

September 1st 2003

JOEY

Face down on a mattress that smelled of piss and freshly spilled tears, I remained completely rigid as awareness claimed me from the sweet escape of sleep.

With my brain foggy and uncooperative, I forced myself to retrace last night's events, trying to link my current surroundings with reality, but came up empty.

"Dada," a familiar voice sniffled, and just like that, I knew where I was.

Like you could be anywhere else.

A small, sticky hand landed on my cheek. "Dada."

Repressing the urge to shudder and scream, I slowly uncoiled my muscles, twisted onto my back, and cracked one swollen eyelid open just as my baby brother climbed on top of me.

Big brown eyes stared down at me. "Dada."

"Jesus Christ," I groaned, grimacing in resignation when his soaking wet pajama bottoms landed on my bare stomach. "Piss through your nappy again, Seany-boo?"

Nodding solemnly, Sean leaned close and pressed his chubby little hand against my cheek. "Dada, ow-ow." Lonesome brown eyes studied my face. "Ow-ow."

"No, Sean," another voice barked. In a tone laced with venom and fury, Tadhg sat up from his makeshift bed on my bedroom floor, and hissed, "For the last fucking time, he's Joey, not Dada. Joey! Your actual Dada beat the shit out of your fake one last night."

"Tadhg, leave him alone. He's only small, and I've been called worse,"

I growled, narrowing my eyes in warning, as I gingerly pulled myself into a sitting position and took stock of the sleeping bodies littered around my room.

Aside from the piss-soaked toddler on my lap, and the mouthy preteen on my floor beside my bed, another brother lay curled up across my legs like a sleeping puppy, while my sister huddled in the corner, with a floral-patterned duvet draped around her small shoulders.

The dresser wedged in front of my bedroom door was a harsh reminder of last night's events, and I was suddenly cold to the bone.

There's no place like home.

What a crock of shit.

"Are you okay?" That was Shannon, who looked like she hadn't slept a wink last night. Deathly pale, she locked her blue eyes on mine and kept them there. "Joe?"

"I'm grand, Shan." Reeling off the sentence of a lifetime, when the truth was that I hadn't been okay since the day I was born, I lifted Sean off my lap, and climbed out of bed, pulling on a pair of sweats as I moved.

Today was Monday; the first day back to school after the summer holidays. No matter how bad any of us felt, staying in this house instead of going to school was not an option.

Fuck that.

Aching in parts of my body I never knew existed, I shoved the dresser aside before unlocking the door.

Inhaling a steadying breath, I quickly yanked open the door before the child inside of me persuaded me to hide under my blanket with the rest of them.

Grow a pair of balls, you prick, I mentally urged myself, as I stepped into the landing, ready to face both the unknown and the inevitable.

The empty landing didn't ease my trepidation one damn bit, because I knew he was still there.

Still in the house.

Like a dark cloud hanging over all of us, but worse.

So much fucking worse.

Loud snoring drifted from behind their locked bedroom door, accompanied by muffled sobbing, and my blood ran cold.

Freezing on the mortal spot, I fought the urge to run to her. To burst through that door and throw my arms around her.

I wanted to protect her from him almost as much as I wanted to protect *me* from *her*.

"Well?" Glancing behind me, I found four wide-eyed faces watching me from the doorway of my bedroom. "Is he gone?"

Adrenalin spiking, and with heat that bordered on lava coursing through my veins, I pushed down the swell of emotion that threatened to break me, to make me weak like her. "No, he's still here."

"He is?"

"Yeah, he's in her bed."

Their faces fell, just like my heart, but again, I pushed it down, needing to get us the fuck out of this house more than I needed to wallow.

"Right, everyone, go back to your own rooms and get yourselves sorted. Wash up and get your uniforms on. I packed the lunches last night; they're in the fridge so don't forget to pack them in your bags," I began to order, knowing that if I didn't, nothing in the house would get done. "Nanny will be here to take Sean and drop you boys to school, and Shan, we'll walk together."

"Okay, Joe."

"Oh, and when I say wash up, I mean clean your ears as well as your teeth, boys," I instructed before stalking into the bathroom for a more likely than not, frigid cold shower.

With the bathroom door slammed shut behind me, I stood in front of the mirror and clutched the rim of the sink, allowing my eyes to assess the damage.

Grimacing at the sight of my swollen face, I forced myself to take a good fucking look.

Black eye.

Bruised cheekbone.

Busted lip.

I couldn't decide what was worse; the fact that I couldn't hide the bruises or the fact that I couldn't stop him from putting them there.

Reaching for the tin that I kept hidden behind the back of the sink, I flipped the lip off and quickly set to work cutting and then snorting a line of coke, feeling some semblance of control return to my body when my head began to function again, and my heart began to thud harder.

Rubbing a hand down my face, I exhaled a sigh of relief before kicking off my clothes and climbing into the shower, willing the water to wash away my sins.

To wash away my pain.

"I don't want to go, Joe," Shannon mumbled, as I practically dragged her ass to school. "Please. It'll be the same this year."

"No, it won't," I lied through my teeth and told her. "You're in second year now. It'll be better."

"I really don't think I can do it."

"Well, I know you can."

"You do?"

"Yeah," I told her. "I promise."

She looked up at me with her big blue eyes. "You really promise?"

She had our mother's eyes and it made it hard to look at her sometimes.

"I promise, Shan."

She smiled and visibly sagged in relief.

The word seemed to comfort something inside of my sister, even if we both knew that I didn't mean it.

She needed the word, and I was more than willing to give it to her if it meant that she was out of the house and away from our father.

"I still can't believe you let somebody do that to your skin," she offered then, reaching over to touch the black ink covering my forearm. "It's so permanent."

Shrugging, I resisted the urge to tell her that the intricate hoops and swivels permanently etched on my forearm helped conceal the huge permanent scar our father had put there when he took a broken bottle to us last Christmas, after too many whiskeys at the dinner table.

There was no point in reminding Shannon of something she was very much aware of. Especially since she was the one who had spent the entire ride to the hospital keeping pressure on my arm, to stop me from bleeding out.

I was just glad it had been my arm and *not* her face that he maimed – like I had a feeling he had been aiming for.

"You're not a fan?"

She scrunched her nose up. "Not at all. I think tattoos are hideous; although, I have to admit that the Celtic crucifix on your back isn't entirely terrible."

"Is that a compliment I hear?" I teased, elbowing her playfully. "Come on, you can say it. 'Joey, my favorite, most amazing, most devastatingly good-looking brother, I love your tattoo'."

"Fine, it's a nice tattoo." Chuckling, she pushed me back and then hurried to catch up with me, her short legs slowing her down. "There, I said it. Are you happy now?"

"I didn't quite hear that." Wrapping an arm around her shoulders, I gently rustled her hair with my knuckles. "Say it."

"Fine, fine," Shannon squealed through fits of laughter. "Joey, my favorite, most amazing—"

"Don't forget the most devastatingly good-looking brother. That's the best part."

"Most *in love with himself* and *vainest* brother," she corrected me with a laugh. "And I love your tattoo – even if it does take up half of your back."

"Good enough," I teased, releasing her from my hold.

"You're such a dope," she giggled, nudging me again with her elbow.

I didn't care what she thought about me as long as she wasn't thinking about how scared she was to go to school.

Her smile was rare, but I was proud to be able to put it there, even after the night from hell we'd been put through.

"It'll be okay, won't it, Joe?" she asked then, as the school came into sight. "When it's all over and done with." She sucked in a sharp breath before whispering, "When we're grown up and gone from this town, we'll get our happy ending, won't we?"

"Yeah, Shan," I replied, hitching my bag up on my shoulder. "You're going to have an epic happy ending."

"So are you, Joe," she replied softly. "I just know it."

It was at that exact moment my eyes landed on the leggy blonde leaning against the school entrance, with a grey beanie hat covering her ridiculously long hair, and a lollypop between her pursed lips.

"Yeah, Shan." I wasn't convinced about happy endings, but when Molloy locked her eyes on me and smiled, I could believe in the possibility of a happy day.

"Welcome back, fifth years," Mr. Nyhan acknowledged from his perch at the podium in the canteen. "It's wonderful to see all of your smiling faces as we embark on a new school year. Now, as you are all well aware, fourth year was a transition year. It was a wonderful opportunity to dip your toes in new waters and try out new hobbies and interests. But that was then, and this is now. Fifth year will see you all taking on new course work, a heavier academic workload than any of you can comprehend. In other words, the next two years of your academic career are going to be the toughest you have ever faced."

"What in the name of Jesus is that fella on?" Podge asked, nudging my shoulder with his. "He's absolutely crackers if he thinks this regurgitated pep talk is going to excite or encourage anyone to come to school."

"Who knows, lad?" I mumbled, arms folded across my chest, as I leaned against the lockers at my back, and listened to Nyhan drone on and on with his usual back-to-school bullshit spiel.

"Rough night?" Podge asked then.

"What?" I narrowed my eyes. "Why?"

"I'll telling you now, lads, the only thing I want to dip is my dick in Aoife Molloy's tight pussy," Alec declared, interrupting us, as he inclined his head to where Molloy was sitting at the opposite side of the canteen.

The minute I locked eyes on her, a surge of heat hit me directly in the dick.

Yeah, she was looking good this year.

I hadn't spoken to her since the weekend when I fitted her new wardrobe for her.

Usually, she came up to me first thing before class for our morning ritual that consisted of a little verbal sparring.

However, I put her absence this morning down to the unfortunate series of events that had led me to almost decapitating her twin.

My eyes scanned the crowd again and landed on the poor scrawny bastard, tucked away in the corner with the rest of the studious, techy fuckers from our year, who would go on to college, and end up with high-paying jobs. Those guys were so smart that they were kept tucked away in honor roll classes, and far away from the rest of us mere mortals; aka the thick fuckers like myself, Podge, and Alec, who would more likely than not end up taking up an apprenticeship and working with our hands.

I never put a lot of thought into the consequences of my flying fists, but I felt terrible for unleashing them on Kevin Molloy. Especially since he hadn't breathed a word of what happened to either one of his parents, meaning that I got to keep my job at the garage. I had a feeling Molloy had a lot more to do with me keeping my job, considering her brother had never been my biggest fan.

My mind drifted back to that weird moment we had in her room on Saturday, and I had to repress a shiver.

Things had been different between us for a while now, *deeper*, since the day of my grandfather's funeral when she surprised the hell out of me by showing up.

Her presence had thrown me, *she* had thrown me, and I wasn't sure if that was a good thing or not.

Either way, having her put some distance between us today couldn't be a bad thing.

The distance helped me to water down some of the fucked-up feelings she evoked inside of me.

"Jesus, did she get taller over the summer?" Alec hissed in a reverent tone, biting down on his fist. "Oh, fuck. Her legs look longer than usual."

"It's the shoes," Podge offered up. "The higher the heel, the longer the leg."

"What?" I chuckled, turning to look at him. "Where'd ya hear that?"

"No, he's right, I've heard that, too," Alec offered. "I think I read it in a magazine."

"At the clinic?" Podge added.

"That's right," Alec agreed, slapping his hands together. "That's where I read it."

"The clinic?" I shook my head. "What the fuck were you two up to over the summer?"

"Same as you, Lynchy, boy," Alec shot back with a wolfish grin. "Scoring and whoring."

Doubtful.

My gaze drifted back to Molloy, and like a hundred times before, I caught her staring back at me.

Instead of the usual comical banter, she offered me a small wave instead.

I winked in response and had to bury my smile when her cheeks turned bright pink. She wasn't blushing, though. It was something else. It was almost like she was excited. To see *me*.

Fuck, she was something else to look at.

"I can't believe she's still with that tosser," Alec groaned, gesturing to Ricey, who was planted on the chair beside her, and all but glued to the girl's hip. "How long have they been together now, three years?"

"Three and a half," I heard myself answer. "On and off."

"Well shit." Alec released a despondent sigh. "He's definitely riding her by now, right? "

Christ, I hoped not.

Christmas wishes and joyrides

December 23rd 2003

AOIFE

"You know, you don't have to buy me a present this year, babe," Paul announced, as he sat across the table from me at The Dinniman, after the lunchtime rush on Tuesday. It was two days to Christmas, and we had been up the walls at work all morning. "All I want for Christmas is—"

"Don't even go there," I warned, reaching across the table to clamp a hand over his mouth. "Seriously, Paul, I have less than two minutes of my lunch break left until I have to get back out there. I have no intention of using them to fight with you."

He threw his hands up. "Who's fighting?"

"Us," I shot back, setting my hand back down. "Or at least we will be, if you bring up the whole sex in lieu of a gift idea again."

"Aoife." He stared hard at me, brown eyes full of barely contained frustration. "Come on, babe. We've been going out forever."

"Three years isn't forever," I replied, taking a sip from my coffee. "It's a drop in the ocean in the grand scheme of things."

"We will be together four years next February," he argued back.

"Not when you add up all of the times during those four years when we've been off," I reminded him. "Take that into account and it's closer to two years than four."

"Aoife!" he snapped, reaching over and snatching my hand up. "Come on. I've been patient. I've done the waiting."

"You've also done the sexing, remember?" I shot back, reminding him of just how much he'd enjoyed our break back in third year.

"Why are you bringing that back up?" He blew out a frustrated breath. "That was *two* years ago. We were off at the time. You said it was okay. I *didn't* cheat on you."

"No, you didn't cheat on me. You were careful to wait a couple of hours after we broke up before sticking your dick inside that black-haired bitch from Tommen," I stuck the knife in by hissing. "What was her name again? Ella something?"

"Bella," he muttered, having the good grace to drop his head. "Bella Wilkinson, and you know that she didn't mean a thing to me. I was drunk and depressed. You had just ended it."

"Last time I checked, needing breathing space because your boyfriend publicly labeled you a slut doesn't constitute as a good enough reason to get drunk and stick your dick in the closest available female. But hey, what do I know about the workings of the male teenage mind."

"I swear to you that it didn't mean anything," he bit out. "It wasn't even that memorable, Aoif. Honestly. It was just sex."

"That's fine, Paul. I believe you," I told him. "But just so we're on the same wavelength, you should know that sex isn't *just sex* to me."

"No," he bit out. "Because sex is just a mythical fucking word in the world of Aoife Molloy. Oral is perfectly acceptable, but God forbid you let a dick inside you!"

I rolled my eyes. "Your tantrum isn't adding any support for your cause, asshole."

"What the hell is it going to take to pry your legs open?" he muttered under his breath, tone laced with resentful sarcasm. "A fucking ring?"

I opened my mouth to give him a piece of my mind, when Garry, my boss, flagged me over with a tap of his watch.

"I need to get back to work, but consider this conversation over," I said, rising from my seat, and re-pinning my apron to my waist. "I'm not discussing it again until I'm ready, but once I am, you'll be the first to know."

"Is it him?" Snatching my wrist, he pulled me back to him and asked, "Is it still about *him*?" He narrowed his eyes in disgust. "Because he doesn't fucking want you, Aoife. He's too busy sticking his dick in half the—"

"No, it's about *me*, Paul. It's about me not being ready," I snapped, yanking my hand away. "I need to get back to work."

"Whatever," Paul grumbled, waving me off. "Enjoy being leered at."

"Hey, Gar," I said, ignoring the big sulking dope behind me, as I hurried behind the bar. "Sorry about that. I lost track of the time."

"You're grand, love," the old man assured me. "The back lounge is after filling up again, so plenty of tables to serve – but only take the food orders and clear away glasses. Whatever you do, make sure you don't take any drink orders, ya hear?" He cast a glance to where my boyfriend was sitting, and muttered, "We don't need any little birdy running home to daddy with tales that his seventeen-year-old girlfriend was serving alcohol."

"Don't worry, Gar. I'm always discreet." I patted him on the shoulder and winked. "And what the Gard's son doesn't know won't hurt him."

"That you are, Aoife," he replied, with a relieved smile on his wrinkly face. "Right you are, so."

With my notepad and pen in hand, I headed into the back lounge, and was immediately bombarded by a surge of both hungry and thirsty punters.

Smiling to myself, I straightened my shoulders, stuck out my chest, and walked towards to a table full of rowdy men. "Hello, gentlemen, what I can get for you today?"

Oh yeah, I was going to make a fortune in tips today.

I ended up staying on at work for a couple of extra hours to help out with the never-ending rush of punters out on the town celebrating Christmas. Instead of finishing at six like I had been scheduled to, it was after nine when I finally left the pub and made my way across town, with the hope of snagging a spin home off my dad.

When I reached the garage, it was in darkness.

"Shit," I muttered, kicking the metal roller door. "This is just perfect."

Groaning loudly, I let my forehead rest against the cool metal while I contemplated my options.

Walk home after an eleven-hour shift in four-inch heels?

Not happening.

Phone up my father, only to have him tell me drive myself?

Nope.

My fingers grazed the car key in my coat pocket, and I instantly rejected the notion, as a ripple of fear coursed through me.

I hated driving.

I literally detested the whole ordeal.

I detested and feared it so much that the rust-bucket of an Opal Corsa that my father had done up and given to me back in September for my seventeenth birthday remained parked at the garage.

That's right; I was so fearful of driving a moving vehicle, that I didn't want it anywhere near my house.

Unlike a lot of other places, the law was pretty relaxed in Ireland regarding learner drivers. Basically, you took a theory test, got your green license from the tax office, and off you went. We didn't need to undertake a shit ton of lessons or abide by a million laws like my cousins in London had to. Hell, my own mam had been driving on her green license for twenty years now. The Gards always looked the other way. It was no biggie.

The only damn reason I had applied for my provisional driving license was so that I would have photo I.D to go out drinking with when I turned eighteen next year.

I didn't want it to *drive*, but that's exactly what my father assumed I would do.

"I hate to point out the obvious, Molloy, but when a shop door's locked, and the lights are out, it means the place is closed."

Joey's familiar voice filled my ears, and I quickly swung around to see him coming from the side of the building.

"Jesus," I whisper-hissed, startled to see him in the darkness. "What are you doing out here?"

"Locking up," he replied dryly. "If you're looking for your old man, you're out of luck," he added, as he used a set of keys to lock the side gate behind him. "He went on the beer with the rest of the lads at lunchtime."

I feigned sadness. "And they didn't take you?"

"Sadly not."

"I suppose you need to turn eighteen to enjoy the full perks of the job, huh?"

He smirked. "I need to turn seventeen first before that can happen."

"That'll be soon, right? Your birthday is close to Christmas, right?"

"Yeah," he agreed, sliding his work keys into his pocket. "Christmas Day."

"That's so shitty," I groaned, feeling a flash of sympathy for him. "I bet you've been cheated out of so many presents down through the years, with the whole two-for-one gift bullshit."

"I can't say that I've ever noticed, Molloy," he replied. "I'm not the present-counting type."

"Well, you're a better person than I am, Joey Lynch, because I would cause ructions if I had to share my birthday with Jesus."

Joey laughed, actually laughed a genuine laugh, as he closed the space between us. "So, are you going to ask me, or are we going to stand out here all night?"

My heart flipped in my chest. "Ask you what?"

"To walk you home."

"Okay." I blew out a shaky breath. "Walk me home, Joey Lynch."

"That's telling," he teased, leaning against the door, as he smiled down at me, green eyes dark and full of heat. "You need to ask nicely."

My god, it was something else when that boy smiled.

He was just so beautiful.

"I have a better idea," I heard myself say, and then I did something incredibly fucking reckless. Reaching into my coat pocket, I withdrew the set of car keys and jingled them in front of his face. "How about you drive me, instead?"

Even though he was the master of concealing his emotions, Joey couldn't mask the excitement that flashed in his eyes. "I won't be seventeen for two more days. I only have a tractor license until then."

"That's true," I agreed, watching his gaze flick from my face to the keys and then back to me. "So that means that we'll be breaking the law, doesn't it?" I taunted, giving the keys a little rattle. "But, then again, when has that ever stopped you?"

Joey stared at me for a long time before releasing a low chuckle. "Give me the keys, Molloy."

Squealing with nervous excitement, I clenched my eyes shut and choked out a laugh, when we took the corner of the local supermarket, after burning the rubber of my tires doing half a dozen donuts around the empty carpark.

"Oh, my Jesus, watch out for the footpath!"

"Relax, Molloy, I've got this."

Yeah, he did.

Joey might not have an official license yet, but he certainly knew how to handle a car. I put it down to years of messing around with motors at the garage with Dad.

With Jay-Z and Beyoncé's ''03 Bonnie & Clyde' blasting from the car stereo, a fitting song given the circumstances, I held on for dear life to the dashboard, as the wild and reckless boy in the driver's seat blew my mind. Sitting in the passenger seat beside him, I felt like I was on a power trip. Like we could take on the whole world in this moment.

It was exhilarating.

"Happy fucking birthday to me," Joey laughed, clearly delighted with life, as he slipped my car into fifth gear, and left the lights of Ballylaggin behind us. "So, where do you want to go, Molloy?"

Anywhere with you. "I don't care, just don't kill me, okay?" I begged, and then screamed out a laugh when we flew over a hump in the back road.

Joey cast a sideways glance at me and grinned. "I'm making no promises.

*

A lot of miles on the clock later, and we were on the back road near the beach, with me in the driving seat, and Joey laughing his ass off at my discomfort.

"I can't do it!" The car chugged and stalled for the third time in a matter of minutes. "It's pointless. I'm never going to figure this shit out."

"Well, you better keep trying," he warned, not one bit sympathetic to my cause, as he balanced my heels on his lap. "Because I heard your father tell Danny Reilly that if you don't pull your finger out, and start actually driving instead of admiring the stereo, he'll sell him the car."

"Fine by me." Flustered and barefoot, I turned the key in the ignition, and attempted to pull off. "I'm entirely the wrong person to be behind the wheel of a potential death machine."

"Yeah, because you're really going to do some damage in first gear," Joey drawled. "Come on, Molloy, you know the drill. Clutch and slide into second."

"I can't."

"You can't."

"I really can't."

"Stop being a princess and just fucking do it."

Deep in concentration, I attempted to do just that, but the gear stick wouldn't comply. "This car hates me," I wailed, yanking on the gear stick and then wincing then the engine roared in protest.

"Jesus, come here. Okay, press the clutch." Reaching across the passenger seat, Joey covered my hand with his, and deftly slid us into second. "Now put a bit of pressure on the accelerator," he instructed, while I repressed a shiver from the feel of his big hand on top of mine. "Good, now clutch again," he added as he switched us into third. "See? You're doing it; driving without conking the engine. It's not as bad as you've built it up in that head of yours."

"Yeah, but it's just so fucking tricky," I wailed, both hands springing up to grip the wheel. "Feet on the pedals, hands on the wheel, hand on the gearstick, eyes on the road . . . " I blew out a frustrated breath. "It's like I tell my dad every time he forces me to get behind the wheel. There are just too many things to do at once."

"I thought females were the ultimate multitaskers."

"Well, not this female," I choked out, twisting the wheel to avoid a pile of sand sludge on the road. "Oh, my Jesus, Joey. I hate this stupid car."

"You don't hate the car," he countered. "You hate the feeling of not being in control. It's new and scary. I get it, Molloy. You're just figuring it all out."

"How do you know so much about this?" I eyed him sitting beside me. "How can you be three months younger than me, and kick my ass at driving?"

"It's not a competition, Molloy," he chuckled, with a shake of his head. "And your dad showed me a lot down through the years."

"Well, good for you," I bit out. "Because he basically showed me nothing until he handed me the keys for this thing and said drive."

"Give it a couple of months. You'll look back at this night and laugh."

"Doubtful," I mumbled, eyes locked on the dark night ahead of me. "Very doubtful."

I don't want to go home

December 24th 2003

JOEY

Pressure was the thing that I was most used to in life. It never normally fazed me, not when I'd spent most of my life with the weight of my father's hands around my neck, threatening to cut off my air supply, but all of that paled in comparison to Aoife Molloy's infinite ability to restrict my breathing.

It was two in the morning and the clock had rolled into Christmas eve. Instead of being home, like I knew I needed to be when there was a full bottle of whiskey at my father's disposal, I found myself spinning around with her, instead.

I felt like a criminal being with her. I had no damn business stepping foot inside the girl's car. A car I had spent a lot of my time working on at the garage. A car I certainly shouldn't have gotten behind the wheel of and driven, but when she dangled those keys in front of me, the temptation had been too strong to resist.

I also didn't understand her reasons for wanting to be here with me. Why she continuously sought me out. But I wasn't about to argue with her tonight because it meant I didn't have to go home and deal with any of my father's bullshit. No, I wasn't about to talk Molloy down from the ledge, because the longer we teetered on the edge of the law, the longer I got to be with her.

Because the truth of the matter was that I *enjoyed* her company.

I *enjoyed* being with her, be it arguing or messing around, flirting or fucking around town in the car her daddy bought for her.

I felt genuine affection towards the girl, which was abhorrently abnormal on my behalf.

But I did.

She could piss me off more than most, and she drove me demented at times, but there was no one else I would prefer to break the law with.

Even as we parked up back outside the garage, with a bag of chips balancing on the dashboard between us, I was having a hard time trying to find the motivation to leave her.

The truth was that staying right here in this car, with the only person whose touch didn't make my skin crawl, seemed like a good idea.

"This one's my favorite," Molloy said, turning up the volume on her stereo when The Pogues' 'Fairytale of New York' drifted from the speakers. "Hands down, the best Christmas song ever." Popping a chip into her mouth, she grinned over at me. "What's yours?"

"Don't know." Shrugging, I reached over and grabbed a chip. "Never really thought about it."

"Ah, come on, Joe," she pushed. "Everyone has a favorite Christmas song."

Not me.

I preferred silence.

I shrugged. "This one, I suppose."

"Good." She nodded her approval. "It reminds me of you."

"Wow," I deadpanned. "Which part?"

"All of it," she teased, tossing a chip at my face. "From now on, this will be our song."

I narrowed my eyes at her. "Oh, yeah, because we really need a song."

"Well, it *is* Christmas Eve, *babe*," she joked, and then went right into a piss-poor rendition of the first verse of the song, before choking out a laugh. "See, it's perfect for us."

"There's only one small problem with your song choice," I offered dryly. "I'm not your *babe*, Molloy."

"Whose fault is that?" she came right back with, not looking away, and not backing down. "Hmm. I wonder."

Christ, she was just so ballsy.

It was seriously impressive.

And sexy as fuck.

I soaked her in, every freckle, every curve, the color of her green eyes, the pale golden streaks in her already blonde hair.

"Yeah, well." Smirking, I shook my head and turned back to stare out the front windscreen. "If tonight's little joyride is anything to go by, then you should be thanking me for that."

"You would think so," was all she replied, as she rummaged around in a stack of discs. "Okay, so, it's clear that you're not sold on the last song, so how's this for hitting the nail on the head?" Molloy asked then, switching up CDs, and pressing track three on her stereo. The Goo Goo Dolls blasted from her stereo.

"'Iris'?" I cocked a brow. "Good song choice, Molloy, but I have to admit that I'm not feeling the festive vibe from it."

"No, asshole, not as a Christmas song," she urged, cranking up the volume. "As *our* song."

I opened my mouth to respond, but she reached across the console and cover my lips with her hand. "Shh. Just humor me and listen, okay?"

Reluctantly conceding to her demands, I nodded once, and kept my eyes locked on hers as the lyrics of the song fucked with my head.

"Well?" she finally breathed, when the song ended. "It's perfect, right?"

"Yeah, Molloy." My voice was thick as I wrestled with a million complicated fucking emotions. "It is."

I care too much

December 24th 2003

AOIFE

If Joey wanted to sit in this parked-up car outside the garage for half the night, then I would gladly sit right there with him.

It didn't matter that it was -2 degrees outside or that I was close to freezing in my work clothes. At least if he was in this car with me, it meant that he was out of trouble.

He wasn't out getting high.

Time passed by much quicker when I was with him, and I didn't notice the hours slipping away as I regaled him with random tales from my life.

You see, Kevin might be the twin that held the lion's share of academic intelligence, but I was the one that could talk the ass off a donkey.

For real. I had been blessed with the ability to make a conversation out of nothing, which was how I had somehow managed to keep this wildly unattainable boy's interest piqued for most of the night.

"And then he said '*oh, baby, my bed smells like you, but it's fading fast, come over and refresh my sheets,*'" I explained, fake gagging at the memory of Paul's ridiculous phone call the other night. "I mean, seriously?" I choked out a laugh, as I rolled up the sleeves of his hoodie that he'd given me to wear. "Get a handle on yourself, man."

"Oh Jesus, the shame," Joey groaned, covering his face with his hand. "I'm actually embarrassed for the prick."

"I know right," I agreed, waving a hand around. "That's exactly how I felt."

"What did you say back to that?"

I grinned deviously. "I told him to spray some perfume on his pillow, turn off the lights, and get reacquainted with his hand."

Joey threw his head back and laughed. "Vicious."

"Yeah, well, he earned it with that line," I laughed. "I mean, come on! What did he think I was going to do? Run over to his house and rub myself all over his mattress like a tomcat scenting its territory? The deluded eejit."

"Probably," Joey offered, still chuckling. "In case it slipped your attention, he's sort of obsessed with you."

"No, Paul is obsessed with *this*," I replied, gesturing to my body. "He has no interest in *this*." I tapped a finger against my temple. "He doesn't even know me, Joey. Not really. He's never taken the time to. It's all about appearances. Honestly, I doubt he would care if I never spoke a word, just so long as I smiled and looked pretty."

"Then what are you doing, Molloy?" he came right out and asked, green eyes clear for a change, and locked on my face. "Do you love him?"

"I have love for him."

"That's not what I asked."

I knew that. "What do you want me to say, Joe?"

"Make it make sense to me."

"Make what make sense?"

"You and him."

"Oh god." I laughed. "How long do you have?"

"All night."

Blowing out a shaky breath, I thought about it for a while, trying to find a diplomatic way of saying '*because if I have any chance of getting over you, I need to be with a boy who's the complete opposite*' before settling on, "I guess, I've always known where I stand with Paul." *Something I've never known with you.*

"Where you stand?"

"Yeah." I nodded slowly. "I mean, don't get me wrong. I know it's not perfect. It's really, *really* far from perfect, but at least I'm navigating our relationship with a clear head and my eyes open." *And most importantly,*

I can't get hurt. "I know his game, and he's not going to be able to pull the wool over my eyes."

"That sounds miserable."

"It's safe." *Safer than you.*

"So, he's your shield."

"My shield?"

"From getting fucked over." Joey's brows furrowed. "Why keep it going this long?"

"I don't know." I shrugged, feeling at a loss. "Probably because it's all I've known since first year. Being with Paul is comfortable. There's no work to it, and besides, he wants to be with me." *And you don't.*

Joey stared at me for the longest time before shaking his head. "It won't last with him."

"No?" *Oh god, I hope not.* "You don't think?"

"No." He shook his head again. "Any relationship that is held together because it's comfortable isn't a relationship worth having."

I huffed out a breath. "Yeah, well, take it from someone with first-hand knowledge of this kind of thing, sometimes comfortable is as good as it gets."

"Bullshit. Comfortable isn't as good as it gets," Joey challenged, narrowing his eyes. "You shouldn't settle for *comfortable*, Molloy. You shouldn't settle for anything less than being in love to the point of madness. The only person that you should be settling for is the person who *unsettles* you the most. The person who drives you to the brink of suicide because he or she makes you feel so fucking much that you can't catch your breath or remotely function without them. And what's more is you won't want to. You won't want to breathe, or feel, or fucking function without them. That's how you'll know that it's a real relationship, Molloy. Only when you're feeling the most discomfort you've ever felt in your entire life, should you even *consider* settling. Because that's when you'll know you're in love, which, sounds to me, like a hell of a lot nicer way to live than settling for someone you have nothing in common with because it's *comfortable*."

Whoa.

My breath hitched in my throat as my heart decided to jackknife in my chest. "You really believe that?"

"For you?" He nodded without a hint of uncertainty. "Absolutely."

"What about you?"

"What about me, Molloy?"

"Is that what you're holding out for?" I whispered, pulse racing. "That kind of epic love?"

"No," he said flatly.

My heart sank. "Why not?"

"Because you have to care about someone to fall in love." He gave me a hardened look. "And I don't care about anyone, remember?"

Now, I was the one to say, "Bullshit." Twisting sideways in my seat, I met his hard look with one of my own. "You care about me, Joe."

"You're my friend," he conceded.

"Yeah, your friend that you care about."

"Molloy."

"It's okay to care about me, Joe."

He glared at me. "I don't care."

I narrowed my eyes. "*Yes*, you *do*."

"Listen, the only one I've ever been able to depend on being there is my shadow, and that's how I like it," he snapped, running a hand through his hair. "I don't care about people because I can't afford to. I don't have the time in my life or the space inside of my head to allow myself to care about anyone other than my family. That's me, okay? That's who I am. I can't *afford* to care, Molloy."

"Well, that sucks because I do," I tossed back, feeling hurt, and flustered, and a million other emotions in this moment. "I care about you, Joey, and I always have."

It had never been my brightest idea.

Too bad I was headstrong and incessantly reckless with my heart.

Too bad I was determined to care about him regardless.

"Don't fucking say it out loud," Joey groaned, dropping his head in his hands. "Christ, Molloy, why do you always have to go too far? Why can't you just keep that shit to yourself, *please*!"

"You mean like you?" I demanded, unflinching. "You know, Joe, one of these days you're going to have to stop lying to yourself and admit how you feel."

"There's nothing to admit."

"Yes, there is, and you know it."

"You're wrong."

"You're just afraid to admit it," I argued, holding a finger up. "Because that means you'll have to acknowledge the fact that there's a girl sitting right in front of you who cares about you for no other reason than that she just does! A girl who isn't depending on you to do anything for her other than be her friend! A girl who sees just how much of an asshole you can be, but cares about you regardless, because I do, Joe. I absolutely fucking care, despite your shit-head tendencies; hell, maybe even *because* of them." I threw my hands up in resignation. "Who the hell knows anymore?"

"If you could just *try* to understand what I'm trying to do," he bit out, and then exhaled a ragged breath. "If you only knew what I was trying to spare you from, you wouldn't push for this."

"Push you for what?" I demanded, heart thudding violently. "Your friendship?"

"Push for anything from me," he roared back. "Fuck!"

Eyes bulging with temper, I went right ahead and pushed him. *Literally*. With both hands. "How's that for a push, you big coward!"

"Don't fucking start," Joey warned, holding an arm up to ward me off. "Don't even think about going there with me. It won't end well."

"Too late." I pushed him again and then I did it twice more for good measure. "Come on, tough guy, at least now I'm pushing for more in the only way you seem to understand!"

"Molloy."

I pushed him.

"I'm warning you."

I pushed him again.

"Goddammit, Molloy." Tossing me onto my back, Joey pinned my hands to my sides, and leaned in close. "You reek of desperation and it's such a fucking turn off."

He was saying the cruelest things, but his eyes told a different story entirely, as he hovered over me, chest heaving against mine, as his body thrummed with tension.

"Why would I care about a girl who offers herself up on a plate for the taking?" Narrowing his eyes, he leaned even closer, and hissed, "You're another fella's girlfriend and yet here you are, on the flat of your back for me like a *slut*."

"Get off me!" I practically snarled, temper frayed, as his words cut me to the bone. "Now, asshole!"

"No fucking problem," he sneered, equally furious, as he jerked back.

"You can be such a fucking bastard!" I screamed, as I flung the passenger door open and jumped out of the car. "The biggest one I've ever met!"

"And you can be such a fucking bitch," he roared back, before quickly climbing out of the car after me. "Wait – where are you going?"

"Away from you!"

"It's your car, Molloy."

Dammit. "I don't care."

"You don't have any shoes on."

Double dammit. "I don't care!"

"Molloy, cop on to yourself, will ya?" His tone was hard and laced with frustration. "You're not walking home in the dark on your own."

"Why not? Afraid I'll be easy pickings since I'm such a slut and all that?"

"Would you just stop moving for a sec—"

"No, now fuck off – and don't even think about coming after me!"

"Don't walk away from me, Molloy."

"Don't tell me what to do, asshole." Upping my pace, I hurried around the street corner, and quickly crossed the road. Because it was so close to Christmas, people continued to spill out from pubs and bars.

"Wait, wait, wait—" His strong arms came around my body, pulling me flush against his chest. "Just hold up, will you?"

"Let go," I warned, shivering when his hands clamped down firmly on hips, keeping my back pressed closely to his chest. "Now."

"I fucked up," came his thick response, as his breath fanned my cheek. "Forgive me."

"No." My heart raced wildly. "You hurt my feelings."

"Be my friend again, Molloy."

"No." Shaking my head, I twisted around to look up at him. "You said that to hurt me, you *knew* it would, and if I forgive you, you'll only hurt me again."

"Yeah, I probably will." Green eyes, so lonesome and full of regret seared me. "But I won't mean to." He blew out a harsh breath. "I won't hurt you on purpose again."

Accidently or on purpose; it hurts just the same.

"I can't." Releasing a shaky breath, I took a step back. "You *really* hurt me with that."

"I care." Reaching out a hand, he grabbed the front of the hoodie I was wearing – *his* hoodie – and fisted the fabric as he pulled me back to him, our bodies flush together. "I care. I care. I care," he repeated, eyes locked on mine, as his hand moved up from my hoodie to cup my neck. "Too much."

"See?" Blowing out a ragged breath, I sagged forward, letting my head fall against his chest. "That's all I wanted to hear."

"I know, Molloy." Resting his chin on my head, he sighed heavily. "I know."

How's your halo?

December 31st 2003

JOEY

My life was a sequence of one disaster after the next.

The first of which happened to be the day I was born.

Yeah, that was a fucking mistake in itself.

I didn't say that because I was suicidal, looking for pity, or depressed. I said it because it was the wholehearted truth. I had been born into a family that never wanted me.

To a weak mother and a wicked bastard of a father.

I was the spare son, the backup, second best to my mother's favored firstborn, and from day one, it had been a shitshow, a train wreck.

More children followed after me, my father's inability to put a condom on his dick the root cause of our household overpopulation – well, that, along with his inability to hear the word *no*.

Growing up in a home like ours made it difficult for me to work right. I didn't mean hold down a job; I'd had one of those since childhood. I meant that I didn't work right in the head, not like other people my age, at least.

There was a whole host of things wrong with me.

Things I was too scared to invest time in trying to figure out.

Truth be told, my brain was a scary place to be, and I didn't want to be anywhere near me most of the time.

How fucked up was that?

The current piss-poor state of my life was a direct result of poor choices.

Choices I had made.

Choices that had been made for me by people who were supposed to love me but either didn't have the capacity to love me or just plain didn't.

I knew I was far from a saint, and I wasn't blaming my wrongdoings on anyone other than yours truly. But fuck, things might have been different if I had been given a different start in life – a start like the prick standing in front me had been given, for example.

Yeah, with a stable family, a nice house, and a few quid tucked away in the bank, Paul Rice had been given a good start in life.

A better one than me.

It must be nice to be able to sleep at night without the fear of being dragged out from under the covers and beaten to within an inch of your life.

Must be nice to not be distracted by the screams of your half-starved siblings, or the low wails of your battered and bruised, not to mention brutally raped, mother on the daily.

Dick.

"Babe, lay off the vodka tonight, yeah?" he told Molloy, as they wandered into Danielle Long's jam-packed parent-free kitchen on New Year's Eve, while her house party was in full swing.

They had spent most of the party in the sitting room. I knew this because I'd legged it out here to get away from them.

I was determined to get off to a good start this year – new year, new me, and all that bullshit – but if I had to watch that prick molest the side of Molloy's face with his tongue a second longer, I would have lost before I even started.

"... I care. Too much."

"... See? That's all I wanted to hear ... "

Blinking away the memory before it took hold and depressed me, I concentrated on the prick in front of me as he spoke down to her like she was a small child.

Seriously, I gave more respect to Sean, and I wiped his ass on the daily.

"You know how you get aggressive after drinking," Ricey continued to put her down by saying. Acting like he owned the air around him, he opened the fridge and retrieved what had to be his seventh can of lager, leaving his girlfriend empty handed. "And I can't stand it when you get sloppy."

Leaning against the back door, I watched as Molloy's cheeks flushed bright pink, but instead of giving him a piece of her mind like she normally would, she just brushed it off.

She just let it go.

She let him speak to her like he was her keeper.

It didn't settle well with me.

Fuck it, though, I wasn't getting involved in anymore of her drama. Last time I tried to defend her, I lost the head so badly that I almost killed her brother.

You spoke to her like shit, too, asshole, my mind reminded me, and I flinched at the horrible fucking mess of things I had made with her before Christmas.

My inability to produce a competent fucking sentence to explain to Molloy how very wrong I was for her, had resulted in me spewing poison and making her cry.

Tearing my eyes off her, I took a deep drag from my joint and held it in my lungs for the longest time, reveling in the burn, in the dizziness, in the momentary release it gave me.

It wasn't enough, though.

It never was.

The little baggie of benzos in the ass pocket of my jeans were proof to that. Mixed in with vodka and vicodin, and I was getting somewhere.

I could forget *her* voice for a while.

I could forget everything

Staring out the back door into the darkness, I found my mind wandering back to the earlier conversation I had with my mother.

"How could they be so cruel?" Mam demanded, holding her head in her hands, as she stared down at Shannon's torn, blood-encrusted jumper strewn on top of the kitchen table. "I just don't understand this, Joey."

"Neither do I," I agreed, *feeling at a complete fucking loss as to what to do for my sister.*

We were on Christmas break from school, and somehow, the bullies from school had managed to follow her home from a walk.

A bloody nose and a torn jumper had been the result.

Since she started second year, the bullying had ramped up to epic proportions. I tried to sort it, I fucking tried to nip it in the bud, but it was like I was fighting against the tide. The more scores I settled; the faster they seemed to keep rising up against me.

It was fucking exhausting, and I was running on empty.

"I thought you said you would look out for her this year," Mam sobbed then, and I couldn't miss the accusation in her tone. *"She looks up to you so much, Joey."*

"No, no, no, don't even think about putting this on me," I warned, holding up a hand. *"I didn't do this to her. And I looked after her last year, too, Mam. I did everything I could for the girl."*

"I know you did," Mam strangled out. *"But couldn't you have done something to stop it today?"*

"Like what?*"* I demanded, throwing my hands up. *"I can't watch her twenty-four-seven, Mam. I have class, and training, and work and—"*

"Something," Mam cried. *"Anything."*

"What do you want me to do, Mam? Go around beating the shit out of her bullies? Because I can't, Mam. They're girls. I'm out of my fucking depth with this as much as she is." Running a hand through my hair, I expelled a harsh breath. *"I can't keep fighting all of Shannon's battles for her, and I can't keep fighting all of yours, either."*

"Steal any more cars lately?" Molloy's familiar voice infiltrated my thoughts, dragging me back to the present, and fuck if my heart didn't take a U-turn in my chest when she sidled up beside me and nudged my arm with her shoulder. "Nice hoodie."

"Nah, just the one," I shot back, returning her nudge. "And nice legs."

"I'm wearing jeans tonight."

"Not in my head."

"Funny." She grinned up at me and I couldn't stop myself from mirroring her actions. ""So, what are we smoking tonight?"

Her disapproval was blatant. "How's your halo, Molloy?"

"In better shape than yours by the smell of it." Standing in the doorway beside me, I watched as she leaned in close and took a whiff of my smoke. "Mm-mm-mm," she said in a tone laced with sarcasm. "Smells like debauchery."

I arched a brow. "You're killing my buzz, Molloy."

"Am I?" She beamed up at me. "That's the best news I've had this whole entire shit-fest of a night."

"Not in the festive spirit?"

"I would prefer to be anywhere than here tonight, Joe, and that's not an exaggeration," she told me with a sigh. "Including that freezer that you guys call a garage. Even *with* my father's hairy ass crack staring me in the face." She blew out a frustrated breath. "I mean, he owns like ten belts. You'd think he'd wear one."

A reluctant smile spread across my face. "Maybe you should have a drink; being as it's New Year's Eve and all." Reaching for the bottle of vodka I'd hidden behind the microwave; I waved it in front of her. "Besides, I've heard it's good for the nerves."

"I've already had three beers," she replied, by way of explanation, as she batted the bottle.

"And?"

"And Paul always gets shitty with me if I have too much to drink?"

"And?"

"And . . . " She cast a glance to the kitchen door behind her and then shook her head. "And fuck him."

That's my girl. "That's the spirit."

Turning to grin at me, she asked, "You got any Coke to go with that?"

I cocked a brow.

Her eyes widened. "I meant the drink, asshole."

I winked back at her. "Grab a glass."

*

"No, no, no," Molloy laughed a couple of hours later, as she sloshed her drink around in her hand, and staggered towards me. "There's no way you can keep this going."

"I can go all night, Molloy," I shot back, feeling a lot more relaxed now that I had half a bottle of vodka in my system.

We were outside the back of Danielle's house, had been for over an hour, playing this fucked game that Molloy referred to as *the one-word game*.

What had started with us joking around, taking turns to add one word to make a sentence, had turned into a fucked-up story.

I'd never played before, but as the vodka kept coming, the story kept getting more inventive.

Knotting her fingers in the front of my hoodie, she pulled me close and grinned up at my face. "Gimme that bottle."

"I don't know, Molloy," I taunted, unscrewing the cap, and drinking straight from the bottle. "Any more *debauchery* and your wings won't take you up to heaven."

"Then I'll just have to stay in hell with you, won't I?" she teased back, swiping the bottle out of my hand and taking a huge gulp.

She wasn't an aggressive drunk.

She was a fucking hilarious one.

Obviously, the girl wasn't keeping the right company on nights out.

"You're my best friend," she blurted out of left field. "But don't tell Casey, because she'll claw your eyes out for that title."

"I'm honored."

"You should be."

"Well, you're mine, too," I agreed with a chuckle. "But don't tell Podge because . . . yeah, he won't give a shit."

"So, we're besties?" she asked, holding her pinkie finger up.

"Fuck it." I shrugged and hooked mine around hers. "Why not?"

"*Yay*. Okay, okay," she laughed, sinking down on the edge of the trampoline, bottle in hand. "Where were we?"

"He was reaching between her legs," I reminded her, sinking down beside her.

"Oh yes," she squealed with delight and flopped on to her back, causing the trampoline to sway beneath us.

"And don't be fucking around with it this time," I warned, swiping the bottle out of her hands to take a swig. "When it gets to the good bit, don't choke."

"I didn't choke," she snickered, pulling herself up on her elbows. "Okay, so he was reaching between her legs . . . " Frowning, she thought hard for a moment, before adding, "when."

I rolled my eyes. "All."

"Of."

"A."

Her eyes widened. "Sudden."

"He."

"Stopped."

She smirked. "To."

I arched a brow. "Slide."

"Her."

"Thong."

"Down."

"Her."

"Legs."

"Full stop," she cackled. "Then."

"His."

Her cheeks flushed bright pink when she added, "Mouth."

"Was."

"There."

"*There?*" I arched a brow. "The fuck, Molloy? Where's there?"

"Okay, okay," she conceded, giggle. "His mouth was *on*."

"Her." Grinning, I gestured to her to go right ahead and take her turn.

"No, I can't, I can't," she choked out through fits of laughter, as she flopped back on the trampoline. "Stop trying to make me."

"Yes, you can," I laughed. "Say it."

"I can't."

"Say it!"

"Pussy!" she screamed at the top of her lungs. "His mouth was on her pussy! There I said it." Choking out another fit of laugher, she strangled out, "I'm going to wet myself."

"Jump the fuck off if you are," I laughed, twisting sideways to watch her roll around on the mat, clutching her side. "If you piss on this trampoline with me on it, I'm going to have to revoke your friendship status, Molloy, and find somebody else to play the one-word game with."

"You wouldn't dare." Twisting onto her hands and knees, she crawled back to me and sighed in contentment. "I'm irreplaceable."

That she was.

"Joey?" A familiar voice called out from the back door. "Are you coming inside?" Danielle asked, as she hovered in the doorway. "I was hoping we could have a dance."

"I don't dance."

"Oh. I was really hoping we could."

"Like I said, I don't dance."

"Well, come inside soon, yeah? I want to ring in the new year with you."

"Yeah, grand, Dan, I'll be inside in a bit."

Snickering when the door closed behind Danielle, Molloy ribbed me with her elbow. "Sounds like she wants to do more than just ring in the new year with you."

Grinning, I shook my head and looked at her. "Is that right?"

"Yep." Bursting out in another fit of giggles, she added, "Sounds like she wants your mouth on her pussy."

My brows shot up. "Bold words coming from the girl who was too shy to say the word pussy two minutes ago?"

"Pussy, pussy, meow-meow," she countered with a fake purr. "How's that for too shy?"

"I take it back," I replied dryly. "You're a wild one."

"And you're the opposite of pussy," she offered with a supportive smile.

"Gee, thanks."

"No, *you're* welcome." Smiling, she reached up to pat my cheek. "Take it down," she instructed then, pulling down my hood. "I wanna see your pretty face."

"Pretty," I snorted. "Jesus, keep those compliments coming, Molloy. You'll do wonders for my ego."

"You are, though," she sighed, hand moving from my cheek to cup the back of my neck. "If I had a packet of Rolos right now, I'd give you my last one."

"Yeah?" I smiled, indulging her. "Well, if I had a packet of Rolos right now, Molloy, I'd give them all to you."

"You would?" Her eyes widened like saucers, as she looked up at me like I'd just offered her the moon on a string. "That's the nicest thing anyone's ever given me."

I shook my head and laughed. "You're such a lightweight."

She grinned. "Okay, okay, how's this for the next word in the story." Pressing her fingers to her temples, she hummed before blurting out, "She."

"Spread."

"Her."

"Legs."

"Wider."

"For."

"Him."

"To."

"Taste."

"Her."

"Throbbing."

"Clit."

She blew out a shaky breath and leaned in closer. "She."

"Used."

"Her."

I felt her shift closer. "Hands."

"To."

"Push"

"His."

"Boxers."

She exhaled a ragged breath and whispered, "Down."

"And."

"Then."

"He."

Her hand tightened around the back of my neck. "Buried."

"His."

"Hard."

Her breath hitched when I whispered, "Cock."

She gripped my neck so tight, her nails dug into my skin. "Deep."

My heart was gunning in my chest, so loud and violently, that I was surprised to still be breathing. I resisted the urge to rest my forehead against hers.

Instead, I held my ground, and watched her watch me.

It was too much – her, the moment, my feelings, the way my heart beat – it was all too fucking much.

And still, I remained completely motionless, watching her watch me. "Inside."

I felt her lips sway dangerously close to mine. "Of."

"His girlfriend," Paul said coldly, startling us. "What's going on out here?"

"Hey Paul, we're in the middle of the one-word game," Molloy chirped, oblivious to the look of murder etched on her boyfriend's face. "Wanna join us?"

"No," he said flatly. "I *want* to spend time alone with my girlfriend, but I haven't been able to find her for the last hour and a half."

"That's because she was out here playing with Joe, silly," she reeled off happily.

"Well, would you mind coming inside and ringing in the new year with me?" he argued. "If it isn't too much of a bother for you to peel yourself away from Lynchy, that is."

"Sure, Paul." Smiling up at me, she tapped my nose with her finger. "And I'll see *you* . . . later."

"I'll be seeing ya, Molloy," I replied, watching her peachy ass as she shimmied into the house.

"You won't," Paul said, when Molloy had gone back inside. "You won't be seeing her, playing games with her, or having anything to fucking do with her."

I laughed. "You've got some serious issues with control, lad."

"I mean it, Lynchy," he warned. "Stay away from her."

"She's the one who keeps coming back to me, lad," I drawled, draining the last remnants of vodka from the bottle. "What does that tell you?"

"It tells me that she's bored and you're the perfect charity case to work on."

"Really?" I shrugged. "That's funny, because it tells me that you're too boring for her, and I'm giving her exactly what you can't."

"And what's that?" he sneered. "A tramp stamp on her ass and a rap sheet the length of her arm?"

"Not yet." I smirked. "But there's always tomorrow."

"Listen, prick, I'm only going to say this one more time; leave my girlfriend alone. Stay out of her face and stay out of her life."

"Whatever you say," I replied, unwilling to brawl with him tonight. Not when I was in such a good mood now.

"Oh, one thing I will say before I go." Swinging around to glare at me, he added, "Thanks for getting her drunk for me."

I narrowed my eyes and his smile darkened. "It's always easier to get her knickers off when she's off her face from drink."

With that, he turned around and disappeared inside the house.

I stood up and moved to go after him, but what could I do?

The fuck could I say to that?

I could hardly stop them.

She *chose* to be with him.

Repeatedly.

He was her boyfriend.
I was her . . . nothing.
I was her nothing.
Fuck my life.

Knocking on Danielle's door

January 1st 2004

AOIFE

"Oh, yeah, babe, that's it," Paul groaned, pressing me deeper into the mattress in the spare bedroom he'd pulled me into.

Instead of being downstairs having a good time at the party like I had been doing, I was currently sprawled out, half-naked, beneath my drunk as a skunk boyfriend, while I sweated vodka and plotted my escape.

"You're so fucking sexy," Paul continued to purr, as he groped and pulled at my bare breasts like they were his personal play toys. "Fuck me, I can't wait to ram my dick inside ya," he added gruffly, trailing his tongue up my neck. "I'm going to fuck you so hard that you won't be able to walk straight for a week afterwards."

Wow.

The words every virgin wanted to hear.

His hands moved to the elastic waistband of my thong, and I clamped up. "Wait."

"No," he groaned, burying his face between my breasts. "No, no, no, don't say wait."

"Wait," I repeated, chest heaving, as I slapped his hand away from my knickers. "Wait."

"It's been three and a half years, Aoif," he whined, pressing sloppy, wet kisses to my neck. "Four in February. Haven't I earned your v-card by now?"

V-card?

"No." I shook my head. "I don't want to do this here."

"Shh, it's fine, here is perfect. It's New Year's Eve. Very romantic."

"It's not happening, Paul," I argued, slapping against his chest, in my bid to get the big, drunk bastard off me. "Now get off me."

"For fuck's sake, Aoife," he snapped, rolling off me and onto his back. "This is bullshit. How is it that I'm the only fella in our year with a long-term girlfriend and still the only fella not fucking getting any."

"I'm not there yet," I explained, sliding to the edge of the bed. "I'm not ready to have sex with you, and I'm not about to be pressured into having sex with you at a shitty New Year's Eve party, either," I bit out, reaching for my bra on the bedroom floor.

"Then at least suck me off."

I glared at him palming his cock. "Put that thing near my face, and I'll bite it off you."

"You wouldn't."

"Try me."

"You're such a bitch."

"If you can't be patient and wait until I am ready, then that's on you, not me."

"Well, what if I can't?" He sat up and glared at me. "What if I'm tired of waiting for you to pry open those Virgin Mary legs?"

I narrowed my eyes at him. "Then we have nothing left to say to each other."

"Fine, then fuck off and find some other misfortunate bastard to walk you home tonight," he snapped, throwing the covers off himself and jerking to his feet. "Because I don't even want to look at you right now."

"Look, I'm sorry, okay?" I strangled out, feeling weirdly emotional at his cold rejection. "I told you that I'm just not ready for sex, okay?"

"And I told you that I don't want to look at ya," he sneered, as he yanked on his boxers. "So, you can fuck me, or you can leave."

The words were no sooner out of his mouth when the bedroom door flew inwards.

"Not here," Danielle purred, as she pulled at the buckle of a shirtless Joey's belt. "Let's go in my room instead."

Pain.

It ricocheted through me like a knife.

Clearly high on whatever concoction he'd taken after I left him earlier, Joey swayed against her, eyes bleary and unfocused, as he reached for her waist and pulled her towards him. "Here's grand."

Ouch.

It hurt.

It hurt so bad that I had to suck in a sharp breath to catch my breath.

"Oh, sorry guys," Danielle squeaked, when she noticed our presence. "We were just . . . " Her voice trailed off as her cheeks reddened. "Well, um, you know . . . "

"It's fine." Swallowing down the bile in my throat, I quickly turned my back to the door as I slipped on my bra and shrugged on my jeans. "We were just leaving."

"See? They're fucking, and I can guarantee that he didn't have to spend three years convincing her either," Paul spat, roughly throwing my t-shirt across the room at me. "Come on, Aoife, this is what lads my age are supposed to be doing."

"Then I mean it both figuratively and literally when I tell you to go fuck yourself, Paul," I hissed as I quickly pulled my t-shirt back on, feeling the stinging threat of tears in my eyes.

"Fuck you," Paul sneered. "Enjoy the walk home in the dark on your own. I hope there aren't any weirdos lurking in the bushes."

"You can have the room, Danielle. I was just leaving," I choked out, face burning, as I slipped my feet into my ballerina pumps and moved for the door, which just so happened to be blocked by Joey, who was slumping against the doorframe.

Great.

This was just epic.

His eyes landed on my face, and I swear I saw a flicker of recognition pass through them before he shook his head and turned away from me.

"Is he okay?" I asked, slipping past his tall frame.

"He's fine," Danielle assured me, as she slung his arm over her shoulder and led him down the hall to her bedroom. "Happy new year!"

Whatever happened between Joey and Danielle in her bedroom had clearly been exactly what she wanted, because when she came back downstairs afterwards, she was so happy with herself that she was practically floating.

Disgusted with myself for the abnormal level of jealousy I had steered towards a girl who had never done anything to me, I tried to pull myself out of my dark mood, but the truth was that I just couldn't.

Numb to the bone, not to mention well and truly sober now, I sat on the couch in her sitting room, and watched as the crowd slowly dwindled, until there were only a handful of us left.

I should have gone home hours ago, but I couldn't seem to get my feet to walk out the front door. Not when he was still upstairs, completely fucking out of it.

I knew it should be Paul I was thinking about, upstairs and alone in the room I'd abandoned him in, but it wasn't.

It was Joey.

I liked that he was a little fucked up.

I adored his sharp edges, and I loved his broken pieces.

I liked him even though I knew he'd just given my classmate everything Paul had tried to give me.

What did that say about me?

I just fucking liked him.

So much that it hurt the skin covering my chest.

Jesus.

Unable to stick the not-knowing a second longer, I sprang to my feet and bolted for the staircase, catching a glimpse of Danielle in the doorway of the kitchen as I went.

Stay put.

Stay put.

Stay put.

Rounding the banister, I hurried past the room I'd shared with Paul a few hours ago and went straight for the door at the end of the hall.

It was cracked open, so when I slipped inside, I didn't make a sound.

"Joey?" I whispered into the darkness, as I felt my way over to the bed. Finding a lamp on the locker, I flicked it on, bathing the room in a soft yellow hue. "Joe?"

"Molloy," he groaned, twisting his face into the mattress.

My heart both cracked and soared at the sound.

Soared because even in his worst state, he knew my voice.

Cracked because he was naked in another girl's bed, with a used condom strewn on the bedroom floor.

"Are you okay?" I heard myself ask, heart racing, as I looked down at where he was sprawled out, I presumed, naked under Danielle's pink floral duvet.

The covers were draped over his hips, leaving the rest of his body exposed, and revealing a huge crucifix tattoo on his back.

"No," Joey groaned, keeping his face buried in the sheets. "Fuck."

Exhaling a shaky breath, I gingerly sat on the edge of the bed next to him. "What did you take?"

"I fucked up, Molloy," he slurred, twisted his head from side to side. "Again."

"Yeah, you did." Sighing heavily, I placed my hand on his shoulder, and watched as the muscles in his back physically tensed under my touch. "What am I going to do with you, huh?"

My breath hitched in my throat at the sight when my gaze landed on a long, five- or six-inch scar going diagonally across his back. It was concealed behind the crucifix tattoo, but if you looked close enough it was plain to see.

"Is that from a belt?" I heard myself whisper, not even trying to stop myself from trailing a finger over the other deep ridges and grooved scars that seemed to be littered across his flesh. Most seemed old, like they had been imprinted on him a long time ago, but some of them were more recent. "And this one?"

"Probably," he mumbled drowsily. "Don't look."

"What happened to your back, Joe?" Heart in my mouth, I continued to trail my fingers over his marred skin, feeling the ache in my chest spread as the seconds passed by. "Where did all these scars come from – and don't say fighting."

"Fighting," he said anyway, before rolling onto his back. "Christ, my head is hopping."

"Yeah," I replied, reaching up to smooth his blond hair back. "I bet it is."

"You're really here." He cracked a lid open and peered up at me. "Thought I dreamt you up." And then he looked at me, completely spaced out of his mind, with lipstick smeared across his mouth and cheek. "Hey."

"Hey." My stomach bottomed out at the sight. "You shouldn't give yourself away to the likes of her," I whispered, giving him back the words he'd spoken to me a long time ago.

A flash of recognition filled his eyes, causing his nostrils to flare. "Molloy."

"It hurts," I admitted softly, reaching down to rub the lipstick off him. "This hurts me."

"I would never hurt you, Molloy," he slurred, his words a lot like his life: a broken mess. "I'd rather die than hurt you."

"Don't say that."

"It's the truth." Releasing a pained groaned, he croaked out, "Only thing I've ever done right in my life is leave you alone."

My eyes filled with tears, and I quickly blinked them away, but not before one lone tear dripped from my cheek and landed on his bare chest.

"You're crying." A bleary sort of anxiety filled his features as he slowly pulled himself up on his elbows. "Why? What did I do?"

"I'm grand." Shaking my head, I tucked my hair behind my ear, feeling his hot breath on my cheek. "I'm okay."

He looked around us then, his eyes raking in the unfamiliar bedroom, as confusion swept over him. "Did I?" His gaze settled back on mine, wild and panicked, as he sat straight up. "Did we?"

"No." Shaking my head, I forced out the bitter truth, "Not us."

"Fuck." His body visibly sagged. "Molloy."

"Don't stay here." My breath hitched in my throat, and I dropped my gaze to the mattress, to where the smell of sex was still in the air. "In this bed." I exhaled a ragged breath, hating the plea as it came stumbling out of my mouth, "With her."

Joey tipped my chin up and forced me to look at him, as he stared so hard the green orbs of his irises darkened to coal.

"Okay," he finally said, thumb stroking over the curve of my bottom lip, as I leaned my cheek into his big hand. "I won't."

A little while later, I was walking the familiar trek back to my house.

With his hood pulled up, and his hands shoved into the front of his hoodie, Joey looked exactly like he always did when he walked me home.

A little pissed off, and a lot sexy.

I didn't have the energy to joke around with him tonight, though, or even speak.

So instead, we walked in silence with a cloud of bitterness hanging over our heads.

"Thanks," I said when we reached my gate. "For walking me home, and, um, well, you know."

"It's grand." He kept his hands in his pockets, as he watched me close the garden gate behind me. "I'll see you at school next week."

"Yeah." Nodding, I lingered in front of the gate, watching him watch me. "I suppose you will."

He nodded stiffly, but made no move to leave, and neither did I.

"I thought I hurt you tonight," he finally said, breaking the heavy silence between us. "When I woke up and saw you there? I thought I did something we couldn't take back. I was so fucking relieved when you told me that we didn't." Exhaling a heavy sigh, he added, "But the way you're looking at me right now makes me wish we had." He shook his head and turned to walk away. "At least if we had, then I could understand the disappointed look in your eyes."

"Joe." I sucked in a sharp breath as he started to walk away. "Joey, wait I—"

"I'll be seeing ya, Molloy," he called over his shoulder.

And then he was gone.

I will always stick up for you

January 7th 2004

JOEY

"Hey, Joe, have you seen your sister?"

Seven words I had learned to fear, especially if they were spoken at school.

Shoulders stiffening to the point of spasm, I stopped unraveling the new grip on my hurley, and glanced up at Danielle.

"Why?" My tone was hard and flat as I crouched on the grass, clad in my school jersey, shorts, socks, and football boots. I was about to head out for training with the rest of the school team. "What happened?"

"She's bawling her eyes out in the bathroom."

Again?

"Why?" I demanded, rising to my feet, and towering over the petite, blue-eyed blonde in front of me.

Chewing on her lip, Danielle gestured towards the school building. "I'm not entirely sure what happened, but I heard she and Ciara Maloney had a few words."

"A few words?" Reaching for the clasp on my helmet, I snapped it open and ripped it off my head. "Any chance these words turned into a few slaps?"

Danielle shrugged, looking nervous. "Listen, I don't want to get involved, okay. I don't want to get on anyone's bad side. I'm only telling you because you're a friend."

Friend?

That was a stretch.

Friends cared about each other.

I could count the people I considered my friends on one hand.

My sister was one.

Podge was another.

Alec, thick as shit that he was, still made the cut.

Tony Molloy, for obvious reasons.

Aside from my sister, there was only one girl that held court in my affections, who held the highest rank of friendship my heart could offer, and it sure as hell wasn't the girl who I lost my virginity to back in third year – the one I had made the mistake of hooking up with on multiple occasions since.

Danielle was a girl I was friendly with, but she wasn't my *friend*, and I had no intention of repeating the mistake I had made on New Year's Eve.

The clingy texts I'd received from her most days since were more than enough of a wake-up call to let me know that particular ship had sailed.

I couldn't remember a whole pile about the night – I had been too fucked up at the time to take stock of anything other than the fantastic fucking feeling of floating away.

The only part of the whole night that I did remember was the condom I'd clumsily rolled on my dick, and her hair.

It was blonde, and long, and smelled like coconuts.

The smell stuck in my nose for days afterwards.

Problem was, I couldn't be sure if it was Danielle's hair and scent that I remembered, or if it was Molloy's.

She'd been there when I came to, had looked at me like I was responsible for breaking her heart clean open in her chest, and, after walking her home that night, hadn't looked at me since.

The look in her eyes that night had complicated everything for me because I was now fully aware that I had the ability to hurt her, whether I was near her or not.

That was a sobering thought, but not as sobering as the scene I had arrived home to after walking her home from said house party.

Yeah, the absolute carnage I had been faced with had quickly killed any notions of girls, and a social life.

Mam had fallen down the stairs while I'd been out and had broken her arm.

How fucking convenient.

I had spent the following twenty-four hours at home alone with the kids to look after, not to mention reeling in my guilt, while my mother sat in the A&E with *him*.

"Did she hit her?" I asked, dragging my thoughts back to the present. "Was it bad? Come on, Dan, just tell me."

"It was bad, Joe," she whispered, reaching up to rub my arm. "There was a lot of shouting and screaming. Apparently, someone cut her hair, too."

My blood ran cold. "Tell me you're joking."

"Your mam is up there now," she added, cringing. "They called her in. She's talking to the principal."

"Jesus fucking Christ." Chest heaving, I cleared the five-foot wall enclosing the pitch in one quick sweep, before storming off in the direction of the school building, football studs clattering against the concrete as I went.

"Don't lose your head, Joey," I heard Danielle call after me, but it was too late for that.

My head was long gone, lost in fucking space, the moment I heard someone had taken a pair of scissors to my sister's hair.

Like a red rag to a bull, I stormed through the school yard towards the main building and slammed my hand against the glass door so hard I was surprised it didn't shatter.

"Where's the fire?" Alec asked when I stormed past him and the rest of the team, who were heading outside for training.

"Lynchy, the pitch is the other way."

"Get fucked!" I roared, losing what little self-control I had left inside of me, as I thundered towards the girls' bathroom.

"You can't go in there, Joseph," Miss Lane, one of the teachers, warned when I stormed past her.

"Oh yeah?" I sneered, shoving the door open. "Fucking stop me."

"Excuse me?" she demanded, tone laced with shock. "You'll be suspended for speaking to me like that."

"Then suspend me," I countered, turning my attention to the group of girls huddling at the communal sinks. "Get the fuck out now!"

"I'm getting the principal," Miss Lane warned in a shaky voice, as she quickly ushered the girls out of the bathroom.

"You do that," I sneered, slamming the door shut in her face.

Blowing out a breath that felt like flames, I walked along the row of a dozen or so toilet cubicles, pushing in each door as I passed, until I came to the last one.

It was locked.

"It's me," was all I said, and then waited, heart rate spiking as I prepared for what I would find on the other side of the door.

Several beats passed before the sound of a lock clicking filled the air, and then the door swung slowly inwards.

Sitting on the closed lid of the toilet, with her knees tucked into her chest, and her eyes bloodshot from crying, my baby sister peeked up at me.

"Hey, Joe."

My heart cracked clean open in my chest at the sight of her.

It didn't matter to me that she was fourteen now.

In my eyes, she was still the tiny girl in pigtails who had followed me around for most of our childhood.

The world was dark and full of disappointments. This wasn't new information to me. I was far too familiar with the shitty side of life. I'd learned that lesson a long time ago, but Christ, nobody wore heartbreak quite like my sister.

Trembling, I forced myself to rein in my temper, something I was surprisingly good at doing around my sister and crouched down in front of her. "Hey, Shan."

Her lip was split, her uniform caked in what, by going off the smell, I could only assume was sour milk, and she was clenching her long dark ponytail in her hand.

Her ponytail that wasn't attached to her head anymore.

I was going to kill them.

I was going to kill them *all*.

"D-don't ask me wh-what happened," she whisper-sobbed, tone pleading. "I d-don't w-want to t-talk about it."

"Okay." Going against every instinct inside of my body, I nodded slowly, careful not to make any sudden move that would scare what was left of her senses out of her. "I won't."

I understood what it felt like to be afraid, I'd spent most of my life drowning in terror until I just stopped caring.

Caring meant feeling.

If I didn't care about what happened to me then I had nothing to fear.

I could survive feeling like that.

I could survive this life.

Shannon stared at me for a long moment, big blue eyes full of unshed tears, and then she bolted forward like a skittish foal, crying hysterically. "I don't w-want to be h-here anymore, J-Joe."

"I know, Shan." Catching her small frame as she barreled into me, I wrapped her up in my arms as tight as I could, wanting to protect her from something that had already happened. "I know."

"I w-want to d-die," she continued to cry, choking hard on her tears. "I w-want to n-not be h-here anymore."

"You can't go dying on me," I tried to coax, as terror filled my veins. "What would I do without you, huh?"

"But I m-make everything w-worse f-for you," she continued to cry. "You k-keep getting in f-fights trying to pr-protect and s-stick up f-for me. It's n-not fair on y-you . . . always h-having to s-save me."

"That's my job, Shan," I said as I pried her ponytail from her small fist. "I'm your big brother. I will *always* stick up for you."

"I l-love you, J-Joe."

"I love you, too," I whispered, wrapping her up in my arms. "I'm going to fix this, okay? I'll make this right for you. I promise."

"Shannon!" Mam's loud cry filled my ears, as she hurried into the bathroom, with our principal hot on her heels. "Oh, Shannon, baby."

"Shannon," Mr. Nyhan, our principal, acknowledged in a gentle tone and then, "Joseph," in a much flatter one.

"What are you going to do about this?" I demanded, rising to my feet and taking Shannon with me. "Did you see this?" Thrusting my sister's ponytail in front of her face, I hissed, "What the fuck are you going to do about this?"

"Joey!" Mam snapped, flushing, as she pulled Shannon out from under my arm and into hers. Looking as pale as a ghost, she pointed her finger in my face. "Don't you dare use that kind of language when you're speaking to your principal."

"Don't worry, Mrs. Lynch," Mr. Nyhan replied in a haughty tone. "We can discuss your son's behavior at a later time. Miss Lane will contact you in due course to discuss the issue."

"Oh, what fucking ever," I sneered, shaking my head. "You're worried about my behavior, but I'm not the one going around hacking anyone's ponytail off."

"Joey!" Mam choked out. "Enough, please."

"I will deal with the students involved as I see fit," Mr. Nyhan replied. "Not how you demand me to, Joseph."

"Meaning that you'll do fuck all," I hissed, tone laced with disgust.

"Keep it up, Joseph," the principal warned. "Because, with an attitude like that, you're on the verge of skipping over suspension and moving straight to expulsion."

"Please," Mam started. "Please try to understand; he's going through a lot right now."

"Don't *beg* for me," I warned, hating the emotion seeping into my voice, when I locked eyes with my mother. "If he wants to expel me then he can go right ahead."

"It's okay, Joe," Shannon sniffled. "I'm o-okay."

"No, it's not okay, Shan." I shook my head. "None of this is okay, and you're not okay, either."

Shaking my head, I walked towards the door, feeling the need to get as far away from these people as I physically could. "I'll fix this, Shannon. I'll make it right."

"Joey?" Mam called after me.

"Joseph." That was Mr. Nyhan. "Where do you think you're going?"

Not bothering to answer either one of them, I shoved the bathroom door open and stalked out.

Eyes scanning the hoard of students in the hallway, I honed in on Podge's carrot-top head.

"Ciara Maloney's brother," I bit out. "Where would I find him?"

"Mike?" Podge's brows shot up. "I think he's having a smoke behind the PE hall."

Nodding stiffly, I headed for the front door.

"Why?" I heard him call after me, but I didn't stop to explain.

With my mood darkened to the point of no return, I rounded the back of the PE hall, not stopping until I had Mike Maloney's jumper fisted in one hand, while I buried my other in his face.

Commotion erupted around us, as several of our classmates cheered and called out "fight, fight, fight . . ."

"What the hell, Joe?" Mike demanded, staggering backwards.

Like a shark tasting blood in the water, I was on the bastard, my fists moving harder and faster than I thought possible.

Dragging him to the ground, I wrapped my hand around his throat and squeezed. "Scary, isn't it?" I seethed, tightening my grip until he began to turn purple. "Being attacked for no reason?"

"Joey," Podge called out, trying and failing to pull me off him. "Come on, lad, you're choking him."

"Good," I roared, spitting with temper. "Maybe this way his whore of a sister will take the fucking warning."

"Joey!" Mr. Ryan, our hurling coach, roared, coming to help Podge drag me off my classmate. "That's enough – let him go! Now!"

"Let that be a warning to your sister," I roared. "If she so much as looks at my sister again, I'll kill *you*." Chest heaving, I pointed straight at the lad bleeding all over the concrete, as Mr. Ryan and several of my teammates dragged me away. "Do ya hear me? I will *kill* you!"

Don't pretend you haven't noticed

January 7th 2004

AOIFE

I heard about the fight after lunch on Wednesday.

It was all anyone could talk about, as the school bustled with gossip and rumors.

Apparently, Ciara Maloney had orchestrated some type of vicious attack on Joey Lynch's younger sister, Shannon, and in retaliation, Joey had pummeled Ciara's brother, beating Mike until his face was unrecognizable.

Both Mike and Shannon had reportedly been taken to the doctor by their respective mothers, while Ciara sat it out in detention, and Joey went on the missing list.

"It has to be his last strike," Paul said, sitting to my left, and looking entirely too happy about the whole horrible situation.

"Lynch has had too many chances," he continued, drumming his fingers on the desk. "Nyhan's definitely going to expel him this time."

Kind of like how you've had too many chances with me. I thought to myself, still feeling salty over how he had tried to pressure me on New Year's Eve.

"I don't know, Paul," Casey replied, from where she was sitting to the right of me, dragging me from my thoughts. "If he expels Joey, then he'll have to expel Ciara, too, for what she did to Joey's sister, and somehow I can't see that happening."

"Even after he almost put Mike in the *hospital*?" Leaning forward in his seat, Paul talked over me, giving my best friend his sole attention. "You weren't there, Case; you didn't see Mike's face. He was *mangled*. Lynchy had to be physically dragged off the lad," he argued. "I don't care how good of a hurler he is, that lad is a liability. A fucking lunatic."

"Hey, I'm not arguing with you about the guy," Casey replied. "Joey Lynch might be sex on legs but he's about two fights shy of a stint in prison."

"Yeah, a stint in prison or a strait jacket," Paul muttered under his breath. "And he's been with so many girls, he's more like a walking sexually transmitted disease on legs."

"Well, he can feel free to infect me any time he likes," Casey replied, waggling her brows.

"That's not funny."

"Ah, would you relax, I'm only joking," Casey shot back with a laugh. "Well, about the infection part, at least. If boys were fairground rides, Joey Lynch would be the rollercoaster." Her eyes danced with mischief as she winked and said, "You can't blame a girl for wanting to take a ride on that bad boy."

Wasn't that the truth.

"Nice analogy," Paul grumbled, looking thoroughly disgusted.

"Ah, don't worry, Paulie boy," Casey teased, reaching over to pat his hand. "You're a definite fairground ride, too."

"I am?" He grinned wolfishly. "Which one?"

"The teacups," she snorted.

"Oh, pack it in, the pair of you," I snapped, annoyed with the entire situation. "You're acting like he's this terrible person when he's not. He's just . . . he was defending his sister who had been *terrorized*."

"Yeah, Aoif, but Mike didn't do it," Casey offered up. "He was just an innocent bystander."

"Oh, you mean the same way his sister was innocent. That didn't stop Ciara Maloney from cutting the poor girl's hair off, now, did it?"

"Get a grip, Aoife," Paul scoffed. "There's a big difference in giving someone a haircut and beating seven kinds of shit out of a person."

"Giving someone a *haircut*?" I balked. "Did I just hear that right? Listen, I'm not condoning what Joey did to Mike, because that was outright insanity. But I'm telling you right now that if anyone tried to hack my hair off with a pair of rusty scissors, then I would take leave of my senses."

"True," Casey reluctantly agreed. "I would lose my shit."

"Exactly," I pressed. "It would be the very last thing they did with scissors, that's for sure. And that's his baby sister that happened to," I added. "You've seen Shannon Lynch walking through the halls between classes; she like a mouse. She couldn't defend herself if she tried."

"So, because his sister can't defend herself, that gives him the right to use his fists to fight her battles?" Paul arched a brow, clearly unimpressed that I had a different opinion on the matter. "He's nothing but a thug. A hot-headed bully. One you should steer clear of."

"Care to say that to his face?" I heard myself toss back heatedly.

"No," Paul drawled in a sarcastic tone. "Because he would try to rearrange my face with his fists – like he already tried to do on several occasions, Aoife. Which is *exactly* the point I'm trying to make about the prick." He shook his head and muttered, "To be honest, I don't know how your father puts up with him at the garage. Tony must be a god honest saint to have stuck it out so long with that waste of space."

"He's a *good* worker," I was quick to point out. "Dad's always praising how dependable and punctual and hardworking Joey is, so maybe you don't know as much about him as you think you do."

"What's this?' Paul growled. "The I-heart-Joey-Lynch club?"

"Well, it sure beats the complain-about-him-until-you've-bored-everyone-to-tears club that you're the founding member of," I shot back, unwilling to back down.

"Why are you *always* defending him?" he demanded, tone laced with annoyance.

"Because you're *always* talking shit about him," I snapped back. "He's my friend, Paul. Deal with it."

"Christ." Paul narrowed his eyes. "If you still like the guy so much then what are you doing with me?"

"Good question," I snapped. "I've been asking myself that exact question a lot these days."

Paul reeled back like I'd struck him. "Are you serious?"

"Whoa, guys, everyone take a chill pill," Casey interjected. "Let's not have a fight over this."

"Who's fighting?" I snapped, very much in fighting form.

"Whatever," Paul grumbled. "That prick doesn't deserve this much airtime. The sooner he's expelled and out of this school, the better for all of us."

"It's so easy for you all to sit there and judge him," Podge erupted, as he shoved his chair back and pushed out of his desk. "When *not one* of you knows what that lad has to deal with. You don't have the slightest inkling."

"We all have shit to deal with, Podge," Paul argued, unapologetically. "That doesn't give any of us the right to walk around like a ticking time-bomb, and it doesn't give him the right to do it, either. He doesn't get a free pass to kick someone's head in every time he loses his temper."

"You've just proven my point exactly," Podge said. "You *don't* have a clue." He turned his disappointed gaze on me. "I thought *you*, of all people, would know better than to judge him."

"What?" I gaped at him. "Me of all people?"

"Don't pretend like you don't know, Aoife."

"I don't," I replied in confusion. "I *don't* know."

"Bullshit," Podge snapped. "You act like his friend, but I guess that's all it is, an act, because the minute the chips are down, you talk shit about him with the rest of them."

"Hey, back off," Casey warned, quickly coming to my defense. "Don't start on her just because your friend fucked up. She's not his cheerleader."

"You know what?" Podge growled, shaking his head. "I don't have time for this shit." Having said that, he shouldered both his and Joey's school bags onto his back and stormed out of the classroom.

Feeling like I had been sucker-punched in the gut, I quickly scooped up my things and hurried after him, ignoring protests from Paul, Casey, and the poor substitute teacher attempting to rein in the class.

"Podge, wait," I called after my redheaded classmate as he stalked off in the direction of the school exit. "Wait a minute, will you?"

"I'm not in the form, Aoife," was all he replied. Not turning around he pushed the glass doors open and walked outside into the latest downpour of January rain. "I'm really not."

"What did you mean back there?" I asked, falling into step alongside him, as he hurried away from the school. "About the crap Joey has to deal with?" I blew out a frustrated breath. "What crap?"

"Like you haven't figured out by now," Podge grumbled. "You're not blind, Aoife, and you're far from stupid, either."

"Humor me," I pleaded. "Come on, Podge, tell me what you meant."

"You've seen the condition he comes into school in," he snapped, losing his cool. "Don't pretend you haven't noticed the bruises, Aoife. Not when they're so fucking obvious that he can't hide them most of the time. Come on, girl, it doesn't take a genius to know that he's getting the stuffing knocked out of him when he's not at school."

And there it was.

It was something I definitely hadn't expected him to say, but in a weird, unsettling way, I also sort of had.

My mind wandered back to the scars I knew he bore beneath his clothes, and further back again, to an altercation I witnessed a couple of years back where, after losing the county final to the neighboring town, Joey had come to blows with who I presumed was his father at the back of GAA Pavilion carpark.

At the time, I'd put it down to his usual hot-headedness and the fact that Ballylaggin had been hammered in the game.

But now, recalling the way the bigger man had pushed and shoved at him before clamping a hand on the back of his neck before physically forcing Joey into the back of a car, it was becoming a lot clearer.

"Oh my god," I whispered, covering my mouth with my hand.

"Don't act so surprised," Podge accused. "He works with your father. Like you didn't know what's been going down."

"I didn't! Wait – Joey told you that?" I demanded, reaching out to grab ahold of his jumper. "He told you that his father is beating him?"

Pausing mid-step, Podge swung around and gave me a look that said *are you crazy?* "No, of course he didn't *tell* me," he spat, tone indignant. "In case you haven't noticed, he's a fair bit closed off. Joey doesn't tell anyone what happens in that house. I've heard enough rumors, and seen him come into school enough times with black eyes, to know that he has it a lot harder than you or that self-righteous asshole you call your boyfriend."

"Hey, that's not fair," I snapped, flushing. "I was trying to defend him back there."

"Yeah, sure you were," he sneered before walking off.

"I *was*," I argued, hurrying after him once more. "I don't have the same opinion of Joey that Paul has. I *don't*. I have my own mind, Podge."

"Well then maybe you should use it sometime," he shot back, "and maybe you should speak up a little louder for the lad, especially considering he's returned the favor a time or two for you."

"What?" I narrowed my eyes. "What's that supposed to mean?"

"Nothing," Podge bit out, upping his pace in his obvious bid to get away from me. "It means nothing at all."

"Where are you going with his school bag?" I called after him, pushing my damp hair out of my eyes, as the rain continued to hammer down on us.

"Taking it to him!" he shouted over his shoulder. "Wherever the hell he might be."

"Let me do it," I heard myself say, as I raced after him in the rain. "I can find him, Podge," I repeated, slipping Joey's bag off his shoulder and onto mine. "Let me do it."

He watched me with mistrustful eyes. "Why?"

"Because I want to."

"Why, though?"

"Because I just do, okay!"

"Fine." He eyed me warily. "You won't tell Joe what I said to you about his uh, his dad, will you? Because he'll lose his—"

"I won't," I promised, cutting him off. Not when I had every intention of having him tell me himself.

He wasn't at the garage with Dad, he wasn't at the GAA grounds, and he wasn't at any of the other local haunts I knew he frequented.

That only left one place.

His house.

The estate I lived on didn't have the best reputation, but it was Disneyland compared to the one he lived on.

With some houses on his street boarded up, and even more covered in graffiti, it was safe to say that Elk's Terrace had a definitive air of misery about it.

There was a burnt-out car at the far end of the dilapidated green near his house, close to where three ponies were roaming freely, grazing on the overgrown grass and weeds.

Jesus.

Inhaling a steadying breath, I rounded his graffiti-clad garden wall, walked up to the front door, and knocked loudly.

Several beats passed before the sound of key jiggling in the lock filled my ears.

A few seconds later, the door opened inwards, but only a crack. "Yes?"

"Hi," I said, smiling brightly at the young girl peeking through the crack in the door. *Shannon*, I quickly noted. "Is Joey here? I need a word with him."

She glanced behind her and then quickly shook her head. "He hasn't come home yet." Red-eyed and sniffling, her skittish gaze flicked to the school bag I was holding, and she slowly opened the door further. "Is that his bag?"

"Yeah," I nodded. "He left it at school. I'm just returning it."

The sound of raised voices drifted from somewhere behind her and she quickly reached for the bag. "Thank you for bringing it home for him. I can give it to him."

"That's okay," I replied, taking a step backwards, hand firmly clamped around the strap as I hoisted it onto my shoulder. "I can wait."

Something was off.

I could feel it in the air the moment she'd opened the door to me.

Podge's earlier words flashed through my mind, and I winced sympathetically, before quickly steeling my resolve.

"Like I said, I need a word with your brother," I added, offering her what I hoped was a warm smile. "I'm Aoife, by the way. Aoife Molloy. Joey works with my dad."

"Yeah," she whispered, keeping her head down as she clutched the door like it was the only thing holding her up. "I know who you are. You were at my Granda Murphy's funeral."

"Yeah, I was. And you're Shannon, right?" I knew that was exactly who she was. "Joey's little sister?" I had seen her around school many times since she joined BCS, but she kept to herself, never making eye-contact with anyone long enough to be noticed.

Looking at her now, it was hard to peg her for older than eleven. She was only a couple of years younger than me, but she had the body of a small child.

"Yes." Nodding, she kept her chin tucked down as she whispered, "I'm Shannon."

"I heard what happened at school today," I added softly, cringing when my eyes took in the sight of her hacked-up, ear-length bob. "I'm sorry that happened to you."

"It's okay," she croaked out. Her hands were shaking. In fact, she looked about two seconds away from passing out on the floor.

"Hey, are you okay?" I asked, tilting my head to the side in my bid to get her to meet my eye.

"Yes."

"You don't look okay." Concern rose to life inside of me. "You're as pale as a ghost."

More shouting filled the air, and I watched as she physically flinched. "You should go." Her voice was small and pleading. "Now. Please."

The door was yanked inwards then and a small blond boy grinned up at me. "Joey's friend," he said in delight. "The pretty girl."

"Hi, Ollie," I replied, smiling down at him. "I haven't seen you in a while. How have you been doing?"

"I'm okay," he replied, tone bright, seemingly oblivious to the very loud argument occurring behind the closed door at the far end of their hallway. "Are you here to play with Joey?" he asked them, all innocence and wide smiles.

"Ollie," Shannon warned in a shaky tone. "Go back inside."

"Yeah, I am," I hurried to say. "Is he here?"

"Uh-huh," Ollie replied, nodding dutifully, and causing Shannon to exhale a shaky sigh. "But he's getting in trouble right now. You wanna come in and wait for him?"

It was the look of pure terror in his sister's eyes that had me answering, "sure," as I took a cautious step inside.

"Joe's in big trouble again," Ollie explained gesturing with his small hand to follow him into the sitting room. "It's a bad one this time."

Bolting past me, Shannon hurried into the sitting room and scooped up a small bundle of what I first thought was a white blanket. Until the white blanket began to squawk and a small blond head popped out from behind said blanket.

"You have yourself a real cute baby on your hands," I said, eyes locked on the wriggling infant in her arms, the one I remembered from the funeral.

"No, no, no," she strangled out, as she rocked him in her scrawny little arms. "He's not *my* baby."

"That's Sean," Ollie explained, climbing onto the worn-looking couch and then patting the space next to him. "He's the newest one of us."

"He's our brother," Shannon clarified, as she tried to soothe the grizzly infant, who was refusing the bottle she was offering him.

"How old is he?" I asked, sinking down on the thread-worn cushion.

"Who, Sean?" Bouncing him in her arms, she tucked a blond curl behind his tiny ear and said, "He just turned two."

"Really?" I found it incredibly hard to believe that the infant in her arms was as old as two. He was dinky in size and reminded me more of a twelve-month-old.

"I've gots four brothers," Ollie added.

My eyes widened. "Four?"

"Yep, and one sister," Ollie added proudly. "Darren's the oldest, and then there's Joe, Shannon, Tadhg, me, and Sean."

"In case you haven't guessed; he's the one who can't keep his mouth shut," Tadhg interjected from his perch on the armchair opposite us. Flicking through channels with the remote control of the television in hand, he cast me a sideways glance before looking back at Shannon. "He's going to flip."

"Who?" I asked.

"Daddy," Ollie said at the same time as Tadhg said, "Joey," and Shannon said, "Nobody."

"Acting the big hard man at school," a dominant male voice roared, causing all of the children around me to flinch and cower. "You're lucky they're not going to the Gards with this. You'd be off the team permanently. Yeah, that's right; they've suspended you from the team, too."

"You think I give a shit about being kicked off the hurling team?" I heard Joey's strained laugh. "Get fucked, old man. That's your dream, not mine."

"Oh, you're still riled up, are ya? Don't worry, I'll knock that out of you, boy."

"What in god's name is wrong with the pair of you? Why do you always resort to using your fists? Why can't you stop being like this?" a woman's voice cried out. "Why do you have to resort to violence at the drop of a hat?"

Uncomfortable, I looked at his siblings, who were all dutifully ignoring the shouting coming from the other room.

"It's too much, Joey. I can't handle you anymore, I really can't."

"Handle me? You don't need to handle me. You don't need to do shit for me, not that you do anyway. I'm grand as I am. And I was trying to protect my sister, if you're so fucking concerned. She's going to end up topping herself if you don't get her out of that school. She can't take any more of them."

"And I can't take any more of your behavior!"

"Then throw me out."

"Don't fucking tempt me, boy."

"Get off him, Teddy!"

"Now, where the fuck is that sister of yours? She's got a hand in this."

A few moments later, the sitting room door was thrown open, and in walked a tall, formidable-looking man.

Their dad, I mentally noted, recognizing the very obvious resemblance he bore to the children littered around the sitting room.

I also instantly recognized him as one of the meaner, sleazier drunks that propped up the bar at work when I worked the afternoon shift on weekdays. He never ordered food, so I never had to personally serve him, but I always got the creepiest vibe from him.

"Who's this?" he demanded, balking at the sight of me sitting on his couch.

"This is Aoife," Ollie said proudly, patting my shoulder with his small hand. "She's my friend."

"Teddy, wait," a woman, who looked an awful lot like Shannon, called out, hurrying into the room after her husband. "Please, just wait . . . " Her voice trailed off when her eyes landed on me, and I swear I saw her sag in relief. "Oh, hello."

"Hi," I replied, quickly standing up. "I'm Aoife."

"Aoife," the mother repeated with a small nod of her head. Sliding the sleeve of her cardigan down in her attempt to conceal the cast on her arm, she forced a small smile and asked, "Are you friends with Shannon?"

Her husband snorted as if it was the most ridiculous thing he'd ever heard. "Take one look at her, Marie." His dark eyes roamed over me in such a way that I felt uncomfortable. "She's not here for the girl."

"Then who ..." the mother's voice trailed off for a brief moment before she nodded her understanding. "Oh, you're here for—"

"Me," an achingly familiar voice said. "She's here for me."

"Joey," I breathed, locking eyes on my furious-looking classmate as he stood in the sitting room doorway.

"What are you doing here, Molloy?" His tone was hard, his eyes blazing with barely contained frustration, as blood trickled from a cut above his eyebrow. "In my house?"

"You forgot your bag at school." I held it up by way of explanation, my gaze honing in on his disheveled hair and the collar of his t-shirt that had been stretched out of shape. "I figured you might need it back."

"You might as well toss that fucking thing away," his father sneered, and the stench of whiskey wafting from the man was as obvious as the smell of cakes in a bakery. "Fat lot of use he gets out of it."

"That was very kind of you," his mother was quick to interject, taking the bag from me with her good hand. "Wasn't that kind of her, Teddy?"

Uninterested, her husband grunted some semblance of a reply before snatching the remote out of Tadhg's hand. "Up out of my chair, ya little shit," he commanded, snapping his finger. "And bring me in my smokes."

I watched as the older child scowled up at his father in such a way that he reminded me of his older brother, but then quickly clambered out of the armchair.

"Come on, Ols," he grumbled, padding out of the room. "You can help me find an ashtray."

"It was nice to see you," Ollie chirped up at me, all brown eyes and innocence, before he climbed off the couch and hurried after his brother.

Yeah," I squeezed out, heart fluttering around nervously, as I watched the little guy hurry out of the room. "You, too."

Shannon, who looked like she had turned to stone on the mortal spot, blinked wildly before rushing from the room, mumbling something about Sean needing a drink as she went.

"Can I make you a cup of tea?" their mother offered, pulling on the sleeve of her cardigan, looking almost as uncertain as her daughter. *Almost as frightened.* "Or would you prefer coffee?"

"No, she's not staying," Joey answered instead, as he inclined his head towards the front door, never taking his eyes off me. "A word."

"I, ah, better ..." my voice trailed off as I watched the front door swing open and Joey stalk outside. "Go," I finished, offering his mother a small smile before stepping around her and moving for the door.

"Thank you for bringing his bag home," she called after me. "It really was very good of you."

"No problem." Offering her a hasty wave, I followed her son out of the house. "Bye."

The minute I had stepped outside and closed the front door behind me, Joey was on me.

"Who the fuck do you think you are?" he demanded in a hushed tone, clearly livid, as he paced around like a madman. "Coming to my home like this?" His green eyes blazed with a mask of anger, but I could see the absolute panic underneath, as his attention kept slipping to the front door behind me. "What were you *thinking* showing up here?"

"I was thinking that you forgot your bag and might need it," I tossed back before reaching a hand up to touch his face. "Did he do that to your eye?"

"Stay out of it," he bit out, snatching my hand up before I could touch him. "I mean it, Molloy." Once again masking his fear with his temper, he met my eyes with a look of pure fury and pushed my hand away. "Stay out of my face and stay out of my fucking life!"

"Listen to me." Closing the space he'd put between us, I reached for his hand, willing him to open up to me. "I know, okay? I get what's happening here. Your dad's a drunk, right?" With my thumb, I gestured behind me. "Gets a little handsy after a few too many glasses of Jameson?" I reached out to touch his shoulder. "Your back? Those scars—"

"You need to leave, Molloy," Joey seethed, chest heaving, as he quickly stepped out of my reach again. "Now. I'm not fucking around here." His gaze flicked to the house again and I could see the anxiety in his eyes. "You need to go," he snarled, stalking down the driveway. "You need to go now, Molloy," he added when he reached the garden wall. "Just fucking go. *Please*."

"I'm not going anywhere until you talk to me," I argued, not giving him an inch, as I stalked towards him and reclaimed the space that he had put between us.

The rain was pouring down on both of us, but I wasn't walking away.

Not now that I knew.

Not ever again.

I had a decent life, and a relatively stable home life. Sure, my father had a roaming eye, which mean that my parents' relationship was off more times than it was on, but neither he nor Mam were abusive to each other or to myself and Kev.

We didn't have a whole pile of money behind us, and we depended on social housing like most of the families on our estate, but we weren't lacking anything, and definitely not love. It was given unconditionally and came from an unlimited supply source.

Most importantly, they didn't beat us or starve us, and we weren't woken in the dead of the night to the sound of glass shattering or flesh pummeling flesh.

We weren't afraid to speak our minds or launch an opinion for fear of physical retaliation like his mother and siblings so obviously were.

"It's okay, Joe," I urged, imploring him to hear me, as I pushed my damp hair off my face. "I get it now."

And I did.

Suddenly all of the aggression and mood swings began to make sense.

The drugs.

The fighting.

The vicious way he attacked both Paul and Kevin when he thought I was under threat.

It was a like a raincloud had lifted in front of my eyes.

He wasn't violent by nature.

He was violent because he wasn't nurtured at home.

"I understand what's happening here, and I'm on *your* side."

"You don't know shit about what's happening here," Joey warned, backing up another step when I reached out to the darkening bruise on his cheek. "Don't touch me."

"Why not?" I closed the space between us once more, pinning him to the garden wall. I reached up and let my fingers graze over the cut on his brow. "Are you afraid I'm going to hurt you?"

"No," he strangled out, shaking from head to toe, as he physically strained his body away from me. "I'm afraid *I'll* hurt *you*."

His words threw us both.

"Hurt *me*?" I repeated and quickly shook my head. "All you've ever done is look out for me, Joey Lynch. You would never hurt me."

"I could," he argued back, running a hand through his soaked hair. "I might."

Wide-eyed and chest heaving, he watched me warily, waiting for my reaction.

Waiting for my rejection, I quickly realized.

"That's not going to happen." With my eyes locked on his, and my heart hammering wildly in my chest, I forced myself not to flinch. Not to turn away at the sight of his bruised face, or the dark circles under his eyes, as I whispered, "Because you're not him."

Joey stiffened. "You don't know that, Molloy. You don't know *me*. I break everything I care about. That's what I do. I fuck it all up."

My heart skipped about three dozen beats.

"It's okay to let yourself care about me, Joe," I whispered, knowing that I was treading on some very dangerous territory right now, but not having the self-control to fall back and retreat to safer surroundings.

Not when the only place I ever wanted to be seemed to be in the middle of one of his breakdowns.

"Don't do that." His voice was gruff, green eyes full of dangerous heat. "Don't look at me like I'm *that* guy, Molloy. Don't look for hidden meanings in the things I say. I'm not the guy for you." He shook his head and blew out a pained breath. "I will break this . . ." he paused to gesture between us, before adding, "Whatever this is; this warped little friendship we've formed over the years? I will fuck it up."

"But will you mean it?" I pushed, refusing to back off. "That's the important part."

"No." His green eyes narrowed on me, studying me with a sharpness that was entirely unnerving and exhilarating all in one breath. "I won't mean it, of course I won't fucking mean it, but that won't stop it from happening—"

His words broke off when I kissed him.

That's right, I lost my head right there in the middle of his street, threw caution to the wind, and slammed my lips to his.

His entire frame froze for a long moment, stiff and unmoving, and I briefly wondered if I had made a terrible mistake, but then he was kissing me back, twisting our bodies around so that I was the one with my back to his garden wall, as his lips moved against mine with an air of expertise that was truly rattling.

My breath came hard and fast, leaving me feeling almost faint, as I swayed against his tall frame.

He wasn't overly big or hugely muscular, even though I knew from watching enough of his fights that he was ridiculously strong.

Instead, he was lean, with muscles that were defined beneath his taut, tanned skin.

Reaching up, I wrapped my arms around his neck, holding on to this boy for dear life, as I kissed him back with everything I had inside of me.

This was our first kiss, and it wasn't the comet-hitting-earth moment I had anticipated from years of binge-watching unhealthy teen sitcoms.

It wasn't anything like what happened in the movies.

It was so much *more*.

This kiss was real, and raw, and gritty, and so full of unspoken emotion that I felt my legs shake from the pressure.

His arms came around my body, with one hand resting on my hip, as he knotted the other in my hair, kissing me back with an intensity that caused jolting shocks of pleasure to ripple through my core every time his tongue brushed against mine.

Drowning in both my senses and the rain hammering down on us, I allowed myself to be completely swept up in the moment, in him.

Nothing else mattered to me in this moment.

All I could see, feel, taste, touch was *him*.

He was everywhere.

Consuming me entirely.

I had three and a half years' worth of kisses with Paul, and a few other boys before him, to prepare me, but nothing could have prepared me for the feelings this particular boy evoked inside of me.

He could have had all of me right there in the rain and I wouldn't have raised a finger in protest. That was how deep the dangerous feelings I had developed for him went.

Joey kissed me like he was starving for me and no one else's lips could sate the hunger overtaking him. I knew the feeling and returned it unconditionally as I kissed him back with an insatiable hunger of my own.

With his lips never leaving me, he lifted me up with effortless ease and set me down on his garden wall. And then his hands were on my bare legs, his experienced fingers gliding over the smooth skin of my thighs, as he pushed them apart and stepped between them.

His hands were in my hair, his tongue in my mouth, his big body cemented to mine, all of his hard edges probing against my soft ones, and even though I knew I was a shitty person for not breaking up with Paul before kissing someone else, all I could think about was how epically *right* it felt to be with Joey.

This kiss was going to have consequences, I realized.

Huge, heart-stopping, feeling-igniting consequences.

Maybe you're the dangerous one

JOEY

I had whiplash from the crazy twists and turns this day had taken.

It had started with a fight with my dad, the middle involved a whole heap of trouble at school, and it was ending in a kiss.

Feeling Molloy's soft lips against mine, as she moaned into my mouth and pushed her body against mine, was entirely too much for me to handle in this moment.

I was reeling; completely fucking thrown by the girl whose hands were knotted in my hair.

Her scent, so fresh and addictive, invaded my lungs, taking me down harder than a punch from my old man ever could.

It's this scent you remember, my brain quickly recognized, *and this hair.*

With my heart racing wilder than any drug had ever provoked, I held her in my arms, fought the feeling of panic that was climbing up my throat, and allowed myself to *finally* stop fighting against the tide of feelings overcoming me.

The feelings that had been drowning me for five years.

When I saw her standing in my sitting room earlier, with that piece of shit leering at her like she was fresh meat, I all but took leave of my senses.

If I had more years on this earth, it still wouldn't be enough time to describe the depth of the fear I'd felt when I watched that bastard train his attention on her.

How I kept the head, I would never understand, but the urge to protect her had been so strong that my need to get her safely away from my father had eclipsed everything else in that moment.

She had power over me, and we both knew it. I'd tried for so long to do the right thing, to steer clear of her, to be a good person for once in my life. She'd caught me in a weak moment though, and my resolve had continued to crumble with every stroke of her tongue.

I couldn't think straight.

My mind came up blank and my body took over.

I couldn't think about the argument I had with my parents, or the suspension I was facing at school. Not my sister's bullies, or the shift at work that I knew I was late for.

I couldn't think about anything other than *her*.

Aoife Molloy consumed me to the point that I didn't feel like everything was completely fucked in the world anymore.

Excitement and fear thrummed through my body. As I allowed myself to feel something other than hopelessness, as I enjoyed the sensation of being inside of my own body, my own head, for once without needing to self-medicate first.

Dangerous fucking lips, I warned myself, *don't get your hopes up.*

Soaked to the skin from the rain pissing down on top of us, I felt a shiver rack through her body, and reluctantly forced myself to pull back. "Are you—"

"Don't even think about stopping," came her flustered reply, as she hooked her fingers into the waistband of my sweats and dragged me back to her. "I'm not shaking because I'm cold," she growled, wrapping her legs around my waist. "I'm shaking because you're making me horny, so stop talking and keep kissing me."

"Jesus," I muttered, finding her blunt-to-the-point-of-outspoken nature even more of a turn-on than usual. "Maybe you're the dangerous one."

"Maybe I am," she agreed, sliding a hand underneath the hem of my t-shirt. "God, you're so hard," she moaned against my lips, as her hand trailed over my stomach.

"My dick's a little further south, Molloy," I teased against her lips.

"Funny," she replied, "I was talking about your stomach, not the beast," and then she raised my t-shirt up a few inches, taking a good long look at what I had to offer. "Yeah, I was definitely talking about those abs."

"Like what you see?"

"What?" She grinned shamelessly. "I always check the product before I make any purchases."

"And?"

She blew out a shaky breath and nodded. "Oh, I've been sold on you for a long time now, Joey Lynch."

Her words did something to me, fucked my head up real good, and when she pulled me back into her embrace, and pressed her lips to mine, I couldn't see beyond her.

Tread carefully, the beating muscle in my chest commanded, *because if you let her in, if you let yourself fall for this girl, you'll never recover.*

Forget that shit, she's already in.

Keep her.

"Oh my god, I think he just got her pregnant," a female voice announced from somewhere behind us. "What did you expect? I told you he doesn't do relationships. Oh my god, hold up! Is that Aoife Molloy?"

Jerking away like my lips had burned her, Molloy flicked her gaze over my shoulder to where the annoying fucking girls' voices had come from. "Aw crap," she strangled out, clamping her thighs around my hips like a vice. "We are so busted."

For fuck's sake.

Clearing her throat, she said, "Uh, hey, Rebecca. Hey, Danielle."

I glanced back at my house and, for the first time in my life, I actually *wanted* to go inside.

Jesus Christ.

Biting back a pained groan, I dropped my head on her shoulder for a moment while I steeled myself for the shitshow that I had no doubt was about to unfold.

This is all on you

January 7th 2004

AOIFE

"Is that seriously Aoife Molloy I'm seeing, with Joey Lynch between her legs?" Rebecca announced in a voice laced with exaggerated admonishment, as she stood underneath a bright-pink umbrella, with her pal in tow. "And behind her boyfriend's back." Giving me a look of snooty superiority, she tutted softly. "On the wall outside his house, no less. Wow, classy girl, Aoife. Real classy."

"Oh, bore off, Rebecca," I growled, unwilling to wither under her snotty judgement. "We were kissing, not riding, so tone down the disbelief. It's not that deep."

"Joey?" Danielle choked out, and I stared in horror as tears filled her eyes. "What are you doing with her?"

"For fuck's sake," Joey muttered. Inhaling a deep, steadying breath, he stepped away from me and turned to face our classmates. "Girls," he acknowledged with a clipped nod, cheeks flushed, and lips swollen from all of our earlier kissing, as he took a stance in front of me. "What are you two doing around my neck of the woods?"

"Danielle was looking for you," Rebecca snapped, gesturing to her tearful friend. "She wanted to make sure you were okay after what happened at school. More fool her, I guess?"

"Yeah, well, I'm fine."

"Oh, yeah," Danielle cried out hoarsely. "We can see just how *fine* you are."

"Don't start," Joey said in a low, warning tone. "I didn't make you any promises."

"You had *sex* with me less than a week ago!" she practically screamed.

"And now you're . . . you're . . . " She shook her blonde head and glared at me. "What the hell, Aoife? You were supposed to be my friend! What are you even doing here?"

I *was?*

I thought we were more classmates and acquaintances than bosom buddies.

"Hey." Jumping down from the wall, I held my hands up. "I didn't know you had anything serious going on with him."

"We don't," Joey was quick to point out. "We have nothing going on, serious or otherwise."

"And I was just . . . " Trailing off, I shrugged. "Checking on him, too."

"Liar," Danielle screamed, face turning an unflattering shade of purple. "You saw us together the other night. You knew exactly what was happening between us."

"Did she?" Joey barked. "Well, that makes one of us."

"You have your own boyfriend to check on," Rebecca hissed, tone accusing, as she joined the fray and pointed a finger at me. "You do remember Paul, don't you?"

"Oh, pack it in, Becks," Joey sneered. "He's far from fucking perfect himself."

"Yeah, does Paul know what you've been up to?" Danielle demanded, planting her hands on her curvy hips.

"Not yet," I drawled calmly, when I felt anything but, resisting the urge to reach into my pocket and grab my phone. "But I'm sure that you'll be only too happy to tell him."

"Oh, you can bet your ass I will." She glared at me. "He's going to flip his lid."

"Bold of you to assume that I care," I shot back, groaning internally when I couldn't stop my mouth from verbally kicking my own foot.

Quiet, Aoife, you're in the wrong here. Now shush.

Narrowing her eyes, Rebecca planted her hands on her hips and glowered at me. "It's bad enough that you don't have any respect for your own relationship, but you could have spared a thought for Danielle's!"

"What relationship?" Joey demanded, throwing his hands up. "Because she sure as shit isn't in one with me!"

"Oh Joey," Danielle sobbed, pressing a hand to her chest. "How could you?"

"No, no, no, don't go there. Don't give me that *oh, Joey, how could you* bullshit," he snapped, shaking his head. "I told you, Danielle, I fucking *told* you that I wasn't interested in anything serious. I told you that it was a one-time thing and you said that you were fine with it!"

"A one-time thing?" She glared at him. "Have you forgotten about the other couple of dozen times?"

Ouch.

"Don't give me that shit," Joey was quick to counter. "I laid it all out for you, said I wasn't interested in anything more than one night, and you said that you agreed with me."

"Well, I lied," she cried out.

"Well, I didn't!" Clearly frustrated, Joey ran a hand through his soaked hair and hissed, "You came on to *me*, remember? You propositioned *me*, and I made my intentions perfectly clear. You knew that I was out of my mind that night. You knew I was unavailable. I was up-fucking-front with you, Dan, so these tears you're spilling are not on me."

"Have a heart, Joey," Rebecca snapped when her friend cried harder. "The girl has feelings for you."

"Then tell her to stop having feelings for me!" Releasing a frustrated growl, he pointed a finger at Danielle and hissed, "You *promised* you wouldn't do this."

"I know, but—"

"No buts," he snapped. "And no promises, either. I'm a free agent."

"You might be," Danielle spat, pointing a finger in my direction. "But she's not."

"What she is or isn't hasn't got a damn thing to do with either one of you," Joey sneered in a menacing tone. "So, why don't you both turn around and walk your asses out of here before this gets messier than it needs to."

"Who are you calling?" I blurted out, attention flicking to Rebecca, who had her phone pressed to her ear, expression smug.

"Hi, Paul, yeah, it's me, Becks."

My eyes widened.

"Yeah, so, I'm up Elk's Terrace, and I thought you should that I just saw your girlfriend, Aoife, with Joey Lynch."

Oh god, oh god.

"Uh-huh, that's right. Yeah, I legit just saw them scoring with each other."

"Jesus Christ," Joey groaned under his breath.

My mouth fell open. "What a bitch."

"Yeah, I swear," Rebecca said, grinning deviously. "No, I'm not lying. She was wrapped around him like ivy."

"Ugh." I dropped my head in my hands and groaned. It felt like my rolling stomach had fallen out of my ass, as I listened on helplessly.

What could I do?

Not deny it, that's for sure.

I'd been caught red-handed.

I planned on owning up to Paul anyway, and it would have sounded a hell of a lot better coming from my mouth than hers.

Yeah, because the instant Joey Lynch reciprocated my kiss, my feelings, I knew there was no going back to pretending.

"Oh my god, Joe," I groaned, screaming on the inside, as the realization of what I had done suddenly dawned on me. "I'm my father."

"What are you talking about, Molloy?"

"Dad," I choked out. "I'm him." I looked at Joey. "He's a cheater, I'm a cheater!" I threw my hands up in dismay. "We're both cheating apples from the same cheating tree. Ugh," I muttered, thoroughly distressed. "And now I'm no better than he is."

"Relax," Joey attempted to comfort me by saying, tone gruff. "It was a kiss, not an affair, Molloy. You're nothing like your father."

"Affair?" I stared at him, unblinking. "What do you mean, *affair*?"

He shrugged, clearly uncomfortable.

"Oh my god, you know, don't you?" I sucked in a sharp breath as my brain quickly twigged. "About the other women? What he gets up to? You know about my dad's affairs?"

Joey didn't respond, but he didn't deny it either.

"You knew?" I shook my head. "You've always known? And you didn't think to tell me?"

"It's not my business," he finally said, jaw clenched tight from the obvious tension that was emanating from him. Catching ahold of my arm, he led me slightly away from the girls before he continued speaking. "I work with the man. I'm not his keeper and I'm not your spy, either. I don't get involved in shit that doesn't concern me."

The rain was beating down on us, plastering his halo of dirty blond hair to his forehead as raindrops trickled from his brow to his nose and then his lips. Yet still, he remained absolutely rigid, eyes locked on mine.

"Don't make it more than it is, Molloy," he said in a heated tone. "It's an omission, not a betrayal."

"Well, it feels like one," I strangled out, looking up at him. "I feel betrayed."

Emotion flashed in his eyes before he quickly schooled his features. "Tony gave me a job, took a chance on me when nobody else would. My loyalties have always been with your father, not your mother."

"What about your loyalties to me?" I pushed the boat out by asking.

His jaw ticked. "That's not fair."

"What about me, Joe?"

"Molloy—"

"Oh my god, are you two having your first fight?" Rebecca interjected with a laugh. "Priceless. That didn't take long."

It was at that exact moment in time that a familiar blue Toyota Starlet came speeding up the street towards us.

Brakes screeching loudly, I watched as the passenger door flew open and Paul climbed out of his brother Billy's car.

Lovely.

Just fecking lovely.

"Is it true?" he roared, red-faced and raging, as he marched towards me. "Did you fuck her?"

"What?" Gaping, I shook my head. "No, I didn't sleep with anyone, calm down." Hurrying over to intercept him before anything happened, I placed a hand on his chest. "Paul, please, if you just give me a second to explain—"

My words broke off when he literally shoved me out of his way in his bid to reach my partner in this particular crime, intent on one thing only: evoking violence.

"You just couldn't leave her alone, could ya?" Paul roared, going chest to chest with his nemesis. "You had to have her. You *had* to mark her off your list."

"List?" Laughing darkly, Joey met his challenge head on, shoving him back with his chest. "The fuck are you talking about?"

"You had no right to touch her." Rearing an arm back, Paul punched Joey in the face. "You had no goddamn right."

Joey's head twisted sideways, and I held my breath, almost afraid to see what he would do in retaliation.

I didn't have to hold that particular breath for long, because in the blink of an eye, Joey had Paul speared to the road.

"Newsflash, asshole, your girlfriend kissed me," Joey snarled, pouncing on Paul like a lion would a gazelle, as his fists rained down on his face.

"Shut up, Joey," I groaned, dropping my head in my hands. "God."

"The truth hurts, Molloy," Joey seethed, laying into Paul. "Yeah, that's right, prick. Your girl over there made the first move."

"And let me guess; you weren't interested?" Paul roared back at him.

"Have you *seen* your girl?" Joey taunted. "Of course, I was interested. In fact, I was very fucking interested. Still am."

"Joey, stop taunting him – Billy, don't you dare!" I warned, only to curse in frustration when Paul's brother ignored me entirely and jumped into the fray.

"Get off my brother, ya dirty junkie—" Grabbing ahold of the back of Joey's t-shirt, Billy dragged him off Paul before knocking him to the ground and driving his boot into Joey's stomach.

Repeatedly.

Over and over.

Jesus.

"Oh my god, stop!" Danielle screamed, covering her face with her hands.

"Are you happy now?" I demanded, glaring at both girls, who were watching on in horror. "Look what you've done!"

"What *you've* done," Rebecca choked out shakily. "This is your fault, Aoife. This is all on you."

"Yeah," Danielle sobbed. "Look at what *you've* done!"

Yeah, I thought to myself, as I raced over to break up the fight, *I know.*

"That's right, ya little prick," Billy continued to taunt, as he held Joey's arms behind his back, rendering him essentially helpless, while Paul kicked and punched at him. "Not so fucking tough now, are ya?"

"Get fucked," Joey half-spluttered, half-laughed, as he grunted and heaved every time Paul's boot connected with his flesh.

Blood was flowing freely from his lip, but he didn't seem to notice or care, as he continued to taunt Paul. "No wonder you're pissed, lad. Letting a girl like that slip through your fingers."

"I'm going to kill you!"

Joey laughed. "You couldn't fight your way out of a paper bag, prick!"

"Stop it," I ordered, pulling at Billy's brick-shit-house-sized shoulders in my feeble attempt to get the older lad to release Joey. "Let go of him."

"Can't say I regret kissing her back, though." Joey spat out a mouthful of blood and grinned. "I'd have her mouth on me again in a heartbeat."

"Oh my god, Joe, stop taunting him!" I practically begged, stumbling backwards when Paul pushed me out of harm's way. "Paul, come on, I'm sorry, okay? I'm sorry I hurt you, but please just stop this."

"Screw you, Aoife," Paul snarled, socking Joey in the gut with his fist, looking angrier than I'd ever seen him. "You'll play the ice-queen card with me, dangling your virginity over my head like a fucking carrot, but the minute this piece of shit crooks his finger, your knickers come off. Is that it?"

"Oh my god, *nothing* like that even happened," I screamed back at him. "It was a kiss, okay. It was just a kiss."

"Nothing's ever just a kiss with him," Paul sneered, hitting Joey again. "I hope you enjoyed it, because when I get done with him, he won't have a face to kiss."

"Hey!" Just then a small, blond-haired boy came bounding out of the Lynchs' house, and rounded the garden wall, with a floor brush in hand. "Get off my brother!"

"Tadhg," Joey roared, chest heaving and eyes wild now, as he thrashed and tried to break free, the sight of his brother igniting his protective instincts. "Go back inside."

"I said get the fuck off my brother!" Tadhg screamed, ignoring Joey's words, as he swung the floor brush at the back of Paul's legs.

"Hey, don't touch him!" I snapped, when Paul roughly shoved Tadhg away. "He's just a little kid."

"Your brother's a scumbag with a serious learning problem, little man," Billy taunted the younger Lynch. "My brother and I are here to teach him a lesson that'll stick."

"How about I teach you a lesson?" Tadhg seethed, taking aim at Billy this time. "On how to fight fair." With that, the little guy rammed the handle of the floor brush into Billy's face. "And how to not be your brother's little bitch boy."

Blood sprayed from Billy's nose, and he quickly released his hold on Joey's arms. "Jesus Christ," he roared, cupping his nose with both hands. "You little lunatic."

Joey and Paul went crashing to the road once more, fists flying back and forth.

"Like that, did ya? Well, here's some more where that came from!" Yielding the floor brush around like he was Master flipping Splinter from the Teenage Mutant Ninja Turtles Tadhg hit him again, this time in the dick.

Falling like a sack of spuds to his knees, Billy cupped his junk and groaned, while the little guy went in for the kill, flaking him on the head with the brush.

The sound of Paul's promises of pain dragged my attention back to where he had Joey on his back, in the middle of the road, while he straddled his chest.

"You couldn't just let it go," Paul snarled. "You could have any girl you want – what am I saying, you've *had* every fucking girl you've ever wanted, but that wasn't enough for you, was it? You had to go and ruin her!"

"Give it all you've got, lad," Joey continued to laugh, as his head snapped sideways from the impact of Paul's fist, clearly exhausted from the hammering he'd just taken. "It's the only free pass that you'll ever get from me."

The sound of sirens filled the air, and flashing blue lights came into view.

"Oh my god, the cops!" I heard Rebecca call out, as the both of them legged it before the squad car reached us.

"Aw crap," I choked out, when my eyes landed on the Garda car coming towards us. "Stop it. Pack it in, the pair of you!" Rushing over, I grabbed at Paul's arm, only to stagger backwards, seeing stars, when his elbow made contact with my face.

"Ouch," I cried out, losing my balance from the brunt of the force, and landing on my arse on the road. Pain coursed through my cheek bone as the stinging sensation of tears filled my poor, wounded eye socket.

"Look at what you did, you prick!" I heard Joey roar. "Look at her."

"Jesus, Aoife," Paul was quick to shout, turning his attention back to me. "Are you alright?"

"I'm fine, I'm fine," I croaked out, holding a hand over my sore eye, as a horrible vibrating ache pounded inside of my head. "Just stop fighting."

"What's going on here?" a Garda demanded, marching into the fold, with two more following close behind him.

Great timing, I thought to myself sourly, *especially now the fight was over.*

Billy and Paul quickly went on the offence, giving the Gards their version of events, which just so happened to completely throw Joey under the proverbial bus.

"That's not how it happened at all," I argued to the female Garda, who was scribbling down notes in her little black notepad. "It was a huge misunderstanding."

"And then he threw the first punch," Paul reeled off, lying through his teeth, while Joey sat on the road, remaining stoically silent, not bothering to defend himself.

"And it's not the first time, either," Billy interjected. "He assaulted my brother before today, too."

"That's right," Paul agreed, nodding. "And he's literally just been suspended for breaking my friend's nose at school today during lunch."

"Liars," Tadhg spat, face turning beetroot red from temper. "*He* was holding him down while *he* . . ." he paused to point an accusing finger Paul, "kicked his face in."

"I was trying to protect my brother," Billy assured the Garda. "Paul's never been in trouble with the law in his life, sir, neither of us have. You can ask our father, Garda Superintendent Jerry Rice."

I narrowed my eyes. "Name dropping, Billy?"

"But this lad keeps bullying him."

"Bullying him?" I gaped. "Stop it, Billy."

"It's true. My brother has been the victim of a vicious smear campaign. I was afraid for his safety," Billy continued, tone convincing. "He's dangerous, Garda. I don't want to think about what could have happened to my brother if I hadn't been here to protect him from this lunatic."

After taking down a whole heap of notes, making a few phone calls, and cajoling between themselves for a few minutes, one of the male Gardas searched us all before finally settling on Joey, gaze stern and unyielding.

Aw crap.

"Shitting on your own doorstop, Lynch?" he asked, inclining his thumb towards the Lynch house. "Have to say, that's a new one for you."

"Yeah, well, what can I say? I like to keep things interesting," Panting breathlessly, Joey flopped back on the ground and held his wrists up. "Let's just get this over it."

I watched in horror as another Garda walked over to where Joey was sprawled out, and roughly dragged him to his feet. "Joseph Lynch, I am arresting you under Section 4 of the criminal law act on the suspicion of assault . . . "

"What?" Tadhg roared, eyes bulging, as he threw his hands up in outrage. "Are you serious? *They* were double-teaming *him*!"

"You are not obliged to say anything unless you wish to do so, but whatever you do say will be taken down in writing and may be given in evidence . . . "

"Mam!" Tadhg hollered then, bolting back towards his house. "Come out, quick! They're arresting Joey again."

"Wait, wait, wait," I blurted out, hurrying over to where they were placing handcuffs on my classmate. "This is all a misunderstanding."

"What's going on here?" I heard Joey's father demand, as he stood at the front door of their house, with a can of beer in one hand, the remote control for the television in the other, and a cigarette balancing between his lips. Squinting, he asked Tadhg, "Which one is that?"

"It's Joey," Tadhg cried out hoarsely, still clutching the floor brush, as he looked up at his father with a pleading expression. "Please, Dad, do something!"

"Your son is under arrest, Teddy," the Garda called back to him. "Under the—"

"Yeah, yeah, yeah," Teddy Lynch interrupted, waving the Gard off. "Don't give me that long spiel. What's he being accused of?"

"Assault," the Garda replied, looking a little uncomfortable.

"Assault, eh?" He turned his gaze on Joey. "Did ya do it, boy?"

"Sure did, *Daddy*," Joey sneered, as tension emanated from his body.

"Then do whatever the fuck you want with the little bollox," his father told the Gard. "Let the courts deal with him. Just don't expect me to come down to the station to bring him home like the last time." He turned back to Joey and called out, "Do ya hear that, ya little fucker? Don't you be phoning your mother up to come save ya, either. You can clean up your own mess this time."

With my mouth hanging open, I watched as his father hauled a tearful Tadhg back inside and closed the door behind them.

I wasn't the only one stunned by his father's reaction, because the Gard leading Joey to the car shook his head and muttered something unintelligible under his breath.

"Wait," I blurted out, jumping into action, as I hurried to intercept them. "Garda, please, you don't understand. He didn't start this."

"Save your breath, Molloy," Joey interrupted, as he was walked compliantly to the car. "It doesn't matter."

"No, no, it does, it does matter," I argued, watching helplessly as he was bundled into the back seat. "Joe—"

The car door slammed shut, cutting me off, and I looked on, helpless, as resigned green eyes stared back at me.

"Joe," I whispered, pressing my hand to the glass.

I watched as he sucked in a sharp breath before turning away from me, jaw set in a hard line, as another Garda climbed into the backseat alongside him.

The other two Gardaí climbed into the front seat and then they were driving away, taking him with them.

This time, the tears filling my eyes weren't caused by my throbbing eye socket.

Spinning around to glare at Paul who was walking back to the car with his brother, I called out, "Are you proud of yourself?"

"Don't you dare talk down to me," he seethed, swinging back to point a finger at me. "This is on you, Aoife. None of this would have happened if you weren't sneaking around behind my back."

Furious, I stalked towards him and shoved at his chest. "Listen here, you big bastard, I might be in the wrong for kissing him, and I'm sorry for hurting you, but what I did pales in comparison to what you just did."

"You cheated on me!" he roared in my face.

"It was just a kiss!"

"Maybe physically that's all it was, but you've been having an emotional affair with him for years!"

"Paul."

"He got what was coming to him." With a look of utter contempt etched on his face, his gaze trailed over me, and his lip curled up in disgust. "And so did you, slut."

"Slut?" I laughed bitterly. "Oh my *god*, I am so glad I didn't lose my virginity to you."

"Nah," he roared, losing his cool. "Because you were saving that up for him, weren't ya? You wouldn't let the fella you've been with for four years go near you, but you're more than willing to be a whore for a junkie!"

"Don't be so ridiculous, Paul—"

"He'll have you on your back with his dick inside you before the week's out," he warned, face red and eyes bulging with temper. "And then you'll be old news to him. Just like Danielle and all of the others. He'll sack you off once he's had his fill of you, and when that day comes, because it *will* come, don't even think about coming crawling back to me."

"I'd rather join a convent than ever let you touch me again, you big prick," I called after at him.

"That's unfortunate," he tossed over his shoulder, as he walked back to his brother's car. "Because once Joey Lynch is done ruining you, not even the nuns will have you."

Willful girls and withering willpower

January 28th 2004

JOEY

The original punishment I received for fighting with Mike Maloney at school had initially started as a week's suspension but had quickly escalated into an extra month once the principal caught wind of my arrest.

Cautioned by the Gards and given a slap on the wrist for the fight I had with Ricey outside my house, I had been *excused* from school until after the February midterm. I was told to return with a new attitude or not return at all.

Fuck them.

They could keep their school.

I didn't want to go back there anyway.

The place was full of snakes and liars.

My only regret about the whole ordeal was that I wasn't at school to protect my sister when she needed me to. And judging by the number of days Shannon had come home in floods of tears since my suspension, it was safe to say that she needed a *lot* of protection.

After all of the drama and tears with Danielle, I had decided to put my dick into semi-retirement, needing another girl bitching at me like I needed a hole in the head.

It didn't stop me from thinking about Molloy, though.

No, she lived rent-free in my head.

Same as always.

The emotion on her face as she watched the Gards take me away that day was sobering.

She cared a hell of a lot more than was good for both of us, and I couldn't handle it.

What she witnessed that day was a small preview of what being with me entailed.

Of how bad a guy like me would be for a girl like her.

A train wreck.

Disgusted with myself for barreling over a line I had vowed never to cross, I forced myself to blank her out of my head, something that was a lot harder to do now that I'd had her mouth on me.

With Tom Petty's 'Free Fallin'' drifting from the radio at work, I shook my head to clear my depressing thoughts. Wiping the oil from my already stained hands with a rag, I reached for the socket wrench that I'd been using to replace the spark plugs on a '97 Golf. Setting it back on the rack with all of the other tools, I locked the car and tossed the keys in the office before grabbing a sweeping brush.

Alone to clean the place up – my penance for once again getting into trouble with the law – I quickly tidied up before switching off the lights and letting myself out the back door of the garage.

I was bolting the door when a familiar voice came from behind me. "So, this is where you've been hiding."

Stiffening, I paused with the key in the lock before forcing my body to relax. "I don't hide, Molloy."

"Well, apparently, you don't call, either," she drawled in the sarcastic tone of voice that I was so used to sparring with.

"Your dad's not here."

"I know." Turning around, I found her leaning against the side of the building, with her arms folded across her chest. "I didn't come here to see my dad."

"Then what did you come for?"

"You."

"What's wrong, Molloy?" I asked, lingering when I knew better. The sensible thing to do would be to walk away from her, but I never seemed to have much sense when she was near.

Clad in dark jeans, a white puffy jacket, a grey scarf, and matching wooly hat, she looked every inch the good girl I knew she wasn't.

"You missing me at school or something?"

"Or something," she replied, not giving me an inch. "So, why didn't you call, Joe? It's been three weeks."

My gaze flicked to the small bruise under her left eyes that she was still sporting, and a pang of guilt churned in my gut. I quickly masked it with indifference. "Why would I call?"

"Again with this bullshit?" She rolled her eyes, not buying the crap I was attempting to sell her. "Answer me."

I shrugged. "I didn't have time."

"Oh, yeah," she drawled. "Because you're *so* busy these days, what with being suspended from school *and* from the hurling team."

"Clearly, I have less time on my hands than you have. Skulking around town in the dark?" I gestured around us. "How'd you get here, Molloy?"

"I used these remarkable new inventions called feet."

"Funny," I deadpanned. "How are you getting home?"

"Believe it or not, the same remarkable inventions can be used to go in two directions."

Yeah, that wasn't happening.

"Come on." I shook my head and stepped around her. "I'm walking you home."

"Don't do me any favors," was her smart-ass response, while she fell into step beside me.

"I'm not," I shot back. "I'm doing your father a favor."

I heard her grumble the word *dickhead* under her breath and I had to bite back a smile.

"Move your ass, Molloy. I have places to be when I get done babysitting your ass."

"Oh, you mean the same ass you enjoyed feeling up outside your house that day?"

"That was a slip."

"Yeah," she agreed. "A slip of *your* tongue in *my* mouth."

"I meant figuratively," I told her, pulling my hood up to hide my amusement.

"Which you displayed literally," she huffed, before adding, "So, when are you coming back to school?"

"After the midterm next month," I replied, shoving my hands into the front pocket of my hoodie. "How's it going over there?"

"Oh, you know," she replied breezily, waving a hand around in front of her. "Pariah number one, meet pariah number two."

"That bad, huh?"

"Ah, it'll blow over once the dust settles," she said with a resigned sigh. "It's only a bit of hazing."

I frowned. "From Paul?"

"And the delightful Danielle, who's still holding on to her grudge with a death grip." Smirking, she cast me a sideways glance. "You sure caused some damage to her pride with your dick, Joe."

"Yeah, well ... " I shrugged, not having a fucking clue of how to answer that. "What can I say?"

"You could explain what you were thinking," she challenged, and I didn't miss the bite in her tone. "Of all the girls in school that you could've messed around with that night, you had to pick the grade-A clinger."

"Yeah, well, she wasn't my first choice that night," I heard myself admit. "If I recall correctly, my first choice was taken."

Stopping in her tracks, she turned and looked up at me. "She's not taken anymore."

"Are you serious?" My eyes widened. "Rebecca's single now?"

Molloy's eyes narrowed. "You dick."

"Relax," I laughed, narrowly avoiding a side swipe. "I'm only messing with you."

"Not funny."

"So, you're finally finished with Paul the prick?"

"Yep."

"For good?"

"Unless hell freezes over."

"Good, he was a prick."

"So you've said a time or twenty." Falling into step alongside me once again, she nudged me with her elbow and asked, "So, what's happening here, Joey?"

Nudging her back gently, I said, "You tell me, Molloy."

She exhaled a ragged breath, causing the cold night air to expel from her lips like a puff of smoke. "You're not going to make this easy for us, are you?"

"No." I shook my head. "No, I'm not."

"Fine. How's this for easy? I like you," she came right out and declared, and fuck if my heart didn't pound in my chest in response. "And before you start with all of your bullshit denials, I *know* you like me back," she was quick to add. "It stands to reason that if we both like each other – which we *both* do . . . " She paused to narrow her eyes and point a warning finger in my face. "Then shouldn't we, you know, continue liking each other on an exclusive basis?"

Slowing my feet to a stop, I tilted my head to one side, and watched her. "Are you propositioning me, Molloy?"

Blowing out another shaky breath, she closed the space between us. "That depends."

"On what?" My tone was low and gruff, and when I felt her hand entwine with mine, I couldn't stop the shiver that racked through me.

"On what you do next," she whispered, leaning up on her tiptoes to press a soft kiss to the curve of my jaw.

Fuck.

This girl.

Pulling back slightly, she locked her green eyes on mine. "You're not running." Leaning in, she pressed another soft kiss to my cheek, lingering a little longer this time. "That's always a good sign."

Jesus.

"Molloy," I half-growled, half-groaned, as she continued to blow my world apart with soft, featherlight kisses to my cheek, getting closer and closer with each one. "It's a bad idea."

"Don't worry," she said in a soft tone, as she reached up and stroked her thumb over my cheekbone. "It'll be safe with me, Joe."

"What will?"

"Your trust."

My survival instinct kicked into gear, demanding I ward this girl off because she was getting way too close to my weak spot. "You think I trust you?"

"Maybe not yet." She cupped my face in between her hands, pressing me to look at her, and Jesus, she took the air clean out of my lungs with that move. "But you will."

Forcing myself to hold my breath and not pant breathlessly like a fucking tool, I absorbed every sensation that trickled through my body, knowing full well that no one had ever affected me like this girl.

"I see you, Joey Lynch," she continued to say, stroking her nose against mine.

"Yeah," I replied in a gruff tone, "I see you too, Molloy."

"No." Shaking her head, she shifted closer, pressing her body flush against mine. "I mean that I *see* you."

My heart thundered wildly in my chest, though on the outside I didn't move a muscle. "If you really saw me, the *real* me, you'd be running by now."

A sad smile pulled at her lips. "You really believe that, don't you?"

I didn't answer.

Didn't need to.

She already knew that she'd hit the nail on the head with that statement.

"You're tired of being alone," she whispered against my lips. "You're tired of being let down." She kissed me again. "Of being hurt."

"Stop," I warned, tensing. "Don't try to psychoanalyze me. Don't play those games with me, Molloy. I don't fucking like them," I added, feeling my walls go flying back up at a rapid pace. "You don't know shit about me, so back the hell off."

"I think I do know you," she argued right back, unwilling to unlock her hold on me, so that I could get some much-needed breathing space. "I think I've finally figured you out."

"Bullshit." Running a hand through my hair in frustration, I jerked away from her touch, feeling completely naked around this girl. "So, you met my family once and think you know it all. You saw a few scratches on my back. Big deal. You don't know shit, Molloy. Not a goddamn thing – stop it!" I warned again, holding a hand up as I backed the fuck away. "Don't look at me like that!"

"Like what, Joe?"

Her voice was soft, her eyes warm, as she closed the much-needed space I'd put between us.

"Hmm?" Reaching up, she cupped the back of my neck. "Don't look at you like you matter?"

With a sharp tug, she dragged my face down to hers and pressed another hot kiss to my lips.

"Because you do."

She kissed me again, harder this time.

"You matter to me, Joey Lynch."

"I shouldn't," I strangled out, forcing my body to remain rigid and not fold into her like a huge part of me wanted to.

"And yet you still do," she whispered, knotting her fingers in my hair. "And what's more is that I matter to you, too." She smiled. "And it scares the hell out of you."

"You don't mean shit to me," I desperately tried to convince the both of us, as my chest heaved. "I don't care about you, Molloy. I never have and I never will."

"You're a terrible liar," was all she replied before crushing her lips to mine.

My words were swallowed up when she pressed her lips to mine, and I didn't even try to resist her this time. I couldn't if I wanted to.

She ran her hands through my hair, and I was thoroughly fucked.

She gently held on to my hips, drawing me closer, as her tongue slid into my mouth.

She was just so fucking sexy.

My hands shot out of their own accord, cupping her rosy cheeks, as I kissed her back with a tenderness that I didn't know I possessed.

No one had ever touched me with this level of affection before.

I could feel how much Molloy cared, it was emanating from her lips, and that made me want to do better, be better, straighten my shit out and be the fella she deserved.

"You need to run."

She shook her head. "I don't run."

"Run," I desperately urged. "Run, Molloy."

"I'm staying right here," she whispered. "With you."

"Molloy."

"I know who you are," she whispered against my lips, taking the lead when I physically couldn't in the moment.

I wasn't seeing straight, couldn't fucking think straight, as a concoction of God only knew what floated through my veins, and yet there she was, crystal clear in front of me, making the rest of the haze, of the whole fucking world, just fade away.

"The quintessential lost boy." Her lips grazed mine as she spoke. "Don't worry, Peter Pan, I'll be your Wendy."

I kissed her.

Shouldn't have done it, knew it was a terrible fucking idea, but still, that didn't stop me. Knowing how jinxed I was couldn't change my mind anymore, either.

I was just too fucking weak to resist the girl a second longer.

Shivering against my will, I let her control me, gave her the power to hurt me worse than my family ever could.

When she kissed me like that, I couldn't take the vulnerable way it exposed me. Like a sheep baring its neck to a wolf, I went willingly, giving it all up to her, knowing that she could hurt me beyond repair.

Oh Jesus.

It was bad.

It was dangerous.

I was the very worst person a girl like her could get tangled up with, and still, she clung to me like I hung the goddamn moon.

I needed to stop it.

And I would.

As soon I summoned up enough willpower to stop kissing her.

That might take a while, the beating muscle in my chest warned.

The One-Word Game

February 20th 2004

AOIFE

"Then."

"He."

"Teased."

I clutched the pillow beneath my head and whispered, "Her."

"Clit."

My legs shook violently. "With."

"His."

"Oh my god."

"Tongue, Molloy." Joey's head poked up from beneath my duvet. "He teased her clit with his *tongue*."

"Oh my god, you can't just stop like that!" I groaned, reaching a hand between my legs to fist his hair. "Get back down there, dammit."

He laughed softly and then my eyes rolled back when I felt his lips back there, his tongue snaking out to taste and tease me in ways I never knew a tongue could make a girl feel.

"I'm, uh . . . " Hips jerking violently, I felt my toes curl up to the point of pain, as white-hot flashes of heat pulsed through me. "Oh shit, Joe."

"Ride it out, Molloy," he coaxed, using his fingers and tongue to touch me in ways that made my body burn and my back arch off the mattress. "Fuck my tongue, baby."

Baby.

Oh Jesus . . .

Clenching my eyes shut, I did exactly that.

*

"You're sort of a babe, Joey Lynch," I teased a little while later, as I watched him climb out of my bed and slip on his grey school trousers. "Has anyone ever told you that?"

"It's definitely a first for me."

Yeah, me too.

"You're staring," he pointed out in his gruff tone, as he shrugged on his now rumpled shirt. "What's up?"

I arched a brow. "So?"

"More than normal," he replied, focusing on re-buttoning his shirt – and stealing from me the glorious image of his bare chest. "Let's have it."

I shook my head. "I'm just thinking."

His gaze flicked to mine. "Sounds dangerous."

You're dangerous.

"Nothing." I flopped back on my bed and sighed. "It doesn't matter."

Releasing a low growl, he closed the space between us. "When a girl says it's nothing, it's never nothing." Sinking down on the edge of my bed, he rested his hands on either side of me and leaned in close. "So, I'll ask again; what's up, Molloy?"

"I'm just thinking about Paul," I admitted with a sigh.

"Nice," he deadpanned. "How's that going for you?"

"Not like that," I grumbled, slapping his arm. "I'm thinking about something he said."

"What did he say?"

"He warned me that you would have me on my back with your dick inside me within a week." Pulling myself up on one elbow, I used the other to gesture to my very naked body beneath the covers. "Um, hello?"

Joey smirked.

"It's not funny, Joe," I huffed. "He said that you would sack me off once you've had your fill of me, and not even the nuns in the convent would take me in."

He threw his head back and laughed.

"Gee, thanks for the reassurance," I grumbled, flopping back down. "I feel so much better now, while I lay naked in a puddle of cum."

"The nuns in the convent wouldn't take you whether I was on the scene or not," Joey laughed, peeling my hands away from my burning face. "Remember Jesus is always watching, Molloy. He sees what you do to yourself with those fingers when you're alone at night."

"Oh, fuck off, you turncoat," I grumbled. "I told you *that* in confidence."

"And I'm so grateful you did," he shot back. "The visual keeps me company when I'm alone with *my* hands at night."

"Okay, that's kind of hot," I admitted, grinning wolfishly up at him.

"Listen, you need to relax and put that prick's bullshit predictions out of your head," he said then. "Because that's all they are, bullshit."

"Yeah?" I blew out a breath. "Really?"

"Really," he agreed, leaning close to press a hot kiss to my mouth. "Besides, it took me three weeks to get you naked, not one like he predicted." Winking, he added, "and it's my fingers and tongue I've been putting inside you, not my dick, so that just shows what lover boy knows."

I narrowed my eyes. "Joey."

"I better get going," he laughed, clearly unsympathetic to my cause. "Before your father gets suspicious and starts wondering why I've been late for work every evening this week."

I smiled sweetly up at him. "Tell my dad that you prefer servicing his daughter than the cars in his garage."

"Yeah, because that would go down well." Frowning, he added, "I've never done that before, you know? Skipped work or been late for a girl. You're becoming a real bad habit, Molloy, and a bad influence, with it."

"Coming from the boy who can scale the side of a two-story house better than a cat," I called out, watching as he tossed both his hurley and helmet out of my bedroom window and onto the shed roof below, before throwing his school bag after them.

"Don't be joining any convents on me now, ya hear?" Joey said, swinging his leg over the ledge. "Contrary to your ex's predictions, I'm not quite ready to sack you off yet."

"Ha-ha-ha," I deadpanned. "Funny."

"I'll be seeing ya, Molloy," he added with a cheeky wink.

And then he was gone.

Honor restored

February 23rd 2004

AOIFE

Late Monday night, when I had bored myself to tears with homework, I decided to change it up by going downstairs and annoying my parents.

Unfortunately for me, the members of my family were in similar mischievous form.

"Well, would you look at Lady Muck herself," Mam said the minute I walked into the sitting room, as she turned down the volume on the TV control, and gave me her full attention. "What happened, Aoife, love? Did your mattress finally spit you out?"

"Ha-ha." I rolled my eyes. "Very funny, but no, nothing so dramatic. I was studying."

"With books?" Kev tossed out from his perch on the couch.

"Yes, Kev, with actual books," I shot back, flopping down on the couch next to him. "Don't act so surprised. I can open a book, you know."

"Ah, but can you read the inscription inside?"

"Don't ye be teasing my little pet," Dad interjected, from the other side of the room, where he sat with Mam in their matching armchairs. "How are you, Aoife, love?"

"Daddy's girl," Kev fake coughed.

"I'm good, Dad," I shot back with a smug grin. "How was work?"

"Ah, grand, love," he replied, resting his slipper-clad feet on the coffee table. "Young Joey was in flying form this evening."

I bet he was.

I grinned. "That's nice."

"Did you hear about our Aoife and Paul breaking up?" Kev interjected then, digging me in the thigh with his foot.

"What did I tell you about touching me with those hooves?" I snapped, batting his foot away with a cushion.

"I heard something about that alright," Mam replied, no doubt having heard it from Katie's mother next door. "A few weeks ago now, isn't that right, Aoife?"

"Yep."

"Really?" Dad's eyes widened. "You never said anything, Aoife, love."

"Oh, um, yeah," I replied, huffing out a breath. "Well, there's not much to say. It's dead in the water."

"For now," Kev snickered.

"Forever," I corrected, smacking him over the head with the cushion. "Asshole."

"Ah, don't you worry, pet," Mam coaxed, setting down her knitting. "I'm sure he's already planning on how to win you back as it stands."

"He'd be flogging a dead horse," I replied, narrowing avoiding a cushion to the head from my brother. "We're done, Mam."

"Sure they'll be back together again in no time," Dad said, turning to look at my mother for help. "They're on and off like the weather, those two."

"Not this time, I reckon," Kev taunted. "I don't think your darling Aoife is too upset about the breakup, either?" He winked knowingly as he climbed to his feet and wandered out of the room. "Isn't that right, Aoife?"

"That's *right*, Kevin," I replied, glaring at his retreating back. "I couldn't give a flying fu—"

"Fig," Mam quickly interjected. "Couldn't give a flying fig, Aoife."

"One of those, too," I shot back with a smirk. "He can go to hell."

"Well good," Dad said with a supportive nod. "He was a right little bollox, Trish, wasn't he?"

Mam laughed. "He was a bit of one, alright, Tony."

"A right uppity little fucker."

"Sure what would you expect from a Garda superintendent's son?"

"That's true, love. To be honest, it used to stand the hair on the back of my neck when you'd bring him over to the house," Dad admitted with a rueful expression. "I was afraid of my life that you would take him into the shed and expose me."

"Ah, here now, Tony," Mam chuckled. "I doubt the Gards would come knocking on the door over a few bottles of home-brewed poitín."

"You'd never know, love," Dad mumbled. "You'd never know."

"So, any new love interests, sister dearest?" Kev asked when he returned a moment later with a bowl of cereal. "Any short-tempered, would-be mechanics in your sights?"

"What's that now?" Mam's ears pricked up. "You've got a new boy-friend already?"

"Yes," Kev mused. "She sure does, Mam."

"No, I don't," I bit out, resisting the homicidal urge I had to throttle my brother. "Kev's just being a little shit-stirrer."

"Oh, come on," he laughed. "It's so obvious."

"What is?"

"Nothing," I strangled out.

"Aoife and Joey."

"Kevin!" I hissed, red-faced. Joey and I were trying to be discreet, and up until now, I thought we had been doing a great job. Apparently, nothing got past my brother, though.

Nosey fucker.

"Joey?" Dad's eyes widened. "My Joey?"

"I think that you'll find he's more Aoife's Joey than yours, Dad," my brother sneered. "At least, that's what I've heard at school."

Oh, you are a dead man.

"Those rumors are a bunch of crap," I choked out, lying through my teeth. "And you, being my brother, should know better than to believe them."

"What rumors?" both Mam and Dad asked in unison.

"There was a fight," I blurted out of nowhere.

"A fight?" Dad's frown matched my brother's. "What fight?"

I looked to Kev to help me, but he came up with an empty shrug.

So much for twins being able to read each other's mind.

My one was a dud.

Thinking on the spot, I quickly reeled off what I hoped was a generic, watered-down version of the truth. "It happened a while back. Remember that black eye I got after Christmas? Well, it didn't happen from falling off Casey's rollerblades like I told you guys."

Mam rolled her eyes. "Obviously."

"What happened to you?" Dad was quick to demand. "Did someone hit you?" His eyes narrowed. "Did Joey—"

"No, no, Jesus, no, Dad," I quickly appeased. "Joey never laid a finger on me." *Well, none I didn't beg him to.* "Basically, Paul was saying a few shady things about me around the place." *Like slut. And whore. And cock tease.* "And when Joey heard about it, he pulled him up on it." Shrugging, I added, "For your benefit, apparently. You know, since I'm your daughter, and he has a lot of time for you ever since you took him on at the garage. That's why Joey got arrested for fighting early in the new year. Remember?"

Dad nodded. "I do."

"Yeah." I blew out a shaky breath. "Well, anyway, I got the black eye from Paul when I tried to break up their fight. In his defense, it *was* an accident," I begrudgingly admitted. "But once the rumor mill got wind of Joey sticking up for me, people started gossiping about us, putting two and two together and coming up with five." I blew out a breath. "Yep, that pretty much sums it all up."

Kev snorted and then quickly buried the sound with a cough when I gave him a look that threatened violence. "Yeah, that sounds about right."

Dad stared at me for a long moment before blowing out a breath. "Well, I hope Joey gave that bollox a good stuffing."

"What was he saying about you, love?" Mam asked, concern etched on her face. "Would you like me to phone his mother, because I will. I'll give her a good piece of my mind—"

"No, Mam, it's grand," I hurried to say. "Paul was just salty because I wouldn't, well . . ." I shrugged. "Because I wouldn't . . ."

"Have sex with him," Kev offered dryly. "He was pissed because Aoife wouldn't have sex with him after four years of stringing him along and treating him like an afterthought."

"I didn't string him along," I snapped. "And it was three and a half years, not four."

Kev cocked a brow. "*Sure* you didn't."

"Fine," I reluctantly conceded. "Maybe there is a teeny tiny bit of truth to that statement, but that doesn't mean that I have to—"

"Lay on your back and spread your legs for him?" Kev shook his head. "Because that's what Paul thinks you're doing for Lynchy."

"More lies," I bit out, glaring at my brother.

"Kevin," Dad barked. "Don't be saying those kinds of things in front of your sister."

"What kinds of things?"

"You know," Dad mumbled, flustered. "Sex type things. She's too young for that sort of talk."

"She's the same age as me."

"Still," Dad huffed, looking incredibly uncomfortable. "It's not right, son."

"Was that it, Aoife?" Mam asked me. "Paul was making up stories about you?"

I shrugged. "Pretty much."

"And there's no truth to the rumors about Joey?"

"None at all," I lied.

"Well, I never." Dad looked to Mam and shook his head. "Fair play to young Joey, having my back like that."

"Yeah," Kev drawled, tone laced with sarcasm. "Let's all raise a glass to the honorable Joey Lynch."

"What a good lad." Dad beamed at my mother. "Defending my daughter's honor."

Kev snorted again, and, this time, he didn't even bother to hide it. "I'm off to bed."

"Yeah," I squeezed out, as the image of Joey's head between my legs filled my mind. "My honor's restored."

Blue eyes and blue balls

March 4th 2004

JOEY

I ended up being almost a half an hour late for work on Thursday evening, the fourth time I'd been late in the past five weeks, because I was too weak to resist stealing an extra twenty minutes under the sheets with Molloy.

Obviously, I couldn't tell her father that, so when he asked about what kept me, I reeled off some bullshit about hurling.

Tony didn't bat an eyelid when I fed him the line that I'd rehearsed all the way from his daughter's bed to his garage.

It was similar to the line I fed him last time, and the time before that – and the time before that.

Tony never questioned me because he *trusted* me.

And I was the lying piece of shit going behind his back, and against his wishes, by messing around with his daughter.

For the past five fucking weeks.

Jesus, I was a piece of shit.

For the rest of the evening, we worked alongside each other in mostly companionable silence.

I didn't have the stomach to pretend with him.

No, because lying to this particular man was something that could never sit well with me.

"Are you alright there, Joey, son?" Tony finally breached the silence when he found me out back having a smoke after I had finished up work.

"Yeah, Tony," I muttered, kicking gravel with my boot, as I stood in the rain.

His eyes flicked to the butt in my hand and a look of resigned disappointment washed over his features. "I hope that's a rollie you're smoking, boyo, and nothing stronger."

"Isn't it always" I lied, exhaling deeply.

"How are you supposed to hurl when you're poisoning yourself with those things?"

The question wasn't how I was supposed to play hurling; it was how was I supposed to survive if I didn't.

"Ah, you know me, Tony." Stubbing it out, I quickly slid the blunt back into the pocket of my work trousers before my boss lost his shit on me. "You can't kill a bad thing."

He looked at me for a long moment and then shook his head. "Well, it's almost nine. You better get on home, lad, before your mother sends out a search party for you. You've school in the morning."

It didn't matter what time I stayed out until.

Nobody was coming to search for me.

"Tony?"

"Yes, Joey, lad?"

"I just . . . " I blew out a breath, as I wrestled with my conscience, with the tsunami of guilt inside of me. Because I knew exactly where I would go when I left him, and it wasn't home. No, I was heading straight for his daughter. "I just wanted to say thanks."

He smiled. "For what?"

For everything. I shrugged. "Just thanks."

"Anytime, boyo," he replied, waving me off.

Sliding my phone out of my pocket, I smirked as I re-read the text Molloy had sent me earlier.

MOLLOY: I'LL SEE YOU AND YOUR HAND (AND YOUR FANTASTIC FINGERS AND YOUR GIFTED TONGUE) AFTER WORK. I FINISH AT 9. SEE YOU THEN, STUD.

Grinning like a dope, I began to tap out a text to let her know that I was on my way, when my phone decided to ring.

My stomach sank into my ass as Shannon's name flashed across the screen.

I didn't want to answer her because I already knew what it was she needed, and I didn't want to be needed tonight.

Skin crawling, I forced myself to press accept and put the phone to my ear.

"Joe," she sobbed down the line. "Can you come home? We need you."

Exhaling a weary sigh, I closed my eyes and let my head fall forward. "I'm on my way."

I was rounding the corner at the bottom of the hill to our road when I saw her.

The minute my eyes landed on her face, my hackles rose, and my blood ran cold in my veins. "What happened?"

"Hi, Joe." She offered me a small wave, as she stood under the street-lamp in the pissing rain. "H-how are you?"

"I'm grand, Shan." On high alert and poised for danger, I closed the space between us, not stopping until I had her chin tipped up. "Jesus Christ."

Her left eye was swollen shut and darkening at a rapid pace.

"I'm ok-kay," she strangled out, shaking from what I presumed was a mixture of fear and the cold. Her teeth chattered violently as I inspected her face with a horrified expression. "It's n-not as b-bad as it l-looks."

"It's not okay, Shan," I choked out, feeling like I was physically inhaling her pain in this moment.

Because she might be wearing the bruises tonight, but I was wearing the shame, along with the absolute fucking guilt of not being here to stop this from happening to her.

Again.

"I know I sh-shouldn't be o-outside this late," she sobbed, throwing her arms around me. "But if I d-didn't get out, he w-was g-going to k-kill me."

"You did the right thing," I assured her, body rigid, as I tried and failed to comfort her. "You absolutely did the right thing. If he puts his hands on you, and I'm not here, then you run, Shannon. You fucking run, ya hear me?"

Sniffling, she looked up at me and nodded. "I h-hear you, Joe."

"Where is he?" I demanded then, striding past her, in my bid to get my hands on the piece of shit we had the misfortune of calling *Dad*.

"D-don't, Joe," Shannon cried out, chasing after me. "I'm n-not w-worth getting h-hurt over."

"You are worth it," I roared back, shoving the front door open. "Of course you're fucking worth it, Shannon. You're worth a thousand of that piece of shit, and don't you ever let him make you feel anything less!"

"Joey, wait!" Mam hurried to intercept me at the front door. "He didn't mean to hurt her—"

"Move," I snarled, stepping around my mother, as I barreled inside, breathing flames of fury. "Get the fuck out here, old man. Come out and hit someone your own goddamn size!"

"Joey," Tadhg cried out from where he was hiding behind the banister. Cowering at his side were Ollie and Sean. "He's after losing it."

Yeah?

Well so had I.

"Where's the fire?" Dad barked, when he stalked out of the utility room that housed the toilet. He fumbled with the zipper of his jeans and then hissed sharply. "Jesus Christ, boy, pack in the roaring, will ya? I nearly cut my cock off."

"Pity you didn't!" I roared, livid, as I stalked towards him, feeling the blood rush to my hands as they clenched into fists of their own accord. Even if my mind wasn't ready for this man, my body sure as hell was. "You put your hands on my sister," I seethed, not stopping until I was in his face. "Did it make you feel like a man?" Shoving his chest with everything I had in me, I watched as he staggered backwards.

"You little bastard!" my father roared, his face reddening with rage.

When he lunged forward with a swinging right hook, I was ready.

Ducking sideways, the bone in my nose narrowly avoided another break.

"Joey, please," Mam wailed.

"You're getting slow, old man," I sneered, as my fist made contact with his jaw. "Or else I've just learned all of your moves off by heart."

"Teddy, please don't."

"You think you can beat me?" He staggered forward, both arms swinging with fists that felt like concrete blocks when they made contact with your flesh. "I'll fucking end you, boy."

"Oh my god, stop it now, both of you!"

"Not if I end you first," I roared, spearing his huge frame to the kitchen tiles. Not an easy thing to do when he outweighed me by at least five stone. "Prick!"

"Yeah, Joe, fucking kill him!"

"Shut up, Tadhg!"

"D-don't, Joe. He's not w-worth it!"

"Shut up, Shannon!"

"Tadhg, go up to your room now!"

"Mammy . . . make it stop!"

"Dada ow-ow."

"Can you hear them?" With my hands around his throat, I squeezed with every ounce of strength I had inside of my body. "That's your family, asshole. And they're scared shitless of you."

"Little cunt!" Reaching up, the bastard fisted my hair and dragged me roughly off his chest. "Think you're a full-grown man?"

"Joey!"

Now it was my turn to have my airwaves restricted when my father's beefy hand clamped around my throat.

He didn't need to use two hands to strangle me, either.

Not when his hands were as big as shovels.

Throwing one good punch, he connected with my eye socket so hard that I felt the vibration down to my toes. "How's that for a taste of your own medicine, pretty boy?"

"Teddy, please stop!" That was Mam. "He's your son."

"You might have come from my prick, but you're no son of mine, boy," he sneered, and then added insult to injury when he hacked up a phlegm ball and spat right in my face. "Little fucking mammy's boy is all you've ever been!"

"Teddy, please!"

"Shut up, whore!" Dad roared. "Or you'll be next."

"Fuck you!" I tried to scream, but it only came out as a strangled whisper.

Sitting on my chest with his full weight pressing down on my already deflated lungs, my father continued to taunt me.

"Come on, tough man, fight back."

Bucking wildly beneath him, I tried to throw him off me, but I knew in my heart that I never could.

Dizziness began to engulf me then, joining the burning in my lungs, as my muscles spasmed erratically.

I was losing consciousness, I realized, and then, all of a sudden, the pain just dwindled away.

The pressure in my eyes and the fire in my throat evaporated.

Just let go, a voice in my head urged, *it'll all be over if you just let go.*

I let my fists fall to my sides and did just that.

"Joe?"

When I came to, a little while later, it was to the sight of my sister's face, as she lifted and pulled at my eyelids.

"It's me, Shan!"

Another finger in the eye.

"Can you hear me?"

Feeling like I was about to hack up a lung, I grabbed at my throat, as I coughed and spluttered violently.

Drawing air into my lungs, I quickly dragged myself into a sitting position, and leaned against the fridge for support.

"Oh, thank god!" Kneeling beside me, Shannon leaned in with a tea-towel and pressed it to the piece of skin above my left eye. "Are you okay?"

Still coughing and spluttering, I held up a hand to ward her off, while I focused on dragging air into my lungs. "Where . . . is . . . "

"He's gone to bed," she whispered, shuffling closer so that her small knees were pressed to my thigh. "I'm so sorry."

"No . . . your . . . fault."

"Oh, god, Joe." Sniffling, she leaned forward and wrapped her small arms around my neck. "I love you so much. I'm so sorry he did this to you again."

I didn't return her hug.

Couldn't if I wanted to.

Worn to the bone, and breathing ragged, I took my time catching my breath before I asked, "Where's Mam?"

Shannon looked down at the floor.

"Shan?"

"Upstairs," she squeezed out, pulling at a thread on the side of my pants. "She had to coax him off you."

With sex.

Yeah, I needed to get out of here.

I couldn't be in this house tonight.

If I had to endure the sound of him grunting and groaning from behind a closed bedroom door, I was going to crack.

"Joe, don't go," Shannon begged, hurrying after me, when I climbed to my feet and staggered to the front door. "Please don't go anywhere."

"It'll be grand, Shan," I choked out, not looking behind me, as I bolted out the door quicker than I'd come in it. "You'll be safe."

Now that he got his pound of flesh.

Do you have a death wish?

March 5th 2004

AOIFE

I was in foul form when I got home from work on Thursday night.

Aside from the fact that my poor toes had been annihilated from spending six hours crammed into a pair of heels that deserved to be thrown into the nearest fire, I was soaked to the bone, too.

None of that would have bothered me, though, I reluctantly admitted to myself, *if he had just shown up.*

Joey had promised to walk me home after my shift finished, and I had waited outside the pub for over an hour, until the cold got the better of me.

In the end, he never showed, and I ended up walking home alone in the pouring rain, which wouldn't have been so bad had my company showed up.

Since then, I'd sent him a couple of text messages, but had heard nothing in response.

Because I was dealing with Joey and not Paul, I found myself in unchartered waters.

When Paul hadn't answered my texts or calls, I'd never given it a second thought.

When Joey didn't answer, it made me want to curl up in a ball and rock.

Pathetic as it seemed, I'd grown ridiculously attached to the boy who refused to put a label on whatever it was that we were doing.

I didn't push because, for the first time in my life, I was afraid to lose.

I didn't feel like I had the upper hand in this relationship, with the advantage being he held my heart in his hands.

If Joey left, if he walked away from me, it would hurt.

It would *cripple* me, and that was a worrying realization.

I'd given so much power over to a boy who refused to call me his girlfriend.

No, instead, I was the friend he liked on an exclusive basis, but nobody could know.

Fuck my life.

Deciding to crack open the books, for once, I managed to do a decent amount of my homework and overdue assignments for school, before I eventually sacked the books off for some Seth Cohen.

At least, when I wanted to see him, all I had to do was switch on the television.

Curled up in a ball on my bed, with a mini pack of Crunchie bars on my lap, I rewatched *The OC* for the hundredth time.

Dozing off a little after eleven, I slept restlessly, tossing and turning for most of the night until I was fully awakened around half one in the morning by the sound of knocking.

Laying perfectly still, I listened in the darkness as the knocking continued on my window, growing louder and then dwindling off for a moment before picking back up again.

Pissed off, because there was only one person that I knew could scale a two-story house, I threw the covers off and stalked over to the window. Pushing it open, I leaned over the sill and glared down at the bastard balancing on the roof of our garden shed like he was Houdini himself.

"What?"

The moment he realized I was up and looking at him, he quickly tossed away from him what I hoped was a cigarette butt, but knew in my heart *wasn't.*

"Molloy." A slow smile crept across his face. "Mol-fucking-loy."

"Are you . . . " I narrowed my eyes, instantly suspicious. "Oh my god, you're high."

"Nuh-uh."

"Uh-huh." I rolled my eyes. "What did you take?"

"Hmm?"

"Drugs, Joey," I snapped, feeling my breath hitch in my throat. "I know you're after taking something."

He shook his head. "No, I'm not."

"I've known you since we were twelve, genius, I think I'd know when you're high," I whisper-hissed. "What did you take?"

"Nice legs."

Not tonight, buddy.

"Fine, if you're not going to be straight with me, you can leave."

"I don't wanna leave, Molloy."

"Then what do you want?"

"What do *I* want?" Swaying from side to side, he held his hands up and shrugged. "Fuck if I know, Molloy."

"Yeah, well, while you go on not knowing what you want, I'm going to sleep," I said flatly.

"Whoa, whoa, whoa – where are ya going?"

"To bed, Joey."

"Why?"

"Why?" I glared down at him. "Because it's the middle of the night, and that's what normal people do at night."

"Oh right." He frowned. "Yeah."

"And because we have school in the morning," I snapped. "You remember that place called school, don't you?"

"Obviously." Still swaying, I watched as his brow furrowed and confusion set in. "Am I in the doghouse again?"

Absolutely. "You tell me."

He stared blankly up at me.

"Forget anything tonight?"

Again, he stared blankly.

"Goodnight, Joey," I sighed in resignation and moved to pull my head back inside, when the mad bastard lunged.

Taking a running jump, he scaled the side of my house like a fucking cat, not stopping until he was holding on to the ledge of my windowsill. "Why am I in the doghouse, Molloy?"

"Do you have a death wish?" I hissed, wide-eyed, as he dangled from the side of my house. "Oh my god, get in here, you eejit." Catching ahold of his arms, I helped to drag him through my window. "That was so fucking stupid," I growled, when he was sprawled on his ass on my bedroom carpet. "Don't ever do that again when you're in this condition."

Holding his thumb up in response, he remained perfectly rigid on the flat of his back on my bedroom floor.

"I'm just going to . . . take a breather down here for a bit."

"Yeah, you go right ahead and do that, asshole," I grumbled, climbing back onto my bed. "From now on, consider my bedroom floor to be your personal doghouse."

"Hmm," Joey slurred. "If you let me come out of the doghouse, I'll let you cum on my face."

"In your condition? Ha. I wouldn't let you put a finger on me," I snapped, pulling the duvet up to my neck. "Now, close your eyes and go to sleep."

"Molloy?"

"Shh."

"Molloy?"

"I'm sleeping."

"Molloy?"

"What?"

"I lied." He exhaled heavily. "I got high tonight."

"Yeah, Joe, I know," I squeezed out, clenching my eyes shut, as the pain in my chest splintered and stretched until I was hurting all over.

There was a long stretch of silence before he slurred, "Molloy?"

"What?"

"Do you hate me?"

No, I love you. "Go to sleep, Joey."

Unable to close an eye, I saw every hour of the clock, as I remained rigid in my bed, with only the occasional soft snore from the boy on my bedroom floor to keep me company.

My heart hadn't stopped pounding since he'd shown up at my window.

I was so mad at him for doing this to himself, but my anger paled in comparison to my concern.

This was serious.

He could die.

It was always a possibility when you played with fire like I knew he did.

I didn't know what he had taken tonight, and I was almost afraid to find out.

Finally, around 05:30 in the morning, I felt myself slip into a fitful sleep.

When I woke up the following morning, it was to the realization that I had somehow managed to sleep through the alarm on my phone.

It was gone half nine when I woke, and I knew school had already started, so I just stayed where I was.

Feeling thoroughly depleted of energy, I remained bundled up under my covers, aimlessly watching the screen of my phone as the time ticked by.

Eventually the sound of a throat clearing filled my ears and I groaned.

"Mam, before you start, I'm sick. I'm on my period," I quickly called out, lying through my teeth, as I thought up the worst, most horrendous temporary ailment I could possibly have. "I'm after bleeding out in the night. It's a blood bath in here. Honest to God, Mam, there isn't a sanitary towel in the bathroom big enough to cope with the flow."

"Yeah, it's me, your mam left the house a while ago."

Springing up, I threw the covers off to find Joey sitting on the chair next to my window, with his hood up and his hands in the front pocket of his hoodie – his usual stance.

I couldn't hide the relief that expelled from my lungs in a shaky breath.

"What are you still doing here?" I couldn't hide the anger in my voice, or the hurt. "I gave you a place to sleep it off. No need to linger."

He didn't blanch at my words.

Instead, he continued to stare back at me. "I was supposed to meet you after work last night. I was supposed to walk you home, and I didn't show up. I remember now."

"Well, good for you." I gestured to the window and glared. "See ya."

"I'm sorry."

"You're not sorry." I stared hard back at him. "You never say sorry, because you're never sorry, remember?"

His green eyes remained locked on mine, unblinking. "I am this morning."

"Well, this morning I'm too mad to accept it," I countered, swallowing down a surge of emotion. "When you didn't show up last night, or answer your phone, I thought you were hurt, or worse." My voice cracked and I quickly steadied myself before adding, "But you weren't hurt or worse. You just had a better offer."

He swallowed the venom in my words, and didn't even try to deny it, or fight with me.

I wasn't sure if that made me feel better or worst.

When he made no move to leave, I shook my head, feeling at a loss.

"I know that you're new to this," I waved a finger between us, "whatever you want to call what we're doing, but this is the part where you either give me some bullshit explanation for why getting high was more important than sending me a goddamn text, or it's the part where you leave."

He didn't budge.

He didn't open his mouth to defend his actions, either.

"You're absolutely right, Molloy." With slow, stiff movements, I watched as Joey slowly dragged himself to his feet. "I should go," was all he replied, and then shook his head. "I will go."

"What?" Throwing off the covers, I sprang out of my bed and stalked towards him. "I wasn't serious, asshole! I was being dramatic. You're not going anywhere until we talk about what happened."

"I'm really not in the mood to talk about it."

"Well, I wasn't in the mood to be woken up by your big, drugged-up ass jumping through my window, but here we are." Planting my hands on my hips, I glowered up at him. "Well?"

"Well, what?" he said flatly, keeping his head down. "I think it's pretty clear that I fucked up."

Giving me his back, he moved for my window.

"Oh hell no." Lunging towards him, I quickly stepped in front of my window and blocked off his escape route. "You don't get to do that," I warned. "You don't get to walk out on me without an explanation for last night."

"I got high!" he snapped. "Is that what you want to hear? Huh? I went out last night and I lost my fucking mind in the bottom of a bottle of vodka and a shit ton of pills."

"*Why*?" I strangled out, feeling his words pierce through me like bullets.

"Why?" he hissed. "*Why?* Because that's what I do, Molloy!" he snapped. "That's fucking why."

"Joey . . ."

"I know I messed up, okay? I know I let you down," he spat. "But this is me, okay?" Knocking his hood down when he roughly dragged both hands through his blond hair, he hissed, "I am who I am, Molloy, and who I am is *not* good for you!"

That's when I saw it.

The bloody eye socket.

The burst lip.

The purple swelling down the entire left side of his cheek.

His beautiful face was completely mangled.

"Jesus . . . " Suddenly starved for oxygen, I sucked in a sharp breath and strangled out, "What happened to your face?"

"Don't ask me to say it," Joey warned, holding a hand up, as he slowly backed away from me. Never once did he take his piercing green eyes off mine as he moved, putting space between our bodies – and hearts. He was thrumming with tension now, visibly shaking with unrestrained fury. "Not when you already know."

"Joey, don't walk away, okay?" I hurried to say, as I rushed to intercept him, stopping him from leaving through my bedroom door this time. "Just stay, okay? Just stay and talk to me."

"I *can't* talk to you," he spat, tensing when I grabbed ahold of his forearm. "That's the whole point. I can't fucking talk about it, okay? I've got too many people depending on me. I can't talk." He blew out a ragged breath. "I don't want to hurt you with my bullshit, but I know that I'm going to."

I shook my head. "Joe . . . "

"You should want me to leave, Molloy," he argued. "You shouldn't be blocking the door, baby; you should be holding it goddamn open."

"I'm not going to do that," I warned, voice thick with emotion. "It's not ever going to happen, so get that bullshit notion out of your head."

"I'm a mess; in case ya haven't noticed."

"Yeah, I've noticed," I shot back, curling my fingers around his wrist, as I pulled him back to me. "Do you see me running?"

"No, and thank fuck for that, because, contrary to how I act sometimes, I *don't* want you to run," he admitted gruffly, chest heaving. "I want time with you, Molloy. I do. I want to be all kinds of right for you. But I have walls and limits and boundaries, and the only way I can be with you, get close to you, is if you stay the fuck behind them!"

I opened my mouth to respond, but he got there before me.

"There are going to be times when I look like this, and I'm not going to be able to give you an explanation. I can't give you the words, Molloy, because those words will cost other people too much." Blowing out a ragged breath, he shrugged helplessly, arms by his sides. "So, you need to decide if you can live with that. Because this is my life. This is me, and I can't change."

Reeling, I absorbed his words, heard his plea, felt his remorse, and drowned in his pain. "I'm willing to do that for you, if you're willing to do something for me in return."

He eyed me warily.

He acted like nothing bothered him, when in truth, he was eaten alive by the pain and insecurity of his home life.

"The drugs, Joey." Heart racing violently, I reached up and pressed my hand to his chest. "You told me once that you wouldn't hurt me on purpose again but seeing you completely out of it last night *hurt*."

"I'm not a saint, Molloy," he replied gruffly. "You've always known what I am. I've never tried to hide it from you. I've never been a—"

"I'm not asking you to be a saint, Joey," I hurried to say. "You're right, I absolutely do know who you are, and I'm in, okay? I am all in with you. All I'm asking for in return is that you try to stay clean."

"Try."

"Yes, try." I nodded slowly. "Just try, Joe. For me. That's all I'm asking for."

He was silent for so long that I thought he wasn't going to answer me. But then, he released a ragged breath and pulled me into his arms. "Okay, Molloy," he whispered, wrapping me up in his arms. "I'll try."

Find you in the dark

April 2nd 2004

JOEY

A cold sweat beaded my brow as I sat in the corner of the lounge in
Biddy's bar on Friday evening after school. I had my phone resting in
one hand, and a vodka and Red Bull in the other.

Unlike most of the other pubs in town, Biddies wasn't unaccustomed
to serving minors. As long as you were discreet, kept your mouth shut,
your drink out of sight, stayed in the back lounge, and didn't cause
trouble, you were welcome.

Which meant that my father wasn't.

Resisting the carnal urge that I had growing inside of me, the one
that demanded I get my hands on something more than just vodka to
take the edge off my racing mind, I forced myself to slide my phone back
into my jeans pocket and sat in my discomfort.

In the horrible fucking feeling of withdrawal.

I hadn't smoked in weeks, hadn't taken anything harder than a few
benzos, and it was showing.

I was *trying* to behave myself, *trying* to keep the head and my shit
together, but it wasn't coming easy to me.

Growing agitated, I drummed my fingers against the table in front of
me and looked around the bar, desperate to find a temporary distraction
from the god-awful burning sensation in my throat.

We were supposed to be celebrating my call up to the minors. The lads
were delighted for me, but my father was also delighted, which meant
that I was anything but.

"Posh pricks," Podge muttered, gesturing to a table of lads in
Tommen College uniforms, sitting at the other end of the lounge. "I

bet you that not one of those rugby-head fuckers has seen a hard day in their lives – or a day's work with it."

"I really couldn't care less what about what they have or haven't seen, lad," I replied, unimpressed by their fancy uniforms, or their table laden down with top-shelf quality liquor.

"That's yer man, isn't it? The lad from that fancy rugby academy," Podge offered, inclining his head to where a tall, dark-haired lad about our age was leaning against the bar, deep in conversation with the owner of Biddies. "What's his name again?"

"Johnny Kavanagh," I filled in, recognizing him the minute he walked through the door earlier, with his army of wealthy pals in tow.

"That's him," Podge agreed with a nod. "I've heard he's going professional soon."

"Lucky fucker," Alec grumbled.

"There's nothing lucky about it," I replied, eyes trained on the back of the lad that resembled a brick shithouse in the physicality stakes. "Look at the size of him. He didn't get that way from luck, lads."

"Well, give me a game of hurling any day of the week over their fancy fucking *rugby*," Alec huffed. "That overgrown bastard might be able to throw a ball around with his posh pals over there, in their blazers and designer jackets, but he'd be eating your dust on a GAA pitch, Lynchy."

"Yeah, he would, Al," I agreed. "But at least he'd be eating."

Alec frowned. "I don't follow, Joe."

"That fella over there is going to finish school, and then make an absolute fortune playing a game he loves," I explained, turning to look at my drinking companions. "The fuck am I going to get from an amateur game? A slap on the back and a few ham sandwiches after a match?"

"Aren't you happy you got called up to play for Cork?"

"Yeah, of course I am, but I just ... " Releasing a frustrated sigh, I added, "Fuck it. It doesn't even matter."

"I'd kill to be in your position, Joe." Alec looked at me like I had grown an extra head. "To have your natural ability and pace. You don't get how unbelievably talented you are, lad. Everyone on our team would gladly change places with you in a heartbeat."

Not if they knew how it really was for me.

Or how it felt to live in my head.

"Hurling isn't my whole future," I tried to explain. "It won't pay my bills like rugby will for that Kavanagh lad. That's all I'm saying. It's not the be-all and end-all of my world."

"Speaking of worlds," Podge chuckled, digging me in the ribs, when a small group of girls sauntered in the lounge. "Looks like yours is about to get rocked."

"A blonde, a brunette, and a redhead walk into a bar. It's like the start of a dirty joke," Alec groaned and then tossed his drink back. "I don't know which one I want more."

"Those are some nice legs, blondie; when do they open?" one of the lads from the rugby table called out.

"Way past your bedtime, little boy."

Instantly, I recognized said legs as the ones that almost cut off my circulation when they were wrapped around my neck the other night.

Fuck . . .

Instantly, my back was up, and a huge part of me wanted to walk over to where she was standing and claim her in front of those pricks. Whatever we had going on, it wasn't exactly public knowledge though. This was mainly due to the fact that Tony would cut my dick off if he found out I was sniffing around the forbidden fruit that was his only daughter. It did mean, however, that I would look even more psychotic than usual if I walked over and started swinging.

Besides, Molloy was more than capable of handling herself against pretty much anyone.

Including me.

The rugby table erupted with *'oohs'* and *'burn, lad'* as another one called out, "You look like a dream."

"Then go back to sleep," Molloy called back, as she waited at the bar with her friends, while the barman prepared their drinks.

"Why don't you come over here and sit on my face, sweetheart?" another one took a swing before striking out in glorious fashion.

"Why?" Molloy said sweetly, as she took her drink from the barman, and sauntered off in the direction of our table. "Is your nose bigger than your dick?"

Laughter erupted from the rugby table, and I couldn't stop the surge of heat that spread in my chest when she looked across the room at me and beamed.

She was something else, that girl.

She fucking beamed at me like I was someone worth being that happy to see.

I'm not.

Her smile caused a dull ache to settle in my chest.

I watched as her redheaded neighbor said her goodbyes to Molloy and Casey before joining the Tommen table and making a beeline for who I thought looked a lot like Shannon's friend's brother.

"Evening, lads," Casey said brightly, taking a seat at our table beside Alec. "Mind if we join ye? Katie's gone off with her fella from Tommen, but we'd rather sit with our own boys."

"Be our guests."

"You're looking well tonight, Al."

Alec's cheeks turned bright red. "Her," he whispered to Podge. "She's my favorite."

Podge smirked. "Of course she is."

"I hear congratulations are in order, Joe. Mack told us that you got the call up to the minors."

"Nice one, Case," I replied, not taking my eyes off Molloy, who was removing her coat, and holy fuck, if my heart wasn't racing before, it gunned in my chest at the sight of her little red dress.

The girl had an unreal body.

Seriously, she was something else entirely.

408 • SAVING 6

Tall and blonde, with curves in all the right places, a nice big ass, and fabulous fucking double-D tits, I didn't blame the lads at the other table for trying their luck.

She had the face of an angel, and the tongue of a devil.

"Lads," Molloy acknowledged as she subtly lowered herself down on the bench next to me. Her gaze flicked to me. "Joey."

My lips twitched. "Molloy."

"Nice shirt."

"Nice legs."

"So, girls, are ye out on the drink or the pull for the night?" Podge asked, making conversation.

"Well, since it's my birthday, I have every intention of pulling," Casey laughed. "If the right fella asks nicely enough."

"Happy birthday," all three of us chorused in unison.

Casey grinned. "Thanks, boys."

"What about yourself, Aoife?" Podge asked. "I heard things are finally over between yourself and Ricey. Have to say, girl, I think you made a smart move."

"Yeah," Casey agreed. "Especially since he started texting Danielle an hour after you broke up."

I watched Molloy's face for any indication that she was still bothered by Paul.

She didn't bat an eyelid at the news.

"Oh, yeah, I heard about the breakup." Alec waggled his brows. "I heard Ricey caught the two of you shifting the faces off each other."

I rolled my eyes. "Lies."

"Yeah," Molloy said in agreement. Grinning devilishly, she used a straw to sip on her bottle of Smirnoff Ice, and then she subtly slid her hand under the table, not stopping until she had her hand between my legs. "All lies."

Jesus Christ.

A deep shiver rolled through my body. She made me weak, this girl. It was insane, but I forgot about things when I was with her.

Things like time, school, hurling, home. She even made me forget about *him*.

"What about you, Molloy?" I replied, quickly snaking a hand under the table to stop her from palming my rapidly hardening dick. "Are you out on the hunt tonight?"

"You know what, Joe," she replied teasingly. "I think I am."

"Well, be careful," I shot back with a smirk. "Because I hear there are some bad pricks out tonight."

"That's good to know," Molloy purred. "I'm thinking of finding myself a bad boy to walk me home later. I hear they hit the *spot* just right."

"He'll hit more than just the right spot, if he gets you alone in the dark," I told her in a low, warning tone. "It's a dangerous move. You should have your daddy come get you."

"Dangerous sounds like just what I'm looking for," she whispered, hand sliding under the table once more to touch me, but I was prepared for her this time.

"Keep it up, Molloy." Snatching her hand up, I leaned in close, lips brushing against her ear, as I said, "He'll look forward to finding you in the dark later."

"I'll keep my window open for him," she whispered, breathing hard.

"You should keep your legs open, too," I whispered, resisting the urge to lean in and kiss those pouty red lips. "I hear he loves eating pussy."

A deep shiver racked through her, and I smiled when she squeezed her thighs together, before dragging in a steadying breath, and standing up. "I'll be right back," she whispered, as her finger trailed down my arm. "I need some fresh air."

"I need a smoke," I replied, not even managing to count to three before I stood up.

"All lies, was it?" Alec grinned as he watched me trail after the fucking fantastic blonde. "Yeah, lad, I believe you."

Interrupted by a flanker

April 2nd 2004

AOIFE

My back hit the wall of the empty corridor outside of the bathrooms, moments before Joey's body came crashing against me.

"You don't get it, Molloy," he growled as his lips claimed mine, hands moving straight to my hips, as he dragged them roughly against his. "I'm broken in the head. I don't work right. I get hooked. I get so fucking addicted, and if we keep this up, I won't let go. I won't be able to."

If he intended to scare me, then he'd failed. His words had the opposite effect.

"Good," I breathed. "Because I don't want you to."

"Fuck, Molloy."

Reclaiming his mouth with mine, I yanked and pulled at the hem of his shirt, knowing that my behavior was beyond reckless, but desperate to feel his skin.

He had been trying so hard to stay on track lately, and I had every intention of rewarding him for his efforts.

Sliding my hands under his shirt, I reveled in the sharp hiss that tore from his lips when my cold hands connected with his hot skin. "Jesus, you're freezing."

"Then warm me up," I breathed against his lips, as I reached out and guided his big hands to my ass. "Because I want you."

"Keep it up," he warned, giving me a tight squeeze. "And you'll have me."

That was a thrilling thought.

"Good."

He rocked against me. "You want me?"

"Uh-huh."

He pushed his knee between my legs, spreading them. "How bad?"

I roughly dragged my nails down his stomach. "*So* bad."

And then his hand was under my dress, brushing the fabric of my thong aside, moments before he slid two fingers deep inside of me. "You want this?"

My breath hitched. "Joe."

He did something with his fingers then, something wonderful that sent a full body tremor straight through me. "Spread your legs."

Shivering, I let my head fall back against the wall, and opened my legs.

"Wider."

"Joe, I—"

He thumbed my clit and growled, "Wider."

Reckless, I hitched one leg up, and, resting my heel on the wall at my back, I completely bared myself to him.

"Good girl."

"Asshole." An illicit shiver rolled through me. "Hey, Joe?"

"Yeah?"

"Don't hurt me, okay?"

His hand stilled inside of me and he frowned. "Am I hurting you now?"

"No. What you're doing feels amazing." Breathless, I shook my head and encouraged him with my hips to keep going. "Just don't hurt me like my dad hurts my mam, okay?"

He stilled again. "Molloy."

"Don't stop," I groaned, rocking into his touch. "I want you."

"I won't do that to you." He pressed a kiss to my lips. "I promise."

"Good." Exhaling a ragged breath against his lips, I bucked my hips and grinned. "Now shut up and make me cum."

"Fuck my fingers," he replied, tongue snaking out to trace my bottom lip before he claimed my mouth with his. "Help me stretch this tight little pussy."

"Oh, Jesus."

"You're beautiful."

"Fuck me, Joe."

"I will."

"Fuck me now."

"I will, Molloy."

"Yes."

"But not tonight."

"Joe."

"You're not ready."

"I am."

Shaking his head, he leaned in close and pressed a kiss to my lips. "We've got plenty of time."

"Then don't stop," I encouraged breathlessly, reaching between my legs to push his fingers deeper inside of my body. "Don't ever stop."

"Howdy, lovebirds. Don't mind me. I'm just on my way to send a salmon up the river."

"Oh my god!" I strangled out, hands moving to push my dress back down, as Joey reluctantly tore his hand away.

Furious, Joey swung around to glare at the huge blond guy, in a Tommen uniform, who was grinning at us. "Do you want popcorn, asshole? Get the fuck out of here."

"No, no, I have everything I need," he replied, still grinning wolfishly at us. "But I may be of some assistance to you." Reaching into his pocket, he pulled out a condom and held it out to Joey. "Because sex is fun and all that, but it's best practiced with a glove on your d—"

"Are you serious?" I laughed, flustered and amused by the strange boy. "We're not having sex."

"Yet," the blond lad chuckled with a wink.

"Listen, prick," Joey snarled, bristling. "I don't know how things work in that posh school of yours, but where I come from, you get your ass kicked for pulling a stunt like this. So if you don't start walking the fuck away from me and my girl, I'm going to rip your head off your shoulders and feed it to your asshole."

"Gibs!" an even taller, dark-haired boy snapped from the doorway, thankfully interrupting us. "Would you leave them alone, ya weirdo. They don't need your running bleeding commentary."

"Hey, Cap," this Gibs lad said in a cheerful tone. "I was only providing some safety precautions."

The dark-haired boy's eyes landed on the condom his friend was holding, and he audibly groaned. "Jaysus."

With a shake of his head, he stalked down the corridor and quickly clamped an arm around his buddy.

"Excuse my flanker," he told us, as he led the blond lad back towards the lounge. "He's like a bleeding Labrador. Completely harmless, with zero awareness of social cues and etiquette."

"I was only being friendly," the blond lad argued as his friend led him away. "It's nice to be nice, Johnny."

"Yeah, I know you were, Gibs, but those people are strangers, and what did we say about you talking to strangers?"

"Don't do it?"

"Exactly."

The lounge door closed behind them, and Joey turned to look at me. "Did that really just happen?"

I choked out a laugh and shrugged. "I think so?"

Casual sex without the sex

April 12th 2004

JOEY

I was in over my head.

What had started with a kiss had developed into several months' worth of kisses, with a whole heap of heavy petting thrown into the mix.

Basically, what Molloy and I had going on was casual sex – minus the sex and multiply the feelings.

Yeah, I'd fucked around and caught feelings.

I was a real genius.

I never wanted to be in a relationship.

I never wanted another person to depend on me for something that I couldn't give, and that's where it got fuzzy, because, somehow, Molloy had become exactly that.

Hearing everyone at school whisper about how we wouldn't last longer than a week, or how my head would turn, only made me more determined to stick with the girl – to stand over my decision to be with her.

Their lack of faith in me only strengthened my determination to *not* fuck this up, whatever the hell this was.

I'd been with girls before Molloy, but I was no hardcore fuck boy like I knew the girls at school made me out to be.

Like I knew she thought I was.

It wasn't like I'd fucked my way through the entire female population at our school.

Only a handful.

And besides, that wasn't what was happening between us.

When we were together, it wasn't because I was out of my mind and trying to float away in the moment.

Being with her made me *want* to keep a clear head, because I *wanted* to remember her.

I wanted to be *in* the moment with her, and not just float through it. Because she was Molloy.

My friend.

Maybe even my best friend.

"Are you going to do something about that?" Podge asked, dragging me back to the present, as he waved a spoon in front of us, gesturing to where Molloy looked to be in a heated discussion with Ricey.

"I'm not her keeper, lad," I replied, leaning back in my chair, as I studied the jam-packed canteen. Molloy was standing in line for the tuck shop, with Ricey breathing down her neck. "She can handle herself."

"You're a better man than him," Podge said. "Because if the shoe was on the other foot, and you were trying your arm with her like that, he would flip."

"That was his mistake," I said, eyes glued to her fucking peachy ass, barely concealed by her scrap of a skirt. "He thought that he could put her in a cage, and slap a label on top saying *look, don't touch*." I shook my head. "That girl is her own person, lad. Believe me. Nobody's going to cage her."

"Except for you," he chuckled.

"No, lad," I corrected, feeling my heart roar to life when she smiled across the room at me. "Especially not me."

The door's always open

JOEY

Trouble.

I was in big fucking trouble and going through some major changes to add to the clusterfuck of a mix.

On the one hand, since I turned seventeen, everything at home had steadily gotten worse.

Dad was drinking more than normal these days, which only meant one thing.

Mam was self-medicating with more Valium than usual – something I had realized the other night when I broke into her stash for my nightly fix and found it almost completely gone.

Shannon was being continuously tormented at school.

The boys were on edge.

And I was beyond agitated.

For as far back as I could remember, my coping mechanism for when the shit hit the fan at home had always been one similar to my mother's.

The only difference was that I didn't have a prescription from a doctor for what I needed.

And I needed it.

Badly.

One the other hand, there was Molloy.

That was it.

She was the only reason I had to *not* lose myself.

Because I told her that I would try.

And I'd been trying, dammit.

I was trying so fucking hard.

To be honest, the only reason I'd managed to hold out as long as I had was the thought of how she would look at me if she found out.

She was a fucking beautiful distraction from a life of bullshit.

But even she couldn't take the edge off how I was feeling tonight.

Not after I'd taken just about all I could at the hands of my prick of a father.

My body was aching in ways that I never knew it could and there was only one thing I knew that could help me.

And I hated myself for being weak enough to need it.

"Well, if it isn't the prodigal prick," Shane announced, when I walked into his sitting room late Friday night. "Where the fuck have you been hiding, Lynchy? I thought that I was going to have to come break your legs for my money."

Pillows of smoke wafted in the air, and the stench of alcohol, mixed with sex, piss, weed, and dog was extreme.

Jesus.

"I've been busy," I replied, tossing a wad of notes on his lap, inclining my head to three older men in the corner. "And you know I'm good for it."

"True that." Shooing one of his three bullmastiffs off the couch, he gestured for me to take a seat. I wasn't stupid – or suicidal – enough to say no so I sank down while he counted and then tucked my money into his jeans pocket.

"So, what's been happening, lad?" he asked. "Why haven't I seen you around lately? You on the straight and narrow again?"

"Something like that," I replied, taking the spliff from his out-stretched hand. "I'm keeping my head down."

"I get you, lad," he replied, nodding as if he understood. "Heard about your sister getting jumped the other week. Sad stuff. Was surprised when you didn't call for a fix, though."

"Like I said." Letting my head fall back, I slowly released the smoke from my lungs. "I'm keeping my head down."

"But you're back now."

I sighed in resignation. "Yeah."

I'm back.

"Fair play, lad," he mused, clearly stoned off his head, as he slid a tin out from under the couch and lifted the lid off. "So, what's new? How's the family?"

"Same old shit," I replied, taking another deep drag, as I watched him rummage around in a stash of pills, "different day."

"You want anything stronger than 512s?" he asked, holding up a bag of brownish powder. Heroin. "Guaranteed to blow your fucking mind."

"No." I shook my head. "Just oxy."

"You know where I am when you need something that hits harder." Humming in contentment, he separated the pills into a small baggie. "So, I heard from one of the boys that you've got yourself some regular pussy."

Stiffening, I resisted the urge to tell him to go fuck himself.

Like I said before, I wasn't suicidal.

"Don't we all, lad."

Shane laughed. "Don't be coy, fucker. I heard you're after setting yourself up nicely with that ride of a barmaid from The Dinniman. The blonde with the legs."

"And?" I stiffened, not fucking liking where this was going one bit. It unnerved me that he knew about Molloy because it meant that he was keeping tabs on me. "What's it to you?"

"Is she interested in a making a bit of side cash? I could use a pair of tits like that to help shift some—"

"Leave her out of your plans," I warned, standing up. "Keep her out of your head, period. She hasn't got a damn thing to do with anything."

"Clearly she has," he taunted, chuckling. "Just ask her," he tried to coax. "Ask the girl, and see if she's open to making some easy money by shifting a few—"

"No," I bit out, seething. "Not fucking happening. She's not like you."

"You mean she's not like *us*?" he mocked.

"I'm no dealer, Shane," I said quietly, taking another deep drag, before handing him his spliff. "Never was and never will be."

"Famous last words," he chuckled, as he watched me move for the door. "Relax, lad, I won't look at your girl."

"She's a hard limit for me," I warned. "Look at her and all bets are off, ya hear."

"Yeah, yeah, it's all good," he chuckled, waving the small bag in his hand. "Have you forgotten something?"

Blowing out a frustrated breath, I snatched it up and quickly shoved it into my pocket. "Thanks."

"Just remember I'm always here for ya," he called after me, as I made my exit. "The door's always open."

"Yeah, I know."

That's the problem.

Weird dreams and wandering hands

April 24th 2004

AOIFE

"So, I had this strange dream last night."

"Did you, Aoife, love?" Dad replied.

"Yeah, I did." Leaning my hip against the side of the jacked-up car that my father was working on, I sighed dramatically. "And when I woke up this morning, I was completely soaked."

The sound a spanner clattering to the ground and then the words, "Jesus Christ," filled my ears.

I grinned in victory.

"Are you alright there, Joey, lad?" my dad asked from where he was rummaging under the bonnet of the car with a dipstick in hand. "How's that undertray coming along, son?"

Joey, whose upper body was hidden beneath the car they were working on, muttered another curse before saying, "Yeah, Tony, it's nearly on there."

"Good lad yourself," Dad said, turning his attention back to me. "You know, Aoife, pet, if you're sweating that much during the night, it's a sign that you're coming down with something."

"Yeah, I certainly felt like I was coming—"

Another loud clatter sounded from beneath the car. "Fuck."

"Down with something at the time." I smiled sweetly at my dad. "But I'm fine now, Dad."

"Good girl yourself." Dad smiled and then turned his attention to the phone ringing in the office. "I better answer that."

"Yeah, you really should, Dad."

"I'll be back in a minute," he muttered, hurrying off in the direction of the ringing phone.

"Take your time, Dad," I called out, when he closed the office door behind him. "Please."

"Fucking with me in front of your dad?" Rolling out from beneath the car, Joey glared up from his perch on the creeper. "That's a new low, Molloy."

"How about I just fuck you, instead," I teased, slowly lowering myself onto his lap. "Hmm, Joe?"

"Please," he groaned, hands moving to my hips to stop me before I could straddle his dick. "Don't do this to me."

"Don't you want me?"

"Molloy."

"We could have so much fun on this thing," I purred, rocking my body enough to make his body roll back and forth on the creeper. "Don't you want to play with me, Joe?"

"Please," he begged, holding firm. "I will play with you later."

"Fine." Huffing out a breath, I climbed off him and resumed leaning against the car. "I really did have a dream about you last night."

"Is that so?"

"Uh-huh. It was epic." I poked his blue overall-clad thigh with my foot and grinned. "And I really was soaking when I woke."

"Okay." Quickly springing to his feet, Joey grabbed a rag off the trolley and wiped his oil-stained hands. "I can't be hearing this when I have to spend the next four hours with your father."

"Casey and I had managed to sneak into an over-eighteen's nightclub in the city," I continued, not listening to a word he said. "She ditched me in the smoking area for some guy, and when I was all alone on the dancefloor, you appeared."

"That's it?" He folded his arms across his chest. "That's your epic dream?"

"Not all of it," I whispered, stepping closer, and then laughing when he took two steps back to put some space between us. "You were flirting with me, and you bought me a beer."

"Wow," he deadpanned. "Aren't I the gentleman?"

"You weren't when you took me into the bathroom and fucked me against the sink."

"Against the sink?" Now, I had his interest piqued. "How was that for you?"

"Epic." I smiled. "Except that it wasn't our first time. In my dream, we had been having sex for months."

"Yeah," he laughed. "In mine, too."

"Funny." I took another step towards him. "You came home with me afterwards. You were so . . . sad."

"Sad?" His brows furrowed. "I'd just fucked you in a nightclub toilet, Molloy. Why would I be feeling anything other than delighted with myself?"

"You wouldn't tell me," I explained, sidling closer to him. "You were just so adamant that you couldn't go home. So, you slept in my bed with me, and we were together the entire night." I blew out a shaky breath. "See? Epic dream."

"Huh. Sounds similar to the dream I had last night," he said with a thoughtful look about him. "But you were fucking me from above and I was far from *sad* about it—"

"Joe, that was Mary Dineen," Dad called out from the office doorway, causing Joey to practically leap away from me. "She's after breaking down by the halfway roundabout."

"He told her about that head gasket," Joey whispered, smirking. "But would she listen?"

"I told the woman that head gasket didn't have another ten miles in it, but would she listen?" Dad growled.

Joey winked; it was slightly unsettling how well he knew my father.

"Well, now she'll be paying a lot more than she would have been." Dad shook his head in frustration and grabbed the keys of the tow-truck. "The tight old biddy."

"Do you need me to come with you?"

"No, lad, you're grand here. Just finish off the oil change on the

Rover, and you can call it a day. I'll be half the day trying to sort this out."

"Fair enough."

"Good lad yourself. Don't forget to lock everything up when you're leaving," Dad called out, as he climbed into his truck. "Aoife, do you want a spin home, pet?"

"No, I'm grand, Dad," I called back, waving my father off as he started the engine. "I have my car with me," I added, knowing that it would delight him.

"Good girl yourself."

He beeped twice before pulling out of the garage.

"Now." Turning back to the boy who looked disgustingly sexy in his overalls, I pounced. "Where were we?"

"*I* was finishing up an oil change," he said, sidestepping me. "If you can behave yourself, you can keep me company until I'm finished."

"Where's the fun in that?"

"Molloy."

"What? It's Saturday. It's my day off."

"Then feel free to go enjoy yourself," he drawled, quickly setting to work like the dutiful apprentice he was, "Because I have to work on Saturdays."

"Joe."

He shook his head. "No."

Reaching for the buttons on my blouse, I flicked the top one open. "I bet I can change your mind?"

"Out." He slammed the hood of the car down. "Get out now."

"Fine, fine," I relented. "I'll be good, I swear."

Keeping Joey company while he worked turned out to be a very un-boring experience. He knew his way around a car almost as well as my father did, and that wasn't an easy feat.

Straddling the creeper, I had spent most of the afternoon wheeling back and forth, while we chatted shit and exchanged banter.

He was explicitly clean, too, I found myself noticing, as I watched while he worked. Tidying everything up and putting every nut, bolt, and tool back in its place before he finished up.

"So, what's the plan?" I asked from my perch on my father's desk. Legs swinging, I reached into the large tub of lollypops, and scooped up a red one. "What do you want to do for the rest of the night?"

"I should probably go home and check on things," he admitted, keeping his back to me, as he scrubbed his hands at the sink. "I've been here since early this morning and I—"

"No," I protested, unwrapping my lollypop and popping it in my mouth. "You can't go home."

He sighed heavily. "Molloy."

"It's Saturday night," I moaned. "And I've waited all day for you to be done."

"I know, and I get that, but I have responsibilities at home." He turned to look at me. "I'll walk you home first."

"I brought the car."

He smiled. "How's that going for you?"

"Shocking," I admitted. "I can't get past third gear."

He laughed.

"Listen." Springing off my perch, I prowled towards him, giving him my best moves, as I tried to look as enticing as possible. "How about if we just—"

"I *have* to go home," he warned, arms coming around my waist when I reached his chest. "It's not a matter of want, it's a matter of need, okay?"

"Fine." Letting my head fall forward against his chest, I muttered a string of curses under my breath. "Or," I quickly added when an idea came to me, "since you're finishing work an hour earlier than usual, you could come to my house and spend that hour with me, and I'll drive you home afterwards."

"You'll *drive* me home?"

"It'll be good practice. And you'll still be home on time to do whatever it is that you need to do."

"I don't know, Molloy."

"Mam's not at home," I hurried to say. "And Kev's at one of those creepy sleepovers."

I could see the temptation in his eyes. "Yeah?"

"Yeah, we would be all alone." I went in for the kill. "In an empty house, with a big bed, and no distractions."

I *felt* his enthusiasm grow against my belly. "You know exactly what you're doing, don't ya?"

Grinning, I reached for his hand and pulled. "Let's go."

My back hit the mattress moments before Joey came crashing down on me.

Laughing against his lips, I pushed myself up on my elbows, and watched as he knelt between my legs and quickly dragged his t-shirt off, before moving for my blouse.

I didn't let it get in my way or sour my mood that he could flick the buttons off a blouse and unsnap a bra quicker than a porn star. I couldn't be mad at him for having a past. Besides, he had the good grace to never mention how experienced he was, while I was more than happy to enjoy the perks of said experience.

See; it was a win-win situation all round.

When we were both topless, he grabbed ahold of my hips and dragged me down the bed to where he was kneeling.

"An hour," he warned, lips claiming mine in the most drugging kiss imaginable. "And then I'm gone."

"Fine, fine, whatever you say, Joe," I whispered, and then moaned loudly, when he reached between my jean-clad thighs and roughly cupped me, causing a jolt of pleasure directly to my clit. "Oh, Jesus."

"Not Jesus; just Joey."

"Shh." With my hands knotted in his hair, and my legs locked around his waist, I kissed the lips off the boy on top of me, needing him more in this moment than I thought humanly possible. "Oh, Joe."

Grimacing in what seemed like a combination of fury and pain, he cupped the back of my head with his big, callused hand, while he reached his free hand between us and deftly popped the button on my jeans.

The zip went down next, and then, by some special sort of magic, he was dragging the fabric down my thighs, while his lips moved to my breasts, tongue flicking over my pebbled nipple, as he licked and suckled me.

When my jeans were off, he kissed a trail back up my body until he found my lips.

Growling into my mouth, he snaked an arm behind my back, and then we were rolling, not stopping until I was the one on top of him.

The move was just so effortless *sexy*.

"You have some serious moves." I blew out a shaky breath and took in our surroundings. "You even got your sweats off without me noticing. It's seriously impressive."

He smirked up below me, hands moving to tangle with the waistband of my knickers. "You're impressive."

"I am so wet for you right now," I admitted, hands moving to rest on his bare chest, as I rocked my hips against his boxer-clad erection. "It's insane."

"I know." He rocked his hips upwards. "I can feel you."

His words caused me to clench *everywhere*.

"So." Trailing a finger down his chest, I stopped when I reached the elastic waistband of his boxers. "What do you want to do now?"

"You tell me, Molloy." His hands moved to my hips, and he gave me a reassuring squeeze. "You're calling the shots here."

"I am?"

"Yeah, you are." Leaning up on his elbows, he pressed an achingly soft kiss to my neck. "You set the pace on this, and I'll fall in line with you."

Fuck me.

I exhaled a ragged breath before asking, "So, if I told you that I wanted us to have sex?"

"Then I'd tell you that I have a condom in my wallet."

"And if I told you that I just wanted to sit on your lap and look at you?"

"Then I'd tell you feel free to look."

My heart bucked around wildly.

"Joe?"

"Molloy."

"Get your wallet."

His eyes blazed with heat. "That's the pace you want to set here, Molloy?"

Nodding slowly, I whispered, "Get the condom," as I climbed off his lap, and settled back down on my bed.

Without a word, Joey did just that. Reaching into his grey sweatpants pocket, and then his wallet, to retrieve a foil wrapper.

Breathless and trembling, I lowered myself onto my back and reached for the hem of my thong.

"Just don't hurt me, okay?" I squeezed out, watching as he sheathed his impressively big dick.

Oh god.

"Seriously," I strangled out, eyes flicking to his, when he closed the space between us, and climbed on top of me. "Be, uh, gentle with me."

Nodding slowly, he pressed a kiss to my lips and then deepened it, kissing me with so much affection and tenderness, that I felt myself relax into the mattress.

Feeling weakened and aroused, I let my legs fall open to take him inside of me.

Settling between my thighs, he kissed me deeply, as he aligned the thick head of his cock against me.

And that's when it happened.

"No, wait!" Like the habit of a lifetime, I clammed up at the pivotal moment and choked out the words, "I'm sorry … I've changed my mind."

I felt his body tense above me, heard the groan when he buried his face in my neck, and I mentally prepared myself for the backlash I fully expected to come.

It didn't.

428 • SAVING 6

However, something much stranger happened.

Instead, of shouting at me and calling me a cock-tease, like I had been so used to hearing from Paul when we had been in similar positions, Joey pressed a kiss to my neck before pulling back to ask, "Do you want me to get you off anyway?"

My eyes widened. "Huh?"

"Get you off, Molloy," he repeated, leaning back in to kiss me. "Do you want me to make you cum?"

"Aren't you mad?"

He frowned. "Why would I be mad?"

"Because I choked."

His frown deepened. "And?"

I shrugged. "And I got your hopes up."

"Jesus." Chuckling softly, he pressed another drugging kiss to my lips before kneeling back on his haunches, his fully erect dick bouncing around proudly. "You seem to be under the illusion that I'm some sex-starved deviant, incapable of spending time with you, unless that time revolves around being between your legs."

"Aren't you?"

"You wound me."

"You want in between my legs, don't lie."

"I absolutely want between your legs," he wholeheartedly agreed. "But that's not what I'm here for."

"Then what are you here for, Joe?"

"Your company."

"Funny."

"Your company," he repeated, unyielding.

"Really?"

"I didn't come here with the expectation of sex," he said. "That's not why I'm here and it's not why I keep coming back, either."

"But you *do* want to?"

"Obviously, I want to." He gestured to his dick. "But I'm not going to force you into doing something that you have the honesty to admit you're not ready for." He blew out a breath and shrugged. "I'd rather you tell me now than regret me after."

"Wow."

He heard the word no, took the meaning, and obliged, without complaint or confrontation.

It was so refreshing.

It was such a turn on that I almost regretted saying it.

"I would never regret you, Joe," I said, sitting up so that our chests were touching. "I couldn't. Not ever. I care too much."

"I know." His eyes burned with heat. "And I know that I'm not good with the words you need to hear from me."

"I know," I whispered, understanding. "It's okay."

"But don't ever think that I don't have feelings," he said, and then pressed a kiss to my mouth. "Because the only time that I allow myself to feel anything is when I'm with you."

It's time to lay your cards down

May 7th 2004

AOIFE

JOEY: THEN.

AOIFE: SHE.

JOEY: FLICKED.

AOIFE: THE.

JOEY: HEAD.

AOIFE: OF.

JOEY: HIS.

AOIFE: THICK.

JOEY: COCK.

AOIFE: WITH

JOEY: HER

AOIFE: TONGUE

"Hello? Earth to Aoife?" Clicking her fingers in front of my face, Casey swiped my phone out of my hand and groaned loudly. "Whoops. On second thought, never mind." Grinning wickedly, she handed me back the phone. "You go right ahead and suck his cock, girl. But doesn't he have Construction class right now? Isn't it a bit risky to be sending the boy messages like that when he's surrounded by sharp saws and power tools?"

Smirking, I slid my phone back into my pencil case and gave my friend my full attention. "So, what's new?"

"What's new?" Casey laughed. "Are we really going to play it like this?"

"I have no idea what you're talking about."

"Oh, come on." She rolled her eyes. "It's been months. Everyone knows you guys are together. It's so bloody obvious. The rumors are rampant around school, and even if they weren't, your lingering stares and his *I-want-to-rip-your-clothes-off* heated glances when you're in the same classroom are a dead giveaway. So, come on. How much longer do you two plan to act like you're not riding like sexy little rabbits behind closed doors."

"Jesus, Case. Say it louder, why don't you?" I hissed, poking her with my elbow. "I don't think Mr. Ryan heard you at the front of the class."

"Actually, I did," our biology/PE teacher confirmed, pushing his glasses up his nose. "Please refrain from discussing the sexual productivity of rabbits until after my class. Your lunch break is in ten minutes, and patience is a virtue, girls."

"Sorry, sir," we both choroused, smothering our laughter behind a textbook.

"So, you admit it?" she whisper-hissed. "You're shagging Joey *the rollercoaster* Lynch."

"No, I'm not shagging anyone," I strangled out through fits of laughter. "And *rollercoaster*?"

"You know," she laughed. "Because every girl wants to ride him." Waggling her brows, she added, "But it's clear by those sexy text messages that you guys are sending each other, you're first in the queue."

"Oh, haven't you heard the news? After I got on my ride, the queue got cancelled."

"Boom, bitch," Casey snickered, making the mic drop gesture with her hand. "And that's how it's done."

"Thanks," I laughed. "But to answer your earlier question; my dad still doesn't know about our little arrangement. I don't see that changing for the foreseeable. He still works with my dad, so it's just better if we, you know . . ."

"Fuck around behind Daddy's back instead?" she offered with a rueful smile.

"I'm not having sex with him, Case."

Her eyes widened. "How is this possible?"

"See, Case, it's actually really easy," I drawled sarcastically. "All you have to do is *not* allow a boy to insert his penis into your vagina."

"Very funny, bitch." Shaking her head, she leaned in closer to whisper, "Seriously, though, you've been messing around for what, at least three months now?" Her eyes bulged. "How are you *not* getting naked with that boy?"

"I never said that I wasn't getting naked with him."

"*Details.*"

"A lady never tells."

"Good thing we both know that you're not one of those." She leaned closer. "Okay, so you're not having sex yet, but there's some heavy petting going on, right? A little kiss here, a little finger there, a little tug-of-war down there?"

"Casey!"

"Oh, don't act all coy with me," she laughed. "I've known you since we were five, remember? We know everything about each other's lives, *remember*? Including the time that you made me go to the after-hours doctor with you, when we were in third year, because you convinced yourself that you might be pregnant. All because Paul had wanked himself off before he tried to put his fingers—"

"Oh my god, I was young and clueless!" I hissed, clamping a hand over her mouth. "And you *swore* that you would never bring that up again."

"Yeah, but it's on *my* medical file for the rest of time," she shot back with a cackle. "You gave the receptionist *my* name and details, remember?"

"Because you had your medical card with you at the time, and my mam keeps mine in her purse," I replied, cringing at the memory of how incredibly naïve I used to be. "God, I was a pure thick back then."

"Back then?"

"Funny."

"Okay, so back to business," Casey said, tapping her hand on the desk to garner my attention. "Give me those sexy details, Molloy. Heavy petting?"

I grinned. "Maybe."

Her eyes widened to saucers. "Oral."

I shrugged, but didn't respond, as my face burned with heat.

"Oh, come on." She grabbed my arm and squeezed. "Who's doing who?"

I scrunched my nose up before admitting, "Both."

"Omigod!" Clapping with a ridiculous amount of enthusiasm for my sex life, my best friend asked, "Okay, okay, okay, so if we're talking in comparisons here, you know, between Paul and Joey."

"Ugh, Joey all day long." I gave her a look that said *please, bitch*. "Hands down, Case. There's no competition."

"Jesus. So, I guess it's true what they say about the boys from my terrace." Casey blew out an impressed breath. "They fuck like they fight; all in and with one hundred percent effort."

"Casey!" I laughed, shoving her arm.

"I disagree," Danielle hissed from the desk behind us, and we both turned to face her. "At least Paul has an actual functioning brain when he's with a girl."

"Yeah. A brain that only functions on one frequency; *me, me, me*," Casey was quick to shoot back.

I tried to strangle my laugh but ended up looking like I had the face of a blow-fish.

Danielle glowered. "How's life on the outskirts treating you, Aoife?"

I grinned in return. "Why it's fantastic, Danielle, thanks for asking."

"Outskirts?" Casey snorted. "Get a handle on yourself, girl. We both know that you'd still be happily skulking around the *outskirts* if Joe hadn't sacked you off for my best friend here."

"No, I wouldn't," she huffed. "And do you want to know why?"

"No, but I'm sure that you're going to tell us," I drawled.

"Because Joey Lynch might be beautiful, and charismatic, and have a million other qualities that draw girls to him, but he's broken in the head. Sure, he might be riding the high life right now, with his bad-boy status at school, and his ability to master a hurley and sliotar, but that's as good as it's going to get for him," she told us. "He's already peaked."

I narrowed my eyes at her. "You don't know what you're talking about."

"I know that you made a huge mistake when you threw away a boy with a bright future ahead of him for a boy with no future."

"Fuck you, Danielle."

"I would say fuck you right back, but you already did that to yourself," she snapped, releasing a frustrated breath. "Listen, Aoife, I'm not nearly thick-headed or spiteful enough to deny that you're a ten around here," she said. "You're clever, and funny, and beautiful and had your pick of the bunch in first year. You could have picked any one of the lads at school, but you made the smart decision when you chose Paul. He is going to be a *solicitor*, Aoife. He is going places, and if you had only managed to keep your head, he would have taken you right along with him. He adored you, Aoife, and he would have given you a good life, with a nice house, and a stable bank account. We both know that kind of a future doesn't come along often for girls who come from where we come from." She shook her head and added, "But you couldn't resist the temptation of the school's bad boy, and now you're screwed." Folding her arms across her chest, she arched a brow and said, "Because boys like

Joey Lynch never go anywhere in life, and girls like you go nowhere right along with them. You only need to look at his parents for proof of that."

"Oh, get a handle on yourself, Danielle," Casey was quick to interject. "It's not that deep."

"Isn't it?" Danielle looked me right in the eye when she said, "Enjoy becoming his mam, Aoife. I doubt you'll make it to sixth year graduation without a baby Joey in your belly."

"Listen, bitch, Aoife is nothing like you," Casey hissed, jumping to my defense, which I was grateful for, because I had been rendered speechless. "She doesn't drop her knickers the second a fella beckons. And she doesn't need Paul Rice or any other fella to give her a leg up in life. She'll do that just fine by herself."

"While she's claiming loan-parent allowance off the government. While her junkie baby-daddy sits it out in a prison cell for finally pushing the law too far," Danielle tossed back dryly.

"Oh, you mean the same *junkie* you've been chasing after since first year?" Casey shot back. "Give it a rest, Danielle. You reek of jealously, girl."

"Yeah, I *was* jealous," she offered. "It hurt me when I saw them together that day." She spoke directly to me now. "But instead of being mad at you, I should have been thanking you."

"For?"

"For swapping futures with me. You're with my ex and I'm with yours." Smiling, she flashed a shiny gold bracelet on her wrist. "And unlike you, I'll be sure to appreciate the upgrade."

"Oh yeah? Well, make sure you appreciate the feeling of being treated like a glorified mannequin while you're at it." Twisting in my chair, I leaned over her desk and said, "All of those expensive dinners and flashy gifts might seem tempting now, Danielle, but the shine will quickly fade. When it does, you'll be left with the knowledge that all you are to him is a pretty face and nice pair of boobs." I hardened my stare when I added, "Because that's all you'll ever be to him. Paul will *never* care about what's inside your head or put your feelings before his. He'll come first in every way, and if that's enough for you, then I'm happy for you, I sincerely am, but it was never enough for me."

The bell sounded then, and I didn't wait around to hear Danielle's smart response.

Instead, I quickly packed up my books and hurried out of the classroom, with only one destination in mind, the front of the line at the tuck shop for my daily fix of a packet of Rolos, and a Roy of the Rover bar.

Yeah, I was in no mood to be beaten by the hordes of lads in our school and get left with only a damn Wham bar instead.

Besides, I needed the sugar rush to steady the tremor in my hands.

Danielle was wrong about Joey.

Yeah, she was so *wrong*.

"I hope you're not letting that pinhead, with only boobs for a brain, get inside of your head," Casey warned, a little while later, when we were sitting in the canteen. "Danielle is full of crap, Aoif. She was only venting because she's still salty over Joey dropping her ass like a bag of coal for you."

"They were never in a relationship to begin with," I argued. "They slept together a few times. That's it."

"My case in point," my best friend agreed. "It's drives Danielle crazy that you can hold his attention effortlessly, when she spent the last five years trying and failing to do just that."

"He lost his virginity to her, you know."

"Pssh." She waved a hand around. "That doesn't mean anything. Losing their virginity doesn't mean the same thing to a fella as it does to a girl."

"That's a fairly sexist statement, Case," I chuckled. "How would you know that?"

"Because, my dear, sweet, summer child," she crooned, pausing to pat my hand, "by the time boys grow hair on their balls, they're desperate to give it away to the first girl willing to take it."

"You're terrible," I laughed.

"Terribly accurate," she pointed out. "It's the truth, Aoif. I'm dead right. It's a matter of getting it out of the way for boys, not holding on to it for dear life like us girls."

"You haven't been a virgin since third year," I reminded her.

"Okay . . . " she drawled, rolling her eyes. "Holding on to it for dear life like *you* then." She waved a hand around aimlessly. "Just like Paul was stupid enough to hand his over to that girl from Tommen, Joey just so happened to be equally stupid when he inserted his virginal pecker in our classmate."

"Girls," Mack interrupted with a friendly smile, as he slid into the seat beside Casey. "How are ye getting on?"

"Speak of the devil," I snickered, offering Casey a knowing wink, you know, just in case she had forgotten who she gave her virginity away to. "Hiya, Mack."

"Yeah, hi, Mack," Casey bit out, giving me her infamous *bring-it-up-and-you're-dead* look. "What's new?"

"No one nearly as lovely as your good self, Case," he replied, nudging my friend's shoulder with his big one. "I was out having a smoke with Podge and the lads, but yer man from Elk's Terrace is sniffing around, so I got the hell out of there."

"Elk's Terrace?" My ears pricked up. "Who?"

"That Holland creep," Mack replied, and my heart sank into my ass. *Shane Holland.*

"He's one bad egg, girls," Mack continued, unwrapping the paper covering his chicken fillet roll. "Skulking around the school carpark when he finished going here years ago."

"Is he with him?"

Mack looked at me in confusion. "Who?"

"Joey?"

"Who?"

"Joey!"

"Ah, you mean Lynchy?" He chuckled to himself. "I was like *who's Joey*? I'm so used to calling him—"

"Focus, Mack. Jesus!" I practically shouted, as I leaned across the table and tapped his forehead with my empty plastic bottle. "Did you see Joey out there with Shane Holland?"

"Yeah, Jesus," Mack grumbled, rubbing his head. "He's outside with him now."

Shoving my chair back, I jerked to my feet, leaving my bag, lunch, and friends behind me, and stormed out of the canteen.

"Aoife, wait up, I'll come with you."

"No! Don't follow me," I warned Casey, as I stormed through the hallway and out the front entrance of the school.

I was going to blow a head gasket.

Joey had been doing so damn well.

No goddamn way was I allowing this piece of shit to throw him off-kilter.

"Hey!" I screamed, when the familiar black Honda Civic came into my focus, parked up at the far end of the school carpark. "Hey!"

Barging through a group of stoners from the year above me, I whipped out my phone, which absolutely did not have a camera on it, and pretended to take a picture of Shane's car.

"Get out of the car, asshole!"

My whatever-the-hell-he-was, who was sitting in the passenger seat of a car full of much older boys, turned to look out the windscreen, with a look of confusion etched on his face.

However, the moment his eyes landed on me, his confusion quickly morphed into recognition before settling on anger.

Oh, be angry, fucker, because I can be angrier.

"I said get out of the car, asshole," I demanded, slamming my hands down on the bonnet, uncaring of how much attention I was drawing on them. "Now!"

"What the fuck do you think you're doing?" Joey snarled, throwing the car door open and climbing out. "Jesus Christ, Molloy!" Rounding the bonnet, he quickly slid between me and the car. "What are you *thinking*?"

"What am *I* thinking?" I strangled out, chest heaving, as I quickly searched his eyes for the familiar signs that he was high. "What are *you* thinking?"

Losing my cool, I shoved him out of the way, and kicked the number plate of Shane's car.

"Hey!" Shane roared, rolling down his tinted window. "Get a handle on your bitch, Lynchy, or I will."

"I'd like to see you try, asshole," I screamed back at the big bastard, and then I flung my phone at his windscreen for good measure. "I'm not afraid of you!"

"Molloy—"

"No!" Pushing Joey when he tried to wrestle me away, I strode back to the car and kicked it again. "He's not interested in what you have to offer anymore. Do you hear me? He's not fucking interested. So back off!"

"Molloy!"

"You said you'd try, Joe!" Feeling my eyes well up with tears, I roughly pushed on his big shoulders. "You fucking *promised* me that you wouldn't—"

"And I haven't!" he snapped, quickly snatching up my flailing arms and pulling me roughly against him. "Do you have a death wish?" Furious – and crystal clear – green eyes glared down at me. "You don't fuck around with guys like him, Molloy." Keeping my arms pinned by my sides, he hissed, "And you definitely don't go around making a scene in public and kicking their goddamn cars."

"I don't care," I screamed back, and I meant every word. "I don't. I don't care about his bullshit threats. What I care about is what you were doing in his car, Joey!"

"I don't answer to you, Molloy, which means I don't need to explain myself either," he was quick to say, eyes burning with frustrated heat. "I'm not fucking around behind your back with other girls. That, you can be rest assured of. I'm with you, and only you. But everything else I do, or who I do it with, when we're not together, is not your business."

"You are my business, asshole!" I strangled out.

Reckless and wild, I broke free of his hold, knotted his jumper in my fist, and dragged his mouth down to mine, kissing him hard and rough.

Pulling back, I hissed, "And if you gave one single shred of a shit about me, then you would understand why you need to walk away from this car."

"Molloy."

"Right now, Joey," I cried out angrily. "It's not a matter of pride, here. It's a matter of laying your cards on the table and proving that I matter to you just as much as you matter to me."

He stared down at me for the longest moment, nostrils flaring and chest heaving with temper.

Finally, *thankfully*, he relented with a stiff nod.

I could feel the fury emanating from him as he muttered something in the car window to Shane, before following me to where I had bravely driven and parked my car at school today.

"Don't talk to me," Joey warned, when I passed him my keys, and slid into the passenger seat.

The fact that he had climbed into the driver's seat beside me wasn't a victory that I could celebrate, not when I could feel the war brewing between us.

"Not a fucking word."

Jump off the deep end

May 7th 2004

JOEY

Fury.

I'd never tasted it quite this bitterly.

Unable to look at Molloy for fear of what I might say, I kept driving away from the school and further out from Ballylaggin, hoping that some distance would help cool me down.

"We need to talk about this."

She was right, we did, but I wasn't ready for a conversation.

I couldn't listen to her words right now.

I couldn't hear her reasoning for doing what she did earlier.

Talking, while I was wrestling with my temper like this, wouldn't do either one of us an ounce of good.

I would lose my head and spit my poison all over her feelings. It wouldn't matter if I meant the words coming out of my mouth or not; they would explode from my lips like bullets intended to decimate my intended target. A self-preservation tactic that had been programed into me since birth.

Right now, my head was telling me that the target for my fury was the girl sitting beside me, which was a stark contrast to my heart. That was warning me to lower the proverbial gun and *don't* shoot.

"Are you sure that the insurance my father put you on at work covers you driving this?"

She was trying to get me to come around with small talk.

It wouldn't work.

"I still can't believe you got your full license before me."

If she couldn't, then she was the only one. Judging by the way she drove – like a ninety-year-old, with poor eyesight, and a serious lack of awareness – I had a feeling Sean would pass his driving test before she did.

"I'm mad at you too, you know."

Yeah, I got that loud and clear when she went batshit and attacked Shane's car.

Parking up at the beach, I killed the engine, and took a deep steadying breath before I turned in my seat to face her.

She was already facing me, with her arms folded across her chest, and her face set in a hard line.

Her blonde hair fell loosely down her shoulders to her elbows.

She looked like an angel, poised and ready to go to war with me, and that was unnerving as fuck.

"You don't get to do that, Molloy," I finally said, when I was sure that I could control the words coming out of my mouth. "You don't get to stamp your feet and throw a tantrum at school when I'm talking to someone you don't approve of."

With her back leaning against the car door, she glared at me sulkily, but didn't respond.

She looked ridiculously sexy, with her full lips set in a pout, and I wasn't sure if I wanted to fight with her or fuck her in that moment.

"I'm serious," I told her. "If any other girl pulled a stunt like that on me, then I wouldn't be sitting in a car with her, trying to talk it out. No, because I would have told her where to go back at school."

"But I'm not any other girl," she said huffily. "That's exactly the point."

So fucking confident.

"You were wrong to do what you did."

"No, *you* were wrong."

"He's not someone you mess with, Molloy. Did you think about that before you decided to kick the shit out of his car?"

"Neither am I. Did *you* think about that before you got into his car?"

"I can talk to anyone I want."

"Not when they sell you drugs, you can't."

"I told you that I didn't take anything."

"That doesn't mean that you weren't tempted."

"You can't tell me what to do, Molloy."

"Even when it's for your own good?"

"Even then. You don't own me."

"Yeah, I do."

"No, Molloy." I blew out a frustrated breath. "You don't."

She glared back at me. "You're here, aren't you?"

"Because you spat the dummy."

"And you came running."

I narrowed my eyes. "Molloy."

She narrowed her eyes right back at me. "Joey."

Jesus, I couldn't deal with this girl.

I shook my head, feeling at a loss. "Well, if people at school didn't know about us before, they certainly do now."

"Good." More bitchy glaring. "I have nothing to be ashamed of; have you?"

I glowered back at her. "*No.*"

"Good," she bit out. "Glad we got that cleared up."

"I don't know what I'm doing here." I threw my hands up. "I really fucking don't."

"You're here for the same reason that I am, asshole," she came right back and then sucker-punched me in the chest with. "Because you're in love with the person staring back at you, the same way I am."

"I'm *not* in love with you," I warned her, tone shaky now. "I'm not, Molloy. I don't love you."

"Don't bullshit a bullshitter, Joey." She had the nerve to roll her eyes and say, "You love me so much that it makes you sick."

"You're so fucking full of yourself," I snapped, completely unnerved by the blonde, who was crawling over the console to sit on my lap. "You don't know what's in my head, Molloy."

"I'm in your head." Straddling my hips, she reached for the hem of her school jumper and quickly yanked it off. "Then, now, always."

"Don't pull this shit with me," I heard myself say, even though I had my hand behind the back of my head to tug my jumper off right along with hers.

Her hands moved to the buttons of her school shirt, and I didn't even pretend not to watch as she deftly flicked each one open, revealing a sexy, pink lace bra constraining her massive tits.

"Jesus," I growled, hardening to the point of pain beneath her.

"Tell me." Shrugging off her shirt, she reached behind her for the clasp of her bra and gave me a teasing smile as she withdrew her hand and settled in on my chest instead. "Tell me what I want to hear."

"Not happening," I replied, hooking an arm around her waist and pulling her roughly to my chest. Reaching a hand up the middle of her back, I quickly unsnapped the clasp of her bra. "Because I don't."

"Because you're scared," she corrected, pressing a featherlight kiss to the corner of my mouth, as she slowly drew the straps of her bra down each arm before tossing it on the floor. "Because you're," pausing, she leaned in and traced my bottom lip with the tip of her tongue, and then whispered, "a pussy."

Making up and making out

May 7th 2004

AOIFE

You know the old saying; don't poke the bear?

Yeah, I poked him.

Furious at my goading, Joey had decided that the best way to prove that he wasn't a pussy was by eating mine.

Strewn over the passenger seat of my steamed-up car, which had been fully reclined to the point that my hair was spilling onto the back seat, I rocked my hips against his face, as my fingers clutched at his hair.

"Don't stop!" As naked as the day I'd been born, and in broad daylight, I gave a grand total of zero fucks, as he drove me to the brink of madness with his fingers and tongue. "Don't fucking stop, Joe!"

"Ease up on the thigh clenching, Molloy," he growled, and I looked down to see my thighs squeezing his neck tightly. "You're cutting off my circulation here."

"Sorry, sorry," I cried out, letting my legs fall to his sides, only to feel them spring back up when his tongue flicked over my clit. "I can't . . . I can't . . ."

"You can either cum or you can kill me," he warned, prying my thighs open. "You can't do both."

"The first one," I quickly replied, breathless. "I can do the second one later."

Joey chuckled. "That's my girl."

Jesus.

My eyes rolled back of their own accord, and I drowned in the sensations and the unimaginably addictive pulsing of pleasure that he conjured up from deep inside of me.

"Fuck me," I heard myself cry out as I came hard, shuddering and shaking as shocks of white-hot heat tore through me. "Fuck me, Joe."

It wasn't my plea that surprised me as much as it was his response.

He. Laughed.

That's right; instead of taking advantage of the opportunity I'd offered no other boy before him, the big, bare-chested bastard laughed.

"Wow. Thanks for laughing," I deadpanned, watching as he flopped back into the driver's seat and ran a hand through his thoroughly mussed hair. "I feel so special."

"You should," he replied, thoroughly amused, as he reached a hand inside his jocks and readjusted his hard-on. "I just spent the past half an hour with my head between your legs, Molloy."

"Which, as you can tell by my earlier screams, I am very grateful for. But I just offered you my virginity on a bloody platter and you laughed at me."

He laughed again.

Louder this time.

"What's so funny?"

"Nothing, nothing," he choked out, trying and failing to sober his features, as he wheezed with laughter. "It's just ... you said bloody ... platter."

"Oh, cop on to yourself!" I flushed bright pink. "You know what I meant."

"Yeah, I do," he chuckled. "It just got me."

"So, come on," I demanded. "Tell me why you laughed?"

"Because you were high and not thinking it through."

My mouth fell open. "I don't take drugs. I'm not you, asshole!"

"Do you still want to give me that virginity of yours?" he shot back, waving a hand around us. "Or have you come down from your *cum-high* enough to remember that fucking me in a car is not what you've held out this long for."

"Oh."

"Yeah." He laughed. "Oh."

"Well." My face flamed as I begrudgingly agreed with his logic. "I suppose I should thank you," I muttered, as I quickly threw my disheveled school uniform back on. "For being so chivalrous when it comes to my protecting my virginity."

"You're welcome," he replied, re-buttoning his school shirt. "Contrary to popular belief, I'm not that guy, Molloy."

"No," I blew out a shaky breath, as I flipped my hair over one shoulder and reached for my seatbelt. "I know you're not, Joe."

"But I'm not a saint either," he warned, when he was fully dressed and had the key turned in the ignition. He cast me a heated look and said, "Next time you beg me to fuck you, I won't say no."

"Yeah." I laughed nervously. "I'll be sure to remember that."

He winked. "You do that."

Oh boy . . .

Phone calls and phonies

June 8th 2004

JOEY

"And then she poured the jug of water over his head and told him to go fuck himself." Molloy laughed down the line. "Can you believe the audacity of that man? He thought he could cop a feel, and Julie would just take it lying down?"

"Julie?" I asked, as I tried to balance my phone between my ear and shoulder, while rolling a tire across the garage floor.

"You know Julie."

I had no clue.

'She's the barmaid that I'm always telling you about."

Nope, still nothing. "Oh, yeah, I remember now." Like I gave a shit about this Julie and her audacious punter. "Good for her," I added, indulging Molloy for the sake a quiet life. "Wait – he didn't touch your tits, did he?"

"No, chill, the only one touching me is you."

"Good." Pausing, to sit the tire against the wall, I moved for the next one. "Listen, I'd love to stay and talk, but I'm still at work." *And so are you.*

"Yeah, me, too," she replied with a sigh. "I'm on my break."

"Well, I'm not," I replied, growing frustrated by the distraction. It was an unfamiliar feeling for me because when I was at work, I was at *work*. I didn't mess about. I put my head down and got shit done. Unlike the deviant on the other line."So, I'm hanging up now."

"No, no, no, don't hang up," Molloy whined down the line. "Stay on the line and keep me company."

"Call Casey to keep you company," I replied. "I have a lot to get done here before I clock out."

"Joe—"

"Do you want to meet up at five?" I growled. "Because that won't happen if you don't let me finish my jobs, Molloy."

"Fine." She huffed out a breath. "I'll call Casey."

"You do that," I replied. "Bye."

"Love you."

"See you at five."

"Say it."

"Jesus Christ, just go the fuck back to work."

"Say it and I will."

"No." I blew out a frustrated growl. "Stop pushing."

"You love it when I push you," she teased, and then her voice took on a flirty purr when she added, "But you love it even more when I pull you."

"What have I gotten myself into?"

"The best relationship of your life."

She wasn't wrong there. "See you at five."

Potty training and pep talks

July 6th 2004

JOEY

I didn't want to be here.

Not in this house, or this family.

Unfortunately for me, God didn't let children pick their parents.

If he did, then maybe there would be less miserable children in the world.

If he did, then I sure as hell wouldn't be anywhere near these people.

No fucking way.

"Okay, kid, let's do this." Shaking my head to clear my pissy thoughts, I focused on the task in hand and gave my little brother two enthusiastic thumbs up. "Give it your best shot."

With big brown eyes, my baby brother stared up at me from his perch on the potty. "Gots no poos, Dada."

Bullshit, I just caught you crouching behind the couch.

"Try," I said instead, clicking into an earlier text from Molloy. "And good fucking job, kid. That was almost an intelligible sentence."

MOLLOY: IT'S SATURDAY. IT'S SUNNY. IT'S OUR SUMMER BREAK FROM SCHOOL. SO, EXPLAIN TO ME WHY I'M SUNBATHING IN THE GARDEN WITH SPUD LICKING HIS BALLS NEAR MY FACE INSTEAD OF LYING ON A BEACH WITH YOUR BALLS NEAR MY FACE INSTEAD?

Grinning, I leaned against the bathroom wall, and quickly tapped out a text and pressed send.

JOEY: GOT THINGS TO DO @ HOME. DON'T WORRY, THOUGH, I'LL CALL OVER TONIGHT AND YOU CAN HAVE MY BALLS IN YOUR FACE AS MUCH AS YOU WANT. I'LL EVEN WASH THEM FIRST.

MOLLOY: WOW. SUCH A GENT! I BET YOU DO THAT FOR ALL THE GIRLS.

JOEY: ONLY THE ONES WHO GIVE EXCELLENT HEAD.

MOLLOY: ALWAYS HAPPY TO PLEASE A FAN.

MOLLOY: SO . . . HOW WOULD YOU FEEL ABOUT SKIPPING TOWN FOR A NIGHT THIS WEEKEND? THERE'S THIS TECHNO RAVE FESTIVAL IN KERRY, AND I REALLY WANT TO GO.

JOEY: CAN'T.

MOLLOY: NO . . . . WHY?? WE DON'T HAVE TO GO FOR THE WHOLE WEEKEND. JUST ONE NIGHT?

JOEY: WISH I COULD. GOT RESPONSIBILITIES @ HOME.

"He's not your daddy, Sean," Ollie called out, dragging my attention away from my phone to see Ollie poking his head around the shower curtain, where he was supposed to be washing himself. "He's Joey, remember? Our big brother."

"O-wee," Sean recited slowly, frowning up at me for a long moment. "O-wee dada."

"No," Ollie corrected, growing irritated. "Stop saying that, Sean."

"Dada."

"No, Sean, stop!"

"Calm down, Ols," I sighed wearily, sliding my phone back in my pocket. "It doesn't matter."

"But it's weird, Joe."

Tell me about it.

"He'll get there in his own time," I replied,

"You're wasting your time with that one, Ols," Tadhg grumbled from the bathroom doorway. "That baby is broken in the head. He's going to be three in October, and he can't even talk yet."

Yeah, because he's been knocked around the head more times than you have fingers to count.

"You'll be broken in the head if you talk about him like that again," I snapped. "Besides, you were almost four before you could wipe your own hole, so don't get all high and mighty on me."

"I was fucking not!" Tadhg huffed, outraged.

"Watch your language, asshole," I warned. "And yeah, you were."

"What?" Tadhg's mouth fell open. "But you just called me an ass—"

"I'm older than you." I smirked. "I can say what I want."

"I was two when I learned to use the toilet," Ollie, chimed proudly. "And you're not 'posed to say the F word, Tadhg."

"Oh look," Tadhg shot back sarcastically, rolling his eyes. "Another brother who can't talk right."

"Oh, yes, I can."

"Say supposedly."

"Su-pose-ably."

"Exactly."

"Pack it in," I warned, tossing a roll of toilet paper at him. "And you," I added, addressing Ollie this time. "Wash yourself properly this time. You could grow cabbages in those ears."

"I could?" His eyes lit up with delight. "Really?"

Jesus.

"No, not really, ya dope," Tadhg replied, verbalizing my thoughts aloud. "Christ, where did he even come from?"

"Mam's privates," Ollie replied with a shrug. "Same as you guys."

"Privates?" Tadhg gaped at our younger brother. "Who the hell says that?"

"Well, it's really called a regina," Ollie replied happily. "Shannon's got one, too, you know. That's what my teacher said girls got down there. And we're 'posed to use the proper word for it."

"Whoa, whoa, whoa. Hold the fuck up." I cocked a brow and stared at my brother. "Your teacher told you that?"

"Uh-huh."

I gaped. "But you're barely nine."

"Yep." He nodded. "She was teaching us all about the reginas at school before the summer holidays. And the penises. They're the birds – the girls, I mean. The boys are the bees, 'cause we sting, you know."

"It's called a vagina, not a regina, ya little freak," Tadhg grumbled, clutching his stomach. "Get out of the way, Joe, I need to puke."

"Seany poos," a small voice squealed in delight, thankfully drawing my attention away from the strangest child I'd ever encountered. "Seany poos, Dada!"

"He's not your dada!" both Ollie and Tadhg said in unison. "He's your brother."

"Please say he did it," I whispered wistfully, as I grabbed the toddler and lifted him off the potty for further inspection. "Oh my god, lads. He fucking did it." I grinned, feeling a mixture of pride and amazement. "Today is a good day, boys."

"Jesus." Tadhg shook his head. "If Sean taking a dump makes you this happy, then you really need to start to get out more often, Joe. Imagine what seeing a pair of—"

"Don't say it," I warned, reaching for the roll of toilet paper. "Good man, Seany-boo. Next thing you're going to learn is how to wipe your own ass."

Tadhg snickered. "Good luck with that."

"It's called a buck-cocks," Ollie chimed in. "That's what teacher says."

"Jesus," I grumbled, shaking my head.

Tadhg was right.

I needed to get out of here.

My phone pinged in my pocket, and I didn't need to read Molloy's latest message to be convinced of anything, as I quickly tapped out a text and pressed send.

JOEY: THAT FESTIVAL AT THE WEEKEND? I'M IN.

Summer loving: I got me a tatt

July 11th 2004

AOIFE

Joey *never* should have let me talk him into going to that damn techno festival in Tralee on Friday night.

If he hadn't, then we wouldn't be here. Two days later, in a shitty B&B, on the side of the road, in the middle of the backend of Kerry. Not a penny in our pockets to rub together and dying slow deaths from the kind of alcohol abuse that turned a man's liver yellow.

We were a disgrace, and my only consolation was the fact that it was all Joey's fault for going along with my idea.

God, he was so damn impressionable sometimes.

"I think I'm hemorrhaging vodka from my dick," he announced when he stepped out of the ensuite bathroom in our room on Sunday morning. "Seriously." Standing in nothing but his boxers, Joey rubbed his hands up and down his arms, as he padded back to the bed. "I just took a piss that lasted a full two minutes without stopping and smelled *exactly* like what we were drinking last night."

"So sexy," I purred, rolling over to snuggle into him when he flopped back down on the mattress. "Hold up." Springing up in the bed, I gaped down at the five-lettered word ink on his chest. "What the hell is that?"

"What?"

"That." I poked the piece of skin covering his heart.

Aoife was written in italic scribe across the left side of his chest.

"What?" he drawled lazily.

"Did you look in the mirror when you were recording your personal best time for the piss-Olympics?"

"Huh?"

"*Look*," I whisper-hissed, and then bit down on my fist in nervous anticipation.

Bleary-eyed, Joey pulled himself up on his elbows, glanced down at his chest, and released a frustrated groan before flopping back down on the pillows.

"Well, I can tell you one thing for sure that I do remember about the past two days, Molloy, and it's that *this* was *your* genius idea."

"What?" I shook my head, at a total drunken, hazed loss. "No, it wasn't."

"That creepy tent with those hippies," he grumbled. "You dragged me in there last night, demanding to be tramp-stamped."

"I *did*?"

"Yeah, you did."

"Well, it looks like you're the one with the tramp stamp, bitch," I cackled, slapping my palm down on his tender chest. "Hard luck."

"That's what you think," he grunted, shrugging me off, and then draping an arm over his face. "Check your ass."

"Huh?"

"Your ass," he mumbled, voice raspy and hoarse. "I'm on it."

"No, you're not."

"Yeah, I am," he replied, yawning. "If you're in my heart, then I'm in your ass."

"Oh, cop on," I growled, narrowing my eyes. "That's not even funny."

"*You're mine now, Molloy*," he mimicked my voice. "*Hard luck*."

Falling off the bed, I staggered over to the mirror on the back of the bedroom door and unceremoniously yanked my knickers down my legs.

"Oh my god," I screamed, eyes glued to the red inked heart on the right cheek of my ass with the name *Joey* in black ink inside it. "Your name is on my ass!"

"Like I said," he shot back with a yawn. "Looks like you're *my* bitch."

"I'm on my period, you idiot!"

"How is you being on your period my fault?" His voice echoed out from under the pillow he'd draped over his face. "I'm not mother nature, Molloy."

"It's *your* fault because *you* should have stopped me," I strangled out, gaping in absolute horror at the reflection of my red and weltered ass cheek. "Jesus Christ, I don't know what's worse," I wailed, reaching around to rip the cling film off, "the fact that I got a tattoo of my boyfriend's name on my ass like some slut, or the fact that I did it with a *tampon* string dangling between my legs!"

"Do you have any painkillers?" was his loving and supportive response. "My head's in pieces."

"Screw your headache!" I wailed, arms flailing. "How could you let this happen to me?" I shook my head and fought back a whimper. "Joe, my dad is going to kill me."

"Why?" he drawled, not one bit fazed by any of this, as he sprawled out and star-fished the mattress. "Does Tony have a habit of checking the cheeks of your ass, Molloy?"

Road trip home

July 11th 2004

JOEY

"You're going the wrong way."

"No, I'm not."

"Yes, you are."

"Do you want to drive?"

"No."

"Then *shut up*!"

She gasped in a loud breath. "I'm offended!"

I shrugged.

"Say sorry."

"No."

She folded her arms across her chest and huffed. "Do it."

I laughed. "No."

"I want an apology."

"And I want a million euro," I laughed. "Tell you what, you'll get your apology when I get my money."

She glared at the side of my face for a few moments longer before her expression softened. "Hey, Joe, do you think I'm dramatic?"

"Only when you're awake."

Her glare made a reappearance. "Now, I want two apologies."

Her phone started to ring then, and she quickly answered the call. "Hello, father, this is your favorite child speaking."

Rolling my eyes, I concentrated on the road ahead of us, while she rambled on to her dad.

"Yeah, we had a great time," she said, ripping off a lollypop wrapper and popping it into her mouth. "Yeah, Casey really enjoyed the festival, too." She paused to wink at me before continuing with her conversation, "Yeah, I'm totally safe, Dad. I'm really getting the hang of driving."

Yeah fucking right.

"Okay, Dad, I'll see you tonight. Yeah, yeah. Okay, love you. Bye."

Hanging up, she tossed the phone on her lap, and twisted in her seat to face me. "So, I had a really good time this weekend, boyfriend."

"I'm not your boyfriend, Molloy."

"Oh yeah, I forgot," she shot back with a grin. "You're my *bitch*."

Meet my dad – I mean, your boss

August 22nd 2004

AOIFE

On Sunday morning Joey had a face like thunder when he stepped out his front door and made a beeline for where I was sitting on his garden wall.

"I told you that I'd meet you on your street," he snapped, quickly snatching me up, and throwing me over his shoulder. "I don't want you anywhere near this house, Molloy."

His bad mood was something I expected, so I didn't let it faze me.

Instead, I laughed at how ridiculous we looked, as he continued to stalk down the footpath, with me over his shoulder, and my ass in the air.

"I'm wearing a skirt," I laughed, which earned me a string of curse-words, as he quickly set me on my feet, and pulled the hem of my skirt down. "It's nice, huh?" Stepping closer, I grabbed his hand, and made him feel the fabric. "It's totally fake leather, but I feel like a pure ride in it."

"You look like one, too," he muttered, rubbing his jaw, as his eyes drank me in. "Jesus, did you go to mass wearing that skirt?"

"I sure did." Batting my eyes I grinned up at him. "But don't worry, I plan on going to confession next week to atone for my sins."

"Atone." Smirking, he slung an arm over my shoulders as we walked. "You don't know the meaning of the word."

"And you do?" Reaching around, I slipped my hand into his back pocket, my favorite place to touch him. "I didn't see you lining up for holy communion."

"Fair point."

"So." Thinking carefully about how I was going to phrase my next question, I said, "we've had fun this summer, haven't we, Joe?"

"Yeah," he replied slowly. "We have."

"I mean, we have, though, right?" Exhaling heavily, I added, "We've spent a lot of time together, had a lot of fun, done a lot of *stuff*."

"Is this the part where you tell me that you've had a great time, and you'll always cherish the memories we've made together, but it's time for me to get the fuck away from you now?'

"What?" I gaped at him. "*No*. Why would you even say that?"

"Not sure," he replied in a curious tone, rubbing his jaw. "Those damn TV shows you make me watch must be making me soft."

"Well, I'd say that I'm the one making you soft, but we both know that never happens when you're around me."

"Nice."

"Thanks. So, listen, I have no plans on ending anything," I hurried to say. "But I *was* hoping that I could run something by you really quick."

"Sounds dangerous."

"Only a little." I laughed nervously and looked up at him. "How would you feel about coming over for dinner?"

"Huh?" Joey stared down at me like he hadn't understood the question.

"Dinner," I repeated, swallowing deeply. "I want you to come over for dinner."

"With *you*?"

"Yeah," I replied with an enthusiastic nod. "And the rest of my family."

"No," he was quick to shut down, as his hand dropped from my shoulder like my skin had burned him. "Not happening."

I rolled my eyes. "Joey."

"I'm not interested," he snapped, running a hand through his hair. "If you wanted a guy that you could take home to meet the family, then you should have stuck with Ricey. I'm clearly not that guy, Molloy. I'm not the kind that mothers want to see with their daughters shacking up with."

"Oh, please," I snapped. "My mam loves you."

"Only because she doesn't know what I do to her daughter when they go to bed at night."

My jaw fell open. "Joe, come on."

"No, no, no, don't look at me like that," he warned. "Don't give me those big eyes, Molloy. It's not happening. You know that I don't want your father finding out about us. I could lose my job. How the fuck am I supposed to explain rolling up to the dinner table with his baby girl in tow?"

I shrugged. "We could just tell them?"

Now he was the one whose mouth fell open. "Tell me you're joking."

"What?" I defended. "Would it be so terrible if our parents knew about us?"

"Yes, it would," he argued right back. "It would be very fucking terrible. I could lose my job."

"He won't fire you for being my boyfriend."

"I'm not your boyfriend, Molloy," he was quick to deny. "I'm just your—"

"Yes, you are, ya big eejit," I snapped, irritated now. "It's been seven months. You're my boyfriend, I'm your girlfriend, and we love each other a lot."

"We absolutely do not!"

"So much in fact that we love to take our clothes off and put our mouths on each other's—"

"Jesus Christ." He blew out a pained breath. "You are hell-bent on getting me killed, aren't ya?"

"It's going to be fine," I coaxed, sliding my arm through his, as I practically dragged him down the road. "They didn't even sound that surprised when I mentioned it."

"What?" He gaped at me. "What did you do?"

"Nothing."

"Molloy."

"Nothing, I swear."

"Molloy."

"Fine." I threw my hands up. "I already told my parents that I invited you over for dinner."

463 • CHLOE WALSH

"*No.*" Joey stopped walking again, and this time, I think he stopped breathing. "Tell me you didn't."

"And I also told them that you said you'd come," I admitted, covering my eyes with my hand and then peeking through my fingers.

His eyes bulged. "*And?*"

"And they said that dinner will be ready at one o' clock," I twisted the knife by adding, "We're having roast beef. Please don't be mad."

"Roast beef?" Running a hand through his hair, he hissed, "Aoife, I'm going to *be* roast fucking beef when your father gets his hands on me."

"Wow," I mused. "You called me Aoife. You never call me Aoife."

"Well, I suppose I better start practicing," he hissed. "You know, for when I meet your *parents*."

I grinned. "As my boyfriend."

"Not your boyfriend," he muttered, and then released a pained groan. "Oh my Jesus, I just realized something."

"What?"

"My boss's daughter is my *girlfriend*."

Laughing, I patted him on the shoulder. "That she is."

Dinner with Tony

August 22nd 2004

JOEY

Molloy snookered me with an invitation to dinner with her family that I couldn't get myself out of.

I'd been in her house countless times over the years, but never as her invited guest for a family dinner.

Unnerved and completely unprepared for what I was about to face, I stood slightly behind her the whole way there, keeping my hands in my jean's pockets.

Don't touch her, I mentally warned myself, as she opened the front door and stepped inside, *and no goddamn fighting.*

"It's okay," she said, with a smug grin, as she gestured for me to follow her into the lion's den.

Yeah, it might be okay for her, I thought bitterly, but I was the one with everything on the line here.

My ability to provide for my family.

My ability to procreate with a functional pair of balls.

Yeah, I had a feeling both were at stake today.

This was all new territory to me.

One minute, I was twelve years old, and locking eyes on her at the school gates, and the next, I was seventeen, standing in her house, about to tell her father that she was mine.

Christ.

I had no fucking clue how to make this work without screwing everything up.

Because, let's face it, I had a gift for fucking up.

Muttering out a string of curse words under my breath, I followed her into the house, feeling my heart rate increase with every step I took closer to the kitchen – a kitchen I knew well, considering I'd helped Tony fit it three summers ago.

"Aoife, is that you, love?" With her back to the door, Trish Molloy reached into the oven and retrieved the nicest smelling joint of roast beef I'd ever had the pleasure of smelling. "Have you any idea what time young Joey is coming over? The meat's just done, and I want to serve it while it's hot."

"Yeah, Mam," Molloy offered, offering me a reassuring nudge with her shoulder. "We're both here."

Here we go.

"Joey, love." Setting the roasting tin on the counter, Trish pulled off her oven glove and shuffled over to us. "How are you?" With a warm smile, she grabbed my arms, reached up, and pressed a kiss to my cheek. "It's lovely to have you over."

Repressing the urge to jerk away from her touch, I forced myself to smile down at the low-sized, blonde.

"It's good to see you, Trish." Feeling a complete fucking loss, I shrugged and added, "Thanks for having me over." Again. "The food smells great."

"Ah, sure you should know by now that you're always welcome in this house," she replied, and then frowned. "But what have I always told you about keeping that hood up and hiding that handsome face." Reaching a hand up, she pulled my hood down. "Now." She smiled and patted my cheek. "Much better."

Jesus.

"Yeah, Joey." Snickering, Molloy trailed after her mam, helping to set the table and lay out the cutlery. "You really need to stop wearing your hood up all the time."

"Force of habit, I guess," I bit out, glaring at the back of her head. "Can I help with anything?"

"No, no, love," Trish said, ushering me over to the table. "You sit down and relax. You're our guest. We'll look after you for a change."

The sound of a throat clearing filled my ears, and I didn't need to look behind me to know that Tony had entered the kitchen.

"Joey," he said with a sniff, as he walked over to the joint of beef. "You're keeping well?"

"Tony." Forcing myself to remain calm, I offered him a small nod. "All good. Thanks for, ah, for having me over."

"It was Aoife's idea." Reaching into the drawer, he retrieved the sharpest-looking carving knife I'd ever had the misfortune of laying eyes on. "She said the two of you had something to discuss with us."

That's how he'll do it, I thought to myself, as I made my peace with God, *that's what he'll use when he cuts my balls off.*

"Dad," Molloy growled in a warning tone. "You promised."

Tony held his hands up. "Have I said a harsh word to the lad?"

"You didn't have to," she snapped back. "The fact that you're glaring at him while yielding a carving knife says it all for you."

Christ.

"Listen, Tony." Knowing that I was going to have to get this over with sooner or later, I pushed my chair back and stood. "Can we talk outside?"

"You want to talk?"

"Yeah, I do." I glanced warily at the shiny piece of steel in his hand. "Preferably without the knife."

"Right so, boyo, let's have that talk."

Reluctantly setting the knife down, my boss nodded stiffly and opened the back door, before stepping outside.

"Aoife, stay here," Trish called out when Molloy attempted to follow me out.

"But—"

"No buts, young lady," her mother replied. "Now be a good girl and mash the spuds for your poor mammy. My arthritis is flaring up."

Worrying on her lip, Molloy offered me a helpless shrug as I walked to my fate.

If I die today, it's on your conscience, I mentally told her, as I stepped outside and closed the back door behind me.

Turning to face her father, who was glaring at me like I had betrayed him, and let's face it I had, I quickly held my hands up. "Before you say a word, just know that I didn't set out to disrespect you in any way, shape, or form."

He sighed heavily. "Joey."

"I know that you've been good to me," I hurried to add. "And this probably feels like the ultimate betrayal, considering you warned me not to go there with her, but I care about your daughter, Tony."

He shook his head. "Joey—"

"I do, Tony," I urged. "I really fucking care about her, okay? This isn't a fleeting notion, either. We didn't get together on a whim. I put a hell of a lot of thought into this," I added, blowing out a breath. "She's my friend, Tony. My best friend – has been for a long time now. I'm not going to lie to you and say that I didn't see it coming, but I can truthfully say that I did everything I could to stop it from happening—"

"Joey!" Tony barked, and I quickly clamped my mouth shut. "I only have two questions for you."

Oh Jesus.

"And take your time answering them," he added. "Because I only want the truth, lad."

I nodded. "Okay."

"First." He eyed me carefully and asked, "Do you love my daughter?"

Heart thumping violently in my chest, I felt myself nod. "Entirely." And then I heard myself say, "For about five years now."

Well shit . . .

"Second," he said slowly. "Do you see a future with her?"

"No," I admitted, hating my words, but needing to give him the truth, because if anyone deserved my honesty it was this man. "I don't see a future for us, but that's not because I don't want one with her. It's because I don't see a future for myself, period."

The hard look on his face softened. "Ah, lad."

I shook off his sympathy.

I didn't want it, and I didn't need it.

"I know that I let you down," I continued, blowing out a harsh breath. "So, there won't be any hard feelings on my end if you need to let me go at work."

"Let you go?" Tony frowned. "Why would I do that?"

I stared back in confusion. "Because I fell in love with your daughter when you told me not to."

"We seem to have our wired crossed, boyo," Tony said with a heavy sigh, as he walked towards me and clamped a hand on my shoulder. "I warned you off my daughter because I didn't want to lose a good worker if it all went pear-shaped, and for no other reason."

I frowned at him. "But I thought ..."

"You're a grand lad, Joey," Tony added, giving my shoulder a squeeze. "A lad I would be happy to see look after my Aoife."

"No." I shook my head, brows furrowed in confusion. "I'm really not, Tony."

"You forget that I've known you since you were a small boy of twelve," he reminded me, as he steered us towards the back door. "I remember looking at this small scrap of a lad standing in the garage, down on his luck and with the weight of the world on his shoulders. That small boy asked me for a chance that day," he added, voice thick with emotion. "I took a chance on that boy, and I'm glad that I did, because the man that small boy turned into is a man who I am damn proud of."

Meeting Mammy and making plans

August 22nd 2004

AOIFE

My parents were far from perfect, but as I sat at the dinner table and watched them embrace Joey, I was glad they were mine.

The only skeptic in the midst was a very wary-looking Kev, who seemed to have a nervous disposition around my boyfriend.

I couldn't blame my brother, not when the same hands that made me feel so good had almost throttled him.

Somehow, through the jigs and the reels, we had managed to broach the subject of what would happen after all three of us finished secondary school next year.

"That sounds lovely," Mam said after dinner, when we were all in the sitting room, with bowls of Vienetta on our laps. Yeah, Mam had brought out the fancy ice-cream. "And you're happy with the qualification you'll get from that course, yeah? You'll get a good job from it?"

"Absolutely. They also have a fantastic campus, and the curriculum seems solid, which is vastly contradictory to what they have on their pamphlets and website," my brother continued to drone on, almost boring me to tears, as I sat on the couch between him and Joey.

The same Joey who looked incredibly uncertain, as he looked from one face to another.

Stretching my leg out, I discreetly nudged his foot with mine.

His wild green eyes flashed to mine, and I gave him a reassuring smile.

"So, Joey, love," Mam said, when Kev finally decided to stop blowing his own trumpet, "Kev's aiming to get into UCC. Aoife's hoping for hairdressing. What are you planning to do after sixth year?"

"What do you mean *what's the plan*?" Dad interrupted, a spoonful of ice-cream held in the air. "He'll complete his apprenticeship and come on fulltime with me at the garage."

"Would you stop, Tony," Mam admonished, reaching over to slap my father's leg. "I was asking the young lad what *he* wanted to do after school, not what *you* want him to do after school."

"I, ah . . . " Roughly clearing his throat, Joey set his bowl on the floor beside him and turned to my mother. "Well, ah, I was hoping that Tony would consider taking me on for an apprenticeship."

"See now, Trish." My father beamed like the cat that got the cream. "And there's no hoping required, son," he added, this time addressing Joey. "I didn't spend the last five years training you up for some other fella to swoop in and steal you off me."

"Holy fuck." The tension in Joey's shoulder seemed to melt away as he looked at my father like he just told him he won the lotto. "Are you serious?"

"I am," Dad replied. "Just finish off this last year of school, do the best you can, keep your head down and out of trouble, and we'll talk business then."

"Jesus." Exhaling a ragged breath, Joey dropped his head and cupped the back of his neck. "Thanks, Tony."

"Don't you go scaring him off now, ya hear?" Dad said, eyes on me. "I can't be losing my apprentice if you two decide to part ways."

"You won't," Joey assured him. "I won't mess this up."

"Yes, good lad," Dad said. "But I was talking to her ladyship alongside you."

"*Me*?" I laughed. "How am I responsible for this metaphorical parting of ways?"

"Probably because you're such a demanding pain in the hole," Kev offered dryly. "And Dad's having a hard time understanding why anyone would *voluntarily* agree to set up house with such a princess."

"Ha fucking ha," I shot back, digging both of my couch buddies in the ribs when they erupted with laughter. "Aren't you all just so *hilarious*?"

"Don't worry, Aoife, love," Mam offered then. "Dad didn't have to pay Joey too much to go out with you."

More eruptions of laughter unfolded.

"Ah, don't you take any notice of them, pet," Dad crooned, through fits of laughter. "It only cost me a fiver."

"I hate you all," I announced dramatically, and then waved a finger in Joey's amused face. "Especially you, turncoat."

SIXTH YEAR

Home by now

August 31st 2004

JOEY

"You need to do something," Shannon all but begged when I stepped through the front door on Tuesday evening after an extra-long training session with the minors in the city. "Please, Joe, please, you have to do something!" With tear-filled eyes, she clung onto my arm like it was a life jacket. "There's so much blood."

"Jesus Christ, calm down," I snapped, dropping my hurley and gear bag on the hallway tiles. "What's after happening?" I demanded, flustered, as I glanced around wildly. "Who's bleeding?"

Hiccupping out a sob, Shannon dragged me up the staircase, stumbling over her own legs, until we were on the landing.

"In there," she choked out, pointing to the bathroom. "In there, Joe."

"Mam," I strangled out, chest-heaving, as I threw the bathroom door open and barreled inside. "Mam!"

"It's not Mam," Shannon cried out. "It's—"

"It's okay," a small voice said, and my legs gave way beneath me.

"No."

"It's okay, Joe."

No, no, no.

"Really, I'm okay."

Please God no.

Sinking to my knees on the blood-encrusted floor, I just stared helplessly at the small child leaning over the side of the toilet, and the steady flow of blood coming from his nose.

Completely fucking reeling, I felt my head grow light as memories from what felt like a lifetime ago bombarded me.

*

"It's okay, Dar," I wheezed, leaning heavily over the toilet bowl, as a mixture of vomit and blood continued to heave from my black and blue stomach. "I'm okay."

"Joey," Darren croaked out, as he knelt beside me and kept a steadying hand to my back. "I'm so sorry I wasn't here. I had training."

"It doesn't matter," I strangled out, as the pain of having my seven-year-old nose broken threatened to consume me. "I don't care," I continued to say over and over, hoping that if I said it enough times, it might come true.

"It's not as bad as it looks," Tadhg tried to comfort me by saying, as he spat a mouthful of clotted blood into the toilet bowl. He pressed a fresh wad of tissue to his clearly broken nose as the skin under his eyes already started turning a yellowish brown. "Really, Joe, it doesn't even hurt."

"He's gone," Shannon hurried to fill in. "I think he left because he knew you would be home soon."

"Home soon," I mumbled, shaking my head.

"Yeah," she replied softly. "You're usually home by now."

"I'm sorry that I wasn't here to protect you," I heard myself whisper, numb to the bone, as I watched him churn in pain. "I had . . . training."

"It doesn't matter," Tadhg replied, giving me a horrible taste of déjà vu. "I don't care."

"What happened?" I strangled out, feeling my heart hammer violently in my chest. "What the fuck *happened*, Tadhg?"

"Dad hit Shannon," Tadhg bit out. "So, I hit Dad." He spat out another globber of bloodied snot. "Dad hits harder."

"Jesus Christ," I choked out, staggering to my feet, when a surge of panic rocketed through me. "Ollie and Sean?"

"Are in your room listening to music," Shannon hurried to say. "I hope that's okay. It's the only place they feel safe."

It wasn't okay.

None of this was okay.

I'd been knocked on my ass again, and I was losing the will to get back up on my feet.

"Are you staying home tonight?" Shannon asked. "Or do you have plans with Aoife?"

"No," I replied, pulling my phone out of my pocket and quickly unlocking the screen. "I don't have any plans."

JOEY: CHANGE OF PLANS. CAN'T MEET UP TONIGHT. I'LL SEE YOU AT SCHOOL TOMORROW.

MOLLOY: ABSOLUTELY UNACCEPTABLE, JOSEPH. I'M OUTRAGED.

MOLLOY: JOKE. HOPE EVERYTHING'S OKAY?

JOEY: ALL GOOD. SEE YOU IN THE MORNING.

MOLLOY: OKAY.

JOEY: I DON'T LOVE YOU. x

MOLLOY: I DON'T LOVE YOU BACK. ♥

Sliding my phone back into my pocket, I pushed all thoughts of Molloy out of my mind and got down to the business of cleaning up my parents' mess.

Favorite exclusive friend

September 1st 2004

AOIFE

"Look, Neasa, it's the boyfriend-stealing bitch herself."

Resisting the urge to laugh out loud in their faces, I pretended to ignore the girls from my class, as they shuffled past me on the footpath outside of school on Monday.

"What a bitch."

"*Such* a bitch."

Grinning to myself, I continued to suck on my lollipop, thoroughly amused by Rebecca's blatant dislike of me.

I had no doubt that the *scarlet woman* label they'd assigned to me back in fifth year would follow me into the months ahead, but I had a hard time caring.

Especially when the scarlet women got to kiss sexy bad boys like Joey Lynch.

Yeah, we had been liking each other exclusively for about nine months now, and while he went into panic mode every time I put a label on us, I considered myself to be his girlfriend.

Whether he liked it or not.

Sure, Joey fought me at every hand's turn. He pissed me off to epic proportions, and drove me batshit crazy at times, but on the other side, I had never felt more alive, and more like, well, *me* than when I was with him.

The truth was that nothing about being with Joey was easy, and yet being with him felt so incredibly *right*.

Like I was exactly *where* I supposed to be, with exactly *who* I was supposed to be with.

Excitement thrummed to life inside of me the minute my eyes landed on him, walking up the road towards the school, with his little sister in tow.

Feeling ridiculously perky, considering it was the first day of a new school year, my last one, I tossed my lollypop in the nearby bin and strolled down to greet them both.

"Nice shirt."

"Nice legs."

Hooking an arm around my waist, Joey pulled me roughly to his chest and kissed me hard.

"Yeah," he said against my lips. "It's going to be a good day."

"Is that an analogy for something dirty?" I teased, pulling back to look at him, only to feel my stomach somersault – and *not* in a good way – when my eyes landed on his face. "No."

A surge of sadness threatened to drown me as I took in the sight of fresh bruises.

It hurt to look at him sometimes.

To see the marks and bruises on his skin.

It made me so utterly depressed to think about the life he lived when he wasn't with me.

I loathed the fact that he had been thrust into playing the role of both mother and father to his siblings because his shitty parents wouldn't do their job.

It sucked.

It pissed me off that they depended on him for every bloody thing.

Especially his mother.

She was the worst one of all.

Sometimes, I wanted to stand in front of him and scream *back off* to his family.

He has a life of his own to lead!

Because I knew in my heart that he would never leave Ballylaggin and take a year out to travel.

Not while those kids were still in that house.

No, because he needed to work to pay for his parents' mistakes.

I knew that I was extremely selfish for wanting his family, kids included, to back off and leave him alone. I mean, they were little kids, for Christ's sake.

They *depended* on him.

Still, that didn't stop me from wanting to snatch him away and keep him safe, from wanting to give him a safe place to fall, to stay, to rest, and recover.

Of course, Joey was as closed off now as he ever was when it came to his home life.

He never wanted to talk about it, and whenever I tried to broach the subject. It usually resulted in a fight, with him storming off with those assholes from the terrace.

And *that* was something that scared me almost as much as when he was at home.

I didn't know what to do, how to help him, or how to exist in his complicated world.

His parents made me feel homicidal.

His siblings made me feel helpless.

His friends at school made me feel uncomfortable.

And his friends from the terrace made me feel entirely unwelcome.

Especially that dickhead Shane Holland.

But I cared enough about him to *want* to stay.

"I'm grand," he was quick to say, reaching up to remove my prying hand from his face. "I'm *grand*, Molloy," he repeated, pressing another hard kiss to my lips.

"Yuck, guys," Shannon groaned from nearby. "Get a room."

"Hey, Shan," I said, repressing a shiver of pleasure when her brother slung his arm over my shoulder as we walked up the footpath towards the school entrance. "How was your weekend?"

"Hey, Aoife," she replied with a small smile. "It was okay."

Better than your brother's I hope, I mentally replied, taking in the sight of her thankfully unmarked skin.

Slipping a hand around into the back pocket of his grey school trousers, I gave his ass a little pinch, and then leaned into his side and resisted the urge to drag him into the bushes so that I could keep him safe – and get him naked.

"Keep on pinching my ass, Molloy, and I'll have to retaliate," he said in a husky tone, lips brushing against my ear as he spoke. "I have behavioral problems, in case ya haven't heard."

"You know, I think I've heard that a time or ten."

"According to my file, I can't control myself when confronted with a physical altercation."

"Is that so?"

"Yeah, that's so." Pulling me flush against his chest, I felt his hand slide up my bare thigh, not stopping until his fingers trailed over the hem of my knickers.

"Oh my god, you did not just do that!" Shannon wailed, covering her eyes with her hand.

"Ah fuck," Joey declared with a dramatic sigh, as he pulled the elastic of my knickers and let it snap back into place. "Period knickers."

I threw my head back and laughed at his forlorn expression. "How would you know anything about my period knickers?"

"Oh my god, you did not just . . . You know what . . . ? Never mind. I'll see you guys later," Shannon groaned, as she clenched the straps of her school bag, and hurried away.

"Come on, Molloy," he said with a lopsided grin. "You've worn granny knickers for a grand total of five days a month, every month, since we've been *special* friends." His voice was low and ridiculously sexy, as his eyes burned with heat. "I know this because those are the only five days each month that you won't let me put my—"

"Okay, la-la-la, I get it. You've got my menstrual cycle down to a tee," I laughed, clamping a hand over his mouth. "But I think that you've just scarred your sister for life in the process."

"She'll recover," he replied, giving my ass a firm tap. "But I won't."

"It's only for a few days." I rolled my eyes. "Get a handle on yourself."

"I'd prefer if you got a handle on me instead." His hand gripped me tighter. "Again."

"Okay, you've officially shamed me into silence." My cheeks flushed bright pink. "You win this round."

"Thanks." Grinning, he caught ahold of my hand, and led us towards the main building. "I look forward to your comeback, Molloy."

"Oh, you better believe it's coming, Joe," I replied, entwining my fingers with his.

We were crossing the teacher's carpark when a familiar Honda Civic flashed its lights.

I felt Joey stiffen beside me, and my heart plummeted into my chest.

No.

No.

No.

"Joey, don't." I tightened my hold on him. "Just ignore him."

"He's clearly here for me."

"So?" I clutched him tighter. "Just keep walking."

"Molloy."

"Please don't."

The sound a car horn beeping erupted.

"I better go see what he wants," he muttered, gaze flicking to where Shane Holland was signaling him over. "I'll meet you in class."

No.

No.

"Joey."

"I'm just going to talk to him," he assured me. "Just talk. That's it, Molloy."

I stared up at his face, soaking in the image of his clear, focused eyes, and made a silent vow to God that I would rain hell down on that asshole Shane if my boyfriend returned to me in any other condition.

"Promise me," I heard myself beg. "Promise me, Joe."

"Everything is *fine*," he soothed, leaning down to press a soft, lingering kiss on my lips. "Stop worrying." He kissed me again. "I'll meet you in class," he added, giving my chin a playful nudge with his fist before he turned on his heels and jogged across the carpark.

Feeling sick to my stomach now, I clutched the straps of my school bag and stomped towards the entrance of the school, growing more agitated with every step I took away from him.

"Is that Shane Holland?" Shannon asked in a small voice, as she stood under a tree near the front door of the school, with a look of concern etched on her face that resembled the one on mine. "I thought he was gone."

"Yeah," I whispered. "So did I."

"Cunt."

Shannon's breath hitched, and she shifted closer to me.

"Yeah, you heard me, cunt!"

I *hated* that word.

There were few words in the English language that I chose to avoid, but that particular one was not included in my vocabulary.

Swinging around, I locked eyes on none other than Ciara Maloney and Hannah Daly.

Two vicious little bitches from the year below me that needed to be taken down a peg or ten.

"Now." Taking a firm stance in front of my boyfriend's sister, I planted my hands on my hips, and arched a brow, "Which one of you thick fuckers has a death wish?"

"We weren't talking to you," Ciara replied, trying to act tough, but withering now that she was faced with someone older, taller, and stronger. "We meant her."

"Her?" I looked around me. "Who's her?"

"Me," Shannon whispered, trembling behind me. "It's me."

"If by her, you're referring to my fella's sister, then I'll give you a five-second head-start to get the fuck out of her face before I cut your ponytail off and strangle you with it."

"Stay out of this, Aoife," Hannah tried to interject, glancing around nervously. "This isn't your fight."

"If you fight her, you fight me," I warned, as unaffected by their bullshit as I was unwilling to back down. "So, are we fighting, or are you bitches keeping your hair for another day? I'm down either way."

They both looked at each other and then Shannon before shaking their heads and stalking off in the direction of the main building.

When they were out of sight, Shannon released a huge breath and clutched the sleeve of my jumper. "You didn't have to do that for me."

"I know."

"They might go after you next."

I rolled my eyes. "I'd like to see them try. And if they go near you again, all you need to do is come and find me. It doesn't matter if I'm in class or not. Just come and find me and I'll help you, okay?"

She looked up at me with the biggest blue eyes I'd ever seen, so full of sadness and uncertainty, and whispered, "Why?"

"Because I love your brother, and your brother loves you. Keeping you safe is important to him, which makes it important to me." Smiling, I threw my arm over her skinny little shoulders and walked her into school. "And who knows? Maybe in time, you'll be coaxed out of that pretty little shell, and we can be friends."

"You want to be my friend?"

"Is that okay with you?"

"Yes." She nodded uncertainly. "Please."

My heart cracked in my chest.

She was so small.

So vulnerable.

So broken.

"Then it's official." I gave her a reassuring hug as I walked her down the corridor to class, making sure that every catty bitch in this school got a good look at us. "We're friends."

Old habits die hard

September 1st 2004

JOEY

I didn't need anyone to tell me what a piece of shit I was my conscience was more than willing to do that, as it screamed *liar* with every step that I took closer to the car.

It had been screaming at me last night, too, when I sent that text.

Now, as I found myself climbing into the passenger seat beside him, I felt a level of self-loathing that I hadn't plummeted to before.

"Lynchy," Shane said the minute I climbed into the car. "You look like hell."

No shit, Sherlock.

"Yeah." Knees bopping restlessly, I blew out a shaky breath. "I feel like it, too."

Last night was the closest I'd come to cracking up in a very long time.

After finally calming the kids down and persuading them to go to bed, I'd necked a few of my mam's Valium to calm me the fuck down and help me get some sleep.

The only problem with that had been the fact that my old man decided to make a reappearance in the middle of the night, which meant that I had been too strung out to defend myself when his fists started swinging.

When I woke up this morning, it was to a body of bruises, and a mind that had hit its limit.

I couldn't fucking do this anymore.

I couldn't.

I *tried*.

I did.

I tried so hard to be good, but it never seemed to matter, because *nothing* was going to change for me.

I was never getting away from that house, not while the kids were still there, which meant that in order to survive another day in hell, I found myself breaking promises and slipping back into old habits.

"Was surprised to get your message last night, kid," he stated. "Haven't heard from you for a while."

Twist the fucking knife, why don't you?

"Thought you switched up suppliers or something."

No, I want to keep my legs.

"Listen, lad, it's like I said last night, I just need some benzos. Same as always. Just something to relax my brain." Reaching into my pocket, I grabbed the folded wad of cash and dropped it on his lap. "It's all there."

He picked it up and counted it before offering me a clipped nod.

I was ashamed to say that I lunged for the glove box to retrieve my poison of choice, only to frown when my eyes landed on some serious bullshit.

"Weed, Shane?" Furious, I tossed the bag back into the glove box and ran a hand through my hair in frustration. "What the fuck am I supposed to do with that?"

"There's been a situation with my carrier," he explained calmly. "A temporary delay in delivery."

"Fine," I bit out, feeling jittery at the prospect of not getting what I'd come for – what I fucking needed. "Got any oxy? Or hydro? A few benzos? Come on, Shane, don't throw me under the bus like this."

"Like I said, kid, there's been an issue with my supplier." Sparking up a cigarette, he inhaled a deep drag and then tossed both the box and my cash on my lap. "Which means it's going to be a while before I have your usual."

"How long are you talking?" I bit out, sparking up a cigarette, as I shakily tucked my cash back in my pocket. "A couple of days? A week? Because I'm fucking drowning here, lad. I can't wait."

"Relax, Lynchy," he interrupted, tone coaxing. "I know you're in a bad way."

"Yeah," I seethed, chest heaving now. "I am."

There was no point in denying it.

Shane had known me since I was a child.

He could read me like a book.

Nodding in understanding, he reached into his pocket. "Which is why this is on me," he added, sliding the small paper fold over to me. "No strings."

Unfolding the neatly wrapped paper, I stared down at the off-white-colored powder in my hands. "That's not coke, is it?"

He shook his head and exhaled a cloud of smoke.

My pulse skyrocketed. "Shane."

Keeping his eyes trained on the windscreen in front of him, he said, "Gear guaranteed to give the desired effect."

"No." I shook my head. "I told you before that I don't want heroin!"

"I know, I know," he coaxed, holding his hands up. "But this shit just hits on a different level. It's cheaper, too, kid."

"How cheap?"

"What you've been paying for one flush of your usual will keep you good for a week in smack."

"No. No goddamn way. I don't do needles," I snapped, running a hand through my hair. "I'm not a fucking junkie."

"You don't have to," he was quick to explain. "You're watching too much television. That's brown sugar. What I'm offering you is pure. The good stuff. You can smoke it or snort it. Whatever you like, lad. It'll make everything else feel like Smarties, kid. Take my word for it."

"I can't," I strangled out, staring down at the temptation in my hands. "It's too fucking risky."

"Not when it's used safely," he encouraged. "Come on, kid. Do you think I'd fuck you over like that? We're from the same terrace. I've known you since you were in nappies."

"Listen, Shane, I just need something to help me get by," I heard myself argue, and I wasn't sure who I was arguing with; him or me. "I'm so fucking *fucked* in the head here. I don't need anything that's going to make my life worse."

"I get it," he said, giving me an understanding nod. "Those GAA trainers are breathing down your neck, you have teachers giving you shit, and that little ride of yours has you strung up by the bollocks. You're under pressure, kid, and need a little release. I get that. They might not understand, but I do. Don't feel bad for needing a little help to get you through that bullshit you have to take from your old man." I glared at him, and he held his hands up. "Your old man's a scumbag, kid. It's common knowledge. I'm not judging you for needing a reprieve from a bastard like that."

That was the problem; I did *need* that reprieve.

I needed it so damn badly that I heard myself relent and say, "Fine, but only until your supplier comes good with my usual."

"Absolutely," he agreed enthusiastically. "Have at it, kid."

"Fuck." Shaking my head, I stared down at the contents of the fold and muttered, "You said I can snort it, yeah?"

"Here." Reaching across the seat, he took the fold from me and quickly went to work on splitting it. "This is enough at a time to get you fucked," he explained, handing me a CD case with a small amount of powder. "Snort it like you would any other line and feel yourself relax, kid."

"The hell am I doing?" I grumbled, as I looked around the empty carpark before taking the rolled-up fiver from his hand and leaning in close. Disgusted with myself for my weakness, I pressed the make-shift straw to my nose and inhaled deeply.

Strung out

September 1st 2004

AOIFE

Joey didn't follow me into class.

In fact, he didn't show up until the class before big lunch.

"What the hell, asshole?" I whisper-hissed when he sank into the chair alongside mine during Business. "Where have you been?"

"I had to go home," he explained quietly, as he withdrew his textbook and pencil case from his bag. "I, uh ..."

"You what?" I asked, waiting for his answer.

Jerking, he shook his head, and mashed a hand against his cheek. "Must be out of credit."

Suspicious, I narrowed my eyes. "Are you high?"

"No."

"Joey."

"No."

"Don't lie."

"I'm not."

"Then what's up?"

"Nothing."

"You look like you've been crying?" I whispered, as concern rose inside of me at a rapid pace.

His nose was red, his eyes were bloodshot and watering.

"I don't cry." Joey released a shaky breath and retrieved a wad of tissue from his pocket. "I'm just ..." He completely spaced out for several long beats before adding, "coming down with something."

"Oh my god, Joe, you're bleeding," I strangled out, when the white tissue he used to dab his nose came back a crimson red. "Your nose is bleeding."

"I am?" He stared down at the blood-stained tissue in an almost trancelike motion. Blood continued to trickle down his face, but he made no move to intervene. "Ah shit."

"Joey," I snapped, grabbing the tissue from his hand and pressing it to his nose. "What did you do?"

"Nothing."

"Nothing?" With one hand cupping the back of his head, I used the other to hold the tissue to his face. "Bullshit. What did he give you?"

"Nothing," he whispered, hands falling limply to his sides, as he watched me watch him. "It's all good, Molloy."

"Don't lie to me," I warned. "You're completely strung out."

"I'm not lying." My heart plummeted out of my ass and on to the floor, where he then kicked it by saying, "I swear."

"You're such a *liar*."

Furious, I quickly pulled him to his feet, and reeled off some spiel to the teacher before ushering him out of the classroom, ignoring the stares and whispers as we went.

"Is Joey alright there, Aoife?" our teacher, Mr. Brolly, called out the classroom door after us.

"Yeah, yeah, sir, he's grand. It's just a nosebleed. Will you ask Casey to pack up our bags for us," I called back, keeping him welded to my side, as I walked him out of school and over to where I had parked my car.

"Don't hate me, Molloy," Joey mumbled, falling into the passenger seat the minute I let him go to open the car door. "You're all I have to wake up for in the morning."

Back to the dog house

September 1st 2004

JOEY

I was back in the doghouse.

Strewn out on her bedroom floor, bollocks-naked, with a fluffy white pillow under my head, and a pink blanket thrown over me, was how I found myself when I came to.

"So he lives," a familiar voice drawled sarcastically.

Shivering violently, I slowly pulled myself up to find a furious pair of green eyes glaring at me.

Sitting with her back to her door, she glowered at me when she asked, "What did he give you?"

I opened my mouth to lie, but she got there first.

"Don't even think about lying to me," she warned, tossing the tea towel that had been resting on her shoulder at my head. "If you saw what came out of your body, what I had to clean off you, then you'd know that lying is pointless."

Disgusted with myself, I looked around her disheveled room, her now stripped bed, and bit back a groan. "Did I . . . "

"Destroy my room in the process of destroying your brain?" she was quick to hiss. "Yep."

"Sorry." I blew out a breath. "I'll clean everything—"

"It's already done," she snapped. "And before you think about running out on me without an explanation, just know that every stitch of clothing you had on is currently in the dryer downstairs. So, no, Joe, I don't want your help to clean. All I want from you is answers."

"What do you want to know?"

"Start with what you took this morning, and we'll go from there."

"Fuck." Reaching up, I cupped the back of my head and sighed before reluctantly admitting, "I had a slip."

"A slip."

There was no point in lying to her, even if lying was my first language, something I'd inherited from my family.

I couldn't do it now, though.

The look in her eyes told me that I had one chance to fix this and only one.

"I'm not going to make excuses," I said. "There's no excusing it."

"No." Her voice was thick with emotion. "There's not."

"Contrary to today, I really have been trying," I added, running a hand through my hair. "More than you know."

"Then *why*?" Her voice cracked, and I watched as a tear trickled down her cheek. "Why do *this*? You've been doing so well. I *know* you have. I know you're not perfect, okay. I know you smoke weed. I know you have your demons and your secrets, but you were *trying*. You weren't getting all fucked up like this!"

"He broke Tadhg's nose last night," I heard myself admit. "And I wasn't there to stop him."

"Your father?" Her breath hitched in her throat. "Your father broke Tadhg's nose?"

"Yeah. He did," I replied flatly, hating myself with every fiber of my being for telling her things that she had no business knowing.

For dragging her deeper into my fucked-up world.

"But he's only a child," she cried, covering her mouth with her hand. "He's just a little kid."

"Doesn't matter," I deadpanned. "Abusive alcoholics see no age or gender. All they see is a punching bag to take aim at when the notion strikes them."

"Joey."

"*Don't* pity me," I warned shakily, holding a hand up. "That's not what I want from you. Not ever."

"I'm not," she whispered. "I won't."

"Anyway, I couldn't handle what happened last night," I admitted. *Still can't.* "So, I did what I usually do when shit gets too heavy at home." I shrugged. "I called Shane."

Tears streamed down her cheeks as she watched me watch her. "And?"

"And." I exhaled a heavy sigh before admitting, "I got what I needed to help me handle it."

"Which was?"

"Something I haven't tried before."

"Something bad?"

Bitter with regret, I nodded my response, which caused Molloy to choke out a huge, gut-wrenching sob.

"You can't do that again." Scrambling onto her hands and knees, she crawled over to where I was sitting and threw her arms around me. "You can't, Joe. You just can't." Crying hard, Molloy clung to me like a baby monkey, holding on to my body like it was something of great importance to her. "I need you. I need you, Joe. You can't do this to yourself."

"It's okay." Rattled by just how deeply her pain affected me, I wrapped my arms around her. "Shh. It's okay."

"We could get out of here," she sobbed against my neck. "You and me. We could just load up the car and leave this shithole town behind us. I would go with you, Joe. I would. I love you," she continued to sob, peppering kisses down my neck. "I love you. I love you. I love you so fucking much, it makes me want to die."

I believed her, and that scared me worse than the prospect of staying.

Because I knew that she was willing to do anything to help me, and, in the end, it wouldn't be enough, because I was too fucking gone in the mind.

She was too good for me, too fucking good for the world. I knew deep down inside that I needed to let her go in order to give her some chance of a future.

But I just *couldn't.*

"I can't leave them, Molloy," I whispered, tightening my arms around her, when her body racked with sobs. *I'm not my brother.* "I have to stay."

Resigned to heartache

September 1st 2004

AOIFE

I never wanted to experience a day like today ever again.

There were no words to describe the level of helplessness I had felt when I watched Joey soar and then roughly crash and burn.

I wasn't stupid.

I could see the red flags shooting up in every direction.

Problem was, I was too in love to take heed.

Because I knew that beneath all of the pain and bullshit, there was someone worth saving in there.

He was a good person who made terrible decisions.

He wasn't trying to hurt anyone.

He was trying to survive in the only way he'd ever known how, by self-medicating.

Even as I watched him sleep it off on my bed, I could see the heartache he represented to me written all over every inch of his skin.

He was going to break my heart, I knew it. I could see it coming from a mile away, and I still couldn't seem to get my self-perseveration instincts to kick in and protect me from the inevitable.

Listening to him talk about his father earlier was the most forthcoming he'd ever been with me.

Sitting in the middle of my bedroom, I couldn't help but feel like my world had been rocked.

It was a monumental breakthrough.

The omission may have been lacking in specifics, and he held many more cards close to his chest, but for the boy lying next to me, it had been a Grand Canyon-sized step closer to me.

I couldn't walk away if I wanted to.

"You're all I have to wake up for in the morning."

That small slip of tongue had cut me to the bone.

And as I lay on my side, running my hand through his hair, and watching him sleep, I made a mental vow that I wouldn't allow him to lose himself to the world he teetered on the edge of.

No matter what, I would be right beside him, ready to pull him back to safety.

Even if it meant that I lost myself in the process.

Birthday celebrations

September 18th 2004

AOIFE

"Well, you made it to eighteen," Casey called over the DJ, as we threw shapes on the dancefloor of The Dinniman. "And with your virginity intact." Laughing, she added, "I don't know which one I'm more surprised about."

"Funny," I shot back, feeling tipsy, as I readjusted my *happy birthday* sash across my chest, and bounced around to The Killers' 'Mr. Brightside'.

Mam, with the help of Casey, had organized this party to celebrate mine and Kev's coming of age, and the entire place was jammed with friends, family, and most of our year from school.

Balloons and banners were hung all around the bar, and I was on such a high to know that *this* many people turned out for us.

I was finally legal, entitled to both order and be served whatever I wanted at the bar, and I was taking full advantage of the new perks.

Cupping her hands around her mouth, Casey asked, "Where's Joey?"

"Where do you think?" I replied, pointing a thumb in a direction to where both Joey and my dad were deep in conversation at the bar.

Dad was nursing a pint of Guinness, while my boyfriend gripped a tall glass of vodka and Red Bull, his drink of choice.

Joey looked incredibly sexy tonight in his jeans and a fitted white shirt, with the sleeves rolled up to the elbow, revealing some mighty fine forearm porn.

He'd gotten a new haircut for the occasion, too. The back and sides were shaved tight, leaving an adorable mop of blond wavy curls on top.

Of course, he was sporting one hell of a shiner under his left eye, but I was determined *not* to ask him about the bruise.

If I did, the chances were that we would end up in a fight, and that was the *last* thing I wanted tonight.

Joey had opened up to me a few weeks ago but had quickly returned to his usual closed-book persona soon after.

As weird as it sounded, and even though I was still plenty mad about the whole ordeal, Joey getting high and puking all over the walls of my bedroom had unintentionally brought us closer.

He'd been on his best behavior since; with his try-mode reactivated, and Shane's number deleted from his phone – courtesy of yours truly.

It was like one of the roadblocks that he used to keep me out had been knocked aside. I was one step closer to getting over the illustrious walls he'd built up to protect himself.

Towering over my dad, I watched as my boyfriend leaned a hip against the bar and bowed his head to listen to whatever it was my father was rambling on about, nodding in response every once in a while.

"I think it's nice that your boyfriend and your dad are such good buddies," Casey laughed. "They've got this cute little bromance going on. It's adorable."

"True," I agreed, linking arms with my bestie, as we stumbled back to our table. "But when he's *bromancing* my dad, it means that he's not *romancing* me."

"So, you're thinking tonight might be the night?"

"Maybe."

"Oh Christ," Casey groaned. "The anticipation is unbearable."

"How are you, Aoife, love?" Mam asked when I flopped down beside her. "How are you, Casey, pet?"

"Hiya, Trish," my best friend sighed happily, as she plopped down beside me and rested her head on my shoulder. "I'm a small bit tipsy, Trish."

"Are you now?" Mam replied, tone laced with amusement. "What about you, Aoife?"

"I'm tone-sold-cober, Mam."

"Stone cold sober, you mean?" Mam eyed me with that look only mothers could master. "I'm sure you are."

"I love you, Mammy." Hooking an arm around her neck, I pulled her close and pressed a kiss to her cheek. "Thanks for my party."

"I love you too, my little rogue." Worrying her lip, she eyed the hem of my white, skin-tight, boob-tube dress and said, "But I don't love that dress. I could see the cheeks of your arse when you were dancing earlier."

"No, you couldn't," I snorted, batting a hand in the air, as I polished off what was left of my Smirnoff Ice. "Because if you had actually seen what's on my ass, you'd have dragged me off the dancefloor."

"What's on your ass?"

I tapped my nose with my finger. "*Nothing.*"

"And Jesus wept," Mam groaned, shaking her head. "I'm warning you now, young lady, I don't care that you're eighteen now. You're not too big for a clip around the ear."

"You'd never clip my ears." I grinned at her. "You're just a big, old softie, aren't ya, Mam?"

"She looks like a model, doesn't she, Trish?" Casey interjected, as she pulled at the top of my dress. "Yourself and Tony must have used the good stuff when ye made this one." With tears welling in her eyes, Casey grabbed my shoulders and stared at me. "You are my bestestest friend in the whole wide world of Ballylaggin, Aoife Molloy."

"And you're mine, Casey Lordan," I wailed back, throwing my arms around her. "You're the biggest ride in school."

"No, *you're* the biggest ride."

"No, no, I insist it's you."

"Okay, then we're both rides."

"Yay!"

"You're both in love with yourselves, that's what you are!" Tutting, Mam held a finger up and said, "Listen to me now, don't be losing the run of yourself with the novelty of buying your own alcohol now, ya hear?"

"I hear you, Mam."

"I mean it. You are both lovely looking girls," Mam urged, addressing us both now. "Which is why you need to keep a handle on yourselves and keep your wits about you. Don't be drinking to the point of intoxication. It's not safe. You never know who's got their eye on you." Frowning, she added, "And don't be leaving your drinks unattended, either. I was here to watch them, but what if I wasn't? The bar is heaving to the rooftops with young fellas. You could have been spiked."

"Relax, Mam," I cooed, waving a hand around. "Everyone here is a friend of ours."

"Exactly," Casey agreed, smiling. "We're totally safe, Trish, relax."

"Famous last words," Mam muttered, unconvinced.

"Omigod!" I squealed, leaping up when 'Maniac 2000' blasted from the DJ booth. "This is our jam, Case." I grabbed her hand and dragged her to her feet. "Let's go."

"Just be careful tonight, okay?" Mam said. "Please girls."

"Okay," we both chorused in unison as we stumbled towards the dancefloor. "We will."

Happy eighteenth, Molloy

September 18th 2004

JOEY

Molloy had a lot of fans.

The entire back bar of The Dinniman was littered with bodies, all here to celebrate her turning eighteen.

I felt bad for her brother, Kev, who was sitting in the corner with his select group of four friends, while his twin drew half the school to her like moths to a flame.

A very sexy flame.

A flame that, if I saw one more lad from our year kissing on the cheek or touching dangerously low on the back, I was going to lose my shit.

I had no problem with Molloy's extroverted nature; it was who she was. It was a huge part of why I had been drawn to her in the first place, but I had a very big problem with her male friends' wandering hands.

"Looks like you've got your hands full there, son," Tony interjected, inclining his head to where his daughter was surrounded by a group of lads from our year, as they danced and jumped around to Kevin Lyttle's 'Turn Me On'.

"Yeah, Tony," I replied, rubbing my jaw. "Looks like I have."

"Ah, nothing to be worried about there, boyo. She's always been like this. Our Aoife has never been in short supply of admirers," Tony explained in an amused tone. "There's something infectious about her personality, you see. It draws people in." Chuckling to himself, he finished off his pint before adding, "Which puts the fear of god in her poor mother."

I watched from a distance until I saw Eoin Caddigan wrap a strand of Molloy's long blonde hair around his finger as he danced up behind her.

"And that's me off, Tony," I announced, tossing back the last of my drink. "It's time to put the fear of god into someone else."

"Ah, first love." Laughing, he waved me off. "Keep the head, young fella."

"Don't count on it," I muttered under my breath, as I pushed through the crowds, not stopping until I was on the dancefloor, with my arm wrapped around her waist.

"Joe!" Molloy smiled up at me as her arms came around my neck. "I thought you said you don't dance?" Reaching up on her high-heeled tippytoes, she pressed a red-lipstick kiss to the corner of my mouth.

"Tonight's an exception." Glowering at the prick from school, who was gingerly backing away from my girl, I pulled her body flush against mine. "Happy eighteenth, Molloy."

Beaming up at me, she let her hands wander to my chest, as she rocked and thrust her hips against mine, grinding herself against me to the rhythm of the music.

Fuck me, I needed a lot more than a vodka and Red Bull to handle this girl.

"I absolutely don't love you, Joey Lynch," she breathed, fist knotting in my shirt, as she tugged my face down to hers. "And I always won't."

Flying high and falling low

September 19th 2004

AOIFE

"Are you okay?" I asked Joey, several hours later, when we arrived back to my house after the most epic birthday party ever.

"Yeah, Molloy, I'm fine," he replied, dropping my heels and a stack of birthday cards on my bed. "It's all good."

Leaning heavily against my closed bedroom door, I watched as my boyfriend shook out his hands and walked over to my bedroom window.

The tension emanating from his frame assured me that he was *anything* but fine.

"You sure, Joe?"

"Yeah," he called over his shoulder, as he leaned against the window-sill and stared out of the pane of glass. "It's all good."

It clearly wasn't and I wasn't nearly drunk enough to believe otherwise.

Moving over to my stereo, I racked my brain to uncover what I might have done to put him in such a weird move, while I pressed play on a random CD.

Britney's 'Everytime' wafted through the air, and I heard myself say, "If you're feeling weird about staying here tonight, then don't. My parents know and they're fine with it." Closing the space between us, I wrapped my arms around his waist, and pressed a kiss to the middle of his back. "I don't love you."

Sighing heavily, he covered my hands with his and whispered, "I don't love you back."

"Tell me what's wrong." Forcing him to turn and look at me, I reached up and cupped his face between my hands. "Why do you look so sad?" I was drunk, but not drunk enough to miss the lonesome look in his eyes. "*Talk* to me."

"I'm not sad, Molloy," he replied, hands settling on my hips. "I'm just . . . "

"You're just what?"

"Worried."

My brows rose in surprise. "About what?"

"My sister," he confessed quietly, and then blew out a pained breath. "My brothers."

My heart sank into my chest. "Oh."

"I don't like leaving them at night."

Depressed at where this was going, I heard myself ask, "Do you want to go home?"

"No," he surprised me by saying. "That's the thing, Molloy." He shook his head, eyes filling with guilt, and said, "Leaving this room is the *last* thing I want to do."

"Then *stay*," I whispered, pulling him close enough to touch his forehead against mine. "Stay right here with me." Stroking my nose against his, I tightened my arms around his neck, and pressed a kiss to his lips. "I need you too, Joe."

I need you safe and unharmed and the only way I can make sure that happens is if you stay right here with me.

His eyes burned with conflicting emotions. "Molloy."

"I do. I need you, too," I choked out, holding on for dear life. "I need you to stay right here with me, because if you leave me now, I won't be able to breathe until I see you again."

The fact that he had necked at least a dozen shots with me tonight gave me a slight advantage against his ridiculously unyielding moral compass when it came to his siblings.

If I was dealing with sober Joey, he would go home, regardless of how much I begged him not to.

But I was dealing with drunk Joey, and drunk Joey was vulnerable to persuasion.

"Please stay," I whispered, hand snaking up to clutch the small silver chain he always wore around his neck, as I slowly backed towards my bed, taking this beautiful boy with me. "It can be my birthday present." The back of my legs hit the bed, and I fell backwards, taking his big body with me. "Please." Breathing hard against his mouth, I pressed a searing kiss to his swollen lips. "I want this face to be this first thing I see when I open my eyes in the morning."

"Okay," he mumbled against my lips. "I'll stay with you, Molloy."

Thrilled that he relented so easily, I threw myself into the moment, into feeling his body on mine, his hard edges against my soft ones, as we touched each other in ways that should have been illegal.

Later that night, as we lay in bed, facing each other, he broke the silence by saying, "I did, you know."

"You did what?"

"Get you a present."

A smile spread across my face. "Yeah?"

Nodding, he quickly rolled out from under the covers and reached for his discarded jeans.

"It's nothing as flashy as you're used to from Ricey," he warned when he climbed back into bed and tossed a small black jewelry box on the mattress between us, along with a half-melted packet of Rolos.

My heart fluttered. "A whole pack just for me?"

He winked. "I told you I would. And if you don't like the other thing, then it's tough shit because Shannon washed the receipt with my clothes."

Excited, I snatched up the box and flipped the lid open.

Resting against the velvet padding interior was a tiny silver locket with the date *30.08.99* on the front.

"That date . . . " I blew out a shaky breath. "It's—'

"The first day of first year," he explained quietly. "The first time I laid eyes on you, and the first time I understood what it meant to have my heart beating for someone outside of my family."

My heart squeezed so tight in my chest it was hard to breathe. "Joe."

"When I say I don't love you," he continued, nuzzling his face in my neck, "it's the furthest thing from the truth."

Love.

He was talking about *loving* me.

"It's okay, Joe," I whispered, fastening the locket around my neck. "I'm used to your denial by now. I already know how you feel."

"Yeah, but you shouldn't have to be used to it, Molloy. I hear you say the words, and I know that I feel it back. I do. But I just . . . " He shook his head in frustration. "I just don't know how to *not* do it."

"Not do what, Joe?"

"Reject human affection."

My heart.

My poor, poor heart.

It's because of your shitty parents.

Because they treat you like a dog instead of a son.

"It's okay," I croaked out, shifting closer until I was snuggled up to his chest. "We can handle the words the same way we handle sex." Pressing a kiss to his chest, I whispered, "Except in this instance *you* set the pace, and I'll fall in line."

"That sounds like a plan," he agreed gruffly.

"Yeah." I closed my eyes and sighed in contentment. "It does."

Coffee with Marie

October 3rd 2004

AOIFE

"This is a bad idea, Molloy. A really fucking bad idea. Jesus, how did I let you talk me into even considering this?"

Standing in his driveway, with my hand firmly clamped in his, Joey glared at the bricks of his house like he was sizing up a mortal enemy.

"Every instinct I have inside of me is demanding that I get you as far away from shithole as possible."

My heart broke.

This wasn't easy for him.

In fact, this was quite possibly the most riled up I'd seen him behave in a while.

It was unsettling, and I offered him a reassuring squeeze. "It's going to be okay."

"No, it's not." He shook his head sadly. "You don't know what you're letting yourself in for with those people."

I looked up at him. "Those people?"

Nodding grimly, he glared down at me. "My parents aren't your parents, Molloy. They won't welcome you with a hug and a roast dinner." A visible shiver racked through his tall frame, and then he was moving, turning away from his house, and doing his very best to take me with him. "Fuck it. Forget it. Let's just go back to your place."

"I'm doing this, Joey," I warned, digging my heels into the gravel. "It's been almost nine months. I'm meeting them whether you take me inside there or I go in alone."

"For fuck's sake!" He blew out a harsh breath. "Why is this such a big deal for you?"

I didn't flinch or shy away when I said, "Because I want to look that bastard in the eyes and show him that you have someone ready and willing to go to war both *with* you and *for* you."

"Jesus." Running a hand through his hair, he muttered, "Now you're definitely not going inside that house."

"You won't talk about what happens inside of that house, and I don't push," I stated calmly. "I *never* push you, Joe, even when I see the bruises, even when you keep me completely in the dark, and especially when every fiber of my being demands that I do something to protect you."

His eyes flashed with fear. "You swore—"

"I know and I won't call them," I hurried to assure him, remembering the epic fight we had the last time he showed up to school with a bloody lip and I made the mistake of asking if we should call the Gards. "I told you I wouldn't, and I won't."

Releasing a shaky breath, he whispered, "Okay."

"But I *will* stand beside you," I told him, reaching up to wrap my arms around his neck. "I will do that, Joey, and there's absolutely nothing you can do to stop me."

He stared back at me for the longest time before relenting with a frustrated growl.

"It doesn't matter what they say, or how they react," I whispered, reaching up to press a kiss to the curve of his jaw. "I won't run."

"He might be home," he warned, tone thick now. "He might . . . "

"I *won't* run," I vowed, stretching up to kiss him. "I'm not leaving you, and there's nothing he can say or do to change that."

"Don't make me do this, Aoif," he whispered then, tone begging.

His plea hurt because he used my first name, and that meant that he was reaching out to tell me just how serious he was.

"It's going to happen someday," I whispered back, stroking his nose with mine, desperate to give him comfort. "It might as well be this day."

After a long moment, the imploring look in his green eyes morphed into reluctant acceptance. "Stay with me," he told me, as he kept a death grip on my hand. "I'll keep you safe."

Fear washed over me.

Jesus, what the hell was he living with?

Sucking in a steadying breath, I followed Joey inside, not stopping until he had walked us past the outdated living room, through the small, run-down hallway, and into the kitchen.

"Is he here?" were the first words he greeted his mother with.

Daydreaming at the kitchen, his mother's head snapped up, and she stared wild-eyed for a moment before schooling her features. "Who?"

"Dad," came Joey's flat voice.

"No," his mother replied softly. "He's not back yet."

I wasn't sure if the shudder that racked through Joey's frame was one of relief or fearful anticipation, but I didn't have much time to think about it, because he quickly pulled me forward.

"Mam, this is Aoife Molloy," he announced, keeping a tight hold on my hand. "Aoife, this is my mam; Marie Lynch."

"Uh, hey?" I offered a small wave with my free hand. "It's nice to see you again, Mrs. Lynch."

"I remember you." Recognition flashed in her big blue eyes. "You were the girl with Joey's school bag."

"Yeah." Nodding, I smiled. "That's me."

Joey roughly cleared his throat before adding, "Aoife is my girlfriend."

"Your girlfriend," his mother repeated with a small shake of her head. "I didn't know that you were in a relationship with anyone."

"Yeah." Joey shrugged, his stance defensive. "Well, now you know."

"Now I know," his mother said, eyeing me carefully. "This is your girlfriend."

"For his sins," I joked, but she didn't laugh.

Ah crap.

Quickly sobering my features, I added, "It really is lovely to see you again, Mrs. Lynch. I've heard a lot about you." God, I was such a bullshitter. "Joey speaks very highly of you."

"It would be nice if I could say the same," she said, before adding quietly, "But Joey doesn't speak about you at all."

"Mam," Joey said in a warning tone.

A small tremor rolled through his body, and I gave his hand a gentle squeeze, desperate to give him reassurance.

That this was okay.

That I could exist in both of his worlds.

That I wouldn't run.

My act of support was awarded with a smile, as his green eyes locked on mine, searching my face for something he would never find.

He was looking for my trepidation.

It didn't exist.

"When did you both meet?" she asked then, dragging my attention back to her.

"First year," I told her. "We've been in the same class ever since."

Her eyes widened. "So, this . . . relationship has been going on for a long time?"

"Well, we've been friends for—" I began to say, but Joey quickly interrupted when he said, "you could say that."

"And is it serious?" She looked at her son. "Are you serious about her?"

"You could say that," was all he replied, but it caused my heart to hammer with pure unadulterated *joy*.

He wasn't denying how he felt.

He didn't play it down or brush it under the rug.

'*You could say that*' was all but a declaration of love when it came to this boy.

"Mam!" a voice screamed from somewhere above us then. "He's blocked the fucking toilet again."

Startled, Mrs. Lynch literally jerked before releasing a small shudder. "Tadhg, mind your language, will you?" she called back, before sinking down on a chair at the table. "We have company."

"Like I give a crap," came the voice again. "That dope of a son you call Oliver doesn't seem to understand that he doesn't need to use an entire toilet roll to wipe his hole."

"Tadhg!" Mrs. Lynch shouted, but it was a pitiful attempt, sounding more like a defeated sigh, as she reached for her cigarettes. "I told you to mind your language."

"Ollie plugged the toilet," Tadhg shouted again. "And I need to take a—"

"I like to make sure I'm clean," a younger male voice called out. "It's high-gleam-ick."

"It's *hygienic*, not high-gleam-ick!" Tadhg screeched. "And you'll be far from *high-gleam-ick* when I take a shit on your—"

"Jesus Christ, I'll sort it," Joey barked. Releasing my hand, he shook his head and moved for the hallway. "Anything to shut the pair of you up."

"Sound, Joe," I heard Tadhg call back.

"See," I heard Ollie cheer. "Told you Joey would fix it."

"I'll be right down," he called over his shoulder, while he bounded up the stairs. "Just give me two minutes to sort these spanners out."

"You're going to need more than two minutes," Tadhg called back. "Ollie might be small, but he sent a man-sized salmon up the river. It's blocked solid."

"Fuck my life," I heard Joey groan, as he disappeared up the staircase.

"Take your time," I laughed. "I'll wait."

When he was gone, I remained by the fridge, feeling a little unsure of his mother and a lot unwelcome.

If I thought Joey was closed off, it was nothing compared to the woman in front of me.

"He doesn't do much of that, you know," Mrs. Lynch said, flicking her cigarette ash into the already overflowing ashtray in front of her. "At least not these days."

"Much of what?" I replied evenly, unsure of what to make of the broken woman in front of me.

I wanted to hate her so bad for allowing Joey to suffer for as long as he had. Instead, all I felt in this moment was pity.

"Smile," she clarified. "He doesn't smile often."

"He's smiling a lot more lately," I told her. "More than he used to, at least."

511 • CHLOE WALSH

Offering me a weary smile of her own, she exhaled softly. "You must mean a great deal to my son."

"I hope so."

"You must." With a small shrug of her frail shoulders, Mrs. Lynch took a deep drag from her cigarette. "He's never brought a girl home before now."

That statement should have thrilled me, knowing that I was the only girl that Joey had brought home, but to be honest, why would he want to bring anyone here?

Certainly not to meet the parents, that was for damn sure.

"Yeah, well, he means a lot of me, too," I told her.

She arched a brow. "A lot?"

"An awful lot," I clarified, unwilling to be ashamed of how I felt. "I'm in love with your son, Mrs. Lynch."

"I thought you might be." Something that looked a lot like sadness flickered in her blue eyes then. "I could see it written all over your face when you walked into the room with him." She blew out a shaky breath before asking, "Are you being safe?"

I just stared at her, unsure of what to say.

"Is he protecting you?" she pushed.

"I'm on the pill," I heard myself admit. "But we're not sleeping together."

She didn't look like she believed me. "Be safe," she replied. "Protect yourself if he won't."

"He always keeps me safe, Mrs. Lynch," I told her, needing her to know how epic her secondborn was. "Your son is an amazing person."

"My *son* is a loose cannon," she corrected sadly. "Just like his father was at that age."

"Yeah, that's not even close to being true," I shot back heatedly, her words irking me. "Joey is *nothing* like your husband."

Surprise filled her eyes.

"Yeah," I bit out, staring right back at her. "I have eyes. I know what happens in this house."

"You don't know anything," she whispered.

"I know a lot more than you think," I shot back. "So don't you dare tar Joey with the same brush as *him*."

"I understand the need to defend him," she whispered sadly. "I understand the temptation. I was your age once. I understand all about the temptation that comes with loving a boy like my son. He's handsome, and talented, headstrong and protective, wild and reckless. But just remember that protectiveness can switch to possessiveness in the blink of an eye. Headstrong can switch to commanding, and, well, recklessness can lead to more than just addiction." She sucked on her cigarette before exhaling a cloud of smoke and asking, "You do know that, don't you?"

"Know what?"

She looked so sad when she said, "That my son has an ongoing battle with addiction."

My heart plummeted.

"He used to," I corrected, thinking about how good of a handle Joey had gotten on things since his slip back in September. "He's okay now, though."

"You don't really believe that," she replied softly. "Someone like my son, with the kind of habit that has been going on for as many years as it has, can't make it go away overnight, and as powerful as first love may seem, it will never be strong enough to overcome his demons. He will never want you more than he wants his next fix, Aoife. That's the sad truth of my son's life."

Instantly, my back was up. "You're wrong."

"I wish with all of my heart that I was," she said. "But I know I'm not. It's only one flick of the switch away at any given time. And if I could give you one piece of advice, it would be to run for cover before my son explodes like his father and you're swallowed up in the riptide."

Stunned, I gaped at the woman in front of me and just shook my head.

How could she think about her son like that?

How could she have so little faith in him?

"You know, I'm really trying hard to think of something diplomatic to say to you, but I'm coming up empty." I shook my head, unable to hide my disgust. "How can you say that about your own flesh and blood? You're supposed to be his mother."

"I *am* his mother," she agreed, weary. "And that's how I know that he will break you." A shiver racked through her slender frame. "He will chip away at your heart, gnawing and gouging at it, tearing away at it strip by strip, until there is nothing left. Until *you* are nothing. He will break you because that's all he knows. It's all he's ever known."

"He *loves* you," I bit out, feeling my eyes burn with tears of devastation for the boy who kept me company at night. "*So much*, and you speak so badly about him."

"I love my son, Aoife. I do." Exhaling a cloud of smoke, she took another deep drag from her cigarette. "I have six children and make no mistake when I tell you that I love each one of them equally. But there's only one of my children that frightens me. Only one of my children is the walking reincarnation of his father."

Horrified, I shook my head. "Why are you telling me this?"

She looked me dead in the eyes and said, "Because nobody told me."

"I managed to unclog the toilet," Joey said then, re-joining us. "But you're going to need to get someone to take a look at that cistern, and the piping behind the bowl, Mam," he continued, moving to the kitchen sink to wash his hands. "That leak is worse than ever and it's starting to rot away at the floorboards beneath the lino in the bathroom."

Grabbing a bottle of generic-branded washing-up liquid from the windowsill over the sink, he soaped up his hands, oblivious to his mother's words of warning.

"If we don't get a handle on it, it's only a matter of time before the floorboards give way." Shaking his hands, he reached for a tea towel. "I could try and replace the piping at the back, but it would be a patch-up job at best."

"Thanks, Joey, I'll get your father to have a look at it later this evening," his mother replied.

"Why?" Joey shot back defensively. "He doesn't know shit about plumbing. I've already told you what the problem is. Once I get paid on Friday, I can get the parts for you."

"And I've told you that I appreciate your help, and your father will sort it when he comes home."

"When he comes home?" Joey sneered, tossing the tea towel down. "You mean when he's pissed off his head and falling through the door, looking for a warm body to either fuck or fight with?"

Moving to stand beside him, I slipped my hand into his, desperate to show him the support he needed.

"That's enough, Joey," Mrs. Lynch whispered. "I don't want to—"

"Hear the truth?" He balked. "Well, you're going to."

"Fight," his mother corrected. "I don't want to fight."

"What's going on?" a soft voice said from the doorway, and I swung my gaze around to see Shannon standing there. "Is everything okay, Joe?"

"Everything's grand, Shan," he was quick to placate. "I was just—"

"About to show me your room," I blurted out, unable to spend another second with his mother, but even more unwilling to run like I'd promised I wouldn't.

Joey swung his surprised gaze on me. "I was?"

His mother watched him as he watched me, and I felt this swelling resentment build up inside of me on his behalf.

"Yeah." Nodding, I squeezed his hand and smiled, letting his mother know that her words had fallen on deaf ears. I would only ever leave this boy if I was dragged from him kicking and screaming. "You were."

I made a point of dutifully ignoring the decaying plaster on the walls, and the general dilapidated condition of their home, as I followed Joey up the staircase and straight into his bedroom.

The minute the door was closed, I watched as he twisted a key in the lock.

"Don't ask," was all he muttered, when he dragged a chest of drawers across the room and set it in front of the locked door.

515 • CHLOE WALSH

"I won't," I whispered, watching as he kept his back to me, with his head bowed, and his hands resting on the chest of drawers.

"I shouldn't have brought you here."

"I'm glad you did."

"Be real here, Molloy." He hissed out a pained breath, giving me his back. "My life is a fucking mess."

Yeah, it was.

I couldn't deny it.

Everything about this home and the people inside of it screamed *messy*.

Still, I chose to remain right here, playing with fire and willing to get burned. "Talk to me," I instructed calmy. "Tell me what you're thinking right now."

"I'm mad," he bit out, keeping his back to me. "I'm pissed the fuck off, Molloy."

"With me?"

"Yes."

"For making you bring me here?"

"Yes."

"Do you want to talk about it?"

"No."

"Because you're afraid you'll blow up?"

"Yes."

"Okay," I replied calmly. "Then you be mad for as long as you need."

Because I'm not going anywhere.

Quietly, I took in my surroundings, eyes wandering around the meticulously clean bedroom that housed a wardrobe, nightstand, chest of drawers, and a metal bunk bed with a double on the bottom and single on top.

Forcing myself to ignore several make-shift bunks scattered around his bedroom floor, I let my gaze land on the big-ass stereo in the corner of the room, and I honed in on it.

Flicking through a bunch of CDs, I waited until he was ready to talk it out.

After another five minutes, he was.

"I hate that you've been here," he finally broke the silence by admitting.

"Because?"

"Because I don't want your pity."

Tough, it's already yours. "Good," I said instead. "Because you don't have it."

"What are you doing?"

"Putting some music on." I slid my chosen disc, Damien Rice's *O* album, into the CD player, and then browsed through the listing on the back of the case until I found the number of the track I wanted to play. 'Delicate'. I pressed play and then I clicked the repeat button, knowing that this was exactly the song I wanted playing when I made my next move.

"Music? Seriously?" He swung around to glare at me. "What kind of game are you playing here, Molloy? It's pretty fucking obvious I don't live in a house we can hang out and listen to music in!"

"I know." Breathing hitching in my throat, I shakily reached for the hem of my t-shirt and tugged it over my head. "I'm not playing any games, Joe." Then I reached behind my back and unhooked my bra. "I swear."

"Then what . . ." He shook his head, and I watched as a look of tormented confusion filled his eyes. "What are you doing?"

"It's okay." Unsnapping the button of my jeans, I pushed them down my legs, and then kicked them off, right along with my knock-off Converse

His eyes burned with heat and his nostrils flared. "Molloy."

"It's okay," I repeated, slowly pushing my thong down until it landed with the rest of my clothes. "I want this."

Joey stood, frozen as a statue, watching me as I walked over to his bed and sat down on the bottom bunk. "You want what?"

"I want you to have me," I told him, heart hammering with nervous anticipation, as I lay naked on his bed. "All of me."

"No." He quickly shook his head, refuting my offer. "You don't want this. Trust me – and especially not here."

"Yes, Joey, I do," I urged. "And it has to be here."

He looked so lost when he choked out the word, "*Why*?"

"Because I want to put one good memory of this house in your head."

"Molloy." Raw emotion flashed in his eyes. "You don't have to do that."

"I *want* you to take my virginity, Joey," I breathed, chest rising and falling rapidly. "I'm offering it to you, right here, on this bed, in this house, just us."

"I told you before," he warned gruffly, running a hand through his hair, "the next time—"

"The next time that I begged you to fuck me, you wouldn't say no." Exhaling a shaky breath. "Yeah, I heard you, and here I am." I patted the mattress. "So, are you going to make good on your promise, or do I really have to beg?"

"Fuck me."

"Exactly, Joe," I breathed. "Fuck me."

I watched him watch me, his gaze trailing down my body. When his eyes locked on mine, I swear I saw something shift inside of him.

His lips tipped upwards, eyes returning to mine, asking me a million unspoken questions.

I answered them all with a small nod.

"Jesus, Molloy." I watched as he reached a hand behind his back and dragged his shirt off, revealing a tanned, toned stomach, with the most gorgeous, indented V on his hips, and a glorious treasure trail of golden-brown hair that disappeared beneath his waistband. His arms were seared with permanent blank ink; more visible to the naked eye than the perpetual mark he had carved inside of me.

My breath hitched in my throat when his hands moved to the button on his jeans, and I watched through hooded eyes as he pushed them down his legs and then kicked them off.

His green eyes were locked on mine as he stood before me, in only a pair of grey boxers that couldn't conceal his bulging erection.

"This isn't one of your TV shows." His tone was laced with heated warning as he closed the space between us. "This is real life, Molloy." I felt the mattress dip and he moved to settle between my legs. "And in real life, it's going to hurt."

"Good." I licked my lips and pulled up on my elbows to press a kiss to his neck. "I want the pain."

Settling between my legs on his knees, Joey placed his hands on the curves of my hips and shook his head. "I can wait."

"I thought you said that you wouldn't try to talk me out of it?"

"Yeah, well, maybe I care enough to give it another shot," he said thickly. "I mean it, though; I *can* wait. I don't have any problem with waiting."

"I know you can wait," I agreed, sitting up so that our chests were flush together. "But I don't want you to."

"You're sure?"

"I'm sure." I exhaled a ragged breath and nodded. "You're what I want."

His lips came down on mine, moving with such certainty, that I just laid there beneath him, my body alight with an illicit trepidation, because I was in no way naïve enough to believe that having him inside of my body wouldn't hurt.

But I wanted this.

I wanted *him*.

His lips were everywhere: my neck, my breasts, my navel, between my legs.

Awakening that familiar yearning that I'd only known with him, I gave my body over to him, trusting him with the only thing that still remained mine, because God knew my heart was his.

"I don't have anything," I heard him growl a little while later, as he knelt between my quivering thighs, and rummaged through his wallet. "Fuck!" Hissing out a pained growl, he tossed his wallet across the room and swore like a sailor. "Jesus fucking Christ, this is not happening." Looking a little devastated, he leaned back on his heels and glared at his naked dick like it had personally insulted him. "Fuck."

"It's okay, Joe, I'm on the pill," I strangled out, reaching up to pull his face back to mine, desperate to have his skin on mine again. "It's all good. I'm covered."

"Molloy." He looked at me with uncertainty. "I don't know." Blowing out a ragged breath, he confessed, "I've never *not* used a condom."

"Good."

Reckless, I wrapped my arms around his neck and forced him to come with me as my back hit the mattress. "Then this is a first for you, too."

Kissing me deeply, I felt his hand come around my thigh, as he hitched my leg around his waist, and settled in deeper between my legs.

I could feel his hard dick probing my wet folds, as he continued to fuck me with his tongue. His hand slipped between us then, guiding his erection to my entrance.

"Just relax, okay?" Joey whispered against my lips.

And then he pushed inside of my body with one sharp thrust of his hips.

And the pain that emerged from the act?

Oh, sweet merciful baby Jesus, the pain was horrendous.

Crying out against his lips, I felt the stem of tears prickling my eyes, as my entire body locked tight from the sheer shock of it all.

"It's okay," he coaxed, claiming my mouth with his once more, as he held perfectly still inside of me. "I've got you," he whispered, nuzzling me with so much affection that I felt like I would drown in him. "I've got you, baby."

Stroking his nose against mine, he leaned in close and pressed a kiss to where a tear was trickling down my cheek.

Inhaling a shaky breath, I wrapped my arms around his neck and clutched onto his big body for all I was worth.

Slowly, the pain began to subside, and the tight pressure eased up enough that he was able to move again.

With my legs spread open, he buried himself to the hilt inside of me, and the horrendous pain from moments before changed to a dull throb which grew stronger and more addictive with every thrust of his hips.

My cries had morphed to moans, and my hands moved wildly, touching every bare inch of his skin, as he continued to ignite the most fantastic ripple of heat inside of my core.

"Fuck me," I heard myself croak out, urging him to chase after that amazing sensation that only grew with each thrust of his cock.

Every time he stopped, the flame would dim, and it was driving me close to madness.

Jerking my hips restlessly, I clawed at his hips, and tried to pull him closer. "Please, Joe."

"Don't beg," he bit out. "You're so tight, and I can feel you so much better without a condom . . . I'm trying really fucking hard not to cum, Molloy. Please don't fucking beg me."

Beyond reasoning, I grabbed the back of his head and dragged his face down to mine. "Don't you dare cum yet." Biting at his bottom lip, I hissed, "Fuck me, Joe, fuck me hard and fast."

"Jesus," he rasped, plunging his tongue into my mouth, as his hips bucked wildly against my inner thighs, and he stretched me to the point of pain.

If the hurling ever failed Joey Lynch, he would make a mighty fine porn star.

The boy certainly fucked like one.

Reveling in the sensations he evoked from my body, I shook and jerked beneath him, feeling my legs tremble uncontrollably, as the familiar roll of pleasure threatened to wash over me.

"I'm coming," I cried out, shivering violently as my entire frame clamped up in ecstasy when he pushed me over the ledge with the most amazing thrust of his hips.

Clenching my eyes shut, I shuddered and shook beneath him, as he upped his pace, fucking me so hard that the headboard clattered loudly against his bedroom wall.

"I'm going to cum," he groaned, hips still thrusting almost manically. "Tell me if you want me to pull out."

"Don't you dare," I groaned, reaching around to grab his ass and drag him in deeper. "Stay in me."

"You sure – ah fuck!" A flood of heat washed through me then as he released the sexiest, guttural groan I'd ever heard in my entire life.

He was emptying himself inside of me, I realized, and the sensation caused several mini ripples of pleasure to wash over me.

"Jesus," Joey panted above me, breathing hard and fast, as he looked down at where our bodies were still joined. "Are you okay?" Breathless, he leaned heavily on one arm, while using the other to push my hair out of my face. "You good, Molloy?"

"I think so?" I nodded weakly as my body continued to tremble beneath his. "Are you?"

"Yeah." Nodding, he leaned in and kissed me. "I'm good."

I could feel him hardening inside of me again and I tensed. "Don't even think about it."

"I'm not," he laughed, still a little breathless, as he slowly pulled out. "It just happens. I can't help it."

"Lovely," I replied and then groaned when my gaze fell on the blood smeared all over my thighs and his dick and pubic hair. "That's not embarrassing at all."

"Huh." He grinned back at me. "I've never taken anyone's virginity before."

"And you'll never take anyone else's," I warned him. "That's your lot, Lynch. Your first, last, and only virgin. You just signed your dick away in a blood oath, buddy."

"You're so strange." He threw his head back and laughed. "I love it."

"You mean you love me," I teased, grinning up at him.

"Yeah, Molloy." His eyes burned with sincerity when he said, "That's exactly what I mean."

Finally!

Whatever makes you happy

October 3rd 2004

JOEY

I held her hand the entire walk from my housing estate to hers. It was the least I could do for the girl considering the monumental sacrifice it must have taken her to let down her walls enough to take me inside of her body.

She played it down, but Tony's extramarital activities had fucked her up good in the head when it came to trusting men.

Sometimes, I liked the fact that she seemed just as broken as I was.

It made me feel a little less fucked up.

It was her dad's wandering eye that had kept her from sleeping with Ricey after a nearly four-year relationship.

And as for us, we'd been together for almost a year now.

Fuck, where had the time gone?

"Slow down," Molloy grumbled, pulling on my hand, as we crossed the bridge over the river that separated her estate from mine. "It's your fault I'm walking like a wide-legged cowboy."

I laughed, because in all honesty, what else could I do?

"It's not funny."

"Do you want a piggyback?"

"How about I wait here while you run back to my house for my car and come get me?" she suggested instead.

"Molloy." I laughed. "We're nearly there."

"Ugh, fine," she relented with a huff as she released my hand only to wrap her arm around my waist, and then slide her hand into my ass pocket. "So, what's the plan for your birthday? It's only a couple of months away, Joe. Which might sound like we have a lot of time, but with all the project work and practical exam prep we have at school between now and Christmas break, we really need to start making a plan."

"No, we don't," I warned. "Because I'm not having a party or any of that bullshit, so put it out of your head right now."

"Fine, you don't want a party, but how about we go out with a bunch of our friends on Christmas eve instead?"

"I need to be home on Christmas Eve."

"Why?" she teased. "Is Santa coming?"

I smirked. "Funny."

"Just hear me out," she said, and then dove into a flamboyant tangent of plotting and planning before finishing it up with, "And after the pub, we can stay at my house, and then we can spend the day lounging around. That night, we can sleep over at your house, and I'll make sure you're tucked up in bed nice and early for Santa. Then, when you wake up the next morning on your birthday, we can celebrate with some very fun and un-Virgin-Mary birthday sex?"

"Sounds tempting."

"Then be tempted," she encouraged, twirling under my arm until she was flush against me. "Say yes." Batting her long lashes, she smiled sweetly up at me. "*Please.*"

"Fine," I gave in and replied. "Whatever makes you happy, Molloy."

She grabbed my face and kissed me, giving me no choice in the matter, no option but to feel her presence, to kiss her back.

"See?" Breaking our kiss, she winked and patted my chest. "I knew you'd get the hang of this boyfriend gig."

"Hm."

"Hey, Joe?"

"Yeah?"

"I'm glad that I waited," she whispered, curling her arm around my neck. "It meant more with you."

What was I supposed to say to that?

We both knew I couldn't say the same.

Blowing out a breath, I went with the truth and said, "It never meant anything before you."

"Aw," she teased. "You're a sweet slut."

I grinned. "Thanks."

I know exactly who I'm talking to

October 18th 2004

AOIFE

Joey didn't show up to school today.

I knew this because I'd waited an abnormal length of time, standing in the rain outside of school, waiting on him to arrive.

All of my calls had gone straight to voicemail, and I wasn't ashamed to say that I was beyond worried.

Shannon wasn't at school either, which put me on red alert.

I knew his sister was having even more problems than usual with some of the girls at school. While I had warned off a group of little bitches when I caught them hassling her in the bathroom, I knew there was a war raging.

By the time school ended, I got in my car and headed straight for Elk's Terrace, with a pain in my chest, and a knot in my stomach.

"Back like a bad smell," his father sneered, when he opened the front door and locked his menacing brown eyes on me. "You're here so often, you should start paying fucking rent."

Asshole.

I'd been here a grand total of three times and had only bumped into him on one of those occasions.

"Funny," I deadpanned. "I could say the same thing about you."

His eyes narrowed. "What did you say to me?"

My hands itched from the urge I had to lunge forward and avenge my boyfriend.

Instead, I offered him a cold stare. "Only that you're here enough that you should be contributing. Instead of having your teenage son shoulder your dead weight."

"You cheeky little whore," he snarled, hand tightening on the door. "Who the fuck do you think you're talking to?"

"Oh, I know exactly who I'm talking to," I snapped right back. Folding my arms across my chest, I let him know in no uncertain terms that he didn't wield an ounce of power or control over me. "Now, is Joey here or not?"

Whatever he saw on my face in that moment caused him to back down. "No, he's down the station with the other one."

"The Garda station?" my heart rate spiked. "With who – Shannon?"

He gave me a clipped nod. "He's missing an important fucking training session for her, too."

"Why?" My eyes widened. "What happened to her?"

"Some young ones gave her a hiding on the way to school." There was no emotion in his voice, no affection or concern. He truly didn't care about his daughter. *About any of his children.* "That girl has never brought anything but hassle to her mother."

No, that's you, dick.

Not bothering to say goodbye, I turned on my heels and made my way back to where I had parked my car.

"You know," he called after me. "If you ever get tired of letting my young fella dick ya, you could always let his old man show you how it's really done?"

"No thanks," I called over my shoulder, repressing the urge to show weakness and shudder. "That *young fella* of yours is more than capable of keeping me satisfied."

"Prick-tease," he muttered after me.

I rolled my eyes. "Scumbag."

Do you think they'll leave me alone now?

October 18th 2004

JOEY

"How are you feeling now, Shan?" I asked, as I sat opposite my sister in the chipper, and watched as she toyed with the same chip that she'd been holding for ten minutes. "Any better?"

"I'm okay, Joe," she replied, voice barely more than a whisper. Her eyes glazed over as she clearly drifted in and out of her thoughts.

She wasn't eating again, and I was fucking terrified of letting it go to a stage where she couldn't come back from it.

I knew all about falling over the edge of bullshit, and I didn't want that for my sister.

"Just eat another five chips," I coaxed, pushing the tray closer to her. "I won't ask for any more than five."

"I'm not anorexic, Joe," she explained weakly, tucking her hair behind her ears. "I'm just ... I'm just ... " she exhaled a ragged breath before whispering, "not well."

Yeah, I knew how that felt.

When I didn't feel well, I self-medicated.

When my sister didn't feel well, she starved herself half to death.

Her reaction to stress was as real to her as mine was to me.

But that didn't make it easy for me to sit back and watch, especially when everything inside of me demanded that I fix this.

That I fix her.

I couldn't blame her for feeling the way she did.

On the way to school this morning, she'd been jumped by Ciara Maloney and Hannah Daly.

I wasn't with her, because I'd hung back to have a smoke with a few of the lads from my road.

I had never felt so goddamn helpless in my life, when I finally caught up with her and saw her getting attacked.

They were accusing her of being with Ciara's fella.

Shannon.

The same Shannon who had never glanced sideways at the opposite sex, let alone robbed someone's fella.

It was beyond absurd, and I couldn't hit them to get them off her.

I couldn't do a damn thing, because as much as I willing to return the favor to their brothers and boyfriends, they were nowhere to be seen in the movement, and I would rather slit my wrists than put hands on a female.

Those bitches knew that which meant that all I could do was drag her out from beneath them and shield her small body with mine.

"Do you think they'll leave me alone now?" she asked, thankfully taking a bite of a chip. "Do you think that'll be the end of it now that we've made a statement to the Gards?"

No, I didn't think it was going to be the end of it, but I certainly wasn't about to tell my fragile sister that.

"Yeah, Shan." Offering her a reassuring smile, I took a bite of the burger she'd left untouched. "The Gards are going to go over to Ciara's house and give her a right good talking to." *Which wouldn't work, just like last time.* "It's going to get better. I promise."

The minute the word *promise* came out of my mouth, Shannon smiled at me, and I knew that I'd fed that demon of insecurity that lived inside of her just enough to keep it at bay for a while.

"Talk to me about something else," she said then, thankfully eating another chip. "Something that's not depressing."

Our whole world was one big depression.

"Like what, Shan?"

"Your girlfriend," she said and smiled knowingly. "Aoife."

"Aoife," I mused, swallowing another bite of my burger. "What do you want to know?"

"She's very beautiful, Joe."

"Yeah, I know, Shan."

"Like seriously stunning," she offered. "The boys in third year are always talking about her."

"The boys in third year have good taste."

"How long have you been together?"

"A few months."

"Is it serious?"

"Define serious?"

"Are you exclusive?"

"Yeah, we are."

"So, no other girls tucked away to one side?"

"No." I shook my head. "No other girls."

"Wow, Joe." She waggled her brows. "It kind of sounds like you might be in *looooove*?"

"I am."

"Oh my god." Her eyes bulged. "I was half expecting you to deny it."

"There's no point." I shrugged. "I love the girl. It is what it is."

"What's it like?"

"What's what like, Shan?"

"Being in love," she sighed, resting her chin on her small hand, thoroughly invested in the conversation now. "What does it feel like?"

I cocked a brow. "Of all the things we could talk about, you want to talk about feelings?"

"Please," she begged. "Just humor me."

"Alright." Shifting around awkwardly, I took a sip from my Coke, while I thought about it for a moment. "It's painful."

Her eyes widened to saucers. "Painful?"

"Yeah." I nodded. "But it's the kind of pain that's *worth* feeling, you know?"

She blew out a breath. "Really?"

"It's like you know you're about to get your ass handed to you by exposing yourself to this person, and you know that you're fucking around on the edge of something that could potentially break and ruin you, but it's just so damn thrilling, so consumingly addictive, that you're willing to take the risk and do just about anything to be with that person."

"Wow," she mused in a dreamy tone. "That's so great, Joe."

"It's actually pretty terrible," I offered dryly. "You should avoid it like the plague."

Shannon laughed and then asked, "So, is Aoife the reason ..." clearing her throat, she said in a much quieter tone, "you decided to, ah, well, you know ... " she cupped her hands around her mouth before whispering, "don't hang out with Shane Holland and those guys?"

She's certainly the reason I've become so good at hiding it.

"Yeah, Shan," I said, feeling like a piece of shit. "She is."

Stay with me

October 31st 2004

AOIFE

It was Halloween night, and, after keeping Joe company while he took his little brothers out trick or treating, we had spent the rest of the night at Biddies bar, necking shots, and having fun with our friends.

Fancy dress had been optional, but I had no doubt that the slutty nurse's outfit I'd been donning had a lot to do with our current status.

Drunk on alcohol, love, and the fantastic taste of his tongue in my mouth, I kissed him back with everything I had in me, as our bodies collided in a heap on his bed.

This was what it was like when we collided.

It either ended in us fighting or fucking.

And I was down for both.

Groaning loudly, we ripped and tore at each other's clothes until we were naked, with him buried to the hilt inside me.

"Fuck, Molloy, I want you so bad, I can't see straight."

That would be the vodka that had hindered his ability to see straight, but I understood the sentiment, even if I was too drunk to say so.

"Give it to me," I hissed, biting down hard on his lip, needing him to be rough and hard with me tonight. "I want it rough."

Gone were the days of gentle touching and nervous missionary positions, where I laid beneath him and prayed his big dick wouldn't break me open.

No, because my boyfriend had been inside of my body enough times that I knew *exactly* what I wanted from him, and he was never less than one hundred percent willing to oblige.

Hooking one of my legs over his shoulder with one arm, Joey grabbed my hip with his free hand and thrust into me so fast and furiously that the familiar sound of my head smacking off the headboard, and subsequently the headboard cracking off the wall, filled the room.

Beyond aroused by the boy between my legs, I reached out and clutched the sheets, needing to find something to ground me, as my body flooded with heat.

"I want that whore out!"

My breath hitched in my throat when I heard the familiar voice bellowing from the other side of his bedroom door.

"I want that cunt out of my house."

Bang, bang, bang.

"Do ya hear me, boy?"

Bang!

"Get that whore out of my house!"

Just like that, every muscle in Joey's body coiled tight with tension, and he was gone from me.

Pulling out, he sat back on his knees, hands resting on my bare thighs. His chest was heaving, his face still swollen and bruised from the last time they'd fought.

"Ignore him," I begged, more for his sake than mine. "Joe."

"I can't," he whispered, shaking his head. "I can't hear that." His voice cracked, and he drew in several sharp breaths. "I'm going to kill him."

"No." Breathing hard, I sat up and cupped the back of his neck with both hands. "It's okay." Dragging his toned body back down on mine, I held his face between my hands and forced him to look at me, "Just concentrate on us."

"Molloy." Trembling, he shook his head and rested his weight on his elbow. "I can't let him say that about *you*."

"I don't care," I hurried to soothe. "Fuck him. I don't give a damn about what he thinks of me."

"But I—"

"Just stay here, Joe," I begged, wrapping my legs tightly around him, desperate to keep him with me.

I knew what would happen if he left this room and my heart couldn't take it.

Sliding a hand between us, I slowly pumped his shaft before guiding him back inside me. "It's okay." Thrusting my hips upward, I used my body to keep him safe. "Just be with me."

A hand clamped down on my hip, tugging me flush against him.

He was so warm.

Smelled so good.

"Get that cunt out of my house, ya little bastard!"

Exhaling a pained groan, Joey clenched his eyes and buried his face in my neck. "Aoif—"

"I love you, Joey Lynch," I whispered, cradling his face to my neck as he thrust inside me, hips moving almost frantically. "I love you so much."

My heart cracked clean open when I felt the first tear land on my collarbone, followed by another and another.

He was still moving inside me, still taking what he needed from me, but he was broken.

And I was terrified that I couldn't fix him.

Stepping out and stepping up

November 30th 2004

JOEY

"Mam."

Standing in the doorway of her bedroom, I resisted the urge to walk over there and tip the mattress and force her to get out of that goddamn bed.

By some small grace of God, the old man had walked out on our mother three nights ago. He declared that we could all burn to death for all he cared because he'd found himself a real woman.

If I could have packed his bags and walked him to the door, I would have.

Instead, I'd been preoccupied with picking my mother up off the kitchen floor.

She'd taken to the bed soon after and hadn't left it since.

"You have to get up," I told her. "I've the rest of them sent off to school, but Sean is downstairs. Nanny's in Beara with Aunty Alice so she can't take him, and I can't miss school again." I'd already missed yesterday. "Please, Mam."

Nothing.

"I have to get my project sorted for Construction."

Not even a twitch.

"It's worth over fifty percent of my leaving cert exam."

Silence.

"Mam!" I said it louder this time, hoping by some small miracle that I would somehow get through to her – wherever the fuck she was in that head of hers. "You're better off without him. Do you hear me? You are better off. Let him fuck off with that barmaid from town. He's her problem now."

Blowing out a frustrated growl when she didn't so much as flinch, I walked into the room I hated most in this house and forced my legs to walk over to the bed.

"Mam."

Crouching down in front of her, I tapped on her lifeless hand.

Nothing.

Dead blue eyes stared back at nothing.

I knew she was alive.

I could see her chest rising and falling, but that was the only sign.

Other than that, she was a glorified zombie.

"Mam, please." Voice softening, I reached over and tucked her hair behind her ear. "You have to get back up."

A lone tear trickled down her cheek.

It was the only response she gave to tell that she could hear me.

"Okay, Mam." Sighing heavily, I pulled the covers over her frail shoulders to keep her warm, and then I headed for the door. "I'll stay home and mind Sean."

"How is she?" were the first words that came out of Shannon's mouth when she walked through the front door after school. "Did she come out?"

"Heard the toilet flush twice, but that's about it," I called over my shoulder, as I tried to save the mince from burning the pan, having made the rare mistake of forgetting I left the ring on. "Shit, fuck, shit."

"Nice language," Tadhg mocked from the kitchen table. "Should I learn how to spell those words too, Joe?"

"Just concentrate on your homework and less of the snark," I shot back, eyeing my sister to come save me.

Smiling, Shannon walked over to the stove and nudged me out of the way. "Need a hand, Joe?"

"Please." Tossing the spaghetti-smeared tea towel over her shoulder, I scooped up the toddler who, I was fairly sure, was contemplating taking a dump in his pants, and headed for the bathroom. "Does Seany have poos for Joe?"

"No poos, o-ee."

Little liar.

"Go on and check for me," I ordered, setting him down in front of the potty in the utility room. "Good lad yourself."

"Hey, Joe? What's a click-or-is?" Ollie called from the other side of the kitchen table.

"The fuck?" Gaping, I stalked back to where he had his homework book open. "Where did you see that word, Ollie?"

"I didn't see it," he explained innocently, smiling up at me. "I heard it."

Jesus Christ. "Where'd you hear that, Ols?"

"In the sexual education talk at school."

What the absolute fuck?

I looked to Shannon for help, but she had turned redder than the bolognaise she was stirring.

At a loss, I turned to Tadhg. "What's this I'm hearing about sexual education?"

Tadhg shrugged. "No clue, Joe. I was away with the school's hurling team." He grinned proudly. "We won, and I scored two goals."

"Nice." Accepting his high-five, I quickly turned my attention back to spawn number five. "You're in fourth class, Ollie. In primary school. You don't need to be taking any sex education class."

"It's cunt-pulse-hairy."

"Compulsory, you dope," Tadhg growled. "Jesus Christ."

Jesus Christ, I needed to get this kid into speech and language. "I'm going to have to call your school," I told them both. "You're too young to be learning about this kind of thing."

"But what is it, Joe?"

"What's what?"

"A click-or-is?"

Shannon choked on her own spit behind me.

"Well, uh, it's like you said, it's something you click," I muttered, having no idea what to do, or how to handle the kinds of questions these kids continued to throw at me.

"Like a button?"

I nodded. "Yeah, that's right."

"Where?"

"Where's what?"

"The click-or-is, silly," Ollie said, and then frowned. "Teacher said that only girls get a click-or-is, but that's not fair, is it, Joe? How comes they get a secret button, and we don't?"

"O-ee poos!" Sean hollered from the utility room, and I had never been so relieved to clean shit up than I was in this moment.

"Coming, Seany," I called back before saying, "Ols, we can pick this conversation back up when you're a teenager."

House calls and domestic disturbances

December 10th 2004

AOIFE

Being in love with someone who was hell-bent on self-destructing was such a lonely place to exist. I felt incredibly helpless, watching on as my boyfriend buried his secrets with lie upon countless lie.

I *wanted* to save him.

I felt like I was watching him drown. That I was desperately reaching my hand out, but his pride was so potent that it meant he would rather go under than let me pull him to safety.

I knew he wasn't clean.

Hadn't been since the day after Halloween when I had made the fatal decision of admitting to him that his father had made another pass at me.

I physically watched the light in his eyes leave that day, and nothing I'd been able to say or do since had been able to reignite that spark.

I could see it on his face every day.

He was slowly slipping back into old habits, and I was afraid to push back against his behavior, for fear that it would make it worse.

Make *him* worse.

I was so afraid of him ending up dead in a ditch somewhere, that I found myself, disgustingly, turning a blind eye when he came back from lunch with bloodshot eyes that had a faraway look.

But there were two things that I was absolutely sure about when it came to Joey.

The first: it wasn't uncommon for him to skip a day or two of school.

The second: when it came to his job at the garage, he was the complete opposite.

Never mind being uncommon, when it came to his job, the boy's rap sheet was virtually nonexistent.

It was for these reasons that I found myself incredibly concerned over the fact that he had missed almost two whole weeks of school *and* work.

To be fair, he had returned all of my text messages and phoned me for a chat every night, fobbing me off with the reason for his absence being *family business*, and *nothing to worry about*.

Of course I was worried.

All I seemed to do nowadays was to worry about him.

The fact that he had refused to meet up or let me come over had unsettled me to the point of blind panic.

Which was why, by the time the second Friday he missed school rolled around, I drove straight to his house after my shift at work. I needed to see with my own eyes what he had been assuring me nightly on the phone – that he hadn't slipped up to the extent he had last September.

What I didn't expect to find when I got there was a Garda car.

Panic immediately setting in, I hastily parked my car at the side of the road and jumped out.

"What's going on?" I asked a group of women, who were standing at the wall in their dressing gowns, smoking cigarettes. "What happened?"

"Domestic disturbance, apparently," one of them said.

"What's new in that house."

"Sure god love them, the poor craters."

"Marie's young fellas gone off the rails again," the first one added. "Pity about it, too, because he's a fine lad if he could only keep ahold of that temper of his."

"Who?" My eyes widened in horror. "Joey?"

It was at that exact moment that the Gards walked out of the house with my boyfriend in handcuffs.

"Ah, that's very sad," one of the women said with a heavy sigh. "Poor old crater."

"Joe!" Feeling like my windpipe had been severed, I bolted towards him. "Are you okay?"

He definitely *wasn't* okay.

His entire face was swollen like a balloon, and there was blood flowing freely from his clearly broken nose. The knuckles of his handcuffed hands were torn open and dripping with even more blood.

"Molloy," he said, when he noticed me running towards him. "What are you doing here?"

"Joe!" Dodging one Garda, and sidestepping another, I didn't stop until I was flung against his chest, with my arms wrapped tightly around his neck. "Oh my god, Joe."

"It's grand," he was quick to soothe. "It's all good, baby."

"Step away," a Garda instructed, as she forcefully removed me from him.

"Don't be worrying, Molloy," Joey called over his shoulder, as he was ushered into the back seat of the squad car. "I'll call you later."

Reeling, I watched on helplessly for the second time as the Gards drove away with him in handcuffs.

"What the hell happened?" I shouted, furious when the remaining Gards completely ignored me, while they made their way out of the garden. "Well?"

Out of the corner of my eye, I spotted a familiar face, and my heart sank into my ass.

"Well, if it isn't young Aoife," Jerry Rice said, as he strolled towards me. "I haven't seen you in a while." He gestured around him before adding, "So, this is how you're keeping yourself occupied these days."

I knew it was a dig.

I also knew that if I opened my mouth and talked back, it would only harm Joey in the long run.

"That young fella you're knocking around with is a bad type," he continued to say. "Attacked his father, so he did. Made an awful job of the poor man." He sighed heavily. "You'd do well to cut your losses with that toe-rag."

Using an ornate amount of self-control, I smiled politely at my ex-boyfriend's highly ranked Garda father, and turned on my heels, making a beeline for Joey's front door.

I didn't knock.

It was incredibly reckless of me, but I walked right inside without invitation.

I wasn't sure what I had expected to see, but the sheer amount of blood on the sitting room floor was sobering.

"Aoife?" Sniffling, Shannon stumbled off the couch and barreled towards me.

"Hey," I soothed, when her small arms came around me. "Are you okay? What *happened*?"

"He left," she cried. "He was g-gone, for almost t-two weeks. Until tonight. He came b-back and they g-got into a huge f-fight . . . "

"Your father and Joey?"

Clenching her eyes shut, she nodded against me. "It was t-terrible. The worst I've ever s-seen them f-fight."

I glanced around at the room, taking in the sight of the broken coffee table and shattered glass and ornaments. There was a poleaxed Christmas tree strewn against the television unit, with festive baubles scattered everywhere.

"The neighbors must have h-heard them and called the Gards, because they showed up and arrested my b-brother."

"Why?" I demanded. "Why'd they arrest Joey?"

"Because he w-won," Shannon cried, holding on to me like I could somehow fix this. "He got the b-better of Dad for once."

"Where's your father now?"

"G-gone to the doctors."

"And the boys and your mam?"

"The b-boys are in next door with Fran," she sobbed. "And Mam . . . she went with D-dad."

"She what?" My brows shot up in surprise. "What about Joey?"

Shannon shrugged and cried harder. "I don't w-want him to g-go to prison, Aoife."

"He's not going to prison," I was quick to reassure her. "I'm going to go down to the station right now and sort this whole mess out."

"You c-can't!" she cried, clutching me tighter. "You c-can't t-tell them."

"I'm not letting him get into trouble for something your father did."

"No, no, no, please, please!" she practically screamed, and then jerked away, her hands moving to claw her hair. "Don't tell!"

"Okay, okay," I tried to soothe. "I won't say a word until I talk to your brother."

"Help him, Aoife," she cried, clutching at her throat. "He's all alone in t-the world."

"No, he's not," I assured her in a shaky tone as I ran for door, with only one destination in mind. "He has me."

No more chances, Lynch

December 11th 2004

JOEY

It was gone nine the following morning before I was released from the Garda station, making last night one of my longest stints in the cells. A stark preview of what would happen once I turned eighteen at the end of this month.

No more chances, Lynch.

This is your last warning.

Beyond exhausted, I stretched out my stiff limbs and stepped through the station doorway, only to halt at the top of the stone steps when my eyes landed on a familiar blonde, curled up under a coat, fast asleep.

"Molloy?" Concern filled me. "Did you stay here all night?"

Blinking awake, she looked around sleepily before her eyes settled on my face.

"Joe." Relief flashed across her face as she sprang up from the step and bolted towards me. "Oh, thank god!" Throwing her arms around me, she squeezed me tight, and then pulled back to slap my chest. "You have some serious explaining to do."

"You're one to talk," I growled, holding her shoulders so that I could get a proper look at her face. "What the hell were you thinking staying out here all night, Molloy? It's the middle of winter?"

"They wouldn't let me talk to you," she snapped back. "And I wasn't going anywhere until I did." Releasing another ragged breath, she pulled me in for another hug. "What happened? What did they say? Were you charged with anything?"

"Everything's fine." Slinging an arm over her shoulders, I led her away from the station, needing to put some space between this girl and my mistakes. "Stop worrying."

"*Stop worrying*? I've been more than just worrying, Joe. God, I feel like I haven't been able to breathe again until just now." With her arm around my waist, she slipped her hand into the ass pocket of my jeans and leaned into my side. "What *happened*?"

I thought about feeding her the same bullshit I'd given to the Gards, but I had too much respect for this girl, and had too many feelings involved, to give her anything other than the truth.

"He walked out on Mam a couple of weeks ago for some barmaid from town that she caught him messing around with," I heard myself explain, unnerved by just how easy it was to be truthful with her.

It didn't happen often.

Shit, it *never* happened.

Not with anyone else.

Just her.

Only ever her.

"Mam was a mess when he left and took to the bed." I grimaced at the memory of trying to spoon-feed the woman a cup of crappy instant soup. "That was the family shit I told you that I was dealing with." Shrugging, I added, "I couldn't leave Sean on his own with her. Not when I couldn't be sure that she would feed him. So, I took a few days off to hold the fort at home, while my mam processed whatever the hell it was that she needed to process."

"And last night?"

"Last night, he decided he had enough of his barmaid and came back, laying down the law and stinking of whiskey." I stiffened at the memory of him sauntering through the front door like he was God's fucking gift. "And it got messy."

"How messy?"

Messy enough that Mam, who had only managed to drag herself out of the bed and put herself back together that day, made the near-fatal mistake of telling him to turn around and leave.

"He beat my mother," I heard myself growl. "So, I beat him."

"He *beat* your mam?"

"Yeah." I nodded stiffly. "And the bastard's always been smart enough to hurt her where nobody will see the marks."

"Jesus, Joe . . . "

"I didn't even know he'd come back. I was upstairs in my room when I heard her screaming my name, so I came running. I was half-way down the staircase when I saw him slap my sister across the face for trying to pull him off our mother. You've seen how small she is. Shan went down like a sack of spuds. So, I lost my head, went for him . . . " Shrugging, I added, "and here we are."

"Here we are," she repeated sadly. "Your poor face . . . "

"I didn't come out the worst," I was quick to assure her. It was the one part of the whole damn mess that had kept me warm last night. I'd gotten the better of him, *finally*, after almost eighteen years of taking his shit, *he* had to be protected from *me*.

He was a lucky man that the neighbors called the Gards over the commotion, because if they hadn't arrived and dragged me off him, I would have been facing murder charges.

Molloy sucked in a sharp breath. "So, what did the Gards say?"

"It was just the usual slap on the wrist and a warning. They called in an emergency social worker and the youth liaison officer. You know, the usual bullshit."

"What does that mean?" Concern filled her eyes. "Are they . . . are you being taken away?"

"No, no, it's grand," I assured her. "I'm used to social workers coming around. I'll handle it."

"Well, I hope you told them everything, Joe," she growled. "Because this can't happen again."

When I didn't answer her, because I couldn't give her the answer she wanted, she lost it.

"Oh, my fucking god!" she screamed, pushing my chest before jerking away from me. "Why didn't you tell them the truth?"

Because I can't!

"It's not your business, Molloy."

"You're my business!"

"It's okay," I attempted to calm her by saying. "It's going to be fine. They'll write up the usual reports, send the usual people around for a home check and Mam will feed them the usual drivel. Then in a few weeks, it will be all brushed under the table."

"*How?*"

Confused, I looked at her and asked, "How what?"

"How can this be brushed under the table?" Her green eyes blazed with fury. "He *beat* you, Joey. You're his son and he broke your damn nose! He hit your mam. He slapped your sister. And Tadhg!" She choked out a sob. "He hurt him not too long ago. That's not normal, okay? Contrary to whatever bull-crap your parents have fed you, this *doesn't* happen in other homes. So, *how* is this going to be fine?"

"It just is, okay!" I snapped, feeling my defensive walls shoot up around me. "Fuck."

"Bull," she shouted, turning back towards the Garda station. "You're being used as a scapegoat for your father's crimes. Your mother just threw you to the wolves to save her abusive husband's skin. She should have been down here with you last night, straightening all of this and telling them that they arrested the wrong person. Instead, she was with him, plotting and scheming up a story to tell the world about how her son has anger management issues, when that couldn't be further from the truth. You're not the instigator in this, he is, and I'm not about to sit back and watch you take the blame."

"Aoife." I held up a hand in warning, feeling like she had just stabbed me through both the chest *and* the back. "If you say a word about this to the Gards, then I swear to god I will *never* talk to you again."

Her mouth fell open. "I'm trying to protect you!"

"You swore you wouldn't," I reminded her. It was why I opened up to her. "You fucking promised me!"

"Well, I have to do something, Joey," she strangled out. "I can't watch this happen to you. I love you!"

"Well, don't!" I roared back at her. "If loving me means betraying my trust, then don't fucking bother! Don't love me and don't get involved. I can take care of my own shit."

"Joey."

"I shouldn't have told you a damn thing," I choked out, shaking now. "Fuck!"

"Joey, wait!"

"No. No. *No!*" Shaking my head, I turned on my heels and walked away from her, needing to put some space between us before I lost the head and said something I couldn't take back. "I mean it, Molloy," I called over my shoulder. "Talk to the Gards and we're done."

Suspensions and cold shoulders

December 17th 2004

AOIFE

Joey and I were on the outs.

Ever since our fight outside the Garda station last weekend, I had been on the receiving end of his cold shoulder.

All week at school, he had walked right by me in the halls like I wasn't there, and even in the classes where we were assigned to sit together, he never once relented.

Of course, neither did I, and I had all but goaded him until I was blue in the face for a reaction.

I didn't get one.

Not when I sat on his lap at lunch.

Not when I stabbed him with a pencil in English.

Not even when I flashed him a boob in PE.

Nada.

It was fairly evident that my threat to talk to the Gards had backfired on me in epic fashion.

Joey was beyond furious with me, and on the rare occasion that I had caught him staring at me, the look of betrayal directed towards me had made me wish I hadn't.

How was I supposed to explain to him that I was trying to help him and not betray him, if he wouldn't speak to me?

It was beyond frustrating.

Like a glutton for punishment, my masochistic mind drifted back to the last time we had been together before shit had hit the fan at home for him.

Drunk as a skunk, Joey held me and mumbled along to The Beatles'

'Don't Let Me Down', *as we swayed against each other on the dancefloor in the back lounge of Biddies.* "My Granda Murphy was a big fan."

"Of The Beatles?"

"Yeah, and of this song." Pulling me close he pressed a kiss to the curve of my jaw and said, "When I was small, I used to ask him what the words of the song meant. He would always say that one day, when I found myself in love with a girl, I wouldn't have to ask him what the words meant, because I would already know." *His arms tightened around me.* "Turns out he was right."

"You look like someone stole your last Rolo," Casey announced when she sank down on the chair beside me during big break on Friday. "Is he still ignoring you?"

"Yep." I nodded glumly and tossed my spoon back in my yoghurt, appetite null and void. "He sure is."

"Jesus, what did you do to piss him off this much?" She blew out a breath. "I've never seen him ignore you like this, not in the six years we've been in school together. Anytime you guys have been on the outs in the past, it's because you've evoked the silent law, not him."

I sighed wearily. "He thinks I've broken his trust and betrayed him."

"Did you?"

"No," I was quick to defend. "I didn't. I thought about doing something that he considers a betrayal, but he freaked out, so I didn't."

"Then there's no harm done, right?" Casey frowned. "What's he still mad for?"

"Because in his mind, the very fact that I *thought* about it is an act of betrayal."

"Jesus, that boy is complicated."

"You have no idea, Case."

"Uh-oh, speaking of complicated . . ." Nudging my arm with her elbow, she inclined her head towards the window to where Joey and some of his friends were getting fairly aggressive with Mike, Paul, and a few others from our year, outside in the yard.

"Oh, for god's sake," I groaned, watching as he balled his hands into fists at his sides. "He better not start a—"

"Too late, it's already started," Casey interjected, watching right along with me as Joey and Mike Maloney started brawling on the ground. "You better go and calm that stud of yours down," she added. "Before he gets himself expelled and I lose my eye candy for the rest of the year."

"Joey!" I screamed, pushing through the hordes of bystanders who had made a large circle around the fight. "Stop! Wait. Would you just stop, Joey, *stop!*"

Joey didn't stop.

Instead, he attacked our classmate with such bloodlust and viciousness that it resembled a dog fight, where Mike was the unknowing Labrador, and Joey was the bared-teeth pit bull.

Out of the corner of my eye, I could see Podge faithfully throwing punches at Paul in his bid to protect his best friend from being double-teamed.

It wouldn't have mattered if he was.

None of the boys in our year could fight like Joey, because, unlike the trivial fights they got into, when my boyfriend fought, it was a matter of life and death.

Because when someone threatened Joe, it sent him right back to that house, where he had to fight for his life against a man who had caused so much post-traumatic stress inside of him that I doubted a lifetime of therapy could fix.

I doubted Joey was even seeing Mike's face as he bludgeoned him with his fists.

All he could see was his father.

"Stop!" I commanded, unafraid to get right up in his face, when nobody else would.

Because as sure as the sun would rise in the morning, I knew he wouldn't harm a hair on my head.

"Joey, *stop!*" Kneeling down on the ground beside a bleeding Mike, I caught ahold of Joey's face between my hands and forced him to look at me. "I told you to stop!"

Wild and unrecognizable black eyes stared back at me.

Great, not only had he lost himself in what I could describe as a violent bout of PTS, but he was strung out, too.

"*Stop*," I commanded, keeping a firm hold on his face, as I kept his gaze. "You're not there, you're at school. With me."

It took a long time for him to process my face, but once he did, I watched as the tension dissipated from his body in a sudden rush, and he slumped forward.

With his bloodied hands hanging limply at his sides, he let his head fall to my shoulder. "They hurt her," he slurred. "They hurt my sister."

"Who hurt Shannon, Joe? What it Mike's sister? Was it Ciara?"

I felt him nod against my shoulder.

"It's okay," I whispered, wrapping an arm around his back, while I cradled his head to my shoulder with the other. "It's okay."

The commotion around us was all too familiar, and I knew what was coming before it even happened.

"Joseph Lynch," Mr. Nyhan bellowed, pushing through the crowds. "My office. Now! The Gards are on the way."

I'm knocking on heaven's door

December 17th 2004

JOEY

Laying on my back, I stared up at my bedroom ceiling and ignored the screaming going on downstairs. I didn't have anything left in me to go down there and be thrown on the front line like I always was.

Instead of her screams, I concentrated on the sound of Bob Dylan's 'Knockin' on Heaven's Door' as it drifted from my stereo.

I was so fucking dead inside that if you cut me open, my insides would spew black.

That's how dark I felt, how truly rotten I felt on the inside.

How far I'd fallen.

Turning my head to one side, I stared at the tinfoil, lighter, and broken pen on my mattress, as my mind drifted in and out of focus, in and out consciousness.

"Another suspension. Do you want to ruin your life?"

"Joey, help me, please!"

"You're off the hurling team. Don't even think about stepping foot on a pitch until your suspension is lifted."

Bang. Bang. Bang.

"Where's your precious son now, whore?"
    "You are such a disappointment . . . "
    "What did you take?"

*

"Why are you the way you are?"

"Oh, Jesus, Teddy, that's heroin!"

"Don't you ever think about anyone other than yourself?"

"Joey, baby, can you hear me?"

"It's okay, Joe. It's okay. I'm here."

"He's off his trolly on drugs, Marie. There's no talking to him when he's like that. Wait until he comes around and I'll give the little prick a good talking to."

"I wish you were never born."
    "I love you, Joey Lynch . . . "
    "Don't leave me, Darren."

"Close the door. I don't want the rest of the children seeing him like this."

"No, Daddy, I'm scared."

Footsteps retreating.
    "I want to die, Joe."

Door closing.
    "Stay with me, Joey. Stay right here with me."

Alone in the dark, I couldn't tell the difference between what was real and wasn't.
    Shadows danced on my bedroom wall.
    I couldn't feel a thing.

I couldn't hurt.
No more pain.
No fucking more . . .

Too stubborn and too in love

December 19th 2004

AOIFE

Joey was escorted from school by the Gards on Friday, and it had been radio silence ever since.

His phone was constantly off, and none of the Lynch family would answer the door to me when I knocked.

And I had knocked.

Repeatedly

From what I had gathered from the gossip spreading around school, Marie Lynch had pulled Shannon out of BCS with immediate effect and had enrolled her to start at Tommen College after Christmas break.

The jury was still out on Joey's future. His latest episode had been taken to the board of management, who, from what I heard, were due to meet up sometime the next week to discuss his possible permanent expulsion from school.

Therefore, when I received a random text message from Joey at half past eight on Sunday night, asking if I wanted to meet him at Biddies for a drink and to talk, I practically cracked my neck in my haste to get ready.

Running late, due to the innate amount of time it took to blow-dry and straighten my hair, I managed to make it to Biddies for just after nine.

I couldn't stop the rattling in my knees when I made my way into the back lounge, and when my eyes landed on him, sitting alone in the corner, it wasn't just my knees that rattled.

Every inch of me shook.

Joey was sitting at our usual table, with his signature vodka and Red Bull in front of him, and a bottle of Smirnoff Ice with a straw poking over the rim on the opposite end of the table.

The minute his eyes landed on me I felt a rush of heat flood my belly that quickly crawled all over my skin.

"Hey," I said, taking a seat opposite him, and unravelling my scarf from around my neck.

"Hey."

"Thanks for the drink," I added, as I shimmied off my coat and set it on the chair beside me.

"Thanks for coming," he replied, watching me warily from across the table. "You look beautiful."

I know. "So, how are you?"

"I'm not too fucking good, Molloy," he admitted quietly. "How are you?"

"Not too good either, Joe."

I watched him watch me for a long moment and soaked in the feeling of having his eyes on me.

"I'm suspended again," he finally broke the tension with.

"I heard." Picking up my bottle, I wrapped my lips around the straw and took a sip. "Have you heard back if they're expelling you?"

Shaking his head, he took a sip from his glass and set it back down. "But Shannon's moving to Tommen after Christmas, so at least something positive has come out of it. She won't have to deal with those girls anymore."

I already know. "She is?"

He nodded slowly. "Mam took a loan out from the Credit Union for the tuition. Herself and Shannon have been over to the school to meet the principal and look around and she seems to be excited." He shrugged. "Could be a life-changer for her."

"Let's hope so, huh?"

"Yeah," he agreed. "Let's."

"So," taking another deep sip from my drink, I forced myself to get down to business, "what's happening here, Joe? I get that you're mad at me over the whole talking to the authorities idea, but it's more than that, isn't it? I feel like there's a distance between us that wasn't there a month ago."

"Yeah," he agreed quietly. "I guess there is."

Oh fuck.

This is it.

This is where he breaks your heart.

Tossing my straw aside, I put my lips around the rim of my bottle and continued to drink until I had every drop in my belly.

For the nerves.

"So," I roughly cleared my throat and met his gaze head on, "what are you saying?"

"I suppose I'm saying that I'm not intentionally trying to put distance between us, Molloy." Knees bouncing restlessly, he reached for his glass and tipped it back. "I'll get us another."

With that, he bolted to the bar, returning a moment later with two new drinks. "Where were we?"

"You were saying you weren't trying to put distance between us, and then you legged it away to the bar," I offered wryly.

He didn't laugh.

Instead, he blew out a frustrated breath and said, "I'm not good at this, Molloy."

"Good at what, Joe?"

"Talking shit through," he admitted gruffly. "Resolving an argument with words."

The Pogues' 'Fairytale of New York' wafted from the speakers above the bar then, as the DJ started his set.

"Remember this time last year?" His lips twitched. "You told me this was our song."

"Yeah, I remember," I drawled. "And it certainly fits us better this year."

"That's fair." He let out a sigh. "I still can't understand how you lasted a whole year without running for the hills."

"I don't run, remember?" I shot back, reaching across the table with my palm up. "And neither do you."

Joey stared at my outstretched hand for a long moment before placing his on top of it and entwining our fingers. "I guess we're both too stubborn for running, huh, Molloy?"

"Or too in love."

"Yeah," he agreed, tone gruff, as he pressed a kiss to the back of my hand. "Or that."

Snuffed out hopes and dreams

December 23rd 2004

JOEY

I knew I was trip-tumbling down a slippery slope with no sight of stopping, no hope of slamming on the brakes, and still, I was too selfish to do the right thing by my girlfriend.

I had the perfect opportunity to let her go the other night, to free her from my bullshit, and I choked.

I couldn't do it.

I couldn't pull the trigger.

It was like I'd inhaled her so deeply inside of me that my head and heart refused to function. I couldn't release the air in my burning lungs without the absolute guarantee that I would get to see her face again.

Whether I deserved to or not.

Sitting across from her at Biddies the other night, it had really hit me just how fucking beautiful she was – and I wasn't talking about the outside, either.

Aoife Molloy had a heart of gold and was hell-bent on handing it over to a piece of shit like me.

She was my momentary escape from all of the fucking dark.

She was the only bit of brightness I had in my life, and it scared me to think of how little else I had going for me.

Without her, I had nothing.

Without her, I *was* nothing.

Weakened and demoralized with life, I had clung to the lifeline she offered me, because that meant I got to keep her for just a little bit longer.

I didn't have a backup plan or a safety net to land on when everything went to hell, and it *would* go to hell on me.

It always did.

People like me didn't get second chances.

When she finally came to her senses and left, which I had no doubt she would, I would be completely alone.

Fuck.

My mind kept drifting back to how she looked the other night when she took me home with her.

"What are you doing?" she whispered, hovering in the bathroom doorway, as I stood with my back to her, a rolled-up tenner pressed to my nose. "Joe?"

Snorting the crushed powder of a D2 up my nose, I clutched the basin and exhaled a heavy breath, preparing for the fight I knew was about to erupt between us.

Wordlessly she walked up behind me and wrapped her arms around my waist. "Come to bed."

Confusion filled me. "But you just saw—"

"I know what I saw," she whispered, kissing my back again. "Just come to bed."

Higher than Everest, I lay on her mattress and watched as she climbed on top of me.

Her face was ingrained in my mind. I was high, in pain, and close to breaking point, but her face.

Jesus, her face was all I could see.

Her smell was all around me, her hair cloaking my face as she leaned into my lips, kissing me, doing all the work.

She was shining.

Fucking shining.

The moon was illuminating her.

Powerful.

She was so fucking powerful.

"Are you mad at me?" I slurred, feeling weak and disorientated by her calmness.

"Yes."

"Then why aren't you shouting at me?" I shook my head in clouded confusion. "I've stopped trying, Molloy. I can't try anymore. Why aren't you kicking me out?"

"Because you might not love yourself, but I do. I love you enough for the both of us," she whispered, fisting my cock in her hand. "And if keeping you here with me means that you're off the streets and safe, then that's what I'm going to do."

And as she lowered herself down on me, the reality of what I'd done to this girl hit me like a fucking wrecking ball.

I was a fucking mess.

Almost as much as the prick who was standing in front of me when I came downstairs on Thursday, freshly showered and ready to meet up with Molloy for my birthday.

Nah, I thought to myself, as I watched him clamp a beefy hand around my mother's arm and press her against the fridge, *I would never be as big of a mess as him.*

I could see them arguing from the kitchen doorway, but unlike every other time I saw him manhandle her, I just didn't seem to have the fight in me to take him on.

Or I just didn't have the strength, I thought dejectedly, as I forced myself to dig deep, and do my duty. I had to protect the woman who bore me from the man who was responsible for fifty percent of my genetic makeup.

"Back off," I warned, stepping in between them, and forcing him to release her arm.

Mam had the cop on to bolt to the other side of the kitchen, but even more shockingly, Dad didn't throw a punch.

"We were only talking," he said, offering me a rare explanation for his shitty behavior.

He's wary, I suddenly realized, *of me.*

"I don't care." My tone resembled how I felt, flat and empty, as I forced him to step aside when I yanked the fridge open. "Keep your hands to yourself and we'll be peachy."

Reaching inside the fridge, I grabbed a can of Coke off the top shelf and quickly snapped it open, feeling dry-mouthed and itchy. "I'm going out tonight," I added, between gulps. "Don't know when I'll be back."

"Suit yourself," Dad replied with a shrug, as he moved towards the kettle.

So, he's on the wagon again, I thought to myself, as I watched him make a cup of coffee. *I give it a week.*

"I plan to," was my response, as I downed the can, and quickly reached for another, feeling an unquenchable thirst inside of me.

"Who are you going out with?" Mam asked, resuming her usual perch at the table. "Are you going right now? Because your father and I wanted to speak to you about a few things."

"Friends, and yeah, I'm going now," I repeated flatly.

"Just sit down and talk to us for a few minutes," she coaxed, pushing a chair out with her foot. "Please, Joey."

Stiffening, I relented and walked over to the table. "What?"

"Sit down."

"Fine. I'm sitting. Now, what?"

She glanced at my father who walked over and took the seat at the head of the table, opposite her. "Your mother is worried about you."

I shrugged. "Okay."

He continued to stir his tea as he spoke. "Thinks you need some counselling, or some nonsense like that."

Mam sighed heavily. "Teddy."

"What?" Dad tossed his teaspoon down and took a sip from his cup. "You know how I feel about that kind of thing, Marie. It's a load of bollox. The young fella is grand. He's stretching his wings a bit."

"With *heroin*!" Mam cried, and then turned to look at me. "I know what you're doing. I *know*, and I want you to stop right this instant, do you hear me, Joey? I want you to stop this!"

"Okay."

She blinked at me. "Okay?"

"Yeah." My hands were shaking. Everything hurt to the point where I could hardly fucking breathe. I needed to get out of this house. I needed an out from the world I'd been cast into. "Whatever you say, Mam."

She didn't care.

She didn't give a damn about me.

All I was good for was holding the fort.

For carrying the burden.

For taking the weight off her shoulders.

She didn't care, and that concept made me want to peel the skin from my bones.

My own mother didn't give a fuck about me.

Hell, *I* didn't give a fuck about me.

But I cared about those kids that spent most of their lives cowering in their beds.

Yeah, I cared a *lot* for them.

The strings that bonded us together, from my siblings' hearts to mine, were so forceful that they kept me bound to this house.

It kept me trapped.

"See, now, Marie?" Dad nodded in approval. "The young fella's grand."

"He's not fine, Teddy," Mam said in a pleading tone. "One look at his eyes, and you can tell that he's not even here with us right now!"

"He's sitting here, isn't he?"

"You know that's not what I mean."

"Can I go now?" I asked, glancing between the two of them.

"I don't want you to go out," Mam said, worrying her lip. "I don't think it's a good idea."

"For fuck's sake, Marie," Dad snapped. "He's going out to celebrate his eighteenth. Don't be such a pain in the hole."

"But I just don't think—"

"Then stop thinking," Dad snapped. "It doesn't suit ya."

"Wait!" Mam called out when I stood and moved for the door. "There's something else we wanted to tell you."

Stiffening, I kept my back to them and waited to hear what I knew in my heart was about to come out of her mouth.

There was always a reason for my father being on the wagon and it usually resulted in the '*we have something to tell you*' speech.

I closed my eyes and waited for my world to shatter around me.

"We're going to have another baby," Mam told me.

And there it was. The last ounce of hope left in my heart being snuffed out.

"Congratulations," I reeled out numbly, as I moved for the door, knowing that even though I was getting out tonight, this baby only tightened the chains around my ankles.

I was completely fucking unravelling and I couldn't stop it from happening.

It *had* happened.

I had finally hit my limit.

I had *nothing* left in the tank.

Nothing left to give these people.

I was done.

Gone.

Dead inside.

Birthday breakdowns

December 23rd 2004

AOIFE

I was in love with an addict.

It was as humiliating as it was heartbreaking.

Joey's incessant need to snort God only knew what up his nose had overtaken his need for me. I felt like I was the other woman in a twisted love triangle between him, my heart, and his latest drug of choice.

I watched him the other night.

He didn't even try to hide it.

And instead of doing the right thing for *me,* I did the safe thing for *him*.

I took him into my bed and into my body.

Because I loved him.

Because I couldn't stop fighting for the boy that I knew was still inside him.

Even now, as I dolled myself up to meet him out in town for his birthday, I couldn't silence the voice inside of me that demanded I have some respect for myself.

I had always considered myself to be a strong girl, but right now, as I tried to look at myself in the mirror, with my head held high, I never felt like such a fake.

So weak.

So small.

So fucking uncertain.

Coming out tonight was a mistake.

I'd known it the moment I caught a glimpse of Joey's black eyes, and I knew it now.

Whatever he'd taken with his asshole buddies in the bathroom earlier had morphed him into a walking, breathing, Duracell bunny.

All he was short of doing was climbing the walls.

"What's he jacked-up on?" Casey asked, slipping her arm through mine, as we sat in the corner of Biddies back lounge, and watched on as my boyfriend buzzed around the room, unable to stand still for longer than thirty seconds at a time. "Jesus, Aoif, he's wired to NASA."

"I know," I squeezed out, watching as he stumbled his way through a conversation with a few of the lads from his hurling team, downing shots and laughing like a maniac. With his arms flying around animatedly, he looked the opposite of his usual self, if that version of him even existed anymore.

"Do you want to leave?" my best friend asked, resting her head on my shoulder. "We can get out of here, leave Tigger and the rest of his pals from The Hundred Acre Wood to it, and have a girly night at my place instead."

"I can't," I replied, watching on nervously, as I waited for him to crash and burn.

"You can't control him, Aoif," she said softly. "He's his own person. Joey Lynch is going to do what he's going to do, regardless of the consequences."

"I don't want to control him, Case," I whispered. "I want to stop him from self-destructing."

"Only he can do that, babe," she said softly. "And no amount of wanting it for him will work until he wants it for himself, too."

"Joey!"

Everything had been going relatively fine until Joey, along with a group of boys from his estate, had all but flipped out and jumped clean over the wall of the outdoor smoking area.

Bleary-eyed and tipsy, I stumbled out the back door of Biddies, pushing past the crowd, and kicking off my high-heels, in my rush to chase him down.

"Aoife, just leave him!" Casey called after me, but I couldn't.

I just *couldn't*.

Running down the alleyway, I quickly cut across the street where I'd last seen him, and kept running, until I turned a corner in town and my feet came to an abrupt stop.

"Joey!" I screamed, mouth hanging open. "What the hell are you doing?"

Laughing like a deranged maniac, my boyfriend stood on the bonnet of a Mercedes Benz parked just outside one of the pubs we *both* knew that his father drank in and rammed his fists into the windscreen.

"Joey!" I screamed, watching in horror as his recently scabbed over knuckles reopened and started bleeding.

Several of his asshole friends from the terrace were watching on and encouraging this absolute madness, clearly delighted with his outburst.

They were laughing, like ruining his life was some big joke to them. *Bastards.*

"Joe, stop!" I screamed, pushing my hair out of my eyes, as I raced up the street towards him. "You're going to get arrested!"

Joey laughed, clearly out of his fucking mind on whatever they'd given him, as he continued to pummel the luxury model with his bloodied knuckles.

The sound of sirens in the distance had my heart thundering in my chest.

"Ah, leave him alone, girl," one of the lads shouted out. "Give the lad a break."

"Go fuck yourself," I snapped, climbing onto the bonnet of the car, knowing full well that my ass was on full display for all of his so-called *friends* and everyone else watching his meltdown, but not giving a damn.

"Stop!" I ordered, catching ahold of his closed fists before he could do any more damage. "Joey." His blood trickled onto my hands as I closed them over his fists and forced him to still. "Stop."

He was breathing hard, still laughing like a crazy person, as tears flowed down his cheeks.

"Stop," he mimicked my voice and then laughed harder. "Stop. Stop. Fucking stop!" His voice cracked and his expression caved. "Stop," he whispered, shaking now, pushing his bloodied hands through his rain-soaked hair. "Make it *stop*."

My heart cracked clean open in my chest at his words.

"Shite, lads, the shades," one of his prick friends called out, as they all ran in opposite directions. "Scatter!"

Panicked, I did the only thing I could do in this moment; I slid off the bonnet of the car, took Joey's bloody hand in mine, and pulled him down to the ground with me.

"Molloy." He looked at me like he was seeing me for the first time. "What are you . . ."

"Come on, Joe," I coaxed, desperately trying to get through to him, as I reached for his hand. "Come with me."

And then, with his hand firmly clamped in mine, I led him away from the scene of the crime, incriminating myself further into this world that I had no business being a part of.

Literally shaking from the adrenalin rushing through my blood-stream, I kept my hand welded to Joey's for the entire stumbling-run back to my house, too afraid to let go out of fear of what he might do next.

"He's left a hole inside of you," I told him, as I dragged him along after me. "It's trauma, Joey." Releasing a pained growl when we reached my street, I found myself desperately trying to reason with the unreasonable. "You're traumatized, and you need professional help."

"I'm fine."

"Joey, you are about the furthest from fine a person can get."

"Leave it alone, Molloy," he muttered. "I don't want to fight with you."

"And I don't want you to die!" I screamed, tears falling freely now, as my emotions got the better of me. There was something so tragic about this boy, something that I wanted to keep. "Don't you care about yourself? Not even a little bit?"

"It doesn't matter." He shook his head. "None of this *matters*."

"Yes, it does," I heard myself shout. "It fucking does."

"Molloy."

"It matters because *you* matter!" I cried, glancing down at my blood-stained hands. "It matters because I *love* you!"

"I'm sorry I fucked your night up," he decided to go with. "I'll make it up to you."

"I don't want you to make it up to me, Joey, I want you to *talk* to me," I begged him. "Just open up to me, Joe. If you tell me what's going on inside of your head, then maybe I can help." I batted a tear from my cheek and cried, "Then maybe we can start getting a handle on this. "

"I'm not okay!" he roared, yanking his hand away from mine "Is that what you want me to admit? Is that what you want to hear, Molloy? That I'm not okay?"

"Yes," I cried, feeling both relief and devastation flood my body. "That's what I want you to admit. I want the words, Joey. I want all of your *words*!"

"Pain," he roared into my face, eyes alight with temper, as his shadow danced with his demons. "On the outside. On the inside. All around me. Pain so fucking strong I'm drowning in it!" He ran his bloodstained hands through his hair, tingeing his blond hair a faint crimson color. "That's what I feel. That's *all* I feel. All the fucking time!"

My heart spliced open. "Joe."

"Do you want to hear about how often I pissed the bed out of fright until he literally beat the piss, blood and snot out of me?" he roared, tears flowing down his cheeks now, too. "Because that happened, Molloy. I was weak. I cried. I begged. I hid. I ran. And then when all of that failed, I fought back. I stood the fuck up and fought back. It didn't work in the beginning. He still smacked the shit out of me, but at least I felt like I was doing *something*!" Chest heaving, he ran his hands through his hair. "And now I feel *nothing*. I feel *nothing*, and I'm *fine* with that!"

"And you are entitled to feel that way!" I screamed back at him. "Your father has put you through hell. None of what happens in that house is on you. Not one bit of it. You've grown up in a war zone. You've done a phenomenal job—"

"Stop!" He held a hand up in warning. "My true colors are ugly, Molloy. Stop looking for the good in me, because it's not there to find. I promise. Because I know that I love you, but in all honesty, if I could forget you, I would."

The words were like a bucket of ice to my face.

I sucked in a sharp breath. "You don't mean that."

"I used to think that I wasn't like him – that I was different, but you can't change DNA." Choking out a sob, he roughly batted his tears away before saying, "Look at me, Molloy. Look at who I am. Look the fuck at what I've done to you! I'm *just* like *him*."

"*No*." Shaking my head, I stalked right over to him and grabbed his face in my hands, roughly, raw, sincerely refuting his deepest fear. "You are *nothing* like him."

"Yes, I am," he strangled out, breaking free from my hold as he staggered away from me. "And if you don't get away from me soon, you're going to end up just like my mother."

It was Christmas Eve, babe

December 24th 2004

AOIFE

Joey disappeared after that and I hadn't been able to get ahold of him since.

By late Christmas Eve night, I was frantic with worry, and, after searching every one of his haunts and hangouts, including his house, I found myself standing at the front door that caused the hairs on the back of my neck to stand on end.

After several rounds of incessant knocking, the door finally swung inwards, and I was greeted with the sight of a man I hated almost as much as Teddy Lynch.

Maybe even more.

"Is he here?" I asked shakily. Adrenalin was pumping through my body at a rapid rate, making me shiver and tremble, but I forced myself to stand tall. I refused to back down from this piece of shit. "What am I saying? Of course he's *here*. It's the only place left for him to go."

Shane smiled cruelly. "Who?"

Bastard.

"You damn well know who," I hissed through clenched teeth, glaring up at his bloodshot eyes. "Send him out."

He smirked.

He actually fucking smirked at me.

"Go home, princess." Catching ahold of the cigarette that was balancing between his lips, Shane stubbed it out with his fingers and placed the long butt behind his ear. "There's nothing left here for you."

Like hell there wasn't.

He moved to shut the door in my face, but I stuck my foot in the doorway to block him.

"You have something that belongs to me," I hissed, chest heaving now. "And I'm not going anywhere until I get him back, you jumped-up, fucking scumbag!"

"Fiery little ride aren't ya?" he mused, taking my measure. "I can see the appeal. No wonder Lynchy lets you burst his balls. You must be a firecracker in the bedroom."

"Listen, prick, you send my boyfriend out here, or I can come in and get him." Narrowing my eyes, I pushed at the door as hard as I could, forcing him to take several steps into his hallway. "Either way, I'm not leaving without him."

Shane's hand shot out faster than I anticipated, fingers wrapping around my throat. "What did you say to me?"

"Let ... go ... of ... my ... throat ... and ... I'll ... say ... it ... again ... asshole," I choked out, clawing my nails into his beefy hand.

"Have you any idea who you're talking to?" he mused, eyes dancing with a mixture of malice and heat. "Hmm?" He squeezed, not tight enough to choke me – more like scare me.

Unwilling to back down, I glared right back at him, daring him with my eyes to do whatever he had to do because I wasn't leaving.

After a tense stare down, a laugh tore from his throat and he released me.

"You're a crazy bitch," he chuckled, swinging the door inwards and gesturing for me to come inside. "By all means, be my guest."

"Joey?" Furious, I barged past him and stalked down the dilapidated hallway, stepping over empty beer cans and cigarette butts, throwing doors open as I went, feeling more frantic with every step I took. "Joey?"

"He can't hear you, princess," Shane chuckled from behind me. "He's not here right now."

"Fuck you," I seethed, rushing in and out of every room downstairs before bolting up the staircase and starting the same process up there.

On the last door, when I'd given up hope, I stumbled upon my worst nightmare.

There was a stained mattress on the floor.

Alongside the mattress was a metal spoon with some dark, syrupy-looking stains, a lighter, and a tiny plastic bag with some brownish powder inside.

Strewn on top of the filthy mattress was my boyfriend, with his eyes rolling back in his head, and a needle dangling from the crook of his arm.

My heart, the same heart I didn't think could be broken any more than it already had, cracked into a bazillion more pieces.

"Joe." My hand sprang up to cover my mouth, as I battled with the image my mind was assuring me wasn't a nightmare, but reality. "Joey!"

Nothing.

"We were supposed to be spending the day together," I cried, stumbling towards him. The smell of his sorrow was all around me and I honestly felt like I was going to die of a broken heart as I felt myself hemorrhage from the inside.

Kicking the contraband away from his body, like it would somehow make everything better, I knelt down beside him and undid the tie that was cutting off the circulation in his arm. "Joe, can you hear me?"

Nothing.

Sniffling back a sob, I gingerly reached out and pulled the syringe out of his arm before throwing it to the other side of the room. "Joe?"

Soft groaning was the only response I got.

"Get up," I begged, pulling on his shoulders in my pathetic attempt to get him up.

"Molloy."

"It's me," I cried, tears falling fast now, as I managed to pull him into a sitting position. "I'm here, Joe."

"Aoife."

"You've got to come with me, okay?" Sniffling back another sob, I managed to get him to drag himself to his feet. "I'm going to take you someplace safe, okay?"

"Molloy."

"I've got you." Hooking one arm around his back, I draped his arm over my shoulder and unsteadily dragged him towards the door. "It's okay, Joe. Just lean on me. I've got you."

How I managed to get us both down the staircase in one piece was beyond me, but I didn't have time to think about it, because Shane and his goons were waiting for us in the hallway, which put me even more on edge than I already was.

"You know, you should really let him sleep it off," Shane offered with a snicker. "Poor lad can't even get high without the missus busting his bollocks."

"For fuck's sake, Holland, don't be a dick. Can't you see the poor girl is in a bad way over her lad," another much bigger, much older, bearded man, with a distinctive Belfast accent said. He then walked over to where I was attempting to hold up a semi-comatose Joey, and hoisted him upright. "Where's your car, love?" he asked. "I'll carry him over to it for you."

As much as I wanted to tell them all to go to hell, I needed the help.

"It's outside," I sniffled, and then moved for the door, only to quickly glance over my shoulder to make sure the man was following me with Joey.

Thankfully, he was.

Hurrying over to my car, I quickly unlocked the passenger door and swung it open.

"W-will he b-be okay?" I heard myself ask, feeling acutely small and young in that moment. "Should I t-take him t-to the h-hospital?"

Here I was, on Christmas Eve night, bawling like a baby on the side of the road, while some beefed-up gangster put my boyfriend in the car for me.

Jesus Christ . . .

"No, love, he'll be grand, so he will," the big man assured me as he settled Joey into the passenger seat. He even went as far as fastening his seatbelt around him. "Take him someplace safe and let him sleep it off."

"Was that . . ." Shaking my head, I exhaled a ragged breath and strangled out, "heroin?"

The man didn't answer.

"What do I do?" Another harsh cry escaped me. "How do I h-help him?"

"He'll be grand," the man told me. "He's not too far gone to be pulled back. And with a lass like you in his corner, he'll come right. Don't you worry."

I stared up at him, feeling a wave of anger, curiosity, and gratitude wash over me. "Why did you help me tonight?"

"Because I was your lad here once upon a time, and I wish somebody had helped my wife before I became what I am, and she became my ex."

And then he turned around and walked back inside the house, leaving me alone with Joey.

Hiccupping out another sob, I rounded the car and climbed into the driver's seat. Shaking like a leaf, I slowly fastened my seatbelt and stuck the key in the ignition.

"She's pregnant," Joey whispered from beside me, lips mashing together clumsily.

"Who?"

"My mother."

Jesus.

I was so reeling that I honestly didn't know what to say.

Groaning in pain, he slurred. "I'm . . . sorry, Molloy. So fucking . . . sorry . . ."

"I know you are," I sniffled, cranking the engine. "I know, Joe."

"I . . . love . . ." I felt my body tense when he clumsily reached across the car and tried to pat my thigh. "You . . . Molloy . . . ."

Tell me when you're sober," I replied, giving his hand a gentle squeeze. "It won't count tonight."

"Why won't it count, Molloy?"

"Because you won't remember it," I whispered sadly.

Reality checks and dawning awareness

December 25th 2004

JOEY

When I opened my eyes, it was to a room full of mid-morning sunshine and a pillow of hair in my face.

Naked as the day I was born, I had my arm thrown over a blonde who had her equally naked back to me.

Pain, undiluted and toxic, instantly flooded my chest, seeping through every vein and artery in my body until I could feel nothing but misery.

Darkness enveloped me.

Sucking in a pained breath when the familiar pang of hunger clawed at my throat, I tightened my fists, locking my muscles into place.

My hunger wasn't for food.

It was for heroin.

Disgusted, I thought about how far I had fallen.

How I had let myself become my father.

I was poisoned on the inside just like he was.

I couldn't get beyond it.

This hereditary weakness, handed down to me by the person I hated most in this world would forever eat me alive from the inside out.

Addiction had settled deep inside of me like a leach attaching itself to a blood-filled carcass.

Frozen to the spot, and with my stomach twisted up in knots, I desperately tried to rake through my hazed thoughts, until the familiar scent of her shampoo flooded my senses.

Molloy . . .

Heaving a huge sigh of relief, I shifted closer to her warm body and pressed a kiss to her bare shoulder.

She sniffled in response.

I froze.

She sniffled again.

Ah fuck.

She choked out a sob.

The last few days' events came trickling back to me, bit by bit, and my blood ran cold as shame enveloped me in its familiar embrace.

No.

No.

Fuck no . . .

"Molloy." My voice was strangled and torn. "Baby, I'm so fucking—"

"You're not *good* for me," she whispered brokenly, clinging to the hand I had wrapped around her. "I get that now." Her fingers dug into my forearm. "But it doesn't stop my heart from loving you, or my head from wanting you."

I could feel her pain.

It was hemorrhaging out of her chest and pouring straight into mine.

She was the only person I'd ever loved that hadn't been produced from between my mother's legs. That was a horrible fucking image, but I meant it. I cared very little about anything or anyone besides the children who shared my bloodline, because those poor defenseless bastards shared my misfortune.

But I cared about the girl in my arms.

I cared an awful lot about this girl.

"You might be the addict in this relationship, but you're also the habit that I need to kick," she strangled out, chest heaving, as she turned in my arms to face me. "Because I feel like I'm dying when I'm with you, and I feel like I'm dead when I'm not."

Her tears were on my shoulder.

I could feel them.

It shook me to my fucking core.

I wanted to make it up to her, show her the better side of me, but I was just so fucking tired.

I was bone-weary, on the inside and out.

Her eyes were red and swollen.

There was no morality in this.

No one needed to love me if it meant that it hurt them this deeply.

"Aoife." What was left of my heart cracked clean open in my chest. "It kills me that I've done this to you."

"And I can't walk away, because I know that there's still a little bit of you left in there," she choked out. Placing her hand over the part of my chest that bore her name, she sniffled another sob and whispered, "Which means that I'm going to keep on loving you, Joey Lynch. So, you might want to start thinking about stopping breaking my heart."

Curling up against me, she buried her face in my chest and continued to cry.

Her long blonde hair was all around us, her shoulders completely slumped, and I forced myself to take a good hard look at the destruction I'd caused.

This is why you don't have nice things, my conscience hissed while my lungs constricted to the point that I couldn't fucking breathe. *Because you break them!*

Feeling my way through the haze of drugs and feelings, I watched her break down right there in my arms, while I wrestled the evil bastard demon inside of my head – the one that refused to let me do right by this girl.

The harder I fought to take control of this piece of shit person I'd morphed into, the stronger the demon became.

"I'm sorry," was all I could whisper, as I held her. "I'm so fucking sorry."

The louder she cried, the tighter my lungs squeezed until she was full-on screaming into my chest, and I was full-on dying on the inside.

And only then did I find the strength to do what needed to be done.

Only then did I find the strength to save her.

From me.

Christmas Morning

December 25th 2004

AOIFE

It was Christmas morning.

It was also Joey's eighteenth birthday.

But instead of celebrating either, I found myself welded to his chest, holding on to his body with all of my strength, because I had a horrible feeling that once he left my bed, he wouldn't come back.

The physical abuse Joey had been subjected to, the emotional neglect, psychological scarring, and sheer pressure he'd endured from a lifetime of holding the fort and raising children that didn't belong to him, had finally broken something pivotal inside of his mind.

He'd given up on himself; I could see it in his eyes last night. The same look was there when he woke up this morning, and it scared me to death.

He was sick, he was so damn unwell, and I was out of my depth trying to help him out of something I didn't understand.

I wanted to rescue him, to shield him from the horrors he had been born into. I wanted to be his armor when he couldn't fight back.

I wanted to wade into battle for him, protect his beautiful soul.

But I'd been so determined to save him that I hadn't noticed I'd lost myself in the process.

Our love was toxic.

"This is toxic," Joey strangled out, voicing my thoughts aloud, as he held me in his arms, squeezing my body just as tightly as I was squeezing his. "I'm *toxic* for you."

"I don't care," I cried, delirious from a horrible concoction of love and heartache. "I still want you."

"That's the point," he croaked out, voice cracking, as he gently dis-sembled our joined bodies and climbed out of my bed. "I'm fucking *toxic* to you."

"What are you doing?" I asked shakily, watching as he quickly reached for his disheveled clothes, which were thrown in a pile, along with mine, on my bedroom floor. "Joey? What are you doing?"

"Please don't make it any harder. We both know that I need to go." Blowing out a shaky breath, he refused to look at me while he dressed, his movement clumsy because of the severe tremor running through him. "This needs to end and you need to let me do this for you, okay?"

"What? No!" Panic seared me. "No, this doesn't have to end. I don't believe that and neither do you!"

"Molloy." Hollow green eyes, paired with circles so dark they could've been mistaken for bruises, locked on mine. Hell, knowing my boyfriend like I did, those probably *were* bruises under his eyes. "I *have* to leave," he choked out. "All of the pain? All of the dumb, fucked-up shit I've put you through—" His voice cracked, and I watched as he dragged in a pained breath, clearly suffering as much in the moment as I was. "I should have ended this a long time ago."

"No!" Springing off the mattress, I quickly closed the space between us, needing him to stay right here with me. "Don't." Wrapping my arms around him, I buried my face in his neck, holding on to his body for all I was worth. "It's okay, it's okay. I'm fine. We're fine! Don't talk like that. God!"

Instantaneously, Joey's arms came around my body, making me feel so fucking safe it hurt.

It didn't make sense how he could do that to me: make me feel like nothing could hurt me when I was in his arms, when the truth was very different.

Silence settled between us then, with so many unspoken words danc-ing on the tips of our tongues, while we just held each other.

I could feel it all in this moment, every hurt word that had been echoed throughout the course of our fucked-up relationship. Every kiss, every touch, every fight, every scream, every midnight flash of madness that had led us to this moment in time.

"Listen, I want you to know something," he said quietly, clenching my hip with his hand. "I want you to know that you've been the best part of my day *every* day since I was twelve years old."

"Don't, Joe," Voice breaking, my heart hammered violently, as tears spilled down my cheeks. "I don't want to hear this."

Not when I knew where it would lead.

"It's true." Tipping my chin up with his free hand, he forced me to look at him. "My life has been a shitstorm from day dot, Molloy, and the whole goddamn town knows it. I've never had calm. But you?" His tear-filled eyes implored me to *hear* him. "You were like an island. Somewhere for me to go and escape. Somewhere safe. Someone to anchor me, if that even makes sense. And I took advantage of that when I had no right to. I was selfish when I dragged you into my world. Now, I need to put you first."

A tear slid down my cheek as his words only enforced what I already knew to be true; that I would never get over this boy. "Then put me first by *not* doing this, because I don't want *this,* Joey. I don't want your goodbyes."

"You might not want me to say goodbye, but you need me to." And then he cut me deeper than a guillotine ever could when he added, "I was always going to fuck this up, Molloy." With a resigned look, he slowly released me and backed away. "I'm only sorry that I didn't put you first sooner."

"Oh my fucking god!" I screamed, throwing my hands up in frustration and panic, as I watched him walk away from me. "You just love ripping the rug out from under my feet, don't you?" When he didn't answer, I screamed, "Fine. Walk away!"

With a small shake of his head, he moved for the window.

"Go on." Desperately trying to save face while my heart shattered to pieces in my chest, I hissed. "Get the fuck out."

My heart hammered as I desperately resisted the urge to stop him from climbing out of my bedroom window.

"Off you go," I spat instead, bawling like a baby, as I watched him leave. "Turning your back on us at the first sign of trouble."

"Because I'm not good for you!" Joey roared, climbing back through my window, and stalking back towards where I was standing. "Fuck, Molloy, don't you get that? I'm not fucking good for you! Last night was just a taster of how it will be, because I can't change, okay—"

Reckless, I grabbed his neck and pulled his face down to mine, kissing him hard and rough and furiously.

He kissed me back with equal passion and hunger, as he fisted handfuls of my hair and clutched my face between his hands.

"Don't do this," I cried against his lips, feeling my tears mix with his. "Please."

He pressed one final kiss to my brow before stepping away from me. "If I don't walk away from you now, I never will."

And then he disappeared out of my bedroom window, dropping onto the roof of the shed below.

"Joey," I cried, leaning out the window. "Don't do this."

With one final glance at me, he pulled his hood up, dropped to the ground, and called out, "I'll be seeing ya, Molloy," over his shoulder.

And then he was gone.

Cut from the same cloth

December 25th 2004

JOEY

Shook to my core, I made my way home on autopilot, barely managing to put one foot in front of the other, while an internal war raged on inside of me.

My heart was demanding that I turn my ass around and go back to her and beg her to forgive me for something that my brain knew I would do again.

Because that's what *would* happen.

I couldn't get out of this.

I couldn't break the fuck free.

And taking her down with me was out of the question.

Feeling worse than I had in a very long time, I ignored multiple groups of children and young families playing out on the streets with their new bikes and scooters, as I crossed through her estate, and headed across the bridge towards mine.

Don't do this.

Don't walk away from her.

She's the only good thing you've got going for you.

She's the only one who gives a shit about you.

With my hood pulled up, I ignored all of my selfish thoughts, urges, and instincts, knowing that I needed to put her first this time.

And putting her first meant that I needed to put space between us.

Do it for her.

Give her a chance at normal.

Don't drag her down with you.

She's too good for you.

"Alright, Lynchy?" Jason O Driscoll, aka Dricko, one of the lads from my terrace, called out, as I walked past him. I smelled the familiar scent of weed wafting from the rollie he was balancing between his fingers. "Happy Christmas."

"Alright, Dricko," I replied, stopping to acknowledge the lad who used to be in my year at BCS until he dropped out after our junior cert in third year. We had hurled together all the way up through underage club level as well, until life caught up with him. "How's the small fella of yours keeping? Did Santa come?"

"Luke? Ah, he's grand," he replied, as he lounged against the side of his baby mama's dilapidated house, in a pink, frilly dressing gown. "He's only a year and a half, so he doesn't have a notion of what's happening." Exhaling a cloud of smoke, he held out the rollie, offering me a drag. "Smoke?"

"Nah, I'm good." I shook my head, and kept my hands firmly clamped in the front pocket of my hoodie. "How's Sam keeping nowadays?" I offered instead, as my thoughts cast to another one of my former classmates. "Are you living here with her now?" I asked, gesturing to the council house I knew she'd been given not long after she had his baby.

"Am I fuck," he choked out a laugh. "I've my own life to be living. Sam handles the kid."

I cocked a brow. "Pretty sure she had one of those too, lad, before you saddled her with your son at sixteen."

"Ah, you know what I mean," Dricko hurried to add, having the good grace to look sheepish. "Don't get me wrong, she's a great mam. Luke's lucky to have her, because I sure as hell don't know what to do with him, but the girl thinks she owns me because she had a kid off me."

Again, I just stared blankly.

"Seriously, it's a fucking nightmare. I can't move without her, Joe. She's constantly breathing down my goddamn neck," he muttered bitterly, casting a narrowing glance to the front door. "I'm surprised she let me come outside for a smoke without chasing after me."

585 • CHLOE WALSH

I shrugged. "Maybe if you did a little more staying, she wouldn't have to do so much chasing."

"That's easy for you to say," he shot back with a chuckle. "When you've got that little ride from Rosewood Estate to stay put for. You were lucky that she was there the night of your eighteenth to hide you after you went nuclear on that car." He continued to give me a dose of my own medicine by adding. "The Gards were scouring the terrace for the culprit."

I didn't answer him.

I couldn't.

Because Molloy's face was instantly at the fore-point of my mind, and my guilt was fucking choking me.

"What have I got to stick around for?" he continued to rant. "Shitty nappies, overdue bills, constant nagging, and a screaming baby?" He shook his head. "Nah, lad, step into my shoes for a week, and you wouldn't be long coming off that high horse." The front door swung inwards then, and Dricko released a pained growl. "See what I mean?"

"He wants his *father*," Sam snapped, red-faced and teary-eyed, as she stood in the doorway, with a small, dark-haired infant balancing on her hip.

"Yeah, well, his father's busy," Dricko tossed over his shoulder. "Tell him that his mother will have to do."

"He's your son, too, Jason. It's Christmas morning. You could at least pretend like you're interested in him for more than thirty seconds," Sam bit out, before her gaze landed on me. "Oh, hey, Joey."

"Sam." Inclining my head in acknowledgment, forcing myself to take in the sight before me.

Take one look at her, asshole. This right here is how you know you did the right thing, my brain hissed. I felt validated as I locked eyes on the girl that I grew up alongside, who had become a mother before her time.

I was no different to Dricko. We shared the similar misfortune of being born to young mothers and asshole fathers. We were cut from the same cloth, but I would make damn sure that Molloy had a different future to the one stretching out in front of Samantha McGuinness. "Happy Christmas."

"Thanks, and the same to you, Joe," she replied, giving me a long lonesome look, before turning her attention back to her fella. "Well? Are you coming inside or not?"

"When I'm ready."

"Jason."

"Keep nagging and you'll be eating dinner on your own with the kid," he warned, exhaling another cloud of smoke. "I'm doing you a favor by being here, Sam. I told you that I'd come round last night to see the kid open his presents, but I'm not your fucking bellboy."

"You did more than come around," she spat, voice trembling. "You spent the night."

"Right, I'm off," I muttered, striding off down the footpath, before I got dragged into their domestic.

I didn't have the heart or the energy to deal with anyone else's drama this morning.

My head was full, and my shoulders were buckling under the pressure of my own shit.

I could feel my phone vibrating in my pocket, but I didn't reach for it. I couldn't.

Because if I glanced at that screen and saw her name flashing, I knew I wouldn't be strong enough to reject her call.

"Joey!" Ollie was standing in the doorway when I stepped foot in the garden a few minutes later. "Santa came, Joe! He's been to our house this year! He came!"

"Did he?" I replied, somehow managing to muscle up the enthusiasm he needed from me in that moment. "That's because you've been washing your ears properly."

"Uh-huh!" Nodding brightly, my little brother grabbed my hand and dragged me inside. "You were right, Joe. You said he would come if I scrubbed them good and he *came*!"

"Good morning," Mam greeted me in the front hall, clad in the

587 • CHLOE WALSH

same old dressing gown she always wore. The one Darren bought her the Christmas before he left. It didn't matter that she'd been given a new one since. She continued to cling to the past, and her firstborn, by wearing the thread-worn robe. "Happy birthday."

"Oh shoots, I forgot!" Ollie yelped, slapping his forehead. "Happy birthday, Joey."

"Cheers, kid," I replied, before asking my mother, "Where is he?"

"Bed."

"Good." Repressing a shudder of revulsion when my eyes landed on my mother's stomach, I focused on the outstretched arms of the toddler on her hip. "How's my Seany-boo?" I asked, lifting him into my arms. "Did Santa come to my Seany?"

"O-ee," Sean babbled, pressing his spit-slobbered hand to my cheek. "O-ee."

Sidestepping my mother, I moved for the sitting room, where Tadhg was sitting under the tree, looking exceptionally dejected in comparison to our younger brothers.

"You didn't come home," he accused, not bothering to look up from the toy train he was holding in his hands.

"I know."

"Where were you?"

"Out."

"Out where?"

"None of your business." My brows furrowed. "You got a train?"

Tadhg nodded stiffly. "Yeah."

"But you're almost twelve."

"I know."

"You haven't played with trains since you were seven."

"I know."

"That's probably for Sean or Ollie," I offered, setting Sean down and reaching for the wrapping paper. "Ma – Santa must have put the wrong name on it."

"It's not," Tadhg replied quietly, holding a gift tag up for me. "It's for me."

Boy, aged 7-11, the blue gift tag read, and I felt sick, suddenly knowing exactly where the sparse amount of presents under the tree had come from.

Ballylaggin's charity Christmas toy appeal.

Because in this town, our family was considered a charity case.

"What did you get?" I forced myself to ask Ollie, striving for all I was worth to keep my tone light.

"Oh, I gots this super cool game," he explained, reaching for a travel-size edition of *Connect Four*.

"Got," Tadhg corrected wearily. "It's *got*, not *gots*."

"Got," Ollie chimed back. "And Seany gots this glowing worm."

"*Got!*"

"Uh-huh, got," Ollie repeated, grinning up at me. "Want to play, Joe?"

No, I want to die.

"Maybe later," I replied, "but you should go check my room. Maybe Santa left something in there."

Three pairs of widened brown eyes locked on me. "Again?"

I shrugged. "You never know."

"You absolute legend!" Tadhg hooted, bolting past me for the staircase. "

"Come on, Sean," Ollie squealed, pulling the baby of the family up the rickety staircase after him. "I bet Santa hid the good presents in Joey's room again this year!"

"Yes!" I heard Tadhg cheer from upstairs. "Deadly!"

Shaking my head, I ignored the vibrating in my pocket and stalked into the kitchen, to where my mother was peeling potatoes. "You couldn't get them anything they wanted?" I demanded in a hushed tone. "Not even a fucking football?"

"I didn't have any money left over after the groceries," she replied, blushing.

"You couldn't spare a tenner?" I demanded, throwing my hands up. "Tadhg was gutted in there. He's not a baby anymore, Mam. He knows where those presents come from and it's fucking humiliating for him. I know. I've been him. I've been the kid whose friends' parents donated their unwanted shit to. It's horrible."

Mam sniffled. "Yeah, well, I'm sure whatever you bought him will save the day."

There was an edge to her tone, and it got my back up.

I narrowed my eyes. "You're pissed with me because I saved your ass? Again?"

"No, I'm not pissed with you. I'm *embarrassed*. I feel bad enough about it, Joey, I really do," she mumbled, keeping her chin tucked down, as she clumsily peeled the potatoes. "So please spare me the third degree."

"You can't afford the kids you already have, so you decided that it would be the perfect time to throw another into the mix?" I couldn't stop myself from throwing at her. "What's going to happen to this one if you can't look after it? Because I'm not doing it again, do ya hear me? I'm not mothering another newborn."

She flinched like I struck her. "There's nothing you can say that will make me feel worse than I already do."

Leaning a hip against the counter, I stared at her and asked, "What about the money I gave you? Couldn't you have bought them something with that?"

She didn't respond.

"Mam?"

Nothing.

"What did you do with the money I gave you?"

"Your father owed some money," she finally admitted, voice barely more than a broken whisper. "It couldn't wait."

"Jesus Christ, that was two hundred euro!" Blowing out a breath, I ran a hand through my hair in frustration. "It was for you and the kids, not his gambling debts and bar tabs! Do you have any idea how long that took me to save up?" I gaped at her. "Mam, that was a week's wage to me. I won't be paid again until the new year – and neither will you."

"I know," she whispered, sniffling. "I'm sorry."

"And if the electric goes in the meantime?" I demanded, feeling panicked. "Or we run out of coal for the fire before either one of us gets paid next? What then?"

"Joey."

"How are we going to heat them, Mam?" I choked out, heart thumping violently in my chest. "How are we going to keep them warm?"

"I'll get paid my children's allowance money next week," she strangled out. "We'll cope until then."

"Your children's allowance money?" I glared at her in disbelief. "You're depending on an income that he has *always* blown on drink to get us by?"

"Your father is off the drink," she was quick to defend. "He swears it this time."

"Just stop." Holding a hand up, I turned and walked out of the kitchen before I lost it. "I can't hear another word."

"Joey, wait!"

"How long are we going to keep living like this, Mam?" I tossed over my shoulder. "Because I'm really running on empty here."

"What are you saying?"

"I'm saying that maybe those kids *would* be better off in care."

Moving for the staircase, I ignored my mother's pleading tone as she begged me to come back and talk to her, and hurried up to my room.

"He didn't leave them under the tree. The silly billy hid our presents in your wardrobe, Joe," Ollie exclaimed, clutching the weird-ass Gizmo-looking creature he had begged Santa for – the one Molloy and I had queued up for hours in the pissing rain to secure. "See?" He held up the creepy doll creature for all to see. "Santa's the best."

"Mind him," I warned. *Fucker cost me a half a week's wages.*

"Yeah." Setting his new hurley down on my bed, Tadhg walked over to where I was standing in the doorway and wrapped his arms around my waist, hugging me tightly. "He really is the best."

"O-ee, O-ee." Pulling on the leg of my jeans, Sean grappled for my attention. "O-ee?" Reaching down, he grabbed his Elmo and held it up for me. "E-mo."

"Good job," I praised, sinking down to his level. "And see this fella?" I held the red teddy up to him. "He uses the potty just like Seany."

"Happy birthday, Joe," Shannon said from behind me, and I swung around just in time to see her produce a homemade cake from behind her back. "I know you're eighteen today," she added with a blush. "But I could only find four candles."

"Make a wish, Joe," Ollie cheered. "And don't tell us what it is, or it won't come true."

"You made me a cake?"

Blushing a deeper shade of pink, my little sister nodded.

I cocked a brow. "An edible cake?"

"Is that so hard to believe?" she laughed. "I've been cooking your dinner for years and I haven't poisoned you yet, have I?"

"Not yet." Standing up, I ruffled her hair. "Thanks, Shan. Did you get the CD Santa left on your nightstand?"

"Yes." She beamed up at me. "He was most generous."

"Come on, Joe," Ollie groaned. "Make a wish and blow out the cangles. I want some cake."

Tadhg sighed. "It's candles, not cangles."

"That's what I said."

"No, it's not."

"Yes, it is."

"Jesus, don't start this shit already." Leaning in, I quickly blew out the candles before looking to my sister and saying, "You didn't have to do this for me."

"I would do so much more if I could," she replied, leaning in for a half-hug, while she batted several small hands away from the cake. "I love you, Joe."

"O-ee," Seany crooned, clutching my leg. "O-ee."

"We all do," Tadhg begrudgingly agreed. "Love you, that is."

"Uh-huh," Ollie added. "So much."

"Yeah." I blew out a pained breath and took stock of the small humans circling me. "Right back at ye."

I was officially eighteen years old.

I could walk right out the front door, and nobody could stop me.

I could leave.

I could be *free*.

But the four small faces staring expectantly up at me were so defenseless, so utterly dependent on my ability to provide for and protect them, that I knew in my heart that I would never leave this house until I could take them with me.

Whether it was love or duty that kept me shackled here, the lines were too blurred to differentiate, but one thing I was sure of was that I would never become to them what Darren had become to me.

I would never abandon them.

If I could do nothing else, then I would spare them *that* pain.

The aftermath

December 27th 2004

AOIFE

The radio was blasting in the kitchen downstairs, tormenting me with the sound of Mary Black's 'Only a Woman's Heart' as her voice drifted up the staircase.

Her melancholy lyrics wrapped around my already breaking heart.

Numb, I curled up on my bed in the smallest ball I could, with my knees pressed to my chest, and fought to calm the hysteria drowning me.

Pain encompassed every inch of my body, both internally and externally.

I felt like I was hemorrhaging tears.

They wouldn't stop falling.

How I managed to survive Christmas dinner with my family without falling apart at the table, I would never know.

I could only assume that it had a lot to do with the shock and adrenalin that had been thrashing through my veins, but that had long since deserted me.

I knew my parents were worried about me. Aside from leaving the house to fulfil my shift at work this morning, I had spent the past forty-eight hours holed up in my room, which was a huge red flag. Especially considering the previous night was the biggest night out of the year – and I *never* missed a St. Stephen's night out on the tiles.

Hell, even Kev had come knocking on my bedroom door, but I couldn't talk to him about it.

If I talked about it, if I verbalized it out loud, then it would be real.

And I was desperately clinging to the hope that I would somehow wake up from my nightmare and have everything go back to the way it was before.

My breath was coming in short, achy gasps that clawed at my throat in protest because my heart didn't want me to breathe.

My heart wanted me to slip into the deepest sleep of my life and wake up when it was over.

The thought only made me cry harder.

Because it *was* over.

It was over and I wasn't ready for it to be.

I wasn't ready for him to leave me.

But he had.

All of my calls had gone unanswered, while my texts went unsent because I couldn't stop my hands from trembling long enough to type out a message.

Breaking up with me had been a knife to the back and ignoring me was just another cruel twist of the blade.

I had spent the bones of four years in a relationship with Paul, and never once in that entire space of time had he provoked such conflicted turmoil inside of my heart like Joey had.

Like he continued to do.

I didn't want to think of what Joey was doing now that we were over. I hoped he was as miserable as I was, but I wasn't going to hold my breath.

He had been quick enough to run out and shit on our relationship, so what was to say he wouldn't drown this version of his sorrows inside another girl.

Bullshit, a voice in my head hissed, *that's your hurt talking, and you know it.*

Yeah, I knew that.

I also knew that he loved me.

It wasn't a matter of there being someone else in this instance.

The only person getting in between us was *Joey.*

Depression had its claws latched deep inside of me.

My throat felt like sawdust, and my heart felt like it had been crushed to pieces. It was disintegrating in my chest, and I couldn't handle the sensation a second longer.

Get up, my pride demanded, *don't you dare lie down like this.*

Forcing myself to unlock my rigid muscles, I slowly clambered off the bed and stood up on shaky legs, surprised that my body could balance itself after the knockout blow I'd taken.

My heart sure as hell felt like it had been KO'd.

My eyelashes felt thick and heavy from the sheer height of crying, and it took a few moments for the blurriness to recede and my vision to clear.

That's it, the voice in my head coaxed, *now stay up.*

Breathing hard and ragged, I moved on autopilot, walking out of my room and into the bathroom.

Locking the door behind me, I wobbled like a newborn foal towards the sink, and then clutched the basin with a death grip, while I clenched my eyes shut and forced myself to smother the scream trying to escape me.

"Argh!" the tearing sound ripped out of me, and I cringed, tightening my fingers on the porcelain rim until my knuckles turned white.

You will not fall apart.

I held my breath to steady the sobbing.

You will not crumble.

Trembling, I reached for my toothbrush and ran it under the cold tap before squeezing a dollop of toothpaste on the brush and shoving it into my mouth.

I scrubbed my teeth with a viciousness that threatened to make my gums bleed.

I didn't care.

I just needed to wash it all away somehow.

Erase everything.

Nothing could do that for me, though.

I kept thinking that if I had handled my emotions differently that morning, then maybe I could have prevented this.

If I had only waited until he was stable enough to have a coherent conversation, then maybe we wouldn't have ended the way we had.

Shaking my head, I pushed the thoughts away and focused on small mundane tasks like rinsing my toothbrush, screwing the cap back on the paste, turning off the tap, setting my toothbrush back in its holder.

Those, I could manage.

When I had regathered some semblance of self-control, I switched on the shower and stripped, peeling off every stitch of clothing before stepping under the blistering spray of scalding water. Yet I was frozen to the bone, trembling from head to toe, with my teeth chattering violently.

I felt violated.

I felt ripped fucking open.

"I want you to know that you've been the best part of my day every *day since I was twelve years old."*

His words continued to circle around in my mind until I felt like climbing into my car, driving to his house, and throttling him.

And then, the image of how he looked on that mattress, with a needle in his arm, and his eyes rolling back in his head, infiltrated my thoughts, and I wanted to hold him to my chest and never let go.

No, scratch that; I wanted to die from the unfairness of it all.

"So, do you have a name, boy-who-can-think-for-himself?"

"Does it matter? We both know that you'll be calling me baby by the end of the day."

Numb, I grabbed a bottle of shampoo from the rack and lathered my hair. Taking a clean facecloth, I soaked it under the water and then pressed it to my face, breathing in the hot steam.

"I'm not okay! Is that what you wanted me to admit? Is that what you want to hear, Molloy? That I'm not okay?"

*

Tearing at my face with the cloth, I roughly washed any residue makeup away, and then stared lifelessly down at the white cloth streaked with a concoction of mascara, foundation, and lipstick.

"He will never want you more than he wants his next fix, Aoife. That's the sad truth of my son's life."

Numb and broken, I switched off the shower and stepped out, wrapping myself in the biggest, fluffiest white towel I could find before padding back to my room.

Music continued to waft from downstairs, and the sound of laughter assured me that my parents had friends over for drinks.

They did this every Christmas, and normally I would be the first one down there, sipping on cheap Prosecco and sharing some lighthearted flirty banter with their friends' sons. Honestly, though, I didn't have the energy left to rustle up a smile, much less a conversation.

I felt *hollow*.

Exhaling a ragged breath when I climbed onto my bed, I reached for my phone, and pressed the redial button.

"This is Joey, you know what to do."

Beep.

"I don't love you," I whispered brokenly into the phone. A tear trickled down my cheek, and I clenched my eyes shut. "I really, *really* don't love you, asshole."

Fresh start
Back to trying

December 28th 2004

JOEY

My father had fallen off the wagon before my mother had finished carving the turkey, and I ended up spending the rest of Christmas Day breaking up arguments and shielding my siblings from his swinging fists.

It was during one of his whiskey tantrums that I found myself taking stock of my life, and I mean *really* taking stock of it.

I felt trapped.

I felt overwhelmed by responsibility.

I felt angry.

I felt hard done by.

I felt wronged.

But all of those feelings paled in comparison to the feeling of shame that had come crashing down around me when I found myself wrestling a bottle of whiskey from my father's hands on Christmas night and saw my future self staring back at me.

I'd been knocked down many times in my life, but the cold, hard reality of knowing that I was turning into Teddy Lynch made me contemplate *staying* down.

Like a wounded dog, I wanted to crawl into a hole and lick my wounds.

Because I *was* wounded.

I was fucking breaking apart piece by piece, fueled further by the knowledge that my mother was right; this *was* my future.

If I didn't do something to turn this around, I would become everything I hated.

I would become another version of my father, of Dricko, of Shane Holland, of Danny Fitz, of Philly Heffernan, of *their* fathers, and every other asshole from our area that had buried his head in Powers, powder, and pussy.

I was a disgrace, and I didn't want to be this person anymore.

I was disgusted with how far I'd fallen.

Above it all, at the top of my ladder of priorities, was Molloy.

The devastation in her eyes, so similar to the pain my mother bore daily, was imbedded in the forefront of my mind, unwilling to dilute or dissipate, no matter how much time passed.

Her heartbroken expression when I climbed out of her window, the hurt in her voice, the angry words she had thrown in the heat of the moment . . . I had caused that pain.

I had put that hurt in her eyes, and those words in her mouth.

Me.

Not my father.

Not my mother.

It was all on me.

The road I was traveling down scared the shit out of me, and the prospect of a future that resembled my parents was the wakeup call that I needed.

It was a wakeup call that had led me to spending an innate amount of time since that night with my head in the toilet.

The horrible familiar sickly cold bead of sweat trickled down the back of my neck, dampening my brow, my lip, and every other inch of my skin, as I fought against the insurmountable demon inside of my head that demanded I stop fighting and just *feed* it.

Trembling violently, I kept my limbs locked tight, my muscles rigid, as I fought what felt like a hopeless battle.

One more hour, I mentally challenged myself. *Give it all you've got for one more hour, and if it still hurts as bad, you can call him.*

Coaxing myself like this was how I had made it through the last seventy-two hours.

The thought of having to feel this way forever was too huge a concept and too fucking demoralizing, so I concentrated on a period of time that I *could* tolerate.

One hour at a time.

I *could* do that.

"Are you *still* sick?" Tadhg asked, dragging me from my thoughts, as he stood in the bathroom doorway, and watched me hug the toilet. "Jesus, lad, you've been puking since Christmas."

"He's still sick?" Shannon appeared in the doorway, her eyes laced with concern. "Oh my god, Joe, should I call the doctor?"

"No, no, no." Cradling the bowl, I continued to wretch and tremble. "I'm . . ." Teeth chattering, I forced myself to swallow down a wave of nausea, before finishing, "I'll be grand."

"What's wrong with you?" Tadhg demanded, sounding anxiously frustrated. "Is it a bug?" He eyed me warily. "Can we catch it?"

"No, it's not contagious." Pausing, I heaved and wretched as another flood of clear liquid ejected itself from my body. "Will one of you do me a favor?"

"Yeah, of course," they both chimed.

Reaching into the pocket of my sweatpants, I retrieved my phone and held it out for them. "Hide it."

"Huh?"

"You want us to hide your phone?" Tadhg asked, tone incredulous. "Why?"

"Please just take it," I bit out through clenched teeth as a wave of nausea washed over me. "Hide it somewhere, fucking break it if you have to, just . . . just don't give it back to me."

"What if you get mad at us?" Shannon asked uncertainly.

"I won't."

"But what if you do?" Tadhg piped up.

"I won't," I snapped. "Fuck!"

"You're getting mad now," he reminded me.

"Please," I whisper-hissed. "Please just do this for me. I'll never ask any of you for anything."

"Can I keep it?"

Shannon sighed heavily. "No, Tadhg, you can't keep his phone."

"But he said that we could break it. Surely that means he doesn't want—"

"He *wants* his phone," Shannon countered.

"But he just—"

"He just doesn't want it right now," she added. "He'll have it back when the time is right."

"Then why don't you take it?"

"Because I'm weak and I'll give it back to him the minute he asks for it."

"So?"

"So, that's not what he needs us to do for him."

"Okay, none of this makes any sense to me."

"Tadhg!" I snapped. "Fuck!"

"Alright, alright." Sauntering into the bathroom, my little brother snatched up my phone and quickly pocketed it. "Consider it gone. But don't come bitching to me when you're out of credit and can't call your *girlfriend*. I plan on taking full advantage of this baby. How do you block your number when you're making a prank phone call? It's #31# right?"

"Tadhg!"

"Fine, Jesus, I won't prank anyone in your phonebook," he grumbled, stalking out of the bathroom. "Enjoy romancing the toilet, Joe."

"Are you sure you don't want me to call a doctor?" Shannon asked when Tadhg had skulked off with my phone. "What about Aoife?" she offered. "I could call her for you."

"No, don't call Aoife," I warned with a shake of my head. "Don't call anyone."

I hadn't told Shannon that I'd broken up with Molloy.

I hadn't told a soul.

Terrorizing my sister with my issues, when she was already laden down with anxiety, was something that I had no intention of doing. She didn't need to be exposed to what I hadn't been able to protect my own girlfriend from witnessing.

Disgust filled me at a rapid pace, and I heaved noisily, expelling another rush of bile.

Besides, I was too ashamed of myself, and too fucking raw, to form the words that were required to explain the latest level of fucking up I had reached.

I might have been the one doing the breaking up, but I wasn't ready to admit it out loud, much less talk about it.

I'd given a year of my life to the girl, and there was a small part of me, a tiny spark of hope still flickering around in my chest. One that allowed me to believe that if I could get a handle on my shit, if I could just overcome this horrible fucking habit I'd fallen into, then maybe, in time, I could win her back.

Maybe, I could become someone deserving of being with her, because the current version of me sure as hell wasn't.

And if I couldn't beat this thing that had crept up on me and sunk its claws in me, then at least I wasn't going to drag her down with me.

Because I loved Aoife Molloy enough to force her hand with a get-out-of-jail card, even if it almost killed me to do it.

I would *not* turn her into another Sam.

Or worse, my mam.

I would rather cut my bollocks off and join the priesthood before I let that happen.

"Are you sure you don't want me to call Aoife for you?" Gingerly padding into the bathroom, my sister lowered herself onto the bathroom floor, opposite me, and rested her back against the bath. Her blue eyes were laced with worry when she said, "If I had a boyfriend, I would want to know if he was sick." Shrugging helplessly, she added, "I would want to help him."

"She can't help me," I bit out, slowly leaning back to rest against the wall. "No one can."

Sadness enveloped her features. "Joe."

I knew that Shannon realised what was really happening here, and that I knew she knew.

Still, neither one of us spoke a word about the elephant in the room, and I was grateful for her in this moment.

She wasn't lecturing me.

She wasn't calling me names and reminding me of what a terrible person I had become.

She was just *here*.

"It's okay." Breathing labored, I forced myself to look her in the eyes. "It's going to be okay."

She blew out a shaky breath. "You promise?"

"Yeah." I nodded stiffly. "I promise."

It's been seventeen hours and six whole days

December 31st 2004

AOIFE

With my world shattered around me, and my heart splintered in my chest, I somehow managed to make it through the next week by committing myself to three methods/modes in order to survive the un-survivable.

Work mode.
Throwing myself at the mercy of my boss, I snatched up every available hour of work at The Dinniman. Desperate for the distraction, and the mundane anonymity that came with waiting tables, until I could crawl back into bed at night and cry myself to sleep.

Revise for the leaving cert mode.
Because I wasn't the scholar that Kev was, I quickly found that this method, as optimistic and productive as it had seemed in my mind when I conjured it up, was a complete bust. I would have to inhale our books if I had a hope of passing our leaving cert. He only had to hear the teacher say it once and it remained in his big old brain forever. Me? The teacher all but had to force it in and stick sellotape over every orifice in my head to stop the information from falling back out. That's how sucky I was at the academic side of school. Unfortunately for me, there was no exam on socializing, which, unlike Kev, I excelled in. Therefore, I swiftly moved on to the third method.

Take a bottle of vodka in the bath with me mode.

Yeah, when I had hashed up my three-step survival guide, I really hadn't thought it through, because similar to method number two, it sounded like a fantastic idea. Then I remembered that Mam had switched our tub out for the fucking power shower.

See? Nothing was going my way.

Regardless of my methods, I found myself going through the motions.

On Sunday, I was numb.

On Monday, I was empty.

On Tuesday, I was hysterically optimistic that everything would miraculously work out.

On Wednesday, I was filled with a deranged obsessiveness, which in turn, had caused me to fill his voicemail with needy messages that made me hate myself, and then angry ones that assured him that I hated him much more.

On Thursday, I was back to being grief-stricken.

And by Friday, I had resigned myself to the fact that I would never willingly celebrate another New Year's Eve again.

Last year had been horrible enough when I had to sit back and endure the knowledge that Joey was upstairs fucking Danielle, but tonight, as I sat alone in my house, I knew that I felt a million times worse.

Sure, I was technically with Paul last year, and Joey was happily servicing half the school, but we still had each other.

Because last year, as messed up and as blurred the five-year-long precipice of our friendship had become, at least I still had *him*.

But now, this year, I was utterly alone.

My parents were gone to the pub, and even Kev, who rarely left the house, had gone with them.

Fresh from a shower, I stood in front of my bedroom mirror, and took a long, hard glance in the mirror.

My eyes were puffy and bloodshot, my lips were red and swollen, and my cheeks were tear-stained.

I looked like shit.

I felt worse.

Sniffling, I reached up and pulled my damp and knotted hair into a make-shift bun on top of my head.

Dressing in a pair of black leggings, ballet pumps, and a chunky, oversized pink jumper, I batted the tears still trickling down my cheeks away with the back of my hand.

My hair was a wet mess piled on top of my head, and my face was void of makeup, but I didn't care.

I didn't have any plans for the night.

To be fair, it wasn't as if I didn't have offers. I had received countless texts and invitations from school pals, not to mention a dozen or so colorful voicemails from Casey. She was begging me to go with her to a Tommen party that Katie had snagged us an invite to, courtesy of her rugby-playing lover-boy.

According to Casey, the boys were *fine,* the drink was free, and she had every intention of snagging herself a fancy-pants, private-school-attending, built-like-a-brick-shithouse rugby-playing ride for the night.

Good for her.

She could have all of the rugby-obsessed boys of Tommen she wanted, because the only boy I wanted to spend tonight with came with a hurley, a BCS uniform, and a truckload of trauma.

Pulling the sleeves of my jumper down over my hands, I shivered from the cold as my gaze raked over my bedroom floor, eyes searching for the familiar keyring.

Don't do it, my pride warned, *don't be so desperate.*

Oh my god, do it! my heart encouraged, *you know he still loves us.*

Eyes landing on my car keys, I quickly snatched them up and hurried out of my room.

Yay, you're going to do it, my heart cheered.

You can leave me at the door, my pride declared, checking out on me, *this is beyond pathetic.*

I knew that I was taking one hell of a risk in doing what I was about to do, and there was a good chance that I would break my heart further, but I would never forgive myself if I didn't release the words that were burning me from the inside.

He needed *help* and I needed to be *heard*.

And even if he refused to let me help him, then he damn sure would hear me.

Babysitting brothers and boycotting bad habits

December 31st 2004

JOEY

"Go the fuck to sleep," I shouted up the staircase. "I swear to Christ, lads, if I have to come back up these stairs, you'll be sorry."

"Yeah right," Tadhg laughed back, daring as ever, as he leaned over the banister and taunted me. "What are you going to do? *Glare* at us to death?"

"Yeah," Billy brave bollox with the purple Furby tucked under his arm, chimed in. "We knows you won't touch us, Joe."

"Don't get lippy with me, fucker," I warned, pointing a finger at number five. "There's a first time for everything."

"Yeah right," Ollie snorted, not one bit flailed by my empty threat.

"I mean it," I told them. "And if ye even think about waking that baby, it won't be me who spends another two hours rocking him back to sleep."

"Oh please," Ollie shot back. "Seany can sleep through anything."

"Yeah," I countered. "Lucky for him since he's living with a pair of foghorns."

"Why can't I come down?" Tadhg whined. "It's New Year's Eve. Shannon gets to stay up – and don't say it's because she's older than me, because that's a cop-out."

"Because if I let you come down, then I have to let Ollie come down, and if I let Ollie come down, I have to let Sean come down," I heard myself tell him for what had to be the seventh time. "And I'm not carrying all of your asses back to bed when ye pass out on the couch."

"But Dad's gone out for the night," Tadhg continued to protest. "And Mam's gone with him. This happens once a year, Joe. Once a damn year."

"*Exactly*," I agreed. "So, fuck off up to bed like a good lad, and let me enjoy the peace and quiet for once."

"This is bullshit," Tadhg grumbled. "It's only half ten."

"We hates it when you babysit," Ollie huffed, tripping over his words. "You're the meanest. And boring."

I rolled my eyes. "Yeah, because babysitting the three of ye is such a thrilling event for me, too."

"Joey, please—"

"Bed," I ordered, holding a hand up. "Keep fighting with me and neither one of you will see the inside of the GAA grounds for a week."

"You can't do that," Tadhg protested. "You can't ground us. You're not our dad."

"Yeah," Ollie added, sidling up to Tadhg. "You're nots the boss of us."

"Oh, no?" I cocked a brow. "Keep pushing and I'll add on another week."

"But—"

"That's three weeks."

"This is bullshit," Tadhg huffed, before disappearing from sight. "I liked you better when you were puking!"

"Yeah," Ollie grumbled, as he hurried after Tadhg. "We hates you."

"Yeah, yeah. Sweet dreams, ye little fuckers," I called back, waiting for the sound of their bedroom door slamming shut before heading back into the sitting room.

"Wow, I am so glad you're here to crack the whip," Shannon chuckled, when I sank down on the couch beside her. "They literally *never* do what I tell them."

"You can't show weakness," I explained, tossing her a bar of chocolate from my pocket. "Boys grouped up like that are like a pack of rabid dogs. They can smell fear a mile away, and the minute you bare your neck to them, they'll go straight for the jugular."

"Wow," she mused, unwrapping her bar. "What an interesting parenting concept."

"Don't eat it like that, you weirdo!" Gaping in horror at the way my sister brutally savaged a KitKat bar, I grabbed the cushion behind my back and tossed it at her. "The fuck kind of serial killer are you?"

"What?" Cackling from her perch at the end of the couch, Shannon took another bite – straight down the middle without splitting it in half first. "It's only chocolate."

Shaking my head in disgust, I took a sip from the cup of tea she had made me earlier and muttered, "You're a little psycho at heart, aren't ya?"

"You're in a lot better shape than yesterday," she shot back approvingly. "I'm proud of you, Joe."

"For what exactly?"

"For getting better." Cheeks blushing, she squirmed in discomfort. "For staying home tonight when being here is the last place you want to be."

That was for damn sure.

And I was far from *better*, but I was still trying, still hanging in there, and I was still clean.

The worst of the DTs had passed, but I knew that I was balancing on thin ice, which meant that going out tonight was a risk that I couldn't afford to take.

I hadn't put myself through hell this past week to throw it all away, because that's exactly what I *would* do.

Unlike my father, alcohol had never been my issue, but it *was* the sneaky fucking sidekick to my main nemesis.

Because with all of the freedom that alcohol provided me, it stripped me of all logic and awareness. It rendered me reckless, before sending me plummeting headfirst down the path of no return.

When I got drunk, I got sloppy, and when I got sloppy, I got high.

It had been that way since I wasn't much older than Tadhg. Hell, maybe even Ollie.

For close to half my life, I had danced with the devil, playing with fire, and it had finally caught up with me.

Worse than catching up with me, it had overtaken me.

The line I had crossed wasn't one many came back from.

Molloy's heartbroken face was still as fresh in my mind now as it had been the week before. It was the driving force behind my decision to park my ass on this couch and stay out of trouble for the night.

I couldn't fuck up again.

I couldn't afford to.

I knew in my heart that if I let myself slip back down that hole, there would be no coming back out.

"You know," Shannon mused, dragging me back to the present, as she polished off her chocolate bar, "I can't remember the last New Year's Eve we spent together."

I could.

"I was in sixth class; you were in third," I reminded her, remembering the night like it was yesterday. "Darren was in sixth year and had just come out to Mam over the Christmas, and the old man had hit the roof."

"Oh, yeah." The light in her eyes dimmed. "I remember."

"He broke up the house, disowned Darren, broke Mam's arm for defending Darren, then broke my nose for defending Mam, before packing a bag and fucking off for a month."

"Yeah," she whispered, chewing on her lip. "That was the last Christmas that Darren spent with us."

"Yeah," I acknowledged quietly. "And that was the last time I spent New Year's Eve at home."

It was the last time I'd spent it sober, too.

"He left the following autumn," she added, clearly thinking back to a time in our lives when it wasn't so complicated. "Once he had his leaving cert results."

"Which were all higher level As because, let's face it, he was a fair bit of a genius," I begrudgingly admitted. "Clever fucker's probably in an office somewhere, sitting behind a big-ass desk, with a fancy computer in front of him, and making a fortune with that big brain of his."

"I hope so," Shannon replied wistfully. "I really do hope he's okay, Joe."

"He's grand," I bit out, feeling my mood sour. "He got out, didn't he?"

"Yeah, I guess." Anxiety filled her eyes. "Do you hate him?"

I nodded stiffly.

Her eyes widened. "Really?"

"Yes, really," I snapped. "I really and truly despise the guy."

For leaving me on my own in this.

For dropping the burden of responsibility on my shoulders when we should be sharing the load.

For snatching my future away from me when he walked out the door.

"I don't." She eyed me nervously. "Hate Darren, that is. I'm still hurt that he left and never came back—"

"He didn't just not come back," I interrupted, feeling my temper rise at the memory. "He didn't pick up the phone, either. Not once in half a decade."

"But I still don't hate him. I could never hate any of my brothers." She nudged my knee with her foot before adding, "And especially not my favorite brother."

I rolled my eyes. "Kiss ass."

"It was a good month though, huh?" she said with a small smile. "When Dad left that Christmas – I mean, aside from Mam's broken arm, and your broken nose, that is."

"You can chalk that down," I shot back. "It was the first Christmas we had with Mam that I can remember her actually being *present*."

"Me too," Shannon agreed. "She was so alive that Christmas." Her eyes lit up as she thought back. "Remember how much fun we had when she took us out singing 'The Wren' on St. Stephen's Day?" Giggling, she added, "She brought us around from door to door, and pub to pub, singing our hearts out. We made so much money, Joe, remember?"

"Yeah," I snorted. "Only because I persuaded her to swallow her pride and let us do it."

"You did?"

"Yeah," I replied flatly. "Dad had fucked off with all of our money, she wasn't getting paid for another fortnight, and her precious Darren was too busy studying for his exams to get a job." Shrugging, I added, "We needed something to get us by. Ollie needed nappies, and there wasn't a scrap of food in the press when Dad left."

"Really?" Shannon squeezed out. "So, that's why you got that job with Tony Molloy that Christmas? Because we didn't have any money?"

I shrugged. "Pretty much."

"Wow." She blew out a breath. "I never knew that."

"There's a lot you never knew, Shan," I muttered, taking another sip of tea. "Be glad."

"I am," she hurried to assure me. "I am glad, Joe – and grateful. Darren might have been the academic son, but you're the survivor." She reached across the couch and squeezed my shoulder with her small hand. "Which is how I *know* that you are going to be okay." She gave me a meaningful look and whispered the words, "I promise."

A small knock sounded on the front door then, and I quickly sprang to my feet, thankful for the break in conversation.

It was getting too deep, and I couldn't handle heavy right now.

"Who is it?" Shannon called after me, when I had barely made it to the hallway.

"Maybe if you give me a chance to answer it, I can tell you," I replied dryly, as I turned the key in the lock and swung the door inwards.

The minute my eyes landed on her face, I felt like the air that been knocked clean out of my lungs.

Fuck.

With her arms wrapped around herself protectively, Molloy stood at my front door, looking more broken and more beautiful than I'd ever seen her look in the six years I'd known her.

"Hi," she whispered.

"Hi." Ignoring my sister as she called out from the sitting room, I managed to string enough words together to ask, "Are you okay?"

The dark circles under her puffy eyes assured me that she wasn't.

With her teeth chattering, I watched as she started to nod before abruptly stopping and shaking her head instead. "Can we talk?"

Fuck.

With my heart hammering violently in my chest, I stepped outside and pulled the front door out behind me, knowing that whatever she had to say was going to hurt, but complying without protest because I deserved everything that she could throw at me and more.

I'm not okay

December 31st 2004

AOIFE

When I knocked on the Lynchs' front door late on New Year's Eve, the very last person I had been expecting to be standing in the doorway was Joey.

But when the door swung inwards, that's exactly who I found staring back at me.

Of course, he was who I had come to see, but in my heart of hearts, I honestly thought that it would be a fruitless trip.

The minute my eyes landed on his, the pain in my chest that I had been walking around with amplified. To the point where I had to physically press my hand against my chest bone to soothe the ache.

My breath hitched. "Hi."

"Hi." He gripped the door tighter. "Are you okay?"

No. "Can we talk?"

He nodded and I exhaled a shaky breath when he stepped outside and quietly closed the door out behind him.

The grey sweatpants he was wearing hung low on his narrow hips, revealing a hint of the black boxer shorts he had on underneath. The plain white t-shirt he had on revealed his tattooed arms and fitted him in such a way that I could see the hint of black ink on his chest.

It hurt.

It fucking scorched me.

Unable to stop myself, I drank in the sight of him, as my body heated, and my heart cracked under the insurmountable effort that it took for me to stand here and face him.

"I, ah . . ." Letting my voice trail off, I studied his face, feeling more confused with every second that passed. "You're here." *You're sober.*

"Yeah." Joey nodded slowly, jaw ticking. "I am."

"Why?" I demanded, tone hoarse and broken. "Why are you *here*?"

"Should I not be?"

"It's New Year's Eve."

"Yeah, I'm aware of the date."

"Answer me."

He blew out a pained breath when he said, "I'm sort of trying to turn over a new leaf."

I stared at him in disbelief. "Why?"

He gave me a hard look. "Why do you think?"

"*Why*?" I repeated, unrelenting. "Why, Joe, why?"

"Because I fucked up!"

"So?" Tears pooled my eyes, and I carefully kept them open, not daring to blink. I knew if I did, the dam would burst. Blinking tears away never worked for me, I had to stare them back to hell. "You've fucked up before and it hasn't stopped you from doing it again." *Over and over again . . .*

"Yeah, well, maybe this time when I fucked up, it cost me more than I was willing to lose."

"What does that mean?"

"You know what it means," he replied, running a hand through his hair.

"Say it," I demanded, as we stood less than two feet apart, with him towering over me. "Give me the words."

His green eyes blazed with heat when he came right out and said, "It cost me you."

"Me?"

"You."

"No." His words knocked me for six, and I shook my head. "Don't say that."

"You asked," he bit out. "I answered."

"But you . . . " Shaking my head, I glared up at him, feeling hopeful and hopeless all in one conflicted breath. "*You* did this, Joey."

"I know."

"No, no, no." I held up a shaky hand, as I mentally batted away the pitiful hope rising up inside of me. "*You* broke up with *me*."

"I know, Molloy." His eyes blazed with heat when he growled, "I *know*."

"Then don't feed me anymore bullshit," I hissed, unable to get a handle on my frazzled emotions. "You were more than willing to lose me when you walked out on me." Tears burned my eyes as I stared up at him. "I was there, remember? I watched you *leave*."

"Because I was trying to do the right thing," he snarled, losing his cool right back with me. "Fuck!"

"For who?" I screamed, throwing my hands up.

"For you!" he roared back, chest heaving, as he mirrored my actions, throwing his hands up wildly. "For you, Molloy. For fucking you. Always you!" Frustrated, his hands clenched at his sides and he spat, "I was willing to walk away because I knew that it was the best thing that I could do *for* you, not because I don't love you!"

"*Love* me?" I choked out a pained, humorless laugh. "So *now* you give me the word? When it's over?" I shook my head, incredulous, as devastation ricocheted through me. "That's just fucking priceless."

He narrowed his eyes. "I'm giving you the truth."

"You know about my parents' relationship," I accused, delirious with grief, and desperate for him to hear my pain. For him to know just how deep the knife he put in my back had cut me. It was wedged in the bone, and I was slowly dying inside. "You know why I have issues with trusting men."

He had the good grace to clamp his mouth shut and nod.

"I never trusted Paul, not once in four years, and I *never* allowed myself to love him either, because I knew what would happen if I did," I strangled out, breath coming in short audible puffs. "I knew that in the end, he would let me down and break my heart – if I gave him the power to. So, I didn't. I kept that power and my heart to myself." Sniffling, I shook my head and forced myself to look at him, when I said, "But I never stood a chance against you, did I?"

He stared at me for the longest time before blowing out a pained breath. "Aoife. I was trying to protect you."

"Well, it didn't work," I heard myself cry, body growing limp as the adrenalin that had been coursing through me quickly deflated. "Because I'm not okay."

He flinched. "I know."

"I'm not okay," I repeated, needing him to hear me, to see me, to fucking help me. "You asked me earlier if I was okay, and I'm telling you that I'm *not* okay."

"I never meant to . . . " His voice broke off and he scrubbed his face with his hand before strangling out, "I *know*, okay? I know. It's the same for me."

"You made me fall," I forced myself to tell him, as every inch of me trembled. "You made me fall, and trust, and believe, and then you took it all away."

Pain encompassed his features. "I know."

"I'm in love with you." I didn't care how weak or pathetic I sounded in that moment, as I continued to let my truth spill from my lips, as I bled open in front of him. "And I'm afraid for you, and I'm completely fucked up in the head because of you." My throat hitched, and I exhaled a broken sob before forcing out, "And I have felt all of these things for you since I was twelve years old."

"Aoife."

"I have turned a blind eye to all of the shady things you do more times than I care to admit. I have thrown friendships away to be with you. I have walked into drug dens for you. I have covered for you, protected you, lied for you, and given my body to you."

"Aoife," he groaned like I was causing him physical pain. "I—"

"I couldn't love you more if I tried, Joey Lynch," I cried, giving up the fight against the tears that were flowing freely down my cheeks now. "I *couldn't*."

I felt like a poisoned snake that was dying, weakened but exceptionally dangerous and venomous.

619 • CHLOE WALSH

I couldn't understand how my heart was so willing to be hurt. To lay down for this boy to walk and trample all over it with no thought or care for the consequences. Without thought for my future, which didn't exist without him.

"But it's never going to be enough for you!" Losing the battle with my emotions, I clutched my head in my hands and released an agonized scream. "I'm never going to be enough for you because my love doesn't come in the form of a powder that you can snort up your nose or inject in your veins—"

"That's *not* how it is," Joey interrupted, voice cracking. "That's *not* how I feel." Exhaling a ragged breath, he closed the space between us and roughly pulled me into his arms. "*I'm* the problem here, Molloy. *I'm* the one who's never going to be enough, not you."

"You are enough!"

"I'm not," he replied. "I'm really not, baby."

"It's too much, Joe." Tears spilled over, falling so fast it was hard to see clearly, as my arms shot out of their own accord, clinging to the person who had inflicted all of this pain on me. "All of it," I strangled out, burying my face in his chest. "I *feel* too much for you."

"I know," he ground out. "That's *exactly* why I did what I did." He pressed a kiss to my damp hair and wrapped me tighter in his arms. "You need to understand that this is a hill that I've been climbing since before we met. This is *my* demon to slay." He released a torn growl and clung to me. "*None* of this is on you."

I'm trying to fix me

December 31st 2004

JOEY

I used to think that *my* words were bullets, but I was wrong. Nothing I could ever conjure up in my mind could inflict as much pain as had been inflicted on me by her words. Each word after soul-destroying word, splintering me and cutting me to the bone.

"Why can't you love me more?" she continued to cry, holding on to me with a vice-like grip. "Why am I not enough for you?"

"I *do* love you more," I choked out, feeling my soul crack in half, as I reeled in the unimaginable fucking horror of what I'd done to her. "You *are* enough for me."

"No, I'm not."

"Yes, you are." Blowing out a pained breath, I added, "I don't want to *be* the way I am. I don't fucking love what I do. I despise it."

"Then why do it?" she begged, trembling in my arms. "*Why?*"

She was asking me to give her the answer to something I couldn't explain.

How did you justify addiction to someone who had never lived through it?

How was I supposed to make her understand that, for most of my life, I had been desperate to escape. That the only solace I'd ever been able to find had been in the soothing drag of a joint, or a mind-altering line of coke, in the numbing effect of benzos, or the thrilling buzz of uppers? How could I forget the euphoric fucking feeling of heroin?

Because Molloy didn't know what it felt like to wake up every morning with a strong inclination to attempt suicide.

She didn't know how it felt to be a helpless child, half-starved from

621 • CHLOE WALSH

hunger, and even more starved for a way out of a home she wasn't wanted in.

She didn't know what it felt like to be that hopeless kid who *finally* found something that helped him through the pain and sheer fucking misery that was his life.

And she had no idea how quickly the shift in balance had happened for that kid, how it had snuck up on him so unexpectedly.

She could never understand the excruciating self-loathing that came with the realization that the *one* vice that had once helped that kid make it through the day had silently morphed into something he couldn't make it through a day without.

She would never understand how it felt to transition from controlling your life with something you once enjoyed to becoming controlled by the very thing you now despised.

I didn't tell her any of that, though.

Because I couldn't.

Because it wasn't fucking good enough.

"I don't know," was all I could say instead. "I don't know why I do it, Molloy."

Sniffling, she looked up at me and whispered, "That's not good enough."

I know. "It's all I have." Cupping her face between my hands, I leaned in close and pressed my brow to hers. "I'm sorry."

Shivering, she closed her eyes and leaned into my touch. "I don't want to be with anyone else."

"Neither do I," I replied hoarsely, and then it almost killed me to add, "But I don't want to hurt you either, which means that I need to stay away from you, and you need to let me."

"No." With tears dripping down her cheeks, she shook her head and tightened her hold on my waist. "I can't."

"You have to," I croaked out, feeling every ounce of her pain because I shared it right along with her. "Because I need to get my head clear before I can trust myself to be near you."

"But you're fine now," she sobbed, clutching on to me. "You didn't go out tonight. You're here. You're here, Joe! You're not strung out, or stoned, or drunk."

"We both know that I'm not fine, baby."

"But—"

"Listen to me."

"No, because you're not saying what I need you to say."

"You want the words?" Roughly clearing my throat, I sucked in a sharp breath before saying, "Fine; I love you, Aoife Molloy."

"Don't."

"I *love* you," I reiterated, eyes locked on hers, as I brushed away a tear from her cheek. "I love you more than I have ever loved another person in my life, and that's not an exaggeration. That's the god honest truth."

"Joe."

"Which is *why* I can never put you in a position like the one I put you in on Christmas Eve." Sniffing back my emotion, I shook my head and expelled a harsh breath before adding, "It's *because* I love you that I will *never* allow that to happen to you ever again."

"You're not supposed to tell me that you love me *after* we've broken up," she cried, burying her face in my chest. "You were supposed to say it when we were still together."

"Before, during, after." I shrugged helplessly. "It still stands."

"I don't want this, Joey," she strangled out. "I don't want to lose you. You're my best friend."

"And you're my best friend," I admitted, torn apart. "Nothing I feel for you has changed, Molloy."

"Then I need something more than just words," she demanded. "If you expect me to walk away, then I need you to give me some sort of guarantee."

"Like what?"

"Like this isn't forever," she whispered, green eyes searching mine. "That this is a temporary break, and as soon as you process whatever it is that you need to process, we're going to get back together."

"And if I can't?"

She shook her head. "That's not an option."

"Molloy." I blew out a breath. "I don't want to make you a promise that I can't keep."

"Then make it and *keep* it," she urged, reaching up to entwine her fingers with mine. "It's as easy as that."

No, it wasn't, and we both knew it.

"How's this?" I offered instead. "I'm going to go and do my thing for a while, clear my head, and get my shit together."

"Without me," she whispered numbly.

For you. "And you're going to go off and do your thing with Casey, and the girls, and you're going to have a fucking epic time," I continued. "And you're not going to worry about what I'm doing or who I'm with, because you already know that you've got my heart in your ass pocket."

Sniffling, she looked up at me expectantly. "And your dick."

It wasn't a question, it was a warning, but I answered her anyway. "And my dick."

She nodded her approval and I swiftly continued.

"And we're going to see each other at school, and it's not going to be fucked up and awkward because we both remember that before we were us, we were . . ."

"Us," she filled in softly.

"Exactly. I'm not replacing *you*, Molloy." *I couldn't.* "I'm trying to fix *me*." *For you.*

THANK YOU SO MUCH FOR READING!

Joey and Aoife's story continues in *Redeeming 6*.

For updates on release dates, check out
chloewalshauthor.com.

Keep reading for an exclusive **bonus chapter**
from *Saving 6*. Find out what happened just
before the chapter called **Summer loving:
I got me a tatt**, on page 455!

Bonus Scene

July 10th 2004

JOEY

The epic rave Molloy was hellbent on us attending consisted of thousands of scantily clad ravers piled into a harvested hay field, while several well-known club DJs played on top of an artic trailer.

Standing around in a field in the pissings of rain, squashed between thousands of sweaty, rain-soaked bodies would never be my first choice of a night out, but Molloy was enjoying herself.

A thunderstorm in July wasn't anything uncommon for Irish weather, but even I had to admit that the lightning forking the sky looked epic mixed in with the strobe lights flashing around us.

The rain was catapulting down on me, and I could hardly feel my face – courtesy of whatever I'd snorted up my nose earlier – but none of it mattered.

Because she was here, and I was free.

For one weekend, at least.

Added to the mix was an overflow of sex, alcohol, and drugs, which made for a very compliable Joey.

Standing out like a sexy little glowworm in the midnight downpour, I watched as my girlfriend thrashed around to the music.

Clad in denim hotpants, a frilly, white bikini top, and yellow wellies, and with neon body paint dripping from her rain-soaked skin, Molloy threw her hands in the air as she danced like no one was watching.

Jesus Christ, yellow wellies never looked so sexy.

Tipping the scales at the higher end of buzzed, I hovered close to my girl, giving her space she needed to throw shapes and enjoy herself, but close enough to step in if any of the countless pervy bastards eyeing her got a little too handsy.

When Gigi D'Agostino's "L'Amour Toujours" blasted from the main stage, it sent everyone within a two-mile radius into a crazed frenzy.

Meanwhile, I swayed back and forth between the jostling bodies and took another hit off my joint, while dutifully ignoring the blonde that had been attempting to dance with me for the last four songs.

With my t-shirt tucked into the waistband of my shorts, and caked in the neon paint my girlfriend had decorated me in earlier, the same shit that matched her, I tried to keep my wits about me.

"You've got a beautiful body."

Aw shit.

When unfamiliar hands came around my body, touching my bare stomach, I felt my good mood sour.

"I love your tattoos."

Buzzed or not, I knew that this one was getting a little too handsy and was in danger of losing her hair if she didn't back the fuck up – courtesy of my sexy glowworm in her yellow wellies.

"I fly with her," I shouted over the music, referencing the song playing, as I slipped out of her hold before Molloy noticed and went full Sarah Connor mode on her ass. Turning to face the handsy blonde, I pointed to where my girlfriend was dancing and added, "Only her," in as cold a tone as I could muster. "So back up."

"Oh, come on, sexy. Why don't you live a little? What your little girlfriend doesn't know can't hurt her." she purred, unwilling to take the hint, as she continued to push into my personal space, going as far as circling my neck with her arms. "You look like the best mistake I could make tonight." She stepped closer. "I've got a tent at the other end of the—"

"Do you have a death wish, bitch?" a familiar voice cut in, causing me to groan internally. "Because putting your hands on my boyfriend is a solid way of signing your own death certificate."

Oh, it was going down.

Fuck my life.

"Chill, sweetie, we were only talking," the blonde replied in a snarky tone, but had the good sense to remove her hands from my neck and take a safe step back. "You don't own him."

"Oh, that's where you're wrong, *sweetie*," Molloy shot back, taking a defensive step in front of me. "I absolutely do own him."

Well, shit.

"Hey, stud?" Turning back to face me, Molloy eyeballed me with such a look that I momentarily sobered and feared for my own safety. "Who owns you?"

My brows shot up in surprise. "Owns me?"

"*Yes.*" Another eyeballing glare that caused my balls to shrivel. "Owns you."

"You, queen," I had the good sense to say, even though it went against my very nature to heel to anyone. *Not anyone,* my heart reminded me. *Only her.*

"Wow," the blonde drawled sarcastically. "You've got him on a tight leash, don't you? What's next? Brand the poor bastard with your name?"

"What a fantastic idea," Molloy countered, taking a menacing step towards her. "Now, off you fuck before I tear clumps out of those ugly-ass extension."

"Psycho bitch," the blonde spat before disappearing into the crowd.

"Peroxide Barbie," Molloy screamed back at her.

"Calm down, Molloy," I growled, snaking a hand around her waist before she could chase after her retreating nemesis. "It's not that deep."

"Not that deep?" Spinning around to glare at me, Molloy jabbed my chest with her finger. "She was all over you, Joe."

"She knew I wasn't interested. I shut it down."

"*Sure* you had."

"Yeah, Molloy, I had it handled."

"Really? Because it looked like she was handling *you.*"

"Nah, I'd say you did a pretty good job of that yourself," I shot back. "You own me?" I glared down at her. "Nobody owns me, Molloy."

"Oh, cop on. It works both ways." She rolled her eyes at me. "You own me, too."

"I *own* you?" I repeated, feeling a fucked-up concoction of possessiveness and lust. "That sounds toxic as fuck, baby."

"Don't you want to own me, Joe?" she purred, stepping closer until her chest was flush against mine. "Hm?" Snaking her arms around my neck, she swiped the baseball cap off my head and placed it on hers instead – backwards, just like I had been wearing it. "Because I want you to own me."

Fuck.

My.

Life.

Divine Inspiration's "The Way" began to play just as the heavens opened above us, drenching us in a torrential downpour.

I should have been cold, but my body was burning up, urged on by the rapid beat of my heart as it thundered in my chest for the girl in my arms.

"You're a little menace," I finally conceded, leaning in to brush my lips against hers. "A pain in my hole."

"Maybe," she teased. "But you love me."

"Molloy."

"You're in love with me."

"Stop it."

"To the point of madness," she continued to tease. "That's what you said, wasn't it, Joe? All those years ago? That's how a person knows they're in love."

"Aoife."

"And you love me to the point of madness."

"You're hard fucking work, do ya know that?"

"You love me so much it makes you crazy."

"Jesus Christ."

"You're going to get a tattoo of my name someday, right?"

"Like fuck I am."

"Across your heart," she continued to goad, as she grinned up at me in victory. I was bowing down, and she knew it. This round was hers. "Because that's where I stay."

"Don't push it," I grumbled, tightening my hold on her waist, as I felt myself grow with the need to be inside her. To fall into her and never come up for air.

"You adore the ground I walk on."

Yeah, I had a feeling she might be right, but I would never verbally admit it.

So, I told her what I couldn't say with my actions.

Sighing heavily, I cupped her face between my hands and rested my brow against hers.

"It's okay if you can't say it yet, Joe," she whispered, lips brushing against mine as she spoke. "I don't have to hear it," she added, resting her hand on my beating chest. "Because I can already feel it."

Acknowledgements

When my son died last year, I never thought I would regather the motivation, enthusiasm, and thick-skin required to survive and navigate the book world that I had made my second home for a decade.

Deadlines, cover reveals, signings, tours, advertising, social media, bestseller lists ... None of it seemed important to me anymore because I had lost, in my mind, the fifth chamber of my heart.

The other four chambers of my heart were still breathing, smiling, and needing their mother to stay present. I could do that for them – for my children; for my heart, and also for my husband; my metaphorical backbone since I was barely more than a child myself.

With a lot of grief counselling, I found that I could keep a handle of my grief and navigate my life with one child buried in a graveyard, but what I couldn't do, I quickly realized, was afford to put myself back in the public eye. My state of mind was too fragile to take another hit.

As time passed by, the emails began to mount, and the questions kept coming. When was I going to release another book? The answer in my mind for a very long time was never. I had no plans to, and, as ironic as this may sound, still don't.

Publishers reached out, loyal fans and readers continued to send me messages of love and support, and then, with a little persuasive shove by a dynamic duo, who reminded me of my commitments, and supported and encouraged by my husband, I found myself back at the desk.

I don't know if my writing is what it was before he died, I don't know if it will ever be again, but I tried. I poured my pain into a character whose pain and mental anguish I felt I could connect with, and let my grief and anger spill out on the pages. Similar to the previous books in the series, it's a chunky one, which is why I had to turn it into two books.

If you are reading this, as a diehard fan of the Boys of Tommen, and feel like I haven't reached the level of writing I was at when I wrote the first two books in the series, then I am sorry for letting you down. If you are reading this, and I reached you, connected with something inside of these characters, then know that I am with you, and I shoulder your pain daily.

In the line of acknowledgements, I come first to my family. To my husband, who shoulders the same grief as I do every day, and with so much heart, humility, and empathy. My father and stepmother, who stepped in to lighten my load of responsibilities during the writing process. My friends, my family, my editor, my readers. I extend a deep level of gratitude to each and every one of you.

Finally, from the bottom of my heart, I want to thank you for your support, kindness, patience, and of course, for reading this story.

Love, Chloe xx

She's the quintessential sunshine girl.
He's the lovable class clown.

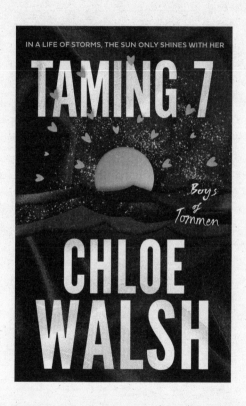

But storm clouds are rolling in, and this
Tommen boy is about to get serious.

Order now!

Epic, emotional and addictive ...

The power and pain of first love has never been more deeply felt than in Chloe Walsh's extraordinary stories about the irresistible Boys of Tommen, which will give you the ultimate book hangover.

Collect them all!